考研英语一本通

考研英语命题研究组　编

中国石化出版社
HTTP://WWW.SINOPEC-PRESS.COM
教·育·出·版·中·心

图书在版编目（CIP）数据

考研英语一本通/考研英语命题研究组编.
—北京：中国石化出版社，2005（2009.3 重印）
ISBN 978 - 7 - 80164 - 776 - 4

Ⅰ．考… Ⅱ．考… Ⅲ．英语 - 研究生 - 入学考试 -
自学参考资料 Ⅳ．H31

中国版本图书馆 CIP 数据核字（2005）第 025851 号

中国石化出版社出版发行
地址：北京市东城区安定门外大街 58 号
邮编：100011　电话：(010)84271850
读者服务部电话：(010)84289974
http：//www. sinopec-press. com
E-mail：press@ sinopec. com. cn
北京奇才晨虹文化发展有限公司排版
北京宏伟双华印刷有限公司印刷
全国各地新华书店经销
＊
787×1092 毫米 16 开本 21.125 印张 538 千字
2009 年 3 月第 1 版第 2 次印刷
定价：38.00 元

目　录

第一部分
考研英语制胜全攻略

俗话说:知己知彼,百战不殆。开始复习考研英语,我们要做到:

一、首先,我们要认真研究《英语考试大纲》,明确试卷考什么

研究生英语入学考试的评价目标有两个方向:一是语言知识的考查,二是语言技能的考查。语言知识包括语法知识和词汇知识,语言技能包括听力、阅读、翻译、写作等方面,语言技能是建立在语言知识的基础之上的。

对于考生来说,熟悉考试的形式和题型无疑会增加获胜的机会。了解考研试题所要考查的各方面,有的放矢地去复习,可以更加胸有成竹地应对考试。

2006			2007			2008			2009		
部 分	题数	分数	部 分	题数	分数	部 分	题数	分数	部 分	题数	分数
1.英语知识运用	20	10	1.英语知识运用	20	10	1.英语知识运用	20	10	1.英语知识运用	20	10
2.阅读理解 Part A(多项选择题)	4篇(20题)	40	2.阅读理解 Part A(多项选择题)	4篇(20题)	40	2.阅读理解 Part A(多项选择题)	4篇(20题)	40	2.阅读理解 Part A(多项选择题)	4篇(20题)	40
Part B(选择搭配题)	5题	10	Part B(选择搭配题)	5题	10	Part B(选择搭配题)	5题	10	Part B(选择搭配题)	5题	10
Part C(英译汉)	5题	10	Part C(英译汉)	5题	10	Part C(英译汉)	5题	10	Part C(英译汉)	5题	10
3.写作 Part A(短文写作)	200词	20	3.写作 Part A(短文写作)	200词	20	3.写作 Part A(短文写作)	200词	20	3.写作 Part A(短文写作)	200词	20
Part B(应用文写作)	100词	10	Part B(应用文写作)	100词	10	Part B(应用文写作)	100词	10	Part B(应用文写作)	100词	10

(一)对英语知识运用的解析

本部分主要测试考生结合上下文的综合理解能力和语言运用能力,即在阅读理解的基础上对篇章结构、语法和词汇知识的运用能力的考查,这是对完形填空的定位。大纲明确指出对完形填空考核的重点:语法、固定搭配、近义词辨析和逻辑关系四大类题型。这种提法针对性更强。考生可从历年真题中按照提示的四类题型去准备和复习有关考研完形填空方面的知识点,这样可以做到事半功倍的效果。同时考虑到完形填空在历年考研中得分较低,大纲明确了考生解答完形填空题的思路,对于考生备考和解题都更具针对性。即:"从上下文的角度来考虑"和"运用逻辑推理",这两点都要求考生大到对文章整体的把握,小到对句子之间和句子内部把握,区别在于前者强调的是文章内容的一致,后者强调的是文章逻辑的一致;"从惯用法和搭配的角度来考虑问题",这点要求考生对惯用法和搭配要有更多积累。

(二)对阅读理解的解析

就多项选择题(Part A)而言,这是一个大家非常熟悉的题型,考试大纲明确表态,文章来源英语国家原版报刊或书籍,绝大多数是评论性的文章(即除文学作品以外的其他类型的短文)。由于新闻记者惯用"引用"的方法,考研的文章经常喜欢正反交替举例,先说作者认同的,然后又是作者要批评的、揭露的,再是用实例来论证作者的观点。这种语篇思维模式会给考生在阅读理解中造成很大的障碍。正因为难,考研命题专家就非常青睐这类语篇来命题。近两年,这种题目每次都有,而且得分率也很低,因为需要大家平时阅读时更多注重阅读一些英美经济文化科技方面的报刊书籍,注重对于作者观点、立足点、态度语气的把握。最后从语言难度来看,阅读文章无论从词汇方面还是从句子方面较往年的难度有所提高,命题和前几年明显不同的是:大量考查了推理和判断题以及细节事实题;文章容易,选项"刁";生词依然存在,但其比例仍然维持在3%左右。

选择搭配题(Part B)要求考生从整体上把握文章的逻辑结构和内容上的联系,理解句子之间、段落之间的关系,对诸如连贯性、一致性等语段特征有较强的意识和熟练的把握,并具备运用语法知识分析理解长难句的能力。2005、2006、2009年考查的是难度相对较大的选择句子搭配题,而2007、2008年则选择了难度相对较低的选择小标题。可以说,此题型是对语言能力和阅读理解能力的综合测试,因此在要求上远远高于这两种题型,考生有必要对这类题型的答题思路多练习,以提高自己在这个部分的应试能力。

英译汉(Part C)考查在准确理解的基础上,按照英语语法结构拆分句子,准确、通顺翻译汉语的能力。翻译考点不变,还是包含对定语从句、状语从句等翻译的考查。纵观往年考研试题,我们发现命题者对于比较复杂的句子结构和文章的考查是加大比重了。这体现在我们各个部分的题型当中,尤其以英翻汉部分最为明显。这也反映出我们的命题者在考虑到各位同学在进入研究生学习之后需要接触大量的专业英语材料,这些材料的特点就是语言结构比较复杂,所以在考研当中考查考生对复杂语言结构和复杂长难句的理解的这种能力就成为了最近几年考试非常明显的特点和趋势。

(三)对写作的解析

短文写作(Part A)的要求是:包含试题规定的所有内容要点;使用丰富的语法结构和词汇;语言自然流畅,语法错误极少;有效地采用了多种衔接手段,文字连贯,层次清晰。平时练习主要注意两个方面:首先,语言是第一要素;其次,结构层次要清晰。在语言方面,应把语言错误降低到最低限度。语言错误大致在如下几个方面:第一,主谓一致;第二,时态;第三,冠词的用法;第四,名词的单复数;第五,搭配问题;第六,单词的拼写。检查的时候,一般不要做内容上的修改。阅卷者根本不会意识到所加的话有多么重要,文章多一句话少一句话是不会改变阅卷者印象的。

根据考试大纲的文字来看,今年的应用文写作(Part B)应依旧是书信的写作,希望考生能够把书信的格式进行进一步的强化。应用文写作能力的提高不可能一蹴而就,必须经过长期的实践锻炼。重点要注意语域和格式两个问题。在复习阶段,应用文的写作,尤其是书信的写作要注意内容的格式安排,首先要熟悉不同类型的应用文写作格式、注意事项、写作特点等。其次要背诵大量的优秀范文。再次,是要多动手写作,要写出属于自己的文章。

鉴于英语考纲的稳定性,各位考生可以继续既定复习思路和计划。当然,千里之外始于足下,各位考生一定要脚踏实地地落实自己的计划,这样才能达到事半功倍的效果。

下面为考生推出了几点复习建议:

1.迅速突破词汇关。大纲要求了5500个考研基本词汇,考生要将它们当作基本常识熟背熟记;严格掌握单词的一词多义及其在句子中的用法;对于一些常考词组更要熟练掌握,并注重平时对这些词汇的积累;对历年真题的阅读、完形填空中出现的高频词汇要加强记忆;学会通过上下文的提示对词汇进行适当推理,加强对词汇用法的掌握。

2.精练历年真题。在考研复习资料中,历年真题最具权威性,其他任何模拟试题都不能与之相比,考生应予以重视。建议先把历年真题练习三遍以上,要特别留意做错的题目,通过分析原因,找出自己的薄弱之处,并总结真题的出题规律,及时调整解题思路。

3.善于抓住文章的主线。考生在掌握了一定词汇辨析知识的基础上,应重点研究段落的内在结构和作者的主要观点。由于历年真题基本上都是“总分结构”的模式,而且大部分文章的第一句就是该段的中心句,因此考生做题需“擒贼先擒王”,确定好文章的主题、核心内容、作者基本观点等主线,在此基础上步步推理,层层深入,才能有效地理解考题,掌握解题技巧。

二、其次,我们要明确自己现有的英语水平以及与考研英语要求的差距

这需要从两个方面考查:一是词汇量的考查,二是综合能力的考查。词汇量的考查可以借助于考试大纲的词汇表进行:从头到尾把2009年《英语考试大纲》的词汇表浏览一遍,标出不熟悉的词和词组,作为日后首先攻克的对象。综合能力的考查要通过做最近2~3年的真题。切忌用模拟题进行考查,因为只有真题才是考试大纲最准确的反映,其权威性和准确性远非市面的模拟题可以比拟。此

外,通过做近几年的真题,可以了解考试的规律性,对后面的复习有很好的指导作用,这不是模拟题所具备的。这也正是编写《考研英语一本通》的意义所在。

要清楚自己目前的水平,需要以下几个能力的考察。

(一)词汇

众所周知,词汇是英语学习的基础。翻开英语大纲,首先看都认识吗?认识多少?都认识的同学不要暗自窃喜以为自己词汇都过关了,其实大纲不再标出词条的具体意义,给了我们一个强烈的暗示,那就是多义现象已经成为考查重点。这对于机械性的背单词是一个根本的否定。所以对词汇方面的检测应该对熟词生义、一词多义现象的认知方面侧重。

(二)语法

许多同学认为语法不重要,还有的人认为许多老外也不懂语法。但我们认为语法有助于中国学生理解英语,我们毕竟没有英语环境让你"水到渠成",还是要脚踏实地的落实好各个语法点。

扎实、系统地掌握语法,而不是孤立地记忆语法的点。例如,动词的系统包括时态、语态、语气、情态动词和非限定动词,他们之间相辅相成,构成了一个整体;从句也是一个系统,它由名词性从句、形容词性从句和副词性从句构成,名词性从句又由主语从句、宾语从句、表语从句和同位语从句几个子系统构成。只有系统地学习语法,才能做到点面结合,不仅要会做语法题,更重要的是应用语法,为英语知识运用、阅读、翻译和写作等单项打下良好的基础。

这一方面的考查最简单的方法就是拿出 50 个长难句,分析一下结构。如果都能分析出来,过关。

(三)阅读能力

考试大纲对阅读能力的要求显然是重中之重。试卷中占 60％的阅读也不得不让我们刮目相看。同学们大都对四六级的阅读很熟,但考研阅读的难度显然不是四六级考试能够比拟的。有的同学平常很少接触原汁原味的外文文章,短时间内接受不了考研的难度。有的同学爱看原文电影、原文杂志,很管用。

(四)写作能力

同学们自己写两篇文章自我检测,让外教或英语教师讲评一下,当然文体是议论文方面。应用文中重点是写信,强调交流能力。

(五)翻译能力

翻译能力是与上述几个方面相互联系的。翻译其实就是一个输入与输出过程。翻译能力中强调的技巧性更多一些。

通过两个例句的翻译,同学们就可以知道自己在理解整合英语意思、输出地道汉语的过程中哪些环节出了问题。

三、备考策略

对自己进行摸底,清楚自己的差距之后,我们应针对自己的不足,明确复习策略。

必须全面地掌握大纲词汇。此处,"全面地"意味着考生不仅要掌握每个单词本身,而且要掌握每个单词的近义词、近形词、衍生和搭配,因为考研英语考查的重点就是词的辨析和搭配。因此,词汇的学习要注意联想记忆法,学习某一个单词时,同时联想到它的近义词和近形词,明晰它们的异同。这样,记忆的过程是一组组、一对对单词同时记忆。这种记忆方法可以在记住单词拼写的同时,还掌握了词与词的区别和各自特殊的用法,于是将平时极易混淆的单词清楚地区别开。例如:学习 accuse 可以联想到它的近义词 charge,二者的用法差异很大:accuse 与 of 搭配,而 charge 与 with 搭配;学习 economic 可以联想到它的近形词 economical,二者的意义差异很大:前者意为"经济的",而后者意为

"会过的,节俭的"。

重视阅读理解训练。阅读理解分值在英语考试中占有最大的比重,自然是复习过程的重要一环。首先,考生一定要细致研究历年真题,把握命题的规律,找出自己的差距,定好复习思路。其次,考生要广泛阅读,尤其是时效较强的英美报刊文摘和杂志,扩大知识面,提高阅读速度,培养浏览、跳读和快读的能力,即抓住关键词、主题句和中心大意的能力。接下来,考生要进行大量的模拟训练,特别注重长句、难句的理解,质和量并重。

写作需要足够的量。从 1997 年后,图表式作文成为作文命题的主要类型,图画作文主要考查考生把握寓意、联想现实、深刻思考、丰富表达的能力。因此,在准备考研的过程中,考生应善于思考各类社会话题,然后将思考的内容用英语写下来,养成用英语思考和写作的习惯。

明确复习策略以后,考生应该安排好自己的备考时间,科学地、分阶段进行复习。我们建议将复习过程分为四个阶段:

基础阶段:(3~5 月)

浏览一些真题,把握复习思路,打好语法、词汇基础。

提高阶段:(6~9 月)

以听力和阅读训练为主,通过泛读提高语感和词汇量,通过做阅读练习题提高阅读速度和答题的准确率;同时,培养回答阅读题的思维模式;开始熟悉写作,及时调整复习思路和重点。

强化阶段:(10~12 月)

单项强化与大量做真题、模拟题并举。注意总结题型和答题规律,并彻底搞明白自己常出错的题目和类型,尽量避免再犯同样的错误。可以通过参加辅导班以求事半功倍。

冲刺阶段:(12~1 月)

坚持每天模拟和反复做真题,研究真题,发现并猛攻薄弱环节。复习已学知识,把重点放在提分幅度高的单项上来;坚持每天做新的练习题,保持思维的敏捷,全面做好应考的准备。

四、应注意的几个问题

(一)英语知识运用

第一,考生在第一遍阅读中,要善于从文章开头的几句话中分析出短文的背景、主题或结构。通常情况下,文章开头的第一二句都是完整的信息,提示着文章的背景知识或主题思想。考生在阅读中一定要仔细研读这几句,以便为后面的阅读扫清障碍。

第二,在答题中,寻找信息词非常重要。所谓信息词,包括上下文中出现过的词、词组、固定搭配、习惯用语和特定句型中的有关词语或者相关句子。有的备选答案在独立的语法条件上看是正确的,但如果结合上下文提供的信息来判断却是错误的。信息词会直接或间接地提示我们寻找正确答案的线索。

第三,词汇是英语知识运用部分考查的一个重点。词组搭配和惯用搭配是每次的必考内容。同义词与近义词的辨析时常出现,形似词或音似词等词汇干扰项也并不少见。这些都值得考生在解题和复习时给予关注。

第四,英语知识运用的题型可分为几种,但无论对于哪种情况,常用的解题方法无外乎验证法、排除法、推理法和对比法四种,而大多数情况下,在解题中还需要考生综合地运用这些方法。

(二)阅读部分

阅读能力的测试是任何一种考试的重心所在,是决定考研英语成败的关键。《新大纲》当中阅读部分没有改变,仍然保持原有的 8 项要求,因为这些要求比较全面,可以考查学生的综合阅读能力。阅读能力是获取信息很重要的途径,也是英语教学的重点,将考研阅读和我们熟悉的六级相比,除了考研阅读明显要难于六级阅读外,我们还可以得出这样的结论:六级是在考阅读速度,而考研则更加侧重于阅读理解的准确性和彻底性;《新大纲》中则对阅读题材做了明确的规定,对体裁也给了很好的提示,比如一定不会考记叙文。

考研的阅读备考不仅仅是语篇的学习。我们常有这样的困惑,即使将文章翻译出来也未必能正确解决所有问题。如何能有信心地面对考试,一方面在于实力,另一方面在于技巧。

阅读实力的培养只能靠精读,建议同学们首先按时间要求做完一篇文章(约15分～20分),然后再精读做一遍,看看哪几个做错了。最后查看答案,将没有做对的题的思路更正过来。

(三)阅读新题型部分

《新大纲》的阅读理解B部分是新增加的题型。试卷中给出一篇总长度为500～600词的文章,其中有5段空白,文章后面有6～7段文字,要求考生根据文章内容从中选择5个分别放进文章中5个空白处。主要考查考生对文章篇章结构的整体把握和句子间的内在逻辑关系。

那么考生该如何准备这个部分呢?

首先,抓住文章的主题。通过重点阅读文章第一段和每段首句尾句迅速确定文章的主要内容、核心概念和作者态度等信息。

其次,阅读给出的选项,注意其中的代词、逻辑副词和核心词汇。做出必要的标记,初步预测前后可能的信息。

然后,认真阅读文章内容,把握文章结构。比如,有些文章是按照总分结构展开的,有些文章是按照正反结构展开的。捕捉到这些信息,将对解题有莫大帮助。

最后,仔细研读文中空格前后的句子,洞察行文逻辑上的连贯性和一致性,依靠这些最贴近的信息判断选择最合适的句子。

(四)英译汉部分

翻译是两种语言之间的转换,是"在准确理解的基础上,用一种语言把另外一种语言贴切地表达出来"。目前,考生常见的翻译问题主要是:不理解,直接开始表达;理解后,表达不到位。那么,如何克服上面这些问题呢?

1.理解的关键是理解句子结构,理清各成分之间的逻辑联系。理解是翻译的前提,只有在准确理解的基础上,才能开始翻译。我们必须纠正那种"一看到英语句子,不是先弄清句子关系,而是先找对等的汉语来翻译"的做法。翻译的时候,首先要做的是理解原文,在弄清句子结构之后,在准确理解的基础上,才开始找合适的汉语来表达。

2.表达的关键在于根据汉语语言习惯做适当的调整。根据汉语习惯,通过"适当调整"就可以做到"贴切表达"。同时,调整的是各个句子的成分,比如,后置定语可以翻译在其中心词前;定语从句如果易于表达、信息量不大,可以提前到先行词前,如果信息量大,放在先行词前表达起来很累赘,可以考虑独立译成一句话;时间、条件和原因状语从句可以翻译在主句之前,等等。在整个翻译的解题过程中,一定要在分析、理清了句子结构之后,在准确理解的基础上用符合汉语语言习惯的句子来翻译。

最后,我们还得重复坊间老调长谈的一句话"要重视真题"。近年来,真题的指导作用以及其在考研英语中的独特作用已被确立。为此我们在重点内容之后重现了部分历年真题,并给出详尽解释。希望对真题的剖析能够让广大考生有豁然开朗的感觉。

下面我们先以2009年考研英语真题为例进行解析。

2009 年全国硕士研究生入学考试英语试题

Section I Use of English

Directions：

Read the following text. Choose the best word(s) for each numbered blank and mark A，B，C or D on ANSWER SHEET 1.（10 points）

Research on animal intelligence always makes me wonder just how smart humans are. __1__ the fruit-fly experiments described in Carl Zimmer's piece in the Science Times on Tuesday. Fruit flies who were taught to be smarter than the average fruit fly __2__ to live shorter lives. This suggests that __3__ bulbs burn longer, that there is an __4__ in not being too terrifically bright.

Intelligence, it __5__ out, is a high-priced option. It takes more upkeep, burns more fuel and is slow __6__ the starting line because it depends on learning—a gradual __7__ —instead of instinct. Plenty of other species are able to learn, and one of the things they've apparently learned is when to __8__ .

Is there an adaptive value to __9__ intelligence? That's the question behind this new research. I like it. Instead of casting a wistful glance __10__ at all the species we've left in the dust I. Q. -wise, it implicitly asks what the real __11__ of our own intelligence might be. This is __12__ the mind of every animal I've ever met.

Research on animal intelligence also makes me wonder what experiments animals would __13__ on humans if they had the chance. Every cat with an owner, __14__ , is running a small-scale study in operant conditioning. We believe that __15__ animals ran the labs, they would test us to __16__ the limits of our patience, our faithfulness, our memory for terrain. They would try to decide what intelligence in humans is really __17__ , not merely how much of it there is. __18__ , they would hope to study a __19__ question: Are humans actually aware of the world they live in? __20__ the results are inconclusive.

1. [A] Suppose   [B] Consider   [C] Observe   [D] Imagine
2. [A] tended   [B] feared   [C] happened   [D] threatened
3. [A] thinner   [B] stabler   [C] lighter   [D] dimmer
4. [A] tendency   [B] advantage   [C] inclination   [D] priority
5. [A] insists on   [B] sums up   [C] turns out   [D] puts forward
6. [A] off   [B] behind   [C] over   [D] along
7. [A] incredible   [B] spontaneous   [C] inevitable   [D] gradual
8. [A] fight   [B] doubt   [C] stop   [D] think
9. [A] invisible   [B] limited   [C] indefinite   [D] different
10. [A] upward   [B] forward   [C] afterward   [D] backward
11. [A] features   [B] influences   [C] results   [D] costs

12. [A] outside   [B] on   [C] by   [D] across

13. [A] deliver   [B] carry   [C] perform   [D] apply

14. [A] by chance   [B] in contrast   [C] as usual   [D] for instance

15. [A] if   [B] unless   [C] as   [D] lest

16. [A] moderate   [B] overcome   [C] determine   [D] reach

17. [A] at   [B] for   [C] after   [D] with

18. [A] Above all   [B] After all   [C] However   [D] Otherwise

19. [A] fundamental   [B] comprehensive   [C] equivalent   [D] hostile

20. [A] By accident   [B] In time   [C] So far   [D] Better still

Section II Reading Comprehension

Directions:

Read the following four texts. Answer the questions below each text by choosing A, B, C, or D. Mark your answers on ANSWER SHEET 1. (40 points)

Text 1

Habits are a funny thing. We reach for them mindlessly, setting our brains on auto-pilot and relaxing into the unconscious comfort of familiar routine. "Not choice, but habit rules the unreflecting herd," William Wordsworth said in the 19th century, In the ever-changing 21st century, even the word "habit" carries a negative connotation.

So it seems antithetical to talk about habits in the same context as creativity and innovation. But brain researchers have discovered that when we consciously develop new habits, we create parallel synaptic paths, and even entirely new brain cells, that can jump our trains of thought onto new, innovative tracks.

But don't bother trying to kill off old habits; once those <u>ruts</u> of procedure are worn into the hippocampus, they're there to stay. Instead, the new habits we deliberately ingrain into ourselves create parallel pathways that can bypass those old roads.

"The first thing needed for innovation is a fascination with wonder," says Dawna Markova, author of "The Open Mind" and an executive change consultant for Professional Thinking Partners. "But we are taught instead to 'decide', just as our president calls himself 'the Decider'." She adds, however, that "to decide is to kill off all possibilities but one. A good innovational thinker is always exploring the many other possibilities."

All of us work through problems in ways of which we're unaware, she says. Researchers in the late 1960 covered that humans are born with the capacity to approach challenges in four primary ways: analytically, procedurally, relationally (or collaboratively) and innovatively. At puberty, however, the brain shuts down half of that capacity, preserving only those modes of thought that have seemed most valuable during the first decade or so of life.

The current emphasis on standardized testing highlights analysis and procedure, meaning that few of us inherently use our innovative and collaborative modes of thought "This breaks the major rule in the American belief system-that anyone can do anything," explains M. J. Ryan, author of the 2006 book "This Year I Will..." and Ms. Markova's business partner. "That's a lie that we have perpetuated, and it fosters commonness. Knowing what you're good at and doing even more of it creates excellence. " This is where developing new habits comes in.

21. The view of Wordsworth habit is claimed by being _____.

　　[A] usual 　　[B] familiar 　　[C] mechanical 　　[D] changeable

22. The researchers have discovered that the formation of habit can be _____.

　　[A] predicted 　[B] regulated 　[C] traced 　　　[D] guided

23. "ruts"(in line one, paragraph 3) has closest meaning to _____.

　　[A] tracks 　[B] series 　　[C] characteristics 　[D] connections

24. Ms. Markova's comments suggest that the practice of standard testing _____?

　　[A] prevents new habits from being formed

　　[B] no longer emphasizes commonness

　　[C] maintains the inherent American thinking mode

　　[D] complies with the American belief system

25. Ryn most probably agree that _____.

　　[A] ideas are born of a relaxing mind

　　[B] innovativeness could be taught

　　[C] decisiveness derives from fantastic ideas

　　[D] curiosity activates creative minds

Text 2

It is a wise father that knows his own child, but today a man can boost his paternal (fatherly) wisdom—or at least confirm that he's the kid's dad. All he needs to do is shell our $ 30 for paternity testing kit (PTK) at his local drugstore—and another $ 120 to get the results.

More than 60,000 people have purchased the PTKs since they first become available without prescriptions last years, according to Doug Fog. chief operating officer of Identigene, which makes the over-the-counter Kits. More than two dozen companies sell DNA tests Directly to the public, ranging in price from a few hundred dollars to more than $ 2500.

Among the most popular: paternity and kinship testing, which adopted children can use to find their biological relatives and latest rage a many passionate genealogists-and supports businesses that offer to search for a family's geographic roots.

Most tests require collecting cells by webbing saliva in the mouth and sending it to the company for testing. All tests require a potential candidate with whom to compare DNA.

But some observers are skeptical,"There is a kind of false precision being hawked by people claiming they are doing ancestry testing," says Trey Duster, a New York University sociologist. He notes that each individual has many ancestors-numbering in the hundreds just a few centuries back. Yet most ancestry testing only considers a single lineage, either the Y chromosome inherited through men in a father's line or mitochondrial DNA, which a passed down only from mothers. This DNA can reveal genetic information about only one or two ancestors, even though, for example, just three generations back people also have six other great-grandparents or, four generations back, 14 other great-great-grandparents.

Critics also argue that commercial genetic testing is only as good as the reference collections to which a sample is compared. Databases used by some companies don't rely on data collected systematically but rather lump together information from different research projects. This means that a DNA database may differ depending on the company that processes the results. In addition, the computer programs a company uses to estimate relationships may be patented and not subject to peer review or outside evaluation.

26. In paragraphs 1 and 2, the text shows PTK'S _____.

　　[A] easy availability

　　[B] flexibility in pricing

　　[C] successful promotion

　　[D] popularity with households

27. PTK is used to _____.

　　[A] locate one's birth place

　　[B] promote genetic research

　　[C] identify parent-child kinship

　　[D] choose children for adoption

28. Skeptical observers believe that ancestry testing fails to _____.

　　[A] trace distant ancestors

　　[B] rebuild reliable bloodlines

　　[C] fully use genetic information

　　[D] achieve the claimed accuracy

29. In the last paragraph, a problem commercial genetic testing faces is _____.

　　[A] disorganized data collection

　　[B] overlapping database building

　　[C] excessive sample comparison

　　[D] lack of patent evaluation

30. An appropriate title for the text is most likely to be _____.

　　[A] Fors and Againsts of DNA Testing

　　[B] DNA Testing and It's Problems

　　[C] DNA Testing outside the Lab

　　[D] Lies behind DNA Testing

Text 3

　　The relationship between formal education and economic growth in poor countries is widely misunderstood by economists and politicians alike progress in both area is undoubtedly necessary for the social, political and intellectual development of these and all other societies, however, the conventional view that education should be one of the very highest priorities for promoting rapid economic development in poor countries is wrong. We are fortunate that is it, because new educational systems there and putting enough people through them to improve economic performance would require two or three generations. The findings of a research institution have consistently shown that workers in all countries can be trained on the job to achieve radical higher productivity and, as a result, radically higher standards of living.

　　Ironically, the first evidence for this idea appeared in the United States. Not long ago, with the country entering a recessing and Japan at its pre-bubble peak. The U. S. workforce was derided as poorly educated and one of primary cause of the poor U. S. economic performance. Japan was, and remains. the global leader in automotive-assembly productivity. Yet the research revealed that the U. S. factories of Honda Nissan, and Toyota achieved about 95 per cent of the productivity of their Japanese countere pants a result of the training that U. S. workers received on the job.

　　More recently, while examing housing construction, the researchers discovered that illiterate, non-English-speaking Mexican workers in Houston, Texas, consistently met best-practice labor productivity standards despite the complexity of the building industry's work.

　　What is the real relationship between education and economic development? We have to suspect that continuing economic growth promotes the development of education even when governments don't force it. After all, that's how education got started. When our ancestors were hunters and gatherers 10,000 years ago, they didn't have time to wonder much about anything besides finding food. Only when humanity began to get its food in more productive way was there time for other things.

As education improved, humanity's productivity potential, they could in turn afford more education. This increasingly high level of education is probably a necessary, but not a sufficient, condition for the complex political systems required by advanced economic performance. Thus poor countries might not be able to escape their poverty traps without political changes that may be possible only with broader formal education. A lack of formal education, however, doesn't constrain the ability of the developing world's workforce to substantially improve productivity for the forested future. On the contrary, constraints on improving productivity explain why education isn't developing more quickly there than it is.

31. The author holds in paragraph 1 that the importance of education in poor countries _____.

[A] is subject groundless doubts

[B] has fallen victim of bias

[C] is conventional downgraded

[D] has been overestimated

32. It is stated in paragraph 1 that construction of a new education system _____.

[A] challenges economists and politicians

[B] takes efforts of generations

[C] demands priority from the government

[D] requires sufficient labor force

33. A major difference between the Japanese and U. S. workforces is that _____.

[A] the Japanese workforce is better disciplined

[B] the Japanese workforce is more productive

[C] the U. S workforce has a better education

[D] the U. S workforce is more organized

34. The author quotes the example of our ancestors to show that education emerged _____.

[A] when people had enough time

[B] prior to better ways of finding food

[C] when people on longer went hung

[D] as a result of pressure on government

35. According to the last paragraph, development of education _____.

[A] results directly from competitive environments

[B] does not depend on economic performance

[C] follows improved productivity

[D] cannot afford political changes

Text 4

The most thoroughly studied in the history of the new world are the ministers and political leaders of seventeenth-century New England. According to the standard history of American philosophy, nowhere else in colonial America was "So much important attached to intellectual pursuits". According to many books and articles, New England's leaders established the basic themes and preoccupations of an unfolding, dominant Puritan tradition in American intellectual life.

To take this approach to the New Englanders normally mean to start with the Puritans' theological innovations and their distinctive ideas about the church-important subjects that we may not neglect. But in keeping with our examination of southern intellectual life, we may consider the original Puritans as carriers of European culture adjusting to New world circumstances. The New England colonies were the scenes of important episodes in the pursuit of widely understood ideals of civility and virtuosity.

The early settlers of Massachusetts Bay included men of impressive education and influence in England. Besides the ninety or so learned ministers who came to Massachusetts church in the decade after 1629, There were political leaders like John Winthrop, an educated gentleman, lawyer, and official of the Crown before he journeyed to Boston. There men wrote and published extensively, reaching both New World and Old World audiences, and giving New England an atmosphere of intellectual earnestness.

We should not forget, however, that most New Englanders were less well educated. While few crafts men or farmers, let alone dependents and servants, left literary compositions to be analyzed, They in thinking often had a traditional superstitions quality. A tailor named John Dane, who emigrated in the late 1630s, left an account of his reasons for leaving England that is filled with signs. sexual confusion, economic frustrations, and religious hope-all name together in a decisive moment when he opened the Bible, told his father the first line he saw would settle his fate, and read the magical words: "come out from among them, touch no unclean thing, and I will be your God and you shall be my people." One wonders what Dane thought of the careful sermons explaining the Bible that he heard in puritan churched.

Mean while, many settles had slighter religious commitments than Dane's, as one clergyman learned in confronting folk along the coast who mocked that they had not come to the New world for religion. "Our main end was to catch fish."

36. The author notes that in the seventeenth-century New England _____.

    [A] puritan tradition dominated political life

    [B] intellectual interest were encouraged

    [C] politics benefited much from intellectual endeavors

    [D] intellectual pursuits enjoyed a liberal environment

37. It is suggested in paragraph 2 that New Englanders _____.

    [A] experienced a comparatively peaceful early history

    [B] brought with them the culture of the Old World

    [C] paid little attention to southern intellectual life

    [D] were obsessed with religious innovations

38. The early ministers and political leaders in Massachusetts Bay _____.

    [A] were famous in the New World for their writings

    [B] gained increasing importance in religious affairs

    [C] abandoned high positions before coming to the New World

    [D] created a new intellectual atmosphere in New England

39. The story of John Dane shows that less well-educated New Englanders were often _____.

    [A] influenced by superstitions

    [B] troubled with religious beliefs

    [C] puzzled by church sermons

    [D] frustrated with family earnings

40. The text suggests that early settlers in New England _____.

    [A] were mostly engaged in political activities

    [B] were motivated by an illusory prospect

    [C] came from different backgrounds

    [D] left few formal records for later reference

Part B

Directions:

In the following article, some sentences have been removed. For Questions 41—45, choose the most suitable one from the list A—G to fit into each of the numbered gaps. There are two extra choices, which you do not need to use. Mark your answers on ANSWER SHEET 1. (10 points)

Coinciding with the groundbreaking theory of biological evolution proposed by British naturalist Charles Darwin in the 1860s, British social philosopher Herbert Spencer put forward his own theory of biological and cultural evolution. Spencer argued that all worldly phenomena, including human societies, changed over time, advancing toward perfection. _____(41)_____.

American social scientist Lewis Henry Morgan introduced another theory of cultural evolution in the late 1800s. Morgan, along with Tylor, was one of the founders of modern anthropology. In his work, he attempted to show how all aspects of culture changed together in the evolution of societies. _____(42)_____.

In the early 1900s in North America, German-born American anthropologist Franz Boas developed a new theory of culture known as *historical particularism*. Historical particularism, which emphasized the uniqueness of all cultures, gave new direction to anthropology. _____(43)_____.

Boas felt that the culture of any society must be understood as the result of a unique history and not as one of many cultures belonging to a broader evolutionary stage or type of culture. _____(44)_____.

Historical particularism became a dominant approach to the study of culture in American anthropology, largely through the influence of many students of Boas. But a number of anthropologists in the early 1900s also rejected the particularist theory of culture in favor of diffusionism. Some attributed virtually every important cultural achievement to the inventions of a few, especially gifted peoples that, according to diffusionists, then spread to other cultures. _____(45)_____.

Also in the early 1900s, French sociologist Emile Durkheim developed a theory of culture that would greatly influence anthropology. Durkheim proposed that religious beliefs functioned to reinforce social solidarity. An interest in the relationship between the function of society and culture—known as functionalism—became a major theme in European, and especially British, anthropology.

[A] Other anthropologists believed that cultural innovations, such as inventions, had a single origin and passed from society to society. This theory was known as *diffusionism*.

[B] In order to study particular cultures as completely as possible, Boas became skilled in linguistics, the study of languages, and in physical anthropology, the study of human biology and anatomy.

[C] He argued that human evolution was characterized by a struggle he called the "survival of the fittest", in which weaker races and societies must eventually be replaced by stronger, more advanced races and societies.

[D] They also focused on important rituals that appeared to preserve a people's social structure, such as initiation ceremonies that formally signify children's entrance into adulthood.

[E] Thus, in his view, diverse aspects of culture, such as the structure of families, forms of marriage, categories of kinship, ownership of property, forms of government, technology, and systems of food production, all changed as societies evolved.

[F] Supporters of the theory viewed as a collection of integrated parts that work together to keep a society functioning.

[G] For example, British anthropologists Grafton Elliot Smith and W. J. Perry incorrectly suggested, on the basis of inadequate information, that farming, pottery making, and metallurgy all originated in ancient Egypt and diffused throughout the world. In fact, all of these cultural developments occurred separately at different times in many parts of the world.

Part C

Directions:

Read the following text carefully and then translate the underlined segments into Chinese. Your translation should be written clearly on ANSWER SHEET 2. (10 points)

There is a marked difference between the education which every one gets from living with others, and the deliberate educating of the young. In the former case the education is incidental; it is natural and important, but it is not the express reason of the association. (46)It may be said that the measure of the worth of any social institution is its effect in enlarging and improving experience; but this effect is not a part of its original motive. Religious associations began, for example, in the desire to secure the favor of overruling powers and to ward off evil influences; family life in the desire to gratify appetites and secure family perpetuity; systematic labor, for the most part, because of enslavement to others, etc. (47)Only gradually was the by-product of the institution noted, and only more gradually still was this effect considered as a directive factor in the conduct of the institution. Even today, in our industrial life, apart from certain values of industriousness and thrift, the intellectual and emotional reaction of the forms of human association under which the world's work is carried on receives little attention as compared with physical output.

But in dealing with the young, the fact of association itself as an immediate human fact, gains in importance. (48)While it is easy to ignore in our contact with them the effect of our acts upon their disposition, it is not so easy as in dealing with adults. The need of training is too evident; the pressure to accomplish a change in their attitude and habits is too urgent to leave these consequences wholly out of account. (49)Since our chief business with them is to enable them to share in a common life we cannot help considering whether or no we are forming the powers which will secure this ability. If humanity has made some headway in realizing that the ultimate value of every institution is its distinctively human effect we may well believe that this lesson has been learned largely through dealings with the young.

(50)We are thus led to distinguish, within the broad educational process which we have been so far considering, a more formal kind of education—that of direct tuition or schooling. In undeveloped social groups, we find very little formal teaching and training. These groups mainly rely for instilling needed dispositions into the young upon the same sort of association which keeps the adults loyal to their group.

Section III   Writing

Part A

Directions:

You have just come back from Canada and found a music CD in your luggage that you forgot to return to Bob, your landlord there. Write him a letter to

1) give your opinions briefly and

2) make two or three suggestions.

You should write about 100 words. Do not sign your own name at the end of the letter. Use "Li Ming" instead. You do not need to write the address.

Part B

Directions:

Write an essay of 160—200 words based on the following drawing. In your essay, you should
1)describe the drawing briefly,
2)explain its intended meaning, and then
3)give your comments.
You should write neatly on ANSHWER SHEET 2. (20 points)

网络的"近"与"远"

2009 年全国硕士研究生入学考试
英语试题参考答案及答案详解

Section I Use of English

1. 答案[B]

　　本题考查动词,后面的宾语是"the fruit-fly experiments described…",suppose 表示"假设",observe 表示"观察",image 表示"想象",Consider"考虑",代入文中表示"考虑已经被描述出来的实验",符合语境。

2. 答案[A]

　　本题考查动词短语,happen to"碰巧",fear to"唯恐……",be threatened to"被恐吓……"。tend to do 表示"有……倾向,往往……",代入文中表示比较聪明的果蝇往往寿命较短。

3. 答案[D]

　　本题考查形容词,lighter"更轻的",thinner"更瘦的",stabler"更稳定的",dimmer"比较暗淡的",本句是前一句推出的结论,即由"果蝇越聪明寿命越短"推出"灯泡越暗使用时间越长"。

4. 答案[B]

　　本题考查名词,由前半句"灯泡越暗使用时间越长"推出"这是不特别亮的灯泡的一个优点"。tendency"倾向",advantage"优势",inclination"倾向",priority"优先权"。

5. 答案[C]

　　本题考查动词短语,turns out"证明是",insist on"坚持",sum up"总结",put forward"提出"。

6. 答案[A]

　　本题考查介词,off 表示离开。代入文中表示离开起点时。

7. 答案[D]

　　本题考查形容词,incredible"难以置信的",spontaneous"自发的",inevitable"不可避免的",gradual"渐进的"。学习是一个渐进的过程,所以选 gradual。

8. 答案[C]

　　本题考查动词词义,本文的主旨是智力需要昂贵的代价。大量的物种会学习,但它们首先学会的是知道什么时候停止学习,与上文的例子灯泡呼应。四个选项中,fight 表示"斗争",doubt 表示"怀疑",stop 表示"停止",think 表示"思考",正确答案为[C]。

9. 答案[B]

　　本题考查形容词,修饰 intelligence。invisible"看不见的",indefinite"不确定的",这两个选项意思不符合,排除。different"不同的",limited"有限的"。因为所有物种的智力都是有限的,所以 limited 符合文意。

10. 答案[D]

本题考查副词词形辨析和用法,cast a glance backward"回顾",固定搭配。

11. 答案[D]

本题考查名词词义,feature"特征",influence"影响",result"结果",cost"代价"。Cost"代价"与文中"事实证明,智力是要付出代价"相呼应。

12. 答案[B]

本题考查介词,on the mind of"为……着想",by the mind"通过思考",outside 和 across 不与mind 的搭配。

13. 答案[C]

本题考查动词,与之搭配的宾语是 experiments,选项中 perform 能与 experiments 搭配,表示"做实验"。deliver"递送",carry"运送",apply"应用"。

14. 答案[D]

本题考查语篇关系,前一句提到 experiments,本句提到一个具体的实验,所以选 for instance"例如"。by chance"偶然",in contrast"相反",as usual"照常"。

15. 答案[A]

本题考查虚拟语气基本形式中连词用法,由后半句中 they would test us to 可推测本句使用了虚拟语气,选项中 if 可以引导虚拟条件句。unless"除非",as"正如",lest"唯恐"。

16. 答案[C]

本题考查动词。所填动词表明实验的目的,并且所填动词的宾语是 limits of our patience, our faithfulness, our memory for terrain,选项中 determine"确定"符合题意,并与下文的 decide 相呼应。moderate"适中的",overcome"克服",reach"达到"。

17. 答案[B]

本题考查介词,空白处语境为:它们会力图确定人类的智力到底_____什么? 本文的主题是聪明的代价,讨论智力的作用,[B]项 for 表示目的,与文意相合,正确;代入空白中,此处句意为"它们会力图确定人类的智力到底有什么真正的用处。"

18. 答案[A]

本题考查逻辑关系。这个句子位于段末,显然起到总结性的作用。四个选项中,Above all"最重要",After all"毕竟",However"然而",Otherwise"否则",故选 Above all。

19. 答案[A]

本题考查形容词,修饰 question。fundamental"基本的",comprehensive"全面的",equivalent"相等的",hostile"敌对的"。由句后问题的内容可推出这是一个最基本和重要的问题,所以选 fundamental。

20. 答案[C]

本题考查副词。空前说"想研究这个问题",空后说"结果还不确定"。四个选项中,By accident"偶然",In time"及时",So far"到目前为止",Better still"更好的是",只有 So far 符合语意。

Section II　Reading Comprehension

Part A

21.答案[C]

事实细节题。意为：Wordsworth 认为以何种方式便能获得文章第二句中提到 We reach for them mindlessly, setting our brains on auto-pilot and relaxing into the unconscious comfort of familiar routine.我们在无意识的状态下就能行成,我们的头脑处于自动导航,放松地进入一种无意识的惯性当中。从这个表述中可以看出习惯的形成过程完全是一种无意状态下的机械活动。

22.答案[D]

事实细节题。事实细节题。意为:研究者发现习惯的形成可以被第二段第二句当中指出当人们有意识的培养新的习惯时,我们就创造出一种相关的轨迹,甚至是全新的脑细胞,这可以使我们的思想进入一个创新的轨道上。由此可见研究人员认为习惯的形成是可以被引导的。

23.答案[A]

词义句义题。意为:不要试图摆脱你的旧习惯;一旦这个过程的进入大脑,它们就会留在脑中。根据上下文逻辑最合上下文语境的为[A]选项"痕迹"。

24.答案[D]

事实细节题。本题问道娜·玛克娃女士最可能同意什么。第五段首句说"创新最重要的是对奇事着迷",故[D]项"好奇可以激发创造性思维"正确。

25.答案[A]

事实细节题。本题问赖恩的观点认为实行标准化测试如何。末段首句说:目前对标准化测试的重视突出了分析和程序化,这就意味着我们根本不太会使用创新与合作的思维方式。提示标准化测试阻碍创新,阻碍新习惯的形成,故[A]项"妨碍新习惯的形成"正确。

26.答案[A]

意为:从第一二段文章表明 PTK 很容易买到。文中第一二段有多处体现,首段最后一句话"只需花 30 美元在地方药房作亲子鉴定……",第二段第一句我们可以看到"自从去年不需要处方即可购买之后,已经超过 6 万人购买了 PTK"。甚至从第二段整段我们可以看出:[B]项关于鉴定价格浮动只在第二段最后一句有所体现,[C]项文中未提到,[D]项属过度推断。

27.答案[C]

事实细节题。意为:PTK 是用来鉴定亲子关系的。从文中第三段可以看到"被收养的孩子可以通过亲子鉴定找到他具有血缘关系的亲属"。[A]选项比较具有迷惑性,从第三段后半句"PTK 最近惹怒了很多谱系学家,他们支持用 PTK 来探寻一个家族的祖籍",可以看出 PTK 没有主要被用来寻找一个人的出生地。选项[B]、[D]文中未提及。

28.答案[D]

事实细节题。意为:持怀疑态度的观察者认为祖先鉴定没有达到声称的准确性。从题干信息我们可以将它定位到文中第五段第一句"那些正在做祖先鉴定的人们所宣扬的(祖先鉴定)精确度其实是错的"。这句话是对这一段的概括,其他三个选项都只是它的细节之一。因此,[D]选项正确。

29.答案[A]

　　事实细节题。意为:最后一段中商业基因鉴定面临的一个问题是数据收集的紊乱。从最后一段第二句我们可以看出"一些公司使用的数据库并不依赖于系统的数据收集而是把不同研究机构收集的信息合在一起。这就意味着处理数据的公司不同,所用 DNA 数据库也会不同"。文中并未提及数据是否重合,[B]无根据,[C]、[D]文中没有体现。

30.答案[B]

　　主旨大意题。意为:本文最合适的题目应是 DNA 测试及它存在的问题。[A]选项"DNA 测试的赞成与反对"从文中我们看不到作者有明显赞成 DNA 测试的倾向。[C]选项,文中没有特别强调实验室内外的问题。[D]选项"DNA 测试背后的谎言",作者只是客观地提出了 DNA 测试存在的不准确性问题,但并没有指明是哪些人的谎言。

31.答案[D]

　　推理判断题目。意为:在第一段作者认为在贫困国家教育的重要性被高估了。作者在首段指出"传统的观点认为在贫困国家对促进经济的快速发展而言,教育是极应优先考虑的要素之一,这是种错误的看法。"教育的优先性和教育的重要性实际上是一个意思,既然文中说优先教育是种错误的看法,由此可推出教育的重要性被过度的重视了即被高估了,因此[D]正确。

32.答案[B]

　　事实细节题。意为:第一段表明建立新的教育体系需要几代人的努力。在第一段作者主要谈论了靠优先发展教育来促进经济发展是错误的看法,而世界各国的工人经过了劳动培训可以获取高产量进而带来更高的生活水平。解答细节题时同样明显背离中心的选项可首先排除,即先可排除 [A]、[C];在依据第一段的倒数第二句可知:通过教育体系来使足够多的人提高经济能力将需要两三代人。由此可知建立教育体系在当前是不可能的,而这种建立需要几代人的努力才能实现。

33.答案[B]

　　事实细节题。意为:日本和美国劳动力的主要区别是日本的劳动力更多产。解答本题可用运排除法。依据文章的第二段,美国劳动力受教育程度差遭到嘲笑并被认为是其经济表现差的原因之一。美国工人接受了职业培训后,本田、丰田的美国公司才达到了日本 95％的产量,由此可知日本工人的生产力比美国工人的生产力高。从文中可知,美国劳动力受教育程度差是个事实也是美国经济表现差的重要原因,由此可排除不符合文意的[C]选项;而 [A]、[D]的信息在文中未提及,由此可得出只有[B]正确。依据文意,既然日本保持了汽车产量的全球领先地位,自然日本的劳动力比美国的劳力更多产也验证了[B]为正确答案。

34.答案[A]

　　推理判断题。意为:作者引用了我们祖先的例子来表明当人们有了充裕的时间时,教育才出现。依据文章倒数第二段的最后两句可知,作者举了我们祖先的例子是来论证最后一句话得出的观点:只有当人们有了更高产的获得食物的方式时,人们才有时间做其他事情。由此可推知,教育是获得食物以外的其他事情,而受教育的前提是人们有剩余时间,由此可知[A]为正确答案。

35.答案[C]

　　主旨大意题。意为:教育的发展受约于产量的提高。文章在最后一段针对上文讨论的教育和生产的关系做出了总结。在本段作者明确指出缺乏正规的教育并不能限制发展极大提高产量的世界劳动力,而反之,对提高产量的限制得以解释了为什么教育发展得没有那么快。由此可见,提高产量优先于发展教育,故[C]为正确答案。而[A]、[D]的表达不符合文章的中心;[B]项的意思和文意相反。

36.答案[B]

　　事实细节题目。[A]选项为原文的篡改。[C]选项从原文的表述中无法推出。[D]选项文章中没有提到"对于知识的追求享有自由的环境"。

37.答案[B]

　　推理判断题。意为:第二段中暗示出新到达英格兰的人带着旧世界的文化。该段中的第二句提到,we may consider the original Puritans as carriers of European culture...,选项中的 New Englanders 对应文中的 Puritans,brought with them the culture of the Old World 对应该文章中的 carriers of European culture,故此选项为此句中的同义替换。

38.答案[D]

　　事实细节题。意为:早期到达马萨诸赛海湾的牧师和政治领导人为新英格兰创造了新的知识环境,对应第三段中的最后一句话 There men wrote and publish ed extensively, reaching both New World and Old World audiences, and giving New England an atmosphere of intellectual earnestness. [A]选项中 in the new world 缩小了原文所表述的范围,[B]选项在文章中没有提到,[C]选项不够全面。[D]为正确答案。

39.答案[A]

　　例证题。[A]选项举例是为了说明文中的观点 their thinking often had a traditional superstitions quality,为正确答案。

40.答案[C]

　　推断题。从文章中可以看出到新英格兰的早期的定居者有政客、牧师、裁缝还有渔夫,由此可见早期的定居者背景多种多样,[C]为正确答案。

Part B

41.答案[C]

　　第一段讲的是 Herbert Spencer 的"生物和文化进化理论",并且出现了 Charles Darwin。我们都知道 Charles Darwin 提出了生物界的适者生存,而这里说人类社会的进化也有适者生存这一特征,所以,我们可以首先确定 41 的答案是选项[C]。

42.答案[E]

　　选项[E]说,在他看来,不同方面的文化随着社会的进化都改变了。我们在读文章的时候,一定要把每一段的关键词划出来,以利于和选项中的关键词对应。读第二段的时候,文章说,在他的作品里,他尽量说明了 how aspects of culture changed together in the evolution of societies,这跟选项[E]的内容不谋而合。所以,我们可以断定,42 题的答案为选项[E]。

43.答案[A]

　　选项[A]主要介绍了什么叫"diffusionism",即它认为文化的革新有一个惟一的起源,并且在社之间传递。因为第五段出现了 diffusionism,所以我们可以判断选项[A]为正确答案。

---

44. 答案[B]

选项[B]的大体意思是:为了尽可能全面地了解特殊的文化,(particular cultures 是关键词),他对语言学和身体人类学都很熟悉。回到文章,我们在第三段找到了 the uniqueness of all cultures,我们可以断定,这个选项中的 he 指的就是 Franz Boas。那 Boas 在第三段和第四段都出现过,所以我们把选项[B]作为 44 的正确答案。

---

45. 答案[G]

选项[G]是一个例子,如果是答案的话应该是用来补充说明前面的观点的,它说,由于信息缺乏,这两位人类学家提出农耕等这些都是起源于古埃及,并且传播到世界各地。事实上,所有这些文化发展在世界不同地方的不同时期都曾分别出现过。通过分析这个例子,我们可以知道,这是两种不同的观点的比较。在第五段我们除了看到"历史特殊论(historical particularism)"外,还看到一种"diffusionism"理论和"diffusionists"这一种人,正好是两种理论的对比。所以我们可以把 45 题的答案轻松的定位到选项[G]。

Part C

46. 【解析】本句考点:宾语从句,of 短语作定语,代词指代,but 引导并列句。结构分析:句子主干是 it may be said that...,but this effect...,it 在句中指代 social institution。

【译文】可以说,任何社会制度的价值在于它对扩大和改进经验方面的影响,但是这种影响并不是它原来的动机的一部分。

---

47. 【解析】本句考点:强调句,分词结构作后置定语,省略。结构分析:强调句的正常语序是 the by-product of the institution was noted。considered as a directive factor in the conduct of the institution 作 this effect 的后置定语。

【译文】一种制度的副产品,只是逐步被注意到的,而这种效果被视为实施这种制度的一个指导性因素更加缓慢得多。

---

48. 【解析】本句考点:比较状语从句,动宾分隔。结构分析:本句主干是 while 引导的一个比较状语从句。in our contact with 作为一个插入成分,分隔了 ignore 和它的宾语 the effect。

【译文】在和他们(年轻人)接触的时候,虽然容易忽略我们的行动对他们的倾向的影响,但是也不像与成年人打交道那么简单。

---

49. 【解析】本句考点:since 引导的原因状语从句,代词指代,宾语从句,宾语从句嵌套定语从句。结构分析:本句主干是 Since... we cannot help considering... 其中 whether or no we are forming the powers which will secure this ability 作 cannot help considering 的宾语,which will secure this ability 作为嵌套定语从句修饰 the powers。

【译文】既然我们的主要任务在于使年轻人参与共同生活,我们禁不住考虑我们是否在形成获得这种能力的力量。

---

50. 【解析】本句考点:插入语,定语从句,同位语从句。结构分析:within the broad educational process which we have been so far considering 作为插入语,which we have been so far considering 作为定语从句修饰 process,本句主干是 We are thus led to distinguish a more formal kind of education。that of direct tuition or schooling 与 a more formal kind of education 是同位语关系。

【译文】因此,我们可以在上面所考虑的广阔的教育过程之内区别出一种比较正规的教育,即直接的教导或学校教育。

Section III　Writing

Part A

Dear Editor,

　　I am writing this letter to comment on the "white pollution" we are facing these days. Despite the government's ban on plastic tableware, disposable plastic bags and food containers are, for various reasons, still prevalent around the country. As we all know, "white pollution" inevitably results in considerable harm to people's health and the environment.

　　To address this problem, I would like to suggest the following. First, newspapers should launch a series of campaigns to discourage the use of plastic bags. Second, we should develop alternative biodegradable products to replace plastic. Finally, enhanced recycling should be the future means of dealing with one-off tableware pollution.

　　I hope you will find these suggestions practical. If you have any questions, please feel free to contact me.

Yours sincerely,
Li Ming

Part B

　　Perhaps no change has characterized the past decade more dramatically than the effect of the Internet on our daily life. The picture bears witness to this: a huge spider web symbolizing the Internet both isolates and unites people of different age, gender, and profession. Even those sitting immediately next to one another are interacting through the Internet, rather than face to face.

　　All the while when I see the tricky cartoon, the doubt flashed through my mind whether the Internet increases or decreases interpersonal contact. While the Internet makes possible our connection to people all over the world, one downside is that it occupies too much of our time with acquaintances. Studies show that excessive usage of the Internet is actually associated with a decline in people's communication with household family members, a decline in the size of their social circle, as well as an increase in depression and loneliness.

　　Based on above-mentioned points, I call this phenomenon the "Internet paradox", because the use of Internet, a technology meant for social contact, has actually led to a reduction in offline social ties. Naturally, the development of society inevitably brings side effects, but if this development has to be based on the cold isolation among people, I think the price is too high. Science and technology should serve the people, and the relationships between human beings should be prominent in society all the time. Couldn't we cherish the warmth between people?

第二部分
考研英语专项突破

第一章 英语知识运用——完形填空

第一节 考研完形填空高分全攻略概述

考研英语知识运用部分采用完形填空的题型,即 Cloze Test。Cloze 一词来源于 Closure. Closure 为西方完形心理学的核心内容,是指读者通过对一些不完全的视觉几何图形的认识和构思以获得完整概念的过程。试题设计者借这个意思,从一段文章中留出若干个单词,让应试者增补上去,以达到考查考生对文章的阅读理解和语言知识综合应用的能力。

根据 2005 年《硕士研究生入学考试英语考试大纲》(非英语专业)的规定,在一篇 240~280 个单词的文章中留出 20 个空白,计 10 分,要求考生从每题给出的 4 个选项中选出最佳答案,使补全后的文章意思通顺,前后连贯,结构完整。它并不完全是测试考生对语法规律和词汇、语义搭配等的识别能力,更重要的是要求考生具有一定的语篇分析能力、良好的语感和逻辑思维能力以及较广泛的背景知识。因此可以说完形填空首先检验的是阅读能力,是阅读理解的变体。

完形填空所选文章的难易程度适中,这样的文章在没有去掉要填的词之前对大多数考生来说阅读起来几乎没有困难。以下是 1990 年~2005 年的完形填空测试题的体裁和题材。

年份	体裁	题材
1990	说明性议论文	未来世界的面貌(the future world)
1991	说明性议论文	电视转播评论员(television commentators)
1992	议论文	美国的宇宙飞船(the US space shuttle)
1993	说明性议论文	室内设计(interior design)
1994	说明性议论文	交谈时遣词的重要性(the importance of the choice of words)
1995	说明文	睡眠的两个阶段(REM sleep and non-REM sleep)
1996	说明文	维生素(vitamins)
1997	说明性议论文	美国人力资源公司及其影响(the US manpower Inc. and its influence)
1998	议论文	英国工业革命(the Industrial Revolution)
1999	说明性议论文	劳动安全规划(industrial safety programs)
2000	说明文	农民的生产与生活(gap between a farmer's consumption and his production)
2001	说明文	国外新闻自由(press freedom)
2002	说明性议论文	通信业的革命(communication revolution)
2003	议论文	帮助青少年适应变化(adjust the change)
2004	议论文	青少年犯罪(juvenile delinquency)
2005	说明文	人类的鼻子(human nose)

从近十五年的完形填空题材来看,内容基本属于科普类或常识类,如:电视、媒体、出版、社会生活、医学、室内设计等。但是所选的文章不会太专业,避免让一少部分人凭常识答题。文章体裁以说明文或论说文为主,其语言特点是时态比较单一,句子结构不太复杂,词的重复率高。考查重点已从原先的语法项目转移到对整体语感的测试。选择词汇的项目增加了,词汇测试也从对基本词义的理解侧重到对次重要词义的理解、同义词辨析和词语搭配等方面的测试。

第二节　完形填空的命题规律

　　英语知识运用的前身是完形填空,从 2001 年后,试题的数量从原来的 10 题增加为 20 题,比重和难度都明显提高。它通常选自一篇长度约为 300 字的短文,覆盖的题材十分宽泛。纵观历年试题,它的内容包括社会、经济、政治、工业、农业、教育、新闻和法律等。

　　英语知识运用是在语篇的层次上考查学生运用英语的综合能力,考查的对象不仅包括语篇的语言要素(如词汇、结构和表达方式),而且还有语篇的上下文逻辑和连贯性,是微观和宏观的有机结合。简要概括起来,英语知识运用主要考查考生以下四种能力:

　　1.阅读理解能力,这主要体现在以下三个方面:从宏观方面看,考生应在短时间内把握短文的主旨和大意、作者的观点和态度;从微观方面看,考生要准确地理解短文的细节,即五大要素(when,where,what,why,how);最后在宏观和微观相结合的基础上,考生可能还需要对短文的某些点进行推断和延伸。

　　2.语篇处理能力,这包括段与段之间、句与句之间的连贯性以及词汇的同现和重现。

　　3.语法知识运用,这可以体现在三个层次:词法、句法和篇章的信息结构。词法主要考查动词的时态、语态、语气和非限定动词以及名词和代词的使用。句法主要考查三大类从句:名词性从句(包括主语从句、宾语从句、表语从句和同位语从句)、形容词性从句(定语从句)以及副词性从句(各类状语从句)。篇章的信息结构主要包括倒装、强调和省略等现象。

　　4.词语应用能力,这包括词语的辨析、搭配和固定搭配。词语的辨析既有近义词的辨析,又有近形词的辨析;词语的搭配包括主谓搭配、动宾搭配、动状搭配、形容词名词搭配以及形容词副词搭配等;固定搭配主要是介词与名词、动词以及形容词连用形成的固定词组。

　　完形填空题所选择的短文,一般语言难度适中、条理清楚。在没有抽掉 20 个词语前,大多数考生阅读起来没有多大困难;但由于命题时有目的地抽取词汇后会留下信息空白,如果语言知识不扎实、语感不强、或者没有掌握正确的答题技巧,就可能比较吃力。选文的条理比较清晰,从表一可以看出近十年来其体裁全部是论说性或说明性、解释性的语体。这是因为这类文章条理清楚,作者思路比较容易把握,估计这种趋势还会延续。

　　完形填空所选短文的题材广泛,但专业性不会太强,其内容应为绝大多数考生所熟悉。据统计,历届考研英语试题中,选文的题材主要取自社会生活、科普知识、经济常识和历史故事等四大类。从表一可以看出,近十年完形填空选材中社会生活题材占 80%,而科普知识只占 20%。

　　完形填空题在所选的短文中留出 20 个空,有 20 个词语被有目的地挖掉。从这些挖掉的词语可以看出英语知识运用对各层次的语言知识技能的考查要求。从表一可以看出,近十年来完形填空考查的词汇有:动词、名词、形容词、介词、连词、副词和代词。其中动词和名词是考查重点,约占一半以上。另外,抽掉的词当中涉及固定搭配的占到 30%～38%,并且呈上升趋势。由此可见,固定搭配也是考研复习的一个重点。

　　从表二可以看出,在完形填空题中,词汇知识的考查约占 70%(20 道题的平均约占 14 道题;10 道题的平均约占 7 道题),而语法、结构知识的考查只占 30%左右。

近十年英语知识运用试题体裁、题材和考点分布情况（表一）

试题分布	2005(20题)	2004(20题)	2003(20题)	2002(20题)	2001(20题)	2000(10题)	1999(10题)	1998(10题)	1997(10题)	1996(10题)	1995(10题)	百分比(%)
体裁	说明文	议论文	议论文	说明文	议论文	说明文	议论文	议论文	说明文	说明文	说明文	议论文60% 说明文40%
题材	人的嗅觉(科普知识)	青少年犯罪(社会生活)	教师教学(社会生活)	信息传播(社会生活)	新闻立法(社会生活)	农业生产(社会生活)	生产安全(社会生活)	工业革命(社会生活)	劳动就业(社会生活)	维生素(科普知识)	睡眠(科普知识)	社会生活80% 科普知识20%
动词	7	5	4	3	8	3	3	3	2	3	4	25%～30
名词	1	6	6	5	6	2	3	1	2	1	1	20%～30%
形容词	4	2	3	4	1	1	1	2	1	1	1	11%～13%
介词	2	1	2	3	2	2	1	2	1	0	2	约13%
连词	3	3	2	2	3	1	1	1	4	2	1	约13%
副词	3	2	2	3	0	1	1	2	1	2	0	7%～11%
代词	0	1	0	0	0	0	0	0	0	1	1	约1%
固定搭配	6	8	8	8	6	4	2	3	2	2	4	30%～38%

近十年英语知识运用试题考点分布情况（表二）

试题分布	2005(20题)	2004(20题)	2003(20题)	2002(20题)	2001(20题)	2000(10题)	1999(10题)	1998(10题)	1997(10题)	1996(10题)	1995(10题)	百分比(%)
词汇知识	15	15	13	14	15	7	7	8	7	7	8	约70%
语法与结构	5	5	7	6	5	3	3	2	3	3	2	约30%

第三节 完形填空的解题步骤

完形填空的基本步骤有三个，首先要通读全文，然后才能着手解题，最后要复读全文。对每部分的重点和要点作者在下文中有详述。

1. 通读全文

完形填空的短文一般都具有完整的主题思想，而且上下文之间有紧密的内在联系，逻辑关系清晰。文中所设的20个空，每一个空都与全文的内容息息相关。因此，考生必须抓住篇章的中心，从全文宏观的角度去分析每一个空。此外，对考生对语篇理解及全文的逻辑关系的考查的比重有逐年增加的趋势,因此掌握段落大意、文章的结构特点和主题思想是考生在做此类题时首先要考虑的问题。要求考生必须树立语篇意识,培养从语篇的全局考虑问题的能力。在通读全文的过程中,应首先仔细推敲文章的第一句,一方面因为,一般情况下,文章的首句中不设空,是一个完整的句子,有助于理解;另一方面,通常文章或者段落的首句是整篇文章的主题思想(Main Idea)或者是段落的主题句(Topic Sentence),对下文的理解有一定的帮助作用。而且,还要仔细研读文章的首段和尾段对了解文章的中心内容也很有帮助。在理清了全文的大概含义之后,要求考生对整篇文章的句法结构和写作风格进行初步判断,从而了解文章的题材、体裁、背景知识甚至于作者的写作手法和风格,这些对选择正确的答案都将会有所帮助。

2. 精读全文

在对文章的内容、题材、体裁和写作手法有所了解之后,结合全文的内容认真阅读四个选项,对那些较难的选项可以使用排除法逐一进行排除,从而选出最有可能的选项,增加答题的准确率。

3. 复读全文

在确定了所有答案之后,最好将各个词填到每个空上,然后再次通读全文。根据文章的主题思想,从整体分析的角度检查文章前后内容是否连贯、时态是否一致、语法结构是否合理等。完形填空题型侧重的是考生对语篇内容的理解,因此考生在学习和综合运用语言知识的同时,更应该注意培养阅读理解的能力,从而培养自己抽象思维的能力。

此外,除了上面提到的各个方面,尤其需要注意从以下几个方面进行检查:(1)文中代词的指代关系是否有误;(2)转折词的使用是否与全文的主题思想相符;(3)选择项前后文是否有重复使用的关键词或同义词。这样在应试的过程中从全局出发可以避免犯一些不应有的错误。

第四节   完形填空解题方法

一、用"无关词排除法"解完形填空题

完形文章一般都有非常明确的中心主线,且整个文章很紧凑,就是紧紧围绕着中心主线展开。因此,理论上正确的选项一定是紧扣文章的主题和中心主线的。故而,一些看上去明显和文章主题和中心主线毫无关系的选项基本上可以排除在正确答案之外。

经典例题 **2001 年考研完形试题的第 35 题**

"bill that will propose making payments to witnesses(34 illegal) and will strictly control the a-mount of ___35___ that can be given to a case"

35. [A]publicity   [B]penalty   [C]popularity   [D]peculiarity

答案:[A]publicity

分析:此题可以应用"无关词排除法"。本题所考查的名词处于这样一个句子结构中:作为 control 的宾语;后边还受到一个定语从句的限制。根据文章的主题,可以发现 3 个选项[B]penalty(惩罚)、[C]popularity(流行度)、[D]peculiarity(古怪度)与文章的主题根本无关,政府不可能去控制这些东西。政府要控制的是选项[A]publicity(公开度)。

二、用"同现"的方法解完形填空题

同现是一种词汇的衔接手段。完形文章由于常常有明确的中心主线,所以作者往往会使用一些重点词汇围绕着中心主线贯穿全文。同现实际上就是一组具有相同倾向性的词语,这些词语所表现的倾向性往往与中心主线中的导向要一致,或者说这些同现词语的任务就是对文章的导向进行展开支持。因此,文章的整体导向这个已知线索可以成为解出这些同现词语的关键信息。

经典例题 **1995 年考研完形试题的第 43 题**

"Sleep is divided into periods of so-called REM sleep, characterized by rapid eye movements and dreaming, and longer periods of non-REM sleep. (41 Neither) kind of sleep is at all well-understood, but REM sleep is ___42___ to serve some restorative function of the brain. The purpose of non-REM sleep is even more ___43___ ."

43. [A] subtle　　　　[B]obvious　　　　[C]mysterious　　　　[D]doubtful

答案：[C] mysterious

分析：此篇文章有非常明确的中心主线。文章首句 — Sleep is divided into periods of so-called REM sleep, characterized by rapid eye movements and dreaming, and longer periods of non-REM sleep.(睡眠分为两种:REM sleep 和非 REM sleep),探讨两种睡眠就是本文的主题。下一句 — 41(答案:Neither) kind of sleep is at all well-understood(两种睡眠都没有被很好地理解),这就是文章的基本导向。

FOUCS (主题):有关两种睡眠的问题。

中心主线 — 文章导向:两种睡眠都没有被很好地理解。

本题考查形容词的辨析,需要考生从 4 个形容词中挑出一个最佳的修饰 non-REM sleep 的目的。但如果仅根据本题所在句子的已知信息是不足以解出题的,还需要在本句之外寻找其他与本题相关的已知信息才可以。这个信息就在本文的总起句所表现的文章导向中:两种睡眠都没有被很好地理解,后面的分述要服从这个导向。所以,本题的 non-REM sleep 既然是两种睡眠中的一种,其目的当然应该不被理解,即 [C] mysterious(神秘的)。本题是很常见的"同现"现象。

三、用"复现"的方法解完形填空题

复现是完形文章中词汇的另一种衔接手段,即表达相同意思的词汇在文章的不同地方出现。复现可以是相同的词重复出现,也可以是用不同的词表示相同的意思。复现的解题意义在于:如果判断出一个未知填空与上下文的那些已知词汇有复现关系,只要从选项中选出与那些词汇同样意义的就是正确答案。

四、用"关联"的方法解完形填空题

关联是完形文章中经常出现的一种结构,即将两个或两个以上的同类别词语,比如两个动词、两个形容词,以连续排比性的结构出现。在这种情况下,两个关联词汇在句子中的语法地位一样,且常常起一样的语法作用,之间又明显具有某种逻辑关系。关联的解题意义在于:出题人一般会将一个关联词语设置成已知信息,另一个是未知的,这样那个已知的词语就会成为破解未知词语的关键线索。

经典例题　1999 年完形试题的第 42 题

"Companies (41with) low accident rates plan their safety programs, work hard to organize them, and continue working to keep them ___42___ and active."

42. [A]alive　　[B]vivid　　[C]mobile　　[D] diverse

答案：[A]alive

分析：从本题所处的句子结构来看,to keep them ___42___ and active,本题的选项受到两个已知信息点的控制:一个是对 them 起修饰作用;再有是与后边的另一个形容词 active 之间形成并列的关联关系,而且形容词 active 同样也是修饰 them。从这两个信息点来看,能够同时满足这两点的选项是[A]alive,表示 them(safety programs 安全制度)是既 alive(有效)又 active(被广泛执行)。选项[B]vivid(栩栩如生的)和[C]mobile(移动的)与被修饰成分 them(safety programs 安全制度)之间根本就没有同质性,构不成修饰关系;而[D]diverse(多种多样的)虽然可以修饰 them,但与 active 没有关联关系。

经典例题　2002 年完形试题的第 33 题

"As time went by, computers became smaller and more powerful, and they became 'personal' too, as well as ___33___ ."

33. [A] institutional　　　[B] universal　　　[C] fundamental　　　[D] instrumental

答案：[A]institutional

分析：本题所考查的形容词用来修饰 they 即 computers,而在本题之前文章中已经有下列 3 个形容词修饰了 computers,本题只是前面 3 个形容词的延续:

$$computers\ became \begin{cases} smaller \\ powerful \\ personal \\ \underline{\quad 33 \quad} \end{cases}$$

实际上前边 3 个已知的形容词就是 33 题的关联成分,通过分析这 3 个已知形容词的特征就可以确定本题的答案。smaller / powerful / personal 这 3 个词首先都是修饰计算机本身的变化,而且其导向都是指计算机变得越来越容易使用(easier to use);因此,33 题我们也要挑选一个具有此特征的词。选项[C]fundamental(根本的,本质上的)和[B]universal(普遍的)不能用来修饰 computers,两者没有同质性。选项[D]instrumental(仪器的)不具有前 3 个形容词的特征,没有表述出计算机变得好用这个概念。只有选项[A]institutional(制度化的)在此处形容计算机变得模块化了,因而有统一的装配和操作标准,也就意味着 computers became easier to use。

五、利用"时间线索"解完形填空题

完形文章中出现的时间信息一般都是非常有用的线索,因为只要通过分析这些时间线索就可以很快把握与这些时间线索联系在一起的信息之间的关系。

经典例题 **1998 年完形试题的第 46 题**

"But they insisted that its(指工业革命) __43__ results during the period from 1750 to 1850 were widespread poverty and misery for the __44__ of the English population. __45__ contrast, they saw in the preceding hundred years from 1650 to 1750,when England was still a __46__ agricultural country, a period of great abundance and prosperity."

43. [A]momentary   [B]prompt

[C]instant   [D]immediate

46. [A]broadly   [B]thoroughly

[C]generally   [D]completely

43. **答案:**[D] immediate

分析:本题考查形容词的词义辨析,关键要注意的已知信息点是后边的一个时间段—during the period from 1750 to 1850。正是这个时间段决定了不可能选择[A]momentary、[B]prompt 以及[C]instant 这三个均表示"时间短"的词。而 immediate 除了立即的含义外,还包括逻辑上的"直接"的意思,本题在这里就是要表达工业革命"直接的结果"这个意思,所以[D] immediate 为最佳选项。

46. **答案:**[D] completely

分析:本题考查副词的词义辨析,主要是在表示绝对性的[B]thoroughly(彻底地)、[D]completely(完全地)和表示相对性的[C]generally(通常地,总体上地)之间做一个选择。解出本题的关键是要根据文章的已知信息分析出"英国是完全的农业国还是总体上的农业国"。做这个分析的关键信息是时间线索。文章给出了两个时间段:

1650   1750   1850

没有发生工业革命(英国社会没有工业因素)	发生了工业革命(英国社会有了工业因素)

此时间段内英国为完全的农业国

根据上述分析,应该选择表示"英国是完全的农业国"的选项。[B]thoroughly 是指细节上的彻底,而[D]completely 是指整体上的完全,显然[D]completely 更为合适。

六、利用"总分结构对照分析法"解完形填空题

由于总分之间的基本关系是互相支持,互相印证的对照关系,而且总述是对分述的总结和概括,而分述是对总述的展开。当一些未知填空出现在总述句时,解出这些填空的相关联已知线索往往可以在与其对应的分述部分找到。

经典例题　2000 年考研试题的第 47 题 — 应用于形容词的例子

"If no surplus is available, a farmer cannot be ___47___ . He must either sell some of his property or (48 seek)extra funds in form of loans. Naturally he will try to borrow money at a low (49 rate)of interest, but loans of this kind are not ___50___ obtainable."

47. [A]self-confident　　　　　　　[B]self-sufficient

[C]self-satisfied　　　　　　　　 [D]self-restrained

答案：[B]self-sufficient

分析：本题处在一个总述句中：If no surplus is available, a farmer cannot be ___47___ 。在此句话之前，文章都是在讲 If surplus is available(有盈余的情况下)，农民的生活如何；实际上，从文章结构来看，从本题开始出现了另一个意群，而 If no surplus is available, a farmer cannot be ___47___ 为这个意群的总述句，即如果没有盈余，农民会怎样？所以，仅仅看本题所在的句子所包含的已知信息是不够的，还要看其他地方的相关已知信息，这个关键的相关已知信息就在分述部分；因为总述部分是对分述部分的高度概括，只要总结出分述部分，本题答案迎刃而解。

总述部分：If no surplus is available, a farmer can not be ___47___

分述部分：... sell some of his properties ...

... loans...

... borrow money at a low ___49___ of interest ...

总结一下分述部分很容易判断出 47 题的答案一定是[B]self-sufficient，因为总述句中的 not be self-sufficient 恰恰是对分述的最佳概括。

经典例题　1999 年考研试题的第 45 题 — 应用于动词的例子

"Successful safety programs may ___45___ greatly in the emphasis placed on certain aspects of the program. Some place great emphasis on mechanical guarding. Others stress safe work practices by (46 observing)rules or regulations. (47 Still) others depend on an emotional appeal to the worker. But, there are certain basic ideas that must be used in every program if maximum results are to be obtained."

45. [A]alter　　　[B]differ　　　[C] shift　　　[D] distinguish

答案：[B]differ

分析：45 题所考查的动词处于本段的总述句中，既然分述所做的是"秉承总述的旨意"，我们通过分析分述的内容可以倒推出总述的意思。

通过分述可以总结出"3 种都是成功的安全项目(主语)"做的动作都是"将重点放置于(谓语)"，"但所放置的点不同(宾语)"。由此分述总结出总述句的主语 Successful safety programs 所要做的动作(45 题)就是"differ"。

经典例题　2002 年考研试题的第 21 题 — 甚至可以应用于介词

Comparisons were drawn between the development of television in the 20th century and the diffusion of printing in the 15th and 16th centuries. Yet much had happened ___21___. As was discussed before, it was not (22) the 19th century that the newspaper became the dominant pre-electronic (23), following in the wake of the pamphlet and the book and in the (24) of the periodical. It was during the same time that the communications revolution (25) up, beginning with transport, the railway, and leading (26) through the telegraph, the telephone, radio, and motion pictures (27) the 20th-century world of the motor car and the air plane. Not everyone sees that process in (28). It is important to do so.

21. [A]between　　　[B]before　　　[C]since　　　[D]later

答案：between

分析：本题所考查的介词处于文章的总述部分 — "作者要在两个时间阶段之间做比较。然后说：但是很多事情发生了"。再去总结分述部分 — "文章首段讲 19 世纪出现了许多信息产品"，正好支持总述的 much had happened，19 世纪处于两个时间段之间，答案一定是 between。

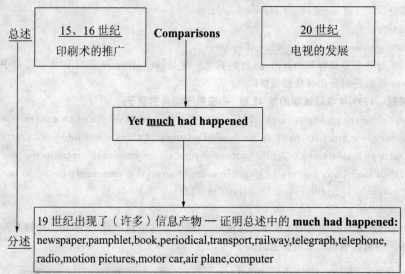

七、使用"对应成分分析法"解完形填空题

由于完形文章的上下文之间，以及句子内部之间往往有着一定的逻辑关系从而句子的各个成分之间形成一定的对应关系，考生可以根据这种逻辑关系找出与未知填空相对应的已知成分作为线索，通过对应的已知成分从而推断出未知填空的答案。

(一)应用于句子内部

经典例题　1996 年完形试题的第 45 题

"Vitamins are similar because they are made of the same elements—usually carbon, hydrogen, oxygen, and ___45___ nitrogen."

45. [A] mostly　　　[B] partially　　　[C] sometimes　　　[D] rarely

答案：[C] sometimes

分析：本题是一个典型的可以应用"对应成分分析法"解出的题：

从上述分析可以看出，45 题与 usually 形成对应关系：因为 usually 是频度副词，所以 45 题起码要选择频度副词，可以马上排除不是频度副词的选项 [A] mostly 和 [B] partially。[D] rarely(很少)虽然是频度副词，但由于 45 题与 usually 之间是 and 并列的逻辑关系，而 rarely 与 usually 是转折对立的

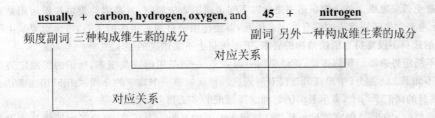

关系,所以不对。只有[C] sometimes,既是频度副词,又可以与 usually 形成并列的逻辑关系。

(二)应用于上下句之间

经典例题　1996 年完形试题的第 46 题

"Vitamins are similar because they are made of the same elements-usually carbon, hydrogen, oxygen, and 45 nitrogen. They are different ___46___ their elements are arranged differently"

46. [A] in that　　[B] so that　　[C] such that　　[D] except that

答案:[A] in that

分析:本题应用"对应成分分析法",分析如下:本题所在的这句话的句子结构与本段的第一句的结构一模一样:

Vitamins are similar　　　　　because　　they are made of the same elements

↓　　　　　　　　　　　　　　　↓　　　　　　　↓

They(指代 Vitamins)are different　　46　　their elements are arranged differently

通过上述分析,可以非常明确地看出 46 题与上句中的 because 形成对应,也就是说 46 题再选出一个表示 because 的选项,答案为[A] in that。

经典例题　1996 年完形试题的第 49 题

"(48 Getting)enough vitamins is essential to life, although the body has no nutritional use for ___49___ vitamins."

49. [A] exceptional [B] exceeding [C] excess [D] external

答案:[C] excess

分析:本题可应用"对应成分分析法",分析如下:本题需要选出一个修饰 vitamins 的形容词,我们发现前边的从句中也有一个修饰 vitamins 的形容词 enough,而且前后两句有着明确的逻辑关系 — 让步关系的主从句。

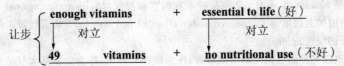

让步 { **enough vitamins** ＋ **essential to life**(好)
　　　　　　对立　　　　　　　　　对立
49　**vitamins**　＋　**no nutritional use**(不好) }

通过上述分析,可以非常明确地看出 49 题与上句中的 enough 形成对应成分,而且两者为对立的关系,所以本题的答案就是去 4 个选项中找一个与 enough 对立的选项即可,[C] excess 是 enough 的对立选项,故为正确答案。

第五节　完形填空得分要领

要做好英语知识运用,以下四个方面是禁忌:

1. 切忌边读边做题。有的考生为了节省时间,边读边做题,如此做法对文章没有宏观的认识,把握不住语篇的连贯性和逻辑关系,结果是断章取义,一错再错,本来想事半功倍,结果适得其反。

2. 避免孤立思维。英语知识运用之所以不同于词汇语法填空,就是因为英语知识运用是在语篇的层次上考查学生运用英语的综合能力。因此,即使选项是对词汇语法的考查,考生也要从上下文入手,对词的选择不仅要符合语法结构的要求,更要满足上下文语义的要求。

3. 不能定势思维。我们知道,英语单词一词多义、一词多用的现象很多,所谓的思维定势就是只知其一,不知其二。翻开《牛津高阶英汉双解词典》,你就知道一个简单的介词:"with"用法多达 16 种,因此在平时的词汇学习中,考生要多了解和掌握词汇的多义和多用现象。

4. 不要忘记复读。做完题目后复读是被很多考生忽视的一个环节,有的考生即使复读也是流于形式,但是不要忘记英语知识运用来源于一篇完整的短文,我们的答案应该还短文以原貌。因此,只有有意识地复读整篇文章,才能感悟出所选答案是否和文章匹配、上下文是否自相矛盾、语篇连贯是否顺畅,复读决定了哪些选项应该重新考虑。

第六节　完形填空常考词汇及语法

真题冲浪

accommodate　　　　　　　　　　　　　　　考点:同义复现

And they also need to give serious thought to how they can best _____ changes. Growing bodies need movement and exercise, but not just in ways that emphasize competition. Because they are adjusting to their new bodies and a whole host of new intellectual and emotional challenges,...(2003−22)

[A]strengthen
[B]accommodate
[C]stimulate
[D]enhance

【解析】选[B]本题是动词词义的辨析,四个词意思分别是:strengthen"加强";accommodate"使适应,调节";stimulate "刺激,激励";enhance"增强,提高"。从空格后的 changes 可知,只有 accommodate 词义符合。实际上,下文中 adjust to (调整)是一个提示线索,accommodate 与该词组构成同义复现。

【题意】他们(教师)同样需要认真考虑他们(学生)怎样才能最好地适应这些变化。发育中的身体需要运动和锻炼,而不仅是为了竞技,因为总是要适应新的身体状况、智力和情感方面的诸多新的挑战。

真题冲浪

against　　　　　　　　　　　　考点:固定搭配、前照后应

He must use this surplus in three ways: as seed for sowing, as insurance _____ the unpredictable effects of bad weather and...(2000−43)

[A]for　　[B]against
[C]of　　[D]towards

【解析】选[B]。insurance 后面的介词可以是 for,表示为某种好事物投保,如:insurance for life(人寿保险);也可以是 against,表示为了防范某种不利因素而投保,如:insurance against accident(事故保险)。本句空格后面的名词短语 the unpredictable effect of bad weather (坏天气带来的难以预料的影响)说明这里的介词应选 against。

【题意】他应该以三种途径使用剩余的粮食:作为播种的种子,作为防备坏天气造成的难以预料的影响……

真题冲浪

against　　　　　　　　　　考点:对比关系

"Benefits"have been weighed _____ "harmful" outcomes.(2002−40)

[A]above　　[B]upon
[C]against　　[D]with

【解析】选[C]。本题测试介词和动词的搭配,解题线索是动词 weigh,weigh... against...是固定搭配,意为"认真考虑,权衡",前后比较的常常是两种不同或相反的东西,例如:weigh one plan against another(权衡一个计划与另一个计划的优劣)。如果考生没有记住这个固定搭配,也可以将空格前后的 benefits 和 harmful outcomes 两个短语作为解题线索。这两个短语意义相对,四个选项中能体现此种相对关系的只有 against。

【题意】利益同有害的后果已经权衡过。

真题冲浪

alive

考点:近义同现

Companies with low accident rates plan their safety programs, work hard to organize them _____ and continue working to keep them and active.(1999-42)

[A]alive　　[B]vivid
[C]mobile　[D]diverse

【解析】选[A]。本题测试形容词辨析,alive"有活力的,有生气的";vivid"生动,逼真";mobile"灵活的,流动的";diverse"不同的,纷杂的"。根据句中线索词 and 可知空白处的词与 active 应是平行并列结构,词义上互为补充,应是 active 的近义词复现,由此能断定选项[A]alive 正确,并且从意义上来说,用 alive 一词修饰 them(programs)更合适。

【题意】事故率低的公司制定自己的安全计划,努力组织好这些计划,并继续努力以确保这些计划不断发挥积极作用。

真题冲浪

although

考点:转折同现

All these conditions tend to increase the probability of a child committing a criminal act, _____ a direct causal relationship has not yet been established.(2004-40)

[A]provided
[B]since
[C]although
[D]supposing

【解析】选[C]。本题考查对上下文逻辑的判断和对连接词的理解,从上下文所列的因素看,都是一些外在因素,而后半部分提到 a direct causal relationship has not yet been established(导致青少年犯罪的直接原因目前还无法确定),由此可判断出上下文的逻辑关系为转折关系,只有 although 一词能连接另外一个句子表示转折的意义。

【题意】虽然一种直接的偶然关系并未成立,但所有的这些条件都有助于增加一个孩子犯罪的可能性。

真题冲浪

although

考点:让步关系

It is generally recognized, however, that the introduction of the computer in the early 20th century, followed by the invention of the integrated circuit during the 1960s. radically changed the process, _____ its impact on the media was not immediately apparent.(2002-31)

[A]unless
[B]since
[C]lest
[D]although

【解析】选[D]。本题测试连词的用法,可根据上下文的逻辑关系来判断。这是一个多重复合句,句子的主干部分是主语从句:it is... that...,其中又包含另一个复合句。由上文中的 radically changed(大大改变)及本句中的 not immediately... 不难看出,连词的前后分句表示相对、相反内容,即电脑大大改变了这一进程,尽管它对媒体的影响没有立刻显现出来,故只有 although 正确。其他选项:unless"除非",引导条件状语从句;since"自从;既然",引导时间或原因状语从句;lest"以防,惟恐",引导目的状语从句。

【题意】然而,人们广泛地意识到,20 世纪初电脑的出现及随后 60 年代集成电路的产生虽然对媒体没有立竿见影的效果,但是也完全改变了这一过程。

真题冲浪

any

There are thirteen or more of them, and if _____ is missing a deficiency disease becomes apparent.(1996-43)

[A]any　　[B]some
[C]anything　[D]something

【解析】选[A]。空白处前面的"thirteen of them"说明空白处的代词代替的是可数名词,而空格后面的 is 又限定了该词应是单数形式,所以只有 any(任何一种)正确,any 后面省略了 of them。"any(of + 名词)"这一结构常用于 if 从句或疑问句中。

【题意】这些维生素有 13 种以上,如果缺少其中 1 种便会出现明显的维生素缺乏症。

真题冲浪

as　　　　　　　　　　　　　　　　　　　考点:结构同现/引导定语从句

One day at a time ____ industrial giants like General Motors and IBM struggle to survive by reducing the number of employees, Manpower, based in Milwaukee, Wisconsin, is booming. (1997-42)

[A]for
[B]because
[C]as
[D]since

【解析】选[C]。本题可根据前后出现的提示词来做出判断,四个选项都可以表示原因,引导原因状语从句。但根据上下文,可知句间不存在因果关系,而是时间上的对比关系,这一点也可从句中的线索词 time 得出结论,所以空白处缺的是一个引导定语从句的词,四个选项中只有[C]as(相当于 when)有此功能。

【题意】当像通用公司和 IBM 这样的工业巨头靠裁员以求生存之时,位于威斯康星州密尔沃基市的 Manpower 公司正在蓬勃发展。

真题冲浪

as　　　　　　　　　　　　　　　　　　　考点:虚拟语气推断

The rats develop bacterial infections of the blood, ____ their immune systems—the self-rotecting mechanism against diseases—had crashed.(1995-50)

[A]if
[B]as if
[C]only if
[D]if only

【解析】选[B]。本题测试连接词,四个选项中的连词都和 if 有关。正确区分这四个连词的含义是本题的关键,as if(似乎,看起来);only if(只有);if only(但愿),用于没有主句的虚拟语气中,表示期望或愿望。根据句子的含义以及主句时态(现在时 develop)和从句中的时态对比(过去完成时 had crashed),这显然是一个虚拟语气,可知 as if 符合题意。

【题意】老鼠患上了病毒感染疾病,看起来它们的免疫系统——自我防御疾病的机制已经被彻底破坏了。

真题冲浪

Because　　　　　　　　　　　　　　　　考点:前因后果

____ they are adjusting to their new bodies and a whole host of new intellectual and emotional challenges, teenagers are especially self-onscious... (2003-24)

[A]If
[B]Although
[C]Whereas
[D]Because

【解析】选[D]。本句的前部分是在重述上文提到的青少年所面临的问题,后半句则提到青少年的普遍的心理状态,由此可推断它们之间的逻辑关系应该是"问题"是产生该"心理状态"的原因。而选项中只有 because 表示因果关系,引导表示原因的从句,符合题意。而如果选 if 引导条件句,则主句的一般现在时态与此不符,逻辑也不符;although 引导的是让步或转折句;whereas(然而;但是;相反)则引导转折句,例如:They want a house, whereas we would rather live in a flat.(他们想要一座房子,而我们宁愿住公寓里。)

【题意】由于他们要不断适应自己新的身体变化和许多智力和情感方面新的挑战,青少年自我意识特别强。

真题冲浪

because　　　　　　　　　　　　　　　　考点:因果关系

Theories centering on the individual suggest that children engage in criminal behavior ____ they were not sufficiently penalized for previous misdeeds.(2004-22)

[A]before
[B]unless
[C]until
[D]because

【解析】选[D]。本题考查考生对上下文逻辑关系的判断和对连词的正确理解。因为上文提到 children engage in criminal behavior(孩子实施犯罪),而紧接着的下文提到 they were not sufficiently penalized for previous misdeeds(对他们以前所犯的过失没有给予严厉惩罚),从这两句的意思来判断,两部分属于因果关系,而后半部分叙述的是原因,所以正确选项是[D]because。

【题意】强调个人影响的理论认为,孩子犯罪是因为他们以前的过失没有受到严厉处罚。

真题冲浪

before　　　　　　　　　　　　　　　　　考点:逻辑时间关系

In a significant tightening of legal controls over the press, Lord Irvine, the Lord Chancellor, will introduce a draft bill that will propose making payments to witnesses illegal and will strictly control the amount of publicity that can be given to a case ＿＿＿ a trial begins.(2001−36)

[A]since
[B]if
[C]before
[D]as

【解析】选[C]。本题测试连接词的用法。这是一个主从复合句。主句很长,句意是"……严格控制案件的曝光程度。"从句很短,意思是"审理开始"。根据主从句的含义可以看出,主句和从句表示时间上的先后关系,因此需要填入一个引导时间状语从句的连词。since(自……以来),as(当……的时候),before(在……之前)都可以引导时间状语从句,但前两个意思不符合,只有 before 可以表示时间上的先后关系。

【题意】为加强对新闻界的法律监督,上院议长艾尔文爵士将提出一项法律草案,提议把向证人付款的行为定为非法,并将严格控制在审理开始前案件的曝光程度。

真题冲浪

between　　　　　　　　　　　　　　　　考点:原词复现

Comparisons were drawn between the development of television in the 20th century and the diffusion of printing in the 15th and 16th centuries. Yet much had happened ＿＿＿.(2002−21)

[A]between
[B]before
[C]since
[D]later

【解析】选[A]。Yet 一词表明了本句是对前一句内容的转折,前一句讲人们对 20 世纪电视的发展和 15 世纪、16 世纪印刷术的传播进行了比较。其中的 between 一词点明了对比的时间,在这期间(而不是以前或以后)又发生了很多事情。同时,上一句中出现的 19 世纪也确定了本题应选择 between。实际上 between 后面相当于省略了时间 the 20th century and the 15th, 16th century。

【题意】人们对 20 世纪电视的发展和 15 世纪、16 世纪印刷术的传播进行了比较。但是,这期间发生了很大的变化。

真题冲浪

capability　　　　　　　　　　　　　　　考点:结构同现

＿＿38＿＿, they can help students acquire a sense of commitment by planning for roles that are within their ＿＿40＿＿ and their attention spans and by having clearly stated rules.(2003−38,40)

38.[A]On the contrary 　　[B]On the average
　　[C]On the whole 　　　[D]On the other hand

40.[A]capabilities 　　　　[B]responsibilities
　　[C]proficiency 　　　　[D]efficiency

【解析】选[A];[A]。这两题考查的内容都同介词短语有关。on the contrary"正相反";on the average "平均";on the whole"大体上";on the other hand"另一方面"。从上文可知,此句和上一句形成对比,所以 on the contrary 符合。第二个空实际上就是考一个固定搭配,即 within one's capability"在某人的能力范围内"(反义词是 beyond one's capability"超过某人的能力")。

【题意】相反,他们能够帮助学生通过制定明确的规则,为他们力所能及和在注意力范围之内的角色做计划,来获得责任感。

真题冲浪

capacity　　　　　　　　　　　　　　　考点:修饰同现

As time went by, computers became smaller and more powerful, and they became "personal" too, as well as institutional, with display becoming sharper and storage ＿＿＿ increasing. (2002−34)

[A]ability
[B]capability
[C]capacity
[D]faculty

【解析】选[C]。本题可以根据特殊用法和习惯搭配来判断,这四个词不仅词形相似,而且词义基本相同,四个词都可以表示"能力"。但是 capacity 一词还有一个特殊含义"容量",正好同空格前的

storage 一词构成习惯搭配,意思是"储存容量"。对于很多同义词的区分,考生可以从其特殊用法和固定搭配来判断。

【题意】随着时光飞逝,计算机变得更小,功能更强大,而随着显示器变得更清晰和储存容量不断增加,它们变得既适用于个人,也适用于公共机构。

真题冲浪

center   考点:同义复现

Many theories concerning the causes of juvenile delinquency (crimes committed by young people) focus either on the individual or on society as the major contributing influence. Theories _____ on the individual suggest that children engage in criminal behavior because they were not sufficiently penalized for previous misdeeds or that they have learned criminal behavior through interaction with others. Theories focusing on the role of society suggest that... (2004—21)

[A]acting
[B]relying
[C]centering
[D]commenting

【解析】选[C]。选项中的四个动词都可以与空格后的 on 搭配。act on"作用于;按照……行事";rely on "依赖";comment on"评价";center on"集中于,以……为中心"。根据句意,只有[C]符合逻辑。实际上,center on 是上一句话和下面这一句话中的同义词组 focus on 的同义复现。

【题意】许多论述青少年犯罪原因的理论都把个人或社会视为其主要影响因素。强调个人影响的理论认为,孩子们犯罪是因为他们以前的过失行为没有受到严厉的处罚,或是由于他们受到其他人的影响而染上了这些行为。强调社会影响的理论认为……

真题冲浪

channel   考点:修饰同现

He may also need money to construct irrigation ___46___ and improve his farm in other ways. If no surplus is available, a farmer cannot be ___47___. 近义同现 He must either sell some of his 语义场同现 property or ___48___ extra funds in the form of loans. Naturally he will try to borrow money at a low ___49___ of interest,...(2000—46,47,48,49) 惯用搭配

46.[A]verssels   [B]routes
   [C]paths   [D]channels
47.[A]self-confident [B]self-sufficient
   [C]self-satisfied [D]self-restrained
48.[A]search   [B]save
   [C]offer   [D]seek
49.[A]proportion   [B]percentage
   [C]rate   [D]ratio

【解析】这四道题都是测试同义词、近义词或形近词的辨析。

46.选[D]。本题考查名词近义词的辨析,可以根据习惯搭配来判断。vessel"船只";route"路线";path"小路,道路";channel"渠道",可指海峡、航道、频道、途径和沟渠。因此,只有 channel 能够和前面的 irrigation 搭配。

47.选[B]。本题考查形容词的形近词辨析。这几个形容词都包含前缀 self-,本题可以根据前后的提示词来判断。四个选项代入句子分别意为"如果没有剩余,农民就不能(自信/自给自足/自我满足/自我克制)"。前面分句中的 surplus 是提示词,根据句意,只有[B]符合逻辑。

48.选[D]。本题测试动词近义词的辨析,可以根据上下文语义和习惯搭配来判断。从本句前一部分的 sell... property 可知,[B]、[C]两项不符合语义。search 和 seek 都可表示"寻找"的意思,但前者侧重指搜寻某物,不与 funds 搭配,而 seek funds 是常用的习惯搭配。

49.选[C]。本题测试名词同义词的辨析,可以根据习惯搭配来判断。这四个名词都含有"比率或比例"的含义:proportion"比例";percentage"百分比";ratio"比率",一般指两方之间的比率。空格后的 of interest 表明只有 rate 符合,因为 rate of interest 是固定短语,表示"利率",其他选项都不能与 interest 形成搭配。

【题意】他可能还需要钱来修建灌溉渠和用其他方式改善农田。如果没有剩余,农民就不能自给自足。他要么出售财产,要么用贷款的方式设法得到额外资金。他自然会设法低息贷款……

真题冲浪

claim 考点:语义场同现	48.[A]comes off [B]turns upe
There can be no question about the value of a safety pro- gram. From a financial standpoint alone, safety ___48___ . The fewer the injury ___49___ , the better the workman's insurance rate. (1999-48,49) **语义场同现**	[C]pays off [D]holds up 49.[A]claims [B]reports [C]declarations [D]proclamations

【解析】

48.选[C]。四个选项词组的意思分别是:come off"(计划,企图)成功";turn up"出现,露面";pay off "还清债务;有收益";hold up"支撑,继续"。前一句中的 value(价值)一词及本句中的关键词 finan-cial 说明空白处所填词汇应与经济价值有关,故 pays off 正确。pay off 与前文的 value,financial 属于同一语义场。

49.选[A]。本句是和保险(insurance)有关的语义,四个选项中只有 claims(索赔)与 insurance 属同一语义概念。其他三项:reports"报告";declarations"宣布,宣告";proclamations"宣言"都不符合。

【题意】安全措施的价值毋庸置疑。单从经济角度来看,安全也会带来效益。因为工伤索赔次数越少,工人的保险率就越高。

真题冲浪

consequently 考点:因果关系,前因后果	[A]contrarily
Families have also experienced changes these years. More families consist of one-parent households or two working parents; _____, children are likely to have less supervision at home than was common in the traditional family structure.(2004-34)	[B]consequently [C]similarly [D]simultaneously

【解析】选[B]。本题的解答要借助于句子间的逻辑关系来确定。上文提到更多的家庭只有一个大人管家或者父母两人都上班,接着说孩子们在家中所受到的监督就比传统家庭结构中所受到的监督少得多。显然,后一句是前一句的结果,为因果关系。所以,只有 consequently(结果,因此)符合文意。其他选项:contrarily"相反地,反之";similarly"同样地";simultaneously"同时地"。

【题意】这些年家庭也经历了变化,更多的家庭只有一个大人管家或者父母两人都上班;结果,孩子们在家中所受到的监督就比传统家庭结构中所受到的监督少得多。

真题冲浪

context 考点:同义复现	[A]context
It was within the computer age that the term "information society"began to be widely used to describe the _____ within which we now live.(2002-37)	[B]range [C]scope [D]territory

【解析】选[A]。本题测试名词的词义,context 是一个多义词,常用的意思是"上下文,前后关系",该词还有另一个不常用的含义,即"(背景事件发生于其中的)环境"。根据句意,该含义符合,正好同前文的 society 构成同义复现,并且和介词 within 构成搭配。其他三个词含义不符:range"范围";scope"范围";territory"地域,领土"。本题考查的正是 context 这个常用的词不常用含义。

【题意】正是在计算机时代,"信息社会"这个词开始广泛地用来描述我们现在所生活的环境。

真题冲浪

contrast 考点:惯用搭配	[A]On
_____ contrast, they saw in the preceding hundred years from 1650 to 1750, when England was still a completely agricultural country, a period of great abun- dance and prosperity.(1998-45)	[B]With [C]For [D]By

【解析】选[D]。本题测试介词短语的固定搭配。四个选项中能和空格后的名词搭配的只有 by。by/in contrast 意思是"相比之下"。

【题意】与此相比,他们视过去的一百年(即从 1650 年至 1750 年这段时期)为繁荣昌盛时期,那时的英国还完全是一个农业国家。

真题冲浪

ensure　　　　　　　　　　　　　考点:动宾搭配

Concerns were raised that witnesses might be encouraged to exaggerate their stories in court to ＿＿＿ guilty verdicts. (2001−50)

[A] assure
[B] confide
[C] ensure
[D] guarantee

【解析】选[C]。本题测试动词同义词的辨析,可以根据同义词的特殊用法来选择。confide 意为"信任,吐露",常用作 confide sth. to sb.,因此在意义上和形式上都不能同 guilty verdicts 搭配。其他三个词是同义词:assure"使……确信",后面一般接人:assure sb. that... 或 assure sb. of...;本题空格后是物(guilty verdicts),ensure 意为"确保,保证",后面一般接物:ensure sth. 或 ensure that...;guarantee 意为"保证,担保",强调"保证产品的质量或保证履行服务或义务"。从这三个同义词的用法可知,本题答案应为 ensure。

【题意】人们担心证人可能会受到怂恿而在法庭上夸大其词,以确保获得有罪判决。

真题冲浪

entitle　　　　　　　　考点:对比关系

...everybody was ＿＿＿ to privacy... (2001−45)

[A] assure　　[B] confide
[C] ensure　　[D] guarantee

【解析】选[C]。本题测试动词与 to 的搭配用法。authorize... to do sth. 意为"授权……做";qualify... to do sth. 意为"使有资格做";credit... to sth. 意为"把……记入;把……归功于";entitle... to sth. 意为"赋予"。其中前两个 to 是不定式形式,后两个 to 是介词。本题中的 to 后接的是名词,可以判断此处 to 是介词,因此[A]、[D]形式不符;而[B]的含义不符;所以只有选项[C]在语法结构和意义上均符合。

【题意】每个人都有隐私权。

真题冲浪

example　　　　　　　　考点:上下义表达,举例说明

However, the typical teenage lifestyle is already filled with so much competition that it would be wise to plan activities in which there are more winners than losers,＿＿＿ publishing newsletters with many student-written book reviews, displaying student artwork, and sponsoring book discussion clubs.(2003−28)

[A] in effect
[B] as a result
[C] for example
[D] in a sense

【解析】选[C]。本题的解答要借助于句子的逻辑关系来确定。本题空格前面谈到应该为他们策划一些多赢少输的活动才是明智的,空格后面接着用了几个并列的现在分词短语 publishing...、displaying...、sponsoring...,它们是用来列举前面提到的 activities,所以空格前后应为列举关系,即选 for example。

【题意】然而,典型的青少年生活方式中已经充满了如此多的竞争,因此为他们策划一些多赢少输的活动才是明智的。例如:出版学生写的书刊评论简报、展示学生的艺术作品以及主办书籍讨论俱乐部。

真题冲浪

excess　　　　　　　　考点:近义复现

Getting enough vitamins is essential to life, although the body has no nutritional use for ＿＿＿ vitamins. (1996−49)

[A] exceptional
[B] exceeding
[C] excess
[D] external

【解析】选[C]。本题涉及语义衔接和近义词辨析两方面的知识。exceptional"例外的,异常的";external"外边的,外部的";exceeding"胜过的,超越的,极度的",该词通常用来修饰由形容词转化的抽象名词 如:darkness, beauty 等;excess"过量的,额外的"。根据全文主题及前半句 enough 的意思,excess 和 exceeding 均符合,是 enough 的近义词复现,但空格后的词是具体名词 vitamins,显然 exceeding 不能修饰。所以,只有 excess 符合。

【题意】尽管维他命摄入过多对身体没有多大的营养价值,但摄取足够的维他命还是必要的。

真题冲浪

follow　　　　　　　　考点:逻辑时间关系

It is generally recoginezed. however, that the introduction of the computer in the early 20th century,＿＿＿＿＿ by the invention of the integrated circuit during the 1960s...(2002-30)

[A]characterized
[B]brought
[C]stimulated
[D]followed

【解析】选[D]。由本句结构来看,空格处的词与后面的 by 并不是构成被动语态,而是一个习惯搭配,followed by 意为“跟随其后的……”。如果考生对这个习惯搭配不了解,完全可以利用相关知识来判断,了解 computer 和 integrated circuit(集成电路)的人都知道这两者出现的先后顺序,即电脑在前,集成电路在后。很显然,只有 followed by 能表达这一意义。

【题意】然而,人们广泛地意识到,20世纪初计算机的出现及随后60年代集成电路的产生……

真题冲浪

for　　　　　　　　考点:因果关系,前果后因

The latter may commit crimes ＿＿＿＿＿ lack of adequate parental control. (2004-27)

[A]on　　　　　　[B]in
[C]for　　　　　　[D]with

【解析】选[C]。本题测试介词短语固定搭配。四个选项中只有 for 可以和 lack of 构成固定搭配,for lack of 意思是“因缺乏……”。

【题意】后者犯罪是因为父母没有很好地管教他们。

真题冲浪

fundamentally　　　　　考点:近义同现

Even though its economy continues to recover, the US is increasingly becoming a nation of part-times and temporary workers. This “＿45＿” workforce is the most important trend in American business today, and it is ＿47＿ changing the relationship between people and their jobs. (1997-45,47)

45.[A]durable　　　　[B]disposable
[C]available　　　[D]transferable

47.[A]instantly　　　[B]reversely
[C]fundamentally　[D]sufficiently

【解析】

45.选[B]。本题中的 this workforce(劳动力)指的是上句的 part-timers and temporary workers(临时工和小时工)。由此可见,这些人干一天算一天,是临时的、经常变动的。也就是说,雇主可以对这些人随意进行安置,即 disposable(用完即可丢弃的,一次性的,可随意处置的)。其他选项:durable “持久的,耐用的”,与文意相反;transferable “可转移的,可转换的,可传递的”,不适合描写无固定工作的就业群体;available “可以得到的”,虽然在意义上可以与上下文相搭配,但由于所填入的选项被加注了引号,而这里的引号具有特殊的意义,所以也不能成为正确选项。

47.选[C]。由上文中的 the most important 可断定这一改变(changing)是最大程度上的改变,所以 fundamentally(根本上)正确。其他选项:instantly “短暂地,迅速地”;reversely “相反地”;sufficiently “足够地”,均不合题意。

【题意】尽管美国的经济持续复苏,但是美国正在加速变成一个兼职工和临时工越来越多的国家。这种“可自由支配的”劳动大军是当今美国商业最重要的发展趋势,这种趋势正在从根本上改变人与工作的关系。

真题冲浪

general

For example, changes in the economy that lead to fewer job opportunities for youth and rising unemployment _____ make gainful employment increasingly difficult to obtain.(2004-31)

[A]in general
[B]on average
[C]by contrast
[D]at length

【解析】选[A]。本题测试介词短语的选择。四个短语的意思分别为：in general "通常，一般而言"；on average"按平均"；by contrast"相比之下"；at length"最后，详细地"。根据句意，只有 in general 符合，表示一般性情况。

【题意】例如，经济上的改变会导致青少年工作机会减少以及失业的增加，这通常使能挣钱的工作机会更难寻找。

真题冲浪

however

It is generally recognized,_____, that the introduction of the computer in the early 20th century, followed by the invention of the integrated circuit during the 1960s, radically changed the process,...(2002-29)

[A]indeed
[B]hence
[C]however
[D]therefore

【解析】选[C]。本题测试副词的用法，可借助于语篇的逻辑关系来确定。由空格前后的标点符号来看，只有选项 however，therefore 适合，因为其他两个副词不用于两个逗号之间。从文章整体来看，每段都谈到了不同的内容。第一段谈到了通讯革命；第二段笔锋一转，指出计算机急剧改变了通讯革命的进程。所以此处应该填入表示转折的副词，即 however。此外，本题也可根据前后出现的提示词来判断逻辑衔接词，however 一词常常与 generally 或 usually 等词同现，本句中含有 generally，所以据此也可判断 however 为正确答案。

【题意】然而人们普遍认识到，20 世纪计算机的出现以及随后 60 年代集成电路的发明彻底改变了这一进程。

真题冲浪

identifiable/availability/incidence 考点:后照前应

Other ___37___ causes offensive acts include frustration 语义场同现 or failure in school, the increased ___38___ of drugs and alcohol, and the growing ___39___ of child abuse and 语义场同现 child neglect. All these conditions tend to increase the probability of a child committing a criminal act, although a direct causal relationship has not yet been established. (2004-37,38,39)

37.[A]assessable [B]identifiable
[C]negligible [D]incredible

38.[A]expense [B]restriction
[C]allocation [D]availability

39.[A]incidence [B]awareness
[C]exposure [D]popularity

【解析】这三个空涉及的内容紧密相关。

第 37 题：选[B]。本题单从修饰关系来看，除 assessable 外(该词一般不修饰 causes)，identifiable、negligible、incredible 三个词均可与 causes 搭配。这时就要结合前后句的具体内容，看哪个词能使上下文语义最连贯顺畅。上文谈到了家庭环境对少年犯罪的影响，接着 other 和 causes 两词表明，作者要讨论其他原因，谈及的三个原因是确实存在的；从下文可知，虽然这些原因和青少年犯罪的关系尚未确定，但还是会增加青少年犯罪的可能性。文中没有任何信息表明这种原因是不予重视(negligible)或难以置信(incredible)的，所以用 identifiable(可确定的)，表明其原因本身是客观存在的，只是它们对青少年犯罪的直接影响尚未确定。

第 38 题：选[D]。第一句话谈到了青少年犯罪的三个原因。第一个原因已给出，即在学校遭受挫折或失败。单从修饰搭配关系来看，该题的四个选项均可放入空格，但这里说的是青少年犯罪的原因，很显然 allocation(分发，分配)不符合常识，不可能给青少年分发毒品和酒精；而 restriction(限制)意义正好相反；毒品和酒精 expense(费用)的增加同犯罪应该没有关系，所以青少年不断 availability

（获得）毒品和酒精符合犯罪的原因。

第39题：选[A]。四个选项中 incidence（发生率）和 awareness（意识到）两项都可放回原文搭配，但这里谈的是犯罪原因，如果用 awareness，意思正好相反，所以应选 incidence。

【题意】其他攻击性行为可以确认的原因包括在学校遭受挫折和失败，不断沾染毒品和酒精，对孩子的虐待和忽视程度不断增加。所有这些情况都趋向于增加孩子犯罪的可能性，但是导致青少年犯罪的直接原因目前还无法确定。

真题冲浪

if　　　　　　　　　　　　　　　　　　考点：条件关系

He can continue to support himself and his family _____ he produces a surplus. (2000-42)

[A] only if
[B] much as
[C] long before
[D] ever since

【解析】选[A]。本题测试连接词的用法。这是一个主从复合句，主句的意思是"他能养活自己及家人"，从句的意思是"生产有剩余"。根据主从句的含义，前后两句应为条件关系，所以应选表示条件关系的连词，即 only if（只有）。其他连词不能引导条件从句：much as"尽管"，引导让步从句；long before"在……很久以前"，引导时间从句；ever since"自从"，引导时间从句。其实，本题还可以根据前后的提示词来做出判断。主句中有情态动词 can，从句中是一般现在时，根据这个特点也可以判断主从句是条件关系。在历届考题中，当情态动词、助动词 will 与动词的第三人称单数（produces）分别出现在两个分句中，通常这两个分句是条件或结果关系。

【题意】只有生产有剩余，他才能养活自己及家人。

真题冲浪

ignore　　　　　　　　　　　　　　　考点：对比关系

Most theories of juvenile delinquency have focused on children from disadvantaged families, _____ the fact that children from wealthy homes also commit crimes.(2004-26)

[A] considering
[B] ignoring
[C] highlighting
[D] discarding

【解析】选[B]。本句中 disadvantaged families 和 wealthy homes, also 表明逗号前后两部分是对照关系。前一部分说的是重点放在贫穷家庭的孩子上，而忽略了富裕家庭的孩子犯罪，因而只有 ignoring 符合。ignoring 和前面的 focused on 构成了反义词复现。

【题意】大多数关于青少年犯罪理论研究的重点放在贫穷家庭的孩子上，而忽视了富裕家庭的孩子同样犯罪的事实。

真题冲浪

impose　　　　　　　　　　　　　　　考点：修饰同现

The phenomenon provides a way for companies to remain globally competitive while avoiding market cycles and the growing burdens _____ by employment rules, healthcare costs and pension plans.(1997-49)

[A] imposed
[B] restricted
[C] illustrated
[D] confined

【解析】选[A]。所填的空是动词的过去分词，作 burdens（负担）的后置定语。四个选项中能与 burdens 搭配的只有 impose，表示"强加于……的负担"；而 restrict, confine 都表示"局限在某一范围之内"；illustrate 表示"以……来说明"，都不符合句意。

【题意】这种现象为各公司提供了一条出路，一方面可保持全球市场的竞争力，同时又可避免市场循环和由用工条例、医疗保健费用和退休金计划所带来的日益沉重的负担。

真题冲浪

influence　　　　　　　　　　　　　考点：动宾搭配

The communications revolution has _____ both work and leisure and how we think and feel both about place and time,... (2002-38)

[A] regarded
[B] impressed
[C] influenced
[D] effected

【解析】选[C]。本题考查动词近义词的辨析，可以根据提示词的词性来做判断。本题空格需要填入一个动词,根据空格后的提示词(宾语部分 work and leisure...)可知需要填入一个表示"影响"意思的词。influence 和 effect 两词均可表示"影响"之意,但是 effect 是名词,该词作动词时的意思是"实现、引起",显然与本题不符。只有 influence 在语法和逻辑意义上都符合。

【题意】通信革命已经影响到我们的工作与休闲,以及我们对时空的看法。

真题冲浪

in   考点:固定搭配、前照后应

Specialists _____ history and economics, have shown two things: that the period from 1650 to 1750 was marked by great poverty, and that industrialization certainly did not worsen and may have actually improved the conditions for the majority of the populace.(1998-48)

[A]at
[B]in
[C]about
[D]for

【解析】选[B]。空格前的 specialist(专家)与后面的词一起表示"……方面的专家",应用介词 in,specialists in 是固定搭配,它源于其动词短语 specialize in...(以……为专业,专攻……)

【题意】历史学家与经济学家已说明了两点:贫穷是 1650 年到 1750 年这段时期的显著特点,工业化肯定没有加剧贫困,反而是改善了大多数人的生活条件。

真题冲浪

institutional   考点:前呼后应、对比关系

As time went by, computers became smaller and more powerful, and they became "personal" too, as well as _____.(2002-33)

[A]institutional
[B]universal
[C]fundamental
[D]instrumental

【解析】选[A]。as well as 是一个并列连接短语,它要求连接两个对等成分。显然四个选项中与 personal 在意思上对等的词只有 institutional,分别指个人电脑和大机构团体用的电脑。universal"普遍的";fundamental"根本的";instrumental"工具性的",这三个词的意思都不符合。institutional 和 personal 属于前后对比、反义复现。

【题意】随着时光飞逝,计算机变得更小,功能更强大,而随着显示器变得更清晰和储存容量不断增加,它们变得既适用于个人也适用于公共机构。

真题冲浪

interaction   考点:结构同现

...or that they have learned criminal behavior through _____ with others.(2004-23)

[A]interaction
[B]assimilation
[C]cooperation
[D]consultation

【解析】选[A]。本题测试以-tion 结尾的形近名词的选择,可以通过上下文的语义和提示词来做出选择。四个选项的意思分别是:interaction"相互作用,相互影响",assimilation"同化,消化",cooperation"合作",consultation "请教,咨询"。根据前文的含义以及本题中的 learned 和 with 表明,interaction 最符合题意,interact 常和 with 搭配。

【题意】由于他们受到其他人的影响而染上了这些行为。

真题冲浪

interpretation   考点:语义场同现

...when he said the _____ of privacy controls contained in European Legislation would be left to judges rather than to Parliament.(2001-41)

[A]translation
[B]interpretation
[C]exhibition
[D]demonstration

【解析】选[B]。选项皆为名词,从语义上看,与 privacy controls(隐私权)相关的话题为保护、解释隐私权。可见,选项中只有 interpretation(解释)正确,指对欧洲立法有关隐私权的解释、说明。本题中 interpretation, privacy controls, legislation 三个词构成了一个同法律有关的语义场。

【题意】……当他说到对欧洲立法中隐私权控制的解释将由法官而不是议会来做出时。

真题冲浪

it

考点：结构同现

Inaccurate or indefinite words may make _____ difficult for the listener to understand the message which is being transmitted to him. (1994-47)

[A]that
[B]it
[C]so
[D]this

【解析】选[B]。本题考查对 it 作形式宾语的用法的掌握。理清本句结构是本题的解题关键,空格前是动词谓语 make,空格后是形容词 difficult,并且还有不定式 to understand...，显然这符合 make 用法中的一个固定结构,即 make＋it＋宾补＋不定式。

【题意】模糊或者不确定的词语可能会使听话者很难理解对其所传达的信息。

真题冲浪

let

考点：近义同现

A variety of activities should be organized so that participants can remain active as long as they want and then go on to something else without feeling guilty and without letting the other participants _____.(2003-37)

[A]off
[B]out
[C]down
[D]alone

【解析】选[C]。本题测试 let 相关的动词短语的用法。let off 意为"放出,准许";let out 意为"泄露";let down 意为"使失望";let alone 意为"不管;更不用说"。句中 and 连接两个由 without 引导的介词短语,前后两个短语应该构成近义或同义同现关系,所以 and 之前的 feeling guilty(感到内疚)这一词组是本题的解题线索。可以看出,四个短语中只有 let down 能和 feel guilty 构成近义同现关系,符合题意。

【题意】应该组织各种不同的活动以便使参加者能长时间保持活跃,然后他们可以继续做其他的事情而不感到内疚,也不使其他人感到失望。

真题冲浪

make

考点：结构同现

The Lord Chancellor said introduction of the Human Rights Bill, which __43__ the European Convention on Human Rights legally __44__ in Britain,... (2001-43,44)

考点：修饰同现

43.[A]changes　[B]makes
　　[C]sets　　　[D]turns

44.[A]binding　　[B]convincing
　　[C]restraining [D]sustaining

【解析】

43. 选[B]。从第 44 题的选项可知,44 题需要填入一个现在分词,空格前面是名词短语"the European Convention on Human Rights"。这就很容易想起"动词＋名词＋宾补(分词)"这个结构,本题的四个选项中只有 make 具有此用法。

44. 选[A]。四个选项的含义是:binding"有约束力的";convincing"有说服力的";restraining"抑制的";sustaining"持续的"。能与空格前的 legally 构成被修饰关系的是 binding,意为"具有法律约束力"。

【题意】大法官说,人权法案的引入使欧洲公约关于人权的内容在英国具有了法律约束力。

真题冲浪

medium

考点：上下同义词复现

As was discussed before, it was not until the 19th century that the newspaper became the dominate pre-electronic _____. (2002-23)

[A]means
[B]method
[C]medium
[D]measure

【解析】选[C]。本题的提示词是句中的 newspaper,显然,该词和 medium(媒介,媒体)是上下义关系,可在同一话题中出现。其他的词同 newspaper 均不能构成复现关系,所以本题应选 medium。

【题意】正如以前所讨论的,直到 19 世纪报纸才成为前电子时代的主要媒体。

真题冲浪

multiple   考点：同义复现

A variety of small clubs can provide _____ opportunities for leadership, as well as for practice in successful group dynamics. (2003—30)

[A] durable
[B] excessive
[C] surplus
[D] multiple

【解析】选[D]。本题测试近义词的选择，可以根据前后搭配来判断。本题中的 excessive，surplus，multiple 三个词都包含"多"之意。前两个词指"过多的，剩余的"，而 multiple 指"多种多样的"。根据空格后的 opportunities，可知 multiple 修饰最合适。durable "持久的"，不能修饰 opportunities。

【题意】各种小俱乐部可以提供多种领导机会，同样也为成功的小组活动提供实践机会。

真题冲浪

nor

They do not provide energy, _____ do they construct or build any part of the body.(1996—41)

[A] either
[B] so
[C] nor
[D] never

【解析】选[C]。本句的前半句是一个否定句，后半句 do 在句首构成主谓倒装"也不……"的结构，在此只有 nor 具有此功能。能引起倒装的还有：only+状语置于句首；含否定意味的词置于句首；so 表示"某人也如何"；neither/nor 表示"某人也不如何"；虚拟语气中条件句 if 省略及 were/should/had 置于句首时，等等。

【题意】它们不提供能量，也不能构成身体的任何部分。

真题冲浪

of

In speaking, the choice of words is _____ the utmost importance. (1994—41)

[A] of
[B] at
[C] for
[D] on

【解析】选[A]。本题测试 be of+名词这一结构的用法，be of+名词相当于 be+相应的形容词。

【题意】在讲话中，词语的选择最为重要。

真题冲浪

on/into   考点：固定句式

It was during the same time that the communications revolution speeded up,beginning with transport, the railway, and leading __26__ through the telegraph, the telephone, radio, and motion pictures __27__ the 20th century world of the motor car and the airplane.

26. [A] on   [B] out
     [C] over   [D] off

27. [A] of   [B] for
     [C] beyond   [D] into

【解析】选[A]；选[D]。本题考查固定句型：beginning with... leading on through... into，意为"由……开始，然后发展到……，最后进入到……"。

【题意】正是在这一时期，通讯革命加快进程。首先发生变化的是运输方式，并以铁路为开始，然后发展到电报、电话、无线电和电影，直到 20 世纪汽车和飞机的普及。

真题冲浪

other   考点：对比关系，反义同现

He must store a large quantity of grain _____ consuming all his grain immediately.(2000—41)

[A] other than
[B] as well as
[C] instead of
[D] more than

【解析】选[C]。本题测试介词短语辨析。四个选项都可以连接并列结构：other than "除了……之外"、as well as "和"、more than "比……更"，这三个连接词的共同点是前后连接的词在语法上一致；instead of "而不是"，前后连接的两个成分在时态、结构上可以不一，后面可以接动名词、名词、介词短语等。本题是 consuming 和 store 平行，所以用 instead of 最确切。instead of 此处表示两种现象的对比。

【题意】他们储存大量的粮食，而不是马上将它们消费掉。

真题冲浪

perspective　　　　　　　　　　考点:结构同现
Not everyone sees that process in _____. (2002-28)

[A]concept　　[B]dimension
[C]effect　　　[D]perspective

【解析】选[D]。本题测试介词和名词的搭配。四个选项中能与 in 搭配的有 effect 和 perspective：in effect"实际上"；in perspective"正确地"。但上文的动词 see 提示，只有 in perspective 正确，因为 see...in perspective 是习惯搭配，意为"正确地认识、看待"。其他两个词 concept"观念，概念"、dimension"尺度，范围"都与本题无关。

【题意】不是每个人都能正确地认识那个过程。

真题冲浪

profit　　　　　　　　　　　考点:反义同现
This may mean the difference between operating at _____ or at a loss. (1999-50)

[A]an advantage　　[B]a benefit
[C]an interest　　　[D]a profit

【解析】选[D]。本题填入的词同 at 构成的短语与 at a loss 是平行结构，由于中间的连接词是 or，再加上前面的介词 between，可判断空白处的意义应与 loss 相反，或是 loss 的同义词，由四个选项可以看出没有 loss(损失)的同义词，只有其反义词 profit(收益)。其他三个选项为：advantage"优势"；benefit"利益"；interest"利益，利息"，都不符合文章。at a profit 和 at a loss 属于反义词复现。

【题意】这就像是蚀本经营和以获利为目的的经营之间的区别一样。

真题冲浪

response　　　　　　　　　　考点:因果关系,前果后因
Theories focusing on the role of society suggest that children commit crimes in _____ to their failure to rise above their socioeconomic status...(2004-24)

[A]return
[B]reply
[C]reference
[D]response

【解析】选[D]。本题测试介词和名词的固定搭配及其含义。从形式来判断 return 不符，因为 return for 才是正确搭配。in reply to 意思是"为答复……"；in reference to 意思是"关于"；in response to 意思是"回应，相应"。本句要表达的意思是"孩子们犯罪是对自己没有实现现有社会经济地位的回应……"，因此，in response to 为最佳选择。

【题意】强调社会影响的理论认为，孩子们犯罪是对自己没有实现现有社会经济地位的回应。

真题冲浪

say　　　　　　　　　　　　考点:结构同现
Up to 19 witnesses were _____ to have received payments for telling their stories to newspapers.(2001-48)

[A]stated
[B]remarked
[C]said
[D]told

【解析】选[C]。本题测试动词的用法。空格前后的内容是本题提示，were 和 to have received 提示这是一个特殊结构：be＋V-ed＋to＋have＋过去分词。这一结构中的动词谓语通常是 said，reported，believed 等(其用法详见第五节固定句型部分)，所以答案应该是 said。be said to have done 含义是"据说……"。本题的另一种表达方式是：It was said that up to 19 witnesses had received payments for telling their stories to newspapers.

【题意】据说有 19 位证人向报纸透露案情而获得报酬。

真题冲浪

small　　　　　　　　　　　考点:修饰同现
They were thought of, like people, in terms of generations, with the distance between generations much _____.(2002-36)

[A]deeper
[B]fewer
[C]nearer
[D]smaller

【解析】选[D]。本题测试形容词比较级的含义以及修饰关系,理清句子的结构是本题解题的关键。空格所在部分是介词 with 引导的复合结构,即 with+名词/代词+宾补(形容词、分词、介词短语等)。因此,填入的词用来修饰名词 distance。比较四个选项,smaller 最符合,smaller 和 distance 构成修饰同现关系。实际上,常用 small、big、great 等来修饰 distance,而不能用 near 或 far,正如 price 不能用 cheap、expensive 修饰,而只能用 low、high 修饰一样。选 near 的考生是受汉语的影响,deeper 和 fewer 更不能修饰 distance。

【题意】它们被认为像人一样,以"代"来划分,"代"与"代"之间的距离更小了。

真题冲浪

something　　　　　　　　　　　　　　　考点:结构同现

... participants can remain active as long as they want and then go on to _____ else without feeling guilty... (2003-36)

[A]everything
[B]anything
[C]nothing
[D]something

【解析】选[D]。这四个词只有 everything 不能和 else 搭配。anything else 常用于否定句中;something 用于肯定句中;nothing else 是否定词,和 without 不符。本句是一个肯定句,所以用 something。

【题意】参加者能长时间保持活跃,然后他们可以继续做其他的事情而不感到内疚……

真题冲浪

still　　　　　　　　　　　　　　　　考点:固定句式

Some place great emphasis on mechanical guarding. Others stress safe work practices by observing rules or regulations. _____ others depend on an emotional appeal to the worker. (1999-47)

[A]Some
[B]Many
[C]Even
[D]Still

【解析】选[D]。参照本句的上文可清楚地发现一条明显的线索,即 Some... Others... Still others... 表示层层递进的固定表达法,由此可见做完型填空时联系上下文的重要性。

【题意】一些安全计划强调机械保障,另一些安全计划强调通过遵守规定或规章来进行安全生产,还有一些安全计划靠感情的力量来打动工人。

真题冲浪

storm　　　　　　　　　　　　　　　考点:修饰同现

Publication of the letter came two days after Lord Irvine caused a _____ of media protest when...(2001-40)

[A]storm
[B]rage
[C]flare
[D]flash

【解析】选[A]。本题测试名词的习惯搭配。四个选项中只有 storm(暴风雨,感情的激烈爆发)与 protest 形成习惯搭配,用来体现媒体抗议的强烈程度。a storm of 的意思是"一阵猛烈的……",所以 a storm of media protest 意为"媒体的抗议风暴"。a storm of 与 protest 构成了修饰同现关系。rage"激怒,激烈"。一般形容人的情绪,如果用于形容物,通常用定冠词 the,例如:the rage of the wind"风的狂暴";flare"闪光",与 protest 不搭界;flash"闪光",也与 protest 不搭界。

【题意】在 Lord Irvine 惹起了一场抗议的风暴后的两天,信发表了。

真题冲浪

structure　　　　　　　　　　　　　考点:原词复现

Changes in the social structure may indirectly affect juvenile crime rates... children are likely to have less supervision at home than was common in the traditional family _____ . (2004-36)

[A]system
[B]structure
[C]concept
[D]heritage

【解析】选[B]。本题测试名词词义的选择。上一段第一句中的 social structure 是本题的解题线索,四个词中应选 structure。family structure"家庭结构"同上一段第一句中的 social structure"社会结构"构成了复现,其中 structure 是原词复现。其他三个词 system"体系"、concept"概念,观念"、heritage"遗产"都不符合题意。不过,本题的原词复现相隔较远,考生解题时要注意上下文线索。

【题意】社会结构变化可能间接地影响青少年犯罪率。……孩子们在家中所受到的监督就比在传统家庭结构中所见到的监督少得多。

真题冲浪

subject　　　　　　　　　　考点:因果关系,前因后果

All theories, however, are tentative and are ＿＿＿＿ to criticism.(2004−28)

[A]immune

[B]resistant

[C]sensitive

[D]subject

【解析】选[D]。本题测试形容词和介词搭配的含义。四个选项都能和空格后的介词 to 搭配,但意义不同。be immune to"不受……影响";be resistant to"对……具有抵抗力";be sensitive to"对……敏感";be subject to"受……制约,易遭受"。实际上,句中的 tentative(试验性的,探讨性的,不确定的)一词是解题的提示线索,试验性的或者说探讨性的理论通常会受到批评,所以只有 subject to 最符合。

【题意】然而,所有这些理论都是探讨性的,都会受到批评。

真题冲浪

such　　　　　　　　　　考点:上下义表达,例证关系

The government is to ban payments to witnesses by newspapers seeking to buy up people involved in prominent cases ＿＿＿＿ the trial of Rosemary West. (2001−31)

[A]as to

[B]for instance

[C]in particular

[D]such as

【解析】选[D]。本题中 the trial of Rosemary West 与空格前面的 prominent cases 是具体案例和泛指的关系,cases 与 the trial 是上下义词的关系,所以选 such as,表示举例,可以用在句中,后接部分是 such as 之前内容的一个方面或者局部。而[B]for instance 虽有"例如"之意,但更多的是表示"举例",后面接句子,或者用逗号隔开放在句中或句尾。本题空格前后无逗号,所以不能用 for instance。

【题意】政府将明令禁止报社通过付给证人报酬而设法收买重大案件(如罗斯马丽维斯特案件的审判)的涉案人员。

真题冲浪

term　　　　　　　　　　考点:语义场同现

They were thought of, like people, ＿＿＿＿ generations, with the distance between generations much smaller. (2002−35)

[A]by means of

[B]in terms of

[C]with regard to

[D]in line with

【解析】选[B]。本题测试复合介词的用法。本题的解题线索是空格前后的 people 和 generations 两个词,也就是说选项要能够反映 people 与 generations 之间的关系。四个短语的含义是:by means of "凭借";in terms of"用……的字眼,从……的观点";with regard to"关于";in line with"与……一致"。句中将计算机的发展比喻为人类的"代",只有 in terms of 能准确地表达此意。

【题意】它们被认为像人一样,以"代"来划分,"代"与"代"之间的距离更小了。

真题冲浪

than　　　　　　　　　　考点:比较关系

Children are likely to have less supervision at home ＿＿＿＿ was common in the traditional family structure.(2004−35)

[A]than

[B]that

[C]which

[D]as

【辨析】选[A]。本题测试连接词的用法,解题的线索是句中的 less 一词,该词提示本句是一个比较结构。很显然,只有连词 than 符合题意。本句是一种特殊的比较结构,即在 than 后的句子中,只有谓语部分,省略了主语部分。

【题意】孩子们在家中所受到的监督比在传统家庭结构中受到的监督少得多。

真题冲浪

that　　　　　　　　　　考点:前后照应,后为目的

A variety of activities should be organized ＿＿＿＿ participants can remain active...(2003−35)

[A]if only

[B]now that

[C]so that

[D]even if

【解析】选[C]。解答本题需要弄清所填词连接的前后两个句子之间的逻辑关系。上文提到的 A variety of activities should be organized（应组织各种活动），而下文则提到参加者能尽量保持活跃、不感到内疚、不让同伴失望等等，可以推测不同的活动是为了使青少年保持活跃而设计的，故两者之间需要一个能表示目的的连接词。选项中表达此意的只有 so that。其他的选项 if only（但愿）、now that（既然）和 even if（即使）都不能正确表达两个分句之间的逻辑关系。

【题意】应该组织各种不同的活动，以便使参加者能长时间保持活跃。

真题冲浪

that　　　　　　　　考点：同位语从句

Concerns were raised ＿＿＿＿＿ witnesses might be encouraged to exaggerate their stories in court to ensure guilty verdicts. (2001－49)

[A]what
[B]when
[C]which
[D]that

【解析】选[D]。本题测试连接代/副词的选择。根据句意，句中所填连接词应引导名词 concerns 的同位语从句，所以只有 that 符合。本题中，中心词 concerns 和其同位语从句被分开了，考生要注意这种用法。在名词 belief，concern，worry，promise，evidence，proof，assumption 等词后面常接 that 引导的同位语从句。

【题意】人们所关心的事便产生了，那就是证人可能被鼓励在法庭上夸大事实，以保证判决有罪。

真题冲浪

that　　　　考点：因果关系，前果后因

That are different ＿＿＿＿＿ their elements are arranged differently. (1996－46)

[A]in that
[B]so that
[C]such that
[D]except that

【解析】选[A]。从空格中连接词前后两半句的意思"各种维生素是不同的"和"每种维生素的元素排列不同"来解析，两者之间构成因果关系，而且是结果在前，原因在后，即所填连接词引导的是表示原因的从句。选项[B]so that 表示"以便"，引导目的状语从句；选项[D]except that 表示"除了"；选项[C]such that 表示"如此……以至于……"，虽然表示因果关系，但所接从句表示结果而非原因。只有 in that 意为"原因是，在于"，所引导的是原因状语从句。

【题意】它们的差异在于它们的元素排列不同。

真题冲浪

though　　　　考点：让步关系

＿＿＿＿＿ its economy continues to recover, the US is increasingly becoming a nation of part-timers and temporary workers.(1997－44)

[A]Even though
[B]Now that
[C]If only
[D]Provided that

【解析】选[A]。空格后的 its 指代 the US，前一分句说明美国经济持续复苏，后一分句则讲美国的兼职者和临时工正在增加。显然两句之间存在着语意上的转折关系，所以选择让步状语从句的连接词 even though。now that 引导原因状语从句；if only 表示"要是……就好了"，接虚拟语气，表达一种愿望；provided that 引导条件状语从句。

【题意】虽然经济继续复苏，美国却越来越成为一个计时工和临时工的国家。

真题冲浪

tighten　　　　考点：修饰同现

In a significant ＿＿＿＿＿ of legal controls over the press, Lord Irvine, the Lord Chancellor, will introduce a draft bill that will propose making payments to witnesses illegal. (2001－32)

[A]tightening
[B]intensifying
[C]focusing
[D]fastening

【解析】选[A]。本题测试动词词义的选择，解题线索是空格后的 of legal controls。四个选项均为动名词，意思分别是：tightening"加强，使严格"；intensifying"加剧"；focusing"集中"，后接介词 on 或 upon；fastening"拴牢，加紧"。其中能与空格后的名词词组 legal control 形成语义衔接的最佳选项是

tightening,表示"加强法律控制"。

　　【题意】为了加强对新闻界的法律监督,上院议长艾尔文爵士将提出一项法律草案,提议把向证人付款的行为定为非法。

until/company	22.[A]after　　　[B]by
As was discussed before, it was not ___22___ the 19th century 考点:结构同现 that the newspaper became the dominant pre-electronic medium, following in the wake of the pamphlet and the book and in the ___24___ of the periodical.(2002-22,24) 考点:同义复现	[C]during　　[D]until 24.[A]process　[B]company [C]light　　　[D]form

【解析】

22.选[D]。句中的 it was... that... 结构表明,这是一个强调句。空格前的 not 一词提示应该用 until 和其搭配,正好构成 not... until 这一结构。It was not until... that... 这一结构是常考的强调句型,考生要格外注意,本题属于结构同现关系。

24.选[B]。本题中 newspaper,pamphlet, book, periodical 都是表示并列含义的词,所以空格处需要一个表示这种关系的词,从而与前面的短语 in the wake of"在……之后"保持一致。因此,选项中符合此条件的只有 in the company of"与……同时"。company 在句中意为"陪伴,伴随",本句表明传单和书出现在报纸之前,而期刊是和报纸同时出现的。其他三个词虽然也可构成 in... of 的短语,但意义不符,in the process of"在……过程中";in the light of"按照,根据,当作";in the form of"以……的形式"。

　　【题意】正如以前讨论的,至19世纪报纸才伴随活页文选和书与期刊杂志一起成为主要的前电子时代的媒体。

真题冲浪

upon	[A]upon　　[B]by
..._____, yet, examination of the dead bodies, the animals look completely normal.(1995-47)	[C]through　[D]with

　　【解析】选[A]。本题测试介词 upon/on＋名词或动名词的用法。

　　【题意】……然而,一经对动物尸体进行检查,动物看起来就完全正常。

真题冲浪

what 考点:主语从句	[A]What little
He claims to be an expert in astronomy, but in actual fact he is quite ignorant on the subject. _____ he knows about it is out of date and inaccurate.(1997-7)	[B]So much [C]How much [D]So little

　　【解析】选[A]。本题测试连接代词/副词的用法。第二个句子使用的是主系表结构,主语由名词性从句担当。[B]和[D]只能用作状语,不能引导从句;how much 可引导从句,但用在这里形成的意思与表语部分无法达成一致;what little 引导从句与题意相符。这里 little 用作名词,与 what 搭配属于"what＋名词"结构引导名词性从句的用法。what 与 little, few 连用,意为"仅有的几个,仅有的一点点"。

　　【题意】他自称是天文学家,可事实上他对这门学问几乎一无所知。他所了解的那点天文知识不是过了时,就是不确切。

真题冲浪

where 考点:定语从句	[A]where
When the work is well done, a climate of accident -free operations is established _____ time lost due to injuries is kept at a minimum.(1999-44)	[B]how [C]what [D]unless

【解析】选[A]。本题要求确定引导从句的关联词,首先就要分析清楚主从句关系,主句的意思是"建立无事故的操作环境",从句的意思是"工伤造成的时间损失可保持在最低限度",结合主从句的意思分析,四个选项中只有 where 可以连接,该词用作关系副词连接的是一个定语从句,修饰 a climate of accident-free operations,用于描述这种情形的特点。how 和 what 常用于引导名词性从句,无论是在形式上还是逻辑上都不符合;unless 在形式上符合,但在逻辑上不符,因为它用于引导条件状语从句,而本句不包含条件逻辑关系。可以说该题的解答关键就在于能够判别分裂式的定语从句,即修饰主句主语的定语从句不是直接跟在先行词之后,而是放在了主句之后;此外,只有理解了上下文,对句子关系的判别才有依据。

【题意】如果这项工作做得很好,就可建立起一种无事故的操作环境,由工伤造成的时间损失便可保持在最低限度。

真题冲浪

wise

考点:因果关系,前因后果

However, the typical teenage lifestyle is already filled with so much competition that it would be _____ to plan activities in which there are more winners than losers... (2003—27)

[A] improper
[B] risky
[C] fair
[D] wise

【解析】选[D]。解本题要注意句中出现的 so... that 结构,that 引导的是结果状语从句,这表明上文的 so much competition(如此多的竞争)是作为原因存在的,有了这个原因,下文出现的 to plan activities in which there are more winners than losers(计划组织有更多人获胜的活动)就成为一种合乎要求的行为。选项中只有 wise 符合这个意思,it is wise to do sth. 的含义是"明智地做某事";而其他选项 improper(不正当的),risky(冒险的)和 fair(公平的)都与题意不符。It+be+*adj.*+(for sb.) to do sth. 是一种常见的结构。

【题意】然而,典型的青少年生活方式中已经充满了如此多的竞争,因此为他们策划一些多赢少输的活动才是明智的。

第七节 历年真题汇编

(1993 年)

Although interior design has existed since the beginning of architecture, its development into a specialized field is really quite recent. Interior designers have become important partly because of the many functions that might be __46__ in a single large building.

The importance of interior design becomes __47__ when we realize how much time we __48__ surrounded by four walls. Whenever we need to be indoors, we want our surroundings to be __49__ attractive and comfortable as possible. We also expect __50__ place to be appropriate to its use. You would be __51__ if the inside of your bedroom were suddenly changed to look __52__ the inside of a restaurant. And you wouldn't feel __53__ in a business office that has the appearance of a school.

It soon becomes clear that the interior designer's most important basic __54__ is the function of the particular __55__. For example, a theater with poor sight lines, poor sound-shaping qualities, and __56__ few entries and exits will not work for __57__ purpose, no matter how beautifully it might be __58__. Nevertheless, for any kind of space, the designer has to make many of the same kind of __59__. He or she must coordinate the shapes, lighting and decoration of everything from ceiling to floor. __60__ addition, the designer must usually select furniture or design built-in furniture, according to the functions that need to be served.

46. [A] consisted   [B] contained   [C] composed   [D] comprised
47. [A] obscure   [B] attractive   [C] appropriate   [D] evident

48. [A] spend	[B] require	[C] settle	[D] retain
49. [A] so	[B] as	[C] thus	[D] such
50. [A] some	[B] any	[C] this	[D] each
51. [A] amused	[B] interested	[C] shocked	[D] frightened
52. [A] like	[B] for	[C] at	[D] into
53. [A] correct	[B] proper	[C] right	[D] suitable
54. [A] care	[B] concern	[C] attention	[D] intention
55. [A] circumstance	[B] environment	[C] surroundings	[D] space
56. [A] too	[B] quite	[C] a	[D] far
57. [A] their	[B] its	[C] those	[D] that
58. [A] painted	[B] covered	[C] ornamented	[D] decorated
59. [A] solutions	[B] conclusions	[C] decisions	[D] determinations
60. [A] For	[B] In	[C] As	[D] With

(1994 年)

The first and smallest unit that can be discussed in relation to language is the word. In speaking, the choice of words is __41__ the utmost importance. Proper selection will eliminate one source of __42__ breakdown in the communication cycle. Too often, careless use of words __43__ a meeting of the minds of the speaker and listener. The words used by the speaker may __44__ unfavorable reactions in the listener __45__ interfere with his comprehension; hence, the transmission-reception system breaks down.

__46__ inaccurate or indefinite words may make __47__ difficult for the listener to understand the __48__ which is being transmitted to him. The speaker who does not have specific words in his working vocabulary may be __49__ to explain or describe in a __50__ that can be understood by his listeners.

41. [A] of	[B] at	[C] for	[D] on
42. [A] inaccessible	[B] timely	[C] likely	[D] invalid
43. [A] encourages	[B] prevents	[C] destroy	[D] offers
44. [A] pass out	[B] take away	[C] back up	[D] stir up
45. [A] who	[B] as	[C] which	[D] what
46. [A] Moreover	[B] However	[C] Preliminarily	[D] Unexpectedly
47. [A] that	[B] it	[C] so	[D] this
48. [A] speech	[B] sense	[C] message	[D] meaning
49. [A] obscure	[B] difficult	[C] impossible	[D] unable
50. [A] case	[B] means	[C] method	[D] way

(1995 年)

Sleep is divided into periods of so-called REM sleep, characterized by rapid eye movements and dreaming, and longer periods of non-REM sleep. __41__ kind of sleep is at all well-understood, but REM sleep is __42__ to serve some restorative function of the brain. The purpose of non-REM sleep is even more __43__. The new experiments, such as those __44__ for the first time at a recent meeting of the Society for Sleep Research in Minneapolis, suggest fascination explanations __45__ of non-REM sleep.

For example, it has long been known that total sleep __46__ is 100 percent fatal to rats, yet, __47__ examination of the dead bodies, the animals look completely normal. A researcher has now __48__ the mystery of why the animals die. The rats __49__ bacterial infections of the blood, __50__ their immune systems—the self-protecting mechanism against diseases—had crashed.

41. [A] Either   [B] Neither   [C] Each   [D] Any

42. [A] intended　　[B] required　　[C] assumed　　[D] inferred
43. [A] subtle　　　　[B] obvious　　　[C] mysterious　　[D] doubtful
44. [A] maintained　　[B] described　　[C] settled　　　[D] afforded
45. [A] in the light　　[B] by virtue　　[C] with the exception　[D] for the purpose
46. [A] reduction　　　[B] destruction　[C] deprivation　　[D] restriction
47. [A] upon　　　　　[B] by　　　　　[C] through　　　[D] with
48. [A] paid attention to　[B] caught sight of　[C] laid emphasis on　[D] cast light on
49. [A] develop　　　　[B] produce　　　[C] stimulate　　[D] induce
50. [A] if　　　　　　[B] as if　　　　[C] only if　　　[D] if only

（1996 年）

Vitamins are organic compounds necessary in small amounts in the diet for the normal growth and maintenance of life of animals，including man.

They do not provide energy，__41__ do they construct or build any part of the body. They are needed for __42__ foods into energy and body maintenance. There are thirteen or more of them，and if __43__ is missing a deficiency disease becomes __44__.

Vitamins are similar because they are made of the same elements—usually carbon，hydrogen，oxygen，and __45__ nitrogen. They are different __46__ their elements are arranged differently，and each vitamin __47__ one or more specific functions in the body.

__48__ enough vitamins is essential to life，although the body has no nutritional use for __49__ vitamins. Many people，__50__，believe in being on the "safe side"and thus take extra vitamins. However，a well-balanced diet will usually meet all the body's vitamin needs.

41. [A]either　　　　[B]so　　　　　[C]nor　　　　　[D]never
42. [A]shifting　　　　[B]transferring　[C]altering　　　[D]transforming
43. [A]any　　　　　[B]some　　　　[C]anything　　　[D]something
44. [A]serious　　　　[B]apparent　　[C]severe　　　　[D]fatal
45. [A]mostly　　　　[B]partially　　[C]sometimes　　[D]rarely
46. [A]in that　　　　[B]so that　　　[C]such that　　[D]except that
47. [A]undertakes　　[B]holds　　　　[C]plays　　　　[D]performs
48. [A]Supplying　　　[B]Getting　　　[C]Providing　　[D]Furnishing
49. [A]exceptional　　[B]exceeding　　[C]excess　　　[D]external
50. [A]nevertheless　　[B]therefore　　[C]moreover　　[D]meanwhile

（1997 年）

Manpower Inc.，with 560,000 workers，is the world's largest temporary employment agency. Every morning，its people __41__ into the offices and factories of America，seeking a day's work for a day's pay. One day at a time. __42__ industrial giants like General Motors and IBM struggle to survive __43__ reducing the number of employees，Manpower，based in Milwaukee，Wisconsin，is booming.

__44__ its economy continues to recover，the US is increasingly becoming a nation of part-timers and temporary workers. This "__45__"work force is the most important __46__ in American business today，and it is __47__ changing the relationship between people and their jobs. The phenomenon provides a way for companies to remain globally competitive __48__ avoiding market cycles and the growing burdens __49__ by employment rules，health care costs and pension plans. For workers it can mean an end to the security，benefits and sense of __50__ that came from being a loyal employee.

41. [A]swarm　　　　[B]stride　　　　[C]separate　　　[D]slip
42. [A]For　　　　　[B]Because　　　[C]As　　　　　[D]Since

43. [A]from [B]in [C]on [D]by
44. [A]Even though [B]Now that [C]If only [D]Provided that
45. [A]durable [B]disposable [C]available [D]transferable
46. [A]approach [B]flow [C]fashion [D]trend
47. [A]instantly [B]reversely [C]fundamentally [D]sufficiently
48. [A]but [B]while [C]and [D]whereas
49. [A]imposed [B]restricted [C]illustrated [D]confined
50. [A]excitement [B]conviction [C]enthusiasm [D]importance

（1998 年）

　　Until recently most historians spoke very critically of the Industrial Revolution. They ___41___ that in the long run industrialization greatly raised the standard of living for the ___42___ man. But they insisted that its ___43___ results during the period from 1750 to 1850 were widespread poverty and misery for the ___44___ of the English population. ___45___ contrast, they saw in the preceding hundred years from 1650 to 1750, when England was still a ___46___ agricultural country, a period of great abundance and prosperity.

　　This view, ___47___, is generally thought to be wrong. Specialists ___48___ history and economics, have ___49___ two things: that the period from 1650 to 1750 was ___50___ by great poverty, and that industrialization certainly did not worsen and may have actually improved the conditions for the majority of the populace.

41. [A]admitted [B]believed [C]claimed [D]predicted
42. [A]plain [B]average [C]mean [D]normal
43. [A]momentary [B]prompt [C]instant [D]immediate
44. [A]bulk [B]host [C]gross [D]magnitude
45. [A]On [B]With [C]For [D]By
46. [A]broadly [B]thoroughly [C]generally [D]completely
47. [A]however [B]meanwhile [C]therefore [D]moreover
48. [A]at [B]in [C]about [D]for
49. [A]manifested [B]approved [C]shown [D]speculated
50. [A]noted [B]impressed [C]labeled [D]marked

（1999 年）

　　Industrial safety does not just happen. Companies ___41___ low accident rates plan their safety programs, work hard to organize them, and continue working to keep them ___42___ and active. When the work is well done, a ___43___ of accident-free operations is established ___44___ time lost due to injuries is kept at a minimum.

　　Successful safety programs may ___45___ greatly in the emphasis placed on certain aspects of the program. Some place great emphasis on mechanical guarding. Others stress safe work practices by ___46___ rules or regulations. ___47___ other depend on an emotional appeal to the worker. But, there are certain basic ideas that must be used on every program if maximum results are to be obtained.

　　There can be no question about the value of a safety program. From a financial standpoint alone, safety ___48___. The fewer the injury ___49___, the better the workman's insurance rate. This may mean the difference between operating at ___50___ or at a loss.

41. [A]at [B]in [C]on [D]with
42. [A]alive [B]vivid [C]mobile [D]diverse
43. [A]regulation [B]climate [C]circumstance [D]requirement
44. [A]where [B]how [C]what [D]unless

45. [A]alter 　　　　　[B]differ 　　　　　[C]shift 　　　　　[D]distinguish
46. [A]constituting 　　[B]aggravating 　　[C]observing 　　　[D]justifying
47. [A]Some 　　　　　[B]Many 　　　　　[C]Even 　　　　　[D]Still
48. [A]comes off 　　　[B]turns up 　　　　[C]pays off 　　　　[D]holds up
49. [A]claims 　　　　　[B]reports 　　　　[C]declarations 　　[D]proclamations
50. [A]an advantage 　　[B]a benefit 　　　[C]an interest 　　　[D]a profit

（2000 年）

If a farmer wishes to succeed，he must try to keep a wide gap between his consumption and his production. He must store a large quantity of grain ___41___ consuming all his grain immediately. He can continue to support himself and his family ___42___ he produces a surplus. He must use this surplus in three ways：as seed for sowing，as an insurance ___43___ the unpredictable effects of bad weather and as a commodity which he must sell in order to ___44___ old agricultural implements and obtain chemical fertilizers to ___45___ the soil. He may also need money to construct irrigation ___46___ and improve his farm in other ways. If no surplus is available，a farmer cannot be ___47___. He must either sell some of his property or ___48___ extra funds in the form of loans. Naturally he will try to borrow money at a low ___49___ of interest，but loans of this kind are not ___50___ obtainable.

41. [A]other than 　　　[B]as well as 　　　[C]instead of 　　　[D]more than
42. [A]only if 　　　　　[B]much as 　　　　[C]long before 　　[D]ever since
43. [A]for 　　　　　　[B]against 　　　　[C]of 　　　　　　[D]towards
44. [A]replace 　　　　　[B]purchase 　　　[C]supplement 　　　[D]dispose
45. [A]enhance 　　　　　[B]mix 　　　　　[C]feed 　　　　　[D]raise
46. [A]vessels 　　　　　[B]routes 　　　　[C]paths 　　　　　[D]channels
47. [A]self-confident 　　[B]self-sufficient 　[C]self-satisfied 　　[D]self-restrained
48. [A]search 　　　　　[B]save 　　　　　[C]offer 　　　　　[D]seek
49. [A]proportion 　　　[B]percentage 　　[C]rate 　　　　　[D]ratio
50. [A]genuinely 　　　[B]obviously 　　　[C]presumably 　　　[D]frequently

（2001 年）

The government is to ban payments to witnesses by newspapers seeking to buy up people involved in prominent cases ___31___ the trial of Rosemary West.

In a significant ___32___ of legal controls over the press，Lord Irvine，the Lord Chancellor，will introduce a ___33___ bill that will propose making payments to witnesses ___34___ and will strictly control the amount of ___35___ that can be given to a case ___36___ a trial begins.

In a letter to Gerald Kaufman，chairman of the House of Commons media select committee，Lord Irvine said he ___37___ with a committee report this year which said that self regulation did not ___38___ sufficient control.

___39___ of the letter came two days after Lord Irvine caused a ___40___ of media protest when he said the ___41___ of privacy controls contained in European legislation would be left to judges ___42___ to Parliament.

The Lord Chancellor said introduction of the Human Rights Bill，which ___43___ the European Convention on Human Rights legally ___44___ in Britain，laid down that everybody was ___45___ to privacy and that public figures could go to court to protect themselves and their families.

"Press freedoms will be in safe hands ___46___ our British judges，"he said.

Witness payments became an ___47___ after West was sentenced to 10 life sentences in 1995. Up to

19 witnesses were ___48___ to have received payments for telling their stories to newspapers. Concerns were raised ___49___ witnesses might be encouraged to exaggerate their stories in court to ___50___ guilty verdicts.

31. [A]as to   [B]for instance   [C]in particular   [D]such as
32. [A]tightening   [B]intensifying   [C]focusing   [D]fastening
33. [A]sketch   [B]rough   [C]preliminary   [D]draft
34. [A]illogical   [B]illegal   [C]improbable   [D]improper
35. [A]publicity   [B]penalty   [C]popularity   [D]peculiarity
36. [A]since   [B]if   [C]before   [D]as
37. [A]sided   [B]shared   [C]complied   [D]agreed
38. [A]present   [B]offer   [C]manifest   [D]indicate
39. [A]Release   [B]Publication   [C]Printing   [D]Exposure
40. [A]storm   [B]rage   [C]flare   [D]flash
41. [A]translation   [B]interpretation   [C]exhibition   [D]demonstration
42. [A]better than   [B]other than   [C]rather than   [D]sooner than
43. [A]changes   [B]makes   [C]sets   [D]turns
44. [A]binding   [B]convincing   [C]restraining   [D]sustaining
45. [A]authorized   [B]credited   [C]entitled   [D]qualified
46. [A]with   [B]to   [C]from   [D]by
47. [A]impact   [B]incident   [C]inference   [D]issue
48. [A]stated   [B]remarked   [C]said   [D]told
49. [A]what   [B]when   [C]which   [D]that
50. [A]assure   [B]confide   [C]ensure   [D]guarantee

(2002 年)

Comparisons were drawn between the development of television in the 20th century and the diffusion of printing in the 15th and 16th centuries. Yet much had happened ___21___ . As was discussed before, it was not ___22___ the 19th century that the newspaper became the dominant pre-electronic ___23___ , following in the wake of the pamphlet and the book and in the ___24___ of the periodical. It was during the same time that the communications revolution ___25___ up, beginning with transport, the railway, and leading ___26___ through the telegraph, the telephone, radio, and motion pictures ___27___ the 20th-century world of the motor car and the airplane. Not everyone sees that process in ___28___ . It is important to do so.

It is generally recognized, ___29___ , that the introduction of the computer in the early 20th century, ___30___ by the invention of the integrated circuit during the 1960s, radically changed the process, ___31___ its impact on the media was not immediately ___32___ . As time went by, computers became smaller and more powerful, and they became "personal" too, as well as ___33___ , with display becoming sharper and storage ___34___ increasing. They were thought of, like people, ___35___ generations, with the distance between generations much ___36___ .

It was within the computer age that the term "information society" began to be widely used to describe the ___37___ within which we now live. The communications revolution has ___38___ both work and leisure and how we think and feel both about place and time, but there have been ___39___ views about its economic, political, social and cultural implications. "Benefits" have been weighed ___40___ "harmful" outcomes. And generalizations have proved difficult.

21. [A]between   [B]before   [C]since   [D]later

22. [A]after	[B]by	[C]during	[D]until
23. [A]means	[B]method	[C]medium	[D]measure
24. [A]process	[B]company	[C]light	[D]form
25. [A]gathered	[B]speeded	[C]worked	[D]picked
26. [A]on	[B]out	[C]over	[D]off
27. [A]of	[B]for	[C]beyond	[D]into
28. [A]concept	[B]dimension	[C]effect	[D]perspective
29. [A]indeed	[B]hence	[C]however	[D]therefore
30. [A]brought	[B]followed	[C]stimulated	[D]characterized
31. [A]unless	[B]since	[C]lest	[D]although
32. [A]apparent	[B]desirable	[C]negative	[D]plausible
33. [A]institutional	[B]universal	[C]fundamental	[D]instrumental
34. [A]ability	[B]capability	[C]capacity	[D]faculty
35. [A]by means of	[B]in terms of	[C]with regard to	[D]in line with
36. [A]deeper	[B]fewer	[C]nearer	[D]smaller
37. [A]context	[B]range	[C]scope	[D]territory
38. [A]regarded	[B]impressed	[C]influenced	[D]effected
39. [A]competitive	[B]controversial	[C]distracting	[D]irrational
40. [A]above	[B]upon	[C]against	[D]with

（2003 年～2005 年真题见第三部分第一章及第一部分）

答案及解析

（1993 年）

46. 答案：[B] contained

[A] consisted 多用于 consist of（由……组成）；consist in（在于）；consist with（与……一致）；[B] contained 包含（符合题意）；[C] composed 组成，常用于 be composed of（由……组成）；[D] comprised 组成，常用于主动语态。[例]Five people comprised the committee. 该委员会由五人组成。

47. 答案：[D] evident

[A] obscure 模糊不清的。[例]obscure meaning/sounds 模糊的含义/声音；[B] attractive 有吸引力的。[例]attractive person 有吸引力的人；[C] appropriate 合适的。[例]appropriate clothes 合适的服装；[D] evident 明显的。[例]evident pride/distress/sarcasm 明显的自豪/沮丧/讽刺。

48. 答案：[A] spend

[A] spend 度过，花费，常和 time 搭配，正确；[B] require 要求；[C] settle 定居；[D] retain 保留，保持。

49. 答案：[B] as

[A] so 是连词，常与 that 连用；[B] as, as ... as possible 为固定搭配；[C] thus 因此，通常引导结果；[D] such 常用于 such as 连用。

50. 答案：[D] each

[A] some 一些；[B] any 任何；[C] this 这；[D] each 原文内容为"我们也希望每个地方都恰如其分。"each 符合此意。

51. 答案：[C] shocked

[A] amused 觉得好笑；[B] interested 觉得有趣，不合题意；[C] shocked 大吃一惊，符合题意；[D] frightened 感到害怕，不合题意。

52. 答案:[A] like

[A] like〔搭配〕look like 看起来像;[B] for〔搭配〕look for 寻找;[C] at〔搭配〕look at 看;[D] into〔搭配〕look into 调查,过问。

53. 答案:[C] right

[A] correct 正确的,无误的。〔例〕correct time,answer,spelling 准确的时间/正确答案/拼写等;[B] proper 恰当的,适当的。〔例〕proper time,place,language 适当的时间/地点/恰当的语言等;[C] right,feel right 意为"感觉正常",符合要求;[D] suitable 适合的。〔例〕books suitable for children 适合儿童读的书。

54. 答案:[B] concern

[A] care 担心,忧虑。〔例〕free from care 无忧无虑;[B] concern 关注(关心)的问题。〔例〕My greatest concern is the economy of China. 我最注意的事是中国的经济问题;[C] attention 注意(力);[D] intention 目的,意图。

55. 答案:[D]space

[A] circumstance 情况,情景(常用复数)。〔例〕in/under the circumstance;[B] environment 环境。〔例〕social/natural environment 社会/自然环境;[C] surroundings(周围的)环境。〔例〕family/social surroundings 家庭/社会环境;[D] space 空间。

56. 答案:[A] too

[A] too few 太少;[B] quite a few 很多。一般不用 quite few;[C] a few 几个。此处不合逻辑;[D] far 不修饰数量形容词。

57. 答案:[B] its

[A] their 形容词性物主代词,与前面代替的词不一致;[B] its 空格要求填入代替 theater 的词。theater 为单数,its 符合此意;[C] those 指代复数名词,与前面代替的词也不一致;[D] that 指示代词,而此处缺一个做定语的物主代词。

58. 答案:[D] decorated

[A] painted 油漆;[B] covered 覆盖;[C] ornamented 装饰,美化。指增添细节使之锦上添花。〔例〕The altar was richly ornamented. 祭坛装饰华丽;[D] decorated 装修,多指房屋建筑。〔例〕Her house was beautifully decorated. 她的房子装修漂亮。

59. 答案:[C] decisions

[A] solutions 解决办法。〔搭配〕solution to;[B] conclusions〔例〕arrive at/reach/draw/make a conclusion 得出结论;[C] decisions〔例〕await/form/make/pass/reach a decision 等待/形成/做出/通过/达成一项决定;[D] determinations 决心。〔例〕make determination。

60. 答案:[B] In

[A] For 为了;[B] In〔搭配〕in addition 此外;[C] As 正如……一样;[D] With 表示伴随状况。

参考译文:

尽管自建筑业出现以来就产生了室内设计,但它发展成一专门领域却是最近之事。室内设计者变得至关重要,其部分原因是在一栋大楼中可以具有多种功能。

当我们意识到有多少时间是在四面是墙的屋子中度过时,室内设计的重要性就显而易见了。我们无论何时需要呆在户内,我们就希望我们的环境尽可能宜人、舒适。我们也希望每个地方都很适用。如果你的卧室内部突然变成像宾馆一样,你可能会大吃一惊。如果办公室搞成像学校的样子,你也会不自在。

很清楚,室内设计者最关注的就是某一特定空间的功能。例如,如果一家剧院的视线不佳,音响效果差、出入口太少,那么无论这家剧院装修多么华丽,也不适合于做剧院。然而,就任何类型的空间而言,设计者都必须作出许多同一的决定。他/她必须协调从天花板到地板所有东西的形状、灯光及装饰。其次,设计者通常应根据必须具有的功能来选择家具或设计内嵌式家具。

(1994 年)

41. 答案:[A] of

此题考查的是 be of＋n. 的用法。be of importance＝be important。[A] of 与抽象名词连用等于其形容词。[例]be of use/value/help/importance;[B] at 不是固定搭配;[C] for 不是固定搭配;[D] on 不是固定搭配。

42. 答案:[C] likely

　　[A] inaccessible 难以到达的,不可获得的,后接 to。[例]inaccessible to traffic;[B] timely 及时的,准时的。[例]timely help/rain 及时的帮助/雨;[C] likely 可能的,与文中 breakdown 连用,符合题意;[D] invalid 无效的,无法律效率的。[例]invalid passport/lease 无效护照/契约。

43. 答案:[B] prevents

　　[A] encourages 鼓励,鼓舞;[B] prevents 阻碍,阻止。符合上下文的逻辑关系;[C] destroy 毁坏,破坏;[D] offers 主动提供。

44. 答案:[D] stir up

　　[A] pass out 分配。[例]pass out tickets/pamphlets 分发票证/小册子;[B] take away 拿走;[C] back up 支持。[例]I will back you up. 我支持你;[D] stir up 煽动,引起。和 reaction 连用,意为"引起反应"。

45. 答案:[C] which

　　interfere with 是谓语动词形式,表明空格处缺少主语,这样初步判断,这个空白处应填关系代词,引出后面的定语从句。这样[D]what 便可排除。what 引导名词性从句,不引导定语从句。如果填入[A]who,先行词就只能是 the listener,而"听话者"不可能干扰"他自己的理解"。如果填入[B]as,代替前面整句话作主语,又无法讲通意思。因此只有[C]which 正确。它的先行词是 unfavourable reactions,这种"不好的反应"会干扰他(听话者)(对讲话者)的理解。

46. 答案:[A]Moreover

　　[A] Moreover 此外,表示递进关系,符合题意;[B] However 然而,表示转折关系;[C] Preliminarily 首先,起初;[D] Unexpectedly 出人意料地。

47. 答案:[B] it

　　由于空格前有 make,空格后有 difficult,而 difficult 后又有 for the listener to understand 这一不定式结构,因此空格处需要填入的词汇为形式宾语 it。make(find)＋it＋adj.＋(for sb.) to do sth. 是一常用句型。[A] that 不能作形式宾语;[B] it 作形式宾语,代替其后的动词不定式,符合题意;[C] so 代替整个句子;[D] this 不能作形式宾语。

48. 答案:[C] message

　　[A] speech 演讲,言语;[B] sense 感官,感觉;[C] message 信息,口信,与文中 transmit(传递)构成"传递信息";[D] meaning 意思,含义。[例]What's the meaning of the word? 这词是什么意思?

49. 答案:[D]able

　　[A] obscure 模糊的,无名的。[例]obscure explanation/writer 模糊不清的解释/无名作家;[B] difficult 困难的,很少用人作主语;[C] impossible 不可能的,不用人作主语;[D] unable 无能力的。主语为人,后接不定式。[例]He seems unable to swim. 他似乎不会游泳。

50. 答案:[D] way

　　[A] case 事例,情况。常用于 in case(连词)以防和 in case of(介词)以防,万一;[B] means 方法,手段,常用于 by all means 想尽一切办法。by no means 决不;[C] method 方法,可用于 in this method,用这种方法;[D] way 方式,其前面常用介词 in,符合搭配。

　　参考译文:

　　就语言而言,可以讨论的首要的和最小的单位是词。说话时,选词是最重要的。适当的选词可以消除交际过程中可能出现的障碍。用词粗心大意往往阻碍说话人和听话人的思想交流。说话人使用的词汇可能引起听话人的不利反应,从而干扰其理解。因此,这发送接受系统就会中断。

　　此外,词义不准确或不明确的词使听话人难于听懂传递给他的信息。说话人的常用词汇中如没有详细而精确词的话,就不可能用听话人能理解的方式进行解释或描述。

(1995 年)

41. 答案：[B] Neither

[A] Either 两者之一；作定语时一般用于肯定句；[B] Neither 两者都不，恰与 at all 搭配；[C] Each 不能与 at all 连用；[D] Any 不能与 at all 连用。

42. 答案：[C] assumed

[A] intended 打算，想要；一般不用于被动语态而且主语一般为人；[B] required，be required to "被要求"，语义不通；[C] assumed，be assumed to"被假定，被设想"符合语义；[D] inferred 推论，推断；其对象应是推导出的结果，而不是此句中的 REM sleep。

43. 答案：[C] mysterious

[A] subtle 微妙的；语义不通；[B] obvious 明显的；与句意相反；[C] mysterious 神秘的；与 not at all well-understood 同义复现；[D] doubtful 可疑的；目的还不明确，无从谈起怀疑。

44. 答案：[B] described

[A] maintained 保持；与 for the first time 矛盾；[B] described 描述的是实验，正合文意；[C] settled 解决，决定；与 suggest 矛盾；[D] afforded 支付得起；不与 experiment 搭配。

45. 答案：[D] for the purpose

[A] in the light of 相当于 according to，"按照，根据"；[B] by virtue of，"依靠，由于"；[C] with the exception of "除了……"；[D] for the purpose 为……的目的；注意 explanation 常与 for 搭配。

46. 答案：[C] deprivation

[A] reduction 减少；与 total 矛盾；[B] destruction 毁坏；一般是指具体的事物；[C] deprivation 剥夺；[D] restriction 限制；与 total 矛盾。

47. 答案：[A] upon

[A] upon/on＋句词/动名词＝when 引导的时间状语从句；[B] by "通过，凭借，靠"，主要表示方法，手段；[C] through "通过，凭借，靠"，主要表示方法，手段；[D] with 用于具体的工具。

48. 答案：[D] cast light on

[A] paid attention to 注意；语义不通；[B] caught sight of 看到；语义不通；[C] laid emphasis on 强调，相当于 emphasize；[D] cast light on 阐明，说明，使清楚；mystery 需要阐明。

49. 答案：[A] develop

[A] develop 得，患病；[B] produce 产生，制造；不与 bacterial infections of the blood 搭配；[C] stimulate 引诱，诱使；与句意不符；[D] induce 引诱，诱使；与句意不符。

50. 答案：[B] as if

[A] if 如果；在此不合逻辑；[B] as if 好像；空格前后时态不一致；[C] only if 只要，引导条件状语从句；[D] if only 一般用来引导感叹句，在此不合逻辑。

　　参考译文：

　　睡眠通常被分为所谓的"快动眼"睡眠阶段（REM＝rapid eye movement）和较长的非快动眼睡眠阶段。前者特点为眼球快速转动并做梦。我们对两种形式的睡眠了解都不多，但是人们设想 REM 睡眠对大脑起某种康复功能。非快动眼睡眠起的作用更神秘。最近睡眠研究协会在明尼阿波利斯举行的会议上，专家们首次描述的一些新实验，对眼球非快速移动睡眠的作用的阐释令人着迷。

　　比如，人们早已了解到，完全剥夺其睡眠对老鼠具有 100％的致命性，然而，在检查老鼠死尸时，这些动物看上去完全正常。一研究人员已阐明这些动物死亡原因的奥秘。老鼠患血液细菌感染，似乎他们的免疫系统——抵御疾病的自我保护机制——已崩溃。

（1996 年）

41. 答案：[C] nor

从本题语法结构来看,应是两个并列分句,表示"既不……也不……",后一个分句为倒装形式。[A]either"或"和[B]so"因而,所以"作连词时不表否定,同时不用倒装;[D]never"永不"虽表示否定,但为副词不属连词,故也应排除;[C]nor"……也不……",既可作为连词与 neither 构成 neither...nor..."既不……也不……"句型,也可放在 not,no,never 等否定词之后表示否定,组成"nor＋助动词＋主语＋动词或 be 动词＋主语"的倒装结构。例如：The day was cold,nor was there any heating in our office.那天天气很冷,办公室又没有暖气。故只有[C]nor"……也不……"能构成本题结构。

译文：维生素属于有机化合物,少量存在于食物中,为包括人在内的动物正常生长和维持生命所必需。它们不提供能量,也不能构成身体的任何部分。

42. 答案：[D] transforming

transform sth. into sth. 意为"将某物转换为另一物",例如：transform heat into power 把热能转换为动力;transform passivity into initiative 变消极被动为积极主动;transform an opponent into an ally 化敌为友。而本题正是意为"将食品转变为能量……";其他选项[A]shifting"移动,替换";[B]trans-ferring"转移";[C]altering"改变,变更"均不能确切表达题意。

译文：人们需要它们来将食物变为能量,维持身体所需。

43. 答案：[A] any

any＋of＋名词表示"有多少,些许",常用于 if 从句、疑问句中,例如：If any of your friends want to go,let me know. 如果你有任何朋友要去,请通知我。在本题句中,由于主句中的主语 them 与 if 从句中主句相同,所以将"any of them"省略为 any,原句应为"and if any of them is missing..."。在其他选项中,[B]some 指"某些"(可数名词),而句子谓语动词为单数形式"is missing";[C]anything 和[D]something 泛指"某物"。与题意不符,故均可排除。

译文：这些维生素有 13 种以上,如果缺少其中 1 种,便会明显地患上某种维生素缺乏症。

44. 答案：[B] apparent

本题意指"如缺少某种维生素,便会明显地患上某种维生素缺乏症"。从逻辑上说,[A]serious,[C]severe,[D]fatal 均意为"严重的,致命的","维生素缺乏症"不会如此"严重",故应排除;[B]apparent"明显的,表面的"能准确地说明这种症状,故应为正确选择。例如：an apparent advantage 表面上的优点;with apparent difference 明显的差别。

译文：参见第 43 题。

45. 答案：[C] sometimes

本题须从逻辑上来加以分析,句中"usually...,and sometimes..."意为"通常……,有时……";如采用[A]mostly"大多数地",则与 usually 相矛盾;如采用[B]partially"部分地",则与事实不符;惟有[C]sometimes 能从句子结构与逻辑上合理地表达题意。

译文：维生素都很类似,因为它们都由相同的元素构成—通常为碳、氢、氧,偶尔有氮。

46. 答案：[A] in that

本题主要测试固定搭配。difference in 意为"在……上的区别",例如：There isn't any difference in structure between the two machines. 这两部机器的构造没有任何差别。He has explained the differ-ence in meaning between the two words. 他解释了这两个词意义上的区别。本题中"in that"应理解为 that 从句作介词 in 的宾语;[B]so that"以致,以便",[D]except that"除了……",[C]such that"如此,这样",均不与 difference 搭配,同时不符合逻辑,故均应排除。

译文：它们的差异在于它们的元素排列不同,而每一种维生素在人体内都有一种或一种以上的特殊功能。

47. 答案：[D] performs

本题主要测试动词近义词的习惯用法。从动词与名词的固定搭配来看,perform functions 意为"行使……功能,尽到职责",function 常与 fulfill,serve,exercise 等动词相搭配,组成动宾结构;[A]un-dertakes"进行",[B]holds"掌握"和[C]play"扮演"均不与 function 构成固定搭配,play 常构成"play a role,play the part of"结构。

译文：参见第 46 题。

48. 答案：[B]Getting

　　从句子逻辑上来说,主语是身体 body,它也是分词短语的逻辑主语,采用[B]Getting 意为"身体获得足够的维生素……";而采用[A]Supplying 则意为"身体提供足够的维生素……";[C]Providing 也为此意;[D]Furnishing 意为"装备,供给",也与原意不符;故后三项均应排除。

　　译文:虽然过量的维生素对身体没有任何营养价值,但获取足够的维生素却是生命所必需的。

49. 答案：[C]excess

　　题句意为过量的维生素对身体无用,[C]excess 作形容词时意为"超过的,过剩的",例如:an excess charge 多收费;an excess rain 过多雨量;an excess demand 过分要求。[A]exceptional"例外的";[B]exceeding"极度的";[D]external"外部的"均不符合题意要求,故均可排除。

　　译文:参见第 48 题。

50. 答案：[A]nevertheless

　　从句子上下文来看,本句应是上句的转折,表达"然而,……"。四个选项中仅有[A]nevertheless 可表达这种关系,例如:He was tired,nevertheless,he kept working. 他很累,然而他继续工作。[B]therefore"因此,为此"表示因果关系;[C]moreover"再者,此外"表示递进关系;[D]meanwhile"同时"表示时间关系,故均不符合题意。

　　译文:然而,许多人出于"安全"考虑而服用过多维生素。不管怎样说,一种搭配很好的饮食通常就能完全满足整个身体对维生素的需求。

　　参考译文:

　　维生素是有机化合物,饮食中必须含有少量维生素以维持动物(包括人)的生存和生长。

　　它们不提供能量,也不构成身体的任何一部分,它们的任务是把食物转变成能量和维持身体健康。至少有13种维生素,若缺其中一种,缺乏症疾病便明显可见。

　　各种维生素都很相似,因为它们由同样的元素构成,一般是碳、氢、氧,有时还有氮。它们的不同之处在于每种维生素内部的元素排列不同,并且每种维生素在人体内都有一种或多种特殊作用。

　　虽然维生素对人体并无什么营养上的用处,但吸收足够的维生素是必要的。尽管如此,有些人出于保险的想法,还是摄入过量的维生素。不过,均衡的饮食一般能够完全满足身体对维生素的需求。

(1997 年)

41. 答案：[A]swarm

　　本题主要测试动词词义理解。文章开始大意是:拥有 56 万员工的人力资源公司是世界上最大的临时就业机构。每天早上,它的员工涌入美国各办公机构和工厂,寻找一天的工作,取得一天的报酬,……swarm 意为"涌往,密集",swarm into"涌入",例如:People swarmed into the exhibition hall. 人群涌进展览馆。stride"迈大步";separate"分开,(使)分离";slip"滑,滑倒";均与题意要求"涌入"不相关,故均可排除。

　　译文:每天早晨,它的员工涌入美国各办公机构和工厂,寻找一天的工作,取得一天的报酬,每天一次。

42. 答案：[C]As

　　从本题句的选项来看,[A]For,[B]Because,[C]As,[D]Since 均可表示原因,表示"因为,由于";而 as 除了表示"由于",还可表示"随着,同时"。从句子的上下文来看,意指"……大公司为了生存而削减雇员,人力资源公司却蒸蒸日上",不存在"因果关系",而是一种同时发生的"时间关系",故应选用[C]as"随着"。例如:As I was walking down the street,an American asked me for directions to the nearest station. 当我走在街道上时,有个美国人问我往最近的车站怎么走。

　　译文:当通用汽车公司和 IBM 等大公司为了生存而进行裁员时,总部在威斯康星州密尔沃基市的人力资源公司却蒸蒸日上。

43. 答案：[D]by

　　通过什么手段或途径去实现某种目的应选用介词 by,意为"用……,借助于……,根据……",例如:You can make the cake by mixing eggs and flour. 把鸡蛋和面粉混合,你就可以做出那种蛋糕。[A] from,[B]in,[C]on 均不具备这种用法。

译文:参见第42题。

44. **答案:**[A] Even though

本题主要测试引起状语从句的几个连词的用法。even though"即使……,纵使……,虽然",引起的从句内容为主句的前提,表示转折,例如:Even though he is poor,she loves him.尽管他很穷,她还是爱他。now that"现在已经……,既然已……",表示原因,例如:Now that I've seen how he lives,I know why he needs so much money.看过了他的生活状况,我现在才知道他为什么需要那么多钱。if only "要是",通常与表示假设的动词连用,省略主句,表示惊讶、愿望,例如:If only John were here with us! 要是约翰和我们一起在这里该多好! provided that"假若,倘若",表示条件,例如:Provided(that)there is no opposition,I will act as representative of our class.倘若没有反对的话,我将担任本班的代表。本题句应为一种转折关系,即指"虽然……经济恢复,但美国却……",故应选择[A]Even though。

译文:虽然经济继续复苏,美国却越来越成为一个计时工和临时工的国家。

45. **答案:**[B] disposable

本题主要测试根据上下文选用适当的形容词。disposable 意指"用完即丢的,可自由使用的",例如 a disposable paper cup 用完即丢的纸杯。在本题句中它用来指计时工和临时工队伍,并加上引号,表示比喻。[A]durable 意为"经久的,耐用的"与题意相反;[C]available"能利用的,有用的",不能准确表达句中"计时工和临时工"的"一次性"特点,也不能加上引号用作比喻;[D]transferable"可转让的,可转移的",也不能准确表达句意,同时不宜加引号用作比喻。经比较,[B]disposable"用完即丢的"最贴近题意。

译文:这种"一次性"劳动大军的出现是当今美国商业发展的最重要的趋势,它从根本上改变了人们与自己工作之间的关系。

46. **答案:**[D] trend

本题主要测试近义词词义辨析。题句意指"这种'一次性'劳动大军的出现是一种潮流(趋势或倾向)……",比较:trend"倾向,趋势",例如:The trend of taxes is still upward. 税金还有提高的趋势。economic trends in China 中国的经济趋势[A]approach 意为"接近,通道";[C]fashion 意为"流行,时髦,时尚,方式";[B]flow 意为"流出,流入",例如:the flow of the traffic 交通流量,不含"趋势"之意。故[D]trend"趋势,倾向"最能表达原意。

译文:参见第45题。

47. **答案:**[C] fundamentally

本题主要测试对副词词义的理解。从内容来看,题句意指:这种趋势从根本上改变了……之间的关系。[A]instantly 意为"立即",不符合题意;[B]reversely 意为"相反地,颠倒地",与题意不相干;[D]sufficiently 指"足够地",也不合乎逻辑;[C]fundamentally 指"根本地,本质地",能恰当地表达题意。

译文:参见第45题。

48. **答案:**[B] while

本题句主要测试连词的选用。句中分词短语 avoiding……应表示与主句谓语动词 provides 同时发生的动作,即"……提供了……,同时避免了……"。[A]but 表示"转折关系",而[C]and 表示"并列关系",故均不适合本题结构;[D]whereas 指"另一方面,反之",用于引导对比、对立的从句,但不引导分词,故也可排除;[B]while 表示"和……同时,另一方面",在引导从句时,如果从句主语与主句相同,从句主语和 be 动词可省略,例如:He watched TV while eating.他边吃边看电视。本题句正属于这种句型,故[B]while 为正确选择。

译文:这种现象为各公司提供了一条出路,一方面可保持全球市场的竞争力,同时又可避免商业周期循环和由用工条例、医疗保健费用和退休金计划所带来的日益沉重的负担。

49. **答案:**[A] imposed

本题主要测试动词近义词辨析。由于所填的动词过去分词是作 burdens"负担"的后置定语,而

[A]imposed 则正是指"使负担，由……强加的"之意，例如：A new tax imposed on food imports was decided by the government. 政府决定对进口食品加以新税。

其他选项，[B]restricted"受限制的"；[D]confined"限制的，监禁的"；[C]illustrated"说明的"；均不能准确表达题意。

译文：参见第 48 题。

50. 答案：[D] importance

本题主要测试名词词义理解。从题中 sense 一词来看，可组成各种词组：sense of humour 幽默感；sense of duty 责任感；sense of direction 方向感；sense of business 经商意识；而本题中 sense of importance 指"重要性，重要感"。[A]excitement"激动"；[B]conviction"确信"；[C]enthusiasm"热情"；此三项在本题题意中均不适宜与 sense 搭配，故只能选用[D]importance。

译文：对于工人们来说，这意味着那种忠实雇员所享有的保障、福利好处和重要感将不复存在。

参考译文：

拥有雇员 56 万人之众的劳务公司，是世界上最大的临时就业机构。每天早晨，公司的员工纷纷涌向美国的机关和工厂，为拿到日工资而寻找一天的工作。一次就一天了，因为一些工业巨头，如通用汽车公司和国际商用机器公司都靠裁员谋求生存，因此，总部设在威斯康星州密尔沃基市的劳务公司得以兴旺起来。

即使美国的经济继续恢复，但是兼职人数和临时工的人数也还是不断增加。这种"一次性"的就业大军是当今美国经济的最重要的趋势，而且它从根本上改变了个人与职业的关系。这种现象为这些公司开辟了一条道路，使其既不失国际竞争力，又可以不受市场周期的冲击，避免就业法规，医疗保健和养老金法案带来的日益增加的负担。对雇员而言，这将意味着不再享有保障、福利，不再具有作为一个忠实雇员的使命感。

(1998 年)

41. 答案：[A] admitted

本题的选择须从上下文逻辑上加以判断，考生切忌孤立地从某一句子进行猜测。从前三个句子来看，第一、二个句子为陈述事实，第三个句子以 but 开头，表示转折："直到最近，大多数历史学家对工业革命仍持强烈批评态度。他们(承认)，从长远看，工业化大大地提高了(普通)人的生活水平。但是他们坚持说……"，从逻辑上看，"承认"表示一种让步关系，而"但是"表示一种转折关系，二者之间是相关联的。而选用[B]believed"相信"，[C]claimed"宣称"，[D]predicted"预言"，则不能恰当地表达这种关系，故正确选择应为[A]admitted"承认"。

译文：直到最近，大多数历史学家对工业革命仍表示强烈的批评。他们承认，从长远来说，工业化大大地提高了普通人的生活水平。

42. 答案：[B] average

本题测试要点为形容词近义词辨析。average"普通的，平常的，一般的"，例如：Is the five-day week the average now? 现在一般人每周工作 5 天吗？He is just an average student. 他只是一个普通的学生。plain"朴素的，平常的"，例如：plain living 俭朴的生活；plain people 平民(与"一般人"意义有所不同)；mean"平均的"，例如：the mean annual temperature 全年的平均温度；normal"标准的，正常的"，例如：normal working hours 正常的工作时间。mean 与 normal 一般不修饰 man，即使修饰，其意义已变；plain 修饰 man 时含"朴素"之意；故只有[B]average"一般的"，最贴近题意。

译文：工业化大大地提高了普通人的生活水平。

43. 答案：[D] immediate

本题测试要点为形容词近义词辨析。四个选词均有"快"的含义，但用法有所不同：immediate"直接的，立即的"，例如：an immediate cause 直接原因；immediate information 直接得到的情报；momentary"瞬间的",例如：a momentary feeling of fear 短暂的害怕；prompt"迅速的，即刻的",例如：make prompt payment 即时付款；a prompt reply 立即的答复；instant"立即的，紧急的",例如：an instant death 猝死；an instant reply 立即回答。本题句意指"工业化带来的直接后果",只有[D]immediate"直接的"能确切表达这个含义。

译文：但他们坚持说,从 1750 年到 1850 年期间,工业化带给英国大多数人口的直接后果是普遍的贫困和苦难。

44. 答案：[A] bulk

本题主要测试名词近义词选择。bulk"主体,大部分",(+of+名),例如：Farmers form the bulk of our population. 我国人口中大部分是农民。The oceans form the bulk of the earth's surface. 地球表面的大部分是海洋。host"一大群,许多",(+of+名),例如：a host of friends 众多朋友；a host of questions 众多问题；gross"总数",例如：the gross amount 总额；gross income 总收入；magnitude 重大,巨大,例如：the magnitude of the universe 宇宙的广大；a decision of magnitude 重大的决定。本题句指的是"英国人口的大多数",bulk 常与定冠词连用表示人口,其他选词不能表达这个含义。

译文：工业化带给英国大多数人口的直接后果是普遍的贫困和灾难。

45. 答案：[D] By

本题主要测试介词短语固定搭配。by contrast 意为"对比起来,对比之下",为固定介词短语搭配,表示两个比较物的反差,例如：By contrast, even the most modern aircraft look clumsy and slow. 对比起来,即使最现代的飞机也显得外表笨拙,飞行缓慢。Back in the drawing room the atmosphere seemed, by contrast, formal. 回到客厅,对比起来,气氛似乎很正式。四个选项中,[A]On,[C]For 一般不与 contrast 搭配,故可排除；[B]With 虽可组成 by contrast with"和(某物)对比起来"或 in contrast with/to"和(某物)形成对比",但 with 后须接比较物为宾语,也不符合本题结构；很显然,by contrast 在本句中可视为插入语。

译文：与此相比,他们视过去的一百年,即从 1650 年至 1750 这段时期,为一个繁荣昌盛时期……

46. 答案：[D] completely

本题主要测试副词词义理解。本句意为"英国还完全是一个农业国家",所填副词修饰形容词 agricultural,比较：completely"完全地,彻底地",例如：I was completely lost in what I should do. 我完全不知道要做什么。She was completely successful in the final examination. 她期终考试取得圆满成功。broadly"概括地,一般地",例如：Broadly speaking, she is right in her judgement. 总的来说,她的判断是对的。thoroughly"彻底地",例如：I feel thoroughly exhausted. 我感到精疲力尽。generally"通常,总体,大致",例如：Banks generally close at three thirty. 银行通常在 3 点半关门。Generally speaking, women cry more easily than men. 一般而言,女人比男人容易哭。在 4 个选项中,broadly"概括地"与 generally"通常地"常用于修饰全句或动词,thoroughly"彻底地"虽可修饰形容词,但要加以选择。这三个副词均不适宜修饰题句中的形容词 agricultural,故只能选[D]completely。

译文：那时,英国还完全是一个农业国家。

47. 答案：[A] however

本题主要测试常用连词、副词。however"然而,可是,但是",连词,表示转折,与 but 意义相同,可置于句首、句末或句中,前后用分号隔开的情形较多。例如：Certainly he apologized, however, I won't forgive him. 他的确道歉了,然而我不会原谅他。meanwhile"同时,在这期间",副词,表示时间,例如：The train won't leave for an hour. Meanwhile, we can have lunch. 火车在 1 小时内不会开走,在这期间我们可以吃午餐。therefore"因此,因而,所以",副词表示因果,例如：He worked day and night, and therefore he was able to buy the sports car. 他日夜工作,所以有能力买那部跑车。moreover"并且,除此以外",副词,表示递进,例如：The new manager is intelligent and hard working, and moreover he is very charming. 那位新任经理才多智广,工作努力,并且也很有人缘。由于本题句是表示转折关系,所以应选用[A]however"然而"；此外 meanwhile,therefore,moreover 很少前后用分号隔开。

译文：然而,这种观点一般被认为是错误的。

48. 答案：[B] in

本题主要测试介词搭配。

表示某一领域或学科的专家(specialist)通常与介词 in(on)连用，例如：a specialist in Oriental history 东方史方面的专家；a specialist in nervous disease 神经病专家；a specialist in modern language 现代语言专家；a specialist in heart(lung) disease 心脏(肺)病专家。其他选项[A]at,[C]about,[D]for 均不构成此种搭配。

译文：历史学家与经济学家已说明了两点：贫穷是 1650 年到 1750 年这段时期的显著特点,工业化肯定没有加剧贫困,反而是改善了大多数人的生活条件。

49. 答案：[C] shown

本题主要测试考生对动词词义的理解,题句指"历史学家与经济学家说明了……"。show"告诉,说明",例如：Please show the meaning of this word. 请说明这个单词的意思。The salesman showed her the various uses of the machine. 那个推销员向她说明那部机器的各种用途。manifest"证明,使……明确",例如：The photograph manifested the truth of what she said. 那张照片证明了她所说的话是真的。speculate"沉思,推测",例如：speculate about the origin of the universe 思索宇宙的起源；approve"批准,赞同",speculate"思索,推断"均不切合题意；manifest 倾向于"思想,感情"的表明,而 show 则常用于"观点、看法"的表达,故[C]最贴近题意。

译文：参见 48 题。

50. 答案：[D] marked

本题主要测试动词的习惯用法。"be marked by"或"be marked with"表示"以……为特点,以……为标志",例如：His face is marked by small-pox. 他的脸上留下了些天花的痕迹。Byron's writings are marked by passionate fire. 拜伦作品的特点是充满火热的激情。noted 意为"记录,注意"；impressed 意为"印象深刻"；labelled 意为"做记号,贴标签"。而题句意指"某一时期的特点",所以[D]marked 最切合题意。

参考译文：

直到最近,多数历史学家对工业革命仍持强烈的批评态度。他们承认,从长远观点来看,工业化的确大大地提高了普通老百姓的生活水平。但是,他们坚持说,从 1750 年到 1850 年期间,工业化的直接结果是广大英国人民的普遍贫困和苦难。对比之下,在此之前从 1650 年到 1750 年的 100 年间,英国还是一个完全的农业国,他们认为是一个富裕和繁荣的时期。

然而,人们普遍认为这种观点是错误的。历史学和经济学方面的专家已经证明了两件事：从 1650 年到 1750 年期间以极度贫困为特征,而工业化显然没有使这种状况恶化；事实上却可能改善了绝大多数平民百姓的生活条件。

(1999 年)

41. 答案：[D] with

本题主要测试介词的搭配用法。选项中[B]in 和[C]on 均不能与其后的名词 rates 构成搭配关系,故可排除。[A]at 与[D]with 均可与 rate 搭配使用,但用法有所不同。at the rate of 表示"以……的比例,以……的速度",rate 应为单数,同时修饰动词,例如：travel at the rate of 100km an hour 以每小时 100 公里的速度行进；with+名词构成介词短语表示"具有……",常作名词的后置定语。题句中的填空位于名词 companies 之后,故只能用 with 构成介词短语作其后置定语,companies with low accident rates 意为"事故率低的公司",符合题意,故应选[D]with。

译文：事故率低的公司制订自己的安全措施,努力实施这些措施,并……

42. 答案：[A] alive

本题主要测试动词短语搭配。keep alive 为固定搭配,意为"使继续下去",例如：The politicians kept the argument alive. 政治家们为这个论点争论不休。句中 them 指 safety programs,即指将"使这些安全措施继续执行下去",与上下文相符。而 keep 不与[B]vivid"生动的",[C]mobile"移动的",[D]diverse"多样的"组成固定搭配,同时从意义上也说不通,故均应排除。

译文:努力实施这些措施,并继续保持执行,使之有效。

43. **答案:**[B] climate

本题句主要测试对抽象名词的正确理解。题句意为:"如果这项工作进行得很好,就可建立起一种无事故的操作环境。"很明显,[A]regulation"规章,规则"和[D]requirement"要求"与题意不符,可先排除。[C]circumstance 指"环境"时一般用复数形式,作单数时表示"一个情况",例如:I was ignorant of one important circumstance. 我忽视了一个重要的情况。[B]climate"气候,气氛,风气"一般只用单数,例如:the present political climate 当前的政治环境。本选项前有不定冠词 a,故选用[B]climate 既符合题意也符合语法结构。

译文:如果这项工作做得很好,就可建立起一种无事故的操作环境,……

44. **答案:**[A] where

本题主要测试关系副词 where 的用法。从本题句的语法结构来看,a climate 是主语,谓语成分为 is established,后面的部分有主语 time lost 和谓语 is kept,可见后面是一定语或状语从句。[C]what 和[B]how 引导主语从句和宾语从句,故应排除;[D]unless"除非"可引导条件状语从句,但从题句意义上说不通;[A]where 可作关系副词引导定语从句,修饰 climate,既符合题意符合语法。where 的这种用法,例如:Let's think of a situation where this idiom can be used. 咱们来想一个可以使用这个习语的场合。

译文:如果这项工作做得很好,就可建立起一种无事故的操作环境,由工伤造成的时间损失便可保持在最低限度。

45. **答案:**[B] differ

本题主要测试表示"不同,差异"一类意义的同义词辨析及搭配。由于所填动词应与介词 in 搭配,[A]alter"改变"为及物动词,后不接介词;[B]differ"不同,有差别",后接介词 in 表示"在……方面不同",例如:differ in opinions 意见不一致;[C]shift 替换,转变,后接 from...to...;[D]distinguish"区别",通常搭配为"distinguish A from B"。很明显,只有[B]differ(in)符合题意。

译文:成功的安全措施在侧重点方面会有很大区别。

46. **答案:**[C] observing

本题主要测试对动词词义的正确理解。题句中所填动词的宾语为 rules"规章,规则"和 regulations"规章,法规",而只有[C]observe"遵守"通常与这两词搭配使用,意为"遵守规章制度";而其他三个动词[A]constitute"构成,组成",[B]aggravate"加重,加剧",[D]justify"证明……公正"均不与这两词相搭配,故均可排除,答案为[C]observing。

译文:某些方面极力强调机械保护,另一些方面则注重以遵守规章制度来实现安全生产。

47. **答案:**[D] Still

本题主要测试上下文逻辑关系及习惯用法。从本段的第二个句子到第四个句子之间的逻辑关系来看,是一种递进关系,三个句子前面使用的过渡词应互相连贯:"Some place... Others stress... Still others depend on..."连贯起来译成:"一些措施重视……另一些强调……还有一些则靠……。" still 在这里意为"还,仍旧,尚"。其他选项[A]some,[B]many,[C]even 均不能构成这种逻辑关系,故应排除。答案只能选[D]still。

译文:还有一些措施则依靠对工人们诚恳的要求来实行。

48. **答案:**[C] pays off

本题主要测试对动词短语的理解。[A]comes off"发生,实现,成功";[B]turns up"出现,来到,(声音)调大";[D]holds up"举起,阻挡";[C]pays off"付清,使……得益,有成效",例如:Our plan paid off. 我们的计划有成效。His hard work paid off. 他的努力没有白费。从题句的意义来看,是指"安全措施起了成效",故只能选用[C]pays off。

译文:安全措施的价值毋庸置疑。单从经济角度考虑,安全生产也能产生效益。

49. **答案:**[A] claims

本题主要测试动词 claim 的正确使用。[A]claims"索赔,要求,声称",与句中 injury 构成词组 injury claims"工伤索赔"。其他同类构成有：damage claims 损失赔偿；territory claims 土地要求。其他选项[B]reports"报告"，[C]declarations"宣布，声明"，[D]proclamations"宣布，声明"均不合题意。

译文：工伤索赔次数越少，工人的保险率就越高。

50. 答案：[D] a profit

本题主要测试修辞上的对称。本题中 at a loss"亏本"应与[D](at)a profit"赢利"搭配才能从意义上对称。[A]an advantage"优势"，[B]a benefit"利益，好处"，[C]an interest"利益，利润"均不能与 at a loss 对称，故均应排除。

译文：这可意味着经营上盈利还是亏本的区别。

参考译文：

安全生产并非始自今日。事故发生率较低的公司往往制订安全计划，尽力安排计划的实施，并不断努力使其保持活力、发挥作用。当上述工作圆满完成时，一个无事故的作业环境便建立起来。在这里，因人员伤害而损失的时间便会保持在最低水平。

各种有效的安全计划其侧重点上很不相同。有些计划注重机械保护，另一些则强调通过遵守各种规章制度来进行安全生产。还有一些计划则主要靠对工人们，晓之以理，动之以情。但是如果要取得最好的结果，每个安全计划都要遵循一定的基本思想。

安全生产的价值毋庸置疑。单从经济角度来看，安全生产也是大有裨益的。伤害索赔越少，员工的保险率就越高。它可能意味着企业经营的盈亏。

(2000 年)

41. 答案：[C] instead of

逻辑衔接题。本题考查短语辨析。此段首句的意思是：一个农民要想成功，就必须努力保持其消费与生产之间较大差距，接着提到 store a large quantity of grain（储存大量的粮食）与 consuming his grain immediately（立即把他所有的粮食消耗完）这两种相反的做法，空格处需要填入一个连词连接语法成分不同的两个结构，因为 store 与空格后 consuming 语法形式上并不一致，这样就排除[A]、[B]、[D]，同时发现 store 与 consuming 属于反义同现，意思相对，能表达此逻辑相对关系的也只有[C]instead of。[A]other than"除了……以外；不包括"，一般用于否定句；[B]as well as "除了……之外还，又……"，表示并列关系[D]more than"多于，不止"语义与逻辑均不符。

42. 答案：[A] only if

逻辑衔接题。注意到空格前分句中用了情态动词"can"，而后面分句中动词为第三人称单数"produces"，据此推测前后两个分句是结果—条件关系，综合句意"有了粮食的剩余才能继续养家糊口"，即 he produces a surplus 是 he can continue to support himself and his family 的条件，四个选项中引导条件状语从句的只有 only if"只要"，相当于 if，但比 if 语气强。[B]much as"尽管"，表示让步关系，相当于 however much，如：Much as she needed the job，she had to refuse.（不管她是多么需要这份工作，她只能拒绝。）[C]long before"在……以前"，表时间关系；[D]ever since"自从……"，与表示时间的词连用，表时间关系。

43. 答案：[B] against

惯用衔接题。insurance 后面的介词有时用 for，有时用 against。当为某种（好）事物设立保险时，应用 for，当投保险是为了防范某种不利因素时要用 against。本句中的 unpredictable effects of bad weather 揭示这里的介词应用 against，与 insurance 形成结构同现。

44. 答案：[A] replace

语义衔接题。注意空格处应补全的是农民 sell 剩余的粮食的目的，同时注意空格所填必须与 old agricultural implements（旧的农业生产工具）照应，[B]purchase"购买"，[C]supplement"补充"；一般情况下人们不会买旧农具更不会补充旧农具，所以排除。[A]replace"替换"旧的生产工具，符合农民卖剩余粮食的目的。而[D]dispose"处理，扔掉"，用卖余粮换得的钱来处理旧生产农具更是说不通。本句句意为他（农民）必须以如下三种方式来利用这些余粮：用作播种的种子，用作不可预测的恶劣天气的防范，用作商品去销售以取代旧家具、买化肥给土壤增加养料。

45. 答案:[C] feed

语义衔接题。空格前的 to 提示所填词与 the soil 构成的短语是 obtain chemical fertilizer"得到化肥"的目的,供给化肥的目的只能是增加土壤肥力 feed the soil 正是习惯上对"增加土壤养料"的表达。enhance"增强,提高",通常用于效力,影响,价值等(如:enhance one's political consciousness 提高政治觉悟);mix"混合",混合土壤显然不是供给化肥的目的;raise"养育;栽培",如:to raise a family(供养一家人)。

46. 答案:[D] channels

语义衔接题。此题关键词为空格前的 irrigation,四个选项中与其属于同一语义场的只有 channels"水渠,渠道",指农民还需要灌溉渠道。[A]vessels"容器,船";[B]routes"海、空以及地图上的路线";[C]paths"乡间小路";均不与 irrigation 属于同一语义范畴。

47. 答案:[B] self-sufficient

语义衔接题。本句句意为"如果没有剩余,农民就不能……",后面一句又讲到他得变卖一些家产或是贷款,可见这里讲的是生存问题,很明显粮食没有剩余,农民就无法养活自己,也就不可能达到自给自足,所以选[B]self-sufficient"自给自足的",sufficient 与 surplus 相照应,近义同现。[A]self-confident"自信的"与[C]self-satisfied"自我满足的"以及[D]self-restrained"自我克制的"均与生存问题无关。

48. 答案:[D] seek

语义衔接题。四个选项均为我们熟悉的动词,到底选哪一个就涉及我们从逻辑语义上分析。所填动词的执行者 he 指的是不能自给自足的农民,因此判断他们不可节约更不可能提供额外的资金,故排除[B]save 与[C]offer。他们只能是以贷款的形式寻求额外的基金,[A]search 后面必须加 for 才能与名词连用,表示"寻找"的意思;[D]seek 后面可直接跟名词,表示"寻求",所以选[D]。

49. 答案:[C] rate

惯用衔接题。上句中提到的 in the form of loans 与本句中的 borrow money 均说明 interest 与贷款有关,是"利息"而不是"兴趣"的意思,而"rate of interest"或 interest rate 是固定的短语,表示"利率",这是 rate 与 of interest 结构同现。

50. 答案:[D] frequently

语义衔接题。本句的前半句指出,"农民自然会努力以低利息借款",转折连词 but 表明后面的内容与前半句的内容相反,也就是"这种低利息贷款并不能够经常获得",故选频度副词[D]frequently"经常地"这里 not frequently 与 naturally 反义复现。[A]genuinely"真诚地,诚实地",不能修饰 obtainable;[B]obviously"明显地";[C]presumably"假定地,可能地"。

参考译文:

农民要想成功,必须在其消费与生产之间努力保持较大的距离。他必须储存大量的粮食,而不是将全部粮食马上消费掉。只有生产有剩余,他才能养活他自己及其家人。农民必须以如下三种方式来使用这些剩余粮食:留作播种用,留作备荒用,留作商品卖掉以更新农具和买化肥用。要修建灌溉沟渠,或以其他方式改善农田,也可能需要钱。没有余粮,农民就不能自给自足。要么卖掉一些财产,要么通过贷款寻求资金。自然他会努力获取低息贷款,但是不能经常借得到这种低息贷款。

(2001 年)

本文论述了英国政府新近的一个措施:政府将禁止媒体出钱收买与重大案件有关的证人。目的在于通过法律程序杜绝因媒体披露或炒作造成的对司法判决的客观性和公正性的干扰。大法官 Irvine 勋爵将提议起草一个法案,法案中将规定付给证人报酬这种行为是违法的,在审判之前必须严格控制有多少案情信息可以披露于众。因为单靠自我约束这一措施并没有能充分控制媒体。下面我们来看一下各题的答案:

31. 答案:[D] such as

此题属于语义搭配题。选项[D] such as 可指对上文的举例说明,意为"像那样的",as 后接名词,例如:I visited several cities such as Shanghai, Beijing and Guangzhou. 也可分开用,即 such...as,例

如：Students such as these（＝such students as these）。空格后的 the trial of Rosemary West（对 Rose-mary West 的审判一案）是对空格前的 prominent cases（重大案件）的举例说明，因此[D]符合上下文的意思，是正确答案。选项[A] as to 意为"关于,至于",例如：As to money, he is indifferent. 在 wh-从句或短语前的 as to 可省略,例如：She was at a loss（as to）what to say. 选项[B] for instance 意为"例如",放在句子中间时,前后常有逗号隔开,例如：There are rare animals in Australia, for instance, koa-las and duckbills.（澳洲有稀有动物,例如考拉和鸭嘴兽。）选项[C] in particular 意为"特别",相当于especially,例如：This boy student, in particular, is good at playing basketball.

全句可译为：政府将禁止报界为买断卷入非常惹人注目的案件的证人而付给证人报酬的这种行为,如 Rosemary West 一案。

32. 答案：[A] tightening

此题属于语义搭配题。选项[A] tightening 意为"拉紧",例如：tighten the rope；其引申义为 to make a rule, law or system more strict. 例如：tighten（up on）measures/controls. 由此可见该选项可与下文中的 controls 搭配,句中的介词 of 表示动宾关系。选项[B] intensifying 意为"增强,变强"（in-crease in degree or strength）,例如：intensify his efforts（加紧努力）. 选项[C] focusing 意为"对准焦距,集中",（pay special attention to）,例如：focus on urgent problems. 选项[D] fastening 意为"系牢,捆绑,集中于",例如：fasten one's coat/one's attention on the swimming children.

33. 答案：[D] draft

此题属于语义搭配题。选项[D] draft 作名词时可意为"草稿,草案",即 sth. not yet finished。例如：a draft for a speech；又如：The plan is in draft.（那计划正在草拟中。）draft 也可转化为动词,例如：to draft a plan/a bill. 考生可能熟悉该词的以上两种词性,而本题则是要求填入一个能修饰名词的定语,于是首先就把[A]给排除了。事实上,draft 可作为形容词使用,例如：a draft proposal；且 bill 后面的定语从句 that will propose... 告诉我们这个议案还没有完全出台,还在草拟的过程中,所以选项[D] draft 正是正确答案。选项[A] sketch 意为"略图,粗略描写"（a short quickly-made drawing or a short written or spoken description）,例如：a sketch of your house（你房子的草图）；又如：a sketch of the author's life（作者的简历）。选项[B] rough 意为"粗糙的,粗暴的",含 not exact 之义,例如：rough paper/ideas/behaviors。选项[C] preliminary 意为"初步的,预备的"（happening before sth. that is more important, often in order to prepare for it）,例如：preliminary rounds of the competition。

34. 答案：[B] illegal

此题属于语义搭配题。四个选项都是加了前缀构成的反义形容词。选项[B] illegal 意为"不合法的"。根据本段落的首句可判断出本文的主题与法律有关,故[B]符合文意,并与上文中的 legal con-trols 相呼应。选项[A] illogical 意为"不合逻辑"的；选项[C] improbable 意为"不太可能的",例如：an improbable story；选项[D] improper 意为"不恰当的,不得体的",例如：improper use of public money。这三个选项都与本文主题不合。

35. 答案：[A] publicity

此题属于语义搭配题。选项[A] publicity 意为"（社会的）注目,宣传",例如：There is a lot of pub-licity about his achievements.（他的成就广受大众的注目。）又如：In spite of bad publicity, the new car sells well. 该选项的语义与上下文,特别是 newspapers, the press 等词相符合,故选[A]。选项[B] penalty 意为"刑罚,处罚",例如：death penalty. 选项[C] popularity 意为"流行,名气",例如：His pop-ularity with teenagers is just surprising. 选项[D] peculiarity 意为"特色,特性"。

36. 答案：[C] before

此题属于语法题。本题中需填入一个引导时间状语的连词。从本文的主题和本句的含义判断,Lord Irvine 主张在案件审判之前不应该对其进行过多的报道,故选项[C] before 是正确答案。选项[A] since 和选项[D] as 都可引导时间状语从句,但从语义上与原文不符。选项[B] if 引导条件状语从句或名词性从句,也不适用于本题。

全句可译为：为了加强法律对媒体的监管,大法官 Irvine 勋爵将提议起草一个法案：付给证人报酬这种行为是违法的,在审判之前必须严格控制有多少案情信息可以披露于众。

37. 答案：[D] agreed

此题属于语义搭配题。本题要求填入一个能与介词 with 搭配使用的动词，而选项[C] compiled 是及物动词，意为"编撰"，例如：compile a dictionary；因此可先排除。选项[A] sided 作动词与 with 连用时，意为"赞成（某）一方"，例如：I will side with you no matter what happens. 选项[B] shared 意为"分享"，例如：Will you share your umbrella with me? 选项[D] agreed 跟上介词 with 意为"同意，支持"，例如：I don't agree with any form of terrorism. 显然[D]符合题意，是正确答案。

38. 答案：[B] offer

此题属于语义搭配题。选项[A] present 作动词时意为"赠送，呈现"，用法为 present sb. with sth. 或 present sth. to sb.，例如：The boy presented the singer with a bunch of flowers. 该选项与本题语法上不符，可排除。选项[C] manifest 作动词意为"证明，表明"(show a feeling, attitude etc.)，例如：They have so far manifested a total indifference to our concerns. 选项[D] indicate 意为"表明，指出"，例如：He indicated the importance of exercises. 这两个选项与句子中的宾语 sufficient control 搭配，不能说明什么。因此选项[B] offer(提供)是正确答案。

全句可译为：Irvine 勋爵在给下议院大众传媒特别委员会主席 Gerald Kaufman 的一封信中说，今年该委员会的一篇报告中指出了单靠自我约束这一措施并没有能充分控制媒体；对于这一点，他很赞成。

39. 答案：[B] Publication

此题属于语义搭配题。选项[B] Publication 意为"出版，发表"，即 the act of making sth. known to the public，例如：the publication of the election results。上文提到了 Irvine 勋爵的一封信，本题所在的句子则提到了媒体抗议以后这封信就被公开发表了，因此[B]符合题意。选项[A] Release 意为"释放"，例如：a release from jail；又如：release of gas。选项[C] Printing 意为"印刷"。选项[D] Exposure 意为"暴露"，尤指"故意揭发，揭穿"某件有损于个人或团体名誉的事情真相，特别是一些罪行、阴谋等，例如：the exposure of political corruption(政府腐败的揭发)。

40. 答案：[A] storm

此题属于语义搭配题。[A] storm 意为"暴风雨"，可引申为"(喝彩、责难等)嘈杂声，骚动"(a situation in which people suddenly express very strong feelings about something that someone has said or done)，例如：a storm of applause/abuse/laughter。[A]符合题意，是正确答案。选项[B] rage 意为"狂怒，愤怒"，例如：fly into a rage；选项[C] flare 作名词时意为"闪耀的火光"，可引申为"(怒气等)爆发"，例如：a flare of anger；选项[D] flash 意为"闪烁，闪现"，例如：a flash of lightning。

41. 答案：[B] interpretation

此题属于语义搭配题。选项[A] translation 意为"翻译"；选项[B] interpretation 可用于意为"口译"，但是也可用于意为"解释，说明"(an attempt to explain the reason of sth.)之意，例如：the interpretation of the law；选项[C] exhibition 意为"展览，展示"；选项[D] demonstration 意为"证明，演示"，例如：a demonstration of the new machine。[B]符合文意，是正确答案。

42. 答案：[C] rather than

此题属于语义搭配题。选项[C] rather than 意为"而不是"，肯定该短语前面的事物，否定后面的事物，例如：I am bored rather than tired. 从原文的意思来判断，应由法官对隐私权的控制做出解释，而不是议会。故选[C]。选项[A] better than 意为"比……好"。选项[B] other than 意为"除了"，相当于 except，例如：Everyone is here other than Tom. 选项[D] sooner than 意为"比……早"。这三个选项都与原文的意思不符。

全句可译为：Irvine 勋爵声称，欧洲立法中包含了对隐私权的控制；对此，应该由法官做出解释，而不是议会。他的这番话引起了媒体的强烈抗议。两天后上述这封信就被公开了。

43. 答案：[B] makes

此题属于词语搭配题。分析整个句子，可看出 the European Convention on Human Rights 是本题所填的动词的宾语，第 14 个空格是宾语补语。据此，可排除选项[A] changes 和选项[D] turns；change 的用法是 change...into，例如：change water into ice；turn 的用法与 change 相同。选项[B] makes 和选项[C] sets 都可跟宾语和宾语补语,但是 make 意为"使某事或某物具有某种特点、性质",例如:Tests help make your new knowledge permanent. set 意为"使……成(状态)",例如:They set all the prisoners free. 两个选项相比,[B] makes 更符合语法和语义的要求。

44. 答案:[A] binding

此题属于语义搭配题。选项[A] binding 意为"有约束力的",例如:a binding contract/agreement。上文提到了 the Human Rights Bill(人权法案),可与 binding 搭配,故[A] binding 是正确答案。选项[B] convincing 意为"有说服力的",例如:His explanation is convincing. 选项[C] restraining 意为"制止,抑制";选项[D] sustaining 意为"支撑,继续";这两个选项一般都不用于这样的结构。

45. 答案:[C] entitled

此题属于词语搭配题。选项[A] authorized 意为"授权",用法为 authorize sb. to do sth.,例如:authorize the man to act as chairman。选项[B] credited 意为"信赖,相信",用法为 credit sb. with sth.,例如:Please credit me with honesty.(请相信我是诚实的。)选项[C] entitled 意为"赋予,使……具有(某)权利",用法为 entitle sb. to sth./to do sth.,例如:You are entitled to a rest. 又如:You are entitled to try once more. 选项[D] qualified 意为"赋予(某人)资格",用法为 qualify sb. for/as sth. 或 qualify sb. to do sth.,例如:Knowledge alone doesn't qualify you to teach. 本题后面是 to privacy,即介词 to+名词,故选项[C]符合本题要求,是正确答案。

全句可译为:大法官声明,人权法案的采用将使欧洲人权公约在英国也具有约束力;它明确规定每个人都有隐私权,公众人物可以用法律来保护自己和他的家人。

46. 答案:[A] with

此题属于词语搭配题。in safe hands with sb. 是固定搭配,意为"由……来处理很安全、妥当",例如:Are you sure your money is in safe hands with the bank? 其余选项:[B] to,[C] from 和[D] by 都不用于这个结构中,故只能选[A] with。

全句可译为:由英国法官来处理新闻自由,这种做法是很妥当的。

47. 答案:[D] issue

此题属于语义搭配题。选项[D] issue 可意指"讨论话题"(a problem or subject that people discuss),例如:We should raise the issue of unemployment. issue 的这个含义与下文提及的 concerns were raised...(人们关注此事)互相呼应,因此是正确答案。选项[A] impact 意为"冲击力",例如:The impact broke the windows of the car. 该词的含义可引申为"影响",例如:My father has a deep impact on me. 选项[B] incident 意为"事件,事变"。选项[C] inference 意为"推理",例如:What inference can you draw from this passage? 它们的词义都不符合文章此处的要求。

全句可译为:1995年 West 被判十项终身监禁后,收买证人就成为人们关注、讨论的话题。

48. 答案:[C] said

此题属于语义搭配题。选项[C] said 在此处意为"据说,据报道",用法为 It is said that... 或 Sb. is said to do sth.,例如:It is said that he was a singer when he was young. 也可以说成:He was said to have been a singer when he was young. 上文提到公众开始关注收买证人这一话题,此处意在说明原因(据传有19位证人夸大其词),故[C]符合上下文的意思。选项[A] stated 意为"陈述,表明",例如:Please state your name and address. 选项[B] remarked 意为"说,评论",例如:remark on the new film. 选项[D] told 意为"告诉"。此三个选项都没有"据说,据报道"的意思。

全句可译为:据说,共有19名证人被收买,向媒体透露他们的经历。

49. 答案:[D] that

此题属于语法题。本句中 Concerns were raised 是主句部分,witness might be encouraged... 是从句,修饰名词 concerns;而从句中主谓齐全,应该是 concerns 的同位语,故只有选项[D] that 可引导同位语从句,是正确答案。选项[B] when 在语义上与本句不符。选项[A] what 不可引导同位语从句,一般引导主语从句或宾语从句,例如:What you have said confused me. 又如:I will tell you what have happened. 选项[C] which 可用于引导主语从句、宾语从句或定语从句,考生应特别注意 which 引导的定语从句和 that 引导的同位语从句,要记住前者在从句中充当主语或宾语,而后者在从句中不充

当成分,试比较:

1) The news which excited us is that our team has won.

2) The news that our team has won excited us all.

50. 答案:[C] ensure

此题属于近义词辨析题。选项[A] assure 意为"使(某人)确信或放心",例如:He assured me that he was able to do that. 选项[B] confide 意为"吐露",例如:confide the truth to one's parents. 选项[C] ensure 意为"保证(某事会发生)"(make certain that sth. happens),例如:I am sorry I cannot ensure you a good post. 选项[D] guarantee 也意为"保证"之意,但是它的英语解释是 promise to make sure that sth. will definitely happen,例如:They have guaranteed that they will repay the money provided by the bank. [C]和[D]在语义上还是有一定差异的,而[C] ensure 更符合文意,是正确答案。

全句可译为:人们担心这样的做法会导致人们受到鼓励而在法庭陈述中夸大其词,致使法庭做出有罪的判决。

参考译文:

报界付款给那些牵扯到大案要案(诸如 Rosemary West 案件)的证人,以图买断。政府对此将要予以查禁。

为了更有效地对新闻界实施合法监控,大法官 Irvine 勋爵将草拟法案。该法案将提出,付款给证人是非法的;在审判开始前,对案件的曝光度要严格控制。

在写给众议院新闻媒体特别委员会 Gerald Kaufman 主席的信中,Irvine 勋爵说,他赞同委员会今年的报告,该报告称,自我约束并未实施足够的监控。

Irvine 勋爵说,对欧洲立法中所包含的关于个人隐私监控权的解释,将留给法官,而不是议会。这招致新闻媒体的一片抗议。此后两天,信被公之于世。

大法官说,引入《人权法案》使得《欧洲人权公约》在英国有了法律效力,按规定,人人都享有个人隐私权,公众人物可以到法庭去保护自己及其家人。

他说"由我们英国的法官来负责,新闻自由将安然无恙"。

1995 年,Rosemary West 被判十项无期徒刑,此后,付款给证人的做法成为争议颇多的问题。据说,足有 19 个人因向报界讲述其经历而获得报酬。人们开始关注:(接受报酬)可能会鼓励证人在法庭上夸大他们经历的事情,来保证(陪审团对被告)做出有罪的裁定。

(2002 年)

本文主要讲述通讯业的革命。人们常常把 20 世纪电视的发展与 15、16 世纪印刷术的普及作比较。15、16 世纪印刷术的普及到 20 世纪电视的发展,从电报、电话到现代社会的电脑、集成电路,通信变革的速度越来越快,对人们各方面的生活也产生了巨大的影响。下面我们来看一下各题答案:

21. 答案:[A] between

此题属于语法题。选项[A] between 表示"在……之间"。考生可能熟悉 between 作介词的用法,却不了解它其实还可作为副词,例如:We have four classes in the morning and two in the afternoon, and we have lunch between. 我们上午有四堂课,下午有两堂课,期间我们进午餐。本题主要考查副词的用法。上文中提到了 20 世纪电视的发展及 15、16 世纪印刷术的传播,下文则讲到了这两个时间之间发生的一些事情。因此,根据上下文的关系,应选择[A] between。选项[B] before 表示"在……之前",既可作介词,也可作连词,例如:Before the class, I went over the lesson. 又如:Before the discussion began, I had a cup of tea. 选项[C] since 表示"既然",可作介词、连词,也可作副词,例如:I haven't written home since Christmas. 又如:I have been at his bedside since he became ill. 再如:Things have not changed very much since. 选项[D] later 表示"后来"例如:a week later. 这三个选项都不符合题意。

全句可译为:然而,在 20 世纪与 15、16 世纪之间发生了很多事情。

22. 答案:[D] until

此题属于词语搭配题。读完此句,考生可以发现本句的主要结构是 it was not until... that...,这是固定搭配,not until 用于强调,例如:It was not until you told me that I knew he was the famous singer. 故选[D] until。其余选项:[A] after,[B] by 和[C] during 都与本题的语意不符。

23. 答案:[C] medium

此题属于语义搭配题。选项[C] medium 表示"媒体"。根据考生的常识不难判断本句中的主语 newspaper 应该属于 medium(媒体)的一种。选项[A] means 表示"方法、手段";选项[B] method 表示"方法";选项[D] measure 表示"措施"。

24. 答案:[B] company

此题属于语义搭配题。上文中的 in the wake of the pamphlet and the book 意为"紧跟随着小册子和书籍的出现",据此可以判断与此相对应的应该是 in the company of the periodical(伴随着期刊的兴起)。所以[B]是正确答案。选项[B]:in the company of 表示"在……的陪同下,伴随着",例如:I traveled Egypt in the company of two teachers. (我在两个老师的陪同下游览了埃及。)选项[A]:in the process 表示"在进行中",例如:The new library is in the process of being decorated. 新图书馆正在进行装修。选项[C]:in the light of 表示"鉴于,依据……看来",例如:In the light of the accident,we have put off the meeting till next week. (鉴于这次事故,我们已经把会议推迟到下个星期。)选项[D]:in the form of 表示"以……的形状",例如:The cookies were in the form of stars. (那些饼干的形状都像星星。)

全句可译为:直到 19 世纪,伴随着小册子、书籍和期刊的兴起,报纸成为前电子时代主要的媒体。

25. 答案:[B] speeded

此题属于词语搭配题。本题主要考查动词短语的含义,这是考查的一个重点。选项[B]:speeded up 表示"加速",例如:The train gradually speeded up. (火车逐渐加速了。)不难看出本句的含义是"在 15 世纪到 20 世纪之间,从火车、电报、电话到汽车、飞机,交通、通信业的变革速度是越来越快",故选[B]。选项[A]:gather+up 表示"收集",例如:gather up one's papers;选项[C]:work+up 表示"逐步发展",例如:work up to a climax(渐至高潮);选项[D]:pick+up 表示"捡起,学会",例如:pick up a few words。

26. 答案:[A] on

此题属于词语搭配题。选项[A] on 可表示"持续地",例如:He coughed on the whole night. lead on 则表示"带头,走在前面",例如:If you lead on,we will follow behind. 原句很长,考生可通过分析句子结构来理解其含义。我们可以发现主句是 communications revolution,而 beginning 与 leading 两个分词是平行结构作状语,因此所填的空格要与 leading 这个关键词有关。因此[A]符合题意,是正确答案。选项[D]off 跟在 lead 之后表示"开始",例如:She led off with a song. (她以唱歌开始。)其他的选项[B] out 和[C] over 都不能与 lead 搭配。

27. 答案:[D] into

此题属于语法题。选项[D] into 表示"进入",强调动态,例如:work far into the night. 上文中有 through the telegraph...,下文是 the 20th century world,说明革命一直持续直到进入 20 世纪,故选[D]。选项[A] of 可表示所有、所属,例如:the legs of a chair. 选项[B] for 表示"为了",例如:Do more exercise for the good of your health. 选项[C] beyond 表示"超越",例如:The town has changed beyond my recognition.

全句可译为:正是在这段时间之内,从火车的发明到电报、电话、收音机、电影的发明,再到 20 世纪汽车和飞机的发明,交通和通讯技术的革命一直占据领先的地位。

28. 答案:[D] perspective

此题属于语义搭配题。本题考查的是介词与名词的语意搭配。选项[D] perspective 意为"透视图,看法";in perspective 意为"正确地,适当地",例如:look at things in perspective(正确地观察事物)。[D]符合题意,是正确答案。选项[A] concept 意为"概念",例如:a concept of space;选项[B] dimension 意为"尺度,维度",例如:The dimension of the window is 150cm long by 120cm wide. 选项[C] effect 意为"效果";in effect 意为"实际上",相当于 in fact,例如:In effect the government has lowered the taxes for the rich and raised them for the poor. (实际上政府已经降低了富人们的税收而提高了穷人们的税收。)此题表明考生应多注意介词与名词构成的搭配词语。

全句可译为:并不是每个人都能正确观察到这个变革的过程。

29. 答案：[C] however

此题属于语篇连接题。选项[C] however 意为"然而"，插入句中，前后要用逗号隔开，例如：Certainly he apologized. However, I won't forgive him. 本题所在的句子很长，又出现了四个空格，这就需要考生同时考虑分析句子的语法关系和关键词语的搭配。上文说到"观察过程本身是很重要的"；本句中又提到"20世纪初电脑的引进……彻底地改变了这个过程"。那么，可以判断上下文应该是转折的关系，所以选[C]。选项[A] indeed 意为"确实，果然"，例如：I am indeed glad to hear the news. 选项[B] hence 意为"所以"，它后面的动词往往省略，例如：Her mother is a singer, hence her love for music. 该选项也可作副词，意为"今后，从此"，例如：What will the world have become a hundred years hence? 选项[D] therefore 意为"所以"，例如：We don't have enough money and therefore we have to give up the plan.

30. 答案：[B] followed

此题属于语义搭配题。上文提到20世纪初电脑的发明，接着就是60年代集成电路的发明，后者应跟随在前者之后，所以正确答案是[B] followed。选项[A] brought 意为"带来"；选项[C] stimulated 意为"刺激，激励"，例如：The desire to become a successful businessman stimulated him to work hard. 选项[D] characterized 意为"以……为特征"，例如：An elephant is characterized by a long trunk. （大象的特征是长鼻子。）

31. 答案：[D] although

此题属于语篇连接题。选项[D] although 可引导让步状语从句。原文从句中出现的否定词 not 可以看做是提示线索的标志词，因此从上下文的逻辑关系来判断，[D]是正确答案。选项[A] unless 意为"除非"（if...not），引导条件状语从句，例如：I won't go to see the film unless I finish my work. 选项[B] since 意为"自从，既然"。选项[C] lest 意为"惟恐，以防万一"，例如：She walked quietly lest she (should) wake up the child.

32. 答案：[A] apparent

此题属于语义搭配题。选项[A] apparent 意为"表面的，明显的"，例如：with apparent indifference（表面上装作漠不关心）；又如：His grief is apparent to me. 选项[B] desirable 意为"值得要的，令人满意的"，例如：a desirable job；该选项可用于 It is desirable for sb. to do sth. 或 It is desirable that... 的句型中，例如：It is desirable for you to be present. （希望你能出席。）选项[C] negative 意为"否定的，消极的"，例如：a negative response. 选项[D] plausible 意为"似是而非的"，例如：His explanation sounds fairly plausible to me. 本题考的是形容词语义的辨析，读懂整个句子后可发现[A]是最佳答案。

全句可译为：尽管一时之间，集成电路对媒体的影响不是很明显。然而，20世纪初发明了电脑，60年代发明了集成电路。人们开始普遍意识到这些彻底改变了这个变革的过程。

33. 答案：[A] institutional

此题属于语义搭配题。本题中需要填入一个与上文中的 personal 相对应的形容词，所以首先要了解 personal 的含义：个人的，个性化的。因此[A]符合题意。选项[A] institutional 意为"制度的，公共机构的"；选项[B] universal 意为"普遍的，通用的"，例如：a universal truth。选项[C] fundamental 意为"基本的，重要的"，例如：fundamental human rights；选项[D] instrumental 意为"仪器的，器械的"。

34. 答案：[C] capacity

此题属于词语搭配题。选项[C] capacity 意为"容量"，例如：The concert hall has a seating capacity of 1000. 可与 storage 搭配，意为"（电脑储存）容量"，因此[C]是正确答案。另外，该选项也可用于意为"能力，理解力"，例如：This book is beyond young children's capacity. （这本书超过了小孩子所能理解的范围。）选项[A] ability 意为"能力"，后面常跟不定式，例如：the ability to deal with the problem；选项[B] capability 意为"能力，资格"，例如：the capability for the job。选项[D] faculty 意为"能力"，后面常跟介词 for 或 of，例如：the faculty of reason. 该选项还可指"（大学的）院系，全体（大学）教员"，例如：the faculty of law(法学院)。不过这三个选项都不能与 storage 搭配。

全句可译为：随着时间的推移，电脑越来越小，功能越来越强，显示速度越来越快，储存容量越来越大，而且变得越来越个性化了。

35. 答案：[B] in terms of

此题属于语义搭配题。本题考查的是介词短语的习惯用法。选项[B] in terms of 意为"按照，在……方面"，例如：A 200-year-old building is very old in terms of American history.（从美国历史来看，一幢有着 200 年历史的房子是很古老的。）根据题意，人们认为电脑与人一样，是一代一代的，故选[B]。选项[A] by means of，意为"通过……的方法"，例如：He can express his thoughts by means of music.（他借音乐来表达思想。）选项[C] with regard to 意为"关于"，例如：He wants to speak to you with regard to your financial situation.（他想就你的经济状况和你谈一下。）选项[D] in line with 意为"与……一致"，如：His idea is not in line with mine.（他的想法与我的不一致。）

36. 答案：[D] smaller

此题属于语义搭配题。本题是以独立主格的形式出现，其逻辑主语是 distance，可指空间的距离或时间的间隔，能与它相搭配的只有选项[D] smaller。注意：选项[C] nearer 本身就表示距离或时间的接近，所以不能修饰 distance。但是我们可以说 The distance is long/short。因此考生在做题时要排除汉语思维方式对英语的干扰。选项[A] deeper 和选项[B] fewer 都与本题题意不符。

37. 答案：[A] context

此题属于语义搭配题。选项[A] context 意为"上下文"，也可指"背景，环境"（situation），例如：I think we need to look at these events in contest. 原句又是一个强调句型，所填空格的后面是一个定语从句，意为"我们所生活的……"，而与空格相对应的是 information society（信息社会），可以判定空格的意思应与 society 相近，故[A]是正确答案。选项[B] range 意为"（气温、价格等浮动的）幅度"，例如：the range of the price。选项[C] scope 意为"（能力、理解等的）范围"，例如：The problem is within the scope of the child. 选项[D] territory 意为"领土"。本题说明考生不仅要注意单词的第一义，即基本意思，还应加强对单词引申义的理解。

全句可译为：正是在电脑时代，"信息社会"这一说法才开始广泛地用于描述我们所生活的这个环境。

38. 答案：[C] influenced

此题属于语义搭配题。选项[C] influenced 意为"影响"，例如：The weather in summer influenced the rice crops. 本题所填的词应与下文中的 implications 相对应；implications 以复数形式出现时，表示 possible effects or results（可能导致的结果，关系）。换句话说，就是影响，所以[C] influenced 是正确答案。选项[A] regarded 意为"看做，考虑"，常与 as 连用，例如：I regarded him as my father. 选项[B] impressed 意为"使（某人）留下印象"，后面往往跟上 sb. 作宾语，例如：His behavior impressed me deeply. 选项[D] effected 作动词时意为"使……产生，改变"，例如：His opinion effected the plan.（他的意见改变了计划。）

39. 答案：[B] controversial

此题属于语义搭配题。选项[B] controversial 意为"有争议的"。下文中提到了通信革命带来的 benefits（利）和"harmful" incomes（弊），可见对于它在经济、政治等方面所产生的结果，人们还是有争议的，因此[B]是正确答案。选项[A] competitive 意为"竞争的"，例如：a competitive society；选项[C] distracting 意为"干扰的"，例如：the distracting noise；选项[D] irrational 意为"非理性的"。

全句可译为：在我们这个时代，在我们这个社会中，通信革命已经影响到了我们的工作、生活、思维和感觉；但是对于它在经济、政治、社会和文化方面所产生的结果，人们还有争议。

40. 答案：[C] against

此题属于词语搭配题。选项[C]：against 与 weigh 连用，意为"权衡（利弊）"，例如：He weighed the advantages of changing his job against the disadvantages.（他把换工作的利弊加以权衡比较。）根据上文"通信革命带来的结果还有争议"，可推断出本句的含义是：我们必须仔细权衡它所造成的利与弊。故选[C]。选项[A]：weigh above 不存在。选项[B]：weigh upon 意为"成为负担"，例如：He's under huge pressure at work and it's really weighing on him.（他的工作压力太大，已成为他的负担。）选项[D]：weigh with sb. 意为"对……很重要"，例如：Access to the railway station weighed heavily with us.（对我们来说，能到火车站是很重要的。）

从 2002 年试题中我们可以总结出以下规律：

① 对词汇的选择可考虑同一语义范围内词语的前后照应。例如：通读之后，我们发现 in the wake of the pamphlet and the book（随着小册子和书籍的出现）与第 24 题 in the company of periodical（期刊的兴起）语义上相互呼应；第 38 题 influenced 则与下文的 implications 相呼应。

② 根据上下文语义判断词汇。有些试题似乎在考查词汇，实际上是考查考生对短文的理解，如第 39 题，考的是人们对通讯革命在政治、经济等方面的看法怎样，下文出现了 benefits 和 harmful incomes（利与弊），显然前面提到的看法是不统一的，是 controversial（有争议的）。

③ 利用固定语言搭配或句子结构。如第 28 题 in perspective（正确地），第 34 题 storage capacity（储存容量），和第 22 题 it was not until...（直到……才……）。

④ 激活相关常识。根据常识，newspaper 应属于 medium（媒体，第 23 题）；随着科技的加速发展，媒体或通讯业的变革也在 speeded up（加速，第 25 题）等。

⑤ 从逻辑性、连贯性考虑语篇的结构。例如：第二段第一句是第一段结尾的转折（第 29 题，however）。

参考译文：

人们曾把 20 世纪电视的发展与 15、16 世纪印刷术的传播进行过比较。然而在这段时间之间还发生过许多事情。正如前面所讨论的，直到 19 世纪，报纸才继小册子和书本之后，与期刊一起，成为电子时代之前最重要的传媒。正是与此同时，通信革命加速发展，从铁路运输开始，发展到电报、电话、无线电和电影，直到 20 世纪的汽车和飞机。并非人人能正确地看到这一进程，而做到这点是很重要的。

然而，人们普遍认为，20 世纪初期出现的电脑，及随后 60 年代发明的集成电路，虽然对传媒没有产生立竿见影的影响，但是却完全改变了发展进程。随着时间推移，电脑变得越来越小，性能越来越强，而且，随着显示（效果）越来越清晰及存储量越来越大，电脑已不只是团体机构的用具，也成了个人的用具。像人一样，电脑也按"代"来划分，而且代与代之间的间距越来越小。

正是在这个计算机时代，"信息社会"这个词开始广泛用来描述我们所生存的环境。通信革命对工作、休闲以及我们思考和感受时空的方式都产生了影响，但是也产生了关于其经济、政治、社会及文化含义的不同看法。"益处"要针对产生的"害处"来权衡。很难一概而论。

(2003 年～2005 年真题解析见第三部分第一章及第一部分)

第二章　阅读理解

第一节　阅读理解综述

全国硕士研究生 2005 年入学考试大纲规定,阅读理解部分要求考生"应能读懂不同类型的文字材料(生词量不超过所读材料总词汇量的 3%),包括信函、书报和杂志上的文章,还应能读懂与本人学习或工作有关的文献,技术说明和产品介绍等"。新大纲对考生的阅读要求依然是原来的八项:

1.理解主要意思;

2.理解文中的具体信息;

3.理解文中的概念性含义;

4.进行有关的判断、推理和引申;

5.根据上下文推测生词的词义;

6.理解文章的总体结构及单句间、段落间的关系;

7.理解作者的意图、观点或态度;

8.区分论点和论据。

新大纲规定阅读理解部分由 A、B、C 三节组成,考查考生理解书面英语的能力。其中 A 部分主要考查"考生理解具体信息、掌握文章大意、猜测生词词义并进行推断等能力"。要求考生根据所提供的四篇(总长度约为 1600 词)文章的内容,从每篇所给出的 4 个选项中选出最佳答案。

阅读理解部分的目的是测试考生通过阅读获取信息的能力,既要求准确,也要求有一定的难度。主要测试以下五方面的能力:

1.掌握所读材料的主旨和大意;

2.了解说明主旨和大意的事实和细节;

3.既理解字面的意思,也能根据所读材料进行一定的判断和推论;

4.既理解个别句子的意义,也理解上下文的逻辑关系;

5.能就文章的内容进行判断、推理和信息转换。

以上五项阅读能力具体表现在以下三个方面:

a.辨别和理解中心思想和重要细节;其中包括理解明确表达的概念或细节;理解隐含表达的概念或细节(如:下结论、作判断、进行推论等);通过判断句子的交际功能(如:请求、拒绝、命令)来理解文章;辨别文章的中心思想(如:找出能归纳文章中心思想的要点);理解作者的观点和态度。

b.运用一些语言技能来理解文章:包括猜测词和短语的意思;句子层次的理解(如:理解句子所表达的原因、结果、目的、比较等);篇章层次的理解(如:运用词汇的、语法的承接手段来理解文章各部分的关系)。

c.运用专门的阅读技能理解文章:通过略读了解文章大意;通过查阅寻找具体信息。

阅读理解短文内容涉及社会科学(主要包括社会学、人类学、教育、心理学、经济、管理、金融等领域)、自然科学(主要包括交通、物理、化学、生物、工程、计算机、医学、农业等领域)和人文科学(主要包括哲学、历史、文学、语言、新闻、艺术等领域)。1996 年以来,上述三类文章所占数目如下表:

	社会科学	自然科学	人文科学
1996	4	0	1
1997	4	1	0
1998	4	1	0
1999	3	1	1

2000	3	1	1
2001	3	1	1
2002	1	2	1
2003	4	0	1
2004	3	0	2
2005	2	1	1

　　根据大纲要求,阅读理解的常考题型主要可归纳为五种:主旨大意型、推理判断型、词汇语义型、事实细节型及观点态度型。1996 年以来,各题型所占数目如下表:

	主旨大意型	推理判断型	词汇语义型	事实细节型	观点态度型
1996	2	8	3	5	2
1997	1	4	1	12	2
1998	3	5	3	7	2
1999	0	4	0	13	3
2000	0	9	0	6	4
2001	1	8	0	10	1
2002	1	6	2	9	2
2003	1	10	2	5	2
2004	0	5	3	10	2
2005	1	9	1	8	1
合计	11	68	15	85	21
占总数百分比	5.5	34	7.5	42.5	10.5

　　而且每篇文章后的几个问题也有大致的规律可循:第一题可能会涉及全文主旨大意;第二题一般是事实细节或词汇语义;第三题往往是推理判断题或观点态度题;最后往往是涉及文章标题(也是主旨型)或写作目的(多是判断型)的题目。

第二节　阅读理解解题技巧概述

一、精读重要句

　　阅读理解大约有五大题型,下面一一给大家讲解一下:

　　1. **细节题很简单,答案定位最关键**。细节题占的比重很大,解答细节题的关键在于能够快速准确地到原文中定位。只要位置确定,基本上答案可以选出。在这里就要培养对题干关键词的敏感度,并熟悉这些关键词的同义或近义词,这样考试时可以省出很多时间给其他题。

　　2. **推理题有点难,通用逻辑跑在先**。推理题虽然难,但是它所用到的逻辑是每个人都知道的最基本的逻辑。而这种逻辑其实是语言方面的,其实质就是“句子水平的同义代换”。一定要在原文中找到作者对所问的相关问题所进行的阐述,然后对那些阐述进行 paraphrase,这种同义代换过程中很容易由于某个小词的替换而影响了全句的意思。比如,原文提到的是 sometimes,而选项中用了 always,那么这个选取项就错误了。很多选项使用如“all nobody,everybody, only”等绝对化的字眼,那么这样的选取项很可能也是错误的。

　　3. **主旨题虽不多,每段句首要看全**。每当问到文章大意时,由于时间紧迫,最高效的办法就是注意首段和尾段,以及其他段落的首句。很多篇章的主要内容在开篇第一句讲明了,推理题的一种就是问作者举某个例子是为了……。这种题跟主旨有很大关系,一般所有的例子都是为了段落的主旨和文章的主旨服务,所以考生了解了这些,就可以斩钉截铁地确定选项了。

4.**语义题不用怕,上句下句帮你选**。每当出现词义题时,如果是生词,那么生词的词义会从上句和上句推断出来。往往帮助你找到词义的是该生词后面的同位语(或同位语从句)、定语从句与生词词性相同、位置成分相同的单词。如果考查的词或词组你认识,而选项中又有你知道的最根本含义,那么此项往往先要排除,因为必然考查引申含义。

5.**态度题只一道,就算错了也过关**。虽然错了也不影响大局,但是还是要争取拿到分数。那么态度题千万要记住的一点就是你自己想的完全不算数,要"置身其外",常见的态度词有:biased 有偏见的;impartial 公正的;puzzling 迷惑的;suspicious 怀疑的;objective 客观的;subjective 主观的;indifferent 漠不关心的;critical 批评的;opposing 反对的;supportive 支持的等。要想选对,往往要注意作者使用词汇的感情色彩,特别是一些形容词、副词。

许多文章有段落主题句或全文中心思想句,找出并抓住这些句子是至关重要的,尤其是段落的叙事结构、整体叙事结构都会因此而一目了然。往往这些句子会出现在段落中的首尾或文章的首尾段中。

经典实例　How is it that we in America have begun to lose this freedom? I believe it has started slipping away from us because of three misunderstandings.

First, the misunderstanding of the meaning of democracy. The principal of a great Philadelphia high school is driven to cry for help in combating the notion that it is undemocratic to run a special program of studies for outstanding boys and girls. Again, when a good independent school in Memphis recently closed, some thoughtful citizens urged that it be taken over by the public school system and used for boys and girls of high ability, that it have entrance requirements and give an advanced program of studies to superior students who were interested and able to take it. The proposal was rejected because it was undemocratic! Thus, courses are geared to the middle of the class. The good student is unchallenged, bored. The loafer receives his passing grade. And the lack of an outstanding course for the outstanding student, the lack of a standard which a boy or girl must meet, passes for democracy.

The second misunderstanding concerns what makes for happiness. The aims of our present-day culture are avowedly ease and material well-being: shorter hours; a shorter week; more return for less accomplishment; more softsoap excuses and fewer honest, realistic demands. In our schools this is reflected by the vanishing hickory stick and the emerging psychiatrist. The hickory stick had its faults, and the psychiatrist has his strengths. But the trend is clear. Do we really believe that our softening standards bring happiness? Is it our sound and considered judgment that the tougher subjects of the classics and mathematics should be thrown aside, as suggested by some educators, for doll-playing? Small wonder that Charles Malik, Lebanese delegate at the U. N. , writes: "There is in the West" (in the United States) "a general weakening of moral fiber. (Our) leadership does not seem to be adequate to the unprecedented challenges of the age. "

The last misunderstanding is the the area of values. Here are some of the most influential tenets of teacher education over the past fifty years: there is no eternal truth; there is no absolute moral law; there is no God. Yet all of history has taught us that the denial of these ultimates, the placement of man or state at the core of the universe, results in a paralyzing mass selfishness; and the first signs of it are already frighteningly evident.

上文中第一段即是全文中心思想句,即 theme sentence,而下述三段中的第一句是每一段的主题句,即 topic sentence。理出这些中心思想句和主题句,文章的叙事结构就非常明确了,主旨就可轻松把握住,这样就更有利于把握其中的细节问题。

二、略读或跳读处理的内容

在首先快速浏览了题干、题肢,初步把握文章大意及叙事结构的基础上,可大胆进行略读与跳读,

这样不但阅读速度快,也更容易居高临下,总体把握原文。在阅读中可略读或跳读处理的内容包括:

(一)繁琐的例证

为了说明问题,作者可借用形象的例子,有时候举例较繁琐,虽能说明问题,但常常很耗费时间,那么在例子所说明的问题不明白之时,可通过略读细读来理解,若例子所说明的问题比较明了,则例子部分可一带而过。如:

经典实例 First, the misunderstanding of the meaning of democracy. The principal of a great Philadelphia high school is driven to cry for help in combating the notion that it is undemocratic to run a special program of studies for outstanding boys and girls. Again, when a good independent school in Memphis recently closed, some thoughtful citizens urged that it be taken over by the public school system and used for boys and girls of high ability, that it have entrance requirements and given an advanced program of studies to superior students who were interested and able to take it. The proposal was rejected because it was undemocratic! Thus, courses are geared to the middle of the class. The good student is unchallenged, bored. The loafer receives his passing grade. And the lack of an outstanding course for the outstanding student, the lack of a standard which a boy or girl must meet, passes for democracy.

文中首句为主题句,其它部分都是举例说明的。如费城一中学校长号召人们起来反对这一错误的观念:为出色的学生开设专门的课程不民主等,举例部分无需精读即可明白其目的和大意。

(二)并列多项列举

有时许多功能相同的项目并列举,那么只读其中一两项即可,无需全读,即使其中有生词也可略读,不用放在心上。如:

经典实例 Preparing for the H. K. C) E. E.

"How can the Organic English Classes prepare students to take the H. K. C) E. E?"you may ask. Our tutors are also concerned about this aspect of course. We have analysed the past H. K. C) E. E. questions. We have to focus on the teaching of words and phrases relating to their real life experiences, **e. g. pastimes, bad habits, useful skills, idols, school studies, extra-curricular activities, family life, etc.**

文中黑体部分不过是实际生活经验——real life experiences中的一些例子,不需要逐项去看,可以略读或只读前一两项即可。

(三)无关大局的生僻字词

阅读中经常会遇到一些生词,而这些生词对于文章总体的把握,关系不大,这时候出题者也不会给这些生词加汉语注释,只要觉得对总体没有影响或影响不大就可略过。

经典实例 Different cultures are more prone to contract certain illnesses because of the food that is characteristic in these cultures. That food is related to illness is not a new discovery. In 1945, government researchers realized that **nitrates** and **nitrites**, commonly used to preserve color in meats, and other food additives, cause cancer. Yet these carcinogenic additives remain in our food, and it becomes more difficult all the time to know which things on the packaging labels of processed food are helpful or harmful.

据上下文可知,文中黑体两词是用来保持肉类鲜亮颜色的东西,而且应属食品添加剂,至于具体是什么,无需费心去弄明白。

经典实例 One may consider the condition of the atmosphere at a given moment and attempt to predict changes from that condition over a few hours to a few days ahead. This approach is covered by the branch of the science called **synoptic meteorology**, which is the scientific basis of the technique of weather forecasting by means of the preparation and analysis of weather maps and aerological diagram.

文中黑体部分学生可能不熟,但上下文在谈论天气预报方面的问题,且其应为一科学分支——气象学分支,具体是什么,汉语怎么叫,都无所谓。

（四）冗长的人名、地名

有许多冗长啰嗦的表示人名、地名等专有名词,阅读时可一扫而过或干脆用其首字母代替法,千万不可试图把整个词读出来。

经典实例　"That is what I came to show you,"Martini answered in his everyday voice. He picked up the placard from the floor and handed it to her. Hastily printed in large type was a black-bordered announcement that:"Out dearly beloved Bishop, **His Eminence the Cardinal, Monsignor Lorenzo Montanelli**"had died suddenly at **Ravenna**,"from the rupture of an aneurism of the heart."

有许多文章(尤其是哲理性议论文)并非用直截了当、简单明了的语言来说明主题,而是常常与所要说明的主题间有一段距离,这就需要读者在两者之间搭桥,透过表象看深层含义。读者应紧扣上下文,本着上下文服务于中心主题这一点进行推测,这种推测包括字、词到句的含义,甚至是一个例子要说明的含义等等。这一点是需要读者经常做到的。

经典实例　John Henderson was driving home late last night from an exhausting business trip.

上句可隐含下列信息:

1. John Henderson may be a businessman because he has just finished a "business trip".

2. John Henderson must be very tired because the trip is "exhausting".

3. John Henderson must be very eager to get home because he is driving "late" a night right after this exhausting trip.

考研阅读中,难句、复杂句经常成为考生的拦路虎,许多考生一遇到复杂长句就慌了手脚,一副无所适从的样子。难句复杂句中经常隐含考点,所以应重点把握。其实,解决办法很简单,就是要去粗取精、化繁为简:先找出主句的主谓宾,其他成分如从句、插入语、定状补语等一概先不理,理出句子的主干之后再慢慢分析一下各成分与从句还有插入语等的关系,理清关系后,句子就自然容易理解了。

三、阅读理解命题重点

（一）双重否定句

经典实例

However, there has hardly been a year since 1957 in which birth rates have not fallen in the United States and other rich countries.

During the years from 1957 to 1976, the birth rate of the United States _____.

A) increased　　　　　　　　　　B) was reduced

C) experienced both falls and rises　　D) remained stable

（二）结尾处有转折关系的句子

经典实例

So far, however, such a form of selection does not seem to have been applied in practice.

Which of the following statements is NOT TRUE?

A) Body temperature may serve as an indication of a worker's performance.

B) The selection of a number of permanent night shift workers has proved to be the best solution to problems of the round-the-clock working system.

C) Taking body temperature at regular intervals can show a person adapts to the changes of routine.

D) Disturbed sleep occurs less frequently among those on permanent night or day shifts.

（三）有言外之意的句子

经典实例

It would have amazed the brightest minds of 18th century Enlightment（启蒙运动）to be told by any of us how little we know and how bewildering seems the way ahead.

It can be inferred from the passage that scientists of the 18th century _____.
A) knew that they were ignorant and wanted to know more about nature
B) were afraid of facing up to the realities of scientific research
C) thought that they knew a great deal and could solve most problems of science
D) did more harm than good in promoting man's understandings of nature

（四）有类比关系的句子

经典实例

Yet，when we ask why the Industrial Revolution was a revolution. We find it was not the machines. The primary reason why it is revolutionary is that it led to great social change. ……. In somewhat similar fashion，computer promises to revolutionize the structure of American life……

According to the author，the introduction of the computer is a revolution mainly because _____.
A) The computer has revolutionized the workings of the human mind
B) The computer can do the tasks that could only be done by people before
C) It has helped to switch to an information technology
D) It has great potential impact on society

（五）有矛盾关系的句子

经典实例

Yet，instead of joy，there is wide spread uneasiness and confusion. Why do food prices keep on rising，when there seems to be so much food about ?

Why is there "wide-spread uneasiness and confusion" about the food situation?
A) The abundance of food supply is not expected to last.
B) Despite the abundance，food prices keep rising.
C) Britain is importing less food.
D) Britain will cut back on its production of food.

真题再现 ▷

 Passage 1 （2001 年）

Specialization can be seen as a response to the problem of an increasing accumulation of scientific knowledge. By splitting up the subject matter into smaller units，one man could continue to handle the information and use it as the basis for further research. But specialization was only one of a series of related developments in science affecting the process of communication. Another was the growing professionalization of scientific activity.

No clear-cut distinction can be drawn between professionals and amateurs in science：exceptions can be found to any rule. Nevertheless，the word "amateur" does carry a connotation that the person concerned is not fully integrated into the scientific community and, in particular, may not fully share its values. The growth of specialization in the nineteenth century, with its consequent requirement of a longer, more complex training, implied greater problems for amateur participation in science. The trend was naturally most obvious in those areas of science based especially on a mathematical or laboratory training, and can be illustrated in terms of the development of geology in the United Kingdom.

A comparison of British geological publications over the last century and a half reveals not simply an increasing emphasis on the primacy of research, but also a changing definition of what constitutes an acceptable research paper. Thus, in the nineteenth century, local geological studies represented worthwhile research in their own right; but, in the twentieth century, local studies have increasingly become acceptable to professionals only if they incorporate, and reflect on, the wider geological picture. Amateurs, on the other hand, have continued to pursue local studies in the old way. The overall result has been to make entrance to professional geological journals harder for amateurs, a result that has been reinforced by the widespread introduction of referring, first by national journals in the nineteenth century and then by several local geological journals in the twentieth century. As a logical consequence of this development, separate journals have now appeared aimed mainly towards either professional or amateur readership. A rather similar process of differentiation has led to professional geologists coming together nationally within one or two specific societies, whereas the amateurs have tended either to remain in local societies or to come together nationally in a different way.

Although the process of professionalization and specialization was already well under way in British geology during the nineteenth century, its full consequences were thus delayed until the twentieth century. In science generally, however, the nineteenth century must be reckoned as the crucial period for this change in the structure of science.

1. The growth of specialization in 19th century might be more clearly seen in sciences such as _____.
   A) sociology and chemistry
   B) physics and psychology
   C) sociology and psychology
   D) physics and chemistry

2. We can infer from the passage that _____.
   A) there is little distinction between specialization and professionalization
   B) amateurs can compete with professionals in some areas of science
   C) professionals tend to welcome amateurs into the scientific community
   D) amateurs have national academic societies but no local ones

3. The author writes of the development of geology to demonstrate _____.
   A) the process of specialization and professionalization
   B) the hardship of amateurs in scientific study
   C) the change of policies in scientific publications
   D) the discrimination of professionals against amateurs

4. The direct reason for specialization is _____.
   A) the development in communication
   B) the growth of professionalization
   C) the expansion of scientific knowledge
   D) the splitting up of academic societies

 ## Passage 2 (2001 年)

A great deal of attention is being paid today to the so-called digital divide—the division of the world into the info(information)rich and the info poor. And that divide does exist today. My wife and I lectured about this looming danger twenty years ago. What was less visible then, however, were the new, positive forces that work against the digital divide. There are reasons to be optimistic.

There are technological reasons to hope the digital divide will narrow. As the Internet becomes more and more commercialized, it is in the interest of business to universalize access—after all, the more people online, the more potential customers there are. More and more governments, afraid their countries will be left behind, want to spread Internet access. Within the next decade or two, one to two billion people on the planet will be netted together. As a result, I now believe the digital divide will narrow rather than widen in the years ahead. And that is very good news because the Internet may well be the most powerful tool for combating world poverty that we've ever had.

Of course, the use of the Internet isn't the only way to defeat poverty. And the Internet is not the only tool we have. But it has enormous potential.

To take advantage of this tool, some impoverished countries will have to get over their outdated anti-colonial prejudices with respect to foreign investment. Countries that still think foreign investment is an invasion of their sovereignty might well study the history of infrastructure(the basic structural foundations of a society) in the United States. When the United States built its industrial infrastructure, it didn't have the capital to do so. And that is why America's Second Wave infrastructure—including roads, harbors, highways, ports and so on—were built with foreign investment. The English, the Germans, the Dutch and the French were investing in Britain's former colony. They financed them. Immigrant Americans built them. Guess who owns them now? The Americans. I believe the same thing would be true in places like Brazil or anywhere else for that matter. The more foreign capital you have helping you build your Third Wave infrastructure, which today is an electronic infrastructure, the better off you're going to be. That doesn't mean lying down and becoming fooled, or letting foreign corporations run uncontrolled. But it does mean recognizing how important they can be in building the energy and telecom infrastructures needed to take full advantage of the Internet.

5. Digital divide is something _____.

　A)getting worse because of the Internet

　B)the rich countries are responsible for

　C)the world must guard against

　D)considered positive today

6. Governments attach importance to the Internet because it _____.

　A)offers economic potentials

　B)can bring foreign funds

　C)can soon wipe out world poverty

　D)connects people all over the world

7. The writer mentioned the case of the United States to justify the policy of _____.

　A)providing financial support overseas

　B)preventing foreign capital's control

　C)building industrial infrastructure

　D)accepting foreign investment

8. It seems that now a country's economy depends much on _____.

　A)how well-developed it is electronically

　B)whether it is prejudiced against immigrants

　C)whether it adopts America's industrial pattern

　D)how much control it has over foreign corporations

Passage 3 （1996 年）

　　With the start of BBC World Service Television, millions of viewers in Asia and America can now watch the Corporation's news coverage, as well as listen to it. And of course in Britain listeners and viewers can tune in to two BBC television channels, five BBC national radio services and dozens of local radio stations. They are brought sport, comedy, drama, music, news and current affairs, education, religion, parliamentary coverage, children's programmes and films for an annual licence fee of £83 per household.

　　It is a remarkable record, stretching back over 70 years—yet the BBC's future is now in doubt. The Corporation will survive as a publicly—funded broadcasting organization, at least for the time being, but its role, its size and its programmes are now the subject of a nation-wide debate in Britain.

　　The debate was launched by the Government, which invited anyone with an opinion of the BBC—including ordinary listeners and viewers—to say what was good or bad about the Corporation, and even whether they thought it was worth keeping. The reason for its inquiry is that the BBC's royal charter runs out in 1996 and it must decide whether to keep the organization as it is, or to make changes.

　　Defenders of the Corporation—of whom there are many—are fond of quoting the American slogan "If it ain't broke, don't fix it." The BBC "ain't broke", they say, by which they mean it is not broken (as distinct from the word 'broke', meaning shaving no money), so why bother to change it?

　　Yet the BBC will have to change, because the broadcasting world around it is changing. The commercial TV channels—ITV and Channel 4—were required by the Thatcher Government's Broadcasting Act to become more commercial, competing with each other for advertisers, and cutting costs and jobs. But it is the arrival of new satellite channels—funded partly by advertising and partly by viewers' subscriptions—which will bring about the biggest changes in the long term.

9. The world famous BBC now faces _____.

　　A) the problem of new coverage

　　B) an uncertain prospect

　　C) inquiries by the general public

　　D) shrinkage of audience

10. In the passage, which of the following about the BBC is not mentioned as the key issue?

　　A) Extension of its TV service to Far East.

　　B) Programmes as the subject of a nation-wide debate.

　　C) Potentials for further international co-operations.

　　D) Its existence as a broadcasting organization.

11. The BBC's "royal charter" (Line 3, Paragraph 3) stands for _____.

　　A) the financial support from the royal family

　　B) the privileges granted by the Queen

　　C) a contract with the Queen

　　D) a unique relationship with the royal family

12. The foremost reason why the BBC has to readjust itself is no other than _____.

　　A) the emergence of commercial TV channels

　　B) the enforcement of Broadcasting Act by the government

　　C) the urgent necessity to reduce costs and jobs

　　D) the challenge of new satellite channels

Passage 4 (1999 年)

It's a rough world out there. Step outside and you could break a leg slipping on your doormat. Light up the stove and you could burn down the house. Luckily, if the doormat or stove failed to warn of coming disaster, a successful lawsuit might compensate you for your troubles. Or so the thinking has gone since the early 1980s, when juries began holding more companies liable for their customers' misfortunes.

Feeling threatened, companies responded by writing ever-longer warning labels, trying to anticipate every possible accident. Today, stepladders carry labels several inches long that warn, among other things, that you might—surprised!—fall off. The label on a child's Batman cape cautions that the toy "does not enable user to fly."

While warnings are often appropriate and necessary—the dangers of drug interactions, for example—and many are required by state or federal regulations, it isn't clear that they actually protect the manufacturers and sellers from liability if a customer is injured. About 50 percent of the companies lose when injured customers take them to court.

Now the tide appears to be turning. As personal injury claims continue as before, some courts are beginning to side with defendants, especially in cases where a warning label probably wouldn't have changed anything. In May, Julie Nimmons, president of Schutt Sports in Illinois, successfully fought a lawsuit involving a football player who was paralyzed in a game while wearing a Schutt helmet. "We're really sorry he has become paralyzed, but helmets aren't designed to prevent those kinds of injuries," says Nimmons. The jury agreed that the nature of the game, not the helmet, was the reason for the athlete's injury. At the same time, the American Law Institute—a group of judges, lawyers, and academics whose recommendations carry substantial weight—issued new guidelines for tort law stating that companies need not warn customers of obvious dangers or bombard them with a lengthy list of possible ones. "Important information can get buried in a sea of trivialities," says a law professor at Cornell Law School who helped draft the new guidelines. If the moderate end of the legal community has its way, the information on products might actually be provided for the benefit of customers and not as protection against legal liability.

13. What were things like in 1980s when accidents happened?

　　A) Customers might be relieved of their disasters through lawsuits.

　　B) Injured customers could expect protection from the legal system.

　　C) Companies would avoid being sued by providing new warnings.

　　D) Juries tended to find fault with the compensations companies promised.

14. Manufacturers as mentioned in the passage tend to _____.

　　A) satisfy customers by writing long warnings on products

　　B) become honest in describing the inadequacies of their products

　　C) make the best use of labels to avoid legal liability

　　D) feel obliged to view customers' safety as their first concern

15. The case of Schutt helmet demonstrated that _____.

　　A) some injury claims were no longer supported by law

　　B) helmets were not designed to prevent injuries

　　C) product labels would eventually be discarded

　　D) some sports games might lose popularity with athletes

16. The author's attitude towards the issue seems to be _____.

　　A) biased　　　　　B) indifferent　　　　　C) puzzling　　　　　D) objective

真题再现答案解析及译文

Passage 1

题材:自然科学——科学史

本文主要是一篇论述科学发展的专业化和职业化的文章,作者客观地描述了这一过程,而文章一半左右的篇幅都在以英国地质学的发展来举例。因此在阅读此文的时候要注意例证对于作者观点的支持。

1. 正确答案 D)。该题问,19 世纪专业化的成长可能在哪一门学科里看得更清楚。文章第二段最后五行指出,19 世纪专业分工的发展以及时间更长、内容更复杂的培训暗示了业余人员参加科学活动遇到更大的障碍。这一趋势在以数学或实验室培训为基础的科学领域尤其明显。A)项"社会学和化学",B)项"物理和心理学"及 C)项"社会学和心理学"均不符合题意。

2. 正确答案 B)。该题问从这一段文章可以推断什么。文章第一段最后两句指出,专业分工是影响信息交流过程的一系列相关科学发展的一个方面。另一个方面是科学活动不断的专业化。由这两句可看出,专业分工和专业化是科学发展的两方面,两者不同,所以 A)"专业分工和专业化之间没有什么差别"不合题意。文章第二段指出专业人员与非专业人员并不享有完全一样的实用价值,第三段指出专业刊物对业余人员的论文的"高标准"及出现了不同刊物和学术团体。由此判断,专业人员对业余人员是持"不相容"态度的,所以 C)"专业人员倾向于欢迎业余人员加入到他们的科学团体中去"是错误的。第三段最后一句明确表示业余科技人员不是倾向于占据地方学会,就是在全国范围内联合起来,其意与 B)相同。

3. 正确答案 A)。该题问,作者写到地质学的发展,用来说明什么问题。文章第三段谈到了在地质研究上业余人员和专业人员的不同研究方法,业余人员在专业刊物上发表论文的困难,以及出现分别以专业读者或业余读者为主要对象的刊物和专业学会与业余学会的形成。这实际是专业分工和专业化形成的过程。另外,第二段最后两行提到:"The trend……can be illustrated in the United Kingdom.""the trend"应指上文中提到的"the growth of specialisation in the nineteenth century"。所以,选择 A)项"专业分工和专业化形成的过程"。B)项"业余者在科研上的困难"和 C)项"科学论文出版政策的改变"都是专业分工和专业化过程中的具体表现,并非作者想要说明的问题。D)项"专业人员对业余人员的歧视"本文未提及。

4. 正确答案 C)。该题问,专业分工的直接原因是什么?根据第一段第一句"专业分工可以看做是对科学知识不断积累这一问题的反映。"选择 C)项"科学知识的膨胀"。A)项"信息传播的发展",B)项"专业化的成长"和 D)项"学术团体的分裂"都不符合题意。

译文

专业化可以视为是对科学知识不断增加的应对之策。把一个课题分解成小的单元,这样一个人就能够处理这些信息,并把它们作为进一步深入研究的基础。但是专业化还只是科学影响交流的过程中产生出的一系列相关现象之一,另外一个现象是科学研究的日益职业化。

在科学研究中,职业和业余之间并没有非常清楚的界限,就像对任何规则都能找到例外情况一样。但是,"业余"一词的确有这样的含义:就是这个人并没有完全融入科学研究的圈子,尤其是,他与这个圈子里的人的价值观可能并不相同。19 世纪职业化的发展要求训练更加复杂,训练时间也更长,这给业余科学研究提出了更大的问题。这种趋势在那些需要以数学或实验室培训为基础的学科中尤其明显,这一点可以从英国的地质学发展中看出来。

对过去 150 年间英国出版的地质学刊物做一个比较,我们不但可以发现对研究的重视加强了,而且对什么是合格的科研论文的定义也改变了。19 世纪时,地方上的地质学研究主要做一些力所能及的有价值的研究;但是,到了 20 世纪时,地方上的研究只有融合了或者反映了更广阔的地质学问题,才会被专业人士接受。而另一方面,业余研究人员继续走着地方研究的老路。结果是,业余研究者的论文想进入专业的地质杂志是越来越难了,尤其是在广泛引入审阅制度之后,这种制度最初在 19 世纪被引入全国性杂志,然后在 20 世纪时进入几家地方性的地质学杂志。结果是,现在不同的杂志分别面向不同的读者群,专业人士有专业人士的杂志,业余人士有业余人士的杂志。同样,全国范围内专业的地质学家都集中在一两个社团内,而业余研究者或者加入当地社团,或者也在全国范围内组织起来。

尽管英国地质学研究的职业化和专业化在 19 世纪就已经在进行了,但是它的结果一直延迟到 20 世纪才完全显现。然而总的来说,在科学领域里,科学结构的这种转变的关键性时期是在 19 世纪。

Passage 2

题材:时文——信息科学

本文讨论的是在信息时代出现的 digital divide,即信息分配的贫富差异,以及互联网(Internet)对消除其中差异的积极作用。此文紧扣作为当前热点的互联网和信息技术,时效性很强。

5. 正确答案 C)。本题要求对信息差的理解给出正确答案。参看文章第一段第一句"如今,人们正在关注着所谓的信息差,即世界上信息资源丰富的地区与信息资源贫乏地区之间的差异。今天,这种差异的确存在。我和妻子二十年前就对当时隐约出现的这种危险做过讲演。"由此得出 C)"全世界都要警惕的东西"为正确答案。A)"由于互联网而变得日益严重",参看第二段倒数第二三句"在未来的二十年内,世界上将有一二十亿人进入互联网。因此,我认为将来信息差异只能缩小,不会扩大。"由此可知,A)与之内容相反。B)"富裕国家应为之负责"文章未提。D)"当今人们认为有利的东西"与内容相反。

6. 正确答案 A)。本题问政府重视互联网的原因是什么。参看第二段第三句"目前,由于害怕自己的国家会落后,越来越多的政府想扩大互联网的使用范围。"和第三段最后一句"但是,其潜力巨大"。所以,答案为 A)"提供经济能力"。B)"能引来外资"与文章内容不符。C)"不久就能消除世界贫困","不久"一词与内容不符。D)"能把全世界所有人连接在一起"与文章内容不符。

7. 正确答案 D)。本题问作者提到美国的发展情况来证明下列哪项政策是正确的。参看第四段第三、四、五句"美国当初建设自己的工业基础设施时,没有足够的资本。因此美国当时的基本设施建设,包括道路、港口、交通干线、码头等都使用外国的投资。英国、德国、荷兰及法国当时都为这一英国前殖民地投了资。这些国家投资外国移居美国的移民建设。"所以,D)"接受外国投资"为正确答案。A)"向海外提供资金援助"文章未提。B)"防止外国资本的控制"与内容不符。C)"建设工业基础设施"文章提到该点,但不是作者提及美国的目的。

8. 正确答案 A)。本题问现在一个国家的经济看来应该依赖什么。参看最后一段倒数第三句"当今是第三次浪潮,即电子基础设施的建设。发展电子设施所拥有的资本越多,将来就越富有。"因此,A)"电子方面怎样发达"为正确答案。B)"该国家对移民是否有偏见"文章未提。C)"该国是否采用美国的工业模式"文章未提。D)"该国对外国公司控制的力度"与文章内容不符。

译文

当今有很多人在关注所谓的"信息分化"的问题——也就是把世界上的人分化为信息富有和信息贫困两大类。这种分化确实是存在着的。我和妻子在二十年前就谈到了这一迫切的危险状况,但在那时,有一件事我们看得还不是那么清楚,这就是一种积极的力量正在对信息分化做出反击。因此我们有理由感到乐观。

技术上的原因有希望能够缩小这种信息分化。随着互联网变得越来越商业化,商业会使互联网的使用更普遍化——毕竟,上网的人越多,潜在的顾客就越多。越来越多的政府,因为害怕自己的国家会被甩在后面,也会扩大互联网的覆盖。在未来的十到二十年里,这个星球上十到二十亿的人会被网络连接在一起。因此,我相信,在未来这种信息分化会缩小而不是扩大。这会是一个好消息,因为互联网是打击世界范围内贫穷的最强大的工具。

当然,网络并不是打击贫穷的惟一方法,互联网也不是我们惟一拥有的工具,但是它具有无比强大的潜力。

为了利用这一工具,一些贫困国家必须克服他们对外国投资的那种过时的反殖民偏见。那些仍然认为外国投资是侵犯其主权的国家,不妨学习一下美国的基础设施建设史(基础设施是指一个社会的基础结构)。美国在进行工业基础设施建设时,并没有足够的资金,因此美国的第二批基础设施——包括公路、海港、高速路、码头等等——都是利用外国投资修建的。英国、德国、荷兰和法国都在这块英国的前殖民地上投资,由他们来资助,美国的移民来建造。猜猜如今谁拥有这一切?是美国人民。我相信同样的事情也可以发生在巴西或其他任何地方。有越多的外国资金来帮助你修建第三批基础设施,也就是今天的电子设施,你将来的生活就会越好。这并不意味着屈从和任人榨取,也不意味着让外国公司自由行动不受控制。但这确实意味着你必须意识到为了能充分利用互联网,让他们修建需要的能源和通讯设施是多么的重要。

Passage 3

题材:社会科学——传播学,大众传媒

本文介绍了英国广播公司的现状以及目前面临的问题。

9. 正确答案 B)。该题问:世界著名的 BBC 现在正面临什么问题。根据第三段第一句"……yet the BBC's future is now in doubt"应选 B)"没有把握的前景"。A)"新闻报道问题"和 D)"观众减少"在文中均未提到。C)"公众质询"在文中虽有提及,但并不是所面临的问题。

10. 正确答案 C)。该题问:关于 BBC,下面哪项未作为主要问题提到。A)项"电视服务向远东的延伸"在开头第一段第一句提到。B)项"作为全国性争论话题的电视节目"在第三段末句中提到。D)项"作为广播机构的存在"在第四段末句中提到。

11. 正确答案 C)。该题问:BBC 的"royal charter"意指什么。charter 的含义是"统治者、政府等给予做某事权力的特许状",又根据"run out"的意义是"期满",所以选 C)(与女王的契约)。B)"女王授予的特权"与 run out 在意思上无法搭配。A)"来自皇室的经济帮助",D)"与皇室的独特关系"都不是 charter 一词的准确含义,并且不能与 run out 在意思上搭配。

12. 正确答案 D)。该题问 BBC 广播公司进行重新自我调整的最主要原因是什么。根据本文最后一段"但是,新增加的卫星频道,其资金部分来自广告收入,部分来自用户费用,从长远来看会带来最大的变化。

译文

随着 BBC 英国广播公司电视节目的开播,亚洲和美洲成百万人现在不仅可以收听该公司的新闻广播而且还可以收看它的新闻报道。

当然,英国听众和观众可以收到两个 BBC 电视频道,五个 BBC 全国广播电台和几十个地方电台。每户每年交 83 英镑收视费即可看到体育、喜剧、戏剧、音乐、新闻和时事、教育、宗教、会议、儿童和电影节目频道。

近 70 年来,BBC 历程辉煌,但它的未来现在还难以判定。公司将作为公众收视费资助的广播机构而存在,至少目前如此,但它的作用、规模和节目如今在英国成了全国争论的话题。

争论是由政府发起的,它邀请了每一位对 BBC 有看法的人——包括普通听众和观众——说出公司好坏之所在,甚至说出他们认为该公司是否值得存在下去。这样做的原因是 BBC 持有的皇家特许证到 1996 年到期。政府必须决定对该公司维持原状还是进行变革。

公司的辩护者——他们中很多人——喜欢引用美国的一个广告口号:"如果还没有坏,就不要修理,"他们说 BBC 公司还没有"broke",意指还没"broken(垮掉)"(与表示"破产"的"broke"意义不同)。所以为什么要找麻烦去改变它呢?

然而,BBC 将不得不进行变革,因为它周围的广播界正在发生变化。作为商业电视频道的独立电视公司和四频道按撒切尔政府广播法案的要求进一步商业化,互相竞争广告业务,降低成本,裁减工作人员。但是,新增加的卫星频道,其资金部分来自广告收入,部分来自用户收视费,从长远来看会带来最大的变化。

Passage 4

题材:社会科学——法律

此类法律方面的文章在历年的考试中并不多见,因此考生最好借助阅读本文熟悉一下美国的法律架构。

13. 正确答案 B）。本题问及事故发生在 20 世纪 80 年代时情况怎样。文中第一段的第二、三句列举了生活中的偶然事故，接着在第四、五句说："如果门垫或炉灶上没有警告字样告诉你可能发生的危害，你或许可以幸运地就自己所受的伤害通过法律诉讼，成功地获得赔偿。大概自 80 年初以来人们不再这样认为，80 年代初陪审团成员开始认为更多的公司应对他们的消费者遭受的不幸负责"。这与选项 B）"受伤的消费者可望得到法律制度的保护"意思相吻合。选项 A）"消费者可能会通过法律诉讼而摆脱灾难"，显然与事实不符。选项 C）"生产商会通过提供新的警告提示而免遭起诉"及 D）"陪审团往往对公司所承诺的赔偿严加挑剔"，均与原意相差甚远，故不能入选。

14. 正确答案 C）。本题问及本文中提到的厂家往往怎样做。本文第二段第一句说："公司感到（赔偿的）威胁，便作出反应，写出的警告标签越来越冗长，以期预测任何可能出现的事故"。这样就可以"逃避法律的责任"（选项 C）这是厂家的真正意图，而不是"为使消费者满意"（选项 A），"诚恳地说出其产品的不足"（选项 B），"把消费者的安全看做头等大事"（选项 D）。

15. 正确答案 A）。本题问及作者在文中援引 Schutt 头盔案例是何用意。本文第三段最后一句说："当受伤的消费者把公司告到法庭后，大约 50％的公司会输掉官司"。接着在第四段列举了一位橄榄球队员戴了 Schutt 体育公司生产的头盔踢球时受伤瘫痪了，要求赔偿。结果陪审团同意该公司的解释：是这种运动的性质，而不是头盔造成运动员的伤害。这与选项 A）"某些因伤提出的索赔再也受不到法律的保护了"意思一致。其他选项均缺乏事实依据。

16. 正确答案 D）。本题问及作者对这个问题的态度如何。综观全文，不难发现作者是站在第三者的角度引用事实论述问题，没有表明自己的主观意图，而是客观地叙述了从 80 年代至今美国法律在这一问题上态度的变化，同时还援引了业内人士对此的看法。因此可以说作者对此的态度是客观的，既不带偏见（选项 A），也未表现出冷漠（选项 B）或疑惑（选项 C）。

译文

　　外面是个危险的世界。如果你走出去，可能会滑倒在门口地垫上，摔伤一条腿。如果点燃炉灶，可能会烧毁整幢房子。如果地垫或炉灶上没有警示字样告诉你可能发生的危害，你或许可以幸运地就自己所受的伤害通过法律诉讼，成功地获得赔偿。大概自 80 年代初以来人们不再这样认为，80 年代初陪审团成员开始认为更多的公司应对他们消费者遭受的不幸负责。

　　公司感到（赔偿的）威胁，便作出反应，写出的警告标签越来越冗长，以期预测任何可能出现的事故。结果，现在的梯子上的警告标签有几英寸长，除了警告你可能发生的其他意外之外，还警告你可能摔下来——这种警告真是莫名其妙。儿童的蝙蝠侠玩具的斗篷上也印有警告词：本玩具"并不能使使用者飞行。"

　　虽然警示语常常是合理的和必要的，如有关药物副作用可能产生的危害的警示语，而且许多是州或联邦法律要求的。但是，如果消费者受伤，这些警示语能否保护产销商免于责任，这还很难说。当受伤的消费者把公司告到法庭后，大约 50％的公司会输掉官司。

　　现在看来这种趋势正在改变。尽管人们依然为产品所造成的人身伤害提出索赔，但有些法院已开始站在被告一边，特别是处理那些即便是有警示语也无法避免伤害的案例时。五月份（美国）伊利诺斯州的 Schutt 体育公司被告，一位橄榄球队员戴了 Schutt 体育公司生产的头盔踢球时受伤瘫痪。该公司总裁 Julie Nimmons 先生辩解说，"他瘫痪了我们非常难过，但是这种头盔设计时不是用来防止这种伤害。"陪审团也认为造成球员受伤的不是头盔，而是橄榄球运动本身（的危险性）。公司因此胜诉。同时，美国法学会——该组织由一群举足轻重的法官、律师和学者组成——宣布的新民事侵害法纲要指出：公司没有必要警告消费者显而易见的危险或者展示给他们一个尽可能长的单子，新纲要起草的法学教授说，"重要的信息可能被埋没在浩如烟海的细枝末节里。"如果该法律组织的这一不太过分的要求能得以实行，产品上提供的警示信息可能实际上是用来保护消费者利益的，而不仅仅是为了保护公司免除法律责任。

第三节　阅读理解题型分类详解

一、主旨题

主旨题的测试要求及题型

主旨题主要测试考生对短文整体理解概括的能力。任何一篇文章都表达了一定的中心思想,为了测试考生对文章整体的理解程度,命题者往往设计一些主旨归纳题来对考生进行考查。要准确地回答这类问题,考生必须通过仔细阅读,了解文章的主旨大意。而要了解文章的主旨大意,就要求考生学会寻找段落或文章的主题句。主旨题的问题一般都出现在第一或最后一个题。同时对不同的题材、体裁,其提问方式及用词也不尽相同,因此要求考生熟悉这些题型,不要为理解题型而花费太多的时间和分散精力。

主题题型分为三种:文章标题题、写作目的题、隐蔽的主旨题等。

二、主旨题解题方法

(一)通过文章逻辑结构解主旨题

把握文章的逻辑结构对于做主旨题很有帮助。因为文章主题出现的位置对应于文章逻辑结构中的一个部分。此外,它对于回答与主旨题密切相关的推测上下文所讨论的主题这一类问题也很重要。阅读理解中的文章主要是说明文和议论文。二者的主要逻辑结构有:

1. 时间顺序　按时间先后说明某一理论的发展,或某一研究成果由过去至现在的情况。属于这种结构的主题通常在首段或末段。下面这篇文章就是属于这种情况。

经典实例

Oceanography has been defined as "The application of all sciences to the study of the sea."

Before the nineteenth century, scientists with an interest in the sea were few and far between. Certainly Newton considered some theoretical aspects of it in his writings, but he was reluctant to go to sea to further his work.

For most people the sea was remote, and with the exception of early intercontinental travellers or others who earned a living from the sea, there was little reason to ask many questions about it, let alone to ask what lay beneath the surface. The first time that the question 'What is at the bottom of the oceans?' had to be answered with any commercial consequence was when the laying of a telegraph cable from Europe to America was proposed. The engineers had to know the depth profile (起伏形状) of the route to estimate the length of cable that had to be manufactured.

It was to Maury of the US Navy that the Atlantic Telegraph Company turned, in 1853, for information on this matter. In the 1840s, Maury had been responsible for encouraging voyages during which soundings (测深) were taken to investigate the depths of the North Atlantic and Pacific Oceans. Later, some of his findings aroused much popular interest in his book The Physical Geography of the Sea.

The cable was laid, but not until 1866 was the connection made permanent and reliable. At the early attempts, the cable failed and when it was taken out for repairs it was found to be covered in living growths, a fact which defied contemporary scientific opinion that there was no life in the deeper parts of the sea. Within a few years oceanography was under way. In 1872 Thomson led a scientific expedition, which lasted for four years and brought home thousands of samples from the sea. Their classification and analysis occupied scientists for years and led to a five-volume report, the last volume being published in 1895.

2. 一般→具体　首段做总的说明,其他段落分别说明或具体论述首段的观点。属于这种结构的文章主题在首段。

经典实例

We find that bright children are rarely held back by mixed-ability teaching. On the contrary, both their knowledge and experience are enriched. We feel that there are many disadvantages in streaming (把……按能力分班) pupils. It does not take into account the fact that children develop at different rates. It can have a bad effect on both the bright and the not-so-bright child. After all, it can be quite discouraging to be at the bottom of the top grade!

Besides, it is rather unreal to grade people just according to their intellectual ability. This is only one aspect of their total personality. We are concerned to develop the abilities of all our pupils to the full, not just their academic ability. We also value personal qualities and social skills, and we find that mixed-ability teaching contributes to all these aspects of learning.

In our classrooms, we work in various ways. The pupils often work in groups: this gives them the opportunity to learn to co-operate, to share, and to develop leadership skills. They also learn how to cope with (对付) personal problems as well as learning how to think, to make decisions, to analyse and evaluate, and to communicate effectively. The pupils learn from each other as well as from the teacher.

Sometimes the pupils work in pairs; sometimes they work on individual tasks and assignments, and they can do this at their own speed. They also have some formal class teaching when this is appropriate. We encourage our pupils to use the library, and we teach them the skills they need in order to do this efficiently. An advanced pupil can do advanced work: it does not matter what age the child is. We expect our pupils to do their best, not their least, and we give them every encouragement to attain this goal.

The author's purpose of writing this passage is to _____.

A) argue for teaching bright and not-so-bright pupils in the same class

B) recommend pair work and group work for classroom activities

C) offer advice on the proper use of the library

D) emphasize the importance of appropriate formal classroom teaching

本文一开始就是一个主题句：We find that bright children are rarely held back by mixed-ability teaching. 优秀学生很少受制于混班教学，接着从正面肯定混班教学，On the contrary, both their knowledge and experience are enriched. 由此可知这道题的答案为 A)，而 B)、C)、D) 均为混班教学的具体方面，所以不对。

3. 具体→一般　前面几段分别说明，末段总结。主题在末段。

4. 对比　进行对比的各事物之间的基本共同点或差异为主题。

(二)通过主题句解主旨题

主题句表达中心思想，其他句子均围绕其展开说明或议论。它通常以判断句的形式出现，在文章中的通常位置为第一段首句、第一段末句和全文末句等地方。

1. 主题句在第一段首句

任何一篇阅读理解文章都有一个中心思想。尽管绝大多数阅读理解文章是从一篇较长的文章中摘选下来的，但不管摘选一段还是几段，不管摘选哪几段，摘选下来的句子必须本身是自成一体的，是有中心思想的。一般说来，绝大多数文章的中心思想是用一个句子表达出来的。其特点是概括性的，观点性的。因此只要抓住中心思想句，就能解答主题大意问题。文章中心思想句到哪儿找？它在文章中的位置比较有规律，一般出现在文章的开头。

许多文章开门见山，一开始就摆出要说明的主要对象或要论述的主要观点。接下去的句子和段落都说明或论述它。这样，文章的结构就属于一般→具体，主题也就在首段首句。

经典实例

Researchers have established that when people are mentally engaged, biochemical changes occur in the brain that allow it to act more effectively in cognitive areas such as attention and memory. This is true regardless of age.

People will be alert and receptive if they are faced with information that gets them to think about things they are interested in. And someone with a history of doing more rather than less will go into old age more cognitively sound than someone who has not had an active mind.

Many experts are so convinced of the benefits of challenging the brain that they are putting the theory to work in their own lives. "The idea is not necessarily to learn to memorize enormous amounts of information," says James Fozard, associate director of the National Institute on Aging. "Most of us don't need that kind of skill. Such specific training is of less interest than being able to maintain mental alertness." Fozard and others say they challenge their brains with different mental skills, both because they enjoy them and because they are sure that their range of activities will help the way their brains work.

Gene Cohen, acting director of the same institute, suggests that people in their old age should engage in mental and physical activities individually as well as in groups. Cohen says that we are frequently advised to keep physically active as we age, but older people need to keep mentally active as well. Those who do are more likely to maintain their intellectual abilities and to be generally happier and better adjusted. "The point is, you need to do both," Cohen says. "Intellectual activity actually influences brain-cell health and size."

本文以引经据典的方法强调了头脑健康,尤其是老年人头脑健康的重要性。这个中心内容在第一段第一句就已指出:人在用脑时,大脑会处于兴奋状态,这时大脑在诸如注意力和记忆力等属于认知领域的能力方面会得到有效发挥。因此,

What is the passage mainly about?

A) How biochemical changes occur in the human brain.

B) Why people should keep active not only physically but also mentally.

C) How intellectual activities influence brain-cell health.

D) Why people should receive special mental training as they age.

这道题的正确答案为 B)。A)与 C)均为原文中的细节,而 D)与原文第三段第 4～5 行 "……Such specific training is of less interest than being able to maintain mental alertness" 相矛盾,所以都不是正确答案。

2. 主题句在第一段末句

首段末句也是主题句常出现的地方。假若如此,这个主题句就不仅是对全文的总结,也是对第一段的总结,而且开启第二段及以后的说明或论述。简而言之,这种文章结构是:具体说明或论述(一段)→总结(一段末的主题句)→后文的具体说明或论述。

这种形式的主题句之前通常有表示总结的提示词,如:in conclusion, to conclude, in summary, to sum up, in short, in brief, in a nutshell;或表示推断的提示词:therefore, thus, as a result, accordingly;或表示转折的提示词,but, however 等。转折之后就出现主题句的情况较多,这种谋篇套路可以用"去旧取新、标新立异"八个字概括。文章中诸如"every parent"、"a popular belief"、"frequently assumed"、"universally accepted"等词句提示作者可能在下文提出一个与之不同的观点标新立异,假若如此,那么作者"标新立异"之处的观点就是主题大意。对于某一现象,过去已有解释,作者提出新的解释,新解释就是主题大意。这体现了上述的"去旧取新"原则。

经典实例

Do you find getting up in the morning so difficult that it's painful? This might be called laziness, but Dr. Kleitman has a new explanation. He has proved that everyone has a daily energy cycle.

During the hours when you labour through your work you may say that you're 'hot'. That's true. The time of day when you feel most energetic is when your cycle of body temperature is at its peak. For some people the peak comes during the forenoon. For others it comes in the afternoon or evening. No one has discovered why this is so, but it leads to such familiar monologues as:'Get up, John! you'll be late for work again!' The possible explanation to the trouble is that John is at his temperature-and-energy peak in the evening. Much family quarrelling ends when husbands and wives realize what these energy cycles mean, and which cycle each member of the family has.

You can't change your energy cycle, but you can learn to make your life fit it better. Habit can help, Dr. Kleitman believes. Maybe you're sleepy in the evening but feel you must stay up late anyway. Counteract (对抗) your cycle to some extent by habitually staying up later than you want to. If your energy is low in the morning but you have an important job to do early in the day, rise before your usual hour. This won't change your cycle, but you'll get up steam and work better at your low point.

Get off to a slow start which saves your energy. Get up with a leisurely yawn (呵欠) and stretch. Sit on the edge of the bed a minute before putting your feet on the floor. Avoid the troublesome search for clean clothes by laying them out the night before. Whenever possible, do routine work in the afternoon and save tasks requiring more energy or concentration for your sharper hours.

这段文章先提出现象:早晨起床困难,接着以不肯定的口吻提出一种解释,然后"but"一转,提出 Kleitman 博士的新解释:各人的精力在一天之中有个周期。这个"but"之后的新解释就是主题句。

3. 文章首末两段均有主题句

主题句到末段才出现的情况较少,常见的情况是文章开门见山提出主题句,中间加以论述,文末 复述首段的主题,这也是写作方法之一。

经典实例

Attention to detail is something everyone can and should do — especially in a tight job market. Bob Crossley, a human-resources expert notices this in the job applications that come across his desk every day. "It's amazing how many candidates eliminate themselves," he says.

"Résumés arrive with stains. Some candidates don't bother to spell the company's name correctly. Once I see a mistake, I eliminate the candidate,"Crossley concludes. "if they cannot take care of these details, why should we trust them with a job?"

Can we pay too much attention to details? Absolutely. Perfectionists struggle over little things at the cost of something larger they work toward. "To keep from losing the forest for the trees,"says Charles Garfield, associate professor at the University of California, San Francisco, "We must constantly ask ourselves how the details we're working on fit into the larger picture. If they don't, we should drop them and move to something else."

Garfield compares this process to his work as a computer scientist at NASA. "The Apollo Ⅱ moon launch was slightly off-course 90 percent of the time,"says Garfield. "But a successful landing was still likely because we knew the exact coordinates of our goal. This allowed us to make adjustments as necessary."Knowing where we want to go helps us judge the importance of every task we undertake. Too often we believe what accounts for others' success is some special secret or a lucky break. But rarely is success so mysterious. Again and again, we see that by doing little things within our grasp well, large rewards follow.

Which of the following is the author's advice to the reader?

A) Although too much attention to details may be costly, they should not be overlooked.

B) Don't forget details when drawing pictures.

C) Be aware of the importance of a task before undertaking it.

D) Careless applicants are not to be trusted.

题干问作者对读者的建议,其实就是问文章的主题。本文开头提出要成就一番大事业,必须从小事做起。中间几段分别从使用沾满墨迹的求职履历表遭淘汰、小事与大事的辩证关系及其例证两个方面论证主题。文章最后呼应文章开头的主题:任何人取得成功都是靠一点一滴做出来的,成功的秘密只有一条:千里之行,始于足下。因此 A)为正确答案,而 B)、C)、D)均无法由文章本身推出,为错误答案。

4. 主题句在文章中间

主题句出现在文章中间的情况也有,而且通常在第二段。倘若如此,文章的逻辑结构通常属于下面两种中的一种:

a. 现象(或问题)→主题→阐述或论证;

b. 一个观点(旧观点或大众观点,为作者要驳斥的观点)→主题(新观点,为作者观点)→阐述或论证。属于这种逻辑结构的,往往伴有表示转折的提示词 but,however 等。

经典实例

For some time past it has been widely accepted that babies — and other creatures — learn to do things because certain acts lead to "rewards"; and there is no reason to doubt that this is true. But it used also to be widely believed that effective rewards, at least in the early stages, had to be directly related to such basic physiological "drives" as thirst or hunger. In other words, a baby would learn if he got food or drink or some sort of physical comfort, not otherwise.

It is now clear that this is not so. Babies will learn to behave in ways that produce results in the world with no reward except the successful outcome.

Papousek began his studies by using milk in the normal way to "reward" the babies and so teach them to carry out some simple movements, such as turning the head to one side or the other. Then he noticed that a baby who had had enough to drink would refuse the milk but would still go on making the learned response with clear signs of pleasure. So he began to study the children's responses in situations where no milk was provided. He quickly found that children as young as four months would learn to turn their heads to right or left if the movement "switched on" a display of lights — and indeed that they were capable of learning quite complex turns to bring about this result, for instance, two left or two right, or even to make as many as three turns to one side.

Papousek's light display was placed directly in front of the babies and he made the interesting observation that sometimes they would not turn back to watch the lights closely although they would "smile and bubble" when the display came on. Papousek concluded that it was not primarily the sight of the lights which pleased them, it was the success they were achieving in solving the problem, in mastering the skill, and that there exists a fundamental human urge to make sense of the world and bring it under intentional control.

这篇文章开始指出人们以往接受的一种观点(老观点):婴儿(其他生物也是一样)学做某些事(动作),是因为做这些事(动作)可以得到"奖赏";随后进一步指出,过去人们普遍认为(老观点):这种"产生预期效果的奖赏"都和满足诸如口渴、饥饿等关于人的"基本生理需要"直接相关。

在第二段一开始,作者指出(新观点):情况并非如此。婴儿学做某种动作,是想让这些动作在周围世界产生结果,而不是为了得到单纯满足生理需要的"奖赏"。

第三段和四段讨论 Papousek 的实验,并得出结论:人类自身存在着一种内在的了解世界并力图对其有意识地加以控制的欲望。

由上可知,本文的结构属于旧观点→主题(新观点)→论证。主题句为第二段的第二句话。

(三)通过概括段落大意解主旨题

1. 分析段落主题句

对于一般→具体结构或分类说明的文章,作者从几个方面论述同一个问题,这样,论述的几个方面加起来就构成全文的主题。各个方面的论述通常自成一段,且以段落主题句阐述该段大意。于是,综合各段主题句的意思就得到本文主题。

经典实例

"Congratulations, Mr. Jones, it's a girl."

Fatherhood is going to have a different meaning and bring forth a different response from every man who hears these words. Some feel pride when they receive the news, while others worry, wondering whether they will be good fathers. Although there are some men who like children and may have had considerable experience with them, others do not particularly care for children and spend little time with them. Many fathers and mothers have been planning and looking forward to children for some time. For other couples, pregnancy was an accident that both husband and wife have accepted willingly or unwillingly.

Whatever the reaction to the birth of a child, it is obvious that the shift from the role of husband to that of father is a difficult task. Yet, unfortunately, few attempts have been made to educate fathers in this resocialization process. Although numerous books have been written about American mothers, only recently has literature focused on the role of a father.

It is argued by some writers that the transition to the father's role, although difficult, is not nearly as great as the transition the wife must make to the mother's role. The mother's role seems to require a complete transformation in daily routine and highly innovative adaptation, on the other hand, the father's role is less demanding and immediate. However, even though we mentioned the fact that growing numbers of women are working outside the home, the father is still thought by many as the breadwinner in the household.

本文讨论的是做父亲的问题。除第一段以外,其余各段的第一句均为主题句:第二段是"Fatherhood is going to have a different meaning and bring forth a different response from every man who hears these words."("做父亲将喻示不同的意义,而且听到这句话的人反应各不相同");第三段是"Whatever the reaction to the birth of a child, it is obvious that the shift from the role of husband to that of father is a difficult task."(不管对于小孩出生的反应如何,从丈夫向父亲的角色转变非常困难,这一点很明显);第四段是"It is argued by some writers that the transition to the father's role, although difficult, is not nearly as great as the transition the wife must make to the mother's role."(有些作家认为向父亲角色的转变尽管困难,但根本不如妻子向母亲角色的转变那么大);把这些主题句的内容综合起来,就是本文的主题——丈夫向父亲角色转变的三个方面:因人而异,非常困难,不如妻子向母亲角色的转变那么大。

2. 概括各段落的主旨大意

有时段落中没有明确的主题句,可以根据句与句之间的逻辑关系推出段落的大意,然后将大意汇总,就得出全文主题。

经典实例

There is a popular belief among parents that schools are no longer interested in spelling. No school I have taught in has ever ignored spelling or considered it unimportant as a basic skill. There are, however, vastly different ideas about how to teach it, or how much priority it must be given over general language development and writing ability. The problem is, how to encourage a child to express himself freely and confidently in writing without holding him back with the complexities of spelling?

If spelling becomes the only focal point of his teacher's interest, clearly a bright child will be likely to "play safe". He will tend to write only words within his spelling range, choosing to avoid adventurous language. That's why teachers often encourage the early use of dictionaries and pay attention to content rather than technical ability.

I was once shocked to read on the bottom of a sensitive piece of writing about a personal experience: "This work is terrible! There are far too many spelling errors and your writing is illegible (难以辨认的)." It may have been a sharp criticism of the pupil's technical abilities in writing, but it was also a sad reflection on the teacher who had omitted to read the essay, which contained some beautiful expressions of the child's deep feelings. The teacher was not wrong to draw attention to the errors, but if his priorities had centred on the child's ideas, an expression of his disappointment with the presentation would have given the pupil more motivation to seek improvement.

The major point discussed in the passage is _____.

A) the importance of developing writing skills

B) the complexities of spelling

C) the correct way of marking compositions

D) the relationship between spelling and the content of a composition

本文共分三段：第一段驳斥了家长们普遍认为学校不重视拼写教学的问题。作者认为问题主要在于如何鼓励学生在写作文时不要因为过多考虑拼写问题而影响自己对内容的表达。

第二段指出教师只注重拼写所造成的后果及正确的做法：重视作文内容。

第三段批评一位教师评阅一篇极富表现力的作文时只注意其拼写是否正确和书写是否工整而忽视内容的做法。

由上面概括的段落大意可知，本文论述的中心思想是单词的正确拼写和写作的内容之间的关系，所以 D)为正确答案。

上面三种找主题的方法表明：文章中有些句子比其他句子重要，阅读时可留意：1. 各段首句；2. 全文末句；3. 第二段第一句。各段首句和全文末句的重要性可以由上面找主题的方法看出，而第二段第一句有两个方面的作用：1. 如果对第一段的意思进行转折，它可能为主题句；2. 与第一段末句结合看，就会对主题有明朗认识。如果第二段第一句顺承第一段末句的意思，那么说明第二段与第一段讨论的为同一内容，而这个内容通常就是文章主题。总而言之，上面所列的三种重要句子有助于了解文章主题，也是考官重要的命题来源。

(四)通过作者论述的重点解主旨题

有时文章主题很不明确，由上述方法较难找到文章主题，此时可以根据文章论述的详略确定主题。

通常与主题有关的部分有较详尽的论述，而与主题关系不够密切的部分论述较简略。

经典实例

It has been thought and said that Africans are born with musical talent. Because music is so important in the lives of many Africans and because so much music is performed in Africa, we are inclined to think that all Africans are musicians. The impression is strengthened when we look at ourselves and find that we have become largely a society of musical spectators. Music is important to us, but most of us can be considered consumers rather than producers of music. We have records, television, concerts, and radio to fulfill many of our musical needs. In most situations where music is performed in our culture it is not difficult to distinguish the audience from the performers, but such is often not the case in Africa. Alban Ayipaga, a Kasena semiprofessional musician from northern Ghana, says that when his flute and drum ensemble is performing. "Anybody can take part". This is true, but Kasena musicians recognize that not all people are equally capable of taking part in the music. Some can sing along with the drummers, but relatively few can drum and even fewer can play the flute along with the ensemble. It is fairly common in Africa for there to be an ensemble of expert musicians surrounded by others who join in by clapping, singing, or somehow adding to the totality of musical sound. Performances often take place in an open area (that is, not on a stage) and so the lines between the performing nucleus and the additional performers, active spectators, and passive spectators may be difficult to draw from our point of view.

The best title for this passage would be _____.

A) The Importance of Music to African People

B) Differences Between African Music and Music of Other Countries

C) The Relationship Between Musicians and Their Audience

D) A Characteristic Feature of African Musical Performances

这是一道主旨题。阅读全文后发现,从第六句话开始,文章一直在讨论非洲音乐活动的一个明显特点——观众积极参与。对于这一点的论述占了文章的大部分,根据主题论述较详细的特点,确定 D)为正确答案。A)音乐对于非洲人的重要性;B)非洲音乐与其他国家音乐的差别;C)音乐家与观众之间的关系,三者均为原文提及的具体细节,没有展开论述,所以都应排除。

论述的详细还体现在重复之中,这种重复可以通过每段主题句实现,也可以在文章的字里行间以同义词复述全文关键词的方式完成。

二、态度评价题

(一)测试要求及题型

一篇文章不可避免地会反映作者的观点、态度和情绪。能否正确地把握作者的观点和态度是体现考生阅读理解能力的一个重要方面。这类题目主要是考查考生能否正确理解作者的写作意图、所持的观点及阐述文章主题时的语气或对他所论述的对象的态度。命题者设计这类题时往往涉及对有争议问题的看法,对事物的评价——作者持什么样的态度? 是赞同还是反对? 是同情、冷漠、失望还是批评、表扬?

作者态度题有两种题型:文章作者态度题和局部作者态度题。

(二)局部作者态度评价题的测试要求

局部作者态度题考查考生对局部细节所体现出的作者态度的理解,因此做此类题时,考生不能再像前一种态度题一样去找"感觉",而应当回到文章局部上,落到实处。

经典实例(1996 年)

In the last half of the nineteenth century "capital" and "labour" were enlarging and perfecting their rival organisations on modern lines. Many an old firm was replaced by a limited liability company with a bureaucracy of salaried managers. The change met the technical requirements of the new age by engaging a large professional element and prevented the decline in efficiency that so commonly spoiled the fortunes of family firms in the second and third generation after the energetic founders. It was moreover a step away from individual initiative, towards collectivism and municipal and state-owned business. The railway companies, though still private business managed for the benefit of shareholders, were very unlike old family business! At the same time the great municipalities went into business to supply lighting, trams and other services to the taxpayers.

The growth of the limited liability company and municipal business had important consequences. Such large, impersonal manipulation of capital and industry greatly increased the numbers and importance of shareholders as a class, an element in national life representing irresponsible wealth detached from the land and the duties of the landowners; and almost equally detached from the responsible management of business. All through the nineteenth century, America, Africa, India, Australia and parts of Europe were being developed by British capital, and British shareholders were thus enriched by the world's movement towards industrialisation. Towns like Bournemouth and Eastbourne sprang up to house large "comfortable" classes who had retired on their incomes, and who had no relation to the rest of the community except that of drawing dividends and occasionally attending a shareholders' meeting to dictate their orders to the management. On the other hand "shareholding" meant leisure and freedom which was used by many of the later Victorians for the highest purpose of a great civilisation.

The "shareholders" as such had no knowledge of the lives, thoughts or needs of the workmen employed by the company in which he held shares, and his influence on the relations of capital and labour was not good. The paid manager acting for the company was in more direct relation with the men and their demands, but even he had seldom that familiar personal knowledge of the workmen which the employer had often had under the more patriarchal system of the old family business now passing away. Indeed the mere size of operations and the numbers of workmen involved rendered such personal relations impossible. Fortunately, however, the increasing power and organisation of the trade unions, at least in all skilled trades, enabled the workmen to meet on equal terms the managers of the companies who employed them. The cruel discipline of the strike and lockout taught the two parties to respect each other's strength and understand the value of fair negotiation.

The author is most critical of _____.

A) family firm owners

B) landowners

C) managers

D) shareholders

[正确答案]D

在谈到 family firms owners 时,作者只是说:"通过雇用一大批专业人员,这一变化适应了新时代的技术要求,防止了效率的下降。而效率的下降通常是家族公司在精力充沛的创立者之后的第二三代破产的原因。"这是很客观的表述,在谈到 landowners 时说:"对资本与企业的如此大规模的非个人运作大大增加了作为一个阶层的持股人的数量及地位的重要性。国民生活中这一现象的出现代表了不由个人负责的财富与土地及土地所有者的义务的分离,这也在同样程度上意味着(不由个人负责的财富)与经营管理责任的分离。"也是很客观的表述,没有表明自己的态度。C 选项在原文中有两处提及,但都是指带薪经理,对经理并没有进行任何批评性评论,因而也不符合题意。只有 D 选项对应原文中 The "shareholders" as such had no knowledge of the lives, thoughts or needs of the workmen employed by the company in which he held shares, and his influence on the relations of capital and labour was not good. "像这样的'持股人'对所持股票公司雇用的工人的生活,思想和需求一无所知,他对资本与劳工关系没有什么好的影响。"显然,作者对这种"持股人"持批判的态度,所以 D 是正确答案。实际上,1996 年第 62 题命题也可以直接以下面的形式出现:

The author's attitude towards shareholders is _____.

A)biased 　　　 B)positive 　　　 C) sympathetic 　　　 D)critical

(三)态度评价题的解题方法

解作者态度(attitude)或语气(tone)题,关键在于把握作者对全文主体事物(与主题有关)或某一具体事物的态度。由于作者态度主要由语言来表达,因此必须弄清有关表达褒义、中性和贬义的手段:

1)加入形容词定语

例如:A) His words were few.

　　　 B) His interesting words were few.

假如 A)为中性叙述的话,那么 B)则体现了说话人对"He"的正面评价。

又如:C) They are all seniors.

　　　 D) They are all premature seniors.

同样,假如 C)为中性叙述,那么由于加入形容词定语"premature",D)表达了一种贬义。

2) 加入副词状语 加入的副词状语通常对动词的叙述加以界定。

例如:He successfully makes the travel plan.(表明一种正面态度); They speak clumsily.(表明一种负面态度)。

3) 特殊动词 英语中有些动词也表明说话者的正负态度,如:fail(未能)、ignore(忽视)、overesti-mate(估计过高)等动词表示一种负态度。由上可知,确定作者态度,可以有两种思路:问全文主体事物的(包括主题),可以根据阐述主题或有关主体事物的相关句中的形容词、副词或动词,确定作者的态度;如果问的是对某一具体事物的态度,则可以定位到具体相关句,然后确定答案。

经典实例

On June 17, 1744, the officials from Maryland and Virginia held a talk with the Indians of the Six Nations. The Indians were invited to send boys to William and Mary College. In a letter the next day they refused the offer as follows:

We know that you have a high opinion of the kind of learning taught in your colleges, and that the costs of living of our young men, while with you, would be very expensive to you. We are convinced that you mean to do us good by your proposal; and we thank you heartily. But you must know that different nations have different ways of looking at things, and you will therefore not be offended if our ideas of this kind of education happen not to be the same as yours. We have had some experience of it. Several of our young people were formerly brought up at the colleges of the northern provinces: they were taught all your sciences; but, when they came back to us, they were bad runners, ignorant of every means of living in the woods……they were totally good for nothing.

We are, however, not the less obliged by your kind offer, though we refuse to accept it; and, to show our grateful sense of it, if the gentlemen of Virginia will send us a dozen of their sons, we will take care of their education, teach them in all we know, and make men of them.

The tone of the letter as a whole is best described as _____.

A) angry   C) polite

B) pleasant   D) inquiring

这道题问的是印第安人信中的语气。只需从文中寻找相关形容词、副词或动词等就可以了:第二段第二句为:……we thank you heartily;第三段第一句指出:We are, however, not the less obliged by your kind offer……。由此可知印第安人回信时很有礼貌,因此 C)为正确答案。其他答案在文中都找不到依据。

三、对比题

(一)对比题的测试要求

议论文和说明文都强调逻辑的严谨性,而转折和对比常常可以用来测试考生在这一方面的阅读理解能力,所以考生对文中的转折和对比关系应高度重视,只要看到标明转折或对比的关系词如 but、however 等,就应当立即在原文上进行圈点。就转折而言:

一般说来转折后的内容多与上文所表达的意思相反,而对比往往是强调其中的一方。

经典实例

The sensation of sound involves a variety of factors in addition to its peak level. Advertisers are skillful at creating the impression of loudness through their expert use of such factors. One major contributor to the perceived loudness of commercials is that much less variation in sound level occurs during a commercial. In regular programming the intensity of sound varies over a large range. However, sound levels in commercials tend to stay at or near peak levels.

Commercials create the sensation of loudness because _____.

A)TV stations always operate at the highest sound levels

B)their sound levels are kept around peak levels

C)their sound levels are kept in the middle frequency ranges

D)unlike regular programs their intensity of sound varies over a wide range

这道题并不难,只要看到 however 这个路标和它后面的句子,就很容易找到答案 B。前面的句子说普通节目的音量变化在很大的范围内,接下来就是一个转折,说广告的音量试图停留在最高音量的位置,转折后刚刚好是本题广告会产生那种声音效果的原因。

(二)转折命题形式的测试要求

经典实例

It is a remarkable record, stretching back over 70 years—yet the BBC's future is now in doubt.

The world famous BBC now faces _____ .
A) the problem of new coverage
B) an uncertain prospect
C) inquiries by the general public
D) shrinkage of audience
[正确答案]B)。

"这是一个了不起的记录,历经长达 70 多年,但目前 BBC 的未来悬而未定。"

But it is the arrival of new satellite channels—funded partly by advertising and partly by viewers' subscriptions—which will bring about the biggest changes in the long term.

The foremost reason why the BBC has to readjust itself is no other than _____ .
A) the emergence of commercial TV channels
B) the enforcement of Broadcasting Act by the government
C) the urgent necessity to reduce costs and jobs
D) the challenge of new satellite channels
[正确答案]D)。

"BBC 不得不重新调整的最主要的原因正是新的卫星频道的挑战。""但是,从长远的观点来看,带来最大变化的将是新的卫星频道的开设——这些频道一部分由广告、一部分由观众的入网费收入提供经费。"

(三)关于比较方面的考点的表现形式

Ⅰ. 比较级与含有比较意义的词汇手段和句型结构:
a) 表示比较级的 more＋形容词(或副词)和形容词(或副词)＋er 形式;
b) 表示最高级的 most＋形容词或副词和形容词或副词＋est 等形式;
c) 表示比较的词汇手段:parallel, rival, match, differ from, like, unlike, different from 等;
d) 表示比较的句型结构:in the same way; as……as;
Ⅱ. 表示绝对意义的字眼:
first (第一),least (最不),always (老是),never (永不),foremost (最),uttermost (最),all (所有),none (一个也不),any (任何)
Ⅲ. 表示惟一性的词汇:only, sole, unique, simply (只要),just (只要)
阅读时最好能圈划表示最高级、惟一性和绝对意义的词汇,便于做题时回原文定位。
经典实例

A rapid means of long-distance transportation became a necessity for the United States as settlement (新拓居地) spread over farther westward. The early trains were impractical curiosities, and for a long time the railroad companies met with troublesome mechanical problems. The most serious ones were the construction of rails able to bear the load, and the development of a safe, effective stopping system. Once these were solved, the railroad was established as the best means of land transportation.

By 1860 there were thousands of miles of railroads crossing the eastern mountain ranges and reaching westward to the Mississippi. There were also regional southern and western lines.

The major problems with America's railroad system in the mid 19th century lay in _____.

A) poor quality rails and unreliable stopping systems

B) lack of financial support for development

C) limited railroad lines

D) lack of a transcontinental railroad

本题问的是 19 世纪中叶美国铁路系统存在的问题。作者在第一段第三句中指出,当时最严重的技术问题是 the construction of rails able to bear the road 和 the development of a safe, effective stopping system,所以答案为 A)。这个问题与该句的比较考点(最高级)相联系 The most serious ones were……。

(四)命题重点分析

只要首段中出现一对处于对比状况的概念,命题专家通常都会就此设置考题,考生应掌握这一规律,在看到文章首段出现转折对比的内容时,应当立即集中注意力,同时还要明白,第一段出现转折关系时,转折后所表述的一定是文章的中心议题,而在首段出现的对照或对比的内容将在下文中进行具体的议论,并在文章最后得出结论。

经典实例

Few creations of big technology capture the imagination like giant dams. Perhaps it is humankind's long suffering at the mercy of flood and drought that makes the ideal of forcing the waters to do our bidding so fascinating. But to be fascinated is also, sometimes, to be blind. Several giant dam projects threaten to do more harm than good.

The third sentence of paragraph 1 implies that _____.(转折)

A) people would be happy if they shut their eyes to reality

B) the blind could be happier than the sighted

C) over-excited people tend to neglect vital things

D) fascination makes people lose their eyesight

[正确答案]C)。

"文中第一段第三句话的意思是过度兴奋的人易于忽略重要的事情。"

首段第三句:"但是,兴奋有时候也表现为盲目。"命题者就转折词"But"后的句子设问,考查考生对转折关系的理解。

四、例 证 题

(一)例证题的测试要求及出题形式

让事实说话往往是最有效的论证方式之一,命题专家在设置题目时往往也会针对文中的事例设问,考查考生对局部结构的理解。

考生们在应用例证原则解题时还应注意常用的例证方式有两种:一是先提出观点、后举例说明;二是先列举事例再做出结论。考生应当学会举一反三,不要被各种原则的变化形式所迷惑。

看见举例说明的情况,我们应该谨记:例子一般是和文章或段落的中心思想紧密相关的,看到举例时要引起一定的警觉,这可能会是考点,而答案往往就在例子前后的总结性话里。而例子本身就可以迅速地扫过,不需要仔细研读。另外还需要注意的是,如果题目问的是例子说明什么,有关例子本身的选项,就不大可能为正确答案,因为它只是一个论据,正确答案一定是超越论据的结论。

阅读理解文章基本上是说明文、议论文。而这类体裁的文章少不了用例子、事实来说明观点。因

此我们往往会碰到要求猜测文章举例的目的——这些例子要说明什么观点的题目。如

The example of……is given to show/illustrate that _____.

What can be inferred from the author's example of ……?

The experiment/study suggests/shows that _____.

　　例子为阅读理解的常考点之一,所以阅读时对于 for example, for instance, such as, as 等引出的例子可以注意,划下这几个提示词,以便做题时查找。这类题的基本结构为 The author provides in Line……(或 Paragraph……)an example in order to……,意思是问文中举出某现象或例子的目的。由于考研英语阅读理解文章大都是说明文和议论文,所以文章中举出一些例子无非是为了说明一定的道理。关键在于这个例子在原文出现的位置,但不管如何,这个例子之前或之后不远处通常都有一句总结说明性的话,这句话就是答案,即被例证的对象。如果例子与全文主题有关,则例证主题,答案为主题句;如果例子与段落主题有关,那就是例证段落主题,则答案为段落主题句;此外,答案为例子前后总结说明性的话。

(二)例证题答案所在句的标志词

　　例证的标志词有:as, such as, for example, for instance 等。

经典实例

　　Taking charge of yourself involves putting to rest some very prevalent myths. At the top of the list is the notion that intelligence is measured by your ability to solve complex problems; to read, write and compute at certain levels; and to resolve abstract equations quickly. This vision of intelligence asserts formal education and bookish excellence as the true measures of self-fulfillment. It encourages a kind of intellectual prejudice that has brought with it some discouraging results. We have come to believe that someone who has more educational merit badges, who is very good at some form of school discipline is "intelligent. "Yet mental hospitals are filled with patients who have all of the properly lettered certificates. A truer indicator of intelligence is an effective, happy life lived each day and each present moment of every day.

It is implied in the passage that holding a university degree _____.

A) does not mean that one is highly intelligent

B) may make one mentally sick and physically weak

C) may result in one's inability to solve complex real-life problems

D) does not indicate one's ability to write properly worded documents

　　解析:作者在后半部分举了一个例子,说精神病医院里有很多病人就有各种各样的证书。可见,有大学学位并不等于智商高。我们只要能判明它是例证,就不难从主旨出发,理解它的含义,就能理解 A)选项实际上是对这些例证的总结与概括,自然就是正确答案。

(三)做例证题时应当注意的问题

　　1) illustrate (例证)、give an example (举例)、verify (证实)等不同表达法在题干或选项中并不影响答案;

　　2)假如题干问的是某一具体事物,其所在的句子就是例证的内容。例子为句段的,通常为两种模式:1)总结说明→例子(例证),总结说明后有时伴有提示词,如 for instance, for example 等;2)例子(例证)→总结说明,总结说明前有时伴有提示词,如 thus, therefore, in conclusion, as a result 等。

　　3)注意例证所在的段落主题句

　　如果例证所在段有概括段落思想的主题句,就首先读这个主题句,看它的意思和问题下四个选择项哪项意思一致。一致的那个就是答案,不要去读具体例证了。因为举例的目的是为了说明观点,而段落中的例子大多是说明段落主题思想的。

经典实例

Faces, like fingerprints, are unique. Did you ever wonder how it is possible for us to recognize people? Even a skilled writer probably could not describe all the features that make one face different from another. Yet a very young child—or even an animal, such as a pigeon—can learn to recognize faces, we all take this ability for granted.

We also tell people apart by how they behave. When we talk about someone's personality, we mean the ways in which he or she acts, speaks, thinks and feels that make that individual different from others.

Like the human face, human personality is very complex. But describing someone's personality in words is somewhat easier than describing his face. If you were asked to describe what a "nice face" looked like, you probably would have a difficult time doing so. But if you were asked to describe a "nice person", you might begin to think about someone who was kind, considerate, friendly, warm, and so forth.

There are many words to describe how a person thinks, feels and acts. Gordon Allport, an American psychologist, found nearly 18,000 English words characterizing differences in people's behavior. And many of us use this information as a basis for describing, or typing his personality. Bookworms, conservatives, military types—people are described with such terms.

People have always tried to "type" each other. Actors in early Greek drama wore masks to show the audience whether they played the villain's (坏人) or the hero's role. In fact, the words "person" and "personality" come from the Latin persona, meaning "mask". Today, most television and movie actors do not wear masks. But we can easily tell the "good guys" from the "bad guys" because the two types differ in appearance as well as in actions.

By using the example of finger prints, the author tells us that _____.

A) people can learn to recognize faces

B) people have different personalities

C) people have difficulty in describing the features of finger prints

D) people differ from each other in facial features

这是一道例证题,实际上考的是对文章首句的理解:Faces, like fingerprints, are unique.（人的面孔像指纹一样独一无二），由此可知 D)为正确答案:各人的面孔各不相同。

4)注意例证上下文、上下句的作者观点

如果例证所在段没有主题句或例证本身就是一段,就要看例证上面一段或句、下面一段或句是否有相关的归纳性的作者观点。如果这个作者观点和问题中的某一个选择项意思一致,那就是答案,也不要去读具体例证了。

五、词汇题

(一)词汇题的测试要求

在阅读理解测试中,词义句意是必考的题型,它包括对单词、词组及句子的理解。词汇测试是要求考生具备推测某个超纲词或短语在特定语言环境中的特定含义的能力。所考词汇或短语具有下列特征:1)生词;2)熟词生义;3)句子中的代词;4)难理解的句子。

因为考研大纲规定试题中可以有3%左右的生词,并且对于大纲中的词汇考生也不一定能够全部掌握或者认知,另外对某些一词多义的单词可能只知其一不知其二,因此生词和一词多义的单词成为很多考生阅读中的难关。搞清文章中的每一个单词对理解文章来说当然是最好不过的,但是由于时间、水平等诸多因素的限制,考生不可能做到这一点,而且我们在解题过程中也无需做到这一点。

对于词义句意题中考查的生词,一般我们可以借助上下文的提示猜测出来,或者借助词的构成猜测出来,关于猜词技巧可以参照本章的第一部分知识必备中的猜测技巧。当题目考查的是我们熟悉的词语,但是很明显不是我们熟悉的含义时,考生应该注意上下文,仔细斟酌,千万不能凭自己对词汇的了解来答题。当题目考查文章中指代词时,一般是考 it、that、they、this 等词的指代对象,而且代词所在的句子一般比较长,逻辑关系会比较复杂,这时考生需要分析句子结构。在考查难以理解的句子时,考生应该注意这句话与上下文的联系,词义句意题的选项中正确选项一般是该词汇的近义词或者同义转述。干扰项一般是和考查词汇相反或者不相干的选项。词义句意题常见的提问方式有:

　　In line..., the word " ... " probably means _____.

　　In line..., the phrase " ... " could be replaced by _____.

　　By " ... " the author means _____.

　　The author uses the word " ... " to mean _____.

　　What is the possible meaning of the word " ... " in line...?

　　Which is the probable definition of the word " ... "?

　　Which of the following is closest in meaning to " ... "?

　　In line..., the word "that / it" stands for _____.

　　Which of the following best defines the word " ... "?

　　The word / phrase " ... " is closest in meaning to _____.

　　From the passage, we can infer that the word " ... " is _____.

　　For any job search, you should start with a narrow concept—what you want to do—then broaden it. "None of these programs do that," says another expert. "There's no career counseling implicit in all of this." Instead, the best strategy is to use the agent as a kind of tip service to keep abreast of jobs in a particular database; when you get E-mail, consider it a reminder to check the database again. "I would not rely on agents for finding everything that is added to a database that might interest me," says the author of a job-searching guide.

　　　　　　　　　　　　　　　　　　　　　　　　　　　　　　(2004—Passage 1)

43. The expression "tip service" (Line 3, Para. 3) most probably means _____.

　　[A]advisory (词性不一致)　　　　[B]compensation(文中未提及)

　　[C]interaction (文中未提及)　　　[D]reminder(进一步补充说明,近义替换)

　　【解析】选[D]语义理解题,本题是对常见词语的不常见搭配提问。tip service 不是固定短语,需要考生从文章中进行猜测。该短语的上下文说搜索代理并不是十分可靠的,也有缺点,所以不妨将其当作一种 tip service," when you get E-mail, consider it a reminder to check the database again"从篇章上看是其同义转述,其中的 reminder 和 tip service 在各自句中的作用相同,所以 tip service 可以解释为 reminder。

　　Railroads justify rate discrimination against captive shippers on the grounds that in the long run it reduces everyone's cost. If railroads charged all customers the same average rate, they argue, shippers who have the option of switching to trucks or other forms of transportation would do so, leaving remaining customers to shoulder the cost of keeping up the line. It's a theory to which many economists subscribe, but in practice it often leaves railroads in the position of determining which companies will flourish and which will fail. "Do we really want railroads to be the arbiters of who wins and who loses in the marketplace?" asks Martin Bercovici, a Washington lawyer who frequently represents shippers.

　　　　　　　　　　　　　　　　　　　　　　　　　　　　　　(2003—Passage 3)

54. The word "arbiters" (Line 6, Para. 4) most probably refers to those _____.

　　[A]who work as coordinators(文中未提)

　　[B]who function a judges (同义替换)

　　[C]who supervise transactions(中文未提)

　　[D]who determine the price(干扰性较强,属偷换概念)

　　【解析】选[B]arbiter 一词超出了考研英语词汇范围,很少有考生认识这个单词,因此解答本题要完全依赖上下文线索。在这个词之前的一句中,作者提到"... but in practice it often leaves railroads in the position of determining which companies will flourish and which will fail.”紧接着该句是一问句：Do we really want railroads to be the arbiters of who wins and who loses in the marketplace? 显然，后句是对第一句表达的内容进行提问，两者意思相同。因此我们可以得出 arbiter 的意思是 one who determines which companies will win and which will fail。显然这是一个仲裁者的角色，在四个选项中[B]“行使法官职能”与之含义最为贴近，故为本题答案。这里作者使用了重复的修辞手段，来强调某个信息或观点。所以，考生猜测词义时不应只局于一个句子，而应从上下文寻找线索。

(二)词汇题的考查重点

1. 生词

对很多考生来说，生词是阅读中的一大难关。

有的同学养成了一种不良习惯，阅读时总希望把文章中每一个词的意思都搞懂，他们对生词花费了太多的注意力，却忽视了对整体意思的把握。这犹如丢了西瓜捡芝麻。搞清文章中每一单词的意思固然对理解以及答案的选择有帮助，但由于时间、水平等诸多因素的限制，我们根本无法、也不可能、同时也没有必要把文章里的词全部搞清楚，而且阅读理解多项选择题中就有猜词义的题，所以要学会和生词打交道。再说，以后工作中的阅读也永远需要和生词打交道，因为英语的词汇量太大了。可以毫不夸张地说，猜测词义是中国人终生有用的英语阅读技能。

2. 熟词僻义

考试中词汇量是有控制的。但众所周知，很多英语单词都是一词多义，而且最常用的词义项最多。比如根据字典，最常用的动词 go 至少有 50 多个义项，这还不算它跟其他词所组成的成语。严格说来一个义项就可以看成是一个单词，所以从原则上说对待熟词僻义的方法跟对待生词的方法相同。

在阅读过程中遇到“熟词”时要念念不忘两条最基本的原则：(1)相信作者所写的东西是有意义的，文章中存在着某种对客观的陈述，此即真实性的原则；(2)相信作者清楚地用文字传达了某种信息，文字中没有混乱，此即合作的原则。因此，如果觉得文章中有混乱、讲不通或违背一般常识，那一定是我们自己没正确理解词义，我们自己没读懂。在多义词词义的选择上这两项原则特别有用。换言之，我们要记住“A word has no meaning, but the meaning lies in the context(词本无义，义随文生)”，即词的意义是由上下文决定的，我们在理解过程中务必使它在上下文中讲得通(make sense)。比如：

(1)Mr. Smith sits on the board of directors.

也许有人会把这句话理解为“Mr. Smith 坐在经理的木板上。”比较爱动脑筋的人也许会将 board 的意思引申为“桌子”“办公桌”，再进一步延伸为“Mr. Smith 成了经理”。但仔细考虑就会发现这样理解有诸多不妥：

① 如果 sit 意为“坐”，通常不会用一般现在时，除非是描述一幅图画，或者是报纸上的标题；

② sit on the board 不会是“坐在木板上”，因为这不符合一般常识；

③ “坐在办公桌前”应该是 sit at the desk；

④ board 是单数，director 是复数，不可能几个经理共用一块木板或办公桌。

所以我们可通过常识和最基本的语言知识排除错误理解。实际上 sit on 在这里是“成为一个成员”之意；board 是“委员会”的意思。所以例(1)意为“Mr. Smith 成为董事会的一名成员。”

再看一个选择多义词正确词义的例子：

(2)The personal chemistry between the men is excellent.

如果把例(2)中的 chemistry 理解为“化学”就无法解读这个句子。遇到这种情况可暂时把它从句子中去掉，即将其视为一个空白。没有“化学”这个先入为主的概念干扰，也许你的思想更自由，很快就会想到“两人之间的个人……情……关系……很好？”对！chemistry 在此处的意思就是“人和人之间的感情关系”。记住：无论如何，一定要使句子讲得通！

经典实例(1997 年)

We live in a society in which the medicinal and social use of substances (drugs) is <u>pervasive</u>: an aspirin to quiet a headache, some wine to be sociable, coffee to get going in the morning, a cigarette for the nerves.

The word "pervasive" might mean _____.

A) widespread　　　　　　　B) overwhelming

C) piercing　　　　　　　　D) fashionable

[正确选项] A)。

"在我们生活的社会里,刺激物被广泛用于医学和社交目的,如:用阿司匹林制止头痛,用酒交际,早晨起来用咖啡提提神,抽支烟定定神。"

"pervasive"属于超纲单词,下文中所举的例子说明的是刺激物用于各个方面,而四个选项的词义分别为:分布广泛的(widespread),势不可挡的、压倒一切的(overwhelming),刺穿、穿透(piercing),时髦的(fashionable),代入原文,只有 A)选项最合适。

经典实例(1998 年)

And the bank has done this even though its advisors say the dam will cause hardship for the powerless and environmental destruction. The benefits are for the powerful, but they are far from guaranteed.

In paragraphs, "the powerless" probably refers to _____.

A) areas short of electricity

B) dams without power stations

C) poor countries around India

D) common people in the Narmada Dam area

[正确答案] D)。

"大坝的建设也许会给有权势的人带来益处,但是即使这一点也根本没有保障。"由上下文中可以得知,powerless 和 powerful 是一对反义词,the powerful 在文中指有权势的人,所以 powerless 必定指普通人。不少考生误以为 powerless 应是缺乏电力的地区而选 A)选项,B)选项是说大坝、C)选项指国家,所以都是干扰选项,只有 D)符合题意。

(三)利用语法和逻辑解词汇题

有时根据上下文提供的线索或者其他方法,仍然不能得到惟一答案,就可以利用语法和逻辑方面的规则来判断,符合语法和逻辑规则的可能为正确答案,反之则不是答案。

经典实例

The cable was laid, but not until 1866 was the connection made permanent and reliable. At the early attempts, the cable failed and when it was taken out for repairs it was found to be covered in living growths, a fact which defied contemporary scientific opinion that there was no life in the deeper parts of the sea.

"defied" in the 5th paragraph probably means _____.

A) doubted　　　　　　　　C) challenged

B) gave proof to　　　　　　D) agreed to

"defied"所在的分句为:……it was found to be covered in living growths, a fact which defied contemporary scientific opinion that there was no life in the deeper parts of the sea. 其中 fact 就是指前半句的内容,由此可知,前半句与 which 引导的定语从句中的宾语通过 defied 发生联系:前半句说的是海底有生物,而定语从句中的宾语及其同位语从句说的是当代科学认为海底没有生命,可见 defied 表示否定的含义,这样只有 A)和 C)符合条件,而由于 A)doubted 通常不能以物作主语,所以只有 C)合适,为正确答案。

六、是非判断题

(一)是非判断题的测试要求

是非判断题是考研英语阅读中测试深层理解能力的重要方式。这种题型主要考查学生对文章中一些似是而非的东西理解得是否全面。其出题方式有两种,一是以不完全句的形式对文中的某种事实和观点的隐含意思进行深层挖掘,以判别正误;二是题干以问句形式出现,让考生判断四个选项的正误。

判断题常见的表达方式有哪些:

Which of the following is NOT mentioned in the passage?

Which of the following would NOT be an example of _____?

All of the following were mentioned in the passage EXCEPT _____.

According to the passage, all of the following are true EXCEPT that _____.

Which of the following statements is NOT mentioned in the passage?

Which of the following statements is NOT true?

Which of the following statements is TRUE according to the passage?

All of the following are reasons for. . . EXCEPT _____.

(二)利用定位法解是非判断题

根据题干或选项中的关键词返回看原文,找到相关句,与选项相比较就能确定答案。

经典实例

Although April did not bring us the rains we all hoped for, and although the Central Valley doesn't generally experience the atmospheric sound and lightning that can accompany those rains, it's still important for parents to be able to answer the youthful questions about thunder and lightning.

The reason these two wonders of nature are so difficult for many adults to explain to children is that they are not very well understood by adults themselves. For example, did you know that the lightning we see flashing down to the earth from a cloud is actually flashing up to a cloud from the earth? Our eyes trick us into thinking we see a downward motion when it's actually the other way around. But then, if we believed only what we think we see, we'd still insist that the sun rises in the morning and sets at night.

Most lightning flashes take place inside a cloud, and only a relative few can be seen jumping between two clouds or between earth and a cloud. But, with about 2,000 thunderstorms taking place above the earth every minute of the day and night, there's enough activity to produce about 100 lightning strikes on earth every second.

Parents can use thunder and lightning to help their children learn more about the world around them. When children understand that the light of the lightning flashing reaches their eyes almost at the same moment, but the sound of the thunder takes about 5 seconds to travel just one mile, they can begin to time the interval between the flash and the crash to learn how close they were to the actual spark.

What is TRUE about lightning according to the passage?

A) Only a small number of lightning flashes occur on earth.

B) Lightning travels 5 times faster than thunder.

C) Lightning flashes usually jump from one cloud to another.

D) There are far more lightning strikes occurring on earth than we can imagine.

由题干可知问的是有关闪电(lightning)的事情,A)、D)与数量有关,B)与速度有关,C)与活动情况有关,可以先找到论述闪电数量的地方:Most lightning flashes take place inside a cloud,and only a relative few can be seen jumping between two clouds or between earth and a cloud. 由此可知D)正确:我们能看到的闪电只是大量闪电中的一小部分。找到正确答案后,不要浪费时间思考其他选项,这是由是非题本身的特点所决定的。

(三)利用关键词回归定位法解是非判断题

这种做题方法主要与三正一误的下列问法相联系:

Which of the following is mentioned in······except······?

Which of the following is not mentioned······?

以这些问法为题干的正确选项所包含的信息通常连续出现在同一段,而且往往无列举标志词,如first,second,third 等。做题时只需阅读有关段落,根据一个正确选项中的关键词在其前后找其他两个正确选项,剩下一个原文中未提到的,为正确答案。这种列举还有其他形式:1)列举项出现在同一句话中;2)列举项分散在全文中。不过做题方法都是一样:带着选项找答案。

经典实例

In our classrooms,we work in various ways. The pupils often work in groups:this gives them the opportunity to learn to co-operate,to share,and to develop leadership skills. They also learn how to cope with(对付) personal problems as well as learning how to think,to make decisions,to analyse and evaluate,and to communicate effectively. The pupils learn from each other as well as from the teacher.

Which of the following is NOT MENTIONED in the third paragraph?

A) Group work gives pupils the opportunity to learn to work together with others.

B) Pupils also learn to develop their reasoning abilities.

C) Group work provides pupils with the opportunity to learn to be capable organizers.

D) Pupils also learn how to participate in teaching activities.

找到文章的第三段,A)所说的"学会合作"(learn to work together with others)对应于此段的第二句:learn to cooperate,to share,and to develop leadership skills。然后在这个句子前后寻找其他选项的原文:C)在第二句;B)体现在紧挨着的第三句中:learning how to think,to make decisions,to analyse and evaluate。这样只剩下 D)在第三段找不到依据,所以以为该题答案。

七、因果与条件关系题

(一)因果题的测试要求

因果句都是指明两个事件之间因果关系的词,尤为命题青睐,因为通过命题可以考查文中两个事件内在的因果关系。此种句型一般出"推断性问题"。除了上述原文有因果关系提示词的显性原因考点之外,隐性原因(两个句子之间为因果关系,但无有关提示词)也是常见考点。不管是显性原因考点,还是隐性原因考点,原文相关句出现的格式都是先说原因,后说结果,而在题干中通常给出结果,就其原因提问。如上所述,因果关系题的答案有时可依据因果关系提示词圈划或定位找,但更多的时候答案中并无因果关系提示词,但仍表达因果关系。有鉴于此,考生平时有必要注意训练自己的因果关系推理。不过,因果关系题的答案以题干中关键词在原文中的前后句或同一段落内为主。

(二)因果题的出题形式

因果题的出题形式有两种:①段落(含首段)第一句如果表达一种因果关系,通常为考点;②文章中细节性的因果关系——通常由一些表示因果关系的词汇手段来表达;

(1)表示因果关系的名词:base,basis(根据),result,consequence,reason;

(2)表示因果关系的动词:cause(原因),result in(结果),result from(由于,由······),follow from

（……结果），base...on...（以……为基础），be due to（由于）；

（3）表示因果关系的连词或介词 because，since，for，as，therefore，so，consequently，thus，why，with；

（4）表示因果关系的副词：as a result，consequently 等。

经典实例（2001 年）

Yet Rosa could not find any evidence that it works. To provide such proof，TT therapists would have to sit down for independent testing—something they haven't been eager to do，even though James Randi has offered more than ＄1 million to anyone who can demonstrate the existence of a human energy field. (He's had one taker so far. She failed.) A skeptic might conclude that TT practitioners are afraid to lay their beliefs on the line. But who could turn down an innocent fourth-grader? Says Emily："I think they didn't take me very seriously because I'm a kid. "

Why did some TT practitioners agree to be the subjects of Emily's experiment?

A) They thought it was going to be a lot of fun.

B) It involved nothing more than mere guessing.

C) They sensed no harm in a little girl's experiment.

D) It was more straightforward than other experiments.

解析：题中问为什么 TT 行医人同意做艾米莉的实验呢？文中第三段最后一句 Says Emily："I think they didn't take me very seriously because I'm a kid. "其中 because 一词提示出这句为因果关系句，所以我们应标记其后的关键词 a kid，不难推出 C)为正确答案。

（三）条件关系题的测试要求以及出题形式

Ⅰ. 以 when、if、as 等连词引导的条件从句；

Ⅱ. 文章中细节性的条件关系——通常由一些表示条件关系的词汇手段表达：如 depend upon（取决于），determine（决定）等。

它在原文出现的模式可以是：条件句＋主句，或主句＋条件句，但题干通常给出主句的意思，问相关条件。

经典实例（1996 年）

British universities，groaning under the burden of a huge increase in student numbers，are warning that the tradition of a free education is at risk. The universities have threatened to impose an admission fee on students to plug a gap in revenue if the government does not act to improve their finances and scrap some public spending cutbacks.

The chief concern of British universities is ＿＿＿＿＿.

A) how to tackle their present financial difficulty

B) how to expand the enrollment to meet the needs of enterprises

C) how to improve their educational technology

D) how to put an end to the current tendency of quality deterioration

解析：文中第一段第二句是主句＋条件句的结构，意思是"英国的大学威胁说，如果政府不采取行动改善高校的财政状况，不废除某些削减公共服务开支的计划，为了弥补经费不足，他们将强行向学生收取学费。"可以得出正确答案为 A)。

经典实例

Even plants can run a fever，especially when they're under attack by insects or disease. But unlike humans，plants can have their temperature taken from 3,000 feet away — straight up. A decade ago， adapting the infrared（红外线）scanning technology developed for military purposes and other satellites, physicist Stephen Paley came up with a quick way to take the temperature of crops to determine which ones are under stress. The goal was to let farmers precisely target pesticide（杀虫剂）spraying rather than rain poison on a whole field, which invariably includes plants that don't have pest（害虫）problems.

Even better, Paley's Remote Scanning Services Company could detect crop problems before they became visible to the eye. Mounted on a plane flown at 3,000 feet at night, an infrared scanner measured the heat emitted by crops. The data were transformed into a color-coded map showing where plants were running "fevers". Farmers could then spot-spray, using 50 to 70 percent less pesticide than they otherwise would.

The bad news is that Paley's company closed down in 1984, after only three years. Farmers resisted the new technology and long-term backers were hard to find. But with the renewed concern about pesticides on produce, and refinements in infrared scanning, Paley hopes to get back into operation. Agriculture experts have no doubt the technology works. "This technique can be used on 75 percent of agricultural land in the United States," says George Oerther of Texas A&M. Ray Jackson, who recently retired from the Department of Agriculture, thinks remote infrared crop scanning could be adopted by the end of the decade. But only if Paley finds the financial backing which he failed to obtain 10 years ago.

Infrared scanning technology may be brought back into operation because of _____.
A) the desire of farmers to improve the quality of their produce
B) growing concern about the excessive use of pesticides on crops
C) the forceful promotion by the Department of Agriculture
D) full support from agriculture experts

根据题干中的关键词组"brought back into operation"找到原文相关句:But with the renewed concern about pesticides on produce, and refinements in infrared scanning, Paley hopes to get back into operation. 但是随着人们重新关注杀虫剂对农产品的影响,以及红外线扫描技术的改进,Paley 希望能重操旧业。由此可以推出 B)为正确答案。这个原因考点与相关句中的原因状语(以 with 引导)相联系。

除了上述原文有因果关系提示词的显性原因考点之外,隐性原因(两个句子之间为因果关系,但无有关提示词)也是常见考点。不管是显性原因考点,还是隐性原因考点,原文相关句出现的格式都是先说原因,后说结果,而在题干中通常给出结果,就其原因提问。

The application of infrared scanning technology to agriculture met with some difficulties due to _____.
A) the lack of official support
B) its high cost
C) the lack of financial support
D) its failure to help increase production

这道题测试的是一个隐性原因考点(原文中没有提示词)。相关句为第三段前两句话:第一句话提到将红外线扫描技术运用于农业遇到困难——Paley 的公司于 1984 年关闭,第二句话叙述了其中的原因:Farmers resisted the new technology and long-term backers were hard to find. 农场主们抵制这项新技术,而且难以找到(投资方面的)长期支持者。由此可知 C)为正确答案。

经典实例

For every course that he follows a student is given a grade, which is recorded, and the record is available for the student to show to prospective employers. All this imposes a constant pressure and strain of work, but in spite of this some students still find time for great activity in student affairs. Elections to positions in student organisations arouse much enthusiasm. The effective work of maintaining discipline is usually performed by students who advise the academic authorities. Any student who is thought to have broken the rules, for example, by cheating has to appear before a student court. With the enormous numbers of students, the operation of the system does involve a certain amount of activity. A student who has held one of these positions of authority is much respected and it will be of benefit to him later in his career.

American university students are usually under pressure of work because _____.
A) their academic performance will affect their future careers
B) they are heavily involved in student affairs
C) they have to observe university discipline
D) they want to run for positions of authority

本题问的是美国大学生通常承受压力的原因。相关句在第二段前两句话——第二句指出：All this imposes a constant pressure and strain of work…… 这一切给学生造成持续的压力和紧张……，由此可知原因在前一句：For every course that he follows a student is given a grade, which is recorded, and the record is available for the student to show to prospective employers. 学生上的每门课都有一个分数登记在册，而分数可以由学生拿给未来雇主看。A)："其学业表现会影响其未来的工作"与上句"分数可以由学生拿给未来雇主看（由其决定是否录用）"意思一致，为正确答案。第二段第一句和第二句之间为因果关系（第一句为因，第二句为果），但没有因果关系提示词，仍然成为考点，这种先因后果（无提示词）的结构值得考生注意。

Some students are enthusiastic for positions in student organisations probably because _____.
A) they hate the constant pressure and strain of their study
B) they will then be able to stay longer in the university
C) such positions help them get better jobs
D) such positions are usually well paid

文中在第二段第三句谈到部分学生热衷于在学生组织中任职：Elections to positions in student organizations arouse much enthusiasm. 接着讨论了任职学生的作用，最后才提到了学生热衷于任职的原因：A student who has held one of these positions of authority is much respected and it will be of benefit to him later in his career. 任职的学生受人尊敬，并在未来工作中获益，由此可知 C) 为正确答案。

八、推理题

（一）推理题的测试要求及出题形式

推理题要求在理解表面文字信息的基础上，做出一定判断和推论，从而得到文章的隐含意义和深层意义。推理题所涉及的内容可能是文中某一句话，也可能是某几句话，但做题的指导思想都是以表面文字信息为依据，既不能做出在原文中找不到文字根据的推理，也不能根据表面文字信息做多步推理。所以，推理题的答案只能是根据原文表面文字信息进一步推出的答案：即对原文某一句话或某几句话做同义改写（paraphrase）或综合。推理题的目的是考识别能力，并不涉及复杂的判断和推理。因此，推理题的主要做法是：速读原文后，根据问题题干中的关键词或选项中的线索找到原文的相关句，读懂后，比照选项，对相关句进行同义改写或综合概括的选项为正确答案。做题时要注意题干的语言形式，如：According to the passage, it can be inferred from the passage that; It can be concluded from the passage that 等，虽然从表面上看是问有关全文的问题，但实际上不用看全篇，仍然只需要根据选项中的线索找到原文中与之相关的一句话或几句话，然后得出答案。

（二）推理题的测试要求及解题方法

（1）假如题干中提到具体线索，根据具体线索找到原文相关句（一句或几句话），然后做出推理；

（2）假如题干中无线索，如：It can be inferred from the passage that; It can be concluded from the passage that 等，先扫一下四个选项，排除不太可能的选项，然后根据最有可能的选项中的关键词找到原文相关句，做出推理；

（3）如果一篇文章中其他题都未涉及文章主旨，那么推理题，如 infer, conclude 题型，可能与文章主旨有关，考生应该定位到文章主题所在位置（如主题句出现处）；假如其他题已经涉及文章主旨，那么要求推断出来的内容可能与段落主题有关，如果如此，应该找段落主题所在处；如果不与段落主题有关，有时与全文或段落的重要结论有关，这时可以寻找与这些结论相关的原文叙述。

题干中含有 infer, conclude 的推理题称为推论题。要求推出的结论可能与文章主旨有关，也可能关系不大，但不管如何，碰到这种推理题，都应尽可能在速读完全文后再做，因为它的综合性较强。与主旨有关的推论题，可以仔细阅读文中表达主旨的相关句；在读完文章后，扫一下选项，排除不太可能的选项（如：与原文明显相矛盾的，提到了原文找不到依据的事实、细节或观点），拿到剩下的选项回原文寻找语言证据，两相对照，能够由原文表面文字信息合理推出来的，即为正确答案。

经典实例

People tend to be more impressed by evidence that seems to confirm some relationship. Thus many are convinced their dreams are prophetic（预言的）because a few have come true; they neglect or fail to notice the many that have not.

Consider also the belief that "the phone always rings when I'm in the shower." If it does ring while you are in the shower, the event will stand out and be remembered. If it doesn't ring, that nonevent probably won't even register（留下印象）.

People want to see order, pattern and meaning in the world. Consider, for example, the common belief that things like personal misfortunes, plane crashes, and deaths "happen in threes." Such beliefs stem from the tendency of people to allow the third event to define the time period. If three plane crashes occur in a month, then the period of time that counts as their "happening together" is one month; if three crashes occur in a year, the period of time is stretched. Flexible end points reinforce such beliefs.

We also tend to believe what we want to believe. A majority of people think they are more intelligent, more fair-minded and more skilled behind the wheel of an automobile than the average person. Part of the reason we view ourselves so favorably is that we use criteria that work to our advantage. As economist Thomas Schelling explains, "Everybody ranks himself high in qualities he values; careful drivers give weight to care, skilled drivers give weight to skill, and those who are polite give weight to courtesy," This way everyone ranks high on his own scale.

Perhaps the most important mental habit we can learn is to be cautious（谨慎的）in drawing conclusions. The "evidence" of everyday life is sometimes misleading.

What can be inferred from the passage?

A) Happenings that go unnoticed deserve more attention.

B) In a series of misfortunes the third one is usually the most serious.

C) People tend to make use of evidence that supports their own beliefs.

D) Believers of misfortunes happening in threes are cautious in interpreting events.

浏览一下选项，B）与 D）在原文找不到依据，而 C）与文章首句 People tend to be more impressed by evidence that seems to confirm some relationship. 意思不符，所以均应排除。文章第一段和第二段各举了一个例子；第一段指出人们因为一些梦想成真而忽视了多数梦想没有变成现实这一事实；第二段指出人们总是抱怨"每次淋浴电话就响"，但却忽视了大多数淋浴时电话并不响这一事实。这两个例子都说明人们易于记住表明某种关系的少数事件，而对多数事件注意不够。因此 A）为正确答案。

经典实例

Exchange a glance with someone, then look away. Do you realize that you have made a statement?

Hold the glance for a second longer, and you have made a different statement. Hold it for 3 seconds, and the meaning has changed again. For every social situation, there is a permissible time that you can hold a person's gaze without being intimate, rude, or aggressive. If you are on an elevator, what gaze-time are you permitted? To answer this question, consider what you typically do. You very likely give other passengers a quick glance to size them up (打量) and to assure them that you mean no threat. Since being close to another person signals the possibility of interaction. You need to emit a signal telling others you want to be left alone. So you cut off eye contact, what sociologist Erving Goffman (1963) calls "a dimming of the lights." You look down at the floor, at the indicator lights, anywhere but into another passenger's eyes. Should you break the rule against staring at a stranger on an elevator, you will make the other person exceedingly uncomfortable, and you are likely to feel a bit strange yourself.

It can be inferred from the first paragraph that _____.

A) every glance has its significance

B) staring at a person is an expression of interest

C) a gaze longer than 3 seconds is unacceptable

D) a glance conveys more meaning than words

浏览一下选项,可以先排除 B)与 C),因为第一段并未讨论这两点;再看一下第一段的逻辑结构,刚开始几句从总的方面论述:Exchange a glance with someone, then look away. Do you realize that you have made a statement? Hold the glance for a second longer, and you have made a different statement. Hold it for 3 seconds, and the meaning has changed again. 每一瞥的含义随时间长短变化而变化,接着举例说明在不同场合中的具体情况。由此可知,A):每一瞥均有其本身的含义(即各种瞥的含义不同)为正确答案,D)所提到的比较,在原文中找不到依据,应该排除。

三、暗示推理题的测试要求及解题方法

凡是题干中含有 imply, suggest 等词的推理题,可以称为暗示推理题,做题思路是:根据题干或选项中的线索回原文定位,仔细阅读找到的相关句,然后比较选项,排除不正确的,找到对相关句进行同义表达或综合的正确答案。既然是暗示推理题,那么答案不能一字不差地照搬原文词句,而应对原文词句做出同义改写。这种改写可以通过利用同义词、改变原句顺序或结构等方式完成。题干中如含有 learn from the passage that 也可视为这种推理题。

经典实例

It has been thought and said that Africans are born with musical talent. Because music is so important in the lives of many Africans and because so much music is performed in Africa, we are inclined to think that all Africans are musicians. The impression is strengthened when we look at ourselves and find that we have become largely a society of musical spectators (旁观). Music is important to us, but most of us can be considered consumers rather than producers of music. We have records, television, concerts, and radio to fulfill many of our musical needs. In most situations where music is performed in our culture it is not difficult to distinguish the audience from the performers, but such is often not the case in Africa. Alban Ayipaga, a Kasena semi-professional musician from northern Ghana, says that when his flute (长笛) and drum ensemble (歌舞团) is performing. "Anybody can take part". This is true, but Kasena musicians recognize that not all people are equally capable of taking part in the music. Some can sing along with the drummers, but relatively few can drum and even fewer can play the flute along with the ensemble. It is fairly common in Africa for there to be an ensemble of expert musicians surrounded by others who join in by clapping, singing, or somehow adding to the totality of musical sound. Performances often take place in an open area (that is, not on a stage) and so the lines between the performing nucleus and the additional performers, active spectators, and passive spectators may be difficult to draw from our point of view.

The author of the passage implies that _____.

A) all Africans are musical and therefore much music is performed in Africa

B) not all Africans are born with musical talent although music is important in their lives

C) most Africans are capable of joining in the music by playing musical instruments

D) most Africans perform as well as professional musicians

文中第二句提到：……music is so important in the lives of many Africans……，由此可知音乐是非洲人生活中的一个重要组成部分；而文章后半部又提到：……but Kasena musicians recognize that not all people are equally capable of taking part in the music……It is fairly common in Africa for there to be an ensemble of expert musicians surrounded by others who join in by clapping, singing, or somehow adding to the totality of musical sound. 由此可知，非洲人中只有一部分人是音乐家，而其他人通常只是参与音乐活动，称不上是音乐家。综合起来，B)表达了这个意思：音乐是非洲人生活的重要组成部分，但并非每个非洲人都是音乐天才，所以 B)为正确答案。

经典实例

Taste is such a subjective matter that we don't usually conduct preference tests for food. The most you can say about anyone's preference, is that it's one person's opinion. But because the two big cola（可乐饮料）companies—Coca-Cola and Pepsi Cola are marketed so aggressively, we've wondered how big a role taste preference actually plays in brand loyalty. We set up a taste test that challenged people who identified themselves as either Coca-Cola or Pepsi fans: Find your brand in a blind tasting.

It is implied in the first paragraph that _____.

A) the purpose of taste tests is to promote the sale of colas

B) the improvement of quality is the chief concern of the two cola companies

C) the competition between the two colas is very strong

D) blind tasting is necessary for identifying fans

扫一下四个选项，A)、B)、D)在原文中均找不到根据，那就只剩下 C)了。第一段第三句指出：But ……the two big cola companies Coca-Cola and Pepsi Cola are marketed so aggressively, 两大可乐公司——可口可乐公司和百事可乐公司极其积极地推销，这就暗示着两大公司之间的竞争非常激烈，那么 C)符合题意，为正确答案。

九、文章出处题

（一）文章出处题的测试要求

文章出处题其实属于推理类的一种。但和一般的推理题目相比，文章出处题有它自己的特点，所以把它另归一类。此类题型强调文章各段落之间的逻辑联系，而这种逻辑联系通常情况下都体现在段落的开头和结尾。这种类型的题目一般要求学生根据所阅读的短文推测出该文章的前一段或后一段的内容。有时候该题型也要求学生在弄清楚文章的中心思想后判断文章的来源或作者的身份。

文章出处题常见的表达方式有哪些：

The passage is most likely to be taken from _____.

The passage is most likely a part of _____.

The paragraph following the passage will probably discuss _____.

The passage is most likely to be taken from the article entitled _____.

The writer/author of the passage is most likely to be a/an _____.

（二）文章出处题的解题方法

这类测试题难度较大，需要学生充分理解测试材料、分析语篇特点、仔细寻找解题依据。如果问题要求考生猜测短文之前的内容,考生就必须注意短文的开头部分;如果问题要求考生猜测短文之后的内容,考生就必须注意短文的结尾部分。如果问题要求学生猜测作者的身份或是文章的出处,考生就必须在领会全文的基础上,做出判断。

　　一篇文章各段落之间都存在着一定的逻辑联系,而这种逻辑联系通常情况下都体现在段落的开头和结尾。这种类型的题目一般要求学生根据所阅读的短文推测出该文章的前一段或后一段的内容。有时该题型也要求学生在搞清楚文章的中心思想后判断文章的来源。在考试中,通常考的是文章的出处及来源。

经典实例

Priscilla Quchida's "energy-efficient" house turned out to be a horrible dream. When she and her engineer husband married a few years ago, they build a $100,000, three-bedroom home in California. Tightly sealed to prevent air leaks, the house was equipped with small double-paned(双层玻璃的)windows and several other energy-saving features. Problems began as soon as the couple moved in, however. Priscilla's eyes burned. Her throat was constantly dry. She suffered from headaches and could hardly sleep. It was as though she had suddenly developed a strange illness.

Experts finally traced the cause of her illness. The level of formaldehyde(甲醛)gas in her kitchen was twice the maximum allowed by federal standards for chemical workers. The source of the gas is from new kitchen cabinets and wall-to-wall carpeting.

The Quchidas are victims of indoor air pollution, which is not given sufficient attention partly because of the nation's drive to save energy. The problem itself isn't new. "The indoor environment was dirty long before energy conservation came along," says Moschandreas, a pollution scientist at Geoment Technologies in Maryland. "Energy conservation has tended to accentuate the situation in some cases."

The problem appears to be more troublesome in newly constructed homes rather than old ones. Back in the days when energy was cheap, home builders didn't worry much about unsealed cracks. Because of such leaks, the air in an average home was replaced by fresh outdoor air about once an hour. As a result, the pollutants generated in most households seldom built up to dangerous levels.

This passage is most probably taken from an article entitled _____.
A) Energy Conservation
B) Air Pollution Indoors
C) House Building Crisis
D) Traps in Building Construction

答案是 B)。文章出处题。问这段文字出自哪篇文章。这段文字的第 1、2 段是讲一对夫妇因室内空气污染而患病。第三段第一句话点明他们是室内空气污染的受害者。下文接着分析了室内空气污染。因此这段文字最有可能出现在"有关室内空气污染"的文章中。

第四节　阅读理解题型真题汇编及答案

全真题 ▷

Passage 1 (1994 年)

　　Exceptional children are different in some significant way from others of the same age. For these children to develop to their full adult potential, their education must be adapted to those differences.

　　Although we focus on the needs of exceptional children, we find ourselves describing their environment as well. While the leading actor on the stage captures our attention, we are aware of the importance of the supporting players and the scenery of the play itself. Both the family and the society in which exceptional children live are often the key to their growth and development. And it is in the public schools that we find the full expression of society's understanding—the knowledge, hopes, and fears that are passed on to the next generation.

Education in any society is a mirror of that society. In that mirror we can see the strengths, the weaknesses, the hopes, the prejudices, and the central values of the culture itself. The great interest in exceptional children shown in public education over the past three decades indicates the strong feeling in our society that all citizens, whatever their special conditions, deserve the opportunity to fully develop their capabilities.

"All men are created equal." We've heard it many times, but it still has important meaning for education in a democratic society. Although the phrase was used by this country's founders to denote equality before the law, it has also been interpreted to mean equality of opportunity. That concept implies educational opportunity for all children—the right of each child to receive help in learning to the limits of his or her capacity, whether that capacity be small or great. Recent court decisions have confirmed the right of all children—disabled or not—to an appropriate education, and have ordered that public schools take the necessary steps to provide that education. In response, schools are modifying their programs, adapting instruction to children who are exceptional, to those who cannot profit substantially from regular programs.

1. In paragraph 2, the author cites the example of the leading actor on the stage to show that _____.

 A) the growth of exceptional children has much to do with their family and the society

 B) exceptional children are more influenced by their families than normal children are

 C) exceptional children are the key interest of the family and society

 D) the needs of the society weigh much heavier than the needs of the exceptional children

2. The reason that the exceptional children receive so much concern in education is that _____.

 A) they are expected to be leaders of the society

 B) they might become a burden of the society

 C) they should fully develop their potentials

 D) disabled children deserve special consideration

3. This passage mainly deals with _____.

 A) the differences of children in their learning capabilities

 B) the definition of exceptional children in modern society

 C) the special educational programs for exceptional children

 D) the necessity of adapting education to exceptional children

4. From this passage we learn that the educational concern for exceptional children _____.

 A) is now enjoying legal support

 B) disagrees with the tradition of the country

 C) was clearly stated by the country's founders

 D) will exert great influence over court decisions

 ## Passage 2 (1993 年)

When an invention is made, the inventor has three possible courses of action open to him: he can give the invention to the world by publishing it, keep the idea secret, or patent it.

A granted patent is the result of a bargain struck between an inventor and the state, by which the inventor gets a limited period of monopoly and publishes full details of his invention to the public after that period terminates.

Only in the most exceptional circumstances is the lifespan of a patent extended to after this normal process of events.

The longest extension ever granted was to Georges Valensi; his 1939 patent for colour TV receiver circuitry was extended until 1971 because for most of the patent's normal life there was no colour TV to receive and thus no hope of reward for the invention.

Because a patent remains permanently public after it has terminated, the shelves of the library attached to the patent office contain details of literally millions of ideas that are free for anyone to use and, if older than half a century, sometimes even re-patent. Indeed, patent experts often advise anyone wishing to avoid the high cost of conducting a search through live patents that the one sure way of avoiding violation of any other inventor's right is to plagiarize a dead patent. Likewise, because publication of an idea in any other form permanently invalidates further patents on that idea, it is traditionally safe to take ideas from other areas of print. Much modern technological advance is based on these presumptions of legal security.

Anyone closely involved in patents and inventions soon learns that most "new" ideas are, in fact, as old as the hills. It is their reduction to commercial practice, either through necessity or dedication, or through the availability of new technology, that makes news and money. The basic patent for the theory of magnetic recording dates back to 1886. Many of the original ideas behind television originate from the late 19th and early 20th century. Even the Volkswagen rear engine car was anticipated by a 1904 patent for a cart with the horse at the rear.

5. The passage is mainly about _____ .

    A) an approach to patents   B) the application for patents

    C) the use of patents   D) the access to patents

6. Which of the following is TRUE according to the passage?

    A) When a patent becomes out of effect, it can be re-patented or extended if necessary.

    B) It is necessary for an inventor to apply for a patent before he makes his invention public.

    C) A patent holder must publicize the details of his invention when its legal period is over.

    D) One can get all the details of a patented invention from a library attached to the patent office.

7. Georges Valensi's patent lasted until 1971 because _____ .

    A) nobody would offer any reward for his patent prior to that time

    B) his patent could not be put to use for an unusually long time

    C) there were not enough TV stations to provide color programmes

    D) the colour TV receiver was not available until that time

8. The word "plagiarize" (Line 5, Para. 5) most probably means "_____".

    A) steal and use   B) give reward to

    C) make public   D) take and change

9. From the passage we learn that _____ .

    A) an invention will not benefit the inventor unless it is reduced to commercial practice

    B) products are actually inventions which were made a long time ago

    C) it is much cheaper to buy an old patent than a new one

    D) patent experts often recommend patents to others by conducting a search through dead patents

态度评价题 ▶

Passage 1 (1999 年)

In the first year or so of Web business, most of the action has revolved around efforts to tap the consumer market. More recently, as the Web proved to be more than a fashion, companies have started to buy and sell products and services with one another. Such business-to-business sales make sense because business people typically know what product they're looking for.

Nonetheless, many companies still hesitate to use the Web because of doubts about its reliability. "Businesses need to feel they can trust the pathway between them and the supplier," says senior analyst Blane Erwin of Forrester Research. Some companies are limiting the risk by conducting online transactions only with established business partners who are given access to the company's private intranet.

Another major shift in the model for Internet commerce concerns the technology available for marketing. Until recently, Internet marketing activities have focused on strategies to "pull" customers into sites. In the past year, however, software companies have developed tools that allow companies to "push" information directly out to consumers, transmitting marketing messages directly to targeted customers. Most notably, the Pointcast Network uses a screen saver to deliver a continually updated stream of news and advertisements to subscribers' computer monitors. Subscribers can customize the information they want to receive and proceed directly to a company's Web site. Companies such as Virtual Vineyards are already starting to use similar technologies to push messages to customers about special sales, product offerings, or other events. But push technology has earned the contempt of many Web users. Online culture thinks highly of the notion that the information flowing onto the screen comes there by specific request. Once commercial promotion begins to fill the screen uninvited, the distinction between the Web and television fades. That's a prospect that horrifies Net purists.

But it is hardly inevitable that companies on the Web will need to resort to push strategies to make money. The examples of Virtual Vineyards, Amazon. com, and other pioneers show that a Web site selling the right kind of products with the right mix of interactivity, hospitality, and security will attract online customers. And the cost of computing power continues to free fall, which is a good sign for any enterprise setting up shop in silicon. People looking back 5 or 10 years from now may well wonder why so few companies took the online plunge.

1. We learn from the beginning of the passage that Web business _____.
   A) has been striving to expand its market
   B) intended to follow a fanciful fashion
   C) tried but in vain to control the market
   D) has been booming for one year or so

2. Speaking of the online technology available for marketing, the author implies that _____.
   A) the technology is popular with many Web users
   B) businesses have faith in the reliability of online transactions
   C) there is a radical change in strategy
   D) it is accessible limitedly to established partners

3. In the view of Net purists, _____.
   A) there should be no marketing messages in online culture
   B) money making should be given priority to on the Web
   C) the Web should be able to function as the television set
   D) there should be no online commercial information without requests

4. We learn from the last paragraph that _____.
   A) pushing information on the Web is essential to Internet commerce
   B) interactivity, hospitality and security are important to online customers
   C) leading companies began to take the online plunge decades ago
   D) setting up shops in silicon is independent of the cost of computing power

Passage 2 (1997 年)

It was 3:45 in the morning when the vote was finally taken. After six months of arguing and final 16 hours of hot parliamentary debates, Australia's Northern Territory became the first legal authority in the world to allow doctors to take the lives of incurably ill patients who wish to die. The measure passed by the convincing vote of 15 to 10. Almost immediately word flashed on the Internet and was picked up, half a world away, by John Hofsess, executive director of the Right to Die Society of Canada. He sent it on via the group's on-line service, Death NET. Says Hofsess: "We posted bulletins all day long, because of course this isn't just something that happened in Australia. It's world history."

The full import may take a while to sink in. The NT Rights of the Terminally Ill law has left physicians and citizens alike trying to deal with its moral and practical implications. Some have breathed sighs of relief, others, including churches, right-to-life groups and the Australian Medical Association, bitterly attacked the bill and the haste of its passage. But the tide is unlikely to turn back. In Australia—where an aging population, life-extending technology and changing community attitudes have all played their part—other states are going to consider making a similar law to deal with euthanasia. In the US and Canada, where the right-to-die movement is gathering strength, observers are waiting for the dominoes to start falling.

Under the new Northern Territory law, an adult patient can request death—probably by a deadly injection or pill—to put an end to suffering. The patient must be diagnosed as terminally ill by two doctors. After a "cooling off" period of seven days, the patient can sign a certificate of request. After 48 hours the wish for death can be met. For Lloyd Nickson, a 54-year-old Darwin resident suffering from lung cancer, the NT Rights of Terminally Ill law means he can get on with living without the haunting fear of his suffering: a terrifying death from his breathing condition. "I'm not afraid of dying from a spiritual point of view, but what I was afraid of was how I'd go, because I've watched people die in the hospital fighting for oxygen and clawing at their masks," he says.

5. From the second paragraph we learn that _____.
   A) the objection to euthanasia is slow to come in other countries
   B) physicians and citizens share the same view on euthanasia
   C) changing technology is chiefly responsible for the hasty passage of the law
   D) it takes time to realize the significance of the law's passage

6. When the author says that observers are waiting for the dominoes to start falling, he means _____.
   A) observers are taking a wait-and-see attitude towards the future of euthanasia
   B) similar bills are likely to be passed in the US, Canada and other countries
   C) observers are waiting to see the result of the game of dominoes
   D) the effect-taking process of the passed bill may finally come to a stop

7. When Lloyd Nickson dies, he will _____.
   A) face his death with calm characteristic of euthanasia
   B) experience the suffering of a lung cancer patient
   C) have an intense fear of terrible suffering
   D) undergo a cooling off period of seven days

8. The author's attitude towards euthanasia seems to be that of _____.
   A) opposition　　B) suspicion　　C) approval　　D) indifference

Passage 3 (1995 年)

Money spent on advertising is money spent as well as any I know of. It serves directly to assist a rapid distribution of goods at reasonable price, thereby establishing a firm home market and so making it possible to provide for export at competitive prices. By drawing attention to new ideas it helps enormously to raise standards of living. By helping to increase demand it ensures an increased need for labour, and is therefore an effective way to fight unemployment. It lowers the costs of many services; without advertisements your daily newspaper would cost four times as much, the price of your television licence would need to be doubled, and travel by bus or tube would cost 20 per cent more.

And perhaps most important of all, advertising provides a guarantee of reasonable value in the products and services you buy. Apart from the fact that twenty-seven acts of Parliament govern the terms of advertising, no regular advertiser dare promote a product that fails to live up to the promise of his advertisements. He might fool some people for a little while through misleading advertising. He will not do so for long, for mercifully the public has the good sense not to buy the inferior article more than once. If you see an article consistently advertised, it is the surest proof I know that the article does what is claimed for it, and that it represents good value.

Advertising does more for the material benefit of the community than any other force I can think of.

There is one more point I feel I ought to touch on. Recently I heard a well-known television personality declare that he was against advertising because it persuades rather than informs. He was drawing excessively fine distinctions. Of course advertising seeks to persuade.

If its message were confined merely to information—and that in itself would be difficult if not impossible to achieve, for even a detail such as the choice of the colour of a shirt is subtly persuasive—advertising would be so boring that no one would pay any attention. But perhaps that is what the well-known television personality wants.

9. By the first sentence of the passage the author means that _____.
   A) he is fairly familiar with the cost of advertising
   B) everybody knows well that advertising is money consuming
   C) advertising costs money like everything else
   D) it is worthwhile to spend money on advertising

10. In the passage, which of the following is NOT included in the advantages of advertising?
   A) Securing greater fame.
   B) Providing more jobs.
   C) Enhancing living standards.
   D) Reducing newspaper cost.

11. The author deems that the well-known TV personality is _____.
   A) very precise in passing his judgement on advertising
   B) interested in nothing but the buyers' attention
   C) correct in telling the difference between persuasion and information
   D) obviously partial in his views on advertising

12. In the author's opinion, _____.
   A) advertising can seldom bring material benefit to man by providing information
   B) advertising informs people of new ideas rather than wins them over
   C) there is nothing wrong with advertising in persuading the buyer
   D) the buyer is not interested in getting information from an advertisement

Passage 4 （1993 年）

In general, our society is becoming one of giant enterprises directed by a bureaucratic（官僚主义的）management in which man becomes a small, well-oiled cog in the machinery. The oiling is done with higher wages, well-ventilated factories and piped music, and by psychologists and "human-relations" experts; yet all this oiling does not alter the fact that man has become powerless, that he does not wholeheartedly participate in his work and that he is bored with it. In fact, the blue-and the white-collar workers have become economic puppets who dance to the tune of automated machines and bureaucratic management.

The worker and employee are anxious, not only because they might find themselves out of a job; they are anxious also because they are unable to acquire any real satisfaction or interest in life. They live and die without ever having confronted the fundamental realities of human existence as emotionally and intellectually independent and productive human beings.

Those higher up on the social ladder are no less anxious. Their lives are no less empty than those of their subordinates. They are even more insecure in some respects. They are in a highly competitive race. To be promoted or to fall behind is not a matter of salary but even more a matter of self-respect. When they apply for their first job, they are tested for intelligence as well as for the right mixture of submissiveness and independence. From that moment on they are tested again and again—by the psychologists, for whom testing is a big business, and by their superiors, who judge their behavior, sociability, capacity to get along, etc. This constant need to prove that one is as good as or better than one's fellow-competitor creates constant anxiety and stress, the very causes of unhappiness and illness.

Am I suggesting that we should return to the pre-industrial mode of production or to nineteenth-century "free enterprise" capitalism? Certainly not. Problems are never solved by returning to a stage which one has already out grown. I suggest transforming our social system from a bureaucratically managed industrialism in which maximal production and consumption are ends in themselves into a humanist industrialism in which man and full development of his potentialities—those of love and of reason—are the aims of all social arrangements. Production and consumption should serve only as means to this end, and should be prevented from ruling man.

13. By "a well-oiled cog in the machinery" the author intends to render the idea that man is _____.

A) a necessary part of the society though each individual's function is negligible

B) working in complete harmony with the rest of the society

C) an unimportant part in comparison with the rest of the society, though functioning smoothly

D) a humble component of the society, especially when working smoothly

14. The real cause of the anxiety of the workers and employees is that _____.

A) they are likely to lose their jobs

B) they have no genuine satisfaction or interest in life

C) they are faced with the fundamental realities of human existence

D) they are deprived of their individuality and independence

15. From the passage we can infer that real happiness of life belongs to those _____.

A) who are at the bottom of the society

B) who are higher up in their social status

C) who prove better than their fellow-competitors

D) who could keep far away from the competitive world

16. To solve the present social problems the author suggests that we should _____.

A) resort to the production mode of our ancestors

B) offer higher wages to the workers and employees

C) enable man to fully develop his potentialities

D) take the fundamental realities for granted

17. The author's attitude towards industrialism might best be summarized as one of _____.

A) approval　　B) dissatisfaction　　C) suspicion　　D) tolerance

 ## Passage 5 （1994 年）

Discoveries in science and technology are thought by "untaught minds" to come in blinding flashes or as the result of dramatic accidents. Sir Alexander Fleming did not, as legend would have it, look at the mold on a piece of cheese and get the idea for penicillin there and then. He experimented with anti-bacterial substances for nine years before he made his discovery. Inventions and innovations almost always come out of laborious trial and error. Innovation is like soccer; even the best players miss the goal and have their shots blocked much more frequently than they score.

The point is that the players who score most are the ones who take the most shots at the goal—and so it goes with innovation in any field of activity. The prime difference between innovators and others is one of approach. Everybody gets ideas, but innovators work consciously on theirs, and they follow them through until they prove practicable or otherwise. What ordinary people see as fanciful abstractions, professional innovators see as solid possibilities.

"Creative thinking may mean simply the realization that there's no particular virtue in doing things the way they have always been done," wrote Rudolph Flesch, a language authority. This accounts for our reaction to seemingly simple innovations like plastic garbage bags and suitcases on wheels that make life more convenient:"How come nobody thought of that before?"

The creative approach begins with the proposition that nothing is as it appears. Innovators will not accept that there is only one way to do anything. Faced with getting from A to B, the average person will automatically set out on the best-known and apparently simplest route. The innovator will search for alternate courses, which may prove easier in the long run and are bound to be more interesting and challenging even if they lead to dead ends.

Highly creative individuals really do march to a different drummer.

18. What does the author probably mean by "untaught mind" in the first paragraph?

A) A person ignorant of the hard work involved in experimentation.

B) A citizen of a society that restricts personal creativity.

C) A person who has had no education.

D) An individual who often comes up with new ideals by accident.

19. According to the author, what distinguishes innovators from non-innovators?

A) The variety of ideas they have.

B) The intelligence they possess.

C) The way they deal with problems.

D) The way they present their findings.

20. The author quotes Rudolph Flesch in Paragraph 3 because _____.

A) Rudolph Flesch is the best-known expert in the study of human creativity

B) the quotation strengthens the assertion that creative individuals look for new ways of doing things

C) the reader is familiar with Rudolph Flesch's point of view

D) the quotation adds a new idea to the information previously presented

21. The phrase "march to a different drummer" (the last line of the passage) suggests that highly crea-

tive individuals are _____.

A) diligent in pursuing their goals

B) reluctant to follow common ways of doing things

C) devoted to the progress of science

D) concerned about the advance of society

Passage (1993 年)

Is language, like food, a basic human need without which a child at a critical period of life can be starved and damaged? Judging from the drastic experiment of Frederick Ⅱ in the thirteenth century, it may be. Hoping to discover what language a child would speak if he heard no mother tongue, he told the nurses to keep silent.

All the infants died before the first year. But clearly there was more than lack of language here. What was missing was good mothering. Without good mothering, in the first year of life especially, the capacity to survive is seriously affected.

Today no such severe lack exists as that ordered by Frederick. Nevertheless, some children are still backward in speaking. Most often the reason for this is that the mother is insensitive to the signals of the infant, whose brain is programmed to learn language rapidly. If these sensitive periods are neglected, the ideal time for acquiring skills passes and they might never be learned so easily again. A bird learns to sing and to fly rapidly at the right time, but the process is slow and hard once the critical stage has passed.

Experts suggest that speech stages are reached in a fixed sequence and at a constant age, but there are cases where speech has started late in a child who eventually turns out to be of high IQ. At twelve weeks a baby smiles and makes vowel-like sounds; at twelve months he can speak simple words and understand simple commands; at eighteen months he has a vocabulary of three to fifty words. At three he knows about 1,000 words which he can put into sentences, and at four his language differs from that of his parents in style rather than grammar.

Recent evidence suggests that an infant is born with the capacity to speak. What is special about man's brain, compared with that of the monkey, is the complex system which enables a child to connect the sight and feel of, say, a toy-bear with the sound pattern "toy-bear". And even more incredible is the young brain's ability to pick out an order in language from the mixture of sound around him, to analyse, to combine and recombine the parts of language in new ways.

But speech has to be induced, and this depends on interaction between the mother and the child, where the mother recognizes the signals in the child's babbling, grasping and smiling, and responds to them. Insensitivity of the mother to these signals dulls the interaction because the child gets discouraged and sends out only the obvious signals. Sensitivity to the child's non-verbal signals is essential to the growth and development of language.

1. The purpose of Frederick Ⅱ's experiment was _____.

A) to prove that children are born with the ability to speak

B) to discover what language a child would speak without hearing any human speech

C) to find out what role careful nursing would play in teaching a child to seek

D) to prove that a child could be damaged without learning a language

2. The reason some children are backward in speaking is most probably that _____.

A) they are incapable of learning language rapidly

B) they are exposed to too much language at once

　　C) their mothers respond inadequately to their attempts to speak

　　D) their mothers are not intelligent enough to help them

3. What is exceptionally remarkable about a child is that _____.

　　A) he is born with the capacity to speak

　　B) he has brain more complex than an animal's

　　C) he can produce his own sentences

　　D) he owes his speech ability to good nursing

4. Which of the following can NOT be inferred from the passage?

　　A) The faculty of speech is inborn in man.

　　B) Encouragement is anything but essential to a child in language learning.

　　C) The child's brain is highly selective.

　　D) Most children learn their language in definite stages.

5. If a child starts to speak later than others, he will _____ in future.

　　A) have high IQ　　　　　　　　　　　B) be less intelligent

　　C) be insensitive to verbal signals　　　D) not necessarily be backward

Passage 1 (2002 年)

　　Since the dawn of human ingenuity, people have devised ever more cunning tools to cope with work that is dangerous, boring, burdensome, or just plain nasty. That compulsion has resulted in robotics—the science of conferring various human capabilities on machines. And if scientists have yet to create the mechanical version of science fiction, they have begun to come close.

　　As a result, the modern world is increasingly populated by intelligent gizmos whose presence we barely notice but whose universal existence has removed much human labor. Our factories hum to the rhythm of robot assembly arms. Our banking is done at automated teller terminals that thank us with mechanical politeness for the transaction. Our subway trains are controlled by tireless robo-drivers. And thanks to the continual miniaturization of electronics and micro-mechanics, there are already robot systems that can perform some kinds of brain and bone surgery with submillimeter accuracy—far greater precision than highly skilled physicians can achieve with their hands alone.

　　But if robots are to reach the next stage of laborsaving utility, they will have to operate with less human supervision and be able to make at least a few decisions for themselves—goals that pose a real challenge. "While we know how to tell a robot to handle a specific error," says Dave Lavery, manager of a robotics program at NASA, "we can't yet give a robot enough 'common sense' to reliably interact with a dynamic world."

　　Indeed the quest for true artificial intelligence has produced very mixed results. Despite a spell of initial optimism in the 1960s and 1970s when it appeared that transistor circuits and microprocessors might be able to copy the action of the human brain by the year 2010, researchers lately have begun to extend that forecast by decades if not centuries.

　　What they found, in attempting to model thought, is that the human brain's roughly one hundred billion nerve cells are much more talented—and human perception far more complicated—than previously imagined. They have built robots that can recognize the error of a machine panel by a fraction of a millimeter in a controlled factory environment. But the human mind can glimpse a rapidly changing scene and immediately disregard the 98 percent that is irrelevant, instantaneously focusing on the monkey at the side of a winding forest road or the single suspicious face in a big crowd. The most advanced computer systems on Earth can't approach that kind of ability, and neuroscientists still don't know quite how we do it.

1. Human ingenuity was initially demonstrated in _____.

A)the use of machines to produce science fiction.

B)the wide use of machines in manufacturing industry.

C)the invention of tools for difficult and dangerous work.

D)the elite's cunning tackling of dangerous and boring work.

2. The word"gizmos"(line 1,paragraph 2)most probably means _____.

A)programs.

B)experts.

C)devices.

D)creatures.

3. According to the text, what is beyond man's ability now is to design a robot that can _____.

A)fulfill delicate tasks like performing brain surgery.

B)interact with human beings verbally.

C)have a little common sense.

D)respond independently to a changing world.

4. Besides reducing human labor, robots can also _____.

A)make a few decisions for themselves.

B)deal with some errors with human intervention.

C)improve factory environments.

D)cultivate human creativity.

5. The author uses the example of a monkey to argue that robots are _____.

A)expected to copy human brain in internal structure.

B)able to perceive abnormalities immediately.

C)far less able than human brain in focusing on relevant information.

D)best used in a controlled environment.

Passage 2 （2002 年）

The Supreme Court's decisions on physician-assisted suicide carry important implications for how medicine seeks to relieve dying patients of pain and suffering.

Although it ruled that there is no constitutional right to physician-assisted suicide, the Court in effect supported the medical principle of "double effect,"a centuries-old moral principle holding that an action having two effects—a good one that is intended and a harmful one that is foreseen—is permissible if the actor intends only the good effcet.

Doctors have used that principle in recent years to justify using high doses of morphine to control terminally ill patients' pain, even though increasing dosages will eventually kill the patient.

Nancy Dubler, director of Montefiore Medical Center, contends that the principle will shield doctors who"until now have very, very strongly insisted that they could not give patients sufficient mediation to control their pain if that might hasten death. "

George Annas, chair of the health law department at Boston University, maintains that, as long as a doctor prescribes a drug for a legitimate medical purpose, the doctor has done nothing illegal even if the patient uses the drug to hasten death. "It's like surgery,"he says. "We don't call those deaths homicides because the doctors didn't intend to kill their patients, although they risked their death. If you're a physician,you can risk your patients' suicide as long as you don't intend their suicide."

On another level, many in the medical community acknowledge that the assisted-suicide debate has been fueled in part by the despair of patients for whom modern medicine has prolonged the physical agony of dying.

Just three weeks before the Court's ruling on physician-assisted suicide, the National Academy of Science(NAS)released a two-volume report, Approaching Death:Improving Care at the End of Life. It identifies the undertreatment of pain and the aggressive use of "ineffectual and forced medical procedures that may prolong and even dishonor the period of dying" as the twin problems of end-of -life care.

The profession is taking steps to require young doctors to train in hospices, to test knowledge of aggressive pain management therapies, to develop a Medicare billing code for hospital-based care, and to develop new standards for assessing and treating pain at the end of life.

Annas says lawyers can play a key role in insisting that these well-meaning medical initiatives translate into better care. "Large numbers of physicians seem unconcerned with the pain their patients are needlessly and predictably suffering," to the extent that it constitutes "systematic patient abuse." He says medical licensing boards "must make it clear……that painful deaths are presumptively ones that are incompetently managed and should result in license suspension."

6. From the first three paragraphs, we learn that _____.

  A)doctors used to increase drug dosages to control their patients' pain.

  B)it is still illegal for doctors to help the dying end their lives.

  C)the Supreme Court strongly opposes physician-assisted suicide.

  D)patients have no constitutional right to commit suicide.

7. Which of the following statements is true according to the text?

  A)Doctors will be held guilty if they risk their patients' death.

  B)Modern medicine has assisted terminally ill patients in painless recovery.

  C)The Court ruled that high-dosage pain-relieving medication can be prescribed.

  D)A doctor's medication is no longer justified by his intentions.

8. According to the NAS's report, one of the problems in end-of-life care is _____.

  A)prolonged medical procedures.

  B)inadequate treatment of pain.

  C)systematic drug abuse.

  D)insufficient hospital care.

9. Which of the following best defines the word "aggressive" (line 4, paragraph 7)?

  A)Bold.

  B)Harmful.

  C)Careless.

  D)Desperate.

10. George Annas would probably agree that doctors should be punished if they _____.

  A)manage their patients incompetently.

  B)give patients more medicine than needed.

  C)reduce drug dosages for their patients.

  D)prolong the needless suffering of the patients.

Passage 1 (1998 年)

Science has long had an uneasy relationship with other aspects of culture. Think of Gallileo's 17th-century trial for his rebelling belief before the Catholic Church or poet William Blake's harsh remarks against the mechanistic worldview of Isaac Newton. The schism between science and the humanities has, if anything, deepened in this century.

Until recently, the scientific community was so powerful that it could afford to ignore its critics— but no longer. As funding for science has declined, scientists have attacked "antiscience" in several books, notably *Higher Superstition*, by Paul R. Gross, a biologist at the University of Virginia, and Norman Levitt, a mathematician at Rutgers University; and *The Demon-Haunted World*, by Carl Sagan of Cornell University.

Defenders of science have also voiced their concerns at meetings such as "The Flight from Science and Reason," held in New York City in 1995, and "Science in the Age of (Mis) information," which assembled last June near Buffalo.

Antiscience clearly means different things to different people. Gross and Levitt find fault primarily with sociologists, philosophers and other academics who have questioned science's objectivity. Sagan is more concerned with those who believe in ghosts, creationism and other phenomena that contradict the scientific worldview.

A survey of news stories in 1996 reveals that the antiscience tag has been attached to many other groups as well, from authorities who advocated the elimination of the last remaining stocks of smallpox virus to Republicans who advocated decreased funding for basic research.

Few would dispute that the term applies to the Unabomber, whose manifesto, published in 1995, scorns science and longs for return to a pre-technological utopia. But surely that does not mean environmentalists concerned about uncontrolled industrial growth are antiscience, as an essay in *US News & World Report* last May seemed to suggest.

The environmentalists, inevitably, respond to such critics. The true enemies of science, argues Paul Ehrlich of Stanford University, a pioneer of environmental studies, are those who question the evidence supporting global warming, the depletion of the ozone layer and other consequences of industrial growth.

Indeed, some observers fear that the antiscience epithet is in danger of becoming meaningless. "The term 'antiscience' can lump together too many, quite different things," notes Harvard University philosopher Gerald Holton in his 1993 work *Science and Anti-Science*, "They have in common only one thing that they tend to annoy or threaten those who regard themselves as more enlightened."

1. The word "schism" (Line 3, Paragraph 1) in the context probably means _____.

    A) confrontation   B) dissatisfaction   C) separation   D) contempt

2. Paragraphs 2 and 3 are written to _____.

    A) discuss the cause of the decline of science's power

    B) show the author's sympathy with scientists

    C) explain the way in which science develops

    D) exemplify the division of science and the humanities

3. Which of the following is true according to the passage?

    A) Environmentalists were blamed for antiscience in an essay.

    B) Politicians are not subject to the labeling of antiscience.

    C) The "more enlightened" tend to tag others as antiscience.

    D) Tagging environmentalists as "antiscience" is justifiable

4. The author's attitude toward the issue of "science vs. antiscience" is _____.

    A) impartial   B) subjective   C) biased   D) puzzling

Passage 2 （1994 年）

The American economic system is organized around a basically private-enterprise, market-oriented economy in which consumers largely determine what shall be produced by spending their money in the marketplace for those goods and services that they want most. Private businessmen, striving to make profits, produce these goods and services in competition with other businessmen; and the profit motive, operating under competitive pressures, largely determines how these goods and services are produced. Thus, in the American economic system it is the demand of individual consumers, coupled with the desire of businessmen to maximize profits and the desire of individuals to maximize their incomes, that together determine what shall be produced and how resources are used to produce it.

An important factor in a market-oriented economy is the mechanism by which consumer demands can be expressed and responded to by producers. In the American economy, this mechanism is provided by a price system, a process in which prices rise and fall in response to relative demands of consumers and supplies offered by seller-producers. If the product is in short supply relative to the demand, the price will be bid up and some consumers will be eliminated from the market. If, on the other hand, producing more of a commodity results in reducing its cost, this will tend to increase the supply offered by seller-producers, which in turn will lower the price and permit more consumers to buy the product. Thus, price is the regulating mechanism in the American economic system.

The important factor in a private-enterprise economy is that individuals are allowed to own productive resources (private property), and they are permitted to hire labor, gain control over natural resources, and produce goods and services for sale at a profit. In the American economy, the concept of private property embraces not only the ownership of productive resources but also certain rights, including the right to determine the price of a product or to make a free contract with another private individual.

5. In Line 7, Para. 1, "the desire of individuals to maximize their incomes" means _____.

　　A) Americans are never satisfied with their incomes

　　B) Americans tend to overstate their incomes

　　C) Americans want to have their incomes increased

　　D) Americans want to increase the purchasing power of their incomes

6. The first two sentences in the second paragraph tell us that _____.

　　A) producers can satisfy the consumers by mechanized production

　　B) consumers can express their demands through producers

　　C) producers decide the prices of products

　　D) supply and demand regulate prices

7. According to the passage, a private-enterprise economy is characterized by _____.

　　A) private property and rights concerned

　　B) manpower and natural resources control

　　C) ownership of productive resources

　　D) free contracts and prices

8. The passage is mainly about _____.

　　A) how American goods are produced

　　B) how American consumers buy their goods

　　C) how American economic system works

　　D) how American businessmen make their profits

Passage 3 (1994 年)

One hundred and thirteen million Americans have at least one bank-issued credit card. They give their owners automatic credit in stores, restaurants, and hotels, at home, across the country, and even abroad, and they make many banking services available as well. More and more of these credit cards can be read automatically, making it possible to withdraw or deposit money in scattered locations, whether or not the local branch bank is open. For many of us the "cashless society" is not on the horizon—it's already here.

While computers offer these conveniences to consumers, they have many advantages for sellers too. Electronic cash registers can do much more than simply ring up sales. They can keep a wide range of records, including who sold what, when, and to whom. This information allows businessmen to keep track of their list of goods by showing which items are being sold and how fast they are moving. Decisions to reorder or return goods to suppliers can then be made. At the same time these computers record which hours are busiest and which employees are the most efficient, allowing personnel and staffing assignments to be made accordingly. And they also identify preferred customers for promotional campaigns. Computers are relied on by manufacturers for similar reasons. Computer-analyzed marketing reports can help to decide which products to emphasize now, which to develop for the future, and which to drop. Computers keep track of goods in stock, of raw materials on hand, and even of the production process itself.

Numerous other commercial enterprises, from theaters to magazine publishers, from gas and electric utilities to milk processors, bring better and more efficient services to consumers through the use of computers.

9. According to the passage, the credit card enables its owner to _____.
    A) withdraw as much money from the bank as he wishes
    B) obtain more convenient services than other people do
    C) enjoy greater trust from the storekeeper
    D) cash money wherever he wishes to

10. From the last sentence of the first paragraph we learn that _____.
    A) in the future all the Americans will use credit cards
    B) credit cards are mainly used in the United States today
    C) nowadays many Americans do not pay in cash
    D) it is now more convenient to use credit cards than before

11. The phrase "ring up sales"(Line 2, Para. 2) most probably means "_____".
    A) make an order of goods   B) record sales on a cash register
    C) call the sales manager   D) keep track of the goods in stock

12. What is this passage mainly about?
    A) Approaches to the commercial use of computers.
    B) Conveniences brought about by computers in business.
    C) Significance of automation in commercial enterprises.
    D) Advantages of credit cards in business.

 是非判断题 ▷

Passage 1 (1996 年)

In the last half of the nineteenth century "capital" and "labour" were enlarging and perfecting their rival organisations on modern lines. Many an old firm was replaced by a limited liability company with a bureaucracy of salaried managers. The change met the technical requirements of the new age by engaging a large professional element and prevented the decline in efficiency that so commonly spoiled the fortunes of family firms in the second and third generation after the energetic founders. It was moreover a step away from individual initiative, towards collectivism and municipal and state-owned business. The railway companies, though still private business managed for the benefit of shareholders, were very unlike old family business. At the same time the great municipalities went into business to supply lighting, trams and other services to the taxpayers.

The growth of the limited liability company and municipal business had important consequences. Such large, impersonal manipulation of capital and industry greatly increased the numbers and importance of shareholders as a class, an element in national life representing irresponsible wealth detached from the land and the duties of the landowners; and almost equally detached from the responsible management of business. All through the nineteenth century, America, Africa, India, Australia and parts of Europe were being developed by British capital, and British shareholders were thus enriched by the world's movement towards industrialisation. Towns like Bournemouth and Eastbourne sprang up to house large "comfortable" classes who had retired on their incomes, and who had no relation to the rest of the community except that of drawing dividends and occasionally attending a shareholders' meeting to dictate their orders to the management. On the other hand "shareholding" meant leisure and freedom which was used by many of the later Victorians for the highest purpose of a great civilisation.

The "shareholders" as such had no knowledge of the lives, thoughts or needs of the workmen employed by the company in which he held shares, and his influence on the relations of capital and labour was not good. The paid manager acting for the company was in more direct relation with the men and their demands, but even he had seldom that familiar personal knowledge of the workmen which the employer had often had under the more patriarchal system of the old family business now passing away. Indeed the mere size of operations and the numbers of workmen involved rendered such personal relations impossible. Fortunately, however, the increasing power and organisation of the trade unions, at least in all skilled trades, enabled the workmen to meet on equal terms the managers of the companies who employed them. The cruel discipline of the strike and lockout taught the two parties to respect each other's strength and understand the value of fair negotiation.

1. It's true of the old family firms that _____.
   A) they were spoiled by the younger generations
   B) they failed for lack of individual initiative
   C) they lacked efficiency compared with modern companies
   D) they could supply adequate services to the taxpayers

2. The growth of limited liability companies resulted in _____.
   A) the separation of capital from management
   B) the ownership of capital by managers
   C) the emergence of capital and labour as two classes
   D) the participation of shareholders in municipal business

3. According to the passage, all of the following are true except that _____.
   A) the shareholders were unaware of the needs of the workers
   B) the old firm owners had a better understanding of their workers
   C) the limited liability companies were too large to run smoothly
   D) the trade unions seemed to play a positive role

4. The author is most critical of _____.
   A) family firm owners   B) landowners
   C) managers   D) shareholders

Passage 2 （2000 年）

Aimlessness has hardly been typical of the postwar Japan whose productivity and social harmony are the envy of the United States and Europe. But increasingly the Japanese are seeing a decline of the traditional work-moral values. Ten years ago young people were hardworking and saw their jobs as their primary reason for being, but now Japan has largely fulfilled its economic needs, and young people don't know where they should go next.

The coming of age of the postwar baby boom and an entry of women into the male-dominated job market have limited the opportunities of teenagers who are already questioning the heavy personal sacrifices involved in climbing Japan's rigid social ladder to good schools and jobs. In a recent survey, it was found that only 24.5 percent of Japanese students were fully satisfied with school life, compared with 67.2 percent of students in the United States. In addition, far more Japanese workers expressed dissatisfaction with their jobs than did their counterparts in the 10 other countries surveyed.

While often praised by foreigners for its emphasis on the basics, Japanese education tends to stress test taking and mechanical learning over creativity and self-expression. "Those things that do not show up in the test scores—personality, ability, courage or humanity—are completely ignored," says Toshiki Kaifu, chairman of the ruling Liberal Democratic Party's education committee. "Frustration against this kind of thing leads kids to drop out and run wild." Last year Japan experienced 2,125 incidents of school violence, including 929 assaults on teachers. Amid the outcry, many conservative leaders are seeking a return to the prewar emphasis on moral education. Last year Mitsuo Setoyama, who was then education minister, raised eyebrows when he argued that liberal reforms introduced by the American occupation authorities after World War Ⅱ had weakened the "Japanese morality of respect for parents."

But that may have more to do with Japanese life-styles. "In Japan," says educator Yoko Muro, "it's never a question of whether you enjoy your job and your life, but only how much you can endure." With economic growth has come centralization; fully 76 percent of Japan's 119 million citizens live in cities where community and the extended family have been abandoned in favor of isolated, two-generation households. Urban Japanese have long endured lengthy commutes (travels to and from work) and crowded living conditions, but as the old group and family values weaken, the discomfort is beginning to tell. In the past decade, the Japanese divorce rate, while still well below that of the United States, has increased by more than 50 percent, and suicides have increased by nearly one-quarter.

5. In the Westerners' eyes, the postwar Japan was _____.

A) under aimless development

B) a positive example

C) a rival to the West

D) on the decline

6. According to the author, what may chiefly be responsible for the moral decline of Japanese society?

A) Women's participation in social activities is limited.

B) More workers are dissatisfied with their jobs.

C) Excessive emphasis has been placed on the basics.

D) The life-style has been influenced by Western values.

7. Which of the following is true according to the author?

A) Japanese education is praised for helping the young climb the social ladder.

B) Japanese education is characterized by mechanical learning as well as creativity.

C) More stress should be placed on the cultivation of creativity.

D) Dropping out leads to frustration against test taking.

8. The change in Japanese life-style is revealed in the fact that _____.

 A) the young are less tolerant of discomforts in life

 B) the divorce rate in Japan exceeds that in the U. S.

 C) the Japanese endure more than ever before

 D) the Japanese appreciate their present life

Passage 3 (1995 年)

There are two basic ways to see growth; one as a product, the other as a process. People have generally viewed personal growth as an external result or product that can easily be identified and measured. The worker who gets a promotion, the student whose grades improve, the foreigner who learns a new language—all these are examples of people who have measurable results to show for their efforts.

By contrast, the process of personal growth is much more difficult to determine, since by definition it is a journey and not the specific signposts or landmarks along the way. The process is not the road itself, but rather the attitudes and feelings people have, their caution or courage, as they encounter new experiences and unexpected obstacles. In this process, the journey never really ends; there are always new ways to experience the world, new ideas to try, new challenges to accept.

In order to grow, to travel new roads, people need to have a willingness to take risks, to confront the unknown, and to accept the possibility that they may "fail" at first. How we see ourselves as we try a new way of being is essential to our ability to grow. Do we perceive ourselves as quick and curious? If so, then we tend to take more chances and to be more open to unfamiliar experiences. Do we think we're shy and indecisive? Then our sense of timidity can cause us to hesitate, to move slowly, and not to take a step until we know the ground is safe. Do we think we're slow to adapt to change or that we're not smart enough to cope with a new challenge? Then we are likely to take a more passive role or not try at all.

These feelings of insecurity and self-doubt are both unavoidable and necessary if we are to change and grow. If we do not confront and overcome these internal fears and doubts, if we protect ourselves too much, then we cease to grow. We become trapped inside a shell of our own making.

9. A person is generally believed to achieve personal growth when _____.

 A) he has given up his smoking habit

 B) he has made great efforts in his work

 C) he is keen on learning anything new

 D) he has tried to determine where he is on his journey

10. In the author's eyes, one who views personal growth as a process would _____.

 A) succeed in climbing up the social ladder

 B) judge his ability to grow from his own achievements

 C) face difficulties and take up challenges

 D) aim high and reach his goal each time

11. When the author says "a new way of being" (Line 3, Para. 3) he is referring to _____.

 A) a new approach to experiencing the world

 B) a new way of taking risks

 C) a new method of perceiving ourselves

 D) a new system of adaptation to change

12. For personal growth, the author advocates all of the following except _____.

 A) curiosity about more chances

 B) promptness in self-adaptation

C) open-mindedness to new experiences

D) avoidance of internal fears and doubts

 ## Passage 4 （1998 年）

Well, no gain without pain, they say. But what about pain without gain? Everywhere you go in A-merica, you hear tales of corporate revival. What is harder to establish is whether the productivity revolution that businessmen assume they are presiding over is for real.

The official statistics are mildly discouraging. They show that, if you lump manufacturing and services together, productivity has grown on average by 1. 2% since 1987. That is somewhat faster than the average during the previous decade. And since 1991, productivity has increased by about 2% a year, which is more than twice the 1978—87 average. The trouble is that part of the recent acceleration is due to the usual rebound that occurs at this point in a business cycle, and so is not conclusive evidence of a revival in the underlying trend. There is, as Robert Rubin, the treasury secretary, says, a "disjunction" between the mass of business anecdote that points to a leap in productivity and the picture reflected by the statistics.

Some of this can be easily explained. New ways of organizing the workplace—all that re-engineering and downsizing—are only one contribution to the overall productivity of an economy, which is driven by many other factors such as joint investment in equipment and machinery, new technology, and investment in education and training. Moreover, most of the changes that companies make are intended to keep them profitable, and this need not always mean increasing productivity: switching to new markets or improving quality can matter just as much.

Two other explanations are more speculative. First, some of the business restructuring of recent years may have been ineptly done. Second, even if it was well done, it may have spread much less widely than people suppose.

Leonard Schlesinger, a Harvard academic and former chief executive of Au Bong Pain, a rapidly growing chain of bakery cafes, says that much "re-engineering" has been crude. In many cases, he believes, the loss of revenue has been greater than the reductions in cost. His colleague, Michael Beer, says that far too many companies have applied re-engineering in a mechanistic fashion, chopping out costs without giving sufficient thought to long-term profitability. BBDO's Al Rosenshine is blunter. He dismisses a lot of the work of re-engineering consultants as mere rubbish—"the worst sort of ambulance-cashing."

13. According to the author, the American economic situation is _____.

　　A) not as good as it seems 　　　B) at its turning point

　　C) much better than it seems 　　　D) near to complete recovery

14. The official statistics on productivity growth _____.

　　A) exclude the usual rebound in a business cycle

　　B) fall short of businessmen's anticipation

　　C) meet the expectation of business people

　　D) fail to reflect the true state of economy

15. The author raises the question "what about pain without gain?" because _____.

　　A) he questions the truth of "no gain without pain"

　　B) he does not think the productivity revolution works

　　C) he wonders if the official statistics are misleading

　　D) he has conclusive evidence for the revival of businesses

16. Which of the following statements is NOT mentioned in the passage?

A) Radical reforms are essential for the increase of productivity.

B) New ways of organizing workplaces may help to increase productivity.

C) The reduction of costs is not a sure way to gain long-term profitability.

D) The consultants are a bunch of good-for-nothings.

因果与条件关系题 ▶

Passage 1 (2003 年)

To paraphrase 18th-century statesman Edmund Burke, "all that is needed for the triumph of a misguided cause is that good people do nothing." One such cause now seeks to end biomedical research because of the theory that animals have rights ruling out their use in research. Scientists need to respond forcefully to animal rights advocates, whose arguments are confusing the public and thereby threatening advances in health knowledge and care. Leaders of the animal rights movement target biomedical research because it depends on public funding, and few people understand the process of health care research. Hearing allegations of cruelty to animals in research settings, many are perplexed that anyone would deliberately harm an animal.

For example, a grandmotherly woman staffing an animal rights booth at a recent street fair was distributing a brochure that encouraged readers not to use anything that comes from or is tested in animals—no meat, no fur, no medicines. Asked if she opposed immunizations, she wanted to know if vaccines come from animal research. When assured that they do, she replied," Then I would have to say yes." Asked what will happen when epidemics return, she said, "Don't worry, scientists will find some way of using computers." Such well-meaning people just don't understand.

Scientists must communicate their message to the public in a compassionate, understandable way-in human terms, not in the language of molecular biology. We need to make clear the connection between animal research and a grandmother's hip replacement, a father's bypass operation, a baby's vaccinations, and even a pet's shots. To those who are unaware that animal research was needed to produce these treatments, as well as new treatments and vaccines, animal research seems wasteful at best and cruel at worst.

Much can be done. Scientists could "adopt" middle school classes and present their own research. They should be quick to respond to letters to the editor, lest animal rights misinformation go unchallenged and acquire a deceptive appearance of truth. Research institutions could be opened to tours, to show that laboratory animals receive humane care. Finally, because the ultimate stakeholders are patients, the health research community should actively recruit to its cause not only well-known personalities such as Stephen Cooper, who has made courageous statements about the value of animal research, but all who receive medical treatment. If good people do nothing there is a real possibility that an uninformed citizenry will extinguish the precious embers of medical progress.

1. The author begins his article with Edmund Burke's words to _____.

A) call on scientists to take some actions.

B) criticize the misguided cause of animal rights.

C) warn of the doom of biomedical research.

D) show the triumph of the animal rights movement.

2. Misguided people tend to think that using an animal in research is _____.

A) cruel but natural.　　　　B) inhuman and unacceptable.

C) inevitable but vicious.　　D) pointless and wasteful.

3. The example of the grandmotherly woman is used to show the public's _____.

A) discontent with animal research.

B) ignorance about medical science.

C) indifference to epidemics.

D) anxiety about animal rights.

4. The author believes that, in face of the challenge from animal rights advocates, scientists should
_____.

A) communicate more with the public.

B) employ hi-tech means in research.

C) feel no shame for their cause.

D) strive to develop new cures.

5. From the text we learn that Stephen Cooper is _____.

A) a well-known humanist.

B) a medical practitioner.

C) an enthusiast in animal rights.

D) a supporter of animal research.

 # Passage 2 (2003 年)

In recent years, railroads have been combining with each other, merging into supersystems, causing heightened concerns about monopoly. As recently as 1995, the top four railroads accounted for under 70 percent of the total ton-miles moved by rails. Next year, after a series of mergers is completed, just four railroads will control well over 90 percent of all the freight moved by major rail carriers.

Supporters of the new super systems argue that these mergers will allow for substantial cost reductions and better coordinated service. Any threat of monopoly, they argue, is removed by fierce competition from trucks. But many shippers complain that for heavy bulk commodities traveling long distances, such as coal, chemicals, and grain, trucking is too costly and the railroads therefore have them by the throat.

The vast consolidation within the rail industry means that most shippers are served by only one rail company. Railroads typically charge such "captive " shippers 20 to 30 percent more than they do when another railroad is competing for the business. Shippers who feel they are being overcharged have the right to appeal to the federal government's Surface Transportation Board for rate relief, but the process is expensive, time consuming, and will work only in truly extreme cases.

Railroads justify rate discrimination against captive shippers on the grounds that in the long run it reduces everyone's cost. If railroads charged all customers the same average rate, they argue, shippers who have the option of switching to trucks or other forms of transportation would do so, leaving remaining customers to shoulder the cost of keeping up the line. It's theory to which many economists subscribe, but in practice it often leaves railroads in the position of determining which companies will flourish and which will fail. " Do we really want railroads to be the arbiters of who wins and who loses in the marketplace?" asks Martin Bercovici, a Washington lawyer who frequently represents shipper.

Many captive shippers also worry they will soon be hit with a round of huge rate increases. The railroad industry as a whole, despite its brightening fortunes still does not earn enough to cover the cost of the capital it must invest to keep up with its surging traffic. Yet railroads continue to borrow billions to acquire one another, with Wall Street cheering them on. Consider the $ 10. 2 billion bid by Norfolk Southern and CSX to acquire Conrail this year. Conrail's net railway operating income in 1996 was just $ 427 million, less than half of the carrying costs of the transaction. Who's going to pay for the rest of the bill? Many captive shippers fear that they will, as Norfolk Southern and CSX increase their grip on the market.

6. According to those who support mergers, railway monopoly is unlikely because _____.

    A) cost reduction is based on competition.

    B) services call for cross-trade coordination.

    C) outside competitors will continue to exist.

    D) shippers will have the railway by the throat.

7. What is many captive shippers' attitude towards the consolidation in the rail industry? _____

    A) Indifferent.　　　B) Supportive.　　　C) Indignant.　　　D) Apprehensive.

8. It can be inferred from paragraph 3 that _____.

    A) shippers will be charged less without a rival railroad.

    B) there will soon be only one railroad company nationwide.

    C) overcharged shippers are unlikely to appeal for rate relief.

    D) a government board ensures fair play in railway business.

9. The word "arbiters" (Line 6, Para 4) most probably refers to those _____.

    A) who work as coordinators.　　　　　B) who function as judges.

    C) who supervise transactions.　　　　　D) who determine the price.

10. According to the text, the cost increase in the rail industry is mainly caused by _____.

    A) the continuing acquisition.　　　　　B) the growing traffic.

    C) the cheering Wall Street.　　　　　D) the shrinking market.

 Passage 1 (1998 年)

　　Few creations of big technology capture the imagination like giant dams. Perhaps it is humankind's long suffering at the mercy of flood and drought that makes the ideal of forcing the waters to do our bidding so fascination. But to be fascinated is also, sometimes, to be blind. Several giant dam projects threaten to do more harm than good.

　　The lesson from dams is that big is not always beautiful. It doesn't help that building a big, powerful dam has become a symbol of achievement for nations and people striving to assert themselves. Egypt's leadership in the Arab world was cemented by the Aswan High Dam. Turkey's bid for First World status includes the giant Ataturk Dam.

　　But big dams tend not to work as intended. The Aswan Dam, for example, stopped the Nile flooding but deprived Egypt of the fertile silt that floods left—all in return for a giant reservoir of disease which is now so full of silt that it barely generates electricity.

　　And yet, the myth of controlling the waters persists. This week, in the heart of civilized Europe, Slovaks and Hungarians stopped just short of sending in the troops in their contention over a dam on the Danube. The huge complex will probably have all the usual problems of big dams. But Slovakia is bidding for independence from the Czechs, and now needs a dam to prove itself.

　　Meanwhile, in India, the World Bank has given the go-ahead to the even more wrong-headed Narmada Dam. And the bank has done this even though its advisors say the dam will cause hardship for the powerless and environmental destruction. The benefits are for the powerful, but they are far from guaranteed.

　　Proper, scientific study of the impacts of dams and of the cost and benefits of controlling water can help to resolve these conflicts. Hydroelectric power and flood control and irrigation are possible without building monster dams. But when you are dealing with myths, it is hard to be either proper, or scientific. It is time that the world learned the lessons of Aswan. You don't need a dam to be saved.

1. The third sentence of paragraph 1 implies that _____.

A) people would be happy if they shut their eyes to reality

B) the blind could be happier than the sighted

C) over-excited people tend to neglect vital things

D) fascination makes people lose their eyesight

2. In paragraph 5，"the powerless" probably refers to _____.

A) areas short of electricity

B) dams without power stations

C) poor countries around India

D) common people in the Narmada Dam area

3. What is the myth concerning giant dams?

A) They bring in more fertile soil.

B) They help defend the country.

C) They strengthen international ties.

D) They have universal control of the waters.

4. What the author tries to suggest may best be interpreted as _____.

A) "It's no use crying over spilt milk"

B) "More haste，less speed"

C) "Look before you leap"

D) "He who laughs last laughs best"

 ## Passage 2　(2000 年)

　　If ambition is to be well regarded，the rewards of ambition—wealth，distinction，control over one's destiny—must be deemed worthy of the sacrifices made on ambition's behalf. If the tradition of ambition is to have vitality，it must be widely shared；and it especially must be highly regarded by people who are themselves admired，the educated not least among them. In an odd way，however，it is the educated who have claimed to have given up on ambition as an ideal. What is odd is that they have perhaps most bene-fited from ambition—if not always their own then that of their parents and grandparents. There is a heavy note of hypocrisy in this，a case of closing the barn door after the horses have escaped—with the educated themselves riding on them.

　　Certainly people do not seem less interested in success and its signs now than formerly. Summer homes，European travel，BMWs—the locations，place names and name brands may change，but such i-tems do not seem less in demand today than a decade or two years ago. What has happened is that peo-ple cannot confess fully to their dreams，as easily and openly as once they could，lest they be thought pushing，acquisitive and vulgar. Instead，we are treated to fine hypocritical spectacles，which now more than ever seem in ample supply：the critic of American materialism with a Southampton summer home；the publisher of radical books who takes his meals in three-star restaurants；the journalist advocating participatory democracy in all phases of life，whose own children are enrolled in private schools. For such people and many more perhaps not so exceptional，the proper formulation is，"Succeed at all costs but avoid appearing ambitious. "

　　The attacks on ambition are many and come from various angles；its public defenders are few and unimpressive，where they are not extremely unattractive. As a result，the support for ambition as a healthy impulse，a quality to be admired and fixed in the mind of the young，is probably lower than it has ever been in the United States. This does not mean that ambition is at an end，that people no longer feel its stirrings and promptings, but only that, no longer openly honored, it is less openly professed. Consequences follow from this, of course, some of which are that ambition is driven underground, or made sly. Such, then, is the way things stand: on the left angry critics, on the right stupid supporters, and in the middle, as usual, the majority of earnest people trying to get on in life.

5. It is generally believed that ambition may be well regarded if _____.

A) its returns well compensate for the sacrifices

B) it is rewarded with money, fame and power

C) its goals are spiritual rather than material

D) it is shared by the rich and the famous

6. The last sentence of the first paragraph most probably implies that it is _____.

A) customary of the educated to discard ambition in words

B) too late to check ambition once it has been let out

C) dishonest to deny ambition after the fulfillment of the goal

D) impractical for the educated to enjoy benefits from ambition

7. Some people do not openly admit they have ambition because _____.

A) they think of it as immoral

B) their pursuits are not fame or wealth

C) ambition is not closely related to material benefits

D) they do not want to appear greedy and contemptible

8. From the last paragraph the conclusion can be drawn that ambition should be maintained _____.

A) secretly and vigorously

B) openly and enthusiastically

C) easily and momentarily

D) verbally and spiritually

 ## Passage 3 (1998 年)

Emerging from the 1980 census is the picture of a nation developing more and more regional competition, as population growth in the Northeast and Midwest reaches a near standstill.

This development—and its strong implications for US politics and economy in years ahead—has enthroned the South as America's most densely populated region for the first time in the history of the nation's head counting.

Altogether, the US population rose in the 1970s by 23. 2 million people—numerically the third-largest growth ever recorded in a single decade. Even so, that gain adds up to only 11. 4 percent, lowest in American annual records except for the Depression years.

Americans have been migrating south and west in larger numbers since World War Ⅱ, and the pattern still prevails.

Three sun-belt states—Florida, Texas and California—together had nearly 10 million more people in 1980 than a decade earlier. Among large cities, San Diego moved from 14th to 8th and San Antonio from 15th to 10th—with Cleveland and Washington. DC, dropping out of the top 10.

Not all that shift can be attributed to the movement out of the snow belt, census officials say. Nonstop waves of immigrants played a role, too—and so did bigger crops of babies as yesterday's "baby boom" generation reached its child-bearing years.

Moreover, demographers see the continuing shift south and west as joined by a related but newer phenomenon: More and more, Americans apparently are looking not just for places with more jobs but with fewer people, too. Some instances —

● Regionally, the Rocky Mountain states reported the most rapid growth rate—37.1 percent since 1970 in a vast area with only 5 percent of the US population.

● Among states, Nevada and Arizona grew fastest of all: 63.5 and 53.1 percent respectively. Except for Florida and Texas, the top 10 in rate of growth is composed of Western states with 7.5 million people—about 9 per square mile.

The flight from overcrowdedness affects the migration from snow belt to more bearable climates.

Nowhere do 1980 census statistics dramatize more the American search for spacious living than in the Far West. There, California added 3.7 million to its population in the 1970s, more than any other state.

In that decade, however, large numbers also migrated from California, mostly to other parts of the West. Often they chose—and still are choosing—somewhat colder climates such as Oregon, Idaho and Alaska in order to escape smog, crime and other plagues of urbanization in the Golden State.

As a result, California's growth rate dropped during the 1970s, to 18.5 percent—little more than two thirds the 1960s' growth figure and considerably below that of other Western states.

9. Discerned from the perplexing picture of population growth the 1980 census provided, America in 1970s _____.

A) enjoyed the lowest net growth of population in history

B) witnessed a southwestern shift of population

C) underwent an unparalleled period of population growth

D) brought to a standstill its pattern of migration since World War Ⅱ

10. The census distinguished itself from previous studies on population movement in that _____.

A) it stresses the climatic influence on population distribution

B) it highlights the contribution of continuous waves of immigrants

C) it reveals the Americans' new pursuit of spacious living

D) it elaborates the delayed effects of yesterday's "baby boom"

11. We can see from the available statistics that _____.

A) California was once the most thinly populated area in the whole US

B) the top 10 states in growth rate of population were all located in the West

C) cities with better climates benefited unanimously from migration

D) Arizona ranked second of all states in its growth rate of population

12. The word "demographers" (Line 1, Paragraph 7) most probably means _____.

A) people in favor of the trend of democracy

B) advocates of migration between states

C) scientists engaged in the study of population

D) conservatives clinging to old patterns of life

 Passage 4 (1994 年)

"I have great confidence that by the end of the decade we'll know in vast detail how cancer cells arise," says microbiologist Robert Weinberg, an expert on cancer. "But," he cautions, "some people have the idea that once one understands the causes, the cure will rapidly follow." Consider Pasteur, he discovered the causes of many kinds of infections, but it was fifty or sixty years before cures were available.

This year, 50 percent of the 910,000 people who suffer from cancer will survive at least five years. In the year 2000, the National Cancer Institute estimates, that figure will be 75 percent. For some skin cancers, the five-year survival rate is as high as 90 percent. But other survival statistics are still discouraging—13 percent for lung cancer, and 2 percent for cancer of the pancreas.

With as many as 120 varieties in existence, discovering how cancer works is not easy. The researchers made great progress in the early 1970s, when they discovered that oncogenes, which are cancer-causing genes, are inactive in normal cells. Anything from cosmic rays to radiation to diet may activate a dormant oncogene, but how remains unknown. If several oncogenes are driven into action, the cell, unable to turn them off, becomes cancerous.

The exact mechanisms involved are still mysterious, but the likelihood that many cancers are initiated at the level of genes suggests that we will never prevent all cancers. "Changes are a normal part of the evolutionary process," says oncologist William Hayward. Environmental factors can never be totally eliminated; as Hayward points out, "We can't prepare a medicine against cosmic rays."

The prospects for cure, though still distant, are brighter.

"First, we need to understand how the normal cell controls itself. Second, we have to determine whether there are a limited number of genes in cells which are always responsible for at least part of the trouble. If we can understand how cancer works, we can counteract its action."

13. The example of Pasteur in the passage is used to _____.

A) predict that the secret of cancer will be disclosed in a decade

B) indicate that the prospects for curing cancer are bright

C) prove that cancer will be cured in fifty to sixty years

D) warn that there is still a long way to go before cancer can be conquered

14. The author implies that by the year 2000, _____.

A) there will be a drastic rise in the five-year survival rate of skin-cancer patients

B) 90 percent of the skin-cancer patients today will still be living

C) the survival statistics will be fairly even among patients with various cancers

D) there won't be a drastic increase of survival rate of all cancer patients

15. Oncogenes are cancer-causing genes _____.

A) that are always in operation in a healthy person

B) which remain unharmful so long as they are not activated

C) that can be driven out of normal cells

D) which normal cell can't turn off

16. The word "dormant" in the third paragraph most probably means _____.

A) dead　　　　B) ever-present　　　C) inactive　　　D) potential

 Passage 5 (1999 年)

An invisible border divides those arguing for computers in the classroom on the behalf of students' career prospects and those arguing for computers in the classroom for broader reasons of radical educational reform. Very few writers on the subject have explored this distinction—indeed, contradiction—which goes to the heart of what is wrong with the campaign to put computers in the classroom.

An education that aims at getting a student a certain kind of job is a technical education, justified for reasons radically different from why education is universally required by law. It is not simply to raise everyone's job prospects that all children are legally required to attend school into their teens. Rather, we have a certain conception of the American citizen, a character who is incomplete if he cannot competently assess how his livelihood and happiness are affected by things outside of himself. But this was not always the case; before it was legally required for all children to attend school until a certain age, it was widely accepted that some were just not equipped by nature to pursue this kind of education. With optimism characteristic of all industrialized countries, we came to accept that everyone is fit to be educated. Computer-education advocates forsake this optimistic notion for a pessimism that betrays their otherwise cheery outlook. Banking on the confusion between educational and vocational reasons for bringing computers into schools, computer-education advocates often emphasize the job prospects of graduates over their educational achievement.

There are some good arguments for a technical education given the right kind of student. Many European schools introduce the concept of professional training early on in order to make sure children are properly equipped for the professions they want to join. It is, however, presumptuous to insist that there will only be so many jobs for so many scientists, so many businessmen, so many accountants. Besides, this is unlikely to produce the needed number of every kind of professional in a country as large as ours and where the economy is spread over so many states and involves so many international corporations.

But, for a small group of students, professional training might be the way to go since well-developed skills, all other factors being equal, can be the difference between having a job and not. Of course, the basics of using any computer these days are very simple. It does not take a lifelong acquaintance to pick up various software programs. If one wanted to become a computer engineer, that is, of course, an entirely different story. Basic computer skills take—at the very longest—a couple of months to learn. In any case, basic computer skills are only complementary to the host of real skills that are necessary to becoming any kind of professional. It should be observed, of course, that no school, vocational or not, is helped by a confusion over its purpose.

17. The author thinks the present rush to put computers in the classroom is _____.
    A) far-reaching   B) dubiously oriented
    C) self-contradictory   D) radically reformatory

18. The belief that education is indispensable to all children _____.
    A) is indicative of a pessimism in disguise
    B) came into being along with the arrival of computers
    C) is deeply rooted in the minds of computer-education advocates
    D) originated from the optimistic attitude of industrialized countries

19. It could be inferred from the passage that in the author's country the European model of professional training is _____.
    A) dependent upon the starting age of candidates
    B) worth trying in various social sections
    C) of little practical value
    D) attractive to every kind of professional

20. According to the author, basic computer skills should be _____.
    A) included as an auxiliary course in school
    B) highlighted in acquisition of professional qualifications
    C) mastered through a life-long course
    D) equally emphasized by any school, vocational or otherwise

Passage 6 (1997 年)

A report consistently brought back by visitors to the US is how friendly, courteous, and helpful most Americans were to them. To be fair, this observation is also frequently made of Canada and Canadians, and should best be considered North American. There are, of course, exceptions. Small-minded officials, rude waiters, and ill-mannered taxi drivers are hardly unknown in the US. Yet it is an observation made so frequently that it deserves comment.

For a long period of time and in many parts of the country, a traveler was a welcome break in an otherwise dull existence. Dullness and loneliness were common problems of the families who generally lived distant from one another. Strangers and travelers were welcome sources of diversion, and brought news of the outside world.

The harsh realities of the frontier also shaped this tradition of hospitality. Someone traveling alone, if hungry, injured, or ill, often had nowhere to turn except to the nearest cabin or settlement. It was not a matter of choice for the traveler or merely a charitable impulse on the part of the settlers. It reflected the harshness of daily life: if you didn't take in the stranger and take care of him, there was no one else who would. And someday, remember, you might be in the same situation.

Today there are many charitable organizations which specialize in helping the weary traveler. Yet, the old tradition of hospitality to strangers is still very strong in the US, especially in the smaller cities and towns away from the busy tourist trails. "I was just traveling through, got talking with this American, and pretty soon he invited me home for dinner—amazing." Such observations reported by visitors to the US are not uncommon, but are not always understood properly. The casual friendliness of many Americans should be interpreted neither as superficial nor as artificial, but as the result of a historically developed cultural tradition.

As is true of any developed society, in America a complex set of cultural signals, assumptions, and conventions underlies all social interrelationships. And, of course, speaking a language does not necessarily mean that someone understands social and cultural patterns. Visitors who fail to "translate" cultural meanings properly often draw wrong conclusions. For example, when an American uses the word "friend", the cultural implications of the word may be quite different from those it has in the visitor's language and culture. It takes more than a brief encounter on a bus to distinguish between courteous convention and individual interest. Yet, being friendly is a virtue that many Americans value highly and expect from both neighbors and strangers.

21. In the eyes of visitors from the outside world _____.
    A) rude taxi drivers are rarely seen in the US
    B) small-minded officials deserve a serious comment
    C) Canadians are not so friendly as their neighbors
    D) most Americans are ready to offer help

22. It could be inferred from the last paragraph that _____.
    A) culture exercises an influence over social interrelationship
    B) courteous convention and individual interest are interrelated
    C) various virtues manifest themselves exclusively among friends
    D) social interrelationships equal the complex set of cultural conventions

23. Families in frontier settlements used to entertain strangers _____.
    A) to improve their hard life
    B) in view of their long-distance travel
    C) to add some flavor to their own daily life
    D) out of a charitable impulse

24. The tradition of hospitality to strangers _____.
    A) tends to be superficial and artificial
    B) is generally well kept up in the United States
    C) is always understood properly
    D) has something to do with the busy tourist trails

 **Passage 7** (1995 年)

Personality is to a large extent inherent—A-type-parents usually bring about A-type offspring. But the environment must also have a profound effect, since if competition is important to the parents, it is likely to become a major factor in the lives of their children.

One place where children soak up A-characteristics is school, which is, by its very nature, a highly competitive institution. Too many schools adopt the "win at all costs" moral standard and measure their success by sporting achievements. The current passion for making children compete against their classmates or against the clock produces a two-layer system, in which competitive A-types seem in some way better than their B type fellows. Being too keen to win can have dangerous consequences: remember that Pheidippides, the first marathon runner, dropped dead seconds after saying: "Rejoice, we conquer!"

By far the worst form of competition in schools is the disproportionate emphasis on examinations. It is a rare school that allows pupils to concentrate on those things they do well. The merits of competition by examination are somewhat questionable, but competition in the certain knowledge of failure is positively harmful.

Obviously, it is neither practical nor desirable that all A youngsters change into B's. The world needs types, and schools have an important duty to try to fit a child's personality to his possible future employment. It is top management.

If the preoccupation of schools with academic work was lessened, more time might be spent teaching children surer values. Perhaps selection for the caring professions, especially medicine, could be made less by good grades in chemistry and more by such considerations as sensitivity and sympathy. It is surely a mistake to choose our doctors exclusively from A-type stock. B's are important and should be encouraged.

25. According to the passage, A-type individuals are usually _____.

    A) impatient   B) considerate   C) aggressive   D) agreeable

26. The author is strongly opposed to the practice of examinations at schools because _____.

    A) the pressure is too great on the students

    B) some students are bound to fail

    C) failure rates are too high

    D) the results of examinations are doubtful

27. The selection of medical professionals is currently based on _____.

    A) candidates' sensitivity

    B) academic achievements

    C) competitive spirit

    D) surer values

28. From the passage we can draw the conclusion that _____.

    A) the personality of a child is well established at birth

    B) family influence dominates the shaping of one's characteristics

    C) the development of one's personality is due to multiple factors

    D) B-type characteristics can find no place in a competitive society

Passage 8 (1995 年)

That experiences influence subsequent behaviour is evidence of an obvious but nevertheless remarkable activity called remembering. Learning could not occur without the function popularly named memory. Constant practice has such as effect on memory as to lead to skillful performance on the piano, to recitation of a poem, and even to reading and understanding these words. So-called intelligent behaviour demands memory, remembering being a primary requirement for reasoning. The ability to solve any problem or even to recognize that a problem exists depends on memory. Typically, the decision to cross a street is based on remembering many earlier experiences.

Practice (or review) tends to build and maintain memory for a task or for any learned material. Over a period of no practice what has been learned tends to be forgotten; and the adaptive consequences may not seem obvious. Yet, dramatic instances of sudden forgetting can be seen to be adaptive. In this sense, the ability to forget can be interpreted to have survived through a process of natural selection in animals. Indeed, when one's memory of an emotionally painful experience lead to serious anxiety, forgetting may produce relief. Nevertheless, an evolutionary interpretation might make it difficult to understand how the commonly gradual process of forgetting survived natural selection.

In thinking about the evolution of memory together with all its possible aspects, it is helpful to consider what would happen if memories failed to fade. Forgetting clearly aids orientation in time, since old memories weaken and the new tend to stand out, providing clues for inferring duration. Without forgetting, adaptive ability would suffer, for example, learned behaviour that might have been correct a decade ago may no longer be. Cases are recorded of people who (by ordinary standards) forgot so little that their everyday activities were full of confusion. This forgetting seems to serve that survival of the individual and the species.

Another line of thought assumes a memory storage system of limited capacity that provides adaptive flexibility specifically through forgetting. In this view, continual adjustments are made between learning or memory storage (input) and forgetting (output). Indeed, there is evidence that the rate at which individuals forget is directly related to how much they have learned. Such data offers gross support of contemporary models of memory that assume an input-output balance.

29. From the evolutionary point of view, _____.

    A) forgetting for lack of practice tends to be obviously inadaptive

    B) if a person gets very forgetful all of a sudden he must be very adaptive

    C) the gradual process of forgetting is an indication of an individual's adaptability

    D) sudden forgetting may bring about adaptive consequences

30. According to the passage, if a person never forgets, _____.

    A) he would survive best   B) he would have a lot of trouble

    C) his ability to learn would be enhanced   D) the evolution of memory would stop

31. From the last paragraph we know that _____.

    A) forgetfulness is a response to learning.

    B) the memory storage system is an exactly balanced input-output system

    C) memory is a compensation for forgetting

    D) the capacity of a memory storage system is limited because forgetting occurs

32. In this article, the author tries to interpret the function of _____.

    A) remembering   B) forgetting   C) adapting   D) experiencing

✿ Passage (1996 年)

Rumor has it that more than 20 books on creationism/evolution are in the publisher's pipelines. A few have already appeared. The goal of all will be to try to explain to a confused and often unenlightened citizenry that there are not two equally valid scientific theories for the origin and evolution of universe and life. Cosmology, geology, and biology have provided a consistent, unified, and constantly improving account of what happened. "Scientific" creationism, which is being pushed by some for "equal time" in the classrooms whenever the scientific accounts of evolution are given, is based on religion, not science. Virtually all scientists and the majority of nonfundamentalist religious leaders have come to regard "scientific" creationism as bad science and bad religion.

The first four chapters of Kitcher's book give a very brief introduction to evolution. At appropriate places, he introduces the criticisms of the creationists and provides answers. In the last three chapters, he takes off his gloves and gives the creationists a good beating. He describes their programmes and tactics, and, for those unfamiliar with the ways of creationists, the extent of their deception and distortion may come as an unpleasant surprise. When their basic motivation is religious, one might have expected more Christian behavior.

Kitcher is a philosopher, and this may account, in part, for the clarity and effectiveness of his arguments. The nonspecialist will be able to obtain at least a notion of the sorts of data and argument that support evolutionary theory. The final chapter on the creationists will be extremely clear to all. On the dust jacket of this fine book, Stephen Jay Gould says: "This book stands for reason itself." And so it does—and all would be well were reason the only judge in the creationism/evolution debate.

1. "Creationism" in the passage refers to _____.
    A) evolution in its true sense as to the origin of the universe
    B) a notion of the creation of religion
    C) the scientific explanation of the earth formation
    D) the deceptive theory about the origin of the universe
2. Kitcher's book is intended to _____.
    A) recommend the views of the evolutionists
    B) expose the true features of creationists
    C) curse bitterly at this opponents
    D) launch a surprise attack on creationists
3. From the passage we can infer that _____.
    A) reasoning has played a decisive role in the debate
    B) creationists do not base their argument on reasoning
    C) evolutionary theory is too difficult for non-specialists
    D) creationism is supported by scientific findings
4. This passage appears to be a digest of _____.
    A) a book review   B) a scientific paper
    C) a magazine feature   D) a newspaper editorial

答案解析及译文

主旨题答案

Passage 1

题材：社会科学——教育学

此文介绍了对于残疾儿童的教育问题，并指出对残疾儿童的教育的重视反映了美国传统的价值观念以及新的思潮。

1.正确答案 A）。文章第二句为"虽然舞台上的主角吸引我们的注意力，我们也意识到了配角以及戏剧布景的重要性。"很显然，作者把特殊儿童比做舞台上的主角，把家庭和社会比做配角和戏剧布景。这一比喻表明,家庭、社会对特殊儿童的成长和发展所起的作用如同配角和戏剧场景对主要演员所起的作用一样。因此,A)"特殊儿童的成长与家庭和社会有很重要的关系"是解。B)"特殊儿童比正常儿童受家庭影响要大"与内容不符,文章并未进行这种比较。C)"家庭和社会最感兴趣的是特殊儿童"文章也未提及。D)"社会的需要比特殊儿童的需要更为重要"文章中无此比较。

2. 正确答案 C)。本题问"特殊儿童在教育中得到如此关注的原因是什么"。文章第三段最后一句指出"在过去的三十年中,公共教育对特殊儿童显示出的极大兴趣表明了我们社会的强烈情感,即所有公民,无论情况怎样特殊,都应该有机会全面发展自己的能力。"这和 C)"他们应该充分发展他们的潜能"一致,因此 C)是解。A)"人们希望他们成为社会的领导人"显然与内容不符,因为"特殊儿童"在此文中特指有缺陷的儿童。B)"他们可能成为社会的负担"文章未提。D)"残疾儿童值得特别关注"属于答非所问。

3. 正确答案 D)。本题问全文的主题。第一段是文章的主题,即特殊儿童有特殊之处,必须对其教育进行调整。而后,作者指出从家庭、社会、法律三方面都应关注特殊儿童的教育。第四段结尾再次强调调整教育的具体方案。由此可知,答案 D)"使教育适应特殊儿童的必要性"为正确答案。A)"儿童学习能力的差异"虽在第一段第一句提到,但未展开。B)"现代社会中特殊儿童的定义"未曾提到。C)"为特殊儿童制定的特别教育计划"在文章最后有稍有涉及,但未展开。

4. 正确答案 A)。本题问,从文章中我们知道,对特殊儿童的教育方面的关注如何。参看最后一段第五句:"近来法院的裁决已认可了所有儿童(无论残疾与否)都有权接受适当教育,并且命令公立学校采取必要步骤提供这种教育。"由此可知,A)"正在得到法律的支持"为正确答案。B)"与本国传统不符"未曾提及。C)"当初国家缔造者们已清楚地说明了这一点"与最后一段第三句不符。第三句指出:"虽然这句话被这个国家的缔造者们用来指法律面前的平等,但也被解释为机会均等。"显然,缔造者们明确指出的是法律面前人人平等,并未明确提及教育。D)"对法院的裁决将施加很大影响"未曾提及。

译文

残疾儿童和同年龄的孩子相比在某些方面有很大不同,要想挖掘出他们的全部潜力,对他们的教育也应当适应这些不同之处。

尽管残疾儿童的需要是我们谈论的重点。但我们也要描述一下他们所处的环境。正如尽管舞台上的主角吸引着观众的目光,但我们也意识到配角和布景的重要性一样,残疾儿童的家庭和他们所处的社会环境在他们的成长和发展中通常起着决定性的作用。正是在公立学校里,我们找到了社会的理解的充分含义,在这里,知识、希望和恐惧从上一代传到下一代。

在任何社会中,教育都是社会的一面镜子。从这面镜子里,我们看到一个文化自身的长处、弱点、希望、偏见和价值观。过去三十年中对学校教育中的残疾儿童的研究表明,在我们的社会里,任何公民(不论其具体情况如何)都有权利充分发展自己的能力。

"人生来是平等的",这句话我们听过很多遍,但它对于民主社会中的教育仍有很重要的意义。尽管这个国家的创始人用这句话来表明法律面前人人平等,但它也意味着机会均等。它表明所有儿童都有权利享受教育——我们应当帮助每个孩子了解自己的能力,不管这种能力是大还是小。近来,法律肯定了儿童(包括残疾儿童)受到适当教育的权利,并规定学校采取适当的措施为儿童提供这种教育。相应的,学校正在做一些调整,如修改课程,调整授课方式来帮助残疾儿童和那些从普通课程中无法受益的儿童。

Passage 2

题材:社会科学——专利权
本文讲述了专利权的意义、作用及相关背景知识。

5. 正确答案 D)。本题问的是文章的主题。从全文看主要是谈如何利用已有的观点进行新的发明创造并取得专利的途径。因此 D)"获得专利的途径"符合主题。A)"申请专利的方法"未展开。B)"申请专利"和 C)"专利的用途"均有所涉及,但不是文章的主题。

6. 正确答案 C)。本题属于正误判断题。文章第二段指出"授予的专利是发明者和国家之间形成的一种契约。根据契约，发明者对自己的发明获得了一定时期的垄断权，垄断期结束后，可把发明的整个细节公布于众。"这和 C)"当专利的法律有效期结束时，专利持有者必须公布发明的细节"意思一致。A)"当专利失效时，如有必要可以重新申请或延续"与第一段第一句不符。D)"人们可以从专利局所属图书馆得到已获专利权的发明的全部细节"缺少条件，即：专利权限结束之后。

7. 正确答案 B)。本题问 Goerges Valensi 的专利延续到 1971 年的原因。文章第四段指出"延续时间最长的专利经批准给了乔治·瓦伦西。他 1939 年的彩电接收机线路的专利一直延长到1971 年，因为在这项专利期内没有彩电节目可以接收，因此该专利无法被采用。"这和 B)一致。A)"在此之前无人愿意奖励其专利"、C)"没有足够的电视台提供彩色节目"和 D)"在那之前没有彩电接收机"均与事实不符。

8. 正确答案 A)。本题属于推测词义题。根据第五段第二句可以推测：plagiarize 意为"剽窃"，即偷来加以利用。

9. 正确答案 A)。本题属于推论题。文章第六段第二句指出"只有把握时代的需求，通过使用新技术，专利才能转化为商业实践，做到名利双收。"这和 A)"除非把发明转化为商业行为，发明不会对发明者有任何益处"一致。B)"产品实际上是很久以前的发明"是对最后一段第一句that most "new" ideas are, in fact, as old as the hills 的误解。C)"购买旧专利比购买新专利更便宜"与内容不符。D)"专利专家通过研究过期专利向其他人推荐专利"与内容不符。

译文

当做出一项发明时，发明者可以采取三种可能的行动：他可以通过出版物把成果公布于世，也可以保密或取得专利。

授予的专利是发明者和国家之间形成的一种契约。根据契约，发明者对自己的发明获得了一定时期的专有权，专有期结束后，即把发明的整个细节公布于众。

只有在极为特殊的情况下，专利期才被延续从而改变事物的正常进程。

延续时间最长的专利经批准给了乔治·瓦伦西。他 1939 年的彩电接收机线路的专利一直延长到 1971，因为在这项专利期内没有彩电节目可以接收，因此该专利没有被采用的希望。

因为一项专利到期后，该专利就永久公开，因此，专利局所属的图书馆的架子上数百万个专利设想，任何人都可免费使用，如超过半个世纪，有时甚至可以重新取得专利。实际上，专利专家们常对希望使用有效专利而又不愿出高额费用的人提出建议，避免侵犯他们专利权的有效方法就是使用过期专利。同样，因为用任何方式公布一种专利设想会使该设想的专利权永久失效，所以使用其他印刷材料上的专利设想从来就是安全的。许多现代技术都是根据这些法律安全的认定而发展起来的。

任何与专利及发明密切相关的人很快就得知，多数新的专利设想实际上已相当陈旧。只有把握时代的需求，跟上新技术的步伐，专利才能转化成商业实践，做到名利双收。利用电磁录音这一理论的最初专利始于 1886 年。电视生成原理的许多原创思路都始于 19 世纪后期和 20 世纪初。甚至1904 年马在车后的马车专利已经预见到了发动机后置的德国"大众"轿车的出现。

态度评价题答案

Passage 1

题材：时文——互联网经济

在近几年的考研文章中，关于网络方面的内容时有涉及。本文讲述了网络技术的发展有可能带来的网络商业模式的变化以及这种变化的经济和社会影响。

1. 正确答案 A)。本题问及通过本文开头我们了解到网上交易这一回事怎样。本文开头第一、二句说："开始网上交易的一两年中，大部分业务活动都围绕着努力开拓消费者市场而进行的。最后，随着网络证明不是一时的时髦后，公司才开始在网上交易产品和提供各种服务。"这与A)"一直努力开拓市场"的意思相吻合；选项 B)"意欲追赶新奇、时髦"，与原意相悖；选项 C)"企图控制市场，但徒劳无获"。第一段仅提到他们的努力，并未提到努力的结果。选项 D)"已经蓬勃发展了一年左右的时间"也无据可查。

2. 正确答案 C)。本题问及谈到网上所采取的销售技术,作者有何用意。在第三段第二、三句中作者指出:"直到最近,互联网上的销售活动主要是把用户'吸引'到自己的网站上来。然而,就在去年,软件公司开发出新的技术,能让公司直接向用户'推销'信息——将销售信息直接传送给特定的用户"。利用国际互联网络进行网上信息传输,并在网上直接进行交易,这种交易策略显然比过去的交易方式发生了很大变化,这与选项 C)意思相吻合。此举是否受用户欢迎,再看本段倒数第四句:"推销策略遭到许多网上用户的鄙视",选项 A)"这种技术受到了许多网络用户的喜爱"与此大相径庭。根据第二段第一句"许多公司由于怀疑网络的可靠性而对网络的使用犹豫不决",选项 B)"公司对在线交易的可靠性充满信心"与题意不符。选项 D)"它仅限于对固定合作伙伴使用",文中没有涉及。

3. 正确答案 D)。本题问及网络净化者对于"网上推销"持何态度。根据第三段最后四句,网上"推销"受到了许多网上用户的厌弃。在线用户们认为,信息应传送给提出需求的用户。一旦商业广告不请自来地充斥了电脑屏幕,网络与电视就没多大差别了。这样的前景是网络净化者所惧怕的。由此推断,选项 D)"没有要求就不应该有在线商业信息"是正确的。选项 A)"在线领域不应该有销售信息"与事实不符,因为网络净化者反对的是销售信息的传送方式,而不是这种信息本身。选项 B)"上网的首要目的应该是为了赚钱"文中没有提到。选项 C)"网络的功能应该像电视一样"是网络净化者所反对的。

4. 正确答案 B)。本题问最后一段告诉我们什么。在最后一段作者指出,商家如能把相互合作、礼貌周到、安全可靠这几方面恰到好处地结合起来,向用户销售他们所需产品,必定能吸引网上客户。因此说,选项 B)符合题意。选项 A)"对网上商业来说,在网上'推销'信息至关重要"从上下文来看与事实恰好相反。选项 C)"一些大公司在几十年前就开始积极尝试在线服务",与第四段最后一句"只要回顾一下过去 5 到 10 年的历史人们很可能会感到奇怪:为什么尝试在线服务的公司这么少"意思相悖。根据第四段第三句"计算机的运算能力成本下降"与"在计算机上建立销售点"这两者是相关的。因此选项 D)"在计算机上建立销售点与计算机的运算能力无关"与事实相悖。

译文

在互联网经济的第一个年头,大多数的行动还只是围绕着开发消费者市场开展的。最近,随着人们逐渐证明网络并不仅仅是一种时尚,公司之间开始互相购买产品和服务。因为商人大都知道他们需要什么样的产品,所以这种 B-to-B 的销售模式是行得通的。

但是,许多公司对使用互联网仍然心存疑虑,因为他们对网络的可靠性仍不放心。Forrester Researcher 的资深分析家 Blane Erwin 说:"商家需要觉得对连接他们和供货商之间的渠道完全值得信赖。"一些公司只和长期的业务伙伴进行网上交易,以此减少风险,只有固定的业务伙伴才能进入公司的内部网络。

网络经济模式的另外一个主要的变化是销售技术的进步。以前,网上销售主要是集中于把顾客"拉"进某个站点里。而最近几年里,软件公司研发出了能让公司把信息直接"推"到顾客面前的工具,使市场信息能够直接到达既定顾客群。其中最有名的有 Pointcast 网络公司,他们使用一种屏幕保护程序,不断将最新的信息和广告传递到订阅者的电脑上。订阅者可以定制希望接受的信息,并直接进入公司的网站。像 Virtual Vineyards 这样的公司已经开始使用类似的技术,把促销、产品推广和其他活动的信息直接推向顾客。但是这种推销手段受到很多互联网用户的轻视。因为网上文化非常看重这样一个理念,那就是电脑屏幕上出现的信息应该是应邀而来的。一旦商业促销任意充斥屏幕,网络和电视就没有什么区别了。这对网络的净化论者来说是可怕的事情。

但是,互联网上的公司并不一定要靠向顾客强行推销来赚钱。Virtual Vineyards,Amazon,Coin 和其他一些先驱者的例子表明,一个网络,如果卖的产品对路,再加上适当的互动性、热情的服务和良好的安全性,就会吸引网上客户。而且计算机的价格不断下降,这对那些在网上开店的企业来说,是个好兆头。五年或十年以后,人们再回头看看今天,一定会奇怪为什么只有那么少的公司上网了。

Passage 2

题材:时文——社会变革

这篇文章很明显是来自于新闻报道,它具有很强的实效性,先介绍了安乐死在澳大利亚一个州被合法化的事件,然后又报道了各方对于这一事件的看法和态度。

5.正确答案 D)。本题问及第二段的段意。该段的第一句是主题句:这一立法的深刻意义可能要过一段时间才能为人们所理解。正好与 D)项"要经过一段时间才能意识到这一法案通过的意义"吻合。A)项"在其他国家对安乐死的反对来得很慢"与原文所说"在美国和加拿大,死亡权利运动正在积蓄力量,观察家正等待着多米诺骨牌开始倒下(即由此产生连锁反应,相继通过类似法案)"相抵触。B)项"内科医生和普通市民对安乐死所持意见相同"与原文"有些人如释重负,另一些人则对此进行了猛烈抨击,并谴责其草率通过"不符。C)项"该法案的草率通过主要是由于日益变化的科技"在文中找不到根据。

6.正确答案 B)。作者说"观察家正等着多米诺骨牌产生效应",这句话的内涵是什么?多米诺骨牌这种游戏的特点是头一张牌倒下,必然导致后面许多牌相继迅速倒下(一个又一个连锁反应)。在此,作者借此暗示类似法案的相继通过。符合 B)"美国,加拿大和其他国家可能会通过类似法案"的意思。A)项"观察家对安乐死的前景持观望态度"与此矛盾。C)项"观察家正等着看多米诺骨牌这种游戏的结果"只拘泥于字面意思。D)项"通过的法案在实施过程中可能最终被终止"在文中毫无根据。

7.正确答案 A)。尼克森死的时候会如何?从文章结尾,可以看出他对安乐死的看法:死亡本身并不可怕,可怕的是像其他患者那样痛苦地死去,而安乐死的合法化让他可以从容地面对死亡了。选项 A)"他将带着安乐死所特有的平静面对死亡"符合这个意思。B)"经历肺癌患者的痛苦"和 C)"非常恐惧极度的痛苦"都是病人原来的担心,与现在事实相反。D)"经历七天的冷静思考时间"与本题不切题。

8.正确答案 C)。作者对安乐死态度如何?本题涉及对全文的归纳推断,从通篇来看,他没有表示 A)"反对"的态度,而说"这是不可逆转的潮流",安乐死可以减轻临终病人的痛苦的折磨。可见,他是 C)"赞同"的态度。B)"怀疑"和 D)"漠不关心"与文中作者所述矛盾。

译文

投票最终进行是在凌晨 3 点 45 分,在经过了 6 个月的讨论和议会 16 个小时的激烈辩论之后,最终澳大利亚的北部地区成为世界上第一个允许医生合法帮助无药可治的病人进行安乐死的地区。这项法案最终是以 15 比 10 的多数票通过。这个消息立刻就在互联网上传开了,在地球的另一边,加拿大死亡权力协会执行主席 John Hofsess 马上把这个消息发到了该组织的网站 Death NET 上。Hofsess 说:"我们整天都在贴帖子,因为这件事并不只是澳大利亚的事,这是整个世界历史上的大事。"

人们还需要一段时间才能了解这整个事件的重要性。澳大利亚北部地区制定的这项关于晚期病人的法律使得医生和普通公民都在考虑它在道德和实际生活方面的意义。有些人放心地松了一口气,有些人,包括教会、生存权力组织和澳大利亚医药协会,则猛烈抨击这项法案,认为它的通过太草率。但是潮流不可能再逆转了。在澳在利亚——那里的人口老龄化问题,生命延长技术,和社会态度的转变,都在分别施加各自的影响——其他地区也将考虑通过类似的有关安乐死的法案。在美国和加拿大,随着死亡权力运动不断发展扩大,观察家们正静候着连锁反应的发生。

新的北部地区法律规定,成年患者可以要求用注射或药片结束自己的痛苦。患者必须由两位医生诊断为患有不治之症,并且在冷静七天之后,病人就可以签署申请书,这之后的 48 小时之后,病人的愿望就可以实现。对于 54 岁身患肺癌的达尔文市居民 Lloyd Nickson 来说,这项法案意味着他不用成天担心因为窒息而痛苦地死去了。他说:"从精神上来说,我并不害怕死亡,但我担心的是将会怎样死去,因为我曾看到过医院里的病人因喘不上气来,抓着氧气面具痛苦地死去。"

Passage 3

题材:社会科学——经济学——广告

本文是一篇论述广告在现代社会经济生活中地位的文章。注意从第一句话开始,作者就全面肯定了广告的作用,因此他对广告的态度可以说是全面肯定的。

9.正确答案 D)。本题问第一句中,作者想说什么。第一句的意思是:"花钱做广告是我知道的最好的花钱方式"。此句是全文的主题。接着,作者指出了广告给厂家和普通人带来的好处。第二段中,作者接着论述广告给消费者带来的益处。由此可以知道,正确答案为 D)"花钱做广告值得"。其余各项均为与第一段第一句不符。

10.正确答案 A)。本题为是非题,可采用排除法。A)"获得更大的声誉"在文中未曾涉及,因此A)正确。B)"提供更多的工作"与文章第一段第四句"通过促进需求的增加,它确保对劳动力的需求,因此是抵制失业的有效方法"一致。C)"提高生活水平"与第一段第三句"通过把人们的注意力吸引到新观念上来,它有助于极大提高生活水平"内容一致。D)"降低报纸成本"与第一段最后一句"它降低了许多服务的成本,如没有广告,日报价格会上涨四倍,"内容一致。

11.正确答案 D)。本题问作者认为电视名人如何。本题关键要体会作者在评论电视名人观点时的用词。电视名人的观点在第四段第二句,他反对广告,认为,广告的目的在于劝说而不在于提供信息。第三、四句中,作者提出了自己的观点:"他分得太细了。当然,广告力求去说服人。"这表明作者不同意电视名人的观点。由此可知,D)"对广告的看法明显有偏见"为正确答案。

12.正确答案 C)。本题问作者的观点。参看第四段最后一句"当然,广告力求去说服人"和最后一段第一句。作者认为:广告应带有说服性。如果广告内容仅限于信息,则广告会令人生厌。由此可知,C)"广告劝购物者购物并没有错"为正确答案。A)"广告不可能通过提供信息给人带来物质利益"与第三段作者的观点相反。B)"广告给人们提供新的观念而不是争取购买者"与作者观点明显不符。D)"购买者对从广告中获取信息不感兴趣"文章未曾提及。

译文

花钱做广告是我们所知道的最好的花钱方式。它直接帮助货物以合理的价格快速地配送出去,以此在国内市场站稳脚跟,并可能以有竞争力的价格提供出口。广告能吸引人们关注新的概念,从而提升生活品质;广告能刺激需求,从而保证对劳动力的需求不断提高,这不失为对抗失业的有效方法。同时它也降低了许多服务的费用:没有广告,报纸的价格会提高三倍,有线电视费会翻番,公共汽车和地铁的费用会上涨 20%。

最重要的是,广告对人所购买的产品和服务提供了一种保障。国会有 27 项法案是针对广告的,此外,正式的广告公司不敢推销那些无法兑现承诺的商品。虚假广告不会长久,因为公众的眼光是敏锐的,他们决不会再上劣质商品的当。如果你看到一个商品在做广告,这就是它名副其实的最好证明,证明它的质量很好。

广告对社会物质利益的贡献比我所知道的其他任何东西的贡献都要大。

还有一点需要指出的是,最近我听说一位著名的电视人宣称他反对广告,因为他认为广告并不是提供信息,而是劝人去购买。他的区分过分精细了,广告当然是劝人买东西的。

如果广告仅仅是用来提供信息——即使这一点能够做到,那也是很困难的。因为即使是一个细节,比如衬衫的颜色,也有劝人购买的因素在里面——那么这样的广告就太乏味了,没有人会注意,但也许那位著名的电视人要的就是这种乏味。

Passage 4

题材:社会科学——经济

本文的中心思想是:作者对官僚主义管理下的今日社会不给人以独立性和个性发展的机会表示不满。

13.正确答案 C)。本题问作者用"机器中润滑良好的小齿轮"想表达什么观点。此处作者把现代社会中的人比作"a well-oiled cog in the machinery"(机器中润滑良好的齿轮),暗指人在社会中所发挥的作用如同大机器中的一个小齿轮一样,虽然发挥功能,但其作用是微不足道 的。这与 C)意思吻合。A)"尽管每个人的作用微不足道,人仍是社会不可分割的一部分"与内容不符。B)"人与社会的其余部分完全和睦相处"文章未提。D)"人是社会中一地位卑贱的零件,特别是工作顺利的时候"与内容不符。

14. 正确答案 D)。本题问工人和职员忧虑的真正原因是什么。文章第二段指出了工人和雇员的忧虑的原因:第一是可能失业(out of job),与 A)相符;第二是对生活不能得到真正的满足和兴趣,与 B)相符。第三也是最深刻的原因,他们一生都没有感受到这一这样一个事实:自己在情感和智力上都是一个独立的、有创造力的人,与 D)"被剥夺了个性和独立性"相符。他们一生没有去面对人类生存中的根本现实,与 C)相反。A)、B)只是部分的原因,而 D)也可能是造成A)、B)的原因,因此表达了这一问题的真正原因。

15. 正确答案 D)。本题问从这段中我们推论出真正幸福的生活属于谁。第三段最后一句指出"这种需要不断证明自己与竞争对手同样优秀或者超过对手从而不断地产生忧虑和压力,这正是不幸和疾病的起因。"也就是说,摆脱竞争所带来的忧虑和压力就可以得到真正的幸福和乐趣。这和 D)"远离竞争的世界"意思一致。其他三类人,即在社会底层的人:A),在社会上层的人,B)和证明比竞争对手好的人,C)均有忧虑(anxiety),因此 ,也就不幸福、不快乐。

16. 正确答案 C)。本题提问的是作者的结论。第四段第四句指出"我建议把我们的社会制度从以最大限度的生产和最大限度的消费为目的的官僚主义管理工业体制变成一个充分发挥人的潜能——如爱和理性的潜能——为目的的人道主义工业体制。"这和 C)"使人能充分发挥自己的潜能"意思一致。A)"求助于祖先的生产方式"、B)"给工人和雇员提高工资"和 D)"接受这些基本现实"三项在文中未提。

17. 正确答案 B)。本题问作者对工业体制的态度。本文作者指出了现代工业社会的种种弊端:第一段,人的地位微不足道;第二段,工人与雇员感到忧虑;第三段,上层社会的人们也感到忧虑。最后作者提出了改变这种社会体制提的建议。因此不难得出,作者认为现行的 industrialism 不好,所以他对其态度不是 A)"赞许"、D)"容忍"和 C)"怀疑"。作者在这里对 industrialism 的态度表达的明白无误,并不迟疑、犹豫,而是 B)"不满"。

译文

总的来说,我们的社会正在变成一个由官僚主义管理方式来统治的大企业。在这一企业中,人成了机器中润滑良好的小齿轮。小齿轮的润滑是通过高薪、通风良好的厂房、管乐及心理学家和人际关系专家来做的。然而,这种润滑并未改变这样一个事实:人已变得无能为力,不再全心全意投入于工作,并对工作感到厌烦。事实上,蓝领和白领工人已经成了伴随自动化机器和官僚主义管理方式的节奏翩翩起舞的经济玩偶。

工人与雇员心情焦虑不仅仅是因为他们可能失业,而且因为他们不能在生活中获得真正的满足和兴趣。他们一生没有作为情感上与智力上独立的、具有创造性的人去面对人类生存中基本的现实。

那些位于社会阶梯高层的人们也很忧虑。他们的生活同其下属一样空虚。在某些方面,他们更觉得不安全。他们如同参加一场高度竞争的竞赛。被提升或降职不仅仅是薪水问题,更是一个人的自尊问题。第一次申请工作时,他们即受到顺从和独立性须表现得恰如其分的综合测验,也受到了智力测验。自那时起,他们就不断受到心理学家和上司的测验。对心理学家而言,测验是他们的生财之道。上司的测验被用来判断他们的行为、社交能力及与人交往的能力等。这种需要不断地证明自己与竞争对手同样优秀或者超过对手,从而不断地产生忧虑和压力,这正是不幸和疾病的起因。

我是否在建议我们应回到工业化前的生产模式或回到十九世纪"自由企业"资本主义时期呢?当然不是。回到原来的时代不是解决问题的办法。我建议把我们的社会制度从以最大限度的生产和最大限度的消费为目的的官僚主义管理产业体制变成一个充分发挥人的潜能——如爱和理性的潜能——为目的的人道主义产业体制。生产和消费只能作为达到这一目的的手段,并应防止其控制人类。

Passage 5

题材:自然科学——创造性思维
本文主要论述了在科学创新中所必备的思维能力和思维方式。

18. 正确答案 A)。本题问第一段中的 untaught mind 是什么意思,即 untaught mind 在此文中的确切含义。词典给了两条词义"未受过教育的，无知的"。通过亚历山在发明青霉素的例子来说明一切发明创造都来自艰辛的劳动，而不像 untaught mind 所想象的那样。因此，那些人的想象只能是无知的表现，A)。而不是未受过教育的人，C)，因为未受过教育的人未必无知。

19. 正确答案 C)。本题问创新者与非创新者的区别是什么。第二段第二句指出"革新者与其他人主要不同之处是方法的不同"。此处的方法指的是处理解决问题的方法，不是陈述其发现的方法。故 C)正确。A)"他们所拥有的各种各样的方法"、B)"他们拥有科研成果"和 D)"他们陈述发现的方法"均未提及。

20. 正确答案 B)。本题问作者为何引用鲁道夫·佛莱切的话。本题关键在于弄懂其话的原意。原句的话表明，日常生活中许多小发明，这些小发明给人们的生活带来极大的便利。但是"以前为什么没人想到呢?"其意义在于说明，有些人能想到这样小发明就是因为他们勇于进行创造性思维，喜欢从新的角度去考虑问题，而不是按老方法去做事。这和 B)一致。A)"鲁道夫·佛莱切是研究人类创造性的专家"与内容不符。C)"读者熟悉鲁道夫·佛莱切的观点"文章未提。D)"引文对以前提出的信息提供新的观点"与内容不符，因为文章并无新观点出现。

21. 正确答案 B)。本题问 march to a different drummer(按不同的鼓点前进)的含义。本句在原文中是一种比喻，把科学研究比作行军。按一个鼓点行军，就显得单调。搞研究如只按传统方法，则很难有创新。这和 B)"不愿意按常规去做事"一致。A)"勤奋追求自己的目标"、C)"致力于科学的进步"和 D)"关注社会的发展"均与引文不符。

译文

一些不了解情况的人以为科学技术中的发现都迅如闪电一般，或者是戏剧性的偶然结果。但 Alexander Fleming 并不是像传说中的那样，看着奶酪上长出的霉，在那一瞬间就想到了青霉素。在这一发现之前，他已经花了九年的时间试验抗生素物质。发明创造总是来自辛勤的试验和不断的错误之后。创新就像踢足球，即使是最好的球员也会失球，球被挡回来的机会总是比进球的机会要多的多。

比赛中得分最多的球员正是那些射门次数最多的，任何领域中的发明创造也是这样。发明家和其他人的主要区别在于对待事情的方法，每个人都会有些点子，但发明家有意识去试验自己的想法，直到最终证明可行或不可行。而普通人认为是奇思怪想的东西，在职业发明家的眼里也许就是极大的可能。

语言学权威 Rudolph Flesch 曾写道:"创造性思维的含义也许就是认识到没有必要总是循规蹈矩地做事情。"这道出了我们对一些发明的反应，如塑料垃圾袋和带轮子的行李箱，它们外表简单，但给我们的生活却带来了极大的方便，我们总是想"为什么以前没有人想到呢?"

创造性源自于认为事情并不像它们表现出来的那样，发明家从不认为做一件事情的方法只有一种。普通人在面临从 A 到 B 的问题时会自动采取最为人熟悉，并且从表面上看起来是最简单的路线，而发明家则会寻找其他可能，这种可能从长远看来会更加简便，而且即使领人走入了死胡同也非常有趣和富有挑战性。

具有创新思想的人的确有与众不同的想法。

对比题答案

Passage

题材:人文科学——语言

本文介绍语言对孩子的影响。

1. 正确答案 B)。本文问 Frederick Ⅱ的实验目的。文中第一段最后一句指出:"为了发现婴儿在听不到母语的情况下会讲什么语言，他要求保育员保持沉默。"这表明了 Frederick Ⅱ实验的目的，与 B)"弄清楚听不到任何人类语言时孩子会讲什么语言"内容一致。A)"证明婴儿生来就有说话的能力"和 C)"查明细心护理在婴儿说话中起什么作用"在第一段未提。D)"证明婴儿不学习语言可能会受到伤害"在第一段虽提到，但不是其实验目的。

2. 正确答案 C)。本文问一些婴儿学习说话晚的主要原因是什么。文中第三段第三句指出:"其原因往往是母亲对大脑已作好快速学习语言准备的婴儿所发出的信号不敏感。"这与 C)"对孩子

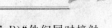

说话所做的努力没有充分的反应"内容一致。A)"他们不能快速学习语言"、B)"他们同时接触的语言太多"和D)"他们的母亲不够聪明,不能教他们"在文章中均未提到。

3. 正确答案 C)。本文问小孩子最杰出的方面是什么。文章第五段最后一句话指出:"更令人难以相信的是婴儿从其周围杂乱的声音中识别语言顺序的能力。以及分析和按新的方式组合与重新组合语言要素的能力。"这和 C)"他能发出自己的句子"一致。A)"他生来具有说话的能力"是第五段第一句提到的事实,但不是婴儿最杰出的方面。B)"他的大脑比动物的大脑复杂"在第五段第二句提到,但也不是作为婴儿特殊之处给出的。D)"他的语言能力应归功于良好的护理"显然不是答案。此题要注意文章措辞:And even more incredible(更令人难以相信)表明此特点为最杰出的方面。

4. 正确答案 B)。本题问,下列哪项无法从文章中推断出来。A)"说话能力是先天的"与第五段第一句:"最新的资料表明,婴儿生来就有说话的能力"一致。C)"婴儿的大脑具有很高的选择性"与第五段第三句"更令人难以相信的是婴儿从其周围杂乱的声音中识别语言顺序的能力,以及分析按新的方式组合与重新组合语言部件的能力"意思一致。D)"多数孩子在一定的年龄学会语言"与第四段第一句"专家们认为,不同语言阶段的发展是按固定的顺序和年龄实现的"意思一致。B)"在婴儿学习语言的过程中,鼓励一点儿也不重要"与文章内容相反。

5. 正确答案 D)。本题问,如果一个小孩子比别的小孩说话晚,将来会怎样。第四段第一句后半句指出"但是在某些情况中,开始说话晚的婴儿后来却有较高的智商。"这与 D)"未必迟钝"意思一致。A)"智商高"不符合逻辑。B)"不聪明"与内容相反。C)"对言语信号不敏感"文章中未提及。

译文

语言是否像食物一样,是人类的基本需要?没有语言,在生命的关键时期孩子是否会挨饿?孩子的身体是否会受损呢?从十三世纪 Fredeick Ⅱ 所做的大量实验中判断,情况也许就是如此。为了发现婴儿在听不到母语的情况下会讲什么语言,他要求保育员保持沉默。

所有婴儿在一年之内都死了。不过很显然,这里缺乏的不仅仅是语言,还缺乏好的母爱。没有好的母爱,生存能力,特别是生命的第一年,会受到严重的影响。

今天,当初 Frederick Ⅱ 所要求的那种严重缺乏的情况已不复存在。然而,一些孩子语言仍然迟钝。其原因往往是母亲对大脑已作好快速学习语言准备的婴儿所发出的信号不敏感。如果这些敏感时期被忽略,获取技能的理想阶段被错过,那么,这些婴儿就可能再也不会如此容易地学习了。鸟在适当的时机很快学会鸣叫与飞翔,但是,一旦错过关键阶段,这一学习过程就会既缓慢又艰难。

专家们认为,不同语言阶段的发展是按固定的顺序和年龄实现的,但是,在某些情况下,开始说话晚的婴儿长大后拥有较高的智商。十二周时,婴儿会笑并会发出元音似的声音;十二个月时,能讲简单的词语,听懂简单的命令;十八个月时,大约有词汇量三到五十个。三岁时,大约认识 1000 个词,并能用这些词造句。四岁时,其语言与父母的不同只表现在风格上而不是语法方面。

最新的资料表明,婴儿生来就有说话的能力。与猴脑相比,人脑的特殊之处在于其复杂的系统。这一复杂系统使婴儿把所见所感联系起来,比如,把玩具熊及其发音联系起来。更令人难以相信的是婴儿从其周围纷乱的声音中识别语言顺序的能力,以及分析和按新的方式组合与重组语言要素的能力。

但是,言语必须加以引导,这取决于母子之间的互动。在母子的互动中,母亲识别出婴儿咿呀学语、抓挠及微笑中的信号,并对信号作出反应。母亲对信号置之不理会削弱母子间的互动。因为孩子得不到鼓励就会只发出那些明显的信号。对婴儿非言语信号的反应灵敏对于婴儿语言的形成和发展是至关重要的。

例证题答案

Passage 1

题材:自然科学——人工智能

本文是 2002 年第一篇科技文章,有一定的难度,它主要介绍了机器人科技的发展,以及机器人和人类在智能上的差距。

1. 正确答案 C）。本题问，人类的创造力最早表现在什么地方。根据第一段第一句"自从人类萌发了创造力，他们就开始设计越来越精巧的工具来处理危险、乏味、累人或令人讨厌的工作"，选择 C）"发明处理困难和危险工作的工具"。A）"使用机器来制作科幻小说"与原文不符。文章第一段只提到科学家还需创造出机器版的科幻小说。B）"机器在制造业的广泛使用"和 D）"精英们对危险和乏味工作的精明处理"是事实，但与该问题不符。

2. 正确答案 C）。本题问"gizmos"一词最可能是什么意思。该词所在段落前一段提到机器人的诞生，该词所在段落谈到机器人的应用所以推断 C）"器械"为正确答案，排除 A）"项目"、B）"专家"和 D）"生物"。

3. 正确答案 D）。本题问，按照该文，现在设计什么样的机器人超出人类的能力。根据第三段第一句"他们（指机器人）的运行在更大程度上不需受人监督，并且至少能够自己作出一些决定"和最后一句"我们还不能给机器人以足够的'常识'使其有把握地与一个不断变化的世界互动"，选择 D）"独立地对不断变化的世界作出反应"。排除 C）"有点常识"。A）"做像大脑手术一样的精细工作"与文章内容不符，因为第二段结尾已经提到机器人具备这方面的能力。B）"用人类语言交流"没有提到。

4. 正确答案 B）。本题问，除了减少人类劳动，机器人还能干什么。根据最后一段第二句"他们制造出的机器人能够在人工控制的工厂环境下识别机器控制面板上不到一毫米的误差"，选择 B）"在人的干预下处理一些误差"。A）"自己作决定"与第三段第一句"他们（指机器人）的运行在更大程度上不需受人监控，并且至少能够自己作出一些决定——这些是具有真正挑战性的目标"，是下一个目标，而不是现在可以实现的。与所提问题不符。C）"改善工厂环境"和 D）"培养人类创造力"没有提到。

5. 正确答案 C）。本题问，作者举猴子一例来论证机器人怎样。根据最后一段结尾一句"这一点连世界上最先进的计算机系统也望尘莫及"，选择 C）"在集中精力于相关信息上远不如人脑"。A）"在内部结构上机器人应模仿人脑"不符合原文内容。第四段指出科学家在这方面已作出努力，但没有成功。B）"能够马上认知异常事物"与所举事例说明的内容相反。D）"在控制环境中利用得最好"不是作者要说明的问题。

译文

自从人类开始发现自己的创造力以来，人们设计出越来越聪明的工具来应付那些危险的、乏味的、繁重的、甚至仅仅是脏一些的工作。这种发明的冲动最终导致了机器人技术的出现——就是将各种人类的能力赋予机器的技术。科学家已经开始接近创造出机械版的科学幻想小说了。

结果是，越来越多聪明的小玩意儿成为现代社会的居民。人们几乎没有注意到它们，但它们的普遍存在节约了大量的劳力。我们的工厂伴随着机械装配手臂的节奏嗡嗡作响。银行自动出纳终端为我们办理银行业务，并用机械的声音礼貌地感谢我们的交易。我们的地铁由不知疲倦的机器人司机操纵。由于微电子技术和微型机械学的不断发展，已经出现了能够进行各种脑部和骨科手术的机器人系统，它们的精确程度能达到亚毫米的级别，再高明的医生仅靠双手也远远无法达到这种精确程度。

但是如果机器人想要进一步实现节省劳力的作用，它们就得减少对人类监督的依赖，至少有些决定得由自己来做——这一目标是一个真正的挑战。NASA 负责机器人技术的 Dave Lavery 说："尽管我们已经知道如何让机器人处理某个特定的错误，我们还无法让机器人有足够的'常识'，来与这个动态的世界进行可靠的互动。"

的确，对真正的人工智能的探索产生了喜忧参半的结果。20 世纪 60 年代和 70 年代曾有一段最初的乐观时期，人们认为到 2010 年，晶体管电路和微处理器似乎就能够复制人类大脑的活动。最近，研究者已经开始把这个期限向后推迟几十年、甚至几个世纪。

在试图模仿人类思维的过程中，研究者发现，人类大脑的大约一千亿个神经细胞比以前想像的更聪明，人类的知觉活动也更复杂。科学家已经造出了在受控制的环境下能够识别极小误差的机器人。但是人类的头脑能对一个迅速改变的场景在一瞥之下，迅速抛弃其中 98%的无关信息，瞬间定位在蜓蜒的林间小路旁的那只猴子或人群中那张可疑的面孔上。世界上最先进的电脑系统也无法达到这种能力,而神经系统科学家目前还不知道我们怎样做的。

Passage 2

题材:社会科学——法律——社会问题——时文

本文是全年试题中最难的一篇,论述的是美国最高法院对于医生帮助身患绝症的病人结束生命的行为作出的道德和法律的裁决。作者援引了一些法律和医学界人士的观点,从而从另一方面表达了作者的观点。

6. 正确答案 B)。本题问,从前三段可以得知什么。本题属于细节题。第二段第一句中的"目前对于安乐死还未从宪法上明确这一权力"这部分内容和答案 B)"医生帮助病人结束生命仍然是违法的"一致。选项 A)"医生过去常通过增加药量来减轻病人的痛苦"范围过宽,与原文第三段中的"减轻重危病人的痛苦"不符。选项 C)"最高法院强烈反对医生帮助下的自杀"与第二段内容不符。选项 D)"宪法没有赋予病人自杀的权力"本文未涉及。

7. 正确答案 C)。本题问,根据全文哪一项选项正确。可通过对照排除法求解。选项 A)"如医生危及到病人生命将被认为有罪。"与第二段内容相反。选项 B)"现代医学已帮助濒危病人在无痛苦中康复。"文中未提。选项 C)"法院裁定认为可以开高剂量的止痛药物。"与第二段中"最高法院支持'双重效果'的医疗原则。这几个世纪以来的医疗道德原则认为,如果一种行为具有双重效果——有以治病为目的的良好效果又有可预见的有害效果——而为了实现治病这一良好效果,允许医生实施治疗而不考虑其有害效果"和第三段中"近几年来,医生们一直在奉行这一原则,大剂量使用吗啡来减轻重危病人的痛苦"内容一致。选项 D)"医生的为病人止痛的目的不能成为大量用药的理由"与第二段中和第三段上述内容相反。

8. 正确答案 B)。本题问,根据国家科学院(NAS)的报告,临终护理存在的问题之一是什么。本题为细节题,比较容易。文章第七段报告标题《接近死亡:加强临终护理》所提到的"undertreatment of pain"和选项 B)"inadequate treatment of pain"属于同义表达法。A)"延长治疗过程"和原文第七段中提到的"坚持见效疗法……延长病人死亡时间"意思不符。C)"蓄意滥用药物"文中未提。D)"医院护理不够"属于范围概括过宽。

9. 正确答案 A)。这是一道词义题。做题关键是分析上下文,猜测该词词义。aggressive 一词并不是难词,属于四级词汇,其词义为:1. 侵略的;2. 过分的,放肆的;3. 敢作敢为的,不缩手缩脚的。根据该词出现的上下句,词义应是第三条,其对应选项应是 A)"bold"译为大胆的,鲁莽的。其他三项的词义均相差甚远。

10. 正确答案 D)。这是一道局部推论题。本题问,如果医生怎样做应受到惩罚。参看最后一段安纳斯所说的话"行医执照颁发机构必须清楚,令人痛苦的死亡可以认定是治疗不当造成的后果,应当吊销其行医执照。"可以得出 D)"延长病人不必要的痛苦"为正确答案。A)"对病人治疗不当",B)"对病人超量用药"和 C)"减少病人的用药剂量"均与文章内容不符。

译文

最高法院对医生协助安乐死这一事件的决定,对医学界应该怎样帮助垂死的病人减轻痛苦有很重要的意义。

尽管法院裁定宪法并没有规定医生有帮助病人自杀的权利,但是它实际上支持了一条医学界古老的道德准则——"双重效果"原则,即:一个行为有两重效果,一个是想要达到的好的结果,一个是可以预见的坏的结果,只要采取这个行为的人的本意是为了达到好的结果,那么这个行为就是允许的。

近年来,医生们已经在用这个原则来为自己使用大剂量的吗啡控制晚期病人的疼痛开脱了,即使增大剂量会最终导致病人的死亡。Montefiore 医疗中心的院长 Nancy Dubler 称,这条原则能保护那些直到现在仍强烈坚持如果大剂量药物会加速死亡,那么他们就无法给病人足够的药来控制疼痛的医生。

波士顿大学卫生法系的主任 George Annas 主张,只要一个医生开的药是为了合法的医疗目的,那么他就没做任何非法的事情,即使病人用他开的药来加速自己的死亡。他说:"这就像动手术一样。

我们不把手术中的死亡叫做谋杀，因为医生并不想杀死自己的病人，尽管他们冒着病人死亡的危险。如果你是个医生，你也可以冒病人自杀的危险，只要你并不想造成他们的自杀。"

另一方面，医学界许多人士承认激起这一场关于医生协助自杀的讨论的部分原因是病人的绝望情绪。对他们来说，现代医学只是延长了他们等待死亡、忍受肉体疼痛的时间而已。

在法院对医生协助自杀做出判决的三个星期之前，国家科学院（NAS）公布了一份长达两卷的报告《临近死亡：改善临终关怀的质量》。报告认为临终关怀的两个重要问题是：对疼痛的治疗不够和过分使用"强制的、无效的医疗手段来延长、甚至污辱死亡的过程"。

医学界正在采取措施，要求年轻医生在收容所里实习，来考验他们用大胆的方法来治疗疼痛的知识，为在医院中开展临终关怀制定医疗保险制度，以及建立新的准则来评定和治疗临终前的疼痛。

Annas说在坚持使这些医学界自发的、本意很好的举动转变成对临终病人更好的关怀方面，律师可以起到很重要的作用。"很多医生对他们的病人所遭受的可以想像的巨大痛苦无动于衷"甚至到了"有系统的虐待病人"的程度。他说行医执照的管理部门"必须明确……痛苦的死亡是治疗不得力造成的，应该暂停医生的行医执照。"

词汇题答案

Passage 1

题材：自然科学与人文科学结合

本文主要介绍了自然科学和人文科学之间的关系，同时透视了科学家们用"反科学"这一标签来攻击他人的行为及动机。

1. 正确答案 C）。此题问"schism"一词在上下文中的含义。从上下文可以作出判断，该词意为"uneasy relationship"即科学与文化其他方法之间这种不和谐的关系，而两者原本属于同一范畴，它们之间的矛盾可视为两方面的分裂、割裂，所以 C）项正确。B）"不满"和 D）"藐视"不符合题意，A）项指"对抗，冲突"，含有敌意，在意思上有出入。

2. 正确答案 D）。作者在第二段和第三段中所陈述的事实旨在证明什么主题？第一段最后一句已经表明自然科学与人文科学之间的差别在加深。第二段第二句用一个事实表明这一分歧：科学家们写了几本书来抨击反科学的观点。第三段指出自然科学捍卫者不仅"笔伐"，还通过集会来表达他们的观点，捍卫科学的尊严。故选项 D）"举例说明自然科学与人文科学之间出现分裂"正确。A）"论述科学力量削弱的原因"与第二段所述大相径庭。B）"表现作者对科学家的同情"也没有事实依据，作者只是在文中陈述客观事实，并未发表主观评论。C）"解释科学发展的方法"不符合事实。

3. 正确答案 A）。本题问依据原文，下面哪种说法正确，宜用排除法。选项 A）"有文章批评环保主义者是反科学的"在第六段第二句可以找到依据。C）"自己比别人高明的人喜欢给别人冠以反科学的称谓"与文章最后一句话有出入。B）"政治家没有被冠以反科学的称谓"与文章第五段矛盾。D）"把环保主义者冠以反科学的称谓是公平的"有悖原意，也与第七段不符。

4. 正确答案 A）。该题问对于科学与反科学的问题，作者持什么态度？在整个篇章中，作者始终在客观公正地从各个角度引用实例向读者展示两派之间的论战及其分歧所在，并未直接发表评论，表明主观意图。故 A）"公平的"正确。B）"主观的"、C）"有偏见的，有偏向性的"和 D）"困惑的，令人费解的"都不对。

译文

科学与其他文化领域的关系一向不睦，比如你可以回想一下 17 世纪伽利略因为其叛逆思想而在天主教会受到审判，或者是诗人 William Blake 对牛顿的机械论世界观的猛烈抨击。到了本世纪，科学和人文学科之间的裂痕愈加扩大了。

以前科学界的势力曾经非常强大，以至于可以忽略它的批评者，但是近来情况发生了变化。随着对科学研究资助的减少，科学家开始写书批判"反科学"，例如比较有名的书有：弗吉尼亚大学生物学家 Paul R. Gross 和 Rutgers、大学数学家 Norman Levitt 所著的《更高级的迷信》，以及康奈尔大学的 Carl Sagan 所著的《鬼魂出没的世界》。

科学的维护者还在一些会议上表达他们的关切,例如1995年在纽约召开的"科学和理智的腾飞"的会议,和去年6月在布法罗附近召开的主题为"信息/错误信息时代的科学"的会议。

反科学对于不同的人来说,意义也不同。Gross和Levitt批判的对象主要是社会学家、哲学家和其他对科学的客观性提出质疑的学者。Sagan反对的对象则主要是那些相信鬼魂、创世论及相信其他与科学观点背道而驰的现象的人。

1996年进行的一次对新书的调查显示,"反科学"的标签也被贴在了很多别的人群的身上,包括提倡根除残余的天花病毒的权威机构,以及提倡削减基础科学研究资金的共和党人。

将"反科学"的标签使用在Unabomber组织身上是无可非议的,他们在1995年发表的宣言中嘲笑科学,并希望回到一个没有科学技术的乌托邦状态。但是,去年五月"美国新闻和世界报道"上的一篇文章称那些对无控制的工业增长表示关切的环境主义者为"反科学",这显然是没有道理的。

对于这样的批评,不用说,环境主义者当然要反唇相讥。斯坦福大学环境研究的先锋Paul Ehrlich评论说:科学的真正敌人,是那些对全球变暖、臭氧层损耗和其他工业增长导致的恶果不愿相信的人。

实际上,观察家们担心"反科学"的头衔正面临着失去意义的危险。哈佛大学的哲学教授Gerald Hilton在他1993年出版的作品《科学和反科学》一书中指出:"反科学一词能包含那么多不同的内容,这些内容只有一点共同的,就是它们能够激怒或者威胁到那些自认为比别人更有知识的人。"

Passage 2

题材:社会科学——经济学

此文是一篇对美国经济结构的简介,从文章的风格来看,可能是从美国大学课本中节选而出。文章主要论述了美国的经济以私营企业为基础,以市场为导向,以及价格决定机制。

5. 正确答案D)。maximize通常有两条词义;一是"把……增加到最大限度,"二是"充分利用……"。maximize profit意为"把利润提高到最大限度",而maximize their income意为"充分利用他们的收入",即用现有的收入买最多的东西。这和D)"美国人想提高收入的购买力"一致,所以,D)是答案。A)"美国人对收入从不满意"和B)"美国人往往对收入过分夸张"内容相差甚远。C)"美国人想提高收入"文中未提。

6. 正确答案D)。第二段前两句译文是"市场型经济中的一个重要因素是由反映消费者需求以及生产者对消费者需求作出反应的机制。美国经济中,这一机制是价格体制决定的,价格随消费者的相对需求与生产者的供应情况而上下起伏。"这和D)"供求调节价格"意思一致。故D)是正确的。A)"生产商能够通过机械化生产满足消费者需求"未提。B)"消费者通过生产者表达他们的要求"与内容不符。C)"生产者决定产品的价格"文中未提。

7. 正确答案A)。文章问"私有企业经济的特点是什么"。在文章最后一段最后一句中作者指出"在美国经济中,私有财产的概念不仅包括生产资料的所有权,也包括某些权利,包括产品价格的决定权或与其他私有个体的自由签约权。"这和A)"私有财产及相关的权利"一致。故A)是正确的。B)、C)、D)三项概括不全。

8. 正确答案C)。本题问文章中心思想。文章第一段从生产者和消费者两方面讲述了美国经济体系的构成;第二段讲市场调节的作用。第三段讲私有企业的特征。第二、三段是对第一段的展开论述。因此只有C)"美国经济体制是如何运作的"概括全篇内容。故C)是解。A)、B)、D)均是生产过程的一个环节。

译文

美国的经济体系是围绕一个基本中心进行组织的,那就是以私有企业为主体,以市场为导向。在这种体系中,消费者通过在市场上消费来决定最需要什么样的产品和服务。私有企业为了获得利润,生产这些产品或提供这些服务,并和其他企业竞争,而这种竞争压力下的谋利动机在很大程度上决定了如何生产这些产品和提供服务。这样,在美国的经济体系下,消费者的个人需求,商人追求利益最大化的欲望,个人对收入最大化的要求,这些加在一起共同决定了生产什么和怎样利用有限的原料来进行生产。

在以市场为导向的经济体制中有一个重要的因素,就是要建立起一种合理的机制使消费者的需求得以体现,并传达到生产者那里。在美国经济中,这一机制是由价格体系来充当的,就是通过价格的涨落来表现供求关系。如果某种产品供不应求,价格就会上涨,某些消费者就会退出市场;相反,大批量生产某种商品导致成本降低,这会造成这种商品的供应增加,而使价格降低,使更多的消费者能够购买。价格就是这样在美国的经济体系中起着调节作用。

在以私有企业为主体的经济体制中,一个重要的因素是,允许个人拥有生产资料,允许他们雇用劳动力,掌握自然资源,来生产产品和提供服务以获取利润。在美国经济中,私有制不光是指生产资料的所属形式,还包括某些权利,比如产品价格的决定权,以及和其他私有个体自由签订协议的权利。

Passage 3

题材:社会科学——经济学

本文若是只读第一段的话极易被理解成关于银行或金融服务的文章,但是如果我们从整体上把握,就可以看出第一段对于银行或金融服务的论述只不过是论述计算机技术在经济领域的广泛应用的一个方面,因此要从这一点出发来把握全文的意思。

9. 正确答案 B)。本题问及"信用卡持有者可以干什么"。第一段作者指出"信用卡持有者可在商店、饭店、宾馆,在当地、外地甚至国外赊购货物,同时还可以使他们得到银行提供的许多服务。越来越多的信用卡可以自动读取,于是持卡人就可以在不同地方存取钱,不管本地支行是否营业。"这和 B)"比其他人享有更多的便利服务"一致。故 B)是解。A)"从银行想取多少钱就取多少钱"显然与事实不符。C)"更能得到店主的信任"文中未提。D)"想在哪儿兑换钱就在哪儿兑换钱"属于概括面太宽。

10. 正确答案 C)。第一段最后一句的意思是:对于我们许多人来说,"无现金社会"不是刚刚兴起,而是早已存在。这和 C)"当今许多美国人不用支付现金"最接近。故 C)是解。从该句中推论不出 A)"将来所有美国人都将使用信用卡",B)"目前信用卡主要在美国使用",D)"现在比过去使用信用卡更方便"三项内容。

11. 正确答案 B)。本题测试判断生词的能力。判断生词词义关键是联系上下文。第二段中作者列举了电子收款机的许多用途。因此 ring up sales 应该指"记录销售额"。这和 B)一致。A)"定货"、C)"呼叫销售经济"和 D)"跟踪库存货物"均与该短语相差甚远。

12. 正确答案 B)。本题问文章中心思想。全文三个自然段。第一段概括讲信用卡为持卡人带来的好处;第二段所用篇幅最多,详细讲述计算机在各种商业活动中给商家带来的好处;第三段讲计算机的应用范围之广。因此,三段文章中,有两段讲述计算机的应用,故 B)"商业使用计算机所带来的好处"是解。A)"商业使用计算机的方法"在第二段有所提及,但概括不全。C)"自动化在商业活动中的重要性"中,自动化一词使用过宽。D)"信用卡在企业中的优势"概括较窄。

译文

一亿一千三百万美国人目前拥有银行信用卡。信用卡使其持有者在商场、饭店、宾馆、家中、国内、甚至国外都拥有信用,同时也能完成许多银行业务。随着越来越多的信用卡可以自动读取,人们可以在不同地方存钱和取钱,即便这些地方没有银行的分支机构也没有关系。对我们大多数人来说,一个"没有现金的社会"已经实现了。

计算机给消费者提供这些便利的同时也给商家提供了很多方便。电子收款机不仅能记录每笔款项,还能记录很多内容,如谁在什么时间卖了什么东西,买方是谁。这些信息使得商家能够跟踪货物信息,了解是什么商品在流动及其流动的速度,从而决定再从哪些供货商那里订货,或将某些货物退还给供货商。同时,计算机也能记录下营业的高峰时间,以及哪些雇员的工作效率最高,从而帮助雇主做出人事的安排,这些记录还能显示促销活动针对的顾客群。也正是因为这些原因,产品制造商也要依赖电脑。电脑分析的市场报告能帮助决定哪些商品是现在的重点,哪些将来要研发,哪些应该淘汰。电脑能够记录库存情况,原材料的多少,甚至生产过程本身。

数不清的其他商业企业,从影剧院到出版社,从电站、气站到牛奶厂,通过电脑向消费者提供更好更高效的服务。

是非判断题答案

Passage 1

题材：社会科学——经济史

本文主要论述了英国19世纪后期劳资关系的变化，重点阐述的是股东作为一个阶层的出现对劳资关系的消极影响。

1. 正确答案C）。该题问对于老的家族式商号，下面哪个论述是对的。根据文章第一段中间部分："很多老商号被有限公司所取代……来满足新时代的技术要求……防止了效益的下降……"应选C）"与现代公司相比，它们缺乏效益"。A）"它们被晚辈们毁掉了"不准确，该选项可使人理解为晚辈们有意地毁掉那些企业。B）"因缺乏创新而垮掉了"与原文内容相违背，企业垮掉了不是因为缺乏创新，而是因为效益下降。D）"它们能对上税人提供充足的服务"未提到。

2. 正确答案A）。该题问有限公司的发展导致什么后果。根据文章第二段前边部分：这种庞大的非个人操纵的资本与企业大大地增加了股东作为一个阶层的数量和重要性……代表了非个人负责的财富及土地所有者应尽义务的分离，而且几乎同样与责任管理相分离。"这里所说的"财富"即"资本"，这与A）"资本与管理的分离"吻合。B）"管理人员对资本的拥有权"与原文内容相反，只有股东对资本有所有权。C）"出现了资方和劳方两个阶层"，D）"土地拥有者股东的参与"在文章中都未提到。

3. 正确答案C）。该题问除了下面哪一项，其余各项都是对的。A）项"股东未意识到工人的需要"在最后一段第一句提到。B）项"老的商号所有者更了解工人的需要"在最后一段第二句提到。D）项"工会似乎起到积极的作用"在最后一段倒数第二句提到。只有C）"有限公司太庞大而难以顺利地运转"未提到。

4. 正确答案D）。该题问作者对谁最持批评态度。本文在第二段和最后一段提到资本与管理的分离，股东未意识到工人的需要等，这都是对股东的批评。A）"家族式商号所有者"，B）"土地拥有者"和C）"管理人员"均不符合题意。"

译文

二十世纪后期，"资本"和"劳动力"两大敌对阵营在更加现代化的条件下，在不断地发展壮大。许多老式的公司被有限责任公司所代替，这些新型公司雇用拿薪水的经理人来进行管理。这种变化是符合新时代的工业需要的，它将职业化元素引入企业，防止了那种在老式家族企业中经常出现的第一代创始人之后的两三代人中工作效率下降，从而妨害公司前途的现象发生。这种机制逐渐摆脱了依靠个人的积极性，而转向集体制和由国家、市政掌管的企业。尽管铁路仍然是为股东牟利的私有企业，但和那些老式的家族企业有很大区别。同时，市政当局入主企业，为纳税人提供电力、交通和其他服务。

有限责任公司的发展壮大和市政企业的介入产生了重要的影响。这种大规模、非个人性质的资金运作大大增加了股东这一社会阶层的人数和重要性，而股东阶层在社会生活中象征着财富与土地及土地拥有者的责任分离开来；同时，财富也与企业经营管理责任分离开来。整个十九世纪，美洲、非洲、印度、澳大利业以及欧洲的部分国家都是在英国的资金扶持下发展起来的，因此英国的股票持有者的腰包就在全球工业化的浪潮中充实了起来。Bournemouth和Eastbourne等城市就居住了一大批"闲适"阶级，他们有收入，又不用工作，除了拿红利和偶尔出席一次股东会议把他们的命令传达给管理人外，他们和社会上的其他人几乎没有什么联系。另一方面，"持有股票"意味着闲适和自由，这也是维多利亚时代很多人对社会文明的最高期望。

这些"股东"并不了解那些在他们持有股份的公司里劳动的工人们的生活、想法和需要，而且他们对资方和劳方之间的关系也没有什么好的影响。经理人受雇替公司工作，他们和工人的接触更直接一些，但即使是这样，现代经理人对工人的了解和过去那种家族式企业中用家长制进行管理的企业主相比，也远远不如。确实，现代企业的规模和工人的数量也使得这种熟悉和了解不可能实现。然而幸运的是，至少在所有技术行业中，工会的组织和力量不断发展壮大，使工人和公司的管理都能在平等的条件下对话。罢工和停工的严重后果使双方谁也不能小看对方的力量,同时也理解了公平谈判的作用。

Passage 2

题材:社会科学——社会学

这是一篇关于当今日本社会变化的文章,作者着重论述了日本目前的道德、伦理以及人们对于工作、生活等态度的变化及其所带来的危机。

5. 正确答案 B)。文章第一句中 Whose 引导的从句"whose productivity and social harmony are the envy of the United States and Europe."表明了西方人对日本的看法,日本的生产率和社会稳定让西方国家感到羡慕,因此战后日本是一个成功的典范,是一个正面的例子,故 B)项正确;注意文中用的是双重否定,"aimlessness"与"hardly"说明战后日本的发展并不是毫无目的,故选项 A)"战后日本处于无目标的发展状态下"不正确,C)"日本是西方国家的劲敌"文中未提及;D)"正在走下坡路"谈的只是现在的情况,并不符合战后日本的情况。

6. 正确答案 D)。第三段末句作者引用教育部长的话"liberal reforms introduced by the American occupation authorities after World War Ⅱ had weakened the Japanese morality of respect for parents.",指出受美国当局自由化的影响,日本人尊重父母的道德观念削弱了;第四段接着陈述了日本人生活方式的变化,主要是受了西方价值观念的影响,所以应该选 D)。A)"妇女参加社会活动受到限制"与第二段首句中"……women into the male dominated job market……"不符;第二段尾句"In addition,far more Japanese workers expressed dissatisfaction with their jobs"虽然指出"更多的工人对自己的工作感到不满",但这只是道德下滑的表现而不能称为原因,所以 B)不可选;C)"过多地注重基础教育"并不是道德下滑的主要原因。

7. 正确答案 C)。文章第三段第一句"……Japanese education tends to stress test taking and mechanical learning over creativity and self-expression."指出日本教育往往只强调应试和机构性学习而不强调创造性与主动性,接着引用 Toshiki Kaifu 的话进一步说明"那些在考试分数中不能表现的东西——个性、能力、勇气或人性——被完全忽略了",故 C)"应该更多地强调创造力的培养"符合作者的观点,同时可以否定 B)"日本教育既强调机构的学习也强调创造力的培养"。从第三段第一句"While often praised by foreigners for its emphasis on the basics"可知,日本教育受到称赞的原因是因为它强调基础的重要性,所以 A)"日本教育受到称赞是因为它有助于年轻人爬上社会阶梯"不符合原文;由"Frustration against this kind of thing leads kids to drop out and run wild.(对考试的反感导致了孩子们的辍学)"可知 D)颠倒了因果关系。

8. 正确答案 A)。文章最后一段中的"……but as the old group and family values weaken,the discomfort is beginning to tell"表明 A)项"年轻人对生活中的不舒服不再持宽容态度"是正确的,C)项是不确切的,和老一辈不同,年轻的日本人不再对生活中的不舒服持宽容态度,也就是说忍耐力减弱;B)与文中提到日本离婚率仍然低于美国的事实不符;D)明显不对,否则不会出现离婚与自杀率的上升。

译文

战后的日本目标明确,生产力水平和社会融洽的程度都令美国和欧洲国家羡慕。但是现在,日本人那种劳动是美德的传统观念逐渐退化了。十年前,年轻人把工作视为生活的主要原因,但现在日本已经基本满足了经济上的需要,年轻人也不知道下一步该做些什么了。

战后婴儿潮时期诞生的婴儿都已经到了工作年龄,再加上妇女如今也进入了本来由男性统治的职业市场,这使得青少年的机会大大缩小了,他们本来就已经抱怨在日本社会里要想上好学校、取得好工作就必须要爬上森严的社会阶梯,所以个人必须做出很多牺牲。在最近的一次调查统计中,只有24.5%的日本学生对学校生活完全满意,而在美国有67.2%的学生表示满意。而且,和其他10个被调查的国家的工人相比,太多的日本工人表示对自己的工作不满意。

尽管外国人经常表扬日本人重视基础教育,但是日本的教育倾向于重视考试和机械式的学习,而不重视培养创造性和表达自己的见解。执政的自由民主党教育委员会主席 Toshiki Kaifu 说:"那些没有反应在考试成绩上的——性格、能力、勇气和仁爱——都被忽略了。由于在这些方面受到挫折，很多孩子辍学或学坏了。"去年,日本就发生了2,125起校园暴力事件,其中包括929起攻击教师的事件。现在许多人在大声疾呼,很多保守党领袖试图回到战前那种重视德育的情况。去年,当时的教育部长Mitsuo Setoyama大为恼火,认为二战后由美国占领引入的自由改革削弱了"日本人尊重父母的道德观"。

但这可能和日本人的生活方式关系更大。教育家Yoko Muro说:"在日本,你是否喜欢你的工作和生活从来不是问题,问题是你究竟能忍受多少。"随着经济发展的集中化,在日本的一亿一千九百万国民中,有76％的人口住在城市里,几代同堂的大家庭和社区已经被独立的、主要由两代人组成的小家庭所取代。城市里的日本人长期忍受着长时间的通勤(乘车上下班),以及居住环境的拥挤,但是随着旧有的家庭观念的削弱,这些不便之处也开始显现出来。在过去十年中,日本的离婚率虽然仍远远低于美国的离婚率,但已经增长了50％还多,自杀的比率也增长了将近25％。

Passage 3

题材:社会科学——心理学

本文讲述的是在心理学上对于个人成长的两种不同的看法,而作者着重强调了视成长为一个过程的优势以及对一个人的影响。

9. 正确答案 A)。本题问,一个人何时被认为取得了成就。首先,要知道成就的定义。参看第一段第二句"人们通常把个人成长看做很容易识别和衡量的外在结果"。由此可知,A)"克服掉了吸烟的习惯"为正确答案。尽管 A)项表达的内容原文并未提到,但我们知道,戒烟是非常不易的,它需要坚定的决心与毅力。正像是一个学生要取得好成绩必须做出努力,最后才能取得成功。B)"工作中尽了很大的努力"和 C)"热衷于学习新知识"都只能表示动作的过程而不是动作的结果。D)"试图确定自己旅行中的位置"也无法看出其结果。

10. 正确答案 A)。本题问在作者看来,视个人成长为过程的人会如何。本文中最后三段都是论述个人成长是过程,同时,作者列举了一些事例对此观点进行了解释。根据作者对个人成长是过程的论述,我们可以确定 C)"面对困难,迎接挑战"为正确答案。A)"提高了社会地位"和第一段提到的"得到提升"一样,属于视成长为结果。B)"判断自己从个人成就中得到的能力"和 D)"要求高,并且每次都实现自己的目标"均属于结果。

11. 正确答案 A)。本题问,a new way of being 指的是什么。本题主要理解 way 和 approach 为同义词。此处的 new way 指第二段最后一句"there are always new ways to experience the world,new ideas to try,new challenges to accept."因此,答案为 A)。

12. 正确答案 D)。本题问,就个人发展而言,哪一项不属于作者所提倡的。本题可采用排除法。A)"对更多机会充满好奇"与第三段第三、四句"我们认为自己敏捷又好奇吗?果真如此,我们会抓住更多的机会,更勇于面对陌生的经历"一致。B)"自我适应快"与第三段最后两句一致。最后两句为"我们认为自己适应或改变得很慢,或是不够精明以适应新的挑战吗?"如果这样,我们可能会采取更消极的态度,或者根本不去尝试",即我们应该快速适应变化。C)"对新的经历能够接受"与第三段第四句"果真如此,我们会抓住更多的机会,更勇于面对陌生的经历"一致。D)"回避内心的恐惧和疑虑"与最后一段第二句不一致。作者指出"如果我们不面对并克服这些内在的恐惧和疑虑,如果我们过分地保护自己,我们就停止了成长"。很显然,作者提倡面对和克服内在的恐惧和疑虑而不是回避。所以,答案为 D)。

译文

对成长的看法基本上有两种:一种把成长看成是结果,一种把它看成是过程。人们大多把个人成长看成是容易识别和衡量的结果,比如:工人得到了提升,学生的学业有了进步,外国人学会了一门新语言——这些例子都是人们取得了能显示出他们努力的结果。

而在另一方面,个人成长的过程却比较难以确定,因为从定义上可以看出,它是一个旅程,而不是旅程中特定的标志或里程碑。而且,这个过程指的并不是脚下的道路,而是人们在遭遇新的体验和预料不到的挫折时的态度和情感,勇气和忧虑。这一旅程永远没有终点,总是有新的体验,新的尝试,新的挑战。

为了实现个人成长,探索新路,人们需要有愿意冒风险的精神,要勇于面对未来的世界,敢于接受开始时可能会碰到的失败。我们在探索新路的时候如何看待自己,这对我们的成长能力是至关重要的。我们是否认为自己头脑灵活、好奇心强?如果是这样,我们会更愿意冒风险,更愿意尝试不熟悉的体验。我们是否认为自己羞怯而缺乏主见?那么胆怯会使我们犹豫,在迈出一步之前总是先要确定路况是否安全。我们是否认为自己不善于应付改变,或认为自己不够聪明,无法迎接新的挑战?这样的话,我们可能会采取比较被动的态度,或者根据就不去尝试新的事物。

在我们成长和改变的过程中,对自己不信任或缺乏安全感这样的感觉是不可避免的,也是必经的。如果无法面对和克服这些恐惧和疑虑,如果我们对自己过分保护,那我们就会停止成长,就会被困在自己编织的茧壳里。

Passage 4

题材:社会科学——经济学——美国经济

本文讲述了当时的美国经济状况,并对经济持续增长的原因进行了分析,同时作者也批驳了流行的关于公司重组能提高生产力的说法。

13. 正确答案 A)。本文首段即道出了文章的主旨"What is harder to establish is whether the productivity revolution that businessmen assume they are presiding over is for real. (很难确定商界自认为正在进行的生产率革命是否名副其实)",这说明作者对美国经济状况的质疑。在第二段中,作者又通过官方的统计数字对美国的经济形势进行了分析:尽管从表面上看生产率有了很大提高,但其部分原因是由于在每个商业循环的同一阶段通常都会出现反弹(usual rebound)造成的,因此还不能以此作为结论性的证据来说明美国经济已呈现出复苏的态势。此处"the trouble"暗示了情况的不乐观,选项 A)"(美国的经济形势)不如表面看上去的那么好"恰恰反映了作者的上述观点。B)"处于转折阶段",文中未提及;C)"比现状要好得多"与作者表述的事实恰好相反,与 A)内容也截然相反,答案只能从二者中择一;D)"几乎要实现全面复苏"正是作者质疑而非真正的观点。

14. 正确答案 B)。依据题干中的关键词"productivity"定位到第二段。该段末句提到财政部长说"There is a'disjunction' between the mass of business anecdote that points to a leap in productivity and the picture reflected by the statistics",即"商业界有关生产率大幅度提高的传闻与官方统计数字所展示的情景并不吻合,是脱节的(disjunction)",可见选项 B)"官方有关生产率提高的调查统计结果并未达到商业家们所期望的目标"是此句的同义表述;而 C)"与商人预想的一致"与此句意正好背道而驰;A)"排除了商业领域里出现的正常反弹"与第二段提到将生产率增长部分原因归结于经济发展周期的反弹的事实不符;D)"没有准确地反映经济的真实情况"与文意相反。

15. 正确答案 B)。本篇开头作者引用了一句谚语"no gain without pain(不劳则无获)"。接着话锋一转,提出反问"But what about pain without gain. (那么要是劳而无获呢?)",这一反问显然是有其寓意的,它与文章的主题有关。文章第二段中,作者通过官方统计数字说明美国的经济形势远非商业家们估计的那样乐观。以后各段作者分析原因认为生产率革命未见效,许多公司的机构重组(reengineering)很不成熟,……这样既不完善又问题重重的改革其结果必然是劳而无功的。选项 B)"他认为所谓的生产力革命并未奏效"正是作者提出反问的寓意所在;A)只是对字面意思的推断,不是作者提出此反问的真正意图;C)"他认为官方的统计数字可能有错"显然与作者用官方数据去说明自己的观点的用意相悖;D)"他有美国经济已经复苏的确凿证据"与文意不符。

16. 正确答案 A)。本题用排除法解答。B)"企业的新组织方法可以提高生产率"与第三段与第二句"New ways of organizing the workplace—all that reengineering and downsizing—are only one contribution to the overall productivity of an economy"相符;最后一段作者引用 Leonard Schlesinger 的话"In many cases, the loss of revenue has been greater than the reductions in

cost."说明 C)"降低成本并不能保证带来长期利润"正确；D)"顾问什么也不是"与最后一段最后一句"He dismissed……consultants as mere rubbish—'the worst sort of ambulance cashing.'（这些顾问们所做的工作多数是垃圾，根本于事无补）"相符。只有 A)项"激进的改革是提高生产率的基础"未提及。

译文

　　人们常说不劳无获，但是假如努力了也没有收获那又怎么样？在美国，到处都流传公司起死回生的故事，但是我们难以确定，生意人认为的他们正在经历的生产力革命是否是真实的。

　　政府的统计数据有些令人失望：如果将生产部门和服务部门算在一起，劳动生产率自 1987 年以来以 1.25% 的平均速度增长，这比前十年的速度要快。自从 1991 年以来，生产率每年增长 2%，这个速度是 1978—1987 年的两倍还多。问题是，造成目前加速增长的原因部分在于经济循环过程中正常的反弹，并不是确实的证据证明复苏是潜在趋势。正如财政部长 Robert Rubin 所说，众多商界传闻显示的生产力大幅度提高和统计数据显示的结果明显不符。

　　有些现象很好解释。对工厂进行调整——例如企业重组和缩小规模——只是改变整个经济中劳动生产率的一方面，影响生产率的还有其他很多因素，例如对机器设备的投资，新的科学技术，对教育和培训的投资等。而且，公司所做的调整大部分都是为了获利，而并不总能带来生产率的提高。转向新的市场和提高产品质量同样也是十分重要的。

　　另外两种解释比较没有事实依据。第一种是近年来开展的企业改组方法不对；第二种是，即使改组是正确的，它所涉及的面也没有人们想像的那么广。

　　Leonard Schlesinger 是一位哈佛大学的学者，并曾担任过一家增长迅速的连锁饮食店的执行长官，他说很多企业进行的重组都是十分粗糙的，在很多情况下，重组造成的财政损失比节省下来的成本还要大。他的同事 Michael Beer 认为，许多企业进行的重组都太机械化了，只是一味地削减成本，而没有足够地考虑长期效益。BBDO 公司的 Al Rosenshine 说话更加坦率，他认为许多企业重组顾问的工作纯粹是一堆垃圾——就知道浪费客户的钱，什么用也没有。

因果与条件关系题答案

Passage 1

　　题材：人文科学——道德伦理

　　文章大意：本文是一篇讨论医学界使用动物做实验是否人道的议论文。文章通过举例说明动物权利运动是一个被误导的事业，号召医学研究者采取有力的行动给动物权利倡导者有力的还击。

1. 正确答案 A)。to call on scientists to take some actions 是"号召科学家们采取行动"。Edmund Burke 原话的意思是"一件不正当的事获得胜利所需要的条件就是好人们不采取任何行动"，言外之意是如果科学家们不采取行动，就会让歪风得逞了。

2. 正确答案 B)。见第 1 段最后两句。这两句中谈到，动物权利运动的领导者们向生化药物研究发难，并且很少有人了解医药研究的过程。听说在研究的环境中残忍地对待动物，许多人都搞不明白为什么人们要故意去伤害动物。句中用了 are perplexed 和 deliberately harm，前者表示"不可接受"；后者表示"不人道"。

3. 正确答案 B)。见第 2 段。这个长得像老祖母似的女人向人们宣传不要吃肉，不要穿毛皮衣服，不要吃药。她并且表示如果疫苗来自于动物研究，她就反对注射疫苗。当问到如果出现瘟疫时怎么办，她说不用担心，科学家们会从计算机里找到答案。这充分暴露了她的无知。许多新药在临床使用前都是要做多次试验的，而这些试验只能在动物身上进行。

4. 正确答案 A)。见第 3 段。本段一开头，作者就说科学家应该与公众多交流，要向公众说清楚动物试验的重要性。不了解动物试验必要性的人才会认为这种试验是一种浪费，并且透着残忍。

5. 正确答案 D)。见最后一段，倒数第 2 句：Finally, because the ultimate stakeholders are patients, the health research community should actively recruit to its cause not only well-known personalities such as Stephen Cooper, who has made courageous statements about the value of animal research,……从 Stephen Cooper 后的定语从句中可以看出他是支持搞动物研究的。

译文

18世纪政治家爱德蒙·伯克说"误导之所以得逞就是因为好人不作为"。现在就有这样一种误导的情形可以诠释这一名言:生物医学将寻求中止,因为有一种观点认为动物有权利拒绝作研究对象。科学家需要对动物权利倡导者做出有力的回答,因为他们的观点正在蛊惑公众,因而阻碍了保健知识和医疗的发展。因为生物医学研究依赖公众资助,而且很少有人理解保健研究的方法,所以动物权利运动领导人把目标盯在生物医学研究上。听说在研究中对动物残忍的做法,多数人会对有人故意伤害动物感到困惑不解。

举例来说,在一个街道市场上,动物权利保护协会的一位老年妇女正在分发小册子,鼓励读者不再使用任何动物或在动物身上试验过的任何食品或制品——包括肉类、药品和毛皮。如果问她是否反对免疫,她想知道疫苗是否来自动物试验。当得到的答案是肯定时,她说:"那么,我会反对的。"当问到如果发生传染病怎么办时,她说:"不用担心,科学家将会用计算机找到一些解决办法"。这样的好心人就是不明白这个道理。

科学家向民众传达信息时应该用富有感情的、容易听懂的方式,也就是说,用通俗的语言而不是用分子生物学的语言讲话。我们需要弄清楚动物研究与祖母的髋骨置换术、父亲的心脏搭桥手术、孩子的免疫接种甚至宠物的防疫之间的联系。对于那些不知道需要动物研究来做这些治疗以及进行新的治疗和研究新的疫苗的人来说,动物研究说得好听一些是浪费,说得难听一些是残酷。

有许多事情是能够做到的。科学家可以以"教授"中学的各年级来向他们介绍自己的研究。他们应该对读者来信迅速回复,以免让动物权利的错误信息畅行无阻,给真理披上一件欺骗性的外衣。研究机构可以对旅游者开放,以此显示供研究用的动物得到仁慈的照料。最后,因为最有利害关系的是病人,保健研究团体不仅要接纳像史蒂芬·库柏这样著名的人物,因为他敢于说出关于动物的研究的价值,而且对任何接受治疗的人都应敞开大门。如果好人不作为,有可能真会使无知的人们扑灭医学进步中珍贵的火种。

Passage 2

题材:社会科学——经济——垄断

本文介绍铁路公司的垄断现象。

6.正确答案 C)。见第 2 段第 2 句:Any threat of monopoly, they argue, is removed by fierce competition from trucks. 此句符合 C)项的意思。

7.正确答案 D)。Apprehensive 是"忧虑的,担心的"。见第 2 段最后一句,句中用了 complain 和 have them by the throat,表明了他们的忧虑。

8.正确答案 C)。见本段最后一句:Shippers who feel they are being overcharged have the right to appeal to the federal government's Surface Transportation Board for rate relief, but the process is expensive, time consuming, and will work only in truly extreme cases. 意思是感觉到被多收费的货主可以起诉,要求降低运费,但是这一程序需要花很多钱,并且可能会旷日持久,而只有在非常极端的情况下才会胜诉。基于这种情况,还有哪个货主会选择起诉呢?

9.正确答案 B)。arbiters 作"仲裁人;裁决者"解,B)项符合本词意思。此词许多人可能不认识,可以从本词所在的句子的上下文中猜测其词义。"Do we really want railroads to be the arbiters of who wins and who loses in the marketplace?"arbiters 后接了"谁赢谁输"。判定输赢的人肯定是裁判、仲裁人、法官等。

10.正确答案 A)。the continuing acquisition 是"不断并购"的意思。见最后一段第 3 句:Yet railroads continue to borrow billions to acquire one another,...

译文

最近几年,各铁路公司一直在进行互相合并而成为超级系统,这引起了人们对垄断的日益关注。在 1995 年四条最大的铁路运输量不到总吨/英里的 70%。第二年经过一系列合并之后,这四条铁路的运输量将大大超过各大铁路货运总量的 90%。

支持新超级铁路的人们争论说这些合并有助于大幅降低费用,更好地协调货运服务。他们认为任何来自垄断的威胁都可以通过来自汽车的激烈竞争加以消除。但许多托运人却抱怨说,对于远途大宗货物而言,如煤、化肥和粮食等货物,汽车货运太昂贵,因此铁路已控制住局面。

铁路业规模空前的合并意味着为托运人服务的铁路公司仅此一家。这样铁路比有竞争对象时向"受制"的托运人一般多收20%～30%的费用。那些觉得运费过高的人有权向联邦政府地面运输委员会投诉要求给予运费补贴,但是过程既昂贵又耗时且只有在极度特殊的情况下才能奏效。

铁路方面认为路方收费差别是合理的,因为从长远看费率不同降低了每个客户的成本。如果铁路对所有客户都平均收费,那些可以选择卡车或其他运输方式的客户就会去选择卡车或其他运输方式。这样一来,剩余的客户就要承担保持铁路运转的费用。这是一个许多经济学家都赞成的理论,但实际上,这样常常使铁路处于决定哪些公司该继续发展哪些公司该倒闭的地位。经常作为托运方代理人的华盛顿律师马丁·伯克威斯问道"难道我们真的要让铁路成为市场上谁胜谁负的仲裁人吗?"

许多受制的托运人也担心将受到费用大幅度增加的打击。就整个铁路业来说,尽管财源大有希望其收入仍然不足以支付为维持运量日益增加而投入的资本。然而由于有华尔街为其打气铁路方面仍然贷款数十亿元去继续并购。考虑一下今年Norfolk Southern和CSX公司出资一百零二亿美元购得联合铁路公司。1996年联合铁路公司的铁路纯收入仅为四亿二千七百万美元,还不到运输成本的一半。那么这笔账的另一半谁来支付呢?许多受制人担心随着Norfolk Southern和CSX公司加强对市场的控制,将由他们来支付。

推理题答案

Passage 1

题材:时文——自然科学——生态学

本文主要论述了人类在水利方面的主要成就,大型水坝的利与弊,作者分析了人类热衷于这一事业的自然和社会原因,而作者本身对于不考虑生态和社会后果的建坝行为提出了批评。

1. 正确答案C)。本题考对文章第一段第三句的含义的理解。该题要结合全段。人类热衷于修建大坝,这是事实。作者对此做出解释:"也许正是由于人类长期听任旱涝之灾的摆布才使得让江水听从人的调遣这种理想如此令人痴迷。"然而,迷恋的结果如何?"有几个巨型大坝颇有弊大于利的趋势。"据此,该句中的fascinated一词显然是指上文提到的对修坝的迷恋,blind一词在此也非"眼睛失明的"之意,而指因迷恋产生的"盲目"。选项B)"盲人可能比看得见的人更高兴"和D)"迷恋使人丧失视力",都是望文生义,应排除。C)项意为"过于兴奋的人有可能忽略至关重要的事"与原文意思吻合。这里over-excited即是文中的fascinated;neglect vital things就是指文中的be blinded to see the fact that several giant dam projects threaten to do more harm than good。选项A)也不对,因为人们并不是高兴对现实视而不见,而是根本没有看清现实。

2. 正确答案D)。本题问的是第五段中的the powerless一词为何意。从文中cause hardship for the powerless来看,hardship应由人来承受;从语法角度判断the+adj.作名词,指一类人。因此,A)项"电力匮乏地区",B)项"没有电站的大坝"和C)项"印度周围的贫穷国家"与"人"无关,不是答案。D)项"纳尔马达河大坝地区的平民百姓"符合要求,也与后文的the powerful(当权者)前后对应。

3. 正确答案D)。本题问关于大坝的神话是什么。文章第四段第一句就告诉我们,这个myth就是controlling the waters,可见,选项D)是正确答案。选项A)"带来更肥沃的土地"违背了第三段所陈述的事实,选项B)"有助于保卫国家"和选项C)"加强国际关系",都不是myth的内容。文章第二段和第四段指出,有些国家建坝是为了证实自己的实力,但并非保卫国家,更非加强国际关系。

4. 正确答案C)。本题要求解释作者的意图。四个选项均为谚语,A)为"覆水难收",B)为"欲速则不达",C)为"三思而后行",D)为"谁笑到最后,谁笑得最好"。文章最后一段表明作者观点:第一,要对建坝造成的危害以及对治水的耗资和收益进行合理的科学研究;第二,不要相信神话,否则,就难以做到合理或科学。第三,世界各国应从阿斯旺大坝的失败中吸取教训。这些都渗透着一个原则:切忌盲目行动。因此,C)最贴切,其余三项不能反映作者的观点。

译文

　　没有什么技术发明像大型水坝这样能抓得住人们的想像力。也许是因为人类长期遭受洪水和干旱的折磨,所以让水听命于人类这个想法特别令人着迷。但有时,令人着迷的东西也会使人盲目。几个大型水坝项目对人们的威胁似乎要大于它们的益处。

　　水坝给我们的一个教训是,大的并不总是美的。建造一个大型水坝,结果却变成向国家和人民展示自己的权威和成就的象征,这样做并没有什么好处。阿斯旺大坝坚固了埃及在阿拉伯世界的领袖地位;土耳其则将塔特克大坝当作一个争取第一世界国家地位的砝码。

　　但是大水坝经常起不到预期的作用。以阿斯旺水坝为例,它阻止了尼罗河的洪水,但埃及再也得不到洪水留下的富含养料的淤泥;与此同时,大坝里因为积满了淤泥,几乎已经无法发电了。

　　然而,对水的控制仍然具有神奇的吸引力。就在这个星期,在欧洲文明的中心,斯洛伐克和匈牙利因为在 Danube 修筑水坝问题上的争端差一点兵戎相见。这一巨型工程可能也会有大型水坝所有的问题,但是斯洛伐克正在和捷克讨论独立,所以需要用一座水坝来证明自己的力量。

　　与此同时,在印度,世界银行批准一项甚至更加执迷不悟的 Narmada 大坝工程,尽管银行的顾问认为建这座大坝会给平民带来苦难,也会给环境造成破坏。大坝的益处很难保证,但即使有利,也是对那些有权有势的人来说的。

　　对大坝可能带来的影响,对治水的成本和收益进行合理的、科学的分析,这样做有利于解决这些矛盾。不用建如此巨型的大坝也可以实现水力发电、控制洪水和灌溉农田,但是当你面临神话般的吸引力时,你就无法进行合理、科学的分析。现在,全世界都应该从阿斯旺大坝身上吸取教训,你并不需要一座大坝来拯救自己。

Passage 2

题材:人文——道德伦理

　　本文是历年考研题目中较难的一篇,全篇围绕 ambition 展开,批判了一些受过良好教育者对 ambition 所抱的虚伪态度,同时也暗示了对 ambition 的追求是一种健康的行为。

5. 正确答案 A)。事实细节题。本题问及抱负在什么条件下可能被看重。根据文章第一句"If ambition is to be well regarded, the rewards of ambition—wealth, distinction, control over one's destiny—must be deemed worthy of the sacrifices made on ambition's behalf.(如果抱负被看重,那么她所带来的回报——财富,荣誉,对命运的主宰——都被认为是值得为之做出的牺牲)"可以得出结论:抱负可以被看重的条件是 A)"收益足足抵得上做出的牺牲时"。金钱、名誉及权力只是抱负所带来的回报,并非其被看重的条件,B)属于答非所问;如果目标只是精神上的而非物质上的,那么为什么还要提到财富做回报呢? 显然,C)"其目标是精神上的而不是物质上的"不符合事实;D)"由富人与名人共有后抱负可能被看重"显然不符和逻辑。

6. 正确答案 C)。推力判断题。本段最后一句以"closing the barn door after the horses have escaped(马跑后才关谷舱门)"为喻,指出了那些在目标达到后否认抱负存在的行为是虚伪的。其中 horse 代表 ambition,riding 代表 ambition 带来的好处;可见 C)"在目标实现后否定抱负是不诚实的"是对这句话的正确理解。A)只是说受过教育的人口是心非,并没有指出它们的虚伪性;B)"抱负一旦被释放出来,就来不及控制",D)"对受过教育的人来说,享受抱负带来的好处是不现实的"与题干不符。

7. 正确答案 D)。事实细节题。文章第二段第三句"lest they be thought pushing, acquisitive and vulgar."说明有些人不肯公开承认他们有抱负的原因是"防止被人认为是爱出风头、贪婪和庸俗的人",选项 D)准确的概括了该句的三个形容词"pushing"、"acquisitive"和"vulgar"。其他选项 A)"他们认为有抱负是不道德的";B)"他们不追求名誉和财富";C)"野心和物质利益不是密切相关的",都不是有些人不公开承认他们有抱负的原因。

8. 正确答案 B)。推理判断题。最后一段中作者谈到人们不愿意公开承认有抱负,但这种做法产生了不良后果,从而推导出人们不应该隐瞒抱负,也就是说人们应该"坦诚而热情的拥有抱负"，故 B）正确。选项 A）"秘密而精力旺盛的"；C）"轻松而暂时的"；D）"口头或存在于精神上的"，这些方式都与作者表达的意思有差距。

译文

　　如果想使人们对野心产生好感，那么必须认为野心获得的回报——财富、名望、对自己命运的主宰——都是值得为其做出牺牲的。如果想使野心这一传统获得活力，那么它必须得到众多人的认可，尤其是得到那些本身就受人羡慕的人的尊敬，特别是其中受过教育的人。然而，令人奇怪的是，正是这些受过教育的人宣称他们放弃了野心，而也正是他们从野心中获益最多——也许不是他们亲身获益，那也是他们的父母或祖父母从中获益。他们的宣称有很重的虚伪成分，就好像等马都跑光了才去关上马厩的门——而骑在马背上的，正是那些受过教育的人。

　　当然，今天的人们和过去相比，对成功及其标志的兴趣并没有减少。度假别墅、欧洲之旅、宝马轿车——这些场所、地名和品牌的名字可能会改变，但对类似东西的需求，在今天和在十年前或者两年前相比，并没有减少。事实是，人们再也无法像以前那样轻易地、坦白地承认自己的梦想，因为怕别人说他们有野心、追求物欲、粗俗。于是，我们带上了精致的伪君子的眼镜，这种眼镜现在比以前更多了，例如：批评美国人过于追求物质利益的批评家，在南安浦顿有座度假别墅；出版激进书籍的出版商经常在三星级饭店用餐；鼓吹在生活各方面都应人人共享民主的记者，却把孩子送进了私立学校。对这些人，还有其他很多更平常一些的人来说，合适的表达应该是"不惜一切获得成功，但不要表现得太有野心。"

　　从各个不同的角度对野心进行的攻击很多，但在公开场合支持它的却很少，也没有给人留下什么印象，虽然这些支持的声音并不是完全没有吸引力。结果，那些支持野心的人，认为它是一种健康的推动力，一种值得钦佩的品质，应该深深地印在年轻人的脑海里的人，比美国历史上的任何时期都要少。这并不意味着野心已经走到了终点，人们再也感觉不到它的激励和鼓动了，只是现在人们再也不公开对它表示敬意，再也不公开承认了。当然，这带来的结果是，野心被赶入了地下，变得偷偷摸摸。于是，事情就变成了这样：左面站着愤怒的批评家，右面站着愚蠢的支持者，而就像通常一样，站在中间的是大多数人，热切地盼望着发迹的那一天。

Passage 3

题材：社会科学——人口学

　　这篇文章主要介绍了美国 1980 年人口普查反映的人口变化，以及美国人口迁移的规律。本文在考研的文章中比较少见，因为它里面包含了大量的数据信息，从一定程度上考查了考生对于数字、地名等细节信息的检索能力。

9. 正确答案 B）。文章第三段"……numerically the third largest growth ever recorded in a single decade."指出 20 世纪 70 年代美国人口从增长数量上来说很大，可见 A）"是历史上人口净增长最低的十年"与原文矛盾；第三段第二句"Even so, that gain adds up to only 11.4 percent, lowest in American annual records except for the Depression years."中"only"，"lowest"等词均说明这次增长形成的增长率很低，所以 C）"有史以来人口增长最快的十年"不正确；第四段"Americans have been migrating south and west in larger number since World War Ⅱ, and the pattern still prevails."说明第二次世界大战以来，美国人不断移居西部和南部，现在这种趋势仍然存在，可见 B）"目睹了人口从西部向南部迁移"为正确答案；而 D）"第二次世界大战以来人口迁移的格局已经停滞不前"与此意大相径庭。

10. 正确答案 C）。在第七段开头作者写道：人口统计学家看到，在不断向南部和西部迁移的趋势中又出现了与之相关却又与往不同的现象：美国人寻找的不再只是能够提供更多工作机会的地方，同时也是人口密度较小的地方，而且这一趋势正变得越来越明显（apparently），在举两例后第十一段又总结到"Nowhere do 1980 census statistics dramatize more the American search for spacious living than in the Far West.（没有哪次调查比历史最高水平 1980 年美国人口普查更能突出显示出美国人迁往最西部是为了找到更广阔的生存空间"，选项 C）正是上面所述的不同于以往的新的现象，其中"pursuit of spacious living"正是"search for spacious"

的同义替换。A)"它强调了气候对人口分布的影响"是过去就反映出来的情况,与题干所问"这次人口普查与以前的人口流动研究的不同之处"不符。C)"它强调了不断的移民潮的影响",D)"它详细地说明了上一轮'生育高峰'的后期效果"虽然在第六段都提到了,但并不能看出是这次人口普查的新特点,故排除。B)项内容是普查中的特有现象,故应排除。

11. 正确答案 D)。题干要求回答哪个选项与普查数据反映的情况相符。第八段的举例"the Rocky Mountain states reported the most rapid growth rate……"与第九段的说明"Among states,Nevada and Arizona grew fastest of all:63.5 and 53.1 percent respectively."指出在这次人口普查中,增长速度最快的地区当数落基山脉周围各州,其中内华达和亚利桑那两州增长最快,分别为 63.5%和 53.1%。可见,亚利桑那的人口增长率仅次于 Nevada,排在第二次,故选项 D)是正确的。文章最后三段均提到加州,但并没有涉及人口稀少的问题,故 A)"加州曾经是美国人口最稀少的州"缺乏事实依据;第九段末句中可以看到:南部的两个州佛罗里达和德克萨斯也排名在前十位,故 B)"人口增长率最高的十个州都在西部地区"是错误的;选项 C)"气候好的城市普遍从人口的迁移活动中受益",文中也无此事实依据。

12. 正确答案 C)。从第七段第一句可见,demographers 所提出的两个数字统计都是在谈人口问题,故他们应是研究人口问题的科研人员。选项 A)"支持民主运动的人",B)"主张在州之间移民的人",D)"坚持旧生活方式的保守分子",都相差太远。实际上本题中 demographer 的词义还可以通过构词法推测,demo 相当于 people,graph 相当于 write,er 指人,因而猜出它是指"记录人口方面数据的人"。

译文

1980 年的人口普查显示,在国内,各地区之间的竞争愈演愈烈,东北部和中西部地区的人口增长几乎处于停顿状态。

这一发展态势表明,在美国的人口普查历史上,南方第一次成为美国人口最稠密的地区,这对美国未来的政治和经济都有很重要的指导作用。

20 世纪 70 年代美国的人口总数增加 2320 万,从绝对人数上来说,是有记录以来,10 年内人口增长位于第三倍的。即使是这样,增加的人口只占总人口的 11.4%,是除了经济衰退时期之外,年增长率最低的。

第二次世界大战以后,大批的美国人开始向南部和西部移民,这种趋势现在仍在继续。

佛罗里达、德克萨斯和加利福尼亚,三个位于阳光地带的州加起来,在 1980 年的人口总数比 10 年前增加了大约一千万。在大城市中,圣地亚哥从第 14 位上升到第 8 位,圣安东尼奥从第 15 位上升到第 10 位,而克利夫兰和华盛顿则被挤出了前 10 位。

人口普查官员说,这种变化并不完全是因为人们搬离冰雪地带造成的。还有其他原因,比如不断到来的外国移民浪潮,还有在前一次生育高峰诞生的婴儿又到达了生育年龄,因此又有大批新生儿出生。

在人口不断向南和向西迁移的同时,人口统计学家也发现了一个新的现象,那就是:越来越多的美国人不光在寻找有更多工作机会的地方,而且也在寻找人口稀少的地方,下面几个例子可以证明:

从地区上来看,洛基山脉附近几个州的人口增长率最快——1970 年,在这片广大土地上的居民只占美国人口总数的 5%,而这里现在的人口速度增长却达到了 37.1%。

在所有的州里,内华达和亚利桑纳的增长速度最快,分别是 63.5%和 53.1%。除了佛罗里达和德克萨斯,人口增长最快的前 10 个州都位于西部,这些州的人口增长了 750 万——大约每平方英里增长 9 个人。

逃离拥挤的人群,这也影响着从冰雪地迁移到气候温和地区的迁移模式。

根据 1980 年的人口普查结果,美国人追求生活空间这一现象在美国西部得以最充分的体现。加利福尼亚在 70 年代人口增加 370 万,比其他任何州的增长都要多。

然后,也是在 70 年代,大批人口也在离开加州,大多数人搬到了西部的其他地方。这些人通常会选择相对比较寒冷的地方,比如俄勒冈、艾达荷和阿拉斯加,这样做是为了逃离烟雾污染、犯罪和都市中的其他烦恼。

其结果是,70年代加州的人口增长率下降至18.5%,这个数字仅仅是60年代的三分之二,比西部其他各州的比率都要低。

Passage 4

题材:自然科学——医学——时文

本文较简单,讲的是医学的进步带来的治愈癌症的前景。

13. 正确答案 D)。本题问文中巴斯特的例子被用来做什么。参看第一段最后一句:"想一想巴斯特吧,他发现了许多传染病病因,但是过了五六十年才有了治疗方法。"此句意味着找到疾病的病因与找到治疗此病的方法还有遥远距离。由此可知,D)"告诫说,在征服癌症之前还有很长的路要走"为正确答案。A)"预言,十年后会发现癌症的秘密"在文中未提及。B)"表明治愈癌症的前景光明"不合文章的调子。微生物学家及癌症专家罗伯特·温伯格的"告诫"一词表明,前景不容乐观。C)"证明癌症会在五十年到六十年内达到治愈"也非罗伯特·温伯格的本意。

14. 正确答案 D)。本题问作者暗示,到2000年下面哪项论述正确。本题可用排除法来做。A)"五年生存率的皮肤癌患者会有大幅度的增加"与内容不符。第二段第三句指出"对于一些皮肤癌患者,目前五年的生存率高达90%",也就是说,不可能会有太大的提高。B)"今天90%的皮肤癌患者将仍然在世"与五年的生存率不符。本题为94年考题,即使该文章为当年所写,数据为当年所统计,距离2000年也还有六年之久,因此,到2000年大部分皮肤癌患者已超过五年生存期。C)"各种癌症患者之间的生存率统计数字将会持平"与第二段内容显然不符。因为各种癌症的生存率相差甚远,五、六年内不可能有太大变化。只有 D)"所有癌症患者生存率不会有大的提高"符合第二段的内容。

15. 正确答案 B)。本题问致癌基因是什么样的引起癌症的基因。参看第三段第二句:"70年代初,研究者们取得了很大进步,当时他们发现在正常细胞中,致癌基因并不活跃。从宇宙射线到辐射甚至饮食等任何东西都可能激活休眠的致癌基因,但这一过程仍然不为人知。如果几个致癌基因被激活,而细胞不能将他们消灭,则会成为癌细胞。"此句表明 B)"只要不被激活,就不会有害"正确。A)"总是活跃在健康人体内"与"当时他们发现在正常细胞中,致癌基因并不活跃"相悖。C)"可从正常细胞中驱赶出去"与"而细胞不能将它们排除"相悖。D)"正常细胞无法排除"虽为句中一个事实,但并无逻辑关系,属定义错误。

16. 正确答案 C)。本题测试 dormant 的词义。本题可从两方面去解:一是根据词根,dorm＝sleep,如 dormitory(宿舍),二是根据上下文。从第三段第二句中可知,致癌细胞一般是不活跃的(inactive in normal cells),第三句中说 Anything from cosmic rays to radiation to diet may activate a dormant oncogene……。activate 意为"激活",则 dormant oncogene 只能译为"不活跃的,休眠的"。故答案为 C)。

译文

　　癌症专家、微生物学家 Robert Wenberg 说:"我充分相信,十年之内我们就能够了解关于癌细胞的大量细节。"但是,他也提醒说:"有些人认为一旦了解了原因,治疗方法很快就能找到。"但是请想一想 Pasteur,他发现了多种导致感染的原因,但是直到五、六十年之后人们才找到治疗的方法。

　　现在,在91万患癌症的病人当中50%的人至少能活5年,国家癌症研究所估计到2000年这个数字将上升到75%。对某些皮肤癌来说,患者能存活5年的几率已高达90%,但是其他一些种类癌症的存活率很低,如肺癌为13%,而胰腺癌只有2%。

　　在已知的120种癌症中找出癌症的致病原因并不是一件容易的工作。20世纪70年代,研究工作取得了重大进展,科学家发现致癌基因在正常的细胞中并不活跃,而很多原因如宇宙射线、辐射甚至饮食都会激发处于休眠状态的致癌基因,至于怎样激发,人们还不清楚。如果几个致癌基因同时被激发,细胞无法控制它们,就发会生癌变。

　　这一过程的确切情况还不清楚,但多种癌症的根源在于基因这一事实表明,我们可能永远无法防止癌症。肿瘤学家 William Hayward 说:"在进化过程中,改变是正常的。"环境因素永远无法排除,正如 Hayward 所说的"我们没法研究出一种药来对抗宇宙射线"。

癌症的治疗,尽管路途仍然遥远,但大有希望。

"首先,我们需要了解正常的细胞是如何自我控制的;然后,我们要决定细胞中是否有有限数量的基因对癌症负责,或至少负部分责任。如果我们能了解癌细胞的活动情况,就能想办法抵消它们的活动结果。"

Passage 5

题材:社会科学——教育学

本文主要阐述了计算机在现代课堂中的地位,同时列举了对于计算机进入课堂的两种代表性意见,作者同时也阐释了自己对于这些观点的看法。

17. 正确答案 B)。作者在开篇句"An invisible border divides those arguing for computers in the classroom on the behalf of students' career prospects and those arguing for computers in the classroom for broader reasons of radical educational reform."中谈到"对于计算机进入课堂教学看法的争论上存在着一条无形的界限:……",可见在此作者已提到了计算机教学目的不清的问题;全文末句作者又总结说:"不管是职业学校还是非职业学校,目标混乱是有害无益的";由此可知只有 B)"目标不明确"符合作者的观点。

18. 正确答案 D)。依据为第二段第五句"With optimism characteristic of all industrialized countries, we came to accept that everyone is fit to be educated(随着所有工业国家所带来的乐观精神,我们逐渐接受了每个人都适合受教育的观点)",可见 D)"起源于乐观的工业化国家的态度",是正确答案。选项 A)是假装悲观的暗示,指代不明;B)"随着计算机的诞生而存在",文中未提到;C)"已深深地扎根于主张计算机教育的人思想里",谈的是计算机教育,与题干中的"education"不符。

19. 正确答案 C)。第三段讲,职业培训的目的是想让学生为自己将来的职业学习一技之长,实际情况是培训并无太大作用。因而选 C)"几乎没有实用价值"。文中并未提学员开始接受培训的年龄,故排除 A);B)"值得在社会各界进行尝试"、D)"对各种专业人员来说都具有吸引力"显然与 C)矛盾,与文意不符。

20. 正确答案 A)。本篇在最后一段倒数第二句给出了本题的答案:In any case, basic computer skills are only complementary to the host of real skills that are necessary to becoming any kind of professional. 本句的重点词是 complementary(补充的),与 A)项中 auxiliary(辅助的)意思接近,本句说明基本的计算机技能只是对成为专业技术人员所需的各种实际技能的补充,故选 A)。而其它几个选择项 B)"在获得专业素质的过程中加以强调"、C)"要花毕生的时间去掌握"、D)"无论是职业学校还是非职业学校都强调计算机基础技能"表达的意义与作者对计算机课程安排的观点不一致。

译文

对于在课堂上计算机教育的问题有两派不同的意见,一种是站在学生未来工作的角度考虑,一种是站在教育改革的大背景下考虑。这两派意见之间存在一种无形的界限。很少有人探讨这一区别——实际上,是这一矛盾——它直指计算机教育运动错误的核心。

目的在于为学生找到一份工作的教育是职业教育,进行职业教育的原因和为什么教育普遍受法律保护的原因有天壤之别。法律规定每个孩子上学必须上到十多岁,这并不仅仅是为了提高个人的就业机会。事实是,我们对美国公民有一种特定的期望,那就是如果一个人无法了解外界的力量能够如何影响他的生活和幸福,那么它的人生就是不完整的。但实际情况并不总是这样,在法律规定孩子到了一定年龄必须入学前,人们普遍认为有些人的资质太差,不适合接受教育。但是和其他工业国家一样,我们有乐观的性格,我们认为所有的人都适合接受教育。但是计算机教育的支持者放弃了这一乐观态度,即使表面上看起来令人振奋,但他们的态度实际上是悲观的。在计算机教育的教育目的和职业训练目的之间,计算机教育的支持者都强调的总是学生毕业后的工作前景,而忽略了教育的成果。

有人支持为学生提供适合他们类型的技术教育,很多欧洲的学校在早期引入职业训练的概念,就是为了确保为孩子将来能够从事他们希望的职业提供合适的训练。然而,你很难说就有那么多的工作机会提供给那么多的科学家、商人和会计。此外,在一个像我们这么广大的国家里,在我们这样一个经济扩展到那么多国家、有那么多跨国公司的国家里,很难保证为各行各业提供数量刚好合适的从业人员。

但是,对人数不多的一群学生来说,职业训练可能是行得通的,因为在其他条件相同的情况下,良好的职业技能决定一个人是否可以得到工作。当然,使用电脑的基础知识很简单,人们并不需要花很长时间来学习使用不同的软件。当然,如果你想成为一名电脑工程师,那就另当别论了。电脑的基本技能最多几个月就能掌握。不论如何,相对于能使人胜任各种职业的真正技能来说,电脑的基本技能只是一个补充。因此,不论是职业学校还是普通学校,都不能混淆电脑教育的目的。

Passage 6

题材:社会科学——文化人类学,跨文化交际

本文主要描述了一种文化现象——美国人对外国人比较友好,易于与他们交友,作者同时也对这个现象做了历史和文化上的解释,并指出这是一种相当复杂的文化现象。

21. 正确答案 D)。文章开篇句"A report consistently brought back by visitors to the US is how friendly,courteous,and helpful most Americans were to them."意思是:"从美国回来的访问者相继带回来一份份报告,说大多数美国人对他们如何友好,如何客气,如何乐于助人……当然也有例外。"D)中"are ready to offer help"正是原句中"friendly","helpful"的改写。而 A)、B)是第一段最后一句话提到的例外;C)与第一段第二句中"To be fair,this observation is also frequently made of Canada and Canadians……"意思不符。

22. 正确答案 A)。一般而言,段首句为段落主题句,设题者往往在此设有关的推断或段落主旨题。最后一段首句"As is true of any developed society,in America a complex set of cultural signals,assumptions,and conventions underlies all social interrelationship(任何发达国家的情况也是一样,在美国,一系列复杂的文化特征、各种设想和各种传统习惯构成了所有社会相互关系的基础)",由此可以推断 A)"文化影响社会关系"正确。B)与文章倒数第二句"It takes more than a brief encounter on a bus to distinguish between courteous convention and individual interest.(仅仅靠在公共汽车上的短暂相遇是不能够区分礼貌习惯和个人兴趣的)"相矛盾,C)"各种各样的美德仅仅表现在朋友关系中",文中未提到;D)"社会关系等同于一系列复杂的文化习俗"显然与本段第一句相矛盾。

23. 正确答案 C)。解此题要注意句子之间的逻辑关系。文章第二段第二、三句提到:"无聊、孤独对住在相互距离很远的家庭来说是家常便饭。陌生人和旅行者也便成为他们转换口味、吸收新信息、受欢迎的根源,"C)to add some flavor to their daily life"给他们自己的日常生活增添风韵"与此意相吻合。选项 A)"改善他们艰难的生活"有点言过其实,而且文章没有依据说他们的生活艰难;B)"考虑到他们的长途跋涉"文章也未提及;D)与文中第三段第三句"It was not a matter of choice for the traveler or merely a charitable impulse on the part of the settlers(这并非是行善的一时冲动)"相矛盾。

24. 正确答案 B)。本文第四段第二句说:"不过,对陌生人殷勤好客的老传统在美国仍很盛行,在远离繁忙的旅游路线的小城市和小城镇情况尤其是这样。"可知,B)"(这种友善的传统)在美国得以保持"为正确答案。至于 A)"是表面应付的、做作的"与文章四段最后一句的描述(neither as superficial nor as artificial)相反;C)与第四段倒数第二句"……but are not always understood properly"意思相反;D)"与一些旅游热线有关"与第四段第二句"Yet,the old tradition of hospitality to strangers is still very strong in the US,especially in the smaller cities and towns away from the busy tourist trails."表述不一致。

译文

旅游者对美国做出的评价经常是:友好、礼貌和乐于助人。公平地说,这一评价对加拿大和加拿大人也适用,因此可以说游客对整个北美地区的印象都是这样。当然,也有例外的情况,比如说美国

官员的心胸狭窄,饭店服务员的态度粗鲁,出租车司机没有礼貌,这些都是众所周知的。然而,既然美国人得到了那么多良好的评价,这就值得我们说上两句。

曾经有很长一段时间,在美国的很多地方,旅行者的来访能打破往日沉闷的生活,因此是很受欢迎的。对于那些居住得比较分散的家庭来说,沉闷和孤独是很普遍的问题。陌生人和旅行者带来了外面世界的信息,解除了生活的烦闷。

同时,边疆地区生活的严酷性也造成了这种好客的传统。当独自旅行的人受到饥饿或伤病威胁时,只有到最近的小屋和居民求助。这并不是说旅行者选择这样做,或者边疆居民一时发了善心,它反应了日常生活的严酷性:如果你不收容和照顾陌生人,就没有人去管他们。而且,记住,总有一天你也会处在和他们一样的处境。

今天,有很多慈善组织专门帮助疲劳的旅行者,但是美国仍然有很强的对陌生人好客的传统,尤其是在远离旅游区的小城镇里。经常可以听到游客对美国这样的评论:"我在旅行中碰到一个美国人,只和他谈了几句,他就邀请我回家吃晚饭了,真奇怪。"旅行者对这种现象的理解往往不正确,很多美国人随意的友善表示并不应该被理解成肤浅或做作的举动,而应该看成是有历史根源的文化传统。

正如在任何发达社会中一样,在美国的一切社会关系背后也有一套复杂的文化符号和传统。当然,会说一门语言并不一定意味着理解社会和文化模式。无法正确翻译文化内涵的旅行者经常会做出错误的结论。例如,当美国人使用"朋友"这个词的时候,其中包含的文化含义可能和旅行者的语言和文化中这个词的含义是不一样的。公共汽车上的简短一词,你是无法分辨出礼貌习惯和个人的真正兴趣的。然而,对人友好是很多美国人很看重的一个优点,他们也期望从邻居和陌生人身上看到这种品质。

Passage 7

题材:社会科学——教育学

本文是一篇教育学的文章,作者最开始就把人的性格分成了两类,分别由 A 和 B 代表。那么通过后面的阅读我们基本上能够知道 A 是指进取心强,在竞争中能获胜的人,而 B 是指生活态度更加从容,不太追名逐利的一类。

25. 正确答案 C)。本题要求回答 A 型性格的特征,因此关键是指出描述 A 型性格的句子。第二段首句出现"One place where children soak up A characteristics is school, which is, by its very nature, a highly competitive institution. ",第三句"in which competitive A-types seem in some way better than their B-type fellows"直接用 competitive"争强好胜的,爱竞争的"一词描述 A 性格的人,而选项中只有 aggressive 与 competitive 一词意思接近,所以选 C) aggressive。A) "缺乏耐心的,不耐烦的",这也许是他们有时候所表现的性格特征但并非其一般性格特征;B) "体贴人的,为人着想的"、D) "和蔼的,易相处的"恰与事实形成鲜明对比。

26. 正确答案 B)。本题要求回答作者强烈反对学校中的考试制度的原因。第三段首句"By far the worst form of competition in schools is the disproportionate emphasis on examinations. "说明学校最糟糕的竞争方式是对考试的过分重视,可见作者在此已经提出自己对考试的否定态度;本段最后一句"The merits of competition by examination are somewhat questionable, but competition in the certain knowledge of failure is positively harmful"又指出"用考试来竞争有无益处很令人质疑(questionable)的,但明知会失败还要去竞争的作法肯定是有害的",也就是说作者认为学校的考试是一种竞争,有人会成功,也必定有人会失败;B)与作者观点一致。文章未提及 A)、C)两项,而 D) "考试结果令人怀疑"显然是对"The merits of competition by examination are somewhat questionable"的曲解。

27. 正确答案 B)。作者在最后一段第二句"Perhaps selection for the caring professions, especially medicine, could be made less by good grades in chemistry and more by such considerations as sensitivity and sympathy"中提到"也许对护理——特别是医疗护理人员——的选择就可能会少注意化学成绩而多关注他们是否敏感、是否有同情心","could be"提示目前还不是这样,也就是说目前医疗工作者的选择依据还是 B) "学术成绩"。A) "申请者的敏感程度"及 D) "更可

靠的价值"正是作者希望重视的方法,不是现状,与题干中的 currently 不符。C)"竞争精神",只是 A 型学生的特点,作者在文中并未说明以此作为选择医疗工作者的标准。

28. 正确答案 C)。文章第一段首句即指出,个性在很大程度上是先天形成的,接着第二句"But the environment must also have a profound effect"用 but 转折说明环境对个性也有深刻影响,环境包括社会、家庭及学校;在随后的段落中,作者主要谈了学校教育对学生的性格形成的影响,由此可以推论 C)"个性的发展受多种因素的影响"与文章内容最为贴切。A)"儿童的个性在出生时就已确立"与首段第二句谈到的环境对个性的形成也有深刻的影响相矛盾;B)"家庭对儿童性格特征的形成起主导作用"中的"dominate"一词过于绝对;作者在第三段"the world need types"和第四段末句"B's are important, and should be encouraged"多次提到世界需要各种性格的人,特别是 B 型性格的人,所以 D)"在竞争的社会中,B 型性格的人不需要"不正确。

译文

性格从很大程度上来说是遗传的——A 性格的父母通常养育的儿女也是 A 性格的。但是,环境的影响也很重要,因为如果竞争对父母是重要的,那么它在子女的生活中也是一个重要的因素。

学校是对孩子性格造成影响的一个场所。从本质上来说,这是一个竞争相当激烈的地方。很多学校把"不惜一切赢取胜利"作为道德标准,并用体育活动中的成绩来衡量这种胜利。现在,学校热情地鼓动孩子们和同学竞赛,或者和时间竞赛,这种行为导致学生两极分化,其中有竞争意识的 A 性格学生似乎在很多方面都优于 B 性格学生。但是,对胜利太热衷也会导致危险的后果,比如第一个马拉松运动员 Pheidippides,在说完"欢庆吧,我们胜利了!"之后,就倒下死掉了。

到目前为止,学校竞争中最糟糕的形式是对考试的过分强调。很少有学校允许学生专注于自己擅长的事情。用考试来竞争,这样做的价值值得怀疑,但是明知道会失败还要参加竞争,这对学生的影响绝对是不好的。

显然,让 A 性格的年轻人全部转变成 B 性格的,这样做既不切实际,也不值得。这个世界需要各种各样的性格,学校的重要职责是使学生的性格能适合他们将来可能的职业,这才是管理的最高境界。

如果学校对学业的关注少一些,而多花些时间来培养孩子的价值观。也许,挑选某些行业的从业人员时,比如说医护人员时,少考虑些化学课的成绩,而多考虑些诸如细心,同情心这样的因素。只从 A 性格的人里挑选医生,这显然不对,B 性格的人也很重要,也要加以鼓励。

Passage 8

题材:社会科学——心理学

本文是较难的一篇关于心理学的文章,其难度不仅在于词汇和语法,同时也在于要求考生有一定的背景知识,了解进化论中适应环境的品性被保留,而不适应自然选择的品性被淘汰这一事实对于理解本文中的 adaptive 非常重要。本文主要论述了在心理学上记忆和遗忘产生的机制和功能。

29. 正确答案 D)。本题要求回答哪一项符合进化论对遗忘的观点,从进化论解释遗忘是第二段的内容。第二段第二句指出,如果我们不及时复习或练习已学过的东西的话,过一段时间,我们可能忘记它,这种情况所造成的适应性(adaptive)后果也许不太明显。A)"缺乏实践的忘记将导致明显的不适应性"与此句的表述不一致;接下来第三句"Yet, dramatic instances of sudden forgetting can be seen to be adaptive."用 yet 转折说明"但是突然遗忘的突出例证可以视为能产生适应性结果",可见 D)"突然遗忘可能带来适应性结果"与此转折处表达的意思一致,故为正确答案。B)"如果人一下子忘掉了所有的东西,他的适应性一定很好"是对第三句的篡改,两个 very 夸大了原文没有的遗忘与适应性之间的比例关系;C)"人们逐渐的忘记事物是他们的适应的表现",与第二段最后一句"Nevertheless, an evolutionary interpretation might make it difficult to understand how the commonly gradual process of forgetting survived natural selection.(进化论的解释说不定会很难让人理解遗忘这个渐进过程是如何在自然选择中幸存下来的)表达的意思相反。"

30. 正确答案 B)。本题要求回答如果一个人从不遗忘会有什么后果,第三段一开始就指出要思考一下记忆不衰退会产生的结果,接着第三句及第四句"Cases are recorded of people who(by

ordinary standards) forgot so little that their everyday activities were full of confusion."论证说忘事少的人日常生活充满了困惑,同时第二段第五句"Indeed, when one's memory of an emotionally painful experience lead to serious anxiety, forgetting may produce relied."也提到感情受到伤害的记忆会使人忧心忡忡,但遗忘可以使人得到解脱,也就是说不忘记就清除不了烦恼,这些都说明 B)"他会有许多麻烦"正确,其中 a lot of trouble 与原文中的"full of confusion"表义相同。A)与第三段第三句"Without forgetting, adaptive ability would suffer"不相符;C)"他的学习能力会得到提高"与第四段第二句 In this view, continual adjustments are made between learning or memory storage(input) and forgetting(output)."在学习或记忆存储(输入)和遗忘(输出)之间要不断进行调整"不符;D)"记忆力的进化就会停止"与第三段不符,而且过于绝对。

31. 正确答案 A)。最后一段的主要内容是:记忆存储系统的能力是有限的,它提供了通过遗忘调整的灵活性。因而,学习或记忆存储与遗忘之间要不断进行调整,以达到出入平衡。A)"遗忘是学习的一种反应"符合文章的含义。而 B)"记忆存储系统是一个非常平衡的输出输入系统",与文章最后一句"Such data offers gross support of contemporary models of memory that assume and input-output balance.(这些数据为假定输出—输入保持平衡的当代记忆模式提供了有力的证据)"不符;C)"记忆就是对忘记的补偿",以及 D)"因为经常遗忘,所以记忆存储系统的能力是有限的",在文中未提到。

32. 正确答案 B)。本文要谈的是遗忘过程的作用(function),它是人生存适应机制的一个很重要的过程,这是文章的第二、三、四段所旨在说明的,对照而言,第一段所谈的内容(remembering)只不过是这个讨论的引子。作者认为从科学的观点上看,没有遗忘就没有记忆,遗忘并非坏事,故 B)项正确。至于其他三项:A)"记忆",C)"适应"和 D)"经历",都不是作者强调的内容,故而都不正确。

译文

　　过去的经历能够影响随后的行为,这种显而易见但却十分重要的行为就叫做记忆。如果没有记忆这种功能,学习行为就不可能发生。不断的练习对记忆产生影响,使我们能熟练地演奏钢琴,背诵诗歌,阅读和理解文字。所谓的智力行为需要记忆,记忆也是推理的基础。解决问题的能力,甚至识别问题的能力,都要依靠记忆。例如,做出穿越马路的决定就是建立在对以前类似经历的记忆的基础之上的。

　　练习(或者复习)能够建立和巩固对事情或对学到的知识的记忆。如果一段时间没有练习,学到的东西就有可能忘掉,这种适应的结果可能并不明显,但是突然性的遗忘就可以看做是适应的结果了。从这个意义上来说,遗忘的能力可能理解成,是在动物的自然选择过程中保留下来的。确实如此,一段令人痛苦的记忆会导致严重的焦虑不安,这时遗忘可以缓解痛苦。然而,这种解释很难真正让人了解普通的缓慢遗忘的过程是怎样从自然选择的过程中保留下来的。

　　在考虑记忆的进化问题时,可以思考一下,如果记忆永远不会淡忘,那会出现什么情况呢?很显然,遗忘有助于时间上的调整,因为旧的记忆会褪色,而新的记忆变得更加明显,使我们能够推测事情发生的时间先后。如果不遗忘,人的适应能力就会受到破坏,比如:十年前正确的行为十年后可能已经不再正确了。在一些病例中,有的人遗忘的太少(和普通人相比),以至于他们的行为充满了混淆。这样看来,遗忘似乎有助于个人和整个人类的生存。

　　另一种猜想是存储记忆的系统的容量是有限的,因此通过遗忘灵活地进行调整。在学习或者记忆存储(输入)和遗忘(输出)之间不断进行着调整。实际上,有证据表明一个人遗忘的速度和他学习的速度是直接相关的,这些数据完全证明了当代的输入—输出平衡的记忆模式。

文章出处题答案

　　题材:自然科学——书评

　　本文是一篇书评,介绍了一位作家对于神造论的批判著作,如果考生有一定的背景知识,在阅读的最开始就能抓住 creationism 和 evolution 之间的矛盾以及作者对于神造说所持的全面否定的态度,那么就能基本理解全文的意思。

1. 正确答案 D）。Creationism 在文中出现多次，是文章的关键词语，可以在阅读完文章后再返回来解答。从第一段第三句"The goal of all will be to try to explain to a confused and often unenlightened citizenry that there are not two equally valid scientific theories for the origin and evolution of universe and life."可知"Creationism"与"evolution"就是宇宙与生命的起源与发展问题的两种理论；该段末句"Virtually all scientists and the majority of non-fundamentalist religious leaders have come to regard 'scientific' creationism as bad science and bad religion."中"scientific"加入了引号表达的是非科学的含义，也就是说将 creationism 描写为拙劣的科学、拙劣的宗教。到了第二段第三句更是指出对一些不了解 creationists 所用花招的人来说，这些人进行欺骗和歪曲的程度使他们感到吃惊，感到不快，根据这些线索，可以判断 creationism 指的是 D）"关于宇宙起源的虚假（deceptive）理论"。A）"有关宇宙起源的真正意义上的进化论（in its true science）"将创世纪论与进化论等同，与文中谈到将二者对立的事实不符，所以排除；既然 creationism 是 bad science，又怎么能够科学地解释地球的形成呢？因此 C）"地球形成的科学解释"不正确；而 B）"宗教产生理论"未在文中提到。

2. 正确答案 B）。文章第二段对该书的前四章进行了介绍，第三句"At appropriate places, he introduces the criticisms of the creationists and provides answers."说明 Kitcher 对上帝造物主义者进行了批评，接下来的第四句"In the last three chapters, he takes off his gloves and gives the creationists a good beating."中"takes off his gloves"形象地说明 Kitcher 在揭露（expose）creationists；接着后一句"He describes……the extent of their deception and distortion"更是说明了 Kitcher 对上帝造物主义者欺骗和歪曲的程度的揭露，由此可以总结得出 Kitcher 写书的目的是 B）"揭露 creationists 的真正面目"，而不是 A）"介绍进化论的观点"；C）"狠狠地咒骂他的对手"，文章无 curse 的证据，所以不正确，D）"对上帝造物主义者进行突然袭击"是对"a good beating"的字面意思理解，曲解了原文的意思。

3. 正确答案 B）。文章末段引用 Stephen Jay Gould 的话"This book stands for reason itself"指出这本书代表理性的东西，接下来的"And so it does（的确如此）"是对引言的强调，那么破折号后面的内容"and all would be well were reason the only judge in the creationism/evolution debate"又是对引言的进一步解释，注意这句话 were 后面省略了 if，是一个带有倒装结构的虚拟语气，也就是说"如果理性是神造论和进化论之间的惟一一裁判，一切问题就解决了"，由此推出 creationists 并未按理性的原则来办事，B）正确。选项 A）"在这场争论中，推理起了决定性作用"以及 D）"科学发现支持了创世纪论"实际上对 creationism 给予了肯定，与文章基调相反；C）"对非专业人士而言，进化论太难"与第三段第二句"非专业人士将至少对支持进化论的数据和论点得以了解"不符。

4. 正确答案 A）。本题要求回答本文是哪种类型文章的摘要，其实质是根据文章内容推断本书题材。文章首段以书开始，接着第二、三段专门介绍 Kitcher 的书的结构内容与突出特点，最后引用 Stephen Jay Gould 的话对此书做出高度评价，由此可以看出本文是一篇典型的书评。B）"科学论文"，C）"期刊的特写"，D）"报纸的评论"，都与本文的写作特点和表达风格有出入。

译文

　　传闻说出版商筹划的二十多本关于创世论和进化论的书中有一些已经出版面世了。这些书的目的都是为了向糊涂和无知的大众解释一个问题，那就是在关于宇宙和生命的起源和进化的问题上，没有两种同样正确的科学理论。宇宙学、地质学和生物学构成了一个连贯而统一的体系，不断完善着对过去发生的事件的解释。有些人试图在课堂里推行"科学"创世论，每当对进化进行科学解释时，他们就开始讲这种理论。科学创世论是基于宗教的基础上的，而非科学。实际上，无论是科学家还是大多数非原教旨主义宗教领袖都开始认为，"科学"创世论既不是科学，也不是宗教。

　　Kitcher 的书在前四章中对进化做了简单的介绍。在合适的地方，他介绍了对创世论者的批判并给出了回答。在最后三章中，他终于显露出本意，给创世论者一顿痛击。他描述了这些人的伎俩，对那些不熟悉创世论者的人来说，这些人对真相的欺骗和歪曲程度让人不快和震惊。因为既然这些人的最初动机是宗教,他们本应该采取更加符合基督教徒的行为。

Kitcher 是位哲学家,这也许部分解释了他的论证为何如此清晰和有效。普通读者至少能够了解什么样的数据和论证是支持进化理论的。他书中最后几章对创世论者的批判非常清楚,所有人都能读懂。在这本书的封面上,Stephen Jay Gould 写道:"这本书是理性的代表。"确实如此,在创世论和进化论的辩论中,理性是惟一合格的评判。

第五节　考研英语阅读理解
正确答案特征规律总结

中心思想是答案。这个特征具有最明显的科学性。首先,一篇论证合理的文章,其使用的每个字词、每一句话都应该是为中心思想服务的,而考研英语考试中所选的文章肯定是写得好的文章,所以文章中的所有细节都应该是服务于中心思想的。其次,大纲要求命题专家在出题时,也得让考生在思考文章中心的基础上答题,所以考题的正确答案必须与中心思想一致,否则就违背了考试大纲。所以,有了这两点依据,我们可以相信,如果某一选项与中心思想(文章的中心思想或段落的中心思想)一致,它很可能是正确答案。

合理选项一般不是答案;不合理选项可能是答案。这与命题策略有关,"围魏救赵"是中国战国时的军事典故,也是孙子兵法的一计,其本质就是"声东击西"。这种策略在考研考试命题时得到了充分运用。在各种干扰项中,用得最多的就是此计策,表现为:A)即文章所论述的是一个内容,而选项是文中的另一个内容,或者根本就是编造出来的相似内容,构成干扰项;B)将两种或多种观点、态度、立场等混淆起来,即把文章作者的看法与文中所引述的他人的看法混为一谈,对作者的观点、态度提问时,用别人的观点去回答,而对他人的观点提问时,则从作者的角度去作答;C)将两种或多种事物的细节掺杂在一起,即对一件事的细节提问时,用其他事物的细节作为选项来应对。此外,出题人为了误导考生,还会特地将干扰项打扮得像真的一样,有时用常识就可以导出,而答案却弄得像假的、不合理。所以我们在这里就得反其道而行之,不要相信那些貌似合理、凭自己的常识就可以推导出的选项,特别重视那些貌似不合理的选项。

照抄原文一般不是答案;同义替换可能是答案。"偷天换日"是出题人常用的又一伎俩,利用考生做题时间紧,很多细节来不及细看,甚至来不及将所有的四个选项看完这一薄弱之处,将干扰项做成与原文句子结构及词汇都几乎一模一样的形式,只略微改动其中的一个词或几个词,从而造成意思上的变化;或者利用原文中的词来伪造选项或断章取义,使干扰项亦真亦假,是非难辨。这种干扰项多半是前半句甚至是前大半句是原文内容,只是换了最后几个词,让人防不胜防。我们在做题时就得心中有数,对照抄原文的选项要小心上当,而对选项中原文词句的同义替换敏感。

含义肯定、绝对的一般不是答案,含义不肯定的可能是答案。前面我们谈到考点"路标"时曾说过:强烈的表达容易成为考点,原因是它们都有一个共同特点:概念绝对,答案惟一,无论是命题还是答题,不会产生歧义和疑问,因此容易命题,答案不会模棱两可。但到了选项之后,情况正好相反,肯定、绝对的选项往往容易把话说过了,而不肯定的选项却因为涵盖面宽,容易成为答案。

表示绝对含义的常见词汇:must,always,never,the most(最高级),all,only,any,none,sole,entirely,every,absolutely,totally 等。有这些词的选项往往是干扰项,但在表示原因、方式、方法时有例外。

表示相对含义的常见词汇:can,could,may,usually,might,most(大多数),more or less,relatively,nearly,possibly,not enough,suggest,seem 等。还有"部分"含义的词汇,也经常作为答案出现,如 part,partial,some(someone,somebody,sometime,something,certain[一定程度上])等。答案选项中常会出现这些词。

含义矛盾或句式复杂的可能是答案。命题人总是想为难考生,所以正确答案往往藏在那些不太容易看得懂的选项中。表现出来要么就是含义矛盾、不知所云;要么就是句式复杂、理解困难。所以我们看到这类选项不要想偷懒放过,反而要想到它们很可能是答案,认真对待。当然如果时间来不及,不妨径直选之。

简单具体、含义肤浅的不是答案,根据抽象、意义深刻的可能是答案。简单、具体、含义肤浅的内容根本不必要写篇文章来说明,值得作者写出一个 passage 来谈的,总有点概括、抽象、意义深刻的味道。我们的出题人也一样,他出的题得围绕作者的写作目的,总不能搞个简单、具体、含义肤浅的答案,这不也显得出题人水平低? 这条常适用于主旨题。

表达基础、基本概念的可能是解,常用词有:basis,be based on,fundamentally 等。如果是社会文化类题的文章,提问中出现 purpose 一词,则选项中含有动词 describe 的一般为正确答案。如果是科普类文章,则选项中含有动词 inform,explain,illustrate 的为正确答案。

示例:

下面,我们从最新考题中抽取了比较典型反映了上述 10 项特征的示例,以具体说明,为避免重复,我们采用的是抽选方式,其实这些规律可以运用到每一道题中,同学们可以自己对照真题加以检验。

经典实例

What is the major weakness of MBA holders according to The Harvard Business Review?

A) They are usually self-centered. (不合理项可能是答案)

B) They are aggressive and greedy.

C) They keep complaining about their jobs. (肤浅的不是答案)

D) They are not good at dealing with people. (肤浅的不是答案)

经典实例

What does the author say about the emic approach and the etic approach?

A) They have different research focuses in the study of ethnic issues. (概括性的是答案)

B) The former is biased while the later is objective.

C) The former concentrates on the study of culture while the latter on family issues. (肤浅的不是答案)

D) They are both heavily dependent on questionnaires in conducting surveys. (含义肯定的一般不是答案)

经典实例

Farming emerged as a survival strategy because man bad been obliged _____.

A) to give up his former way of life(简单具体的一般不是答案)

B) to leave the coastal areas(简单具体的一般不是答案)

C) to follow the ever-shifting vegetation(简单具体的一般不是答案)

D) to abandon his original settlement(概括性的是答案)

The message the author wishes to convey in the passage is that _____.

A) human civilization remains glorious though it is affected by climatic changes(合理项不是答案)

B) mankind is virtually helpless in the face of the dramatic changes of climate(含义相对的是答案)

C) man has to limit his activities to slow down the global warming process(合理项一般不是答案)

D) human civilization will continue to develop in spite of the changes of nature(合理项一般不是答案)

经典实例

The author's opinion of child adoption seems to be that _____.

A) no rules whatsoever can be prescribed（含义不确定的可能是答案）

B) white families should adopt black children

C) adoption should be based on IQ test results（含义绝对的一般不是答案）

D) cross-racial adoption is to be advocated

 # Passage

Historians of women's labor in the United States at first largely disregarded the story of female service workers—women earning wages in occupations such as salesclerk, domestic servant, and office secretary. These historians focused instead on factory work, primarily because it seemed so different from traditional, unpaid "women's work" in the home, and because the underlying economic forces of industrialism were presumed to be gender-blind and hence emancipatory in effect. Unfortunately, emancipation has been less profound than expected, for not even industrial wage labor has escaped continued sex segregation in the workplace.

To explain this unfinished revolution in the status of women, historians have recently begun to emphasize the way a prevailing definition of femininity often determines the kinds of work allocated to women, even when such allocation is inappropriate to new conditions. For instance, early textile-mill entrepreneurs, in justifying women's employment in wage labor, made much of the assumption that women were by nature skillful at detailed tasks and patient in carrying out repetitive chores; the mill owners thus imported into the new industrial order hoary stereotypes associated with the homemaking activities they presumed to have been the purview of women. Because women accepted the more unattractive new industrial tasks more readily than did men, such jobs came to be regarded as female jobs. And employers, who assumed that women's "real" aspirations were for marriage and family life, declined to pay women wages commensurate with those of men. Thus many lower-skilled, lower-paid, less secure jobs came to be perceived as "female."

More remarkable than the origin has been the persistence of such sex segregation in twentieth-century industry. Once an occupation came to be perceived as "female", employers showed surprisingly little interest in changing that perception, even when higher profits beckoned. And despite the urgent need of the United States during the Second World War to mobilize its human resources fully, job segregation by sex characterized even the most important war industries. Moreover, once the war ended, employers quickly returned to men most of the "male" jobs that women had been permitted to master.

1. According to the passage, job segregationby sex in the United States was _____.

   A) greatly diminlated by labor mobilization during the Second World War

   B) perpetuated by those textile-mill owners who argued in favor of women's employment in wage labor

   C) one means by which women achieved greater job security

   D) reluctantly challenged by employers except when the economic advantages were obvious

2. According to the passage, historians of women's labor focused on factory work as a more promising area of research than service-sector work because factory work _____.

   A) involved the payment of higher wages

   B) required skill in detailed tasks

   C) was assumed to be less characterized by sex segregation

   D) was more readily accepted by women than by men

3. The passage supports which of the following statements about the early mill owners mentioned in the second paragraph?

A) They hoped that by creating relatively unattractive "female" jobs they would discourage women from losing interest in marriage and family life.

B) They sought to increase the size of the available labor force as a means to keep men's to keep men's wages low.

C) They argued that women were inherently suited to do well in particular kinds of factory work.

D) They thought that factory work bettered the condition of women by emancipating them from dependence on income earned by men.

4. The passage supports which of the following statements about hiring policies in the United States?

A) After a crisis many formerly "male" jobs are reclassified as "female" jobs.

B) Industrial employers generally prefer to hire women with previous experience as homemakers.

C) Post-Second World War hiring policies caused women to lose many of their wartime gains in employment opportunity.

D) Even war industries during the Second World War were reluctant to hire women for factory work.

5. Which of the following best describes the relationship of the final paragraph to the passage as a whole?

A) The central idea is reinforced by the citation of evidence drawn from twentieth-century history.

B) The central idea is restated in such a way as to form a transition to a new topic for discussion.

C) The central idea is restated and juxtaposed with evidence that might appear to contradic it.

D) Recent history is cited to suggest that the central idea's validity is gradually diminishing.

答案解析及译文

题材:社会科学——社会问题

本文主要介绍了服务行业的女性工作者。

1. 正确答案 B)。工作中性别歧视在美国有什么特点？A 项说很大程度上被二战时情况弱化了，但事实相反，二战时此点仍很严重。B 项正确,被那些赞成雇佣妇女的作坊主永久化了。C 项妇女借此获得更多工作保护。D 项除非有经济利益,雇主不愿改变它。

2. 正确答案 C)。研究妇女劳动的历史学家关注工厂劳动,认为是更有用的领域,而不关注服务行业妇女,因为工厂劳动:A 项报酬高。B 项需要细活。C 项正确,被认为较少有性别歧视特征。D 项更多妇女。

3. 正确答案 C)。哪一个关于第二段说的早期作坊主的观点正确？A 项让妇女不要失去对结婚、家庭的兴趣。B 项为扩大劳动力规模,控制男工工资在低水平。C 项正确,他们认为妇女天生就适合一些工厂工作。D 项"工厂劳动将妇女从依赖男人中解放出来。"不是这些人观点,而是第一段所提一些历史学家的观点。

4. 正确答案 C)。关于美国的雇佣政策,哪个正确？A 项危机过后,很多以前"男性"工作变为"女性"工作。B 项喜欢雇佣有家务劳动经验的妇女。C 项正确。战后政策使妇女失掉许多他们在战时得到的工作。D 项即使二战时战时工业也不愿雇妇女。易混。不是不雇佣妇女,而是在工作中进行男女有别对待。

5. 正确答案 A)。最后一段和文章前面有何关系？A 项正确。中心论点被 20 世纪一个例证加强。作者引用二战中的例子,来说明制造业中男女歧视的情况。B 项 From a transition to a new topic。C 项可能反驳中心观点的证据。D 项削弱中心论点。

译文

　　美国研究妇女劳工的历史学家最初严重忽视了服务行业女性工作者的情况——如从事诸如售货员、保姆、办公室秘书等职业而赚取工资的妇女。这些历史学家关注工厂劳动，主要是因为它看上去与传统的无酬的家庭"妇女工作"差异很大，还因为工业化形成的基本经济压力被设想为没有性别差异，故而在事实上有利于妇女解放。不幸的是，妇女解放没有想象中那么深入，因为即使工业工资劳动者在劳动场所也未能从男女分隔中摆脱出来。

　　为解释这一关于妇女地位的不彻底革命，历史学家们最近开始强调，对女性特点的常见定义常常会决定分配给妇女的工作种类，即使这一分配在新条件下不合适。例如，早期纺织厂的企业主在确定如何雇佣女劳工时，做了许多假设：妇女天生擅于做细活，对做重复性杂事有耐心。这些厂主给新工业秩序引入了与他们认定是妇女本职的家务劳动相联系的古老的陈腐观念。因为妇女更爽快地接受了那些不太吸引人的新工业工作，这些工作就被认为妇女的工作。而那些设想妇女"真正的"渴望是婚姻和家庭生活的雇主从不愿付给妇女与男子相等的工资。就这样，许多低技术、低收入、安全性低的工作被认为是"女性的"。

　　性别分隔的存留在20世纪中比其开端时更为明显。一旦一种职业被认为是"女性的"，雇主对改变这种认识所表现出的兴趣就令人吃惊地少，即使更高的利润会随之而来。尽管二战时美国极需彻底利用其人力资源，可就是在最重要的军工生产中性别分隔仍很严重。而且，一旦战争结束，雇主很快就让男子回到妇女曾被允许的"男性"工作中。

第三章 填空式阅读

第一节 完形填句概述及应试策略

一、大纲要求

阅读理解选择搭配题型是2005年考研英语试卷中新增加的一种题型。该题型主要考查考生对连贯性、一致性、逻辑联系等语篇、语段整体性特征的理解,即要求考生在理解全文的基础上搞清楚文章的整体和微观结构。

该题型分为两个部分:主干部分和选项部分。主干部分的文章原文约600词,其中有5段空白处。空白处的位置可能在段首、段落中间或段末,但不会是语篇的第一句,一般情况下也不会是最后一句。选项部分为6或7段文字,每段可能是一个句子,可能是两三个短句,也可能是一个完整的段落。选项中的5段文字分属于主干部分的空白处。要求考生依据自己对于文章的理解,从选项中选择5段文字放回到文章中相应的5段空白处。考生需要认真阅读主干部分,搞清楚主干的内容、段落关系和结构布局。还应分析选项部分的结构和内容,分辨出它们应属于文章的哪个部分,所选段落要与空白处的上下文衔接起来。试题在一般情况下不可能有特别明显的词汇、句子等语言方面的提示,也并不要求考生过分关注某一具体的细节;而是要求考生着眼于全文,在理解全文内容、语篇结构、逻辑关系(如时间、地点、因果关系、从属关系等)的基础上做出正确选择。

二、出题形式

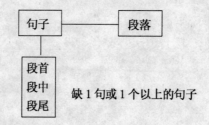

三、文章的结构

1. 描述性结构　主要介绍事物、问题或倾向的特点,对人物的描述如传记,包括人身体特征、家庭背景、成长过程、个性爱好、成就贡献等内容,因此时间、地点往往是出题重点。
2. 释义性结构　解释某一理论、学科、事物,主要用例子、比喻、类比阐述。
3. 比较性结构　把两个人或事物功能、特点、优缺点进行对比。
4. 原因性结构　这种结构主要分析事物的成因,客观的、主观的、直接的、间接的。
5. 驳斥性结构　这种结构主要是先介绍一种观点,然后对其评论或驳斥,然后分析其优缺点、危害性,最后阐明自己的观点。

四、解题步骤

1. 阅读文章题目附近的句子,锁定目标答案可能的特征
2. 阅读选择项,寻找特征词
①抓主干,猜大意,弄清是个啥东西:定义、因果、例子、措施
②不要放过特征词:代词、专用名词、连接词、数字、复数名词填表

③小词帮你出大力,时态帮助你理顺序,标点解决大问题

④用代入法通读全文,检查答案是否合理

4. 回头再去看原文,明确 1～5 位置

①开头常是主题句,莫忘掉头看标题,还有上、下主题句,不行再看前和尾

②中间不忘主题句,前瞻后望找启示

③末尾常是下结论,也可排比和例子

五、完形填句题的注意事项

1. 就近原则寻找信息点

2. 判断句往往是文章或段落的中心思想句,判断句中的名词必定是信息线索

3. 选项中出现时间年代时,往往要注意与原文中年代的前后对应关系

4. 选项中出现代词时,往往该选项不能放在首句,往往要注意指代成立的条件

　　it 可指代前面的单数名词或整个句子;

　　they 或 them 指代前面的复数名词;

　　one 指代前面的单数可数名词;

　　that 指代前面的不可数名词或句子;

　　this 指代前面的单数名词或句子

5. 绝对常是干扰项,意思太泛太窄要小心

6. 警惕无关离题词,两项相近有答案

7. 选项对比原文时,与原文重复或同义改写的字越多的就是选项

8. 填进句子的主语可能是上句的客体(宾语,表语)

9. 总体观、相互补,做题不用按顺序,先做易后做难,莫忘近邻上下文

10. 选项中如果出现专有名词,那么一定要先做

11. 放在段首的句子的特点

①当选项为某段段首会含有 between... and, eithe... or, not only... but also;

②复数名词时,那么该段将是总分结构,其中提到的名词必定是线索;

③会有标点符号":"或";"

12. 放在段尾的句子有时也会有提示词:

①因果连词

therefore、thus、as a result、for this reason、hence

②总结性连词

in short、to sum up、to conclude、in a word

③转折性连词

but、nevertheless

13. 解题方法

①主旨解题法 { a:首尾呼应(段首、段尾)　b:与首句或尾句呼应(段中)

②句子对应成分分析法:(使用在排比语境中)

③同现关系

④复现关系

⑤逻辑关系与解题法

⑥数单词个数解题法

14. 你的路障是单词,更是思维和心境。

六、完形填句题常考的逻辑关系词

(一)并列和递进关系

1.标志词

and、indeed、also、besides、almost、even、similarly、like、correspondingly、accordingly、in the same way、meanwhile、furthermore、moreover、too

2.前后句子的名词或意思具有同指性

(二)转折或让步的对立关系

1.标志词

but、yet、however、although、though、while、wheres、despite、by、contrast、on the contrary

2.前后句子的名词同指,但句意对立,往往出现以下情况

a 褒贬对立

b 句式结构对立,前肯后否、前否后肯

(三)例证关系

①标志词 :for example、for instance、for one thing、to illustrate、as an illustration、that is、name-ly、verify

②出题模式

a 总结说明→例子(例证),总结说明后往往伴有表例证关系的提示词:

for example、for instance →此时前面往往有复数名词或表述概念句子。

b 例子(例证)→总结说明,总结说明提前往往伴有提示词:

thus、therefore、in conclusion、as a result.

(四)定义关系

①有定义或释义关系的句子往往是文章或段落主题句,所以放段首或段尾

②下定义的方式有:

a 判断句:A is B

b 名词(被定义对象)+定语从句(定义内容)

c 名词 +同位语

d 名词+be called+名词

e:by+名词(被定义对象)+be meant+名词(定义内容)

③下定义时所伴随的过度词:

namely、in other words、that is to say、or rather

七、大纲样题解读

本样题出自考研新大纲,考生要仔细研读,掌握解题规律。

Directions:

In the following article, some sentences have been removed. For Questions 41—45, choose the most suitable one from extra choices, which do not fit in any of the gaps. Mark your answers on AN-SWER SHEET 1. (10 points)

Long before Man lived on the Earth, there were fishes, mammals. Although some of these animals were ancestors of kinds living today, others are now extinct, that is, they have no descendants alive now. [41]_____.

Very occasionally the rocks show impression of skin, so that, apart from color, we can build up a reasonably accurate picture of an animal that died millions of years ago. The kind of rock in which the remains are found tells us much about the nature of the original land, often of the plants that grew on it, and even of its climate.

[42]_____. Nearly all of the fossils that we know were preserved in rocks formed by water action, and most of these are of animals that lived in or near water. Thus it follows that there must be many kinds of mammals, birds, and insects of which we know nothing.

[43]_____. There were also crab-like creatures, whose bodies were covered with a horny substance. The body segments each had two pairs of legs, one pair for walking on the sandy bottom, the other for swimming. The head was a kind of shield with a pair of compound eyes, often with thousands of lenses. They were usually an inch or two long but some were 2 feet.

[44]_____. Of these, the ammonites are very interesting and important. They have a shell composed of many chambers, each representing a temporary home of the animal. As the young grew larger it grew a new chamber and sealed off the previous one. Thousands of these can be seen in the rocks on the Dorset Coast.

[45]_____.

About 75 million years ago the Age of Reptiles was over and most of the groups died out. The mammals quickly developed, and we can trace the evolution of many familiar animals such as the elephant and horse. Many of the later mammals, though now extinct, were known to primitive man and were featured by him in cave paintings and on bone carvings.

[A]The shellfish have a long history in the rock and many different kinds are known.

[B]Nevertheless, we know a great deal about many of them because their bones and shells have been preserved in the rocks as fossils. From them we can tell their size and shape, how they walked, the kind of food they ate.

[C]The first animals with true backbones were the fishes, first known in the rocks of 375 million years ago. About 300 million years ago the amphibians, the animals able to live both on land and in water, appeared. They were giant sometimes 8 feet long, and many of them lived in the swampy pools in which our coal seam, or layer was formed. The amphibians gave rise to the reptiles and for nearly 150 million years these were the principal forms of life on land, in the sea, and in the air.

[D]The best index fossils tend to be marine creatures. These animals evolved rapidly and spread over large areas of the world.

[E]The earliest animals whose remains have been found were all very simple kinds and lived in the sea. Later forms are more complex, and among these are the sea-lilies, relations of the star-fishes, which had long arms and were attached by a long stalk to the sea bed, or to rocks.

[F]When an animal dies, the body, its bones, or shell, may often be carried away by streams into lakes or the sea and there get covered up by mud. If the animal lived in the sea its body would probably sink and be covered with mud. More and more mud would fall upon it until the bones or shell become embedded and preserved.

[G]Many factors can influence how fossils are preserved in rocks. Remains of an organism, may be replaced by minerals, dissolved by an acidic solution to leave only their impression, or simply reduced to a more stable form.

文章导读:本文主要通过化石来了解生命的进化历程

41. **答案**:[B]。
策略:理清脉络,顺理成章。
解析:本题既然是在段落的尾部,就可以在前面所给的句子中找出线索,推出文章随后应该表达的思想。根据这条线索解析:原文告诉我们,早在人类以前就有很多爬行类和哺乳类动物在地球上生存了。有些……而其他物种都灭绝了。这段文字以 they have no descendants alive now 结尾。那么,正确的选项应该顺着这一脉络,继续以 they 为中心词而展开论述。选项 B 符合这一要求。

B项大意为:不过,我们对许多绝种的动物了解仍然很多,因为它们的骨骼和外壳形成了化石,保存在岩石中,根据这些化石我们能够……。

42. 答案:[F]。

策略:回光返照,分总结合。

解析:本题既然是在段落的开头,就可以在后面所给的句子中找出线索,推出文章前面的大致内容。然后根据这条线索解析:从后文我们知道,几乎所有的我们知道的化石都是在水运动(water action)的作用下形成的,……。这段文字是对前文的总结,由此我们可以推断出前文是对这一话题的分述:选项 F 恰恰从两方面进行阐述:(1)When an animal dies, the body, its bones, or shell, may often be carried away by streams into lakes or the sea;(2)If the animal lived in the sea its body would probably sink and be covered with mud. 由此可见,从分述到总述是本段行文规则,我们采用回光返照的思路可以快速解题。

43. 答案:[E]。

策略:前后呼应,找寻标记。

解析:本题是在段落的开头,就可以在后面所给的句子中找出线索,推出文章前面的大致内容。句中的 also 是个标志词,可以从这条线索解析:从后文我们知道,还有(also)蟹类动物,它们的身体……。由此我们可以推断出前文一定是和这一话题并列的叙述,即某种动植物。选项 F 符合行文规则:最早期的动物残骸已经被发现,这些动物是十分简单的物种,生活在海洋里,后来物种日趋复杂,海百合就是其中的一种。从 also 出发寻找并列结构,是这道题的解题突破口。依据并列标记词搜寻前后呼应句。

44. 答案:[A]。

策略:前指代词,总分例释。

解析:本题是在段落的开头,就可以在后面所给的句子中找出线索并推出文章的大致内容。句中的 Of these, the ammonites……是标志词,指示代词 these 这条线索,我们可以推知 the ammonites 和前面某个名词应存在从属关系,如果这个词不认识,可看后文:They have a shell composed of many chambers, each representing a temporary home of the animal. 这里的 shell 可以暗示前面某个词的特征,由此我们可以推断出前文一定是一个总的叙述,即:岩石中甲壳类动物化石历史悠久,种类繁多。它可能是此段的主题句,后文则举例说明这一主题。即:菊石不仅让人饶有兴趣,而且十分重要。它们都有一个贝壳,分别代……。选项 A 符合行文规则,是这道题的解题突破口。

45. 答案:[C]。

策略:理清脉络,顺理成章。

解析:本题是独立的一段,这段可能是总结前文,也可能是引起下文,或者二者兼而有之。通过快速浏览我们发现文章中最后的语段是以 About 75 million years ago 这一时间标志词:375 million years ago,About 300 million years ago,nearly 150 million years,而且降幂排列,文章中的 About 75 million years ago 恰好符合这一规律。再大致浏览一下文章的内容,文章在大量枚举事例,选项 C 符合行文规则。

第二节　实　战　演　练

 # Passage 1

As more and more material from other cultures became available, European scholars came to recognize even greater complexity in mythological traditions. Especially valuable was the evidence provided by ancient Indian and Iranian texts such as the Bhagavad-Gita and the Zend-A-vesta. From these sources it became apparent that the character of myths varied widely, not only by geographical region but also by historical period. ___(1)___ He argued that the relatively simple Greek myth of Persephone reflects the concerns of a basic agricultural community, whereas the more involved and complex myths found later in Homer are the product of a more developed society.

Scholars also attempted to tie various myths of the world together in some way. From the late 18th century through the early 19th century, the comparative study of languages had led to the reconstruction of a hypothetical parent language to account for striking similarities among the various languages of Europe and the Near East. These languages, scholars concluded, belonged to an Indo-European language family. Experts on mythology likewise searched for a parent mythology that presumably stood behind the mythologies of all the European peoples. ___(2)___ For example, an expression like "maiden dawn" for "sunrise" resulted first in personification of the dawn, and then in myths about her.

Later in the 19th century the theory of evolution put forward by English naturalist Charles Darwin heavily influenced the study of mythology. Scholars researched on the history of mythology, much as they would dig fossil-bearing geological formations, for remains from the distant past. ___(3)___ Similarly, British anthropologist Sir James George Frazer proposed a three-stage evolutionary scheme in The Golden Bough. According to Frazer's scheme, human beings first attributed natural phenomena to arbitrary supernatural forces (magic), later explaining them as the will of the gods (religion), and finally subjecting them to rational investigation (science).

The research of British scholar William Robertson Smith, published in Lectures on the Religion of the Semites (1889), also influenced Frazer. Through Smith's work, Frazer came to believe that many myths had their origin in the ritual practices of ancient agricultural peoples, for whom the annual cycles of vegetation were of central importance. ___(4)___ This approach reached its most extreme form in the so-called functionalism of British anthropologist A. R. Radcliffe-Brown, who held that every myth implies a ritual, and every ritual implies a myth.

Most analyses of myths in the 18th and 19th centuries showed a tendency to reduce myths to some essential core—whether the seasonal cycles of nature, historical circumstances, or ritual. That core supposedly remained once the fanciful elements of the narratives had been stripped away. In the 20th century, investigators began to pay closer attention to the content of the narratives themselves. ___(5)___

A. German-born British scholar Max Muller concluded that the Rig-Veda of ancient India—the oldest preserved body of literature written in an Indo-European language—reflected the earliest stages of an Indo-European mythology. Muller attributed all later myths to misunderstandings that arose from the picturesque terms in which early peoples described natural phenomena.

B. The myth and ritual theory, as this approach came to be called, was developed most fully by British scholar Jan Ellen Harrison. Using insight gained from the work of French sociologist Emile Durkheim, Harrison argued that all myths have their origin in collective rituals of a society.

C. Austrian psycholanalyst Sigmund Freud held that myths—like dreams—condense the material of experience and represent it in symbols.

D. This approach can be seen in the work of British anthropologist Edward Burnett Tylor. In Primitive Culture (1871), Tylor organized the religious and philosophical development of humanity into separate and distinct evolutionary stages.

E. The studies made in this period were consolidated in the work of German scholar Christian Gottlob Heyne, who was the first scholar to use the Latin term myths (instead of fabula, meaning "fable") to refer to the tales of heroes and gods.

F. German scholar Karl Otfried Muller followed this line of inquiry in his Prolegomena to a Scientifie Mythology, 1825.

Passage 2

Mobile phones should carry a label if they proved to be a dangerous source of radiation, according to Robert Bell, a scientist. And no more mobile phone transmitter towers should be built until the long-term health effects of the electromagnetic radiation they emit are scientifically evaluated, he said. "Nobody's going to drop dead overnight but we should be asking for more scientific information," Robert Bell said at a conference on the health effects of low-level radiation.　(1)

A report widely circulated among the public says that up to now scientists do not really know enough to guarantee there are no ill-effects on humans from electromagnetic radiation. According to Robert Bell, there are 3.3 million mobile phones in Australia alone and they are increasing by 2,000 a day.　(2)

As well, there are 2,000 transmitter towers around Australia, many in high density residential areas.　(3)　The electromagnetic radiation emitted from these towers may have already produced some harmful effects on the health of the residents nearby.

Robert Bell suggests that until more research is completed the Government should ban construction of phone towers from within a 500 metre radius of school grounds, child care centers, hospitals, sports playing fields and residential areas with a high percentage of children.　(4)　He adds that there is also evidence that if cancer sufferers are subjected to electromagnetic waves the growth rate of the disease accelerates.

　(5)　According to Robert Bell, it is reasonable for the major telephone companies to fund it. Besides, he also urges the Government to set up a wide-ranging inquiry into possible health effects.

A. He says there is emerging evidence that children absorb low-level radiation at rate more than three times that of adults.

B. By the year 20004 it is estimated that Australia will have 8 million mobile phones; nearly one for every two people.

C. "If mobile phones are found to be dangerous, they should carry a warning label until proper shields can be devised," he said.

D. Then who finances the research?

E. For example, Telstra, Optus and Vodaphone build their towers where it is geographically suitable to them and disregard the need of the community.

F. The conclusion is that mobile phones brings more harm than benefit.

G. The mobile phone also causes a lot of problems while offering people great convenience.

Passage 3

Until about two million years ago Africa's vegetation had always been controlled by the interactions of climate; geology, soil, and groundwater conditions; and the activities of animals. The addition of humans to the latter group, however, has increasingly rendered unreal the concept of a fully developed "natural" vegetation—i. e., one approximating the ideal of a vegetational climax.　(1)　Early attempts at mapping and classifying Africa's vegetation stressed this relationship: sometimes the names of plant zones were derived directly from climates. In this discussion the idea of zones is retained only in a broad descriptive sense.

　(2)　In addition, over time more floral regions of varying shape and size have been recognized. Many schemes have arisen successively, all of which have had to take views on two important aspects:

the general scale of treatment to be adopted, and the degree to which human modification is to be comprehended or discounted.

(3)　Quite the opposite assumption is now frequently advanced. An intimate combination of many species—in complex associations and related to localized soils, slopes, and drainage—has been detailed in many studies of the African tropics. In a few square miles there may be a visible succession from swamp with papyrus, the grass of which the ancient Egyptians made paper and from which the word "paper" originated, through swampy grassland and broad-leaved woodland and grass to a patch of forest on richer hillside soil, and finally to juicy fleshy plants on a nearly naked rock summit.

(4)　Correspondingly, classifications have differed greatly in their principles for naming, grouping, and describing formations: some have chosen terms such as forest, woodland, thorn-bush, thicket, and shrub for much of the same broad tracts that others have grouped as wooded savanna (grassy plain with many trees) and steppe (treeless grassy plain). This is best seen in the nomenclature, naming of plants, adopted by two of the most comprehensive and authoritative maps of Africa's vegetation that have been published: R. W. J. Keay's Vegetation Map of Africa South of the Tropic of Cancer and its more widely based successor, The Vegetation Map of Africa, compiled by Frank White. In the Keay map the terms "savanna" and "steppe" were adopted as precise definition of formations, based on the herb layer and the coverage of woody vegetation; the White map, however, discarded these two categories as specific classifications. Yet any absence of savanna as in its popular and more general sense is doubtful.

(5)　However, some 100 specific types of vegetation identified on the source map have been compressed into 14 broad classifications.

A. As more has become known of the many thousands of African plant species and their complex ecology, naming, classification, and mapping have also become more particular, stressing what was actually present rather than postulating about climatic potential.

B. In regions of higher rainfall, such as eastern Africa, savanna vegetation is maintained by periodic fires. Consuming dry grass at the end of the rainy season, the fires burn back the forest vegetation, check the invasion of trees and shrubs, and stimulate new grass growth.

C. Once, as with the scientific treatment of African soils, a much greater uniformity was attributed to the United States.

D. The vegetational map of Africa and general vegetation groupings used here follow the White map and its extensive annotations.

E. African vegetation zones are closely linked to climatic zones, with the same zones occurring both north and south of the equator in broadly similar patterns. As with climatic zones, differences in the amount and seasonal distribution of precipitation constitute the most important influence on the development of vegetation.

F. Nevertheless, in broad terms, climate remains the dominant control over vegetation. Zonal belts of precipitation, reflection latitude and contrasting exposure to the Atlantic and Indian oceans and their currents, give some reality to related belts of vegetation.

G. The span of human occupation in Africa is believed to exceed that of any other continent. All the resultant activities have tended, on balance, to reduce tree cover and increase grassland; but there has been considerable dispute among scholars concerning the natural versus human-caused development of most African grasslands at the regional level.

Passage 4

It is hardly necessary to point out that we live in a world of increasing industrialization. Whilst this process enables us to raise our standard of living at an ever—accelerating rate, it also leads to a corresponding growth of interdependence between the different regions of the world.

____(1)____

What, then, is to be done? Although it is difficult to know where to begin to deal with such a large subject, the first is perhaps to consider the main economic difficulties an underdeveloped or emerging region has to face.

____(2)____ A number of quite common occurrences are there sufficient to cause immediate and serious interference with this export roduction: unfavorable weather conditions, plant or animal epidemics, the exhaustion of soil fertility or mineral deposits, the development of substitute products in the industrialized regions, etc. The sensitivity of the economy is greatly intensified in cases where exports are confined only to one or two products—"monocultures" as they are sometimes called.

____(3)____ This also applies to the manufactured goods required to provide their populations with the "necessities of life". This economic structure makes it difficult for them to avoid being politically dependent on the countries which absorb their exports and provide their essential imports.

Since, under modern conditions, a rapid rise in population is a phenomenon closely associated with underdevelopment, This cause alone can subject the economy to severe and continuous stress.

____(4)____ In the first place, to set up modern industries necessitates capital on a large scale, which only industrialized regions are able to provide; secondly, they lack the necessary trained manpower; thirdly, their industries—when established—are usually not efficient enough to compete with foreign imports, and any restriction on these imports is likely to lead to counter-action against their own exports.

From another point of view, it is necessary to bear in mind that there are invariably political, educational, social and psychological obstacles which tend to interfere seriously with any measures taken to deal with the economic difficulties outlined above.

____(5)____

To conclude, it seems clear that if we are to succeed in solving the many inter-related problems of underdevelopment, only the fullest and most intelligent use of the resources of all branches of science will enable us to do so.

A. For example, the economies of such countries are orientated primarily toward the production of raw materials, i. e. agricultural and mineral products; these are then exported to the industrialized countries.

B. Given these conditions, it is easy to see that any permanent economic or political instability in one area is bound to have an increasingly serious effect upon the rest of the world. Since the main source of such instability is underdevelopment, it is clear that this now constitutes a problem of international dimensions.

C. As far as "necessities of life" are concerned, they represent a concept which is continually being enlarged through the mass media of communication such as newspapers, films, the radio and advertising.

D. Although it is obvious that industrialization is the key to development, it is usually very difficult for emerging countries to carry out plans of this nature.

E. Being under-industrialized, these countries are largely dependent on imports to supply the equipment needed to produce the raw materials they export.

F. To consider only one point: it is obviously useless to devote great efforts and expense to education, technical training and planning if, for psychological reasons, the population as a whole fails to turn theory into effective action.

G. This sudden increase in the population of the underdeveloped countries has come at a difficult time.

Even if their population had not grown so fast they would have been facing a desperate struggle to bring the standard of living of their people up.

Passage 5

Marketing is "the process f planning and executing the conception, pricing, promotion, and distribution of ideas, goods, and services to create exchanges that satisfy individual and organizational goals."This means that marketing encompasses everything you have to do in a company for coming up with a needed product or service, making potential customers aware of it, making them want it, and then selling it to them.

Is sales considered "marketing"? Is advertising "marketing"? Often, you'll hear sales fuctions rferred to as "maketing,"but sales is ust a part of the larger marketing process as is advertising. In the olden days (back 30 or 40 years), marketing did consist primarily of sales. (1)

Things began changing as companies grew larger and began offering product lines that required their own brand managers, market segment managers, market segment managers and specialized positions that addressed the needs of their particular markets. (2)

The thing to remember is that, in reality, the marketing department crosses over into the entire company. Everyone in your company should be aware of the marketing message, visions, and goals of the company, and should reflect that message in everything they do this is related to the product and your customers. (3)

Any bad experience a customer has with your company can affect future sales from that customer, as well as the people they tell about the experience. (4)

The marketing department must therefore act as a guide and lead company development. But good communication is vital. The marketing department should not act independently of product development or customer service. Marketing should be involved, and there should be a meeting of the minds, whenever discussions are held regarding new product development or any customer-related function of the company.

(5) Not only does providing input the rest of the company understand marketing efforts, it also provides invaluable insight into what customers want and new ideas that mya have slipped past the rest of the company. Service technicians and customer service reps, for exmple, will have great insights into customer opinions and needs.

A. The need for a marketing department began to be seen as a vital art of business. The marketing department also takes most of the blame if a product (or company) isn't successful, regardless of whether or not the fault actually lies there.

B. This means that every contact with customers and potential customers, whether it's through advertising, personal contact, or other means, should carry a consistent message about the company and product. In effect, every employee is a sales person, and every employee is a customer service representative. If they give mixed messages about what your business is, customers and potential customers will have a distorted picture.

C. To illustrate this, assume a company has implemented a direct mail program and has placed key codes on the mailing labels to track the source of the mailing lists from which customers who place orders are coming. If the employees who take the orders don't ask for and record those codes, then the marketing department has no way of knowing which lists are working and which lists are bombing. Cooperation among departments and support of upper management to enforce necessary procedures is often critical.

D. Ressearch and analysis are critical because they lead you to identifying your product's target audience, as well as its strengths, weaknesses, threats and, most importantly, opportunities.

E. Rather than having marketing departments, companies had sales departments with an advertising manager and someone who did market research. Sometimes they added a promotions manager or hired an agency to handle advertising and promotions.

F. Don't get the idea that marketing should make these plans and recommendations alone. It is very important that the marketing department get input from many people within the company.

G. This bad experience can be anything from a rude receptionist, to poor packaging of a product. There are so many variables that effect whether a potential customer becomes a customer, or a current customer remains a customer, that the marketing departent shouldn't always be held accountable for the total success of a product. But in many companies, that is the case.

 ## Passage 6

Did you ever see the movie Honey, I Shrunk the Kids? It's about wacky dad (who's also a scientist) who accidentally shrinks his kids with his homemade miniaturizing invention. Oops! __(1)__

For older people, shrinking isn't that dramatic or sudden at all. It takes place over years and may add up to only an inch or so off of their adult height (maybe a little more, maybe less). And this kind of shrinking can't be magically reversed, although there are things that can be done to stop it or slow it down. __(2)__

There are a few reasons. As people get older, they generally lose some muscle and fat from their bodies as part of the natural aging process. Gravity (the force that keeps your feet on the ground) takes hold, and the bones in the spine, called vertebrae, may break down or degenerate, and start to collapse into one another. __(3)__ But perhaps the most common reason why some older people shrink is because of osteoporosis.

Osteoporosis occurs when too much spongy bone tissue (which is found inside of most bones) is broken down and not enough new bone material is made. __(4)__ Bones become smaller and weaker and can easily break if someone with osteoporosis is injured. Older people-especially women, who generally have smaller and lighter bones to begin with-are more likely to develop osteoporosis. As years go by, a person with osteoporosis shrinks a little bit.

Did you know that every day you do a shrinking act, too? You aren't as tall at the end of the day as you are at the beginning. That's because as the day goes on, water in the disks of the spine gets compressed (squeezed) due to gravity, making you just a tiny bit shorter. Don't worry, though. __(5)__

A. They end up pressing closer together, which makes a person lose a little high and become shorter.

B. Once you get a good night's rest, your body recovers, and the next morning, you're standing tall again!

C. Over time, bone is said to be lost because it's not being replaced.

D. Luckily, there are things that people can do to prevent shrinking.

E. The kids spend the rest of the movie as tiny people who are barely visible while trying to get back to their normal size.

F. But why does shrinking happen at all?

G. It's surprising that the process can't be changed by environment.

 ## Passage 7

In the 1980s, there was a steady decline in the use of alcohol and other drugs among teenagers. After a decade of porgress, however, a recent survey indicates that this trend has leveled off, leaving the rate of alcohol and some other drug use in the United States still high. The reasons for drg use are varied. Children may use drugs to satisfy their curiosity, confrom to peer pressure, relieve anxiety, or have an adventure. But, whatever tempts them, we must teach children to reject grugs becase drug use is illegal, harmful to their health, and interferes with academic and social development.

　　(1)　Parents, as the prime nurturers of their children's development, play a prominent role in preventing drug use. Schools, communities, social service organizations, religious groups, law enforcement agencies, the media, and local businesses also play vital roles.

Parents hav many opportunities to foster healthy, drug—free lifestyles in their children, playing a sominant role in their children's emotional and interpersonal development from infancy. Children are taught ethical values and responsibility through what social scientists call"modeling" or demonstrating acceptable behaviors for children to follow.　(2)

A basic reality is that children will have to make their way in a world that is filled with opportunities to use drugs, but parents can prepare their children to make positives. High self—esteem sometimes helps children resist peer pressure to use drugs, but not always.　(3)

They also need to appropriately supervise their children. For example, parents should know their children's friends and be aware of what their children are doing. They also need to ensure that there is proper supervision of after-school and weekend activities and that all parties are chaperoned by responsible adults.　(4)

In their classroom practice, teachers can exert significant influence on the beliefs, attitudes, and opinions of their students and complement other drug prevention activities.　(5)

Parents play an important role, but they cannot do it alone. Schools can increase children's awareness of the negative effects of drug use and equip them with skills to resist drug and alcohol use. When parents and schools work together within the context of the larger community, they gain the consensus that will strengthen drug prevention efforts.

A. For example, teachers can hone the problem-solving and decision-making skills of students by incorporating drug prevention strategies into daily lesson plans that are geared to ward the social and intellectual needs of their students. In middle school, for instance, peer pressure can be intense. Middle school teachers may use role-playing to help small groups of students practice ways to resist peer pressure to use alcohol and other drugs.

B. Parents who have responsible habits and attitudes regarding drug use send a healthy message and strongly influence their children's ideas about alcohol, tobacco, and other drugs. Parents are models for their children, and even the use of legal drugs my send the wrong signal

C. Some schools require students and parents to sign a form agreeing that all drug-related offenses will be referred to the police and that students who use drugs, including alcohol, will get counseling.

D. Schools can add a crucial component to the drug prevention efforts of parents by prevention strategies within the context of health, science, and family life curricula. Schools also provide an organized peer group setting in which children can develop communication and decision-making skills.

E. Research is unclear about the relationship between self-esteem and drug use. However, all children need opportunities to practice decision-making and to become aware of the consequences of bad decisions. Parents need to provide clear factual information about drugs and their effects.

F. Drug information programs, while important, cannot stand alone as a deterrent to drug use. Current literature has focused on a "holistic" approach to preventing drug use. A holistic approach emphasizes a prevention strategy that takes into account the wide range of forces that affect children's lives.

G. When community members are asked to provide input into the school's strategy to combat drug abuse, they can make valuable contributions and, in turn, add legitimacy to the schools drug prevention program.

Passage 8

When do people decide whether or not they want to become friends? During their first four minutes together, according to a book by Dr. Leonard Zunin. In his book, "Contact: The first four minutes", he offers this advice to anyone interested in starting new friendships: "___(1)___ A lot of people's whole lives would change if they did just that."

You may have noticed that the average person does not give his undivided attention to someone he has just met. ___(2)___ If anyone has ever done this to you, you probably did not like him very much.

When we are introduced to new people, the author suggests, we should try to appear friendly and self-confident. In general, he says, "People like people who like themselves."

On the other hand, we should not make the other person think we are too sure of ourselves. It is important to appear interested and sympathetic, realizing that the other person has his own needs, fears, and hopes.

Hearing such advice, one might say, "But I'm not a friendly, self-confident person. That's not my nature. It would be dishonest for me to that way."

___(3)___ We can become accustomed to any changes we choose to make in our personality. "It is like getting used to a new car. It may be unfamiliar at first, but it goes much better than the old one."

But isn't it dishonest to give the appearance of friendly self-confidence when we don't actually feel that way? Perhaps, but according to Dr. Zunin, "total honesty" is not always good for social relationships, especially during the first few minutes of contact. There is a time for everything, and a certain amount of play-acting may be best for the first few minutes of contact with a stranger. That is not the time to complain about one's health or to mention faults one finds in other people. It is not the time to tell the whole truth about one's opinions and impressions.

___(4)___ For a husband and wife or a parent and child, problems often arise during their first four minutes together after they have been apart. Dr. Zunin suggests that these first few minutes together be treated with care. If there are unpleasant matters to be discussed, they should be dealt with later.

The author says that interpersonal relations should be taught as a required course in every school, along with reading, writing, and mathematics. ___(5)___ That is at least as important as how much we know.

A. In reply. Dr. Zunin would claim that a little practice can help us feel comfortable about changing our social habits.

B. Much of what has been said about strangers also applies to relationships with family members and friends.

C. In his opinion, success in life depends mainly on how we get along with other people.

D. Every time you meet someone in a social situation, give him your undivided attention for four minutes.

E. He keeps looking over the other person's shoulder, as if hoping to find someone more interesting in another part of the room.

F. He is eager to make friends with everyone.

G. It is also noticed that eye-contact shows something special related to the friendship.

 ## Passage 9

When I began teaching computer science only four years ago, only a fraction of my students, maybe 10%, owned their own computers. Today the situation is reversed: probably 90% of my students own computers. It has been phenomenal to witness the rise in computer literacy among those I teach. I rarely have a student who has no experience at all with computing. Almost all of my students can at least connect to the Internet and type a document. We have come a long way in a very short time.

　　(1)　 I predict that as technology continues to improve and prices continue to drop, computers will become nearly as commonplace among college students as telephones or televisions. Just in the last year, several Internet Service Providers have even offered free computers to individual who sign up for their service!

　　(2)　

　　(3)　 I have witnessed a class of 5th graders (10-year-olds) creating multi-media presentations that incorporated text, sound, and graphics! My own daughter, who is only three, can already manipulate objects on the screen using a mouse. As a result, by the time they get to college, students are no longer intimidated by computers, but simply view them as a tool.

　　(4)　 In addition, many of our highest paying jobs are in the technical field: database designers, programmers, systems analysts, and network administrators. Demand exceeds supply in these highly competitive job markets. Here in the Pacific Northwest, opportunities in technical fields are particularly plentiful. In fact, graduates from Highline Community College's two-year Computer Information System program are having no difficulty finding challenging and high-paying jobs upon graduation, even without experience!

　　(5)　 During college, the primary uses of computers are word processing and internet research. Once students learn how to navigate the Internet, they discover an incredible resource for up-to-date information on just about any topic. But computers are also used for preparing charts, balancing personal budgets, preparing presentations, and communicating with each other and with instructors. E-mail, which is available at no cost at the college, is a very convenient way for students to contact hard-to-reach teachers. Many instructors also have their own Web pages set up, containing pertinent course information.

A. In the introductory computer class I teach, students learn computer terminology and how computers work.

B. Computer skills have become essential for virtually any job there is. It is becoming increasingly difficult to find work without basic computer literacy. Mst jobs at least require applicants to be able to word-process a document, access the Web, enter data into a database, or create a spreadsheet.

C. In addition to increasing their job marketability, students are interested in learning computers as an aid to college study.

D. For students without their own computers, there are computers available in the library. These are connected to the Internet as well as to other research databases. The library also offers free Interent classes. Students taking computer classes also have access to computers, printers and scanners in a computer lab on campus.

E. Computer skills are being taught at the elementary school level as an aid to learning.

F. Because computers are continually dropping in price, I find that many of my students can now afford high-speed computers equipped with modems, sound cards, CD-ROM drives and color printers. Some even possess ZIP, DVD and CD-R drives.

G. Games are popular among students, but what is even more popular is "surfing the Web". Their pastimes include listening to their favorite music groups, looking up scores for their favorite sports team, finding people in on-line chat rooms who share interests and hobbies, reading the news, and on-line shopping. For our many international students, the Internet has become a life-line to their home country. They can correspond with friends and family, as well as read about current events taking place at home.

Passage 10

When you eat, your body, takes the sugar from food and turns it into fuel.   (1)   Your body uses glucose for energy, so it can do everything from breathing air to playing a video game. But glucose can't be used by the body on its own-it needs a hormone called insulin to bring it into the cells of the body.

Most people get the insulin they need from the pancreas, a large organ near the stomach. The pancreas makes insulin; insulin brings glucose into the cells; and the body gets the energy it needs. When a person has insulin-dependent diabetes, it's because the pancreas is not making insulin. So someone could be eating lots of food and getting all the glucose he needs, but without insulin, there is no way for the body to use the glucose for energy.   (2)

You may have heard older people talk about having diabetes, maybe people of your grandparents' age. Usually, this is a different kind of diabetes called non-insulin-dependent diabetes. It can also be called Type 2 diabetes, or adult-onset diabetes.   (3)

When a kid diagnosed with juvenile (insulin-dependent) diabetes, he will have that type of diabetes for his whole life. It won't ever change to non-insulin-dependent diabetes when he gets older.

Scientists now think that a person who has juvenile diabetes was born with a certain gene or genes that made the person more likely to get the illness.   (4)   Many scientists believe that along with having certain genes, something else outside the person's body, like a viral infection, is necessary to set the diabetes in motion by affecting the cells in the pancreas that make insulin.

But the person must have the gene (or genes) for diabetes to start out with-this means you can't get diabetes just from catching a flu, virus, or cold. And this type of diabetes isn't caused by eating too many sugary foods, either. Diabetes can take a long time to develop in a person's body -sometimes months or year. Another important thing to remember is that diabetes is not contagious.   (5)

A. Genes are something that you inherit form your parents, and they are in your body even before you're born.

B. This sugar-fuel is called glucose.

C. It may be possible to beat insulin resistance through lifestyle changes.

D. you can't catch diabetes from people who have it, no matter how close you sit to them or if you kiss them.

E. The glucose can't get into the cells of the body without insulin.

F. When a person has this kind of diabetes, the pancreas usually can still make insulin, but the person's body needs more than the pancreas can make.

G. But it is nature for us to realize such a danger.

Passage 11

Although, recent years have seen substantial reductions in noxious pollutants from individual motor vehicles, the number of such vehicles has been steadily increasing consequently. There is a growing realization that the only effective way to achieve further reductions in vehicle emissions—short of a massive shift away from the private automobile is to replace conventional diesel fuel and gasoline with cleaner burning fuels such as compressed natural gas, liquefied petroleum gas, ethanol, or methanol.

   (1)   These molecules burn more cleanly than gasoline, in part because they have fewer carbon-carbon bonds, and the hydrocarbons they do emit are less likely to generate ozone.

(2)　　These reactions increase the probability of incomplete combustion and are more likely to release uncombusted and photochemically active hydrocarbon compounds into the atmosphere.

　　　(3)

　　Ethanol and methanol, on the other hand, have important advantages over other carbon-based alternative fuels; they have a higher energy content per volume and would require minimal changes in the existing network for distributing motor fuel. Ethanol is commonly used as a gasoline supplement, but it is currently about twice as expensive as methanol, the low cost of which is one of its attractive features.　　(4)

　　Like any alternative fuel, methanol has its critics. yet much of the criticism is based on the use of "gasoline clone" vehicles that do not incorporate even the simplest design improvements that are made possible with the use of methanol.

　　　(5)　　Vehicles incorporating only the simplest of the engine improvements that methanol makes feasible would still contribute to an immediate lessening of urban air pollution.

A. Methanol's most attractive feature, however, is that it can reduce by about 90 percent the vehicle emissions that form ozone, the most serious urban air pollutant.

B. All of these alternatives are carbon-based fuels whose molecules are smaller and simpler than those of gasoline.

C. The combustion of larger molecules, which have multiple carbon-carbon bonds, involves a more complex series of reactions.

D. On the other hand, alternative fuels do have drawbacks. Compressed natural gas would require that vehicles have a set of heavy fuel tanks—a serious liability in terms of performance and fuel effeciency and liquefied petroleum gas faces fundamental limits on supply.

E. It is true, for example, that a given volume of methanol provides only about one-half of the energy that gasoline and diesel fuel do; other things being equal, the fuel tank would have to be somewhat larger and heavier.

F. However, since methanol-fueled vehicles could be designed to be much more efficient than "gasoline clone" vehicles fueled with methanol, they would need comparatively less fuel.

G. More than 100 cities in the United States still have levels of carbon monoxide, particulate matter, and ozone (generated by photochemical, reactions with hydrocarbons from vehicle exhaust) that exceed legally established limits.

Passage 12

　　By refusing to take essential medication after a kidney transplant, a 49-year-old woman drives her doctors and nurses to distraction—to no avail, because the organ has in the end to be removed.

　　　(1)　　Patients refusing to cooperate with medical professionals cause damage not only to themselves but also impose substantial costs on the community. The pharmaceutical company Glaxo Welcome estimates the costs to the German taxpayers of this kind of negative behaviour at around five billion dollars a year.

　　A recent conference of medical professionals, health insurers, the pharmaceutical industry and patient representatives revealed a wide range of factors behind non-compliance. Not all defiant behaviour in a patient can be characterized as non-compliance. Greater stress should be placed on psychology during medical training, delegates said.　　(2)

　　Psychologist Sibylle Storkebaum told of an eight-year-old boy who ran amok in a hospital before undergoing a heart transplant, threatening to rip out his drip tubes.　　(3)　　"Doctors and nurses failed to see that they had downgraded a boy already conscious of his own responsibilities into a small child,"

Storkebaum said, explaining that the boy merely wanted to be taken seriously and to be involved in his own treatment. "Once this was acknowledged, the anger attacks subsided. ____(4)____ "Jan-Torsten Tews of Glaxo Welcome highlighted the problem of excessive medication, with patients having to take a wide range of medicines at short intervals. Educating patients and self-management were the key to treating patients with chronic conditions, he said.

Health insurers also expressed interest in better cooperation between doctor and patient. "The fact that non-compliance exists is a resulf of patient dissatisfaction with their treatment," Walter Bockemuehl, a senior executive in the statutory medical insurance scheme, said. According to one study, half of all patients did not want medication, but had drugs prescribed nevertheless. ____(5)____

A. However, there are still some medical professionals who don't believe in psychological therapy.

B. He became noticeably quieter and turned into a good patient.

C. "In these cases we should not be surprised if the advice is ignored," he said.

D. This case of medical non-compliance is not an isolated example.

E. There was evidence that psychological therapy for insecure patients could improve cooperation between doctors and patients, they added.

F. His fits of rage were subsequently seen as an attempt to assert his rights as a patient.

G. Eventually this kind of relationship between doctor and patients became more complexed.

 # Passage 13

Public schools in the United States are becoming steadily more segregated, isolating blak and Hispanic students in poor, largely minority schools, according to a new study released April 5, 1997.

The study found that between 1991 and 1994 there was the largest backward movement toward school segregation since 1954, when the Supreme Court of the United States ruled that laws enforcing segregated education under the "separate but equal" doctrine were unconstitutional. Researchers at Harvard University in Cambridge, Massachusetts, and Indiana University in Bloomington conducted the study.

____(1)____ "In American race relations, the bridge from the 20th century may be leading back into the 19th century……We may be deciding to bet the future of the country once more on separate but equal," the study concluded.

In 1972, after a 1971 Supreme Court decision mandated school busing to desegregate school systems, 63.6 percent of black students went to predominantly minority schools. That percentage remained almost the same through the mid—1980s. ____(2)____

Nearly 75 percent of HIspanic students — the fastest growing segment of the school population — attend predominantly minority schools, the study found.

Schools in the South and along the Mexican border were leading the nation in the trend toward the segregation of black students. In the South, the proportion of black students in integrated, mostly white schools dropped from a high of 44 percent in 1988 to 39.2 percent in 1991 and 36.6 percent in 1994.

The nation's ten largest inner city school districts are predominantly black and Hispanic, the study found. But even in the suburbs, where minorities have moved in increasing numbers, the pattern of segregation for black and Latino students continued. By 1994 most Latino students living in suburbs went to schools that were 64 percent nonwhite.

The study found "the relationship between segregation by race and segregation by poverty is exceptionally strong." Only 5 percent of the nation's segregated white schools face conditions of concentrated poverty, while more than 80 percent of segregated black and Latino schools do. "If the growing community of Latino students is increasingly isoalted in inferior schools, there could be a vicious cycle of declining opportunity,"the report found.

The study concluded that poor, segregated schools are unequal in a number of different ways that affect students' academic achievement. Among other things, high－poverty schools have to devote more time and resources to family and health crises and security. ___(3)___

The focus is more often on remediation, rather than advanced, demanding classes. ___(4)___

___(5)___ "More and more minority parents, when asked what they care about for their kids' schools, no longer say they care about the skin color of the kid in the next seat,"said Chester Finn, a prominent conservative analyst of education. "They care if their child is going to a safe school that teaches them to read and write."

A. Some education experts disagree with the study's conclusions, arguing instead that the trend toward school segregation reflects housing patterns and the search for ethnic identity on the part of minority parents.

B. Despite vigorous resistance for many years by many southern states, by 1980 the federal courts had largely succeeded in eliminating the system of legalized segregation in southern schools.

C. But by 1995 the percentage of black students isolated in minority schools had risen to 67.1 percent.

D. Although there are exceptions, students attending high－poverty schools face a lower level of competition regardless of their own interests and abilities, according to the study.

E. Segregation usually resulted in inferior education for blacks, whether in the North or the South. Average public expenditures for white schools routinely exceeded expenditures for black schools.

F. The study, "Deepening Segregation in American Public Schools,"concluded that the trend toward segregation was accelerating, in large part because court cases in the 1990s have made it easier for school districts to abandon desegregation plans.

G. They tend to attract less qualified teachers and are unable to hold on to qualified teachers for as long as wealthy schools do.

Passage 14

Many scientists have wondered whether there is some quirk in the way depression is inherited, such that a depressed parent or grandparent is more likely to pass on a predisposition for the disorder to female than to male descendants. Based on studies that trace family histories fo depression,the answer to that question appears to be no. ___(1)___

Simply tracing family histories, though, without also considering environmental influences, might not offer a complete picture of how depression is inherited.

Indeed, Kenneth S. Kendler and his colleagues at the Medical College of Virginia found in a study of 2,060 female twins that genetics with and without a family history of depression; some twins in both groups had recently undergone trauma,such as the death of a loved one or a divorce. The investigators found that among the women who did not have a family history of depression, stressful events raised their risk for depression by only 6 percent. ___(2)___

In other words, these women had seemingly inherited the propensity to become depressed in the wake of crises.

A similar study has not been done in men, leaving open the question of whether environmental stress and genetic risk for depression interact similarly in both sexes. But research is being done to determine whether men and women generally experience similar amounts and types of stress. Studies of key hormones hint that they do not. Hormones are not new to depression researchers. Many have wondered whether the gonadal steroids estrogen and progesterone—whose cyclic fluctuations in women regulate menstruation—might put women at a greater risk for depression. Thlere are at least two ways in which they might do so.

First, because of differences between the X and Y chromosomes, male and female brains are exposed to different hormonal milieus in utero. ___(3)___

Indeed, animal experiments show that early hormonal influences have marked behavioral consequences later on, although the phenomenon is of course difficult to study in humans.

Second, the fact that postpubertal men and women have different levels of circulating gonadal steroids might somehow put women at higher risk for depression. Research shows girls become more susceptible to depression than boys only after puberty, when they begin menstruating and experience hormonal fluxes. ___(4)___

For example, Peter J. Schmidt and David R. Rubinow of the National Institute of Mental Health recently reported that manipulations of estrogen and progesterone did not affect mood, except in women who suffer from severe premenstrual mood changes.

It now appears, however, that estrogen might set the stage for depression indirectly by priming the body's stress response. During stressful times, the adrenal glands—which sit on top of the kidneys and are controlled by the pituitary gland in the brain—secrete higher levels of a hormone called cortisol, which increases the activity of the body's metabolic and immune systems, among others. ___(5)___

Evidence is emerging that estrogen might not only increase cortisol secretion but also decrease cortisol's ability to shut down its own secretion. The result might be a stress response that is not only more pronounced but also longer-lasting in women than in men.

A. But the same risk rose lamost 14 percent among the women who did have a family history of depression.

B. To figure out why depression is more common among women, scientists have to study how genetics and environment divide the sexes—and how the two conspire to produce the symptoms we describe as depression.

C. In the normal course of events, stress increases cortisol secretion, but these elevated levels have a negative feedback effect on the pituitary, so that cortisol levels gradually return to normal.

D. Despite their importance, estrogen and cortisol are not the only hormones involved in female depression, and stress is not the only environmental influence that might hold more sway over women than men.

E. These hormonal differences may affect brain development so that men and women have different vulnerabilities—and fifferent physiological reactions to environmental stressors—later in life.

F. Even so, scientists have never been able to establish a direct relation between emotional states and levels of estrogen and progesterone in the blood of women.

G. Women and men with similar heritage seem equally likely to develop the disorder.

Passage 15

The stars... isn't it strange that not one photo taken by Apollo 11 astronauts on the moon's surface shows even a single star in the lunar sky? The moon is airless, so why did the flag ripple? Why didn't the lunar excursion module blast a crater into the surface when it landed? ___(1)___

___(2)___ To some, the only possible answer is that the "moon landing" on July 20, 1969, was pure flimflam. The millions who drank in the liftoff on their TV screens didn't realize the crew was pitched into Earth's orbit, circling for eight days while the public watched faked scenes from a movie shot by Stanley Kubrick on a huge set in Nevada, or perhaps California or Alabama or Canada. Chosen for his skills in 2001, he was told to cooperate or his brother's Communist past would be exposed. The lips of

Neil Armstrong, Buzz Aldrin and Michael Collins were forever sealed with money—and fear. Can the long list of astronauts and Apollo insiders who have died under suspicious circumstances be only coincidence?

_____(3)_____ They have written books and articles, created Web sites, put together videos. NASA tries to ignore them. "For the agency to engage in debate," says spokesman Bob Jacobs, "is disrespectful to the hundreds of thousands who worked on that program."

Just say may. So the naysayers preach undeterredly. Their putative leader is 80-year-old Bill Kaysing, a former publications analyst for Rocketdyne, which built the engines for Apollo 11s Saturn rocket in 1975, he published We Never Went to the Moon: America's Thirty Billion Dollar Swindle. The impetus came from a homeless, drug-addicted Vietnam vet who urged him to write an expose of the government. Looking into the Apollo missions, he soon realized they were technically impossible.

_____(4)_____ "I was definitely primed from the time I was 10 years old to be suspicious of the government," he says. "By 1974, when I began working on the book, I was strongly anti-government, largely due to Vietnam."

_____(5)_____ But his massed evidence takes on a shadowy if-there's-smoke-there-must-be-fire credibility. Television and radio appearances fan the flame, and the craggy, white-haired Kaysing has a genial persuasiveness made for TV. Last year he was prominent in Conspiracy Theory: Did We Land on the Moon? —an hour long Fox Network special that aired in February and again in March, drawing more than 15 million viewers. Then in August he made his case on the Today show as part of a "Truth or Conspiracy" series. "Well, it's certainly an interesting notion and fun to talk about," concluded Katie Couric, not risking offense by actually taking sides.

A. Kaysing's disciple and self-taught engineer Ralph Rene published his own book (NASA Mooned America!) in 1992. Kaysing's book had made Rene a doubter several years before.

B. Questions, so many questions.

C. That meshed with Kaysing's mind-set.

D. If the sun was the only light source why did the LEM's legs cast multiple shadows?

E. Kaysing's book is not so much written as jotted down—the would be publisher rejected it with the comment: "seemed more like random notes."

F. For more than 25 years, moonlanding disbelievers have been connecting dots few others even see.

Passage 16

Known as a successful architect, entrepreneur, and general design consultant to the who's who of Asia, Kenneth Ko may have what many would consider an enviable lifestyle. But this native of China, living in Hong Kong, is anything but the typical professional. In fact, Ken is paradoxically down to earth: "Success is something that comes from within. _____(1)_____"

"Inspiration flows, but it is not something which can be turned on and off, which is why I think about my work 24 hours a day."

When asked about that inspiration, the answer is straight and simple: People. "As a designer I am inspired by people... they never let me down. A cocktail party isn't boring unless you allow it to be. A party for 200 saves me a lot of time, I don't have to take those people out to lunch..."

_____(2)_____ You need to read people's minds and see into their futures. There is a lot of thinking behind every design detail.

"If I have a client who wears three layers of eye make-up, I know without asking that it will be important to design her a practical dressing table with natural light." _____(3)_____

Ken might be working "twenty-four hours a day", but he looks more like he's stepped off a yacht than out of press conference, "... my mind never stops... which is why I feel I have to balance that mental state with something more physical. "

　　__(4)__ Two years ago, at an age when many people put their health last on the priority list, Ken made a mental decision to turn his clock back. "I need t be physically fit, so I decided to take up a rigorous weight lifting routine and a healthy diet of horrible tasting supplements. " __(5)__

Kenneth measures success not in inches, or in buildings, or in having the luxury of a personal trainer, but simply in knowing he has achieved the best he can. He seems proudest of one of his latest projects that, he admits, might never make it off the drawing board. "I created a whole new look and interior for the 'Golden Gate Hotel' in Shanghai. They didn't ask me to, and I wasn't paid anything. I just wanted to do it. I was born in that hotel when my father was the manager. Who knows, maybe they'll accept my ideas... someday. "

But with an international business to run, how do such "personal ambitions" make it off the sheff? "Timetables give me a structure in which to work—whenever someone complains to me about not having enough time I am inclined to think that either abilities do not match their jobs or they haven't yet learnt to allocate their work load. "

"Time is all in the mind, and that's why a lot of people use it as an excuse to impress others with how busy they are. I prefer to impress people with what I've done. "

A. Ken knows only too well that consistent creativity is stressful.

B. Balance is a recurring theme for the man and his design, his second inspiration.

C. It's not based on the number of awards I have won.

D. "Not for the punishment, but because I like to test myself and create a balance between my mind, body and soul. "

E. To be a successful designer you have to be able to interpret a client's needs.

F. "Success is important, but it all comes down to how you use it. "

 # Passage 17

　　__(1)__ Scientists at the Meteorological Office's Hadley Centre for Climate Prediction and Research said yesterday that, on average, the world's temperature is 1℃ higher than in 1860, when measurements were first properly recorded.

The United Nations team of climate scientists charged with advising governments about the myth of reality of global warming recently concluded that the world is in the grip of greenhouse effect thatis at least partly attributable to mankind's carbon emissions.

They said: "the balance of evidence suggests a discernible human influence on global climate through emissions of carbon dioxide and other greenhouse gases. "

The official figures for 1995 confirm their fears that, by 2050, the world could be 2℃ hotter unless urgent action is taken. While this may not appear a huge increase, a permanent shift in global temperatures of this magnitude could have devastating effects on agriculture, wildlife and water supplies. Dr. Phill Jones of the University of East Anglia's Climate Research Unit in Norwich, which has helped the Meteorological Office to compile the figures, said yesterday: "the way to understand it is by comparision with last year's temperature in Britain. It was 10.5℃ or one degree above the average. A lot of people thought it was very hot last year. " __(2)__

　　__(3)__ The missing links are the levels of rainfall likely over different continents, and whether the Gulf Stream, which warms Britain, might shift south, causing cooling rather than heating.

Some research indicates that amounts of rainfall in northern latitudes will remain the same but will fall in sudden downpours, triggering landslips, contaminating rivers with run-off from the land and making it harder for water companies to collect enough to meet supplies.

The new figures show that, on average, surface temperature last year was 0.4℃ above the 1961-1990 average, which is the 30-year yardstick against which measurements are made. Previously, 1990 had been recorded as the warmest year, with temperatures climbing to an average 0.36℃ above the 30-year level.

(4)　In parts of Siberia, where scientists have been chronicling changes in plant life and a northward shift in the tree line consistent with global warming, temperatures were 3℃ higher than normal.

Ocean surface temperatures near the Azores were 1℃ above normal.

The gradual warming of the Earth's surface was slowed down by the eruption of Mount Pinatubo in the Philippines in June 1991. The volcano pumped thousands of tons of dust into the atmosphere, creating a veil that filtered the Sun's rays.

(5)　Dr. Jones said: "1995 was the warmest year and we would expect gradually to get more and more of these. They will go on. It's all down to burning fossil fuels and the release of carbon dioxide into the atmosphere from power stations. To slow it down, we have really got to do something and that is where the political side of things comes in."

While Britain and Germany are pushing hard for cuts in emissions beyond 2000, scientists are concerned that America, the most important country in climate negotiations, is being overwhelmed by lobbying from industry and big business.

A. Some parts of the world were, as predicted by computer climate models, significantly hotter than the average in 1995.

B. What might they think if years became two degrees higher, which is a lot warmer?

C. Our planet has changed a great deal.

D. The Earth last year was at its hottest since records began.

E. Researchers say the dust effect has now disappeared and warming has recommenced.

F. Scientists still cannot say for certain how the world's climate will behave.

Passage 18

A pond can be dug on flat ground or a gentle slope. Earth dig by the bulldozer is used to make a low dam or bank. The dam must not leak. So the bulldozer drivers push clay into the middle. Clay stops water from seeping through.　(1)

Ponds lose water by evaporation. The sun and wind take water from ponds, just as they dry out clothes on the line. Thus, every pond must have a water supply. Often the water comes from a spring. Sometimes it is piped from a stream of a well. Or the water may drain from the surface of the ground in heavy rains.

(2)　We have almost an acre of water. The greatest depth is about five feet. But in a very dry summer the spring stops running. Then the pond goes down a foot or more. We can see the muskrat holes that are usually under water. We can see the tracks of birds and raccoons in the soft mud.

Some ponds existed long before people did. Hollows were left in many places as the earth's crust took shape. Some were scraped out by glaciers or blown out by the wind. Others were made when the surface of the land moved. The earth's crust is still changing, although very slowly.

The early settlers of the United States built thousands of ponds by damming streams. Water from the pond was turned into a ditch, called a millrace. The water spilled onto a great wheel and made it turn. The turning wheel made smaller wheels turn inside a mill.　(3)

But more ponds are being made than ever before. Where streams are many miles apart, ranchers build dams to catch rainfall that has run off. Thirsty cattle come to these ponds for water. People build other ponds for fishing and swimming and for the pleasure of looking at water.

____(4)____ A pond is a food factory and a restaurant and open 24 hours a day. Millions of plants and animals make the food. Some of the animals in a pond eat nothing but plants. Some eat nothing but other animals. Some eat both plants and animals, depending on what's handy.

Pond water has more living thing than you would ever imagine. A teaspoonful may look like pure water. Actually it contains thousands of plants and animals, so tiny they can be seen only with a microscope. They are called plankton, like the plankton of the oceans. Plankton is food for many little creatures.

____(5)____ Without sunshine, pond plants would die and many creatures would starve. The sun puts in motion a wonderful manufacturing activity called photosynthesis. This takes place in plants that have a green color, which comes from a substance named chlorophyll.

A. No matter why the pond was built, one thing is certain: All kinds of plants and animals will soon move in.

B. Our pond is about 200 feet across and is fed by a spring.

C. The bottom of the pond must have clay, too. A sandy bottom would let the water drain way.

D. The marvelous thing about pond life is the way plants and animals depend on one another. All of them depend on sun, water, air, and soil.

E. The sugar and starch made by photosynthesis are food for the plant. They are food, too, for any animal that eats the plant.

F. Water-powered mills made flour from grain. They sawed boards from logs. They ran many kinds of machines. Few of these mills are still running today. Electricity has put them out of business.

Passage 19

For two hundred years the United States government operated on the assumption that, given time and the proper kind of encouragement, indians would gradually assume the "American" way of life. It seemed inconceivable that the Indian could continue to live as he once did after having seen the advantages of "civilization."

____(1)____

Borrowing elements from other societies was not something new for most Indian groups. For example, the Navajo people of the Southwest borrowed the idea of farming from Pueblo groups along the Rio Grande in the 1500's. In the Navajos borrowed the practice of sheep raising from the Spanish. Many different Indian groups in the Plains, particularly those in the western Plains, learned from the Spanish how to domesticate horses. This borrowed knowledge ultimately changed the Plains Indians' whole way of life. ____(2)____

Indians are not hard and fast enemies of industry, but many are not willing to assume ass of the work habits accepted by most American factory workers. The Sioux realized that informal work procedures were best for them. This decision made their existence more comfortable and secure.

Elements of American government have also been borrowed selectively. Some Indian groups have applied the principles of American politics to tribal problems. ____(3)____

The North American Indians, through group pride, Pan—Indianism, and selective borrowing, entered the 1970's with dignity and strength. They were not, of course, precisely the same kinds of people who had populated America two hundred, or even one hundred years earlier but the cultural heritage of the past still persisted. Indians were persecuted unrelentingly by white settlers and their government for two centuries. Yet they managed to endure.

(4)

In technology, Indian contributions appear in the manufacture of cloth and pottery and of gold, silver, and copper products. Dams, canals, and other irrigation devices of the Indian groups were copied by white settlers, particularly in the arid Southwest. The canoe, certain kinds of fish traps, and hunting and fishing techniques were also part of the Indians' contribution to "American" technology.

(5)

Many names of states such as Illinois, Massachusetts, Minnesota, Connecticut, Utah, and Delaware are also taken from Indian languages. And when names were given to cities and towns, ideas frequently came from Indian words. Consider, for example, such names as Chicago, Miami, Omaha, and Peoria.

A. In borrowing ideas from American society, Indian groups were careful to select only those ideas that would be beneficial; all others were rejected. Selective borrowing produced some interesting results. For instance, some Indian groups incorporated certain Christian symbols into their traditional ceremonies. Television receivers are often present in houses built according to ancient designs.

B. When white Americans finally realized that most Indians preferred their own cultures to that of the United States, they concluded that the Indians were strange people indeed. What they did not realize, however, was that the Indians had in fact examined American society and had selectively borrowed from it those ideas that seemed useful.

C. Physicians and psychiatrists sensitive to the intricate balance between mental and physical disorders began to investigate the role of medicine man, or shamans, in Indian societies.

D. The English language now includes hundreds of words derived from Indian sources. Among them are names for foods, names for animals, and other familiar words, such as hickory, toboggan.

E. Indians have made a significant contribution to the development of American society. Indian customs and practices affected agricultural development, technology, food habits, language, religion, and philosophy. For example, cotton was a crop important to many Indian societies long before the arrival of the Europeans. The corn-belt region of the United States possibly would not exist in its present form if American Indians had not discovered and developed corn as an agricultural crop.

F. For example, local leaders are now frequently elected by group members. But in groups in which clans are important, voting is often conducted on the basis of clan membership, not on the basis of the platforms of the candidates.

G. The influence of the Indians on the actual settlement of America has been significant. Indians provided the European explorers with gifts and information, and they helped the early settlers to survive on the New England coast. Indian trails were used by frontiersmen, and Indians acted as guides and scouts when settlers moved west.

Passage 20

Albert Einstein, whose theories on space, time and matter helped unravel the secrets of the atom and of the universe, was chosen as "Person of the Century" by *Time* magazine on Sunday.

(1) He has come to represent more than any other person the flowering of 20th century scientific thought that set the stage for the age of technology.

"The world has changed far more in the past 100 years than in any other century in history. The reason is not political or economic, but technological—technologies that flowed directly from advances in basic science," wrote theoretical physicist Stephen Hawking in a *Time* essay explaining Einstein's significance. (2)

Time chose as runner-up President Franklin Roosevelt to represent the triumph of freedom and democracy over fascism, and Mahatma Gandhi as an icon for a century when civil and human rights became crucial factors in global politics.

"What we saw was Franklin Roosevelt embodying the great theme of freedom's fight against totalitarianism, Gandhi personifying the great theme of individuals struggling for their rights, and Einstein being both a great genius and a great symbol of a scientific revolution that brought with it amazing technological advances that helped expand the growth of freedom," said *Time* Magazine Editor Walter Isaacson.

Einstein was born in Ulm, Germany in 1879. In this early years, Einstein did not show the promise of what he was to become. __(3)__ He could not stomach organized learning and loathed taking exams.

In 1905, however, he was to publish a theory which stands as one of the most intricate examples of human imagination in history. __(4)__ Everything else—mass, weight, space, even time itself—is a variable. And he offered the world his now-famous equation: energy equals mass times the speed of light squared—$E=mc^2$.

"Indirectly, relativity paved the way for a new relativism in morality, art and politics," Isaacson wrote in an essay explaining *Time*'s choices. "There was less faith in absolutes, not only of time and space but also of truth and morality."

Einstein's famous equation was also the seed that led to the development of atomic energy and weapons. In 1939, six years after he fled European fascism and settled at Princeton University, Einstein, an avowed pacifist, signed a letter to President Roosevelt urging the United States to develop an atomic bomb before Nazi Germany did. Roosevelt heeded the advice and formed the "Manhattan Project" that secretly developed the first atomic weapon. __(5)__

Einstein died in Princeton, New Jersey in 1955.

A. In his "Special Theory of Relativity," Einstein described how the only constant in the universe is the speed of light.

B. The Theory of Relativity was dedicated to President Roosevelt.

C. It is generally accepted the name of Einstein is synonymous with scientific genius.

D. Einstein did not work on the project.

E. "Clearly, no scientist better represents those advances than Albert Einstein."

F. He was slow to learn to speak and did not do well in elementary school.

G. It is said that Einstein's success lies in the fact that few people can understand his theories.

答案及解析

Passage 1

1. **F** 空格前面的句子说:From these sources it became apparent that <u>the character of myths varied widely</u>,not only by <u>geographical region</u> but also by <u>historical period</u>. ,空格后面的句子说He argued that the relatively <u>simple Greek myth</u> of Persephone reflects the concerns of a <u>basic agricultural community</u>, whereas the <u>more involved and complex myths</u> found later in <u>Homer</u> are the product of a <u>more developed society</u>. ",由此可知:所填的句子应该是在讲神话的特点,并且会提到某位学者。选项 F 中说German scholar Karl Otfried Muller followed <u>this line of inquiry</u> in his Prolegomena to a Scientific Mythology, 1825. ",这与前后句子的意思连贯,所以应该选 F。虽然选项 A、C、D 中也都提到了学者,但是,其意思与前后句子不连贯,所以不能选用。

2. A　空格前面的句子说"These languages, scholars concluded belonged to an Indo-European language family……",空格后面的句子说"For example, an expression like 'maiden dawn' for 'sunrise' resulted first in personification of the dawn, and then in myths about her.", 由此可知:所填的句子应该会提到"Indo-European language",并且会说明人们的误解。选项 A 中说"German-born British scholar Max Muller concluded that the Rig-Veda of ancient India—the oldest preserved body of literature written in an Indo-European language…… Muller attributed all later myths to misunderstandings that arose from the picturesque terms in which early peoples described natural phenomena.", 这与前后句子的意思连贯,并且也提了"Indo-European language",所以应该选 A。

3. D　空格后面的句子说"Similarly, British anthropologist Sir Jame George Frazer proposed a three-stage evolutionary scheme in The Golden Bough.", 由此可知:所填的句子应该是在讲学者们的研究方法。选项 D 中说:"This approach can be seen in the work of British anthropologist Edward Burnett Tylor…., Tyor organized the religious and philosophical development of humanity into separate and distinct evolutionary stages.", 这与后面句子的意思连贯,所以应该选 D。

4. B　空格后面的句子说"This approach reached its most extreme form in the so-called functionalism of British anthropologist A. R. Radcliffe-Brown, who held that every myth implies a ritual, and every ritual implies a myth.", 由此可知,前面的句子应该会介绍某种理论,并且提到"myth"和"ritual"。选项 B 中说"The myth and ritual theory, as this approach came to be called, was developed most fully by British scholar Jan Ellen Harrison….",这与后面句子的意思连贯,所以应该选 B。选项 D 虽然也提到了某种方式,但是与后面句子的意思不连贯,所以不能选用。

5. C　空格前面的句子说"In the 20th century, investigators began to pay closer attention to the content of the narratives themselves.", 由此可知:所填的句子应该是讲现代的研究。只有选 C 中表达的"Austrian psycholanalyst Sigmund Freud held that myths—like dreams—condense the material of experience and represent it in symbols."是现代的研究,所以应该选 C。

Passage 2

1. C　"空 1"应该填入与 low-level radiation 有关的内容,例如 low-level radiation 究竟有害还是无害。所以,C 是合适的选项。此外,直接引语也佐证了选择的合理性。

2. B　"空 2"前面一句介绍了澳大利亚拥有手机的现状。选项 B 的内容是对到 2000 年年底之前手机发展前景的预测,内容连贯,是正确答案。

3. E　这一段的第一句说的是,许多微波发射塔建在人口稠密的居民区。选项 E 的内容涉及微波发射塔的地点选择只考虑到地理位置,而不顾及社区的安全。选项 E 扩展了第一句表达的信息。此外,选项 E 中出现 tower 这个词,与第一句的 tower 相呼应,也佐证了选择的合理性。

4. A　"空 4"前面一句说的是 Robert Bell 建议政府应该禁止在学校操场、儿童日托中心、医院、运动场所以及儿童占比例较高的居住场所方圆 500 米范围内建造发射塔。选项 A 说明要这样做的原因,因而是答案。

5. D　"空 5"后面一句说的是 major telephone companies 出钱资助研究项目的问题,提示了 D 是正确答案。

Passage 3

1. F　空格前面的句子说"Africa's vegetation had always been controlled by the interactions of climate；... The addition of humans to the latter group, however, has increasingly rendered unreal the concept of a fully developed "natural" vegetation...",空格前面的句子说:"Early attempts at mapping and classifying Africa's vegetation stressed this relationship...",由此可知:所填的句子应该是会讲气候影响植被的问题,并且会提到某种关系在。选项 F 中说"Nevertheless, in broad terms, climate remains the dominant control over vegetation. Zonal belts of precipitation, reflection latitude and contrasting exposure to the Atlantic and Indian oceans and their currents, give some reality to related

belts of vegetation."这与前后句子的意思连贯，所以应该选 F。虽然选项 E 中也提到了某种关系，但是并没有谈到气候影响植被的问题，所以不能选用。

2．A　空格后面的句子说"In addition, over time more floral regions of varying shape and size have been recognized..."，由此可知：所填的句子应该是在讲人们取得的成就。选项 A 中说"As more has become known of the many thousands of African plant species and their complex ecology, naming, classification, and mapping have also become more particular..."，这与后面句子的意思连贯，所以应该选 A。

3．C　空格前面的句子说"... all of which have had to take views on two important aspects：the general scale of treatment to be adopted, and the degree..."，由此可知：所填的句子应该是在介绍重要的方面，并且会提到"treatment"。选项 C 中说"One, as with the scientific treatment of African soils..."，这与前面句子的意思连贯，所以应该选 C。

4．G　空格前面的句子说"Correspondingly, classifications have differed greatly in their principles ..."，由此可知：所填的句子应该是在讲学者们的分歧。选项 G 中说"... but there has been considerable dispute among scholars"，这与后面句子的意思连贯，所以应该选 G。

5．D　空格后面的句子说"However, some 100 specific types of vegetation identified on the source map have been compressed into 14 broad classifications."，由此可知：所填的句子应该会提到有关地图。选项 D 中说"The vegetational map of Africa and general vegetation groupings used here follow the White map and its extensive annotations."，这与后面的句子的意思连贯，所以应该选 D。

Passage 4

1．B　本题要求选择一个段落填入空白，使上下文加贯、一致解题步骤是分析上下文，划出关键信息词，然后通过关键词的连接找出符合上下文逻辑的选项。第 1 段论述，世界工业化进程的发展，一方面提高了我们的生活水平，另一方面也导致了世界不同地区之间的依赖性随之增加。选项[B]中的 these conditions 即指在上述情况下，一个地区的任何永久的经济或政治不稳定性必然会对世界其他地区产生越来越严重的影响。这一点正具体说明了第 1 段中的关键信息词"interdependence"。可见，选项[B]与第 1 段在逻辑意思上是连贯的。选项[B]中的第 2 句告诉我们，由于这种不稳定性的主要根源是不发达，所以很清楚，这就构成了国际范围内的大问题。这一句与第 3 段第 1 句"那么应该怎么办呢？正好构成逻辑上的一致性。故正确答案非[B]莫属。"

2．A　本题要求选择段落起始句填入空白，使上下文连贯、一致。第 3 段第 2 句说，虽然很难了解从何处开始处理这样一个重要的课题，但是第 1 步或许是考虑一个不发达地区或叫新兴地区必须正视的主要经济困难。选项[A]所起的段落正好以具体事例来说明这些经济困难，从而构成了逻辑上的连贯性。

3．E　本题要求选择段落起始句填入空白，使上下文连贯、一致。第 5 段进一步从工业不发达的角度来论述新国家所面临的经济困难。选项[E]告诉我们"由于工业不发达，这些国家主要靠进口货来提供生产他们出口的原材料所需要的设备。"下文是："这一点也适合于向他们的老百姓提供生活必需品所需要的工业制品。…………"可见，上下文逻辑一致。

4．D　本题要求选择段落起始句填入空白，使上下文连贯、一致。选项[D]告诉我们，"虽然很明显，工业化是发展的关键，但是通常新兴国家很难执行这种性质的计划。"这是段落的论点，接着作者以 3 个方面的论据来论述，为什么很难执行这种性质的计划。可见，选项[D]与下文在逻辑上是一致的。

5．F　本题要求选择段落结尾句填入空白，使上下文连贯、一致。倒数第 2 段说："从另外一个观点来看，必须牢记，总是存在一些政治的、教育的、社会的和心理的障碍，这些障碍往往严重地干扰了为解决上述种种经济困难所采取的任何措施。"这个句子起到承上启下的作用。它一方面总结了 4、5、6、7 段的内容，即兴国家遇到的各种经济困难；另一方面又是本段的主题句，而下一句是段落的扩展句。通过关键信息词"psychological"连接起来，以便保持逻辑上的一致性。然后与全文结论段相连结，保持了文章的完整性。

Passage 5

1. E　选项 E 是(正确答案)选项 E 继续探讨了销售的情况以及过去公司设立销售部门而没有营销部门的原因。空白前面的句子强调销售只是营销的一个组成的一个组成部分,而在过去,销售占据着主导地位。只有选项 E 正确,E 使用衔接词"rather than"(而不是)将题继续下去,紧接着对过去的营销进行了介绍。

2. A　选项 A 是(正确答案)公司的形势发生了变化迫切需要开拓市场,因此有必要建立起专门的营销部门。

3. B　只有选项 B 是合适的答案。选项 B 继续讨论了营销与顾客之间的关系以及个人接触在传达公司理念中的重要意义。

4. G　选项 G 是正确答案,该选项继续讨论了顾客的不良体验。文章前面指出如果顾客没有良好的购物体验,未来的销售将受到负面影响,而选项 G 进一步描述了顾客不良体验的可能情形

5. F　选项 F 是最佳答案。前面一段强调营销部门负有重大责任,选项 F 则强调营销部门应该听取公司其它部门的意见,"减轻"了营销部门的重任。

Passage 6

1. E　文章一开头讲到,在《亲爱的,我把孩子们缩小了》这部电影中,一位古怪的父亲不小心把自己的孩子们给缩小了,接下来的句子还应该与这部电影有关。

2. F　从第三段的第一句话可以判断,此处应为询问原因的问句。

3. A　前一句讲,脊椎骨有可能退化并套缩在一起,接下来应选表明这种行为结果的句子。

4. C　前一句讲到,当太多松软的骨组织坏掉并且没有足够的新的骨组织生成时骨质疏松就发生了。接下来应首选表明这种现象结果的句子。

5. B　此段讲的是:一个人到了晚上的时候就不如他在早起的时候高,但他不必为此着急。接下来应首选表明不必着急之原因的句子。

Passage 7

1. F　学生如果没有完成 2～5 的选择,本部分可能会比较困难。完成了 2～5 之后,就容易看出,选项 F 显然是(正确答案)该选项介绍了影响青少年的那个"全面的"方法。选项 F 认为父母与老师单独完成这一任务,所以 F 是本文的主题。

2. B　只有选项 B 可以入选:本段的主题是父母应该做到那些东西,以身作则,培养孩子拒绝毒品的品质。同时继续讨论并运了刚刚引入的"modeling"(模仿)这一概念。

3. E　文章对自尊进行了讨论,只有选项 E 将自尊和吸毒联系起来,故应入选。

4. D　在讨论了父母的作用后,学生应当阅读空白(4)后面的段落,文章接下来给出一个例子,说明老师能够给青少年什么样的影响。选项 A 不能入选,因显 A 给出的例子所说明的问题文章还没有提及。同样,选项 C 也不能入选。选项 D 引入学校能够做到的事情,故 D 为正选。D 的末尾给出的是青少年同龄人群的活动背景,即课堂。

5. A　(5)前面的主题句谈到了教师在课堂上可以动用的活动。选项 A 讨论的是教师可以利用的课堂策略,故为正确答案。

Passage 8

1. D　本文主要讲与人初次见面头四分钟对于人际交往的重要性。文章开头以自问自答的形式提出主题,然后说 Leonard Zunin 博士在书中向任何想交新朋友的人提出一条建议。什么建议呢? 比较一下只有把 D 放在这里最合适,因为人们常用祈使句向别人提建议,D 是一个祈使句,它的意思是:"每次在社交场合遇到什么人时,全神贯注地与他交流四分钟。"和上下文意思连贯。

2. E　承接上一段作者在本段第一句话告诉我们有人并不按他建议的那样做。那么这些人怎么做呢? E 说:"他不停地往对方身后看,好像要在屋里其他地方找到更有趣的人似的。"显然此处选 E 最合

适。

3．A　文章第三、四段建议当被引见给陌生人时,态度应当友好而自信,还应掌握好分寸。对此有人会说友好和自信非我本性,如果硬要装出如此态度就是不诚实。这是一种反驳意见,我们期待作者的回答。A 说:"作为回答,Zunin 博士说只要我们稍加练习就可以轻松地改变社交习惯。"下文是对此的进一步解释。

4．B　到此为止作者主要谈与生人相处要注意头四分钟。从其他句子来看,本段谈的是家庭成员之间在交往中也应注意在一起的头四分钟,那么选 B 是最合适的句子。

5．C　本段强调人际关系的重要性,C 说:"在他看来,成功主要依赖于如何与他人友好相处。"意思符合本段主题,后一句的主语 this 指的就是与人友好相处这件事。

Passage 9

1．F　本题是在文章第二段首,应考虑第一、二段的段落关系,以及本段句群关系。文章第一段告诉读者 90％的(美国)大学生拥有计算机。原文第二段空白后的首句说"我预测随着科技的不断发展和价格的继续降低,计算机对大学生会像电话或电视机那样普遍。"可以推断,选项应是关于大学生电脑购买力的内容。F 选项符合要求,F 项大意为:因为计算机不断降价,我发现我的学生中有许多现在都能得起配置有调制解调器、声卡、光驱和彩色打印机的高速计算机。

2．D　本题是整个段落的插入,看清前段内容,分析后段语篇,从内容和结构上把握文章主线是关键。此段前面一段讨论介绍了大学生拥有计算机的情况,后段谈论的是非常小的孩子也具有计算机技能。浏览比较除 F 外的几个选项,发现选项 D 谈论的正是文章开篇首段提到的 10％没有自己的计算机的学生使用计算机的情况,选项 D 放在第三段正好与第二段形成并列分述关系。故选 D。D 项大意为:对于自己没有计算机的学生,他们可以使用图书馆的计算机,这些计算机能连接到因特网和其它研究资料库。图书馆还提供免费的因特网培训班。上计算机课的学生也能使用学校计算机实验室的计算机、打印机和扫描仪。

3．E　本题是在文章第四段段首,应考虑段落句群关系,看是否为段首主题句。本题只是考查主题句的选择,较为简单。从原文第四段中得知一个班的五年级学生(十岁)居然会制作了包括文字、声音和图形的多媒体演示文件;很小的孩子也用鼠标,这些为他们上大学掌握和使用计算机打下了基础。所以,提到小学计算机能力课程的 E 选项为正确答案。E 项大意为:在小学阶段,就开始有教计算机能力的课程,以作为学习的辅助。

4．B　本题是在文章第五段段首,应考虑第四、五段的段落关系,或是段落句群关系。还要看是否为段首主题句。第四段谈到小学生就有了一定的计算机技能。原文第五段说美国许多工资最高的工作都是属于技术领域的,在竞争性很强的职业市场上,计算机专业人才供不应求。第五段空白后的首句里用了递进关联词"in addition",这表明此句之前的内容也在谈计算机能力的重要性。故选项 B 为答案。B 项大意为:计算机能力事实上已经成为一切工作所必需的。没有基本计算机知识的人找工作越来越困难了。大部分工作都要求申请人至少能够进行文字处理、上网、向数据库输入数据,或制作电子表格。

5．C　本题是在文章第六段段首,应考虑第五、六段的段落关系,或是段落句群关系。也要考虑是否为段首主题句。文章第五段告诉我们计算机能力事实上是一切工作所必需的,计算机专业技术越强找到的工作薪水越高。原文第六段谈到了大学生在校园里把计算机当作了很好的学习与交流沟通的工具。C 选项"In addition to increasing their job marketability, students are interested in learning computers as an aid to college study."作了很好的承上启下,是本文末段的总说主题句。C 项大意为:学生们对计算机感兴趣不仅是为了提高找工作的竞争力,还为了辅助大学学习。

Passage 10

1．B　文章的第一句讲,一个人进食后,身体便会从食物中获得糖并将其转化成燃料。接下来应首选对这种糖燃料加以解释的句子。

2．E　前两句讲到,患胰岛素依赖型糖尿病的病人,其胰腺不能生成胰岛素,因此,尽管某人进食大量食物并获取所需的全部葡萄糖,但没有胰岛素,身体就无法利用这些葡萄糖获取能量。也就是说,没有胰岛素,葡萄糖就不能进入身体的细胞内。

3.F　此段的前几句主要讲非胰岛素依赖型糖尿病,并指出它不同于胰岛素依赖型糖尿病。两者之间的主要区别是什么呢? 回答这个问题的句子应当首选。

4.A　前一句讲,科学家们现在认为,患少年型糖尿病的人出生时就具有某个或者某些使其易患此病的基因。基因是什么呢? 回答这问题的句子当然应该首选。

5.D　前一句说明了糖尿病不具有触染性,接下来应当是对该句加以阐释的句子。

Passage 11

1.B　作为段首句,一般多具有承上启下的作用,所以先仔细理解上下文。上一段介绍了几种代用燃料,这一段则理所当然应详述它们的情况。而下文中有 These molecules... 字样,正好与 B 选项中的 whose molecules 相呼应,且语义顺畅,所以选项 B 为正确答案。B 项大意:所有这些可供选择的替代物均是碳基(carbon-based)燃料,其分子要比汽油的分子来得更小,更简单。

2.C　本题依然是段首句,所以还是要从上下文衔接上寻找突破点。首先看下文,有 These reactions increase... 这样的明确指代,这样的指代不会凭空出现,我们可以推测前文可能与 reaction 有关,而前文是从分子角度介绍新型燃料与传统燃料相比的优点,综合考虑以上两点,不难看出 C 为正确答案。C 项大意:较大分子的燃烧,由于具有多重碳一碳键,涉及一系列更为复杂的反应。

3.D　注意本题是一个独立的段落,难度较大,需要结合整篇文章综合考虑。前文介绍了四种新型燃料 compressed natural gas, liquefied petroleum gas, ethanol, or methanol,而注意下一段的首句 Ethanol and methanol, on the other hand, have mportant advantages over other carbon-based alternative fuels...,其中的 other 应有所指,此时我们不难看出 other 即指 compressed natural gas 和 liquefied petroleum gas。D 项符合要求,是正确答案。D 项大意:从另一方面来说,可供选择的替代燃料也有其缺陷。压缩天然气要求车辆备有一整套笨重的燃料箱——这在车辆的表现和燃料效率方面不啻是一个严重的不利因素。而液化石油气所面临的是根本上的供应量限制。

4.A　本题是段的结尾句,一般而言起着总结上文的作用。文中提到 ethanol 虽较为常用,但与 methanol 相比却较贵,而低成本是 methano 的优点之一,言外之意 methanol 还有着其他无法比拟的优点,而 A 项正好说出了这层意思,所以推断出 A 为正确答案。A 项大意:然而,甲醇最吸引人的特点是,它能将形成臭氧的车辆尾气这一最严重的城市空气污染物数量降低 90%。

5.F　本题是文章末端的首句,依然会与前文有着千丝万缕的联系,同时又会对全文作出一定的总结概括。前一段大意是 methanol 作为一种新型燃料,在投入实际使用上还有些问题。本段末句大意是一旦 methanol 普遍使用,将会极大改善因使用传统汽车燃料而带来的空气污染的现状,两段意思有着明显的转折,F 项中的 However 再恰当不过,而且这样的段落安排也符合科技类短文结尾展望美好前景的一段思路。F 项大意:然而,以甲醇为燃料的车辆效率可比被设计成以甲醇为燃料的“汽油系列”车辆效率更高,因而它们所需的燃料相对较少。

Passage 12

1.D　空白处的前一句举了一位 49 岁妇女在肾移植手术以后拒服必要的药物。空白处的后一句说拒绝与医务人员合作的病人会给自己、给社会带来什么害处。我们必须注意到后一句的病人是泛指的,当然应该包括这位 49 岁的妇女在内,因此将 D(指出“这种不合作不是孤立的例子”)填入空白处可以将上下文更完美地连接起来。

2.E　空白处的前一句说到应该更多地强调心理学在医疗培训中的作用。E 说有证据表明,对(情绪)不稳定的病人进行心理治疗可增加医患之间的合作。前后两句话是连贯的,而且 they added 还在一定程度上起到了提示作用,故 E 为最佳选择。

3.F　空白处的前一句讲了一个小男孩在做心脏移植手术前脾气非常暴躁的故事。空白处的后面几句叙述了如何解决这个小男孩的心理障碍问题,F 说:“后来这种愤怒被认为是他要争取作为一个病人的权利”,正好起着承上启下的作用。由于医务人员有这种认识才有后面的良好结果。

4. B　空白处的前一句说"一旦他的想法被认可,他的怒气就消退了",所以 B 项所说的"他明显地安静多了,并且变成了一个服从治疗的好病人"是自然而然的结果。

5. C　空白处的前一句说"根据一项调查,有一半的病人并不想吃药,但仍然开了很多药",C"在这种情况下医嘱被置之脑后也就不足为怪了",这种连接是顺理成章的事了。

Passage 13

1. F　在文章的第一和第二段,作者指出"Public schools in the United States are becoming steadily more segregated,"即美国的公立学校种族隔离现象日益严重,导致大多数少数民族学生不得不在条件较差的学校里学习,这是最新的一项研究所表明的。在第三段中,选项之后,这项研究又总结说美国的种族关系现在又从 20 世纪时的状况快速地到退回 19 世纪时的状况,这句话表明,种族隔离不是得到了遏制,而是加速了倒退了,所以,根据逻辑关系,该外的选项作为一段的开始应是对这种现象的一种概括或总结。在这几个选项中,只有[F]的内容说"that the trend toward segregation was accelerating,"与其后的一句话表达的是一个意思。因此,[F]符合逻辑关系。

2. C　在第四段中,在选项之前作者说,63.6%的黑人学生在少数民族学校中学习,而且这一比例"remained almost the same through the mid-1980s."表明在整个八十年代中期,这个比例没有改变,但是在选项之后的一句话却说"Nearly 75 percent of Hispanic students……attend predominantly minority schools."很显然这里提供的数字比前一个数字显著地上升了,按照逻辑上的关系,此外的选项应与它前面的句子形成转折的关系,说明在少数民族学校上学的孩子的比例不再保持不变,而是显著上升。所以,在这几个选项中,[C]是一个明显的带有转折连词 But 的句子,而且也表明了黑人学生人数的增加,因此,[C]符合逻辑关系。

3. G　在第七段中,该项研究指出,贫困的种族隔离的学校在许多方面都与其他学校不平等,这些不等的因素会影响到孩子的学业,然后在选项之前,举例说明了哪些因素会影响学生的学业,如"……have to devote more time and resources to family and health cries and security."等,在选项之后又说,这样的学校的重点只是放在各种补救措施上,而不是用于发展,或建设班级(The focus is more often on remediation,rather than advanced, demanding classes.),所以在文章的这一部分,讨论的重点是贫困的种族隔离学校的劣势,[G]应为正确答案。

4. D　在第七段中,如上所述,该段讨论的彼一时点是贫困的种族隔离学校的劣势,[D]中的"students attending high-poverty schools"表明改选项也应属于这一段的内容,只不过是该段前部分讨论的是学校的劣势,而这一句表明了处在这样的学校中的学生的劣势,[D]符合逻辑关系。

5. A　在最后一段中,在选项之后作者引用了一名教育分析家的话来说明少数民族学生的家长的态度,从这句话中可以看出,当被问到最关心孩子学校的哪方面的时候,越来越多的家长说他们现在不关心孩子的同桌是什么肤色,而是关心孩子们在这样的学校能够学到真正的本民族的东西,可见,这是一种与前面的调查截然不同的观点;调查表明的是越来越多的少数民族学生不得不进入贫困的少数民族学校学习,而且这些学校与其他学校相比有许多不利条件。而这句话表达的却是家长们是自愿将孩子送入这些学校,因为在这样的学校里孩子们可以学到属于他们自己民族的东西。所以,在这些选项当中,[A]的内容说明了这一点,提出了一个不同的观点,符合逻辑关系。

Passage 14

1. G　文章第一段说,许多科学家都对抑郁沮丧的遗传特殊倾向感到好奇,比如说一对抑郁沮丧的父母或祖父母很容易将这种特质遗传给他们的女性后代而不是男性后代。在选项之前,作者又说:"追溯家族的历史,答案似乎不是这样的。"也就是说,父母将这种特质遗传给女性后代和男性后代的几率是均等的。在选项之后作者又说:"不考虑环境因素,只追溯家族的历史,似乎看不出抑郁沮丧是如何遗传的。"可见,作者在此想要表达的意思是虽然抑郁沮丧的遗传是有特殊倾向的,但追溯家族的历史似乎看不出这一点,所以,此处的选项也应与此有关。在这几个选项当中,[G]说男性和女性似乎同样会遗传这种特质,这与本段的说法相一致,符合逻辑关系。

2. A　第二段主要讲述了 Kenneth S. Kendler 和他的同事们所做的一个试验,研究人员将有家族沮丧史和没有家族沮丧史的两组女子进行比较,其中有一些人新近受到了感情上的创伤,如挚亲朋的去世或离婚等,结果研究人员发现,有没有家族沮丧史的那些人中,这种外界的压力沮丧度只提高了百分之六。在选项之后,作者说,那些有沮丧倾向的人在危机来临时变得非常沮丧。很显然,此处的选项应该是关于那些有家族沮丧史的人在危机来临时他们的沮丧度提高了多少个百分点,即与"……that among the women who did not have a family history of depression, stressful events raised their risk for depression by only 6 percent."这句话相对应。A 项说"但是在有家族病史的一组这种患病几率提高了 14%",因此选[A]符合逻辑关系。

3. E　在第三段中作者说没有在男人中做类似的试验,但却做了另一个试验:男人和女人是否感受同样程度的沮丧,对于荷尔蒙的研究表明,他们感受沮丧的程度是不一样的。在此之后,作者就这一现象进行了分析,首先是男人和女人的 X 和 Y 染色体的不同。在选项之前,作者说男人和女人的 X 和 Y 染色体的不同使两者的大脑处于不同的荷尔蒙环境中;在选项之后又说,对动物的实验也表明不同荷尔蒙环境会影响后天的行为。那么,不同的荷尔蒙环境是如何影响男人和女人对于沮丧的感受的呢? 此处的选项应与此有关。而[E]解答了这个问题,即不同的荷尔蒙环境会影响大脑的发育,从而使男人和女人在日后的生活中有不同的弱点,如对环境压力的生理反应不同等,因此,[E]符合逻辑关系。

4. F　在选项之前,作者谈到,青春其后男性和女性有不同水平的性生殖腺类固醇,这也许能解释为什么女性较容易沮丧。研究表明女孩儿在青春期后往往比男孩儿变得敏感,更容易沮丧。在选项之后作者又举了一个 Peter J. Schmidt 和 David R. Rubinow 的例子研究表明对于雌激素和孕酮的控制并不能影响情绪。这就与选项之前的内容互相矛盾。显然,此处的选项应是这两句话的一个衔接,即与前面的内容形成转折关系。在这些选项当中,[F]是一个以"even so……"开始的句子,能够与选项之前的句子形成转折关系,所以,该选项符合逻辑关系。

5. C　在第六段中,作者说刺激素可能会间接地激发身体对于沮丧的反应,在感受到压力的时期,肾上腺(adrenal glands)就会分泌出高水平的被称为皮质醇(cortisol)的荷尔蒙,这种皮质醇会增加身体新陈代谢和免疫系统的活动从这些分析中我们可以看出,本段主要说的是皮质醇的分泌与感受压力进而沮丧之间的关系。在这几个选项当中,选项[C]的内容与此有关,大意是在正常的事情进展中,压力增加了皮质醇的分泌,但这种高水平的皮质醇对于脑垂体有负面的反应,以至于皮质醇的水平又逐渐恢复到正常水平。这句话正说明了皮质醇的分泌管理层沮丧之间的关系,符合逻辑关系,因此,[C]正确。

Passage 15

1. D　本文的首段通过一系列问题导入全文主题,并吸引读者的目光,所以结尾声处依然是一个问题。D. If the sun was the only light source why did the LEM's legs cast multiple shadows?

2. B　第一段为一系列问题,第二段进行了回答,所以二者之间的过渡句为 B. Questions, so many questions. 其作用是承接上文,引起下文。

3. F　本段讲述的是持怀疑态度的人的做法,所以主题句应为 F。

4. C　通过上下文可知,此两种观点一致,所以两者之间的过渡句选 C. That meshed with Kaysing's mind-set. "这与 Kaysing 的观点不谋而合"。

5. F　本句应和下文"但是他大量的证据证明了'无风不起浪',是可信的"形成对比,且是对 Kaysing 观点的评论,因此选 E。

Passage 16

1. C　本句需和上句 Success is something that comes from within. 内容上衔接,语气一致,因此 C. It's not based on the number of awards I have won. 最为合适,它与上文形成了"不是……而是……"结构。

2. A　通过后文"需深入了解人们的思想""预测未来","每个细节都要很多心思"可判断,本段主题句为 A. "一直保持创造性是很有压力的"。

3. E 本句话的前文是一个事例:通过顾客的过分修饰打扮可知给她设计梳妆台十分重要。这个例子说明了一个道理:了解顾客所需是至关重要的。所以本段的总结性话语为 E。

4. B 上文提到了 balance,下文进一步论述了此问题,所以此处需填上一个承上启下的句子 B. Balance is a recurring theme for the man and his design,...。

5. D 本句话应是本段的结论或总结,前文提到 Ken 要举重并吃味道难吃的东西补充营养,保证健康饮食,对它的总结是 D. Not for the punishment, but because I like to test myself and create a balance between my mind, body and soul. 其中前半句承接"举重"、"难吃"之意,后半句又回到本段主题"balance"上来。

Passage 17

1. D 综观全文,可判断本文讨论全球变暖问题。第一段第二句话具体指出全球温度比 1860 年高了 1 度,因此第一句话应是全文的主旨或与第二句内容一脉相承的具体事例。在 A—F 选项中,只有 D. The Earth last year was at its hottest since records began 可与第二句并列,导入全文主题。

2. B 上文提到比平均温度高出 1 度,人们就认为很热了。此处可选 B"要是高出 2 度,天更热些,他们会怎么想?"与前文从语义上形成递进关系,且引出下文"气候会如何变化"。选项 B 在这里起到承上启下的作用。

3. F 从下文可总结出研究者们正探讨世界气候可能出现的变化,因此本句话要做这几段的概述,只有 F. Scientists still cannot say for certain how the world's climate will behave 能综合这几段之意。

4. A 通过后文 In parts of Siberia... temperatures were 3℃ higher than normal 这一事例可知,有些地方的温度更高,所以本段主题句选 A。

5. E 前一段指出火山喷发的尘土进入大气层,过滤了太阳的射线,从而延缓了全球变暖的速度。本段的内容却是全球依然变暖。因此本段第一句话既是全段主题句,又能承接上文,只有 E. Researchers say the dust effect has now disappeared and warming has recommenced 既能揭示本段主题又能顺延上文之意。

Passage 18

1. C 文章第一段空前的文字指出人们通常在平地或缓和的坡地上挖掘池塘,并在池塘的周边筑上不高的坝且四周用粘土覆盖以防止水的流失。C 项指出为防止水的流失,池塘底部同样也用粘土加以覆盖。由此可看出 C 项是对前文的进一步阐述,因此为正确答案。

2. B 第二段指出池塘中的水有可能因为蒸发、日照而减少,因此每个池塘都必须有供水来源,例如泉水或井水。第二段空后文字叙述了我们的池塘的情况:水域面积,水深及水的来源。而 B 项介绍了我们池塘的水域宽度及水的供给来源——泉水,能够在此部分的上下文起到了很好的衔接作用,即由介绍普遍的池塘供水问题转移到具体的池塘供水问题(我们的池塘)。由此可得出 B 项为正确答案。

3. F 第五段空前文字阐述了美国早期的开拓者通过堵截小溪或小河建造了成千上万的池塘,然后将池塘中的水引入沟渠再通过水车将水产生的动力传输到磨坊。而 F 项则阐述了以这种形式产生动力可用于磨坊磨面,还可用于锯木或者带动其他机器运转,但如今由于电力在商业中的应用,这样的磨坊已很少存在了,这些正是对第五段空前文字的进一步阐述。因此正确答案为 F。

4. A 上一段指出在那段时期建造的池塘要比以往的都多,牧场主造池塘是为了给牲畜提供饮水的地方,还有人修建池塘是为了钓鱼或游泳,整段介绍了建造池塘的种种不同的原因。而 A 项由"No matter"引导的从句表明不管是什么原因修建池塘,有一点是明确的,即有了池塘后,池塘周围会出现各种不同的植物和动物。由此可看出 A 项很好的承接了上文。空后文字紧接着介绍了池塘是一个 24 小时营业的工厂和餐馆,滋养了无数的植物及动物。由此可看出 A 项也很好的引出了下文。因此 A 项在此部分起到了承上启下的作用。其中"No matter"是解题的关键。

5. D 最后一段空后的文字表明如果没有太阳,池塘中的植物会死去,动物会饿死,同时也提到了光合作用。即阐述了太阳与生物之间的关系。而 D 项内容指出池塘内的生物互相依赖而生存,但是它们都离不开太阳、空气及土壤。由此可看出 D 项很好地引出了下文。

Passage 19

1. B　文章开篇提到,美国政府认为,假使给予一定时间和一定的鼓励,印第安人会采纳"美国式"的生
活方式。而空白下文又提到对大部分印第安群体来说,从其他社会中借鉴元素并非什么新鲜事。
这和第一段的内容有很大的转折。因此,这时空白处的文字应该提到印第安人借鉴其他的文明这
一点。选项[B]与此一致。

2. A　上文提到印第安人对其他文明有所借鉴,接下来是举的例子。而下文讲的是印第安人对于工业
文明的态度,这属于另外一个具体方面了。由此,可以判断空白处应该还是讲印第安人对于其他文
明的借鉴。选项[A]与此对应。

3. F　上文提到了印第安人对于美国政治规则的借鉴。而下文则是提到了北美印第安人的情况。空
白处前一句说"一些印第安部落把政治原则应用于处理部落内的问题",显然接下来应该是具体就
这一点展开阐述。选项[F]符合要求。

4. E　上文一直讲的都是其他文明对于印第安人的影响。细读下文可以发现,下文描述的是印第安人
对于其他文明的影响。由此判断,空白处应该是能衔接这两点的内容。选项[E]符合这一点。下文
的首句很重要。由"Indian contributions"可以判断接下来讲的是印第安人对其他文明的贡献,由"in
technology"可以判断前文应该还讲到印第安人在其他方面对人类的贡献。

5. D　上文主要讲了从技术上说印第发人对于其他文明的贡献。而空白处下文提到的是美国许多州
的名字都来源于印第安语。由此可以推测空白处应该讲印第安语言对于其他文明的影响。选项
[D]符合这一点。

Passage 20

1. C　选项 E 也有可能是答案,但 those advances 没有着落。除 C 之外,没有一个选项意思上能与本段
第二句匹配的。

2. E　选项 E 中有 those advances,本段第二句有"... that flowed directly from advances in basic science",选项 E 中的 those advances 就是指第二句的 advances。所以,"空 2"应该选 E。

3. F　这一段介绍 Einstein in his early days 并没有显示出很高的天赋。第一句提示,"空 3"不太可能
涉及天赋高的内容。所以,选项 F 是很自然的选择。

4. A　本段第一句说,Einstein 提出一个人类科学史上最富有想像力的理论。选项 A 具体介绍 Einstein 的相对论,所以应该是答案。

5. D　"空 5"前面一句是 Roosevelt heeded the advice and formed the "Manhattan Project" that secretly
developed the first atomic weapon。关键词是 the "Manhattan Project",提示我们要选 D。

第四章 英 译 汉

第一节 考研英译汉高分全攻略概述

英译汉短文内容大体上涉及当前人们普遍关注的社会生活、政治、经济、历史、文化、科普等方面的一般常识或社会、自然科学与技术常识的题材。体裁多为议论文。科学常识性的题材占了相当大的比重。

1991～2005 年英译汉短文主题

1991 年:能源与农业(444 词)

1992 年:智力评估的科学性(406 词)

1993 年:科学研究方法(443 词)

1994 年:天才、技术与科学发展的关系(308 词)

1995 年:标准化教育与心理评估(364 词)

1996 年:科学发展的动力(331 词)

1997 年:动物的权利(417 词)

1998 年:宇宙起源(376 词)

1999 年:史学研究方法(326 词)

2000 年:科学家与政府(381 词)

2001 年:计算机与未来生活展望(405 词)

2002 年:行为科学发展的困难(339 词)

2003 年:人类学简介(371 词)

2004 年:语言与思维(357 词)

2005 年:欧洲电视媒体(405 词)

平均值:短文词数 370 词;要求翻译的词数 160 词。

从英译汉试题内容分析,考生就应明确认识到,要想在英语考试中取得成功,必须在基本训练上狠下工夫。首先要扩大知识面,提高自身文化素质。考生如果熟悉试题内容,将有助于对短文的深入理解,增强信心,提高翻译水平。考生应利用各种渠道,特别是通过大量浏览中、英文报纸杂志,扩大相关的知识面。

从题型改革后、特别是 1996 年以后的试题分析,命题组更侧重考生综合运用语言的能力,考题难度加大,趋向稳定。考题要求考生在理解全句、全段或全文的基础上,把语法、词汇的意思和上下文结合起来理解,表面看上去画线的句子语法不很复杂,词汇似乎也不陌生,但翻译时很多考生觉得难以动笔。难度增大体现在:不能采用就词论词、就句子论句子的简单直译方法,而要求把词和句子放在篇章里去理解,强调英语习惯用法、语感和翻译技巧的掌握。这样,仅靠熟悉语法规则和孤立地背单词已远远不够了。这也是考生得分普遍不高的主要原因。

近年来英译汉试题主要特点如下:

1.反映自然科学、社会科学的常识性、科学类和报刊评论文章占很大比例;

2.考题难度加大;

3.语法现象难度有所降低;

4.突出简单翻译技巧,如:词、词组的省略及补译,译出 it,they,this,that 等代词的真正代表的含义,词义选择、引申、词性转换,长句的拆句与逆序翻译法等。

考生应针对这些特点认真做好适当的准备。

第二节　翻译技巧

一、在翻译过程中词义的选择

英汉两种语言都有一词多类、一词多义的现象。一词多类就是指一个词往往属于几个词类，具有几个不同的意思。一词多义是说同一词在同一词类中，有几个不同的词义。词义的选择可以从以下三方面着手。

(一) 根据词在句中的词类来选择词义

经典例题 The earth goes round the sun.（介词）

参考译文 地球环绕太阳运行。

经典例题 The food supply will not increase nearly enough to match this, which means that we are heading into a crisis in the matter of producing and marketing food.（动词）

分析：market 可以既作名词又作动词。在作名词时，可译为"市场"、"行业"、"需求"等等。例句中的 market 是作动词用的，可以译为"买，卖"或"销售"，根据句中描述的情形，用"销售"更妥当。

参考译文 食品供应无法跟上人口增长的步伐，这意味着在粮食的生产和销售方面我们将陷入危机。（1993 年真题）

(二) 根据上下文和词在句中的搭配关系选择词义

经典例题 Power can be transmitted over a long distance.

参考译文 电力可以被输送到很远的地方。

经典例题 A car needs a lot of power to go fast.

参考译文 汽车高速行驶需要很大的动力。

经典例题 Explosive technological development after 1990 gave the medical profession enormous power to fight disease and sickness.

参考译文 1990 年以来，随着技术的迅速发展，医学界大大提高了战胜疾病的能力。

(三) 根据可数或不可数来选择词义

经典例题 After their interview, he compares not their experience, but their statistics……（不可数）

参考译文 面试以后，他并不比较他们的经验，而是比较他们的统计数字。

经典例题 Our journey to Tibet was quite an experience.（可数）

参考译文 我们的西藏之旅真是一次难忘的经历。

二、在翻译过程中词义的引申

引申是指从原词的内在含义出发，结合语境以及表达习惯，在译文中对某些词作一定的语义调整，以达到忠实、通顺的目的。英译汉时常常会遇到许多单词，按词典上给的词义来翻译，译文就会生硬难懂，甚至造成意思上的曲解。因此，需对词义进行必要的变动，引申出能表达词语内在含义的新的表达方式。

引申既可化具体为抽象，也可化抽象为具体。

(一)具体——→抽象

经典例题 Were it left to an American to decide whether they should have a government without newspapers or newspapers without a government, he should not hesitate a moment to prefer the latter.

参考译文 如果让一个美国人决定要没有言论自由的政府还是要言论自由而无政府的国家,他会毫不犹豫地选择后者。

经典例题 There were times when emigration bottleneck was extremely rigid and nobody was allowed to leave the country out of his personal preference.

分析: bottleneck 本指"瓶颈",由于具有使缓慢和阻滞的效果,因而被抽象地引申为"限制"。

参考译文 过去有过这种情况:移民限制极为严格,不许任何人出于个人考虑而迁居他国。

(二)抽象——→ 具体

经典例题 While there are almost as many definitions of history as there are historians, modern practice most closely conforms to one that sees history as the attempt to recreate and explain the significant events of the past.

参考译文 几乎每个史学家对史学都有自己的界定,但现代史学家们的观点都趋向于认为史学是试图重现并阐明过去发生的重大事件。(1999 年真题)

经典例题 When the Jones were little, they were forbidden to set foot there, because of the revolting language and of what they might catch.

参考译文 琼斯家里的人,小时候是不允许走进那里的,生怕学到一些下流话,或沾染上什么毛病。

经典例题 All the irregularities of the students in that university resulted in punishment.

参考译文 那所大学的学生作出的任何越轨行为都会受到处罚。

三、使用"增补法"进行翻译

英汉两种语言,由于表达方式不尽相同,翻译时既可能要将词类加以转换,又可能要在词量上加以增减。增补法就是在翻译时按意义上和句法上的需要增加一些词来更忠实通顺地表达原文的思想内容。这当然不是无中生有地随意增词,而是增加原文中虽无其词而有其意的一些词。

(一)词汇加词

1.增加名词

经典例题 According to scientists, it takes nature 500 years to create an inch of topsoil.

参考译文 根据科学家们的看法,自然界要用 500 年的时间才能形成一英寸厚的表面土壤。

经典例题 From agreement on this general goal, we have, unfortunately, in the past proceeded to disagreement on specific goals, and from there to total inaction.

参考译文 遗憾的是,过去我们在总的目标方面意见是一致的,但涉及各个具体目标时,意见就不一致了,因而也就根本不能采取什么行动。(1987 年)

2.增加动词

经典例题 In the evening, after the banquets, the concerts and the table tennis exhibitions, he would work on the drafting of the final communique.

参考译文 晚上在参加宴会,出席音乐会,观看乒乓球表演之后,他还得草拟最后公告。

经典例题 The cities utilize these funds for education, police and fire departments, public works and municipal buildings.

参考译文 市政府将这些资金用于兴办教育事业,加强治安消防,投资公共建筑和市政工程。

3. 增加形容词

经典例题 With what enthusiasm the Chinese people are building socialism.

参考译文 中国人民正在以多么高的热情建设社会主义啊!

经典例题 The plane twisted under me, trailing flame and smoke.

参考译文 飞机在我下面旋转下降,拖着浓烟烈焰掉了下去。

经典例题 What a sight!

参考译文 多美的景色啊!

4. 增加副词

经典例题 The crowds melted away.

参考译文 人群渐渐散开了。

经典例题 Theory is something, but practice is everything.

参考译文 理论固然重要,实践尤其重要。

经典例题 He was fascinated by the political processes—the wheeling and dealing of presidential politics, the manipulating, releasing and leaking of news, the public and private talks.

参考译文 一幕幕政治花招使他看入了迷:总统竞选活动中的勾心斗角,尔虞我诈;对新闻消息的幕后操纵,公开发表和有意透露,以及公开和秘密的谈话。

5. 增加表示名词复数的词

经典例题 When the plants died and decayed, they formed layers of organic materials.

参考译文 植物腐烂后,形成了一层层有机物。

经典例题 Things in the universe are changing all the time.

参考译文 宇宙中万物总是在不断变化的。

经典例题 There is enough coal to meet the world's needs for centuries to come.

参考译文 有足够的煤来满足全世界未来几个世纪的需要。

6. 增加语气词

经典例题 Don't be childish. I'm only joking.

参考译文 别孩子气了嘛,这只不过是开玩笑罢了。

经典例题 As for me, I didn't agree from the very beginning.

参考译文 我呢,从一开始就不赞成。

7. 增加量词

经典例题 A red sun rose slowly from the calm sea.

参考译文 一轮红日从风平浪静的海面冉冉升起。

8. 增加概况词

经典例题 It leads the discussion to extremes at the outset; it invites you to think that animals should be treated either with the consideration humans extend to other humans, or with no consideration at all.

参考译文 这种说法从一开始就将讨论引向两个极端,使人们觉得要么就像关心自身一样关心动物,要么就完全不顾它们的死活。(1997 年真题)

经典例题 The thesis summed up the new achievements made in electronic computers, artificial satellites and rockets.

参考译文 论文总结了电子计算机、人造卫星和火箭三方面的新成就。

经典例题 We have got great achievements militarily, politically and economically.

参考译文 我们在军事、政治、经济等方面取得了巨大的成绩。

(二) 逻辑加词

1.增加连接词

经典例题 Could you imagine what a fool I would make myself without that sum of money on me?

参考译文 你能想象我要是身上没带那笔钱,该显得多傻吗?

2.增加承上启下的词

经典例题 Yes, I like Chinese food. Lots of people do these days, sort of the fashion.

参考译文 不错,我喜欢中国菜。现在很多人喜欢中国菜,这种情况算是有点赶时髦吧!

(三) 语法加词

增加表示时态的词

经典例题 Humans have been dreaming of copies of themselves for thousands of years.

参考译文 千百年来,人类一直梦想制造出自己的复制品。

经典例题 The high-altitude plane was and still is a remarkable bird.

参考译文 高空飞机过去是而且现在仍还是一种了不起的飞行器。

四、使用"重复法"进行翻译

重复法实际上也是一种增词法,只不过所增加的词是上文刚刚出现过的词。

(一) 为了明确

1.重复名词

经典例题 I had experienced oxygen and/or engine trouble.

参考译文 我曾碰到过,不是氧气设备出故障,就是引擎出故障,或两者都出故障。

经典例题 Water can be decomposed by energy, a current of electricity.

参考译文 水可由能量来分解,所谓能量也就是电流。

2.重复动词

经典例题 They wanted to determine if he complied with the terms of his employment and his obligations as an American.

参考译文 他们想要确定,他是否履行了受雇条件,是否履行了作为美国公民所应尽的职责。

经典例题 He supplied his works not only with biographies, but with portraits of their supposed authors.

参考译文 他不仅在他的作品上提供作者传记,而且还提供假想作者的画像。

3.重复代词

经典例题 Big powers have their strategies while small countries also have their own lines.

参考译文 强国有强国的策略,小国有小国的路线。

经典例题 He hated failure; he had conquered it all his life, risen above it, despised it in others.

参考译文 他讨厌失败,他一生中曾战胜失败,超越失败,并且蔑视别人的失败。

(二) 为了强调

1.英语原文中有词的重复,译成汉语有时可以保持同样的词的重复。

经典例题 Work while you work, play while you play.

参考译文 工作时工作,游戏时游戏。

2.英语原文中有词的重复,译成汉语有时可以用同义词重复。

经典例题 They would read and re-read the secret notes.

参考译文 他们往往一遍又一遍地反复琢磨这些密件。

(三) 为了生动

1.运用两个四字词组

经典例题 He showed himself calm in an emergency situation.

参考译文 他在情况危急时,态度从容,镇定自若。

2.运用词的重叠

经典例题 I wasn't evasive in my reply.

参考译文 我的回答并不躲躲闪闪。

3.运用四字对偶词组

经典例题 The trial, in his opinion, was absolutely fair.

参考译文 据他看来,这次审判是绝对公平合理的。

五、使用"减词法(省略法)"进行翻译

省略是指原文中有些词在译文中不译出来,因为其在译文中是不言而喻的。换言之,省略是删去一些可有可无的,或者有了反嫌累赘或违背译文语言习惯的词。但省略并不是把原文的某些思想内容删去。

(一) 冠词的省略

经典例题 Because the body's defense system is damaged, the patient has little ability to fight off many other diseases.

参考译文 由于人体的免疫系统遭到破坏,病人几乎没有什么能力来抵抗许许多多其他疾病的侵袭。

经典例题 Any substance is made up of atoms whether it is a solid, a liquid, or a gas.

参考译文 任何物质,无论它是固体、液体或气体,都是由原子构成的。

(二) 代词的省略

经典例题 The desert animals can hide themselves from the heat during the daytime.

参考译文 沙漠中的兽类能躲避白天的炎热天气。

经典例题 We all took it for granted that he would attend the meeting, but in the end he never turned up.

参考译文 我们都想当然地以为他会来开会,但直到最后他也没有露面。

经典例题 We live and learn.

参考译文 活到老,学到老。

(三) 连词的省略

经典例题 Like charges repel each other while opposite charges attract.

参考译文 同性电荷相斥,异性电荷相吸。

经典例题 He looked gloomy and troubled.

参考译文 他看上去有些忧愁不安。

经典例题 If winter comes, can spring be far behind?

参考译文 冬天来了,春天还会远吗?

(四) 介词的省略

经典例题 The density of air varies directly as pressure, with temperature being constant.

参考译文 温度不变,空气的密度和压力成正比。

经典例题 Smoking is prohibited in public places.

参考译文 公共场所不许吸烟。

经典例题 A body in motion remains in motion unless acted on by an external force.

参考译文 如果没有外力的作用,运动的物体仍然保持运动状态。

(五) 同位语前置名词的省略

经典例题 Behaviorists, in contrast, say that differences in scores are due to the fact that blacks are often deprived of many of the educational and other environmental advantages that whites enjoy.

分析:在同位句中,the fact 就是指 that 所引导的 blacks are often deprived of …… that whites enjoy. 在翻译成汉语时,就可以省略 the fact,以免显得累赘。

参考译文 相反,行为主义者认为,成绩的差异是由于黑人往往被剥夺了白人在教育及其他环境方面所享有的许多有利条件。(1990 年真题)

(六) 同义词或近义词的省略

经典例题 Technology is the application of scientific method and knowledge to industry to satisfy our material needs and wants.

分析:例句原文中的 needs and wants 是近义词,在英语中常一起出现,但从中文的角度来看,表达的是同一个意思。所以译文可以简洁一些。

参考译文 技术就是在工业上应用科学方法和科学知识以满足我们物质上的需求。

经典例题 Insulators in reality conduct electricity but, nevertheless, their resistance is very high.

分析:but, nevertheless 是近义词,在文中都表示"但是"。

参考译文 绝缘体实际上也导电,但其电阻很高。

六、翻译过程中,进行词类转换

在英译汉过程中,有些句子可以逐词对译,有些句子则由于英汉两种语言的表达方式不同,就不能用"一个萝卜一个坑"的方法来逐词对译。原文中有些词在译文中需要转换词类,才能使汉语译文通顺自然。

(一) 转译成动词

1. 名词转换成动词

经典例题 Interest in historical methods has arisen, less through external challenge to the validity of history as an intellectual discipline and more from internal quarrels among historians themselves.

分析:interest 在原文中是名词,而在译文中为了符合中文的表达方式,在不改变意思的前提下,将它改成动词。

参考译文 人们之所以关注历史研究的方法,主要是因为史学家们内部分歧过大,其次才是因为外界并不认为历史是一门学科。(1999 年真题)

经典例题 With the click of a mouse, information from the other end of the globe will be transported to your computer screen at the dizzying speed of seven-and-a-half times around the earth per second.

参考译文 只要一点鼠标,来自世界另一端的信息便会以每秒绕地球七周半的惊人速度传输到你的电脑屏幕上。

2.形容词转换成动词

经典例题 Additional social stresses may also occur because of the population explosion problems arising from mass migration movements—themselves made relatively easy nowadays by modern means of transport.

参考译文 由于人口的猛增或大量人口流动(现代交通工具使大量人口流动变得相对容易)所造成的种种问题也会增加社会压力。(2000 年真题)

经典例题 Doctors have said that they are not sure they can save his life.

参考译文 医生们说他们不敢肯定能否救得了他的命。

Success is dependent on his effort.

参考译文 成功与否取决于他的努力。

3.副词转换成动词

经典例题 She opened the window to let fresh air in.

参考译文 她把窗子打开,让新鲜空气进来。

4.介词转换成动词

经典例题 Many laboratories are developing medicines against AIDS.

参考译文 许多实验室正在研制治疗艾滋病的药物。

经典例题 "Coming!" Away she skimmed over the lawn, up the path, up the steps, across the veranda, and into the porch.

参考译文 "来了!"她转身蹦着跳着地跑了,越过草地,跑上小径,跨上台阶,穿过凉台,进了门廊。

(二) 转换成名词

1.动词转换成名词

经典例题 The university aims at the first rate of the world.

参考译文 学校的目标是世界一流。

经典例题 The net and electronic commerce will foster a large number of free-lance, and this will affect social structure in a big way.

参考译文 网络和电子商业将会造就一大批自由职业者,从而将对社会结构产生深远的影响。

经典例题 Numerous abstentions marked the French elections.

参考译文 这次法国选举的特点是弃权的人多。

2.形容词转换成名词

经典例题 They did their best to help the sick and the wounded.

参考译文 他们尽了最大努力帮助病号和伤员。

经典例题 The different production cost is closely associated with the sources of power.

参考译文 生产成本的差异与能源密切相关。

3.代词转换成名词

经典例题 According to a growing body of evidence, the chemicals that make up many plastics may migrate out of the material and into foods and fluids, ending up in your body.

分析:your body 直译是"你的身体",而细读原文,我们发现其实 your body 是泛指人体。作者为了引起与读者的共鸣,用了与读者更息息相关的 your。在翻译时,应将此代词转换成名词,体现其真实含义。

参考译文 越来越多的证据表明,许多塑料制品的化学成分会移动到食物或流体上去,最终进入人体内。

经典例题 Though we can't see it, there is air all around us.

参考译文 虽然我们看不见空气,可我们周围到处都有空气。

4. 副词转换成名词

经典例题 The new type of machine is shown schematically in Figure 1.

参考译文 图一所示是这种新型机器的简图。

经典例题 Internally the earth consists of two parts, a core and a mantle.

参考译文 地球的内部由两部分组成:地核和地慢。

(三) 转换成形容词

1. 副词转换成形容词

经典例题 The engineer had prepared meticulously for his design.

参考译文 工程师为这次设计做了十分周密的准备。

经典例题 When tables and other materials are included, they should be conveniently placed, so that a student can consult them without turning over too many pages.

参考译文 当书中列有表格或其他参考资料时,应当将这些内容编排在适当的位置,以便使学生在查阅时,不必翻太多的书页。

2. 名词转换成形容词

经典例题 Most teenagers feel no difficulty in learning and operating computers.

参考译文 绝大部分青少年在学习和操作电脑方面并不觉得困难。

经典例题 The instrument has been welcomed by users because of its stability in serviceability, reliability in operation and simplicity in maintenance.

参考译文 该仪器性能稳定,操作可靠,维护方便,因而受到用户的欢迎。

(四) 转换成副词

形容词转换成副词

经典例题 The wide application of electronic machines in scientific work, in designing and in economic calculations will free man from the labor of complicated computations.

参考译文 在科学研究、设计和经济计算方面广泛地应用电子计算机可以使人们从繁重的计算劳动中解放出来。

经典例题 By dialing the right number, you may be able to select a play, golf lesson or lecture in physics, from a pretaped library in a remote city, for showing on your home screen.

参考译文 只要拨对了号码,你就可以在家里电视机上选看到由远方城市一座图书馆发出的预先录制的一出戏,一堂打高尔夫球的讲课,或者一次物理学讲演。

七、在翻译过程中,进行结构转换

结构转换着眼于句子成分的相互转换和基本句型的改变。句子成分的相互转换主要在主语与宾语,补语与表语,主语与定语,定语与状语,状语与主语之间进行。

（一）句子成分的转换

1. 非主语译成主语

　　经典例题 Since the invention of the transistor at the Bell Telephone Laboratories in 1984，it has found its way into varied applications in the commercial，industrial and military fields.

参考译文 自从 1984 年贝尔电话研究所发明晶体管以来，晶体管的种种应用已遍及商业、工业和军事各个领域。（状语译成主语）

　　经典例题 Television is different from radio in that it sends and receives pictures.

参考译文 电视和无线电的不同点在于电视能收发图像。（表语译成主语）

　　经典例题 Matter is usually electrically neutral，that is，it has as many protons，as electrons.

参考译文 物质通常是不带电的，就是说，它的质子和电子数量是相等的。（宾语译成主语）

2. 非谓语译成谓语

There is a need for improvement in your study habits.

参考译文 你的学习习惯需要改进。（主语译成谓语）

3. 非宾语译成宾语

　　经典例题 He is admired by everybody.

参考译文 大家都很钦佩他。（主语译成宾语）

　　经典例题 Materials to be used for structural purpose are chosen so as to behave elastically in the environmental condition.

参考译文 用于结构上的材料必须选择得使它们在周围环境条件下具有弹性。（状语译成宾语）

4. 非状语译成状语

　　经典例题 He drew a deep breath.

参考译文 他深深地吸了一口气。（定语译成状语）

　　经典例题 Pictures show him in the company of men like Churchill，Einstein and Gandhi.

参考译文 在这些照片中我们可以看到他和邱吉尔、爱因斯坦、甘地这些人的交往。（主语译成状语）

（二）基本句型的转化

1. 简单句转换成复合句

　　经典例题 At the slightest improvement in my work they would show warm approval.

参考译文 我工作稍有进步，他们就热情肯定。

2. 复合句转换成简单句

　　经典例题 This causes the construction of gigantic buildings where too large masses of human beings are crowded together.

参考译文 这样就盖起了许多人聚居的高楼大厦。

八、在翻译过程中，进行倒译与顺译

　　按照原句语序进行翻译便是顺译。然而，英汉两种语言的语序经常出现差异，翻译时需重新调整语序，包括词序与句序，尤其当英语出现后置及倒装情况时。倒译是语法上的需要，有时由于意思的需要也要将原文的叙述顺序颠倒。这种将原文叙述顺序进行前后调整的翻译技巧便是倒译。

（一）顺译法

　　经典例题 Computers can work through a series of problems and make thousands of logical decisions without becoming tired.

参考译文 计算机能解决很多问题,做出成千上万个符合逻辑的决定,而不感到疲倦。

经典例题 From a long-term perspective, Internet shopping is but a low-level aspect of the Net, and it is not likely to become the most important trend.

参考译文 从长远来看,网上购物仅仅是低层次的网络化,未必会成为最主要的趋向。

经典例题 We are taking steps to prevent stream and air pollution.

参考译文 我们正采取措施防止河流和空气污染。

(二) 倒译法

经典例题 Every living thing has what scientists call a biological clock that controls behavior.

参考译文 每一种生物都有控制自己行为的时钟,科学家们称之为生物钟。

经典例题 The moon is completely empty of water because the force of gravity on the moon is much less than on the earth.

参考译文 月球的引力比地球的引力小得多,所以月球上根本没有水。

经典例题 That energy and mass are equal and interchangeable is known to every student of science.

参考译文 理科学生人人都懂得能量和质量是相等而且是可以互相转换的。

九、在翻译过程中,进行反译

反译即通常所说的反面着笔译法,是指突破原文形式的束缚,变换语气,把原文中肯定的表达形式译成否定形式,把原文中否定的表达形式译成肯定形式。

(一) 否定译成肯定

经典例题 It's not easy to talk about Dolly in a world that doesn't share a uniform set of ethical values.

参考译文 世界各地的伦理观念不同,因此就多利羊展开讨论很难达成一致意见。

经典例题 Ice is not as dense as water and it therefore floats.

参考译文 冰的密度比水小,因此能浮在水面上。

(二) 肯定译成否定

经典例题 Bicycles offer the perfect eco-friendly method of traveling around the vast and beautiful and flat countryside that surrounds Cambridge.

参考译文 骑自行车在剑桥大学周围宽广、美丽而又平坦的乡村旅行,是不会对环境造成危害的理想旅游方式。

经典例题 We should stop treating the sea as a dump for human and industrial effluent (污水).

参考译文 我们不应当再把海洋当成人类生活污水和工业污水的垃圾场了。

十、在翻译过程中,进行分译与合译

所谓分译是指把原文的一个简单句译成两个或两个以上的句子。所谓合译是指把原文两个或两个以上的简单句或一个复杂句在译文中用一个单句来表达。

（一）分译

1.词语搭配分译

英语词语的搭配关系与汉语有较大差别，比如，英语词语可以同两个以上的词搭配，而相应的汉语词语却无法实现。有效的解决办法之一是根据原义和汉语搭配习惯把该词相应地译成两个词，然后分别同原来的两个（或更多）搭配对象组成词组。

经典例题 This military maneuver strained the government's principles as well as their budgets.

参考译文 这种军事演习使政府的原则无法自圆其说，也使其预算捉襟见肘。

2.词语脱句分译

在英语句子中有一种情况，即修饰性词语是作者的主观评论，而被修饰的词语是对事实的客观描述。这种搭配关系不适合汉语的表达方式。需要将修饰词从句子中拆出，另外扩展成单独的子句。

经典例题 The Chinese seemed justifiably proud of their speedy economic development.

参考译文 中国人为他们的经济发展速度感到自豪，这是无可非议的。

3.句子分译

经典例题 The law of universal gravitation states that every particle of matter in the universe attracts every other with a force which is directly proportional to the product of their masses and inversely proportional to the square of the distance between them.

参考译文 根据万有引力定律，宇宙中每个质点都以一种力吸引其他各个质点。这种力与各质点的质量的乘积成正比，与它们之间距离的平方成反比。

经典例题 The research work is being done by a small group of dedicated and imaginative scientists who specialize in extracting from various sea animals substances that may improve the health of the human race.

参考译文 一小部分富有想像力和敬业精神的科学家正在进行这项研究，他们专门研究从各种海洋动物中提取能增进人类健康的物质。

（二）合译

经典例题 He was very clean. His mind was open.

参考译文 他为人单纯而坦率。

经典例题 There are men here from all over the country. Many of them are from the South.

参考译文 从全国各地来的人中有许多是南方人。

十一、在翻译过程中，进行语态转换

由于在英汉两种语言当中都有主动和被动两种语态，在英译汉时，人们常常会简单地认为只要按照原句的语态处理就行了，事实上并非如此。在英语中被动语态的使用频率要远远高于汉语。如果一味按照英语的语态来翻译，往往会使译文显得十分别扭，带有明显的翻译腔，甚至出现文理不通的情况。

（一）主动句转换成被动句

经典例题 There are more than 60,000 prosecutions a year for shoplifting.

参考译文 每年有六万多人因在超市偷窃而被起诉。

（二）被动句转换成主动句

1.转换成含被动义的主动句

汉语译文的句型从形式上看是主动语态，但其中被动的含义不言而喻。在翻译英语被动句时，一般不用改变原句的结构,直接译出即可。

经典例题 If understanding prevails, UNCTAD is in a position to replace confrontation with agreement; it cannot be put off.

参考译文 若能普遍形成谅解,联合国贸发会议就能用协议取代对抗;这项工作不能再拖延下去了。

经典例题 Most of the questions have been settled satisfactorily, only the question of when the transplanting will take place remains to be considered.

参考译文 大部分问题已圆满解决,只剩下何时进行该移植手术问题有待讨论。

2. 转换成带表语的主动句

英语中许多表示某种结果或状态的被动结构一般应转换成汉语的系表结构,把原句中的有关状语或施事方移到汉语的表语之中。

经典例题 A dialect is known by every linguist in this room.

参考译文 有一种方言是在座的每一位语言学家都懂得的。

3. 转换成无主句

无主句是汉语特有的句子形式,其作用和效果相当于英语中无施事方的被动句,因而可以用来翻译某些英语被动形式。

经典例题 It must be admitted that only when we get a taste of its abuse will we feel the full meaning of cloning.

参考译文 必须承认,只有当我们尝到克隆被滥用的恶果之后,我们才会彻底明白其价值所在。

经典例题 It is reported that robots, instead of human beings, are doing jobs as to assemble parts in dangerous environment in our country.

参考译文 据报道,我国已用机器人代替人去做危险环境下的零件组装工作。

4. 转换成以施事方为主语的主动句

经典例题 Our plans have been completely wrecked by bad weather.

参考译文 恶劣的天气使我们的计划完全落空。

练习

Researchers investigating brain size and mental ability say their work offers evidence that education protects the mind from the brain's physical deterioration.

(61) It is known that the brain shrinks as the body ages, but the effects on mental ability are different from person to person. Interestingly, in a study of elderly men and women, those who had more education actually had more brain shrinkage.

"That may seem like bad news," said study author Dr. Edward Coffey, a professor of psychiatry and of neurology at Henry Ford Health System in Detroit. (62) However, he explained, the finding suggests that education allows people to withstand more brain tissue loss before their mental functioning begins to break down.

The study, published in the July issue of Neurology, is the first to provide biological evidence to support a concept called the "reserve" hypothesis, according to the researchers. In recent years, investigators have developed the idea that people who are more educated have greater cognitive reserves to draw upon as the brain ages; in essence, they have more brain tissue to spare.

(63) Examining brain scans(脑部扫描的 X 光片) of 320 healthy men and women aged 66 to 90, researchers found that for each year of education the subjects had, there was greater shrink age of the outer layer of the brain known as the cortex(脑皮层). Yet on tests of cognition and memory, all participants scored in the range indicating normal.

"Everyone has some degree of brain shrinkage," Coffey said. "People lose (on average) 2.5 percent per decade starting in adulthood."

There is, however, a "remarkable range" of shrinkage among people who show no signs of mental decline, Coffey noted. Overall health, he said, accounts for some differences in brain size. Alcohol or drug use, as well as medical conditions such as diabetes and high blood pressure, contribute to brain tissue loss throughout adulthood.

In the absence of such medical conditions, Coffey said, education level helps explain the range of brain shrinkage exhibited among the mentally-fit elderly. The more-educated can withstand greater loss.

(64) Coffey and colleagues gauged shrinkage of the cortex by measuring the cerebrospinal fluid(脑脊液) surrounding the brain. The greater the amount of fluid, the greater the cortical(脑皮层的) shrinkage.

Controlling for the health factors that contribute to brain injury, the researchers found that education was related to the severity of brain shrinkage. For each year of education from first grade on, subjects had an average of 1. 77 milliliters more cerebrospinal fluid around the brain. Just how education might affect brain cells is unknown. (65) In their report, the researchers speculated that in people with more education, certain brain structures deeper than the cortex may stay intact to compensate for cortical shrinkage.

答案及解析

文章大意：调查大脑体积和智力的人称，他们的研究提供的证据表明，接受教育能保护智力免受大脑自然衰退的影响。通过对脑脊液的观察测量，专家发现接受教育多的人脑脊液要多于那些教育层次低的人，这意味着他们脑皮层萎缩得快，表面看来这似乎不利，但实际上接受较多教育的人，他们能承受较多的脑组织萎缩。专家们推测这可能因为人脑中还有某些比脑皮层更深层次的结构，对大脑的退化起更关键的作用。

(61)**结构分析**：句子框架是 It is known that the brain shrinks as the body ages, but the effects……are different from person to person. 这是由 but 连接的两个并列句，意思转折，前一句是个主语从句，it 是形式主语，that 引导的从句是真正的主语，it is known 翻译为"众所周知"。

参考译文：众所周知，大脑随着年龄的增长而萎缩，但是这对智力方面的影响却因人而异。

(62)**结构分析**：句子框架是 However, he explained, the finding suggests that education allows people to withstand……before their mental functioning begins to break down。he explained 是插入语。that 引导宾语从句。在此从句中包含了一个由 before 引导的时间状语从句；suggest 这里意思是"表明，显示"，break down 翻译为"崩溃"。

参考译文：然而，他解释说，这项研究成果表明的是，接受过教育的人在大脑功能开始崩溃之前更能经受得住大脑组织的丧失。

(63)**结构分析**：句子框架是 Examining brain scans……, researchers found that……there was greater shrink age of the outer layer of the brain known as the cortex(脑皮层)。examining……是现在分词结构作时间状语，that 引导宾语从句。此从句是个 there be 句型；the subjects had 作为定语从句修饰 education；known as the cortex 作定语，修饰 the outer layer of the brain。

参考译文：研究人员对 320 名年龄在 66 岁到 90 岁的身体健康的男子和女子的脑部扫描 X 光片研究后发现，受试者的受教育经历每多一年，其大脑外层叫做脑皮层的部位就多一份萎缩。

(64)**结构分析**：句子框架是 Coffey and colleagues gauged shrinkage of the cortex by measuring the cerebrospinal fluid(脑脊液) surrounding the brain. The greater the amount of fluid, the greater the cortical(脑皮层的)shrinkage. 前一句是个简单句，直译即可，其中介词 by 引导的部分作方式状语；surrounding the brain 现在分词作定语修饰 fluid；后一句是 the more……, the more……句型。

参考译文：科菲和同事们通过测量大脑周围脑脊液的体积而测算出大脑皮层的萎缩程度。脑脊液越多，脑皮层萎缩得就越多。

(65)**结构分析**：句子框架是 In their report，the researchers speculated that……，certain brain structures ……may stay intact to compensate for cortical shrinkage. 本句中含有一个宾语从句，宾语从句中，比较级 deeper than the cortex 修饰主语 certain brain structure；compensate for 翻译为"弥补"。

参考译文：研究人员在报告中推测，在接受过较多教育的人的大脑中，某些比脑皮层更深层次的结构可能完好无损，从而弥补脑皮层萎缩带来的损失。

第三节　英语长难句

1. 什么是英语长句？

英语长句一般指的是各种复杂句，复杂句里可能有多个从句，从句与从句之间的关系可能包含、嵌套，也可能并列，平行。所以翻译长句，实际上我们的重点主要放在对各种从句的翻译上。从功能来说，英语有三大复合句，即：①名词性从句，包括主语从句、宾语从句、表语从句和同位语从句；②形容词性从句，即我们平常所说的定语从句；③状语从句。

2. 英语长句的特点是什么？

一般说来，英语长句有如下几个特点：

1) 结构复杂，逻辑层次多；

2) 常须根据上下文作词义的引申；

3) 常须根据上下文对指代词的指代关系做出判断；

4) 并列成分多；

5) 修饰语多，特别是后置定语很长；

6) 习惯搭配和成语经常出现。

3. 英语长句的分析方法是什么？

1) 找出全句的主语、谓语和宾语，即句子的主干结构；

2) 找出句中所有的谓语结构、非谓语结构、介词短语和从句的引导词；

3) 分析从句和短语的功能，例如，是否为主语从句、宾语从句、表语从句或状语从句等，以及词、短语和从句之间的关系；

4) 分析句子中是否有固定词组或固定搭配、插入语等其他成分。

长句翻译的步骤举例：

经典例题

In Africa I met a boy，who was crying as if his heart would break and said，when I spoke to him，that he was hungry because he had had no food for two days.

分析：第一，拆分句子：这个长句可以拆分为四段：In Africa I met a boy/ who was crying as if his heart would break/ when I spoke to him，that he was hungry because/ he had had no food for two days.

第二，句子的结构分析：(1)主干结构是主语＋过去式＋宾语：I met a boy……。(2) crying 后面是壮语从句"as if his heart would break"。(3)"when I spoke to him"是介于"said"和"that he was hungry because"之间的插入语。

第三，难点部分的处理："crying as if his heart would break"应译为"哭得伤心极了"。

参考译文 在非洲，我遇到一个小孩，他哭得伤心极了，我问他时，他说他饿了，两天没有吃饭了。

一般来说，长句的翻译有顺序法、逆序法、分译法和综合法四种。现将各种方法举例说明如下：

1. 怎样用顺序法来翻译长句？

有些英语长句叙述的一连串动作按发生的时间先后安排，或按逻辑关系安排，与汉语的表达方式比较一致，可按原文顺序译出。例如：

经典例题 To fuse atoms together on earth requires much higher temperature than in the sun in order to compensate for the lack of the sun's crushing gravitational pressure.

分析：按意群的关系，该句可以拆分为三部分：To fuse atoms together on earth/ requires much higher temperature than in the sun/ in order to compensate for the lack of the sun's crushing gravitational pressure. 上述三层意思的逻辑关系以及表达顺序基本上与汉语一致，只是第二部分里形容词的比较级根据汉语的表达习惯把"in the sun"前置。

参考译文 在地球上把原子熔聚在一起，要求比太阳内的温度高的多的温度，以补偿它所缺少的在太阳内的起决定性作用的引力。

经典例题 Combined with digital television sets, videodiscs can not only present films but also offer surround sound which provides theatre quality—amazing reality by which the viewers may have an illusion that they were at the scene and witnessed everything happening just around them.

分析：按意群的关系，该句可以拆分为五部分：Combined with digital television sets/ videodiscs can not only present films but also offer surround sound/ which provides theatre quality—amazing reality/ by which the viewers may have an illusion/ that they were at the scene and witnessed everything happening just around them. 除了必要的增减词，原文各句的逻辑关系，表达次序与汉语基本一致，因此可以按原文译出。

参考译文 与数字式电视机相结合，图像光盘不仅可以演电影，还提供环境声音，产生电影院效果——令人吃惊的真实感，使观看者产生一种错觉，以为他们在现场目睹他们周围发生的一切。

2. 怎样用逆序法来翻译长句？

"逆序法"又称"倒置法"，主要指句子的前后倒置问题。有些英语长句的表达次序与汉语习惯不同，甚至语序完全相反，这就必须从原文的后面译起，逆着原文的顺序翻译。考研英语中这样的例子很多，许多句子都需要作这样的调整。逆序法在长句的翻译中，我们可根据不同的情况按意群进行全部逆序或部分逆序。例如：

经典例题 There are many wonderful stories to tell about the places I visited and the people I met.

分析：该句可以拆分为三部分：There are many wonderful stories to tell about/ the places I visited/ the people I met. 这句英语长句的叙述层次与汉语逻辑相反，所以采用逆译法。

参考译文 我访问了一些地方，遇到不少人，要谈起来，奇妙的事可多着呢。

经典例题 There was little hope of continuing my inquiries after dark to any useful purpose in a neighborhood that was strange to me.

分析：该句可分为三部分：There was little hope/ continuing my inquiries after dark to any useful purpose/ in a neighborhood that was strange to me.

第一、二层次是表示结果，第三层次表示原因，按照中文的表达习惯，常把原因放在结果前面。这句英语长句的叙述层次与汉语逻辑相反，因此要打破原句的结构，按照汉语造句的规律重新加以安排。

参考译文 这一带我不熟悉，天黑以后继续进行调查，取得结果的希望不大。

3. 怎样用分译法来翻译长句？

"分译法"又叫"拆译法"，有些英语长句的主句与从句或主句与修饰语间的关系并不十分密切，可把长句中的从句或短语化为句子分开来叙述，这符合汉语多用短句的习惯。为使意思连贯，有时还可适当增加词语。考生必须注意的是，分译的目的是化长为短、化整为零，消除译文的阻塞；分译后的译文必须连贯，有整体感。例如：

经典例题 He became deaf at five after an attack of typhoid fever.

分析：这个英语句子，有两个介词短语，代表两层意思，表示什么时候，生了什么病。翻译时打破原句的结构，按汉语造句的规律重新安排。

参考译文 他五岁的时候，生了一场伤寒病，变成了聋子。

经典例题 I was on my way home from tramping about the streets, my drawings under my arm, when I found myself in front of the Mathews Gallery.

分析：这句英语长句的叙述层次与汉语逻辑相反，因此要打破原句的结构，按照汉语造句的规律重新加以安排。

参考译文　我夹着画稿，在街上兜了一番，回家的路上无意中发现自己逛到了马太画廊的门口。

　　4．怎样用综合法来翻译长句？

　　有些英语长句顺译或逆译都不合适，分译也有困难，单纯的使用一种译法不能译出地道的汉语时，就应该仔细推敲，或按时间先后，或按逻辑顺序，有顺有逆地进行综合处理。例如：

　　经典例题 The phenomenon describes the way in which light physically scatters when it passes through particles in the earth's atmosphere that are 1/10 in diameter of the color of the light.

分析：该句可以分解为四个部分：The phenomenon describes the way/ in which light physically scatters/ when it passes through particles in the earth's atmosphere/ that are 1/10 in diameter of the color of the light. 其中，第一、二和三四部分之间是修饰与被修饰的关系。总体考虑之后，我们可以使用综合法来处理这个句子，即合译第一、二和第三部分，第四部分用"分译法"，这样译出来的句子就非常符合汉语的表达习惯。

参考译文　这种现象说明了光线通过地球大气微粒时的物理散射方式。大气微粒的直径为有色光直径的十分之一。

　　经典例题 When Hetty read Arthur's letter she gave way to despair. Then, by one of those conclusive, motionless actions by which the wretched leap from temporary sorrow to life-long misery, she determined to marry Adam.

分析：该句可以分解为五个部分：When Hetty read Arthur's letter/ she gave way to despair/ by one of those conclusive, motionless actions/ by which the wretched leap from temporary sorrow to life-long misery/ she determined to marry Adam. 首先，第四部分是修饰第三部分的，对第四部分采用"分译法"，然后再适当地根据汉语的表达习惯调整语序，增减词语，对句子进行综合处理。

参考译文　海蒂读过阿瑟的信后陷入绝望之中。后来，她采取了一个不幸者常常采用的那种快刀斩乱麻的行动：嫁给了亚当，从而陷入了终身的痛苦，为的不过是跳出那一时的悲伤。

　　语序调整是保证句子通顺的关键所在。由于长句的翻译大多需要将原句拆分成多个较短的句子，并且要通过多个短句表达出原来长句的修饰关系和意思，汉语句子的逻辑关系在很大程度上依靠各语法单位在句中的顺序得以表现。所以语序的调整是长句翻译中极其重要的一个环节，直接关系到意思是否完整，句子是否通顺。语序调整是各类词语翻译方法和各种特殊句型翻译的综合运用。

历年真题分析

　　经典例题 This will be particularly true since energy pinch will make it difficult to continue agriculture in the high-energy American fashion that makes it possible to combine few farmers with high yields. （1991 年）

结构分析：句子的框架是 This will be particularly true since... 。since 引导原因状语从句。此从句中又套嵌一个由关系代词 that 引导的定语从句，修饰 the high-energy American fashion。this 指代前句中提到的这种困境。energy pinch 译为"能源的匮乏"；in... fashion 译为"用……方法、方式"。

参考译文　这种困境将是确定无疑的，因为能源的匮乏将使农业很难以高能量消耗这种美国耕种方式继续下去，而这种耕种方式使投入少数农民就可获得高产成为可能。

　　经典例题 Now since the assessment of intelligence is a comparative matter, we must be sure that the scale with which we are comparing our subjects provides a "valid" or "fair" comparison. （1992 年）

结构分析：句子的框架是 since... , we must be sure that... 。since 引导原因状语从句。主句中又有 that 引导的原因状语从句。此宾语从句中又套嵌一个由介词 with＋which 引导的定语从句修饰先行词 the scale。scale 在此处意为"尺度、衡量标准"。

参考译文 既然对智力的评估是比较而言的，那么我们必须确保，在对我们的对象进行比较时，我们所用的尺度能提供"有效的"或"公平的"比较。

经典例题 In general，the tests work most effectively when the qualities to be measured can be most precisely defined and least effectively when what is to be measured or predicted can be well defined.（1995 年）

结构分析：句子的框架是 the tests work most effectively when...and least effectively when...。and 连接两个并列分句，每个并列分句中皆有一个 when 引导的时间状语从句分别说明 work most effectively 和 and（work）least effectively。第二个时间状语从句中还有一个主语从句 what...predicted。the tests 是主句的主语，work 为动词做谓语，不能译作"这些测试工作"，应译成"起作用"或"奏效"。most effectively 不译成"（测试）效率最高"，least effectively 不应译作"无效，失去效果"，应译为"效果最差"；qualities 在此处是可数名词，不译为"质量"，而译为"特征"。defined 不能直译为"被定义为"，而应译为主动态"界定"。

参考译文 一般地说，当所需要测定的特征能很精确地界定时，测试最为有效；而当所测定或预测的东西不能明确地界定时，测试的效果则最差。

经典例题 For example，they do not compensate for gross social inequality，and thus do not tell how able an underprivileged youngster might have been had he grown up under more favorable circumstances.（1995 年）

结构分析：句子的框架是 they do not compensate...，and thus do not tell how...。and 连接两个并列分句，第二个并列分句中由 how 引导的宾语从句是一个带有虚拟条件句的主从复合句，其中 had he grown up...（= If he had grown up...）是省略了连词 if 的非真实条件句，译成汉语时，通常译在主句之前。主句主语的 they，在此代指上文提到的 tests，应译为"测试"、"这些测试（验）"、"这些测试手段"；compensate for 译为"补偿，弥补"；gross 在此句中不能译为"总的"或"整个的"，而应译为"明显的，显著的"；able 应译为"有能力的"或"能干的"，在句中作 might have been 的表语。underprivileged 在此不能译为"没有特权的"，而译为"没有地位的"或"物质条件差的"。

参考译文 例如，测试并不能弥补明显的社会不公；因此，它们不能说明一个物质条件差的年轻人，如果在较好的环境中成长的话，会有多大才干。

经典例题 It leads the discussion to extremes at the outset：it invites you to think that animals should be treated either with the consideration humans extend to other humans，or with no consideration at all.（1997 年）

结构分析：句子的框架是 It leads the discussion to extremes at the outset：it invites you to think that...。冒号后的复合句是对冒号前部分作进一步说明。复合句中 that 引导宾语从句，从句中有 either...or...引导的两个并列的介词结构作状语，修饰动词 be treated，其中第一个 with 介词结构中还有一个省略了关系代词 that 或 which 的定语从句 humans extend to other humans，修饰 the consideration。it 代指上文的观点，即如果对人权没有达成一致看法，而谈论动物的权力是徒劳的，译为"这种说法"或"这种观点"。介词短语 at the outset 译为"从一开始"。动词 invites 应转译为"使"、"让"或"促使"。动宾结构 extend consideration to 应意为"给予关怀或关心"，consideration 不应译为"考虑"。

参考译文 这种说法从一开始就将讨论引向极端，它使人们认为应该这样对待动物：要么像对人类自身一样关怀体谅，要么完全冷漠无情。

经典例题 But even more important，it was the farthest that scientists had been able to look into the past，for what they were seeing were the patterns and structures that existed 15 billion years ago.（1998 年）

结构分析：句子的框架是 it was the farthest that...。但 It was...that...在本句中不是强调句型，因此将句子译为"更重要的是，正是这种最远的距离使得科学家们能够研究过去，因为……"是错误的。it 为一个有具体指代意义的实义词，it 应是指上句中所提到的 150 亿年前形成的巨大云团（a strip of enormous cosmic clouds some 15 billion light-years from earth）；that 引导的应是一个定语从句，修饰先行词 the farthest。for 引导的是原因状语从句,从句中还有 that 引导的定语从句,修饰 the patterns and structure。

参考译文 但更重要的是,这是科学家们所能观测到的最遥远的过去的景象,因为他们看到的是 150 亿年前宇宙云的形状和结构。

熟能生巧

经典例题 Thus it happened that when the new factories that were springing up required labor, tens of thousands of homeless and hungry agricultural workers, with their wives and children, were forced into the cities in search of work, and any work, under any condition, that would keep them a-live.

结构分析:句子的框架是 it happened that... 。it 做形式主语,that 引导的从句做真正的主语。主语从句中,又有一个由 when 引导的时间状语从句,主句为 tens of thousands of homeless and hungry agri-cultural workers... were forced... ,时间状语从句中从句主语 the new factories 又带有一个定语从句 that were springing up;that would keep them alive 做 work 的定语从句。spring up 意为"发生,出现,建立"。

参考译文 于是就出现了这样的情况:正当新办的工厂纷纷建立,需要劳动力的时候,成千上万无家可归、饥肠辘辘的从事农业的劳动者携家带口,被迫流入城市;他们要找活干,不管什么活儿,不讲什么条件,只要不使他们饿死就行。

经典例题 As a result of two or three centuries of scientific investigation we have come to believe that Nature is understandable in the sense that when we ask her questions by way of appropriate obser-vations and experiments, she will answer truly and reward us with discoveries that endure.

结构分析:句子的框架是... we have come to believe that... 。that 引导的从句做 believe 的宾语从句;此从句中有一个 that 从句作 the sense 的同位语从句;同位语从句中又套嵌一个由 when 引导的时间状语从句;此时间状语从句又套嵌一个定语从句 that endure,修饰其先行词 discoveries。by way of 意为"经由,通过……方法";reward sb. with 意为"以……报答,酬劳";endure 此处应译为"持久,持续",不要译为"忍受,容忍"。

参考译文 由于两三个世纪以来科学研究的结果,我们逐渐相信,如果运用合适的观察和实验方法向大自然探究问题,她会真心实意地给我们答复,并且以永垂不朽的发现来报答我们。从这个意义上来说,大自然是可以认识的。

经典例题 These new observational capabilities would result in simply a mass of details were it not for the fact that theoretical understanding has reached the stage at which it is becoming possible to indi-cate the kind of measurements required for reliable weather forecasting.

结构分析:句子的框架是 These new observational capabilities would result in simply a mass of de-tails... 。后面紧跟省略了 if 引导的虚拟条件句 were it not for the fact that... ,即 if it were not for the fact that... ;that 从句作 the fact 的同位语从句。此从句中又套嵌一个定语从句,修饰其先行词 the stage;required for reliable weather forecasting 为过去分词短语修饰 the kind of measurements。simply 译为"只不过,仅仅",不应译为"简单地"。

参考译文 理论上的认识已达到了这样的阶段——现在已能指出需要哪种测量方式才能可靠地预报天气,如果做不到这一点,那么上述这些新的观察能力只不过提供了一大堆细节而已。

经典例题 The story of the discovery of what is now generally called the principle of Archimedes, namely that a solid body when immersed in a liquid loses a portion of its weight of the liquid it dis-places, has many different versions, of which the following is one.

结构分析：句子的框架是 The story... has many different versions... 。what is now generally called the principle of Archimedes 为名词性从句做介词 of 的宾语。namely that a solid body... 作 the principle of Archimedes 的同位语；when immersed in a liquid 是省略了主语的过去分词短语，句子补充完整为 when the solid body is immersed in a liquid，修饰其主句 a solid body loses a portion of its weight of the liquid... ；it displaces 是省略了关系代词 that 的定语从句修饰 the liquid，it 代指前面提到的 the solid body；同时，of which the following is one 又构成先行词 versions 的定语从句。displace 意为"排（水）"；version 不译为"版本"，此处指"根据个人观点的（对事件等的）说法，看法"；句尾的 one 代指 a version。

参考译文 当固体浸没到液体中时，固体会失去它所排出的液体的那部分重量，这就是现在通常所谓的阿基米德原理。有关这一发现的故事有很多说法，下面的故事就是其中之一。

经典例题 We assumed that there were forces of attraction between molecules which varied rapidly with the distance so that the attraction between molecules that were more than a few ten-millionths of a millimeter apart was very small but became considerable when the molecules approached more closely.

结构分析：句子的框架是 We assumed that there were forces of attraction... 。that 引导宾语从句。此宾语从句中套嵌一个由 which 引导的定语从句修饰先行词 forces of attraction；so that the attraction between molecules... 是 so that 结构引导的结果状语从句；在此状语从句中，除主干结构 the attraction... was very small but became considerable... ，又有 that were more than a few ten-millionths of a millimeter apart 做定语从句修饰先行词 molecules 和 when the molecules approached more closely 做状语从句，修饰... but became considerable。considerable 译为"相当大（或多的）"。

参考译文 我们曾经假定，分子之间存在着引力，这种引力随着分子之间距离的不同而有显著的变化，因而，在间距为千万分之几毫米的分子之间的引力是很小的，但是分子靠得很近时，这种引力会变得相当大。

经典例题 This need is enshrined in the concept of sustainable development, which means that we must, for the benefit of coming generations, leave enough environmental space so that these generations will be able to address their needs and fulfill their aspirations.

结构分析：句子的框架是 This need is enshrined in the concept of sustainable development... 。其后紧跟着一个 which 引导的定语从句，修饰先行词 sustainable development。此定语从句的谓语动词 means 又套嵌一个 that 引导的宾语从句，即 we must... leave enough environmental space。此宾语从句中又有 so that 结构做此从句的目的状语。be enshrined in 意为"被深深地珍藏（或铭记）在……"，此处转译为主动态"纳入到"。sustainable development 译为"可持续发展"。

参考译文 这一需要能纳入到可持续发展的概念之中。所谓可持续发展是指：为了子孙后代的利益，我们必须保留足够的生存环境空间，以满足他们的需要，施展抱负。

经典例题 Painting lacks only the means to represent movement in time and space, which is the special property of sculpture and architecture, since a painting is designed to be seen from one point at one time, whereas sculpture and architecture are created to be seen from various points of view, thus supplying movements in space and time.

结构分析：句子的框架是 Painting lacks only the means... , since... 。since 引导的原因状语从句修饰主句；关系代词 which 引导的定语从句修饰 the means to represent movement in time and space；property 在此处应译为"性质，特性"，不译为"财产，资产"。

参考译文 绘画仅仅缺少的是表现空间与时间变化的手法，而这正是雕塑与建筑的特性。一幅画在绘制时就只要求在某一时刻，从空间的一点来欣赏，而雕塑和建筑的创造要求从各个角度来欣赏，这样就表现出了空间，时间的变化。

经典例题 Once intimidated by arguments that their children would feel more at home in bilingual classes, and that they might lose their heritage in regular classes, these women have since given voice, loudly and persuasively, to what they know from experience that unless they are fluent in the language of their adopted country, their children will never attend college or land any but the most menial of jobs.

结构分析：句子的框架是 these women have... given voice... to what they know from experience that...。that 从句做 what they know 的同位语从句；此从句中又套嵌一个 unless 引导的条件状语从句；Once intimidated by arguments 是过去分词做状语修饰 these women，其施动者 arguments 又有两个 that 引导的同位语从句修饰限定它。intimidated by arguments 意为"被论点搞得惊慌害怕"；feel at home 不能直译为"感到在家"，而译为"感到自在"；give voice to 意为"表达，表露"；land jobs 译为"找到工作"。

参考译文 有人说，孩子们在双语课堂里会感到更加自由自在，而在正规班级会丧失其传统文化。这几位母亲曾被这一论点搞得惶恐不安，现在发表了最响亮、最有说服力的意见。从他们自身的经验中，他们深知：如果孩子们不熟练掌握他们所移居国家的语言，除了那些最简单的体力活儿外，根本谈不到上大学，也谈不到找到理想的工作。

　　经典例题 The presumption on which human cloning rests is that all these cells, though now specialized, still contain exact copies of the original set of genetic instructions needed to make an entire individual—and can do so if a way is found to switch them back on.

结构分析：句子的框架是 The presumption is that all these cells... contain ... genetic instructions... and can do so...。其中介词 on 加 which 引导定语从句修饰主语 the presumption；that 从句为表语从句；此表语从句中 contain 和 can do 并列做 all these cells 的谓语；表语从句中又插入一个 though 引导的省略了主语 all these cells 的让步状语从句，补充完整为 though these cells are now specialized；needed to make an entire individual 为过去分词短语做 genetic instructions 的后置定语；并列谓语 can do so 又有 if 条件句修饰。rest on 意为"依赖，仰赖"。为避免重复 do so 代替前文提到的 make an entire individual。

参考译文 人类无性生殖赖以存在的假想是：虽然所有的细胞现已全部特化，但却仍然包含有发育为完整个体所需的与母体完全一致的全部遗传指令；如果能找到一个方法使失去作用的部分恢复作用，这些细胞就能发育成为完整的个体。

　　经典例题 Thus, a regularity for which there are general theoretical grounds for expecting it will be more readily called a natural law than an empirical regularity that cannot be subsumed under more general laws or theories.

结构分析：句子的框架是 a regularity... will be more readily called a natural law than an empirical regularity...。介词 for 加关系代词 which 引导定语从句修饰 a regularity。an empirical regularity 后又有定语从句 that cannot be subsumed under more general laws or theories 修饰。grounds 意为"根据，理由"；subsume 意为"把……归入，纳入"。

参考译文 因此，与一条不能被归入更普遍的法则或理论而是基于经验的规律相比，一条具有普遍的理论依据支持的规律很可能被认可为一条自然法则。

　　经典例题 It is because of the close association in most people's minds of tools with man that special attention has always been focused upon any animal able to use an object as a tool, but it is important to realize that this ability, on it's own, does not necessarily indicate any special intelligence in the creature concerned.

结构分析：句子的框架是 It is because of... that..., but it is important to realize that...。but 连接两个并列句，but 前的并列分句为 It is... that... 强调结构，强调 because of 引导的状语。but 后的并列分句又有 that 引导的宾语从句做 realize 的宾语。the close association in most people's minds of tools with man 中注意 in most people's minds 把 the close association of tools with man（工具与人类的密切联系）分隔开来。两个并列句中分别有 able to use an object as a tool 和 concerned 分别做其前面名词 animal 和 the creature 的后置定语。man 根据上下文在此处指"人类"，而不是"男人"；not necessarily 译为"不一定、未必"；on it's own 意为"独立地，凭自己力量"，在此转译为"就其自身而言"。

参考译文 正是由于在大多数人头脑中工具与人类的密切联系，人类才特别关注可以把物体当工具使用的任何一种动物,但值得注意的是,这种能力就其自身而言并不表明这种动物有什么特别的智慧。

经典例题 The point at which tool-using and tool-making acquire evolutionary significance is surely when an animal can adapt its ability to manipulate objects to a wide variety of purposes, and when it can use an object spontaneously to solve a brand-new problem that without the use of a tool would prove insoluble.

结构分析:句子的框架是 The point...is...when...and when....两个 when 引导的从句为并列的表语从句。at which tool-using and tool-making acquire evolutionary significance 为定语从句修饰主语 the point;第二个 when 引导的表语从句中也有 that 引导的定语从句修饰 a brand-new problem。ability to manipulate objects 译为"操纵物体的能力";...a brand-new problem that without the use of a tool would prove insoluble 中 without 和 insoluble 为双重否定可译成肯定句。

参考译文 当一种动物能够使自己操纵物体的能力适用于更广泛的目标范围,并且能够自发地使用物体解决只有通过工具才能解决的崭新问题时,工具的使用和制造就肯定达到了具有进化意义的阶段。

经典例题 It was the desire to be scholarly that brought about a wave of Latin terms which appeared in the 16th century when the humanist movement brought new impetus to learning throughout Europe.

结构分析:句子的框架是 It was the desire...that brought about a wave....it is...that...是强调句型,强调主语 the desire to be scholarly。关系代词 which 引导定语从句,修饰 Latin terms;关系副词 when 引导定语从句,修饰 century。句中 scholarly 作"博学多才"讲;humanist movement 译为"人文主义运动";impetus 意为"动力,促进"。

参考译文 在 16 世纪的时候,人文主义运动促进了欧洲各国的学术运动,人们都想显示自己的博学多才,从而出现了一股使用拉丁字词的潮流。

经典例题 So don't be surprised if you never encounter some of the expressions that still appear in school textbooks; and next time you hear somebody using a strange word you haven't heard before, you can comfort yourself that there may well be a native speaker somewhere who doesn't know it either.

结构分析:句子的框架是...don't be surprised if you...; and next time..., you can comfort yourself that....分号连接两个并列分句。在前面句子中,if 引导状语从句;关系代词 that 引导定语从句,修饰 expressions。在后面句子中,you hear...是省略了关系副词 when 的定语从句,修饰 next time;you haven't heard before 又是省略了关系代词 which 的定语从句,修饰 strange word;主句是 you can comfort yourself that...,这里的 that 引导宾语从句,而关系代词 who 引导定语从句,修饰 native speaker。may 和 well 连用表示有充分的理由,译为"(完全)能,(很)可能"。

参考译文 因此,如果在某些教科书里你碰到某些词组是你从未见过的,你不必惊讶。如果下次你听到有人用一个你以前从未听到过的新词,你可以这样安慰自己说,很可能在什么地方有一个讲英语的本地人也不认识这个字呢!

经典例题 Despite the saying that one never knows if lightning strikes him, a person can sometimes feel the bolt coming and if quick enough, take protective action in time.

结构分析:句子的框架是 a person can...feel the bolt and...take protective action....and 连接两个并列的谓语动词。句首 despite 是介词引导介词短语作状语,此短语中 that 引导的名词性从句做 saying 的同位语,此同位语从句中,if lightning...是一个名词性从句,作 know 的宾语,if 在句中相当于 whether。主句中 if quick enough 补充完整为 if he is quick enough,是条件状语从句,为 take action 的前提条件。句中 bolt 译为"闪电"。

参考译文 尽管人们常说一个人从来不知道是否遭到闪电的袭击,但是一个人有时能感觉到闪电的到来,如果动作快,就能及时采取保护措施。

经典例题 Part of the reason for the ambiguity of the term "law of nature" lies in the temptation to apply the term only to statements of one of these sorts of laws, as in the claim that science deals solely with cause and effect relationships, when in fact all three kinds are equally valid.

结构分析：句子的框架是 the reason...lies in the temptation....。as 引导状语从句,此状语从句中又有 that 从句做 claim 的同位语。此同位语从句中又套嵌一个 when 引导的时间状语从句。ambiguity 意为"意义不明确,模棱两可";equally 在此处不要译为"平等的",而应译为"同样地"。

参考译文 "自然法则"这一术语之所以模糊不清,部分原因在于人们企图把这个术语仅用于表达这些法则中的某种法则。正如有人认为科学仅研究因果关系,但实际上它对三种都同样适用。

经典例题 Aluminum remained unknown until the nineteenth century, because nowhere in nature is it found free, owing to its always being combined with other elements, most commonly with oxygen, for which it has a strong affinity.

结构分析：句子的框架是 Aluminum remained unknown until..., because...。until the nineteenth century 做主句的状语;because 又引导原因状语从句,修饰主干结构;此状语从句中的主句 nowhere in nature is it found free 又是倒装句,正常语序为 nowhere in nature it is found free。owing to 为表原因的介词短语修饰 nowhere in nature it is found free。介词 in 加关系代词 which 引导定语从句修饰 oxygen。

参考译文 铝总是跟其他元素结合在一起,最普遍的是跟氧结合;因为铝跟氧有很强的亲和力,由于这个原因,在自然界找不到游离状态的铝。所以,铝直到 19 世纪才被人发现。

经典例题 When a journalist recently accused the company of lacking integrity in its testing of beauty products, the company overtly appealed to the public by citing its corporate brand, which was firmly associated in people's minds with strong ethical standards concerning animal rights.

结构分析：句子的框架是 When..., the company overtly appealed to the public...。when 引导时间状语从句。主句中关系代词 which 引导定语从句修饰 corporate brand, 此定语从句中 in people's minds 把 associated with 分隔开来。beauty products 译为"美容产品"。

参考译文 有一名记者近日指责该公司在美容产品的测试上缺乏整体性,该公司公开利用其公司品牌求助于公众,而该品牌在公众的心目中已同关系到动物权利的道德标准息息相关。

经典例题 However, the criminal fraternity quickly came to realize that the real value in the computers is in the chip which is remarkably portable and unidentifiable, so even when caught the police have trouble proving the theft.

结构分析：句子的框架是 the fraternity...came to realize that...so...the police have trouble....。这是一个并列复合句,两个句子由 so 连接。在前面句子里 that 引导宾语从句,作 realize 的宾语;此从句中又有 which 引导的定语从句修饰 the chip;so 后面句子里 when caught 是过去分词作状语,when caught 即 when the thief was caught;proving 是现在分词,修饰 trouble。句子中 criminal fraternity 译为"偷盗贼们"。

参考译文 但偷盗者认识到,电脑中真正值钱的东西是芯片(或叫集成电路片),这是可以随身携带和无法识别的,即使当场被抓住,警察也难以证明那是偷来的。

经典例题 Although perhaps only 1 percent of the life that has started somewhere will develop into highly complex and intelligent patterns, so vast is the number of planets that intelligent life is bound to be a natural part of the universe.

结构分析：句子的框架是 Although..., so vast is the number of planets that....。主句为 so...that...结构引导的结果状语从句,因强调 vast,so vast 放在句首进行倒装,正常语序为 the number of planets is so vast that...。although 引导让步状语从句。此从句中套嵌一个关系代词 that 引导的定语从句修饰 life。be bound to 意为"一定,必定"。

参考译文 虽然在某处已经开始的生命中可能仅有百分之一会发展成高度复杂、有智慧的形式,但是行星的数目如此之多,以致有智慧的生命一定是宇宙的一个天然组成部分。

练习

The proportion of works cut for the cinema in Britain dropped from 40 percent when I joined the

BBFC in 1975 to less than 4 per cent when I left. But I don't think that 20 years from now it will be possible to regulate any medium as closely as I regulated film.

The internet is, of course, the greatest problem for this century. (61) The world will have to find a means, through some sort of international treaty or United Nations initiative, to control the material that's now going totally unregulated into people's homes. That said, it will only take one little country like Paraguay to refuse to sign a treaty for transmission to be unstoppable. Parental control is never going to be sufficient.

(62) I'm still very worried about the impact of violent video games, even though researchers say their impact is moderated by the fact that players don't so much experience the game as enjoy the technical manoeuvres (策略) that enable you to win. But in respect of violence in mainstream films, I'm more optimistic. Quite suddenly, tastes have changed, and it's no longer Stallone or Schwarzenegger who are the top stars, but Leonardo DiCaprio-that has taken everybody by surprise.

(63) Go through the most successful films in Europe and America now and you will find virtually none that are violent. Quentin Tarantino didn't usher in a new, violent generation, and films are becoming much more pre-social than one would have expected.

Cinemagoing will undoubtedly survive. The new multiplexes are a glorious experience, offering perfect sound and picture and very comfortable seats, things which had died out in the 1980s. (64) I can't believe we've achieved that only to throw it away in favour of huddling around a 14-inch computer monitor to watch digitally-delivered movies at home.

It will become increasingly cheap to make films, with cameras becoming smaller and lighter but remaining very precise. (65) That means greater chances for new talent to emerge, as it will be much easier for people to learn how to be better film-makers. People's working lives will be shorter in the future, and once retired they will spend a lot of time learning to do things that amuse them-like making videos. Fifty years on we could well be media-saturated as producers as well as audience: instead of writing letter, one will send little home movies entitled My Week.

答案及解析

文章大意:本文作者曾经长期担任英国电影分级委员会主任,掌管电影的生杀予夺的大权。尽管从电视发明之日起,就曾有人预言有朝一日电视将会取代电影,但作者对电影的前景却非常乐观,他说,在高级影院看电影和在家里看电视是完全不同的两种感受,根本不存在取代问题,并且将来人人都可能有机会过一把当电影制片人和电影演员的瘾。

(61)结构分析:句子的框架是 The world will have to find a means, ..., to control the materials that...。句子的主语是 the world,谓语是 have to find,宾语是 a means,介词词组 through some sort of... initiative 作状语,而动词不定式短语 to control... into people's homes 作目的状语,不定式短语中又包含了 that 引导的定语从句修饰先行词 the material。句中的 initiative 的动词形式是 initiate,意思是"发起",这里 initiative 的意思是"(发起的)行动,计划";unregulate 的意思是"不控制,不管理"。

参考译文:网上的东西目前正毫无管制地进入人们的家中,世界各国得找出一种办法,通过某种国际条约或联合国行动,对此加以控制。

(62)结构分析:句子的框架是 I'm still worried about...,even though researchers say their impact is... by the fact that players do not so much... as...。even though 引导了让步状语从句,而状语从句中又包含了一个由 that 引导的宾语从句(that 省略了)作谓语动词 say 的宾语;宾语从句中的 moderated by the fact that... 又是被动又是名词同位语从句,不便按原文结构译,拆除 the fact that,把后面的从句视为 say 的宾语,然后把被动转为主动,添补"这"作为 moderate(减弱)的主语,译成"这就减弱了这类游戏的影响";同位语从句中同时含有句型 not so much... as...,是"与其……不如……"或"不是……更多的是……",另外,此结构中还包含了 that 引导的定语从句修饰先行词 the technical manoeuvres。

参考译文:尽管研究人员说,玩暴力电子游戏的人并不是在体验游戏本身,更多地是在享受使他们能取胜的技术操作,这就减弱了这类游戏的影响。然而我对这种影响仍然忧心忡忡。

(63) **结构分析:**句子的框架是 Go through... and you will find ... none that...。这是典型的句型:Do..., and you will...,等同于 If you..., you will...,主句的宾语是代词 none,并且后面跟了一个 that 引导的定语从句修饰它,副词 virtually 是"几乎,差不多"之意。

　　参考译文:纵观目前欧美最成功的电影,几乎找不出哪一部是暴力的。

(64)**结构分析:**句子的框架是 I can't believe we've achieved that... in favor of huddling... to watch...。句中谓语动词 believe 后面跟了一个宾语从句 we've achieved that... at home,从句中的 achieved that 中的 that 指代前文的 multiplexes(多幕影院),可以译为"建造了那么好的设施",或者抽象地译成"取得了那样高的成就";only to 表示结果与预料的相反,可译成"到头来却";in favor of 的意思是"情愿,更愿意";digitally-delivered 属于构词法中的 adv. + p. p.(过去分词)构成复合形容词,意思是"数码传送的"。

　　参考译文:我无法相信,取得了那样高的成就,到头来却弃而不用,情愿挤在十四英寸电脑显示屏前,在家里观看数码传送的电影。

(65) **结构分析:**句子的框架是 That means..., as it will be...。句中 as 引导了原因状语从句;主句中的 that 指代前面的整个句子 It will become... but remaining very precise,new talent 是"新人才"的意思,根据上下文可译成"电影新秀"。

　　参考译文:这意味着电影新秀会有更多机会脱颖而出,因为人们会更容易学会怎样把电影拍得更好。

第四节　　英译汉历年真题

1994 年英译汉试题

　　According to the new school of scientists, technology is an overlooked force in expanding the horizons of scientific knowledge. (71)Science moves forward, they say, not so much through the insights of great men of genius as because of more ordinary things like improved techniques and tools. (72) "In short", a leader of the new school contends, "the scientific revolution, as we call it, was largely the improvement and invention and use of a series of instruments that expanded the reach of science in innumerable directions."

　　(73)Over the years, tools and technology themselves as a source of fundamental innovation have largely been ignored by historians and philosophers of science. The modern school that hails technology argues that such masters as Galileo, Newton, Maxwell, Einstein, and inventors such as Edison attached great importance to, and derived great benefit from, craft information and technological devices of different kinds that were usable in scientific experiments.

　　The centerpiece of the argument of a technology-yes, genius-no advocate was an analysis of Galileo's role at the start of the scientific revolution. The wisdom of the day was derived from Ptolemy, an astronomer of the second century, whose elaborate system of the sky put Earth at the center of all heavenly motions. (74) Galileo's greatest glory was that in 1609 he was the first person to turn the newly invented telescope on the heavens to prove that the planets revolve around the sun rather than around the Earth. But the real hero of the story, according to the new school of scientists, was the long evolution in the improvement of machinery for making eyeglasses.

　　Federal policy is necessarily involved in the technology vs. genius dispute. (75) Whether the Government should increase the financing of pure science at the expense of technology or vice versa(反之) often depends on the issue of which is seen as the driving force.

1995 年英译汉试题

The standardized educational or psychological tests that are widely used to aid in selecting, classifying, assigning, or promoting students, employees, and military personnel have been the target of recent attacks in books, magazines, the daily press, and even in Congress. (71) The target is wrong, for in attacking the tests, critics divert attention from the fault that lies with ill-informed or incompetent users. The tests themselves are merely tools, with characteristics that can be measured with reasonable precision under specified conditions. Whether the results will be valuable, meaningless, or even misleading depends partly upon the tool itself but largely upon the user.

All informed predictions of future performance are based upon some knowledge of relevant past performance: school grades, research productivity, sales records, or whatever is appropriate. (72) How well the predictions will be validated by later performance depends upon the amount, reliability, and appropriateness of the information used and on the skill and wisdom with which it is interpreted. Anyone who keeps careful score knows that the information available is always incomplete and that the predictions are always subject to error.

Standardized tests should be considered in this context. They provide a quick objective method of getting some kinds of information about what a person learned, the skills he has developed, or the kind of person he is. The information so obtained has, qualitatively, the same advantages and shortcomings as other kinds of information. (73) Whether to use tests, other kinds of information, or both in a particular situation depends, therefore, upon the evidence from experience concerning comparative validity and upon such factors as cost and availability.

(74) In general, the tests work most effectively when the qualities to be measured can be most precisely defined and least effectively when what is to be measured or predicated can not be well defined. Properly used, they provide a rapid means of getting comparable information about many people. Sometimes they identify students whose high potential has not been previously recognized, but there are many things they do not do. (75) For example, they do not compensate for gross social inequality, and thus do not tell how able an underprivileged youngster might have been had he grown up under more favorable circumstances.

1996 年英译汉试题

The differences in relative growth of various areas of scientific research have several causes. (71) Some of these causes are completely reasonable results of social needs. Others are reasonable consequences of particular advances in science being to some extent self-accelerating. Some, however, are less reasonable processes of different growth in which preconceptions of the form scientific theory ought to take, by persons in authority, act to alter the growth pattern of different areas. This is a new problem probably not yet unavoidable; but it is a frightening trend. (72) This trend began during the Second World War, when several governments came to the conclusion that the specific demands that a government wants to make of its scientific establishment cannot generally be foreseen in detail. It can be predicted, however, that from time to time, questions will arise which will require specific scientific answers. It is therefore generally valuable to treat the scientific establishment as a resource or machine to be kept in functional order. (73) This seems mostly effectively done by supporting a certain amount of research not related to immediate goals but of possible consequence in the future.

This kind of support, like all government support, requires decisions about the appropriate recipients of funds. Decisions based on utility as opposed to lack of utility are straight forward. But a decision among projects none of which has immediate utility is more difficult. The goal of the supporting agencies is the praisable one of supporting "good" as opposed to "bad" science, but a valid determination is difficult to make . Generally, the idea of good science tends to become confused with the capacity of the field in question to generate an elegant theory. (74) However, the world is so made that elegant systems are in principle unable to deal with some of the world's more fascinating and delightful aspects. (75) New forms of thought as well as new subjects for thought must arise in the future as they have in the past, giving rise to new standards of elegance.

1997 年英译汉试题

Do animals have rights? This is how the question is usually put. It sounds like a useful, ground-clearing way to start. (71) Actually, it isn't, because it assumes that there is an agreed account of human rights, which is something the world does not have.

On one view of rights, to be sure, it necessarily follows that animals have none. (72) Some philosophers argue that rights exist only within a social contract, as part of an exchange of duties and entitlements. Therefore, animals cannot have rights. The idea of punishing a tiger that kills somebody is absurd, for exactly the same reason, so is the idea that tigers have rights. However, this is only one account, and by no means an uncontested one. It denies rights not only to animals but also to some people—for instance, to infants, the mentally incapable and future generations. In addition, it is unclear what force a contract can have for people who never consented to it: how do you reply to somebody who says "I don't like this contract?"

The point is this without agreement on the rights of people, arguing about the rights of animals is fruitless. (73) It leads the discussion to extremes at the outset: it invites you to think that animals should be treated either with the consideration humans extend to other humans, or with no consideration at all. This is a false choice. Better to start with another, more fundamental question: is the way we treat animals a moral issue at all?

Many deny it. (74) Arguing from the view that humans are different from animals in every relevant respect, extremists of this kind think that animals lie outside the area of moral choice. Any regard for the suffering of animals is seen as a mistake—a sentimental displacement of feeling that should properly be directed to other humans.

This view, which holds that torturing a monkey is morally equivalent to chopping wood, may seem bravely "logical. " In fact it is simply shallow: the ethical equivalent of learning to crawl—is to weigh others' interests against one' s own. This in turn requires sympathy and imagination: without which there is no capacity for moral thought. To see an animal in pain is enough, for most, to engage sympathy. (75) When that happens, it is not a mistake: it is mankind's instinct for moral reasoning in action, an instinct that should be encouraged rather than laughed at.

1998 年英译汉试题

They were by far, the largest and most distant objects that scientists had ever detected: a strip of enormous cosmic clouds some 15 billion light-years from earth.

(71) But even more important, it was the farthest that scientists had been able to look into the past, for what they were seeing were the patterns and structures that existed 15 billion years ago. That was just about the moment that the universe was born. What the researchers found was at once both amazing and expected: the US National Aeronautics and Space Administration's Cosmic Background Explorer satellite—Cobe—had discovered landmark evidence that the universe did in fact begin with the primeval explosion that has become known as the Big Bang(the theory that the universe originated in an explosion from a single mass of energy).

(72) The existence of the giant clouds was virtually required for the Big Bang, first put forward in the 1920s, to maintain its reign as the dominant explanation of the cosmos. According to the theory, the

universe burst into being as a submicroscopic, unimaginably dense knot of pure energy that flew outward in all directions, emitting radiation as it went, condensing into particles and then into atoms of gas. Over billions of years, the gas was compressed by gravity into galaxies, stars, plants and eventually, even humans.

Cobe is designed to see just the biggest structures, but astronomers would like to see much smaller hot spots as well, the seeds of local objects like clusters and superclusters of galaxies. They shouldn't have long to wait. (73)Astrophysicists working with ground-based detectors at the South Pole and balloon-borne instruments are closing in on such structures, and may report their findings soon.

(74)If the small hot spots look as expected, that will be a triumph for yet another scientific idea, a refinement of the Big Bang called the inflationary universe theory. Inflation says that very early on, the universe expanded in size by more than a trillion trillion trillion trillion fold in much less than a second, propelled by a sort of antigravity. (75)Odd though it sounds, cosmic inflation is a scientifically plausible consequence of some respected ideas in elementary-particle physics, and many astrophysicists have been convinced for the better part of a decade that it is true.

1999 年英译汉试题

(71)While there are almost as many definitions of history as there are historians, modern practice most closely conforms to one that sees history as the attempt to recreate and explain the significant events of the past. Caught in the web of its own time and place, each generation of historians determines anew what is significant for it in the past. In this search the evidence found is always incomplete and scattered; it is also frequently partial or partisan. The irony of the historian's craft is that its practitioners always know that their efforts are but contributions to an unending process.

(72)Interest in historical methods has arisen less through external challenge to the validity of history as an intellectual discipline and more from internal quarrels among historians themselves. While history once revered its affinity to literature and philosophy, the emerging social sciences seemed to afford greater opportunities for asking new questions and providing rewarding approaches to an understanding of the past. Social science methodologies had to be adapted to a discipline governed by the primacy of historical sources rather than the imperatives of the contemporary world.

(73)During this transfer, traditional historical methods were augmented by additional methodologies designed to interpret the new forms of evidence in the historical study.

Methodology is a term that remains inherently ambiguous in the historical profession.

(74)There is no agreement whether methodology refers to the concepts peculiar to historical work in general or to the research techniques appropriate to the various branches of historical inquiry. Historians, especially those so blinded by their research interests that they have been accused of "tunnel method," frequently fall victim to the "technicist fallacy." Also common in the natural sciences, the technicist fallacy mistakenly identifies the discipline as a whole with certain parts of its technical implementation.

(75)It applies equally to traditional historians who view history as only the external and internal criticism of sources. And to social science historians who equate their activity with specific techniques.

2000 年英译汉试题

Governments throughout the world act on the assumption that the welfare of their people depends largely on the economic strength and wealth of the community. (71)Under modern conditions, this requires varying measures of centralized control and hence the help of specialized scientists such as economists and operational research experts. (72)Furthermore, it is obvious that the strength of a country's economy is directly bound up with the efficiency of its agriculture and industry, and that this in turn rests upon the efforts of scientists and technologists of all kinds. It also means that governments are increasingly compelled to interfere in these sectors in order to step up production and ensure that it is utilized to the best advantage. For example, they may encourage research in various ways, including the setting up of their own research centers; they may alter the structure of education, or interfere in order to reduce the wastage of natural resources or tap resources hitherto unexploited; or they may co-operate directly in the growing number of international projects related to science, economics any industry. In any case, all such interventions are heavily dependent on scientific advice and also scientific and technological manpower of all kinds.

(73)Owing to the remarkable development in mass-communications, people everywhere are feeling new wants and are being exposed to new customs and ideas, while governments are often forced to introduce still further innovations for the reasons given above. At the same time, the normal rate of social change throughout the world is taking place at a vastly accelerated speed compared with the past. For example, (74)in the early in industrialized countries of Europe the process of industrialization—with all the far-reaching changes in social patterns that followed—was spread over nearly a century, whereas nowadays a developing nation may undergo the same process in a decade or so. All this has the effect of building up unusual pressures and tensions within the community and consequently presents serious problems for the governments concerned. (75)Additional social stresses may also occur because of the population explosion or problems arising from mass migration movements—themselves made relatively easy nowadays by modern means of transport. As a result of all these factors, governments are becoming increasingly dependent on biologists and social scientists for planning the appropriate programs and putting them into effect.

2001 年英译汉试题

In less than 30 years' time the Star Trek holodeck will be a reality. Direct links between the brain's nervous system and a computer will also create full sensory virtual environments, allowing virtual vacations like those in the film Total Recall.

(71)There will be television chat shows hosted by robots, and cars with pollution monitors that will disable them when they offend. (72)Children will play with dolls equipped with personality chips, computers with in-built personalities will be regarded as workmates rather than tools, relaxation will be in front of smell-television, and digital age will have arrived.

According to BT's futurologist, Ian Pearson, these are among the developments scheduled for the first few decades of the new millennium(a period of 1,000 years), when supercomputers will dramatically accelerate progress in all areas of life.

(73)Pearson has pieced together the work of hundreds of researchers around the world to produce a unique millennium technology calendar that gives the latest dates when we can expect hundreds or key breakthroughs and discoveries to take place. Some of the biggest developments will be in medicine, including an extended life expectancy and dozens of artificial organs coming into use between now and 2040.

Pearson also predicts a breakthrough in computer-human links. "By linking directly to our nervous system, computers could pick up what we feel and, hopefully, simulate feeling too so that we can start to develop full sensory environments, rather like the holidays in Total Recall or the Star Trek holodeck," he says. (74)But that, Pearson points out, is only the start of man-machine integration: "It will be the beginning of the long process of integration that will ultimately lead to a fully electronic human before the end of the next century."

Through his research, Pearson is able to put dates to most of the breakthroughs that can be predicted. However, there are still no forecasts for when faster-that-light travel will be available, or when human cloning will be perfected, or when time travel will be possible. But he does expect social problems as a result of technological advances. A boom in neighborhood surveillance cameras will, for example, cause problems in 2010, while the arrival of synthetic lifelike robots will mean people may not be able to distinguish between their human friends and the droids. (75) And home appliances will also become so smart that controlling and operating them will result in the breakout of a new psychological disorder—kitchen rage.

2002 年英译汉试题

Almost all our major problems involve human behavior, and they cannot be solved by physical and biological technology alone. What is needed is a technology of behavior, but we have been slow to develop the science from which such a technology might be drawn. (61) One difficulty is that almost all of what is called behavioral science continues to trace behavior to states of mind, feelings, traits of character, human nature, and so on. Physics and biology once followed similar practices and advanced only when they discarded them. (62) The behavioral sciences have been slow to change partly because the explanatory items often seem to be directly observed and partly because other kinds of explanations have been hard to find. The environment is obviously important, but its role has remained obscure. It does not push or pull, it selects, and this function is difficult to discover and analyze. (63) The role of natural selection in evolution was formulated only a little more than a hundred years ago, and the selective role of the environment in shaping and maintaining the behavior of the individual is only beginning to be recognized and studied. As the interaction between organism and environment has come to be understood, however, effects once assigned to states of mind, feelings, and traits are beginning to be traced to accessible conditions, and a technology of behavior may therefore become available. It will not solve our problems, however, until it replaces traditional pre-scientific views, and these are strongly entrenched. Freedom and dignity illustrate the difficulty. (64) They are the possessions of the autonomous (self-governing) man of traditional theory, and they are essential to practices in which a person is held responsible for his conduct and given credit for his achievements. A scientific analysis shifts both the responsibility and the achievement to the environment. It also raises questions concerning "values". Who will use a technology and to what ends? (65) Until these issues are resolved, a technology of behavior will continue to be rejected, and with it possibly the only way to solve our problems.

(2003 年~2005 年翻译题见第三部分第一章及第一部分)

答案及解析

1994 年英译汉真题详解

71. Science moves forward, they say, not so much through the insights of great men of genius as because of more ordinary things like improved techniques and tools.

结构分析:是一个简单句。主干是主谓结构 Science moves forward, they say 是插入语, not so much...as... 构成一个比较结构,修饰谓语动词 moves forward 作状语。

参考译文:科学向前发展,新学派科学家们说,与其说是因为天才伟人的真知灼见,不如说是因为更为普通的事物,比方说改进了的技术和工具。

72. "In short," a leader of the new school contends, "the scientific revolution, as we call it, was largely the improvement and invention and use of a series of instruments that expanded the reach of science in innumerable directions."

结构分析:这是一个复合句。主句是 a leader of the new school contends,这是一个主谓结构。主句之外是直接引语；in short 是介词短语作状语，修饰整个直接引语；the scientific revolution was the improvement and invention and use of a series of instruments 是直接引语中的主句，它是主系表结构；that expanded the reach of science 是修饰名词 improvement... 的定语从句，其结构为主谓宾；in...directions 是介词短语作状语，修饰动词 expanded。

参考译文："总之"一位新学派的领导说，"我们所谓的科学革命主要是一系列器具的改进、发明和使用，这一系列器具的改进、发明和使用使科学能够到达的范围朝着数不清的方向发展。"（或……使科学发展的范围无所不及。）

73. Over the years, tools and technology themselves as a source of fundamental innovation have largely been ignored by historians and philosophers of science.

结构分析：这是一个简单句。over the years 是介词短语作状语，修饰整个句子。主干是 tools and technology... have been ignored...，是使用了被动语态的主谓结构，其中 as a source of fundamental innovation 是介词短语修饰名词 tools and technology，by historians and philosophers of science 是介词短语作状语。

参考译文：多年来，工具和技术本身作为根本革新的源泉在很大程度上被历史学家和科学哲学家所忽略。

74. Galileo's greatest glory was that in 1609 he was the first person to turn the newly invented telescope on the heavens to prove that the planets revolve around the sun rather than around the Earth.

结构分析：这是一个多重复合句。主句是主系表结构 Galileo's greatest glory was that...，其中 that 引导表语从句。表语从句后面有两个不定式：一是 to turn...，它修饰前面的名词 person 所以是定语；二是 to prove，它修饰动词 turn，所以作状语。prove 后面的 that 从句显然是宾语从句。

参考译文：伽利略最伟大的成就是，1969年他第一个把新发明的望远镜对准太空，以证明行星围绕太阳转，而不是围绕地球转。

75. Whether the Government should increase the financing of pure science at the expense of technology or vice versa often depends on the issue of which is seen as the driving force.

结构分析：这也是一个多重复合句。whether...or... 是介词短语作状语，修饰主语从句的谓语动词 increase，depends on 是主句的谓语，宾语 issue 带 of 结构修饰语，which 则引导宾语从句作介词 of 的宾语。

参考译文：政府是应该以技术为代价增加对纯科学的投入，还是反之亦然，经常取决于哪一方被看作是驱动力的问题。

译文

新学派的科学家认为，技术是扩大科学知识的范围中被忽视的力量。(71)科学向前发展，新学派科学家们说，与其说是因为天才伟人的真知灼见，不如说是因为更为普通的事物，比方说改进了的技术和工具。(72)"总之"一位新学派的领导说，"我们所谓的科学革命主要是一系列器具的改进、发明和使用，这一系列器具的改进、发明和使用使科学能够到达的范围朝着数不清的方向发展。"（或……使科学发展的范围无所不及。）

(73)多年来，工具和技术本身作为根本革新的源泉在很大程度上被历史学家和科学哲学家所忽略。为技术而欢呼的现代学派争辩说，像伽利略、牛顿、麦克斯韦尔、爱因斯坦这样的科学大师和像爱迪生这样的发明家十分重视科学实验中能使用的各种不同的工艺信息和技术装置并从中受益匪浅。

鼓吹技术第一、天才第二的论据的核心是分析了科学革命初期伽利略的作用。那时的聪明才智取自第二世纪的天文学家托勒密；他精心创立的太空体系把地球置于所有天体运动的中心。(74)伽利略最伟大的成就是，1969年他第一个把新发明的望远镜对准太空，以证明行星围绕太阳转，而不是围绕地球转。但是，在新学派科学家看来，这件事中真正重要的因素是制造镜片的机械长期以来不断的改进和发展。

联邦政府的政策必然要卷入到技术与天才之争中去。(75)政府是应该以技术为代价增加对纯科学的投入，还是反之亦然，经常取决于哪一方被看作是驱动力的问题。

1995 年英译汉真题详解

71. The target is wrong, for in attacking the tests, critics divert attention from the fault that lies with ill-informed or incompetent users.

结构分析：这是一个复合句主句 The target is wrong 是主系表结构，for 不是介词而是连词，引导原因状语从句 critics divert attention from the fault，in attacking the tests 是修饰原因状语从句的状语（参见 1998 年第 71 题结构分析），that lies with... 则是修饰名词 fault 的定语从句。

参考译文：把标准化测试作为抨击的目标是错误的，因为在抨击这些测试的过程中，批评者们没有注意到一个错误，而这个错误是由消息不灵通或者能力不够的使用者造成的。

72. How well the predictions will be validated by later performance depends upon the amount, reliability, and appropriateness of the information used and on the skill and wisdom with which it is interpreted.

结构分析：这是一个复合句。How well 引导主语从句，depends upon... and on 并列构成主句的谓语，with which 引导定语从句修饰名词 the skill and wisdom。

参考译文：这些预测将在多大的程度上被后来的表现所证实取决于所使用的信息的数量、可靠性和适用性，同时还取决于解释这些信息的技巧和智慧。

73. Whether to use tests, other kinds of information, or both in a particular situation depends, therefore, upon the evidence from experience concerning comparative validity and upon such factors as cost and availability.

结构分析：这是一个简单句。其主要结构是主谓宾。whether... or... 引导不定式作主语，depends upon... and upon... 并列作谓语，concerning... 是介词短语作定语，修饰名词 experience。

参考译文：是使用测试，或是其他种类的信息，还是在特定情况下两者都使用因此就取决于关于相对效度的来自经验的证据，同时还取决于诸如成本和可获得性这样的因素。

74. In general, the tests work most effectively when the qualities to be measured can be most precisely defined and least effectively when what is to be measured or predicted cannot be well defined.

结构分析：这是一个复合句。In general 是介词短语作整个句子的状语，主句是 the tests work most effectively... and least effectively...，两个 when 引导的从句都是时间状语从句，第一个 when 从句中主语 qualities 带不定式作后置修饰语，第二个 when 从句中主语是由 what 引导的主语从句。

参考译文：一般来说，当所要测定的特征能够最为精确地定义时，测试效果最好；当所要测定或者预测的特征不能很好地定义时，测试效果最差。

75. For example, they do not compensate for gross social inequality, and thus do not tell how able an underprivileged youngster might have been had he grown up under more favorable circumstances.

结构分析：这是一个复合句。For example 是整个句子的状语，they do not compensate for... and thus do not tell... 是主句，how 引导的从句作动词 tell 的宾语，had he grown up... 是一个倒装的条件状语从句，修饰 how 引导的宾语从句。

参考译文：例如，测试并不能弥补明显的社会不公，因此就不能说明一个物质条件很差的年轻人，如果在更加有利的条件下长大，会有多么的能干。（或：例如，测试并不能弥补明显的社会不公，因此就不能说明，如果在更加有利的条件下长大，一个物质条件很差的年轻人会有多么能干。）

译文

标准化教育测试或心理测试广泛应用于协助选拔、委派或提拔学生、雇员和军事人员；这些测试一直是某些人近年来在书本、杂志、日报，甚至国会中进行抨击的目标。(71)把标准化测试作为抨击的目标是错误的，因为在抨击这些测试的过程中，批评者们没有注意到一个错误，而这个错误是由消息不灵通或者能力不够的使用者造成的。这些测试本身只是一种工具。它的各种特性可以在规定条件下用适当的精度来测定。测试的结果是有价值的、无意义的、还是误导的,部分取决于这种工具本身,但主要取决于测试使用者。

所有对未来表现的有见识的预测都是以在某种程度上了解有关过去的表现为基础的:学校学习成绩、研究效益、销售记录或任何符合需要的信息。(72)这些预测将在多大的程度上被后来的表现所证实取决于所使用的信息的数量、可靠性和适用性,同时还取决于解释这些信息的技巧和智慧。任何仔细记分的人都知道,所得到的信息总是不完全的,而且这些预测也总是会有错误的。

应该根据这种观点去考察标准化测试。标准化测试提供了快速、客观地得到某些信息的方法,这些信息是有关一个人所学到的知识、他所获得的技能,或者他是属于哪一类型的人。这样得到的信息,从性质上讲,与其它种类的信息一样具有优点或缺点。(73)是使用测试,或是其他种类的信息,还是在特定情况下两者都使用因此就取决于关于相对效度的来自经验的证据,同时还取决于诸如成本和可获得性这样的因素。

(74)一般来说,当所要测定的特征能够最为精确地定义时,测试效果最好;当所要测定或者预测的特征不能很好地定义时,测试效果最差。这些测试如能恰当使用,就能提供一种快速的方法来获得有关许多人的可比性信息。有时这些测试能鉴别出一些学生,他们很高的潜在能力过去一直没有被承认。但是也有许多事情这些测试是不能胜任的。(75)例如,测试并不能弥补明显的社会不公,因此就不能说明一个物质条件很差的年轻人,如果在更加有利的条件下长大,会有多么的能干。(或:例如,测试并不能弥补明显的社会不公,因此就不能说明,如果在更加有利的条件下长大,一个物质条件很差的年轻人会有多么能干。)

1996 年英译汉真题详解

71. Some of these causes are completely reasonable results of social needs. Others are reasonable consequences of particular advances in science being to some extent self-accelerating.

结构分析:这是两个简单句。在所有英译汉真题中,划线部分都是一个句子,要么是一个简单句,要么是一个复合句,由两个简单句构成一个考题这是惟一的一次。这两个简单句都是主系表结构。

参考译文:其中一些原因完全是社会需求的必然结果,其他原因则是由于科学在一定程度上自我加速而取得特定发展的必然结果(第二句也可以拆译成:其他原因则是科学领域当中一些特定发展的必然结果,科学在一定程度上是自我加速的)。

72. This trend began during the Second World War, when several governments came to the conclusion that the specific demands that a government wants to make of its scientific establishment cannot generally be foreseen in detail.

结构分析:这是一个多重复句。This trend began 是主谓结构的主句,during the Second World War 是介词短语作状语修饰主句,when several governments came to the conclusion 是定语从句修饰 the Second World War,that the specific demands cannot be foreseen 是名词 conclusion 的同位语从句,而 that a government wants to make 是修饰 the specific demands 的定语从句,of its scientific establishment 是修饰 make 的状语,in detail 是修饰 foreseen 的状语。

参考译文:这种趋势始于二次世界大战期间,当时一些政府得出了这样的结论:一个政府想要对其科研机构提出的具体要求通常是无法详细预见的。

73. This seems mostly effectively done by supporting a certain amount of research not related to immediate goals but of possible consequence in the future.

结构分析:这是一个简单句。This seems...done 是句子的主干,by supporting... 是介词短语作方式状语,not...but... 结构作后置定语修饰名词 research。

答案译文:通过给一定数量的研究以支持,这些研究与直接目标没有关系,但是在未来却有可能产生结果,似乎基本上能有效地解决这个问题。

74. However, the world is so made that elegant systems are in principle unable to deal with some of the

world's more fascinating and delightful aspects.

结构分析:这是一个复合句。The world is so made 是主句,that 引导的是结果状语从句。其中 elegant systems are...unable to deal with...aspects 是从句的主干,in principle 是介词短语作状语,some of the world's more fascinating and delightful 都是定语,修饰名词 aspects。

参考译文:然而,世界就是如此,完美的体系一般而言无法解决世界上一些更加引人入胜和令人高兴的问题。

75. News forms of thought as well as new subjects for thought must arise in the future as they have in the past, giving rise to new standards of elegance.

结构分析:这是一个复合句。New forms of thought as well as new subjects for thought must arise in the future 是主句,as they have in the past 是方式状语从句,giving rise to new standards of elegance 是现在分词短语作状语表伴随动作。

参考译文:新的思维方式和新的思维内容将来一定会出现,正如它们过去已经出现过一样,从而给完美以新的标准。

译文

科学研究的各种领域的相关发展,存在若干原因。(71)其中一些原因完全是社会需求的必然结果,其他原因则是由于科学在一定程度上自我加速而取得特定发展的必然结果。(第二句也可以拆译成:其他原因则是科学领域当中一些特定发展的必然结果,科学在一定程度上是自我加速的。)然而,有些发展速度的差异其原因就不尽合理,这是因为某些权威人士对科学理论研究应采取何种形式有先入为主的想法,这些想法起了改变不同科学领域的发展模式的作用。这是一个新问题,也许并非是不可避免的问题,但其趋势却令人担忧。(72)这种趋势始于二次世界大战期间,当时一些政府得出了这样的结论:一个政府想要对其科研机构提出的具体要求通常是无法详细预见的。然而,人们可以预见,往往会出现一些问题要求科学做出具体的回答。因此,将科研机构视为一种资源或一台机器,应维持其良好的运行状态。这样做通常是很有价值的。(73)通过给一定数量的研究以支持,这些研究与直接目标没有关系,但是在未来却有可能产生结果,似乎基本上能有效地解决这个问题。

此种资助也与所有政府资助一样,需要决定合适的投资对象。根据某一项目是否有效来做出决策是明确无误的。但是在几个都没有直接效用的项目中,要做出抉择就特别困难。资助机构的目标是支持"好"的科学,而不资助"坏"的科学,那是值得赞扬的。然而要做出正确的抉择却是困难的。人们往往将好科学与该科学是否有能力提出一套完美的理论混淆起来。(74)然而,世界就是如此,完美的体系一般而言无法解决世界上一些更加引人入胜和令人高兴的问题。(75)新的思维方式和新的思维内容将来一定会出现,正如它们过去已经出现过一样,从而给完美以新的标准。

1997 年英译汉真题详解

71. Actually, it isn't, because it assumes that there is an agreed account of human rights, which is something the world does not have.

结构分析:这是一个多重复合句。Actually 是副词作状语,修饰整个句子,it isn't 是主句,在 because 引导的原因状语从句中,that 引导宾语从句,which 引导非限定性定语从句修饰名词 agreed account, 而 the world does not have 是省略了从句引导词 that 的定语从句,修饰名词 something。

参考译文:事实上,这种提问并不能把问题讲清楚,因为它假设关于人权有一个共识,而这个共识是世界上所没有的。

72. Some philosophers argue that rights exist only within a social contract, as part of an exchange of duties and entitlements.

结构分析:这是一个复合句。Some philosophers argue 是主句,that rights exist only within a social contract 是宾语从句, as part of an exchange of duties and entitlements 是介词短语作非限定性定语,修饰名词 rights。

参考译文: 一些哲学家认为,权利作为责任与权益相交换的一部分只存在于社会契约当中。

73. It leads the discussion to extremes at the outset: it invites you to think that animals should be treated either with the consideration humans extend to other humans, or with no consideration at all.

结构分析: 这是一个复合句。句中用冒号把整个句子分成了两部分:前面部分是个简单句,后面部分是个复合句,后面部分是对前面部分的说明。冒号后的主句是 it invites you to think,that 引导的是宾语从句,either...or... 引导两个介词短语作状语修饰动词 treat,在 either 引导的介词短语中,humans extend to other humans 是省略了从句引导词 that 的定语从句,修饰名词 consideration。

参考译文: 这种观点从一开始就把讨论引向极端,它使你认为动物应该被这样对待:要么带着人给予其他人的关怀体谅,要么完全不带关怀体谅。

74. Arguing from the view that humans are different from animals in every relevant respect, extremists of this kind think that animals lie outside the area of moral choice.

结构分析: 这是一个复合句。Arguing from the view 是现在分词短语作状语,that humans are... 是名词 view 的同位语从句,extremists of this kind think 是主句,that animals lie outside... 是 think 的宾语从句。

参考译文: 这类持极端看法的人认为,人跟动物在每一个相关的方面都不相同,因此他们认为对待动物无须考虑道德问题。

75. When that happens, it is not a mistake: it is mankind's instinct for moral reasoning in action, an instinct that should be encouraged rather than laughed at.

结构分析: 这是一个复合句。像73题一样,冒号将句子分成两个部分:前面部分是复合句,When that happens 是表时间的状语从句,it is not a mistake 是主句;后面部分也是复合句,it is mankind's instinct for moral reasoning in action 是主句,an instinct 是前面 instinct 的补充说明,后面的 that 从句是修饰它的定语从句。

参考译文: 当人们产生同情心的时候,这并不是一个错误,这是人类用道德观念进行推理的本能在起作用,这种本能应该受到鼓励,而不应该受到嘲笑。

译文

动物有权力吗?问题通常就是这样提出的。这种提法听起来似乎有助于把问题讲清楚。(71)事实上,这种提问并不能把问题讲清楚,因为它假设关于人权有一个共识,而这个共识是世界上所没有的。

然而一种权利观点认为,动物是没有权利的。(72)有些科学家论证说,权利只存在于社会契约中,是责任和权利相交换的一部分。因此动物不能有权利。因老虎吃了人而惩罚老虎是荒谬的。正因为同样的原因,认为老虎有权利也是荒谬的。然而,这只是一种观点,而且这种观点并不是无懈可击的。这种观点不仅否定了动物的权利,而且也否定了某些人的权利,如幼儿,他们是不会用脑力来思考问题的未来一代人。此外,如果有人从来就不同意某种契约,那么这一契约还能有多大的效力?如果有人说:"我不喜欢这个契约"。那你又作何回答呢?这些问题尚不清楚。

问题的症结是,如果人们对人的权利没有一致的看法,那么争论动物的权利是徒劳无益的。(73)这种观点从一开始就把讨论引向极端,它使你认为动物应该被这样对待:要么带着人给予其他人的关怀体谅,要么完全不带关怀体谅。这是一处错误的选择。最好换一种更为根本性的提法:我们对待动物的方式是道德问题吗?

许多人否认这种提法。(74)这类持极端看法的人认为,人跟动物在每一个相关的方面都不相同,因此他们认为对待动物无须考虑道德问题。任何关心动物疾苦的想法都是错误的,因为它把应该用来关心其他人的同情感用到关心动物的身上。

这种观点认为,折磨猴子从道义上讲无异于劈柴。这种看法似乎是大胆的"逻辑推理"。实际上,这种看法是非常肤浅的,道德推理的最初级形式,和学习爬行的论理一样,是针对自身利益去权衡他人利益。这就需要同情心和将心比心的想象力,没有这两点就无法用道德观念来进行思考。看到动物受苦足以使大多数人产生同情感。(75)当人们产生同情心的时候,这并不是一个错误,这是人类用道德观念进行推理的本能在起作用,这种本能应该受到鼓励,而不应该受到嘲笑。

1998 年英译汉真题详解

71. But even more important, it was the farthest that scientists had been able to look into the past, for what they were seeing were the patterns and structures that existed 15 billion years ago.

结构分析:这是一个复合句。But even more important 是整个句子的状语,it was the farthest 是主句,that scientists had been able to look into the past 是修饰 the farthest 的定语从句,for 引导表原因的状语从句(参见 1995 年第 71 题结构分析),在这个状语从句中,what they were seeing 是主语从句,were the patterns and structures 为状语从句的系表结构,that existed... 是修饰名词 patterns and structures 的定语从句。

参考译文:但是更为重要的是,这是科学家所能观测到的最遥远的过去宇宙云(或景象),因为他们看到的是存在于 150 亿年前的宇宙云的形状和结构。

72. The existence of the giant clouds was virtually required for the Big Bang, first put forward in the 1920s, to maintain its reign as the dominant explanation of the cosmos.

结构分析:这是一个简单句。The existence of the giant clouds 是主语,was... required 是谓语,for the Big Bang to maintain its reign 是带逻辑主语的不定式作状语,as the dominant explanation of the cosmos 是介词短语作名词 reign 的后置修饰语,first put forward in the 1920s 是过去分词短语作插入语或非限定性定语,说明或修饰前面的名词 the Big Bang。

参考译文:巨大的宇宙云的存在实际上是 20 世纪 20 年代首次提出的大爆炸论保持其在解释宇宙方面的主导地位所要求的。

73. Astrophysicists working with ground-based detectors at the South Pole and balloon-borne instruments are closing in on such structures, and may report their findings soon.

结构分析:这是一个简单句。Astrophysicists 是句子的主语,working with ground-based detectors at the South Pole and balloon-borne instruments 是现在分词短语作 astrophysicists 的后置定语,are closing in on..., and may report... 并列作谓语,structures 和 findings 并列作宾语。

参考译文:使用南极陆基探测器和球载仪器的天体物理学家正越来越靠近地观察这些云系,不久就有可能报告他们的观测结果。

74. If the small hot spots look as expected, that will be a triumph for yet another scientific idea, a refinement of the Big Bang called the inflationary universe theory.

结构分析:这是一个复合句。If the small hot spots look as expected 是条件状语从句,that will be a triumph 是主系表结构的主句,for yet another scientific ideas 是介词短语作状语,a refinement of the Big Bang 是 another scientific idea 的同位语,called the inflationary universe theory 是过去分词短语做 a refinement of the Big Bang 的后置定语。

参考译文:如果那些小热点看上去与预计的一致,那将是又一科学思想的胜利,这个科学思想是一种更加完美的大爆炸论,人们称之为(或即所谓的)宇宙膨胀说。

75. Odd thought it sounds, cosmic inflation is a scientifically plausible consequence of some respected ideas in elementary-particle physics, and many astrophysicists have been convinced for the better part of a decade that it is true.

结构分析:这是一个复合句。Odd thought it sounds 是个倒装的让步状语从句,cosmic inflation is a... consequence..., and many astrophysicists have been convinced... 是两个并列句构成的主句,其中 scientifically plausible 和 of some respected ideas 是 consequence 的定语,in elementary-particle physics 是 ideas 的定语,for the better part of a decade 是修饰 have been convinced 的时间状语,that it is true 则是 have been convinced 的宾语从句。

参考译文:尽管听起来很奇特,宇宙膨胀说是基本粒子物理学当中一些公认的理论在科学上看似可信的推论,许多天体物理学家七八年来一直相信宇宙膨胀说(或这一理论)是正确的。

译文

　　离地球大约150亿光年的一块狭长的巨大宇宙云系是科学家在目前所发现的最大、最遥远的物体。(71)但是更为重要的是,这是科学家所能观测到的最遥远的过去宇宙云(或景象),因为他们看到的是存在于150亿年前的宇宙云的形状和结构。那大约就是宇宙形成的时候。研究人员发现的宇宙云既令人惊讶,又是人们所期待的,因为美国国家航空航天局的宇宙背景探测者Cobe号卫星已经发现了划时代的证据,证明宇宙确实起源于最早的一次爆炸,即人们一直所称的“大爆炸”(此理论认为宇宙起源于一大块能量)。

　　(72)巨大的宇宙云的存在实际上是20世纪20年代首次提出的大爆炸论保持其在解释宇宙方面的主导地位所要求的。根据这一理论,宇宙的形成是由一团亚微观的、极其稠密的纯能量团朝四面八方向外发散,随着放出辐射线,浓缩成粒子,然后形成气体原子。数十亿年来,这种气体受引力的压缩形成星系、恒星、行星,并最终甚至产生人类。

　　Cobe卫星设计的目的就是观察这些最大的物体结构,但宇航员还想看到更为微小的热点,即像星纱中的星团和超星团这样一些局部物体的粒子。看来他们不必长期等待。(73)使用南极陆基探测器和球载仪器的天体物理学家正越来越靠近地观察这些云系,不久就有可能报告他们的观测结果。

　　(74)如果那些小热点看上去与预计的一致,那将是又一科学思想的胜利,这个科学思想是一种更加完美的大爆炸论,人们称之为(或即所谓的)宇宙膨胀说。膨胀说告诉我们,早在很久以前,宇宙的体积在不到一秒钟内被一种反引力驱动而发生了无数倍的膨胀。(75)尽管听起来很奇特,宇宙膨胀说是基本粒子物理学当中一些公认的理论在科学上看似可信的推论,许多天体物理学家七八年来一直相信宇宙膨胀说(或这一理论)是正确的。

　　注:1. 第4句中的 at once 意为“既,又”,如:The story is at once amusing and instructive.(这个故事既有趣又有教育意义。)

　　2. 第1段最后一句中的 a mass of 意为“一大块(团,堆)”。

　　3. 第3段最后一句中的 close in on 原意为“从四面八方紧压过来”。例如:She had a queer feeling that the room was closing in on her.(她有一种奇特的感觉,仿佛那房间从四面八方把她紧紧围住了。)

　　4. 第3段第2句中的 should 表示“推测”的意思。

　　5. (71)题中的 look(=see)意为:看见,作及物动词用,其宾语是关系代词 that。into the past 意为“对过去”。可见...it was the farthest that scientists had been able to look into the past...直译为:……它是科学家对过去所能看到的最遥远的东西……。

1999 年英译汉真题详解

71. While there are as many definitions of history as there are historians, modern practice most closely conforms to one that sees history as the attempt to recreate and explain the significant events of the past.

　　结构分析:这是一个复合句。While there are as many definitions of history as there are historians 整个这部分是让步状语从句,其中第一个 as 是程度副词,第二个 as 是连词,引导比较状语从句 there are historians; modern practice most closely conforms to one 是主谓宾结构的主句;that sees history as the attempt 是修饰代词 one 的定语从句,to recreate and explain the significant events of the past 是不定式短语作名词 attempt 的后置定语。

　　参考译文:虽然关于历史的定义和历史学家一样多,现代实践最符合这样一个定义:把历史看做是(尝试着)重现和解释过去的重要事件。

72. Interest in historical methods has arisen less through external challenge to the validity of history as an intellectual discipline and more from internal quarrels among historians themselves.

　　结构分析:这是一个简单句。Interest 是主语,in historical methods 是修饰 interest 的后置定语,

has arisen 是谓语，less through... and more from... 是两个并列的介词短语作状语，修饰谓语动词 arisen。

参考译文：人们对历史研究方法产生了兴趣，这与其说是因为外部对历史作为一门知识学科的有效性提出了挑战，不如说是因为历史学家内部发生了争吵。

73. During this transfer, traditional historical methods were augmented by additional methodologies designed to interpret the new forms of evidence in the historical study.

结构分析：这也是一个简单句。During this transfer 是介词短语放在句首作整个句子的状语，traditional historical methods were augmented by additional methodologies 是句子的主干，designed to interpreted the new forms of evidence 是 additional methodologies 的后置定语，in the historical study 是 new forms of evidence 的后置定语。

参考译文：在这个转变过程中，传统的历史研究方法中增加了新的（研究）方法，这些新方法是用来解释历史研究中一些新的证据的。

74. There is no agreement whether methodology refers to the concepts peculiar to historical work in general or to the research techniques appropriate to the various branches of historical inquiry.

结构分析：这是一个复合句。There is no agreement 是主句，whether... or... 引导状语从句，其中 refers to.... or (refers) to... 并列作 methodology 的谓语，peculiar to historical work 和 appropriate to the various branches 都是形容词短语，分别修饰名词 concepts 和 research techniques，in general 和 of historical inquiry 则分别是 historical work 和 the various branches 的后置定语。

参考译文：方法论究竟是指一般历史研究中独有的概念，还是指历史研究中适合各个分支的研究方法，人们对此还没有一致意见。

75. It applies equally to traditional historians who view history as only the external and internal criticism of sources and to social science historians who equate their activity with specific techniques.

结构分析：这是一个复合句。It applies equally to traditional historians and to social science historians 是主句，两个 who 引导的定语从句分别修饰 traditional historians 和 social science historians。

参考译文：这个错误同样存在于传统历史学家和社会科学历史学家，传统历史学者（或前者）把历史仅仅看做是外部和内部对历史资料的批评，社会科学历史学家（或后者）则把他们的研究活动看做是具体的方法的研究。

译文

（71）虽然关于历史的定义和历史学家一样多，现代实践最符合这样一个定义：把历史看做是（尝试着）重现和解释过去的重要事件。由于受时间和地点的限制，每一代史学家都要重新判断过去哪些史料对其有重要价值。在这种探索中所发现的证据总是不完整的、零碎的，而且常常是有偏见的或带有派别意识的。实际从事历史研究的人总是知道，他们的努力只不过是为永无止境的探索过程添砖加瓦，这就使其工作颇具讽刺意味。

（72）人们对历史研究方法产生了兴趣，这与其说是因为外部对历史作为一门知识学科的有效性提出了挑战，不如说是因为历史学家内部发生了争吵。尽管历史学曾经崇尚它与文学和哲学的相似性，但新兴的社会科学似乎为人们提出新问题和提供了解过去的有效途径开辟了更为广阔的天地。社会科学研究的方法必须改变以适应这样一条指导，即以史料为基础，而不是为当代社会之需。（73）在这个转变过程中，传统的历史研究方法中增加了新的（研究）方法，这些新方法是用来解释历史研究中一些新的证据的。

在历史学界，方法论这个词从来都是模棱两可的。（74）方法论究竟是指一般历史研究中独有的概念，还是指历史研究中适合各个分支的研究方法，人们对此还没有一致意见。史学家，尤其是那些局限于他们的研究兴趣，以致被指责为"单方面研究法"的史学家，常常成了"单纯技术方法论"的牺牲品。这种谬论在自然科学领域里也是屡见不鲜的，它错误地把整个学科与学科研究的某些操作方法等同起来。（75）这个错误同样存在于传统历史学家和社会科学历史学家，传统历史学者（或前者）把历史仅仅看做是外部和内部对历史资料的批评，社会科学历史学家（或后者）则把他们的研究活动看做是具体的方法的研究。

2000 年英译汉真题详解

71. Under modern conditions, this requires varying measures of centralized control and hence the help of specialized scientists such as economists and operational research experts.

结构分析：这是一个简单句。Under modern conditions 是介词短语作整个句子的状语，this requires 是主语和谓语，measures 和 help 并列作 requires 的宾语，两个 of 结构分别作两个宾语的后置定语，such as... 则是名词 scientists 的后置定语。

参考译文：在现代条件下，这就要求有不同的中央控制，因此就要求有专业科学家的帮助，比方说经济学家和操作研究专家。

72. Furthermore, it is obvious that the strength of a country's economy is directly bound up with the efficiency of its agriculture and industry, and that this in turn rests upon the efforts of scientists and technologists of all kinds.

结构分析：这是一个复合句。Furthermore 是副词放在句首作整个句子的状语，it is obvious 是主句，其中 it 是形式主语，两个 that 引导的从句并列作真正的主语。

参考译文：此外，显而易见的是，一个国家的经济实力直接与其工农业生产的效率密切相关，而工农业生产的效率又依赖（或取决）于各类科学家和技术人员的努力。

73. Owing to the remarkable development in mass-communication, people everywhere are feeling new wants and are being exposed to new customs and ideas, while governments are often forced to introduce still further innovations for the reasons given above.

结构分析：这是一个复合句。Owing to the remarkable development in mass-communication 是介词短语作状语修饰整个句子，people everywhere are feeling new wants and are being exposed to new customs and ideas 是主句，while 则引导状语从句。

参考译文：由于大众传播的显著发展，各地的人们正感觉到有新的需求，并且他们正不断接触到新的习俗和思想，而政府由于上述原因经常不得不推出更进一步的革新。

74. in the early industrialized countries of Europe the process of industrialization—with all the far-reaching changes in social patterns that followed—was spread over nearly a century, whereas nowadays a developing nation may undergo the same process in a decade or so.

结构分析：这是一个复合句。介词短语 in the early industrialized countries of Europe 是整个句子的状语，the process of industrialization was spread over nearly a century 是主句，其中 with all the far-reaching changes in social patterns that followed 是插入语，whereas 则引导一个对比状语从句。

参考译文：在早期实现工业化的欧洲国家，工业化进程——以及所有随后发生的社会结构当中的意义深远的变化——持续了将近一个世纪，而如今一个发展中国家有可能在十年左右的时间里经历同样的过程。

75. Additional social stresses may also occur because of the population explosion or problems arising from mass migration movements—themselves made relatively easy nowadays by modern means of transport.

结构分析：这是一个简单句。Additional social stresses may also occur 是主谓结构的主干，because of the population explosion or problems 是介词短语作状语，arising from mass migration movements 是现在分词短语作名词 problems 的后置定语，themselves made relatively easy nowadays by modern means of transport 是独立主格结构，补充说明 migration movements。

参考译文：由于人口爆炸或者由于大量的人口流动带来的种种问题——人口流动本身由于现代交通工具如今已经变得相对容易——新的社会压力有可能产生（或有可能产生新的社会压力）。

译文

世界各国政府都认为，人民的幸福主要依赖于社会的经济实力和财富。(71)在现代条件下，这就要求有不同的中央控制,因此就要求有专业科学家的帮助,比方说经济学家和操作研究专家。(72)此外,显而易见的是,一个国家的经济实力直接与其工农业生产的效率密切相关,而工农业生产的效率又依赖(或取决)于各类科学家和技术人员的努力。这就意味着,各国政府得越来越多地干预这些部门以便提高产量并确保产品会得到最好的利用。例如,政府可以用各种方法来鼓励研究,其中包括建立自己的研究中心;政府可以改革教育结构,或以政府干预来减少自然资源的消费量、开发迄今未被利用的资源;或者政府可以在日益增加的与科学、经济学和工业有关的项目中直接进行协作。无论如何,所有这些政府干预主要有赖于科学方面的咨询和各种类型的科技人才。

(73)由于大众传播的显著发展,各地的人们正感觉到有新的需求,并且他们正不断接触到新的习俗和思想,而政府由于上述原因经常不得不推出更进一步的革新。而同时,全世界的正常的社会变革速度与过去相比大大加快了。例如,(74)在早期实现工业化的欧洲国家,工业化进程——以及所有随后发生的社会结构当中的意义深远的变化——持续了将近一个世纪,而如今一个发展中国家有可能在十年左右的时间里经历同样的过程。这一切所带来的后果是增加了社会内部异乎寻常的压力和紧张气氛,从而给有关政府提出了若干严重问题。(75)由于人口爆炸或者由于大量的人口流动带来的种种问题——人口流动本身由于现代交通工具如今已经变得相对容易——新的社会压力有可能产生(或有可能产生新的社会压力)。由于这些因素的结果,政府正越来越多地依靠生物学家和社会科学家来安排适当的规划,并付诸实施。

2001 年英译汉真题详解

71. There will be television chat shows hosted by robots, and cars with pollution monitors that will disable them when they offend.

　　结构分析:这是一个复合句。There will be television chat shows hosted by robots and cars with pollution monitors 是主句,其中 hosted by robots 是过去分词短语作 television chat shows 的后置定语,with pollution monitors 是介词短语修饰名词 cars;that will disable them 是定语从句,修饰 pollution monitors;when they offend 是时间(或条件)状语从句,修饰动词 disable。

　　参考译文:将来会有由机器人主持的电视访谈节目,还会有带污染监控器的汽车,当汽车违规(或污染超标)时,污染监控器将使汽车停驶。

72. Children will play with dolls equipped wit personality chips, computers with in-built personalities will be regarded as workmates rather than tools, relaxation will be in front of smell-television, and digital age will have arrived.

　　结构分析:这是一个简单句。句中三个逗号和一个 and 连接四个并列的分句,其中 equipped with personality chips 是过去分词短语修饰名词 dolls,with in-built personalities 是介词短语修饰名词 computers。

　　参考译文:孩子们将会和装有个性芯片的娃娃玩耍,带有内置个性(芯片)的计算机将被看作是工作伙伴而不是工具,人们将在气味电视面前休闲,到这时数字(化)时代就已经到来。

73. Pearson has pieced together the work of hundreds of researchers around the world to produce a unique millennium technology calendar that gives the latest dates when we can expect hundreds of breakthroughs and discoveries to take place.

　　结构分析:这是一个复合句。Pearson has pieced together the work 是主谓宾结构的主句,of hundreds of researchers 是介词短语作定语修饰名词 work,around the world 则是介词短语修饰名词 researchers,to produce a unique millennium technology calendar 是不定式短语作结果状语,that 引导定语从句修饰名词 calendar,when 引导定语从句修饰 dates 。

　　参考译文:(未来学家)皮尔森汇集了世界上数百个研究者的工作成果,(结果)制作出了一个独一无二的千年技术日历,这个日历提供最迟的日期,通过这些日期我们就能预测数百个重大突破和发现的发生时间。

74. But that, Pearson points out, is only the start of man-machine integration:"It will be the beginning

of the long process of integration that will ultimately lead to a fully electronic human before the end of the next century.”

结构分析：这是一个复合句。But that is only the start of man-machine integration 是主句,其中有一个插入语 Pearson points out. It will be the beginning of the long process of integration 是直接引语中的主句,that 引导定语从句修饰名词 integration，before the end of the next century 是介词短语作状语。

参考译文：但是这个突破,皮尔森指出,仅仅是人机一体化的开始:“它将是人机一体化漫长过程的一个开端,人机一体化将在下个世纪末之前导致完完全全的电子人的出现。”

75. And home appliances will also become so smart that controlling and operating them will result in the breakout of a new psychological disorder—kitchen rage.

结构分析：这是一个复合句。And home appliances will also become so smart 是主句,that 引导表示程度的状语从句,kitchen rage 是 a new psychological disorder 的补充说明。

参考译文：家用电器也变得如此智能化,以至于控制和操作它们将导致一种新的精神混乱的爆发,那就是厨房愤怒。

译文

再过不到 30 年“星球旅行”太空平台将成为现实。大脑神经系统与计算机的直接连接也将创造出完全传感的实际环境,使得实际的度假和电影“全面回顾”中的度假一模一样。

(71)将来会有由机器人主持的电视访谈节目,还会有带污染监控器的汽车,当汽车违规(或污染超标)时,污染监控器将使汽车停驶。(72)孩子们将会和装有个性芯片的娃娃玩耍,带有内置个性(芯片)的计算机将被看作是工作伙伴而不是工具,人们将在气味电视面前休闲,到这时数字(化)时代就已经到来。

根据英国电讯公司的未来学家伊恩·皮尔逊的看法,上述种种科研成就均属新千年的最初几十年内的开发项目之列,届时超级计算机将大大加快人类生活各个领域里的进步。

(73)(未来学家)皮尔逊汇集了世界上数百个研究者的工作成果,(结果)制作出了一个独一无二的千年技术日历,这个日历提供最迟的日期,通过这些日期我们就能预测数百个重大突破和发现的发生时间。一些最重大的开发将会发生在医学中,其中包括延长人的估计寿命和从现在到 2040 年间将投入使用的几十种人造器官。

皮尔逊预言了电脑与人各种连接的突破。通过直接与我们的神经系统相连接,电脑能够了解到我们的感情并且有望激发我们的情感,这样我们就能着手开发完全传感的环境,更类似于电影“全面回顾”或“星球旅行”太空平台中的度假。(74)但是这个突破,皮尔森指出,仅仅是人机一体化的开始:“它将是人机一体化漫长过程的一个开端,人机一体化将在下个世纪末之前导致完完全全的电子人的出现。”

经过研究,皮尔逊确定可以预测到的大多数突破的日期。然而,仍然不能预报快于光速的旅行何时到来,或何时将完成克隆人,或何时可以实现邀游过去或将来的时间旅行。但皮尔逊确实预料到技术进步所引起的社会问题。例如,邻里电子监控摄像机的飞速推广将在 2010 年引起许多社会问题,而栩栩如生的人造机器人的问世将意味着人们可能无法把他们的真人朋友和这类机器人区别开来。

(75)家用电器也变得如此智能化,以至于控制和操作它们将导致一种新的精神混乱的爆发,那就是厨房愤怒。

2002 年英译汉真题详解

61. One difficulty is that almost all of what is called behavioral science continues to trace behavior to states of mind, feelings, traits of character, human nature, and so on.

结构分析：这是一个复合句。One difficulty is 是主句的主语和谓语,that 引导表语从句,其中 all 作主语,what is called behavioral science 是介词 of 的宾语从句,of what... 共同修饰主语 all, continues to trace behavior to... 是表主语从句的谓语部分。

参考译文:一个问题是,几乎所有所谓的行为科学都继续从心态、感情、性格特征、人的本性等方面研究行为。

62. The behavioral sciences have been slow to change partly because the explanatory items often seem to be directly observed and partly because other kinds of explanations have been hard to find.

结构分析:这是一个复合句。The behavioral sciences have been slow to change 是主句,两个 because 引导的从句并列作原因状语。

参考译文:行为科学一直发展很缓慢,部分原因是对行为的解释似乎经常是直接观察到的,部分原因是其他种类的(对行为的)解释一直很难找到。

63. The role of natural selection in evolution was formulated only a little more than a hundred years ago, and the selective role of the environment in shaping and maintaining the behavior of the individual is only beginning to be recognized and studied.

结构分析:这是一个简单句。这个简单句中包含两个并列句,这两个并列句都以 the role 作主语,并且两个句子中都使用了了被动语态。

参考译文:自然选择在进化中(所起到)的作用只是在一百多年前才得到阐明(或解释),而环境在形成和保持个人行为的过程中(所起到)的选择作用则刚刚才开始得到承认和研究。

64. They are the possessions of the autonomous (self-governing) man of traditional theory, and they are essential to practices in which a person is held responsible for his conduct and given credit for his achievements.

结构分析:这是一个复合句。主句是由两个并列的分句构成:They are..., and they are...; in which 引导定语从句,修饰名词 practices,其中 is held responsible for... and given... 并列作定语从句的谓语,given 前面省略了助动词 is。

参考译文:自由和尊严是传统理论中自治者(自我管理者)拥有的财富,它们(或自由与尊严)是实践活动中必不可少的,在这些实践活动中,一个人必须对他的行为负责,取得成绩他也必须受到表扬。

65. Until these issues are resolved, a technology of behavior will continue to be rejected, and with it possibly the only way to solve our problems.

结构分析:这是一个复合句。Until these issues are resolved 是条件状语从句,a technology of behavior will continue to be rejected 是主谓结构的主句,并列连词 and 后面首先是个介词短语 with it,接着是名词短语 possibly the only way 及它的修饰语 to solve our problems。从结构上看,and 后面主要是状语加名词短语,它与前面的主谓结构表面上是无法并列的,而英译汉句子又不存在语法问题,惟一的解释是这是一个省略句。省略句一般省略相同的部分,前面的句子有名词短语作主语,and 后面的名词短语应该也是作主语,前面的句子有谓语,and 后面却没有谓语,因此省略部分肯定是谓语,经过补充,and 后面的句子应该是:possibly the only way to solve our problems will continue to be rejected with it。

参考译文:除非这些问题得到解决,(不然)行为科学将继续遭到拒绝,随着行为科学的被拒绝(或随之)解决问题的惟一方法也可能会继续遭到拒绝。

译文

我们遇到的几乎所有重要问题都涉及人的行为,而且仅靠物理技术和生物技术是无法解决这些问题的。我们所需要的是一种行为技术,但是可能产生这种技术的科学一直发展缓慢。(61)一个问题是,几乎所有所谓的行为科学都继续从心态、感情、性格特征、人的本性等方面研究行为。物理学和生物学一度模仿类似的做法并且只有当它们抛弃这些做法后才得到发展。(62)行为科学一直发展很缓慢,部分原因是对行为的解释似乎经常是直接观察到的,部分原因是其他种类的(对行为的)解释一直很难找到。环境因素显然是重要的,但是它的作用仍然是模糊不清的。它既不推动也不阻碍行为科学的发展,它具有选择作用,因而这种作用是很难发现和分析的。(63)自然选择在进化中(所起到)的作用只是在一百多年前才得到阐明(或解释),而环境在形成和保持个人行为的过程中(所起到)的选择作用则刚刚才开始得到承认和研究。然而，由于人（生物）和环境之间的相互作用已经逐渐被人们所认识，所以现在正开始从已知的环境去寻找一度认为是心态、情感和性格特征所造成的影响其根源所在。因此就可以建立一门行为技术。但是，如果行为技术代替不了传统的科学发展以前的观点，那它将无法解决我们的难题。而这些传统的观点是根深蒂固的。自由和尊严是难处之所在。(64)**自由和尊严是传统理论中自治者（自我管理者）拥有的财富，它们（或自由与尊严）是实践活动中必不可少的，在这些实践活动中，一个人必须对他的行为负责，取得成绩他也必须受到表扬。**科学的分析把责任和成绩归因于环境。它还提出有关"价值观念"的种种问题。谁会使用一门技术？其目的何在？(65)**除非这些问题得到解决，（不然）行为科学将继续遭到拒绝，随着行为科学的被拒绝（或随之）解决问题的惟一方法也可能会继续遭到拒绝。**

(2003 年～2005 年翻译题答案及解析见第三部分第一章及第一部分)

第五章 写 作

第一节 考研英语写作高分全攻略概述

一、考纲分析

从 2005 年起，写作将考查两篇文章。两篇文章各有侧重，双管齐下。主要变化来自于增加一篇应用文，其实，2003 和 2004 年的大纲都强调了要会写应用文，如书信、简历摘要和备忘录，只不过在 2005 年才开考，考生已经有了两年的心理准备。从其它考试中看，四六级考试、雅思、全国 MBA 联考、BEC 一直都在考查书信写作，也就是说，写作方面并没有出现新题型。所谓的大纲变化在写作部分只是增加了篇目，调整了分数而已。考查两篇文章的形式类似于雅思考试，已经不是什么新鲜事。

从分值变化来说，以往的写作部分为 20 分，多数考生得分在 6 到 14 分之间，得分曲线呈正态分布。写作题型容易拉开分数差异，但不是非常明显。2005 年写作所占分数将由 20 分提高到 30 分，从而更能考查考生的语言输出能力、语言应用能力和实际英语水平，由于考生在考场上发挥的效果有强有弱，参差不齐，实际考试中也就更容易拉开分数档次。不易分出高低胜负的听力题型被放到复试中，也就意味着难得高分的阅读、翻译、综合运用和写作今后更具挑战性。

改革之后的写作评分标准也随之发生了变化。根据《新大纲》，写作包括 A 节和 B 节两部分，对考生写作能力的要求基本相同。

综合归纳，以下几个方面将成为判断分数标准的因素：

1. 字数要求：A 节的信件要求 100 字，B 节的作文要求 160～200 字。

2. 信息点完整性：作文是否能够覆盖到要求中所有的信息点。

3. 文章的内容：文章是否紧扣主题，严格按照提纲内容和隐含主旨论述。

4. 文章的结构：是否参照提纲几个方面分别展开论述，议论段有没有主题句。

5. 表达准确性：能否尽量避免语法错误、拼写错误、搭配错误、用词不当和汉语思维。

6. 格式和语域：书信的基本格式，以及是否使用了标准的议论文书面语语言，衔接是否利用了议论文中的启承转合。

7. 表达多样性：语法结构和词汇表达是否丰富多变。

8. 对提示语的处理：可以利用提示语中的关键词，但不能照搬提示语中的词组和句子。

9. 标点使用：视其对交际的影响程度来决定是否扣分。

10. 书写效果：要求字迹工整，如果影响了交际，则分数降低一个档次。

实际阅卷时采取的手段是 global scoring，但合格的阅卷者会综合考虑其中的几个主要标准，并确定合理的分数档次。

A 节 应用短文写作

根据大纲要求，A 节可能考查一篇简短的书信，要求的字数为 100 词，长度低于四六级要求的 120 词和 150 词，我们不必太感惊慌，可以泰然处之。从形式上看应该侧重考查事务信函，也只有事务信函才能用到书面语的正式语体。大纲已经强调对信函的格式不会过于苛求，所以考生不用花很多时间研究信封地址写法和信体格式，不用考虑书写属于齐头式还是缩进式。但基本的 Dear XXX，以及 Yours sincerely 还是需要一步到位。

到了这个层次，事务信函已经基本等同于一篇普通的提纲作文，我们还是按照提纲要求的若干内容发挥，把每一点扩充成一段。尽管大纲样题中列出的内容为写信向书店购书，内容上很容易把握，我们还是需要了解掌握各种各样的书信作文。可以分为：订购信、退货信、投诉信、感谢信、申请信、建议信、安排信、咨询信、通知信、求职信和辞职信。在新东方考研课堂上，我会重点分析订购信、咨询信、建议信和投诉信四种类型,其它不同功能的信件都可以根据规律类推。

　　虽然短信好写,还是建议考生参考一些写作书中关于应用文的介绍,了解模式,熟悉套话。毕竟也是书面语语体,要注意语言正式、词汇多变,如前面提到了 reference books,后面不妨修改成 reference (reading) materials. 还要保留一些客气礼貌的用语,如 I do appreciate your kind consideration to my request 或 I am grateful to your kind assistance. 另外,千万不要把前面的提示语(情景说明)照搬到自己的作文中用来凑字数,要利用同义词、同义表达加以改造,否则会有抄袭之嫌。

　　B 节　短文写作

　　B 节写作作为延续了十几年的传统考法,仍然占 20 分,但要求的字数已经减少到 160～200 个词汇。可考查的题型分别为"简单提纲作文"、"图表作文"、"图画作文"、"情景作文"。按照历年考查的趋势,为了使写作能够尽量拉开分数档次,图画作文已经成为主流题型,连续考查了 6 次,分别是 1998 年的"如此承诺",2000 年的"世界商业捕鱼简史",2001 年的"爱心是一盏灯",2002 年的"民族文化与世界文化",2003 年的"温室中的花朵经不起风雨",2004 年的"终点又是新的起点",主题变化多样,考法越来越成熟。

　　图画作文在命题上可以采取三维立体式,即提纲＋图画＋情景说明的组合,需要在审题和创作时面面俱到。在图画构造上又可以采取两图对比式,如 2000 和 2003 年考题。但万变不离其宗,语言第一位,结构第二位,内容第三位。

　　审题构思要注意提纲要求、图画寓意和情景说明,三个角度都考虑到位了,再通过象征联想原则,把画面信息放大,联想到画面细节所象征的特殊意义。创作时往往采取三段式结构,结合提纲严谨创作。第一段为图画描述段,详细描述图画信息,争取能把各种细节一网打尽,但不能随意联想到画面以外的东西。第二段往往为意义阐释段,要点出画面信息所象征的抽象意义,指出图画/讽刺画所传达出的真正涵义。如 2002 年的照片传达出"民族的就是世界的"意义;2003 年的花朵和风雨暗示出青少年必须要经受风吹雨打以及各种磨练才能在竞争中生存;2004 年的作文进一步体现出"发展就是硬道理"这个深刻的思想。第三段往往是建议措施段或者举例论证段。如果画面抨击了过度捕捞或滥砍滥伐等不良现象,最后一段需要考生提出两个以上的建议来解决问题。如果画面比较抽象,并且说明了一个道理,如"爱心是一盏灯"或"终点又是新的起点",则需要考生给出具体的例子来加以论证。

　　不管是哪一种段落,都需要考生写出精确地道的语言,尽量在语法上保证精确,再考虑用词丰富多变,设置各种有特色的词、词组和句型,甚至结合主题引发出一系列的主题相关表达。只有讲究了语言的设置和包装才能在大批考研作文中文采飞扬,脱颖而出,赢得高分。过去我们强调"考研英语的成败看阅读",现在写作已经被提高到了相当重要的地位,两篇文章确实就决定出了高低胜负。因此考生一方面要做更多的写作训练,另一方面还要增强自信,毕竟每篇文章都减少了字数,相对来说难度降低了。总之不管大纲如何变化,我们从容而充实地准备,全力以赴,征服考研英语就指日可待!

　　考研大纲关于写作要求的历次变化如下表:

1991-1996 年	简单提纲式作文
1997 年	复杂图表式作文
1998 年	简单图画作文
2000 年	两图对比作文
2001 年	150 字增加到 200 字;分数由 15 分增加到 20 分
2002 年	两点提纲;开放式议论。
2003 年/2004 年	大纲要求考生会写应用文,包括信函、简历、摘要等材料
2005 年	一篇增加到两篇,加了一篇 100 字小作文;分数由 20 分增加到 30 分

二、写作技巧分析

(一)精心构造全文的引言段

　　阅卷老师所处的特殊环境迫使他们不可能用很多时间去仔细看作文全文。在考研写作三段式中究竟是哪一段最能吸引他们的目光和注意力呢?答案当然是第一段。因为考研作文采用的是总体评分法(Global Scoring),作文评卷老师往往主要凭借第一段的总体印象打分。有人把文章的第一段说成是黄金段落,说老师就是在这一段中不断地"淘金"。这一说法是很有道理的。因此,作文要想得高分,一定要精心构造全文的第一段,最大限度地满足阅卷老师的期待心理,力争给他留下良好的第一印象。经验告诉我们,阅卷老师在看完文章的第一段后就已基本上给文章定了分数档次,即使在第二、第三段中发现一些美中不足之处,他也只是微调几分,总体分数还是比先定的档次低的文章要好得多。总之,引言段在全文三段中的重要性再怎么强调也不过分。如果要按重要性依次递减的顺序来排的话,那么首先应是引言段,其次是结尾段,再次是拓展段。

(二)多多制造语言的闪光点

"言之无文,行而不远",语言干瘪平淡,让人看了面目可憎,读后味如嚼蜡。要想攫住阅卷老师匆匆的一瞥,留住他们的兴奋点,就非得在语言上猛下工夫,多制造些表达上的闪光点。有句话说得好:"It is not what you say but the way you say it",意思是,你说什么并不太重要,重要的是你说的方法(形式)。语言是思维的外壳,语言的好坏直接影响到实际作文分数的高低。国内考试阅卷老师往往更注重的是考生的语言表达,其次才是思想内容。也就是说,语言是第一位的,内容是第二位。这是国内考试作文与国外考试作文的最大差别。

语言表达的亮点体现在小到一个词,大到一个短语甚至句子。高分作文往往是"锱铢必较",几乎字字计较。很多人作文分数很低往往是因为用词面太窄。有人曾讽刺这种文章说,200 个词左右的文章重复的词如只算一个,整篇文章大概不重复的单词不超过 60 个;而且绝大部分是初高中词汇,很少是大学学过的词汇。很多同学一提到"我想""我认为"之类的话,脑中一个反应就是"I think",此外别无其他表达。殊不知,阅卷老师每天要改成百上千作文,要是人人都写"I think",恐怕这位老师改卷回来后三天也没胃口吃饭了! 其实,英语中这类表达俯拾皆是:I think/ believe/ maintain/ argue/ assert/ insist/ hold/ claim/ emphasize/ point out/reckon/ assume/ cling to the idea that 等等。表达法如此丰富,怎么会就用一个"I think"呢! 当然,词汇的积累是有个过程的。可惜的是,很多同学只能认识这些词,却不能在写作时想起并运用这些词。

大多数考生在考研写作时,似乎对下面几对词"情有独钟"。如一提到"越来越多人"便是"more and more people"。尽管这种表达方式没有错误,但往往不能形成表达中的"亮点"。如能改成"people in growing/ increasing/ expanding/ mounting numbers",那效果可就另当别论了。再如表达"为了,目的是"意思时,很多人往往使用"in order to","so as to"。诚然,这样的表达无错,可太 colloquial 了! 不妨试试其他更好的表达:in an attempt to, in a bid to, with a view to, aim to, aim at, for the purpose of 等等。

多种句型的交替使用,文章脉络的层次分明,观点论据的充分合理等在写作中都应引起足够的重视,这里不再多言。"Easier said than done",要想把作文写好,要想在考研写作中得高分,平时一定得多阅读背诵优秀的范文,特别是一些漂亮精彩的句型。同时也有必要掌握一些写作模式和技巧,不断地模仿练习,最终才能真正打造出高分作文。

三、其它应注意的问题

深谙阅卷老师的期待心理。考研作文阅卷老师每天工作量很大,工作时间也较长,因此长时间批改水平参差不齐、质量高下不一的作文难免感到疲劳、厌倦,甚至气恼。据测试统计,一口气读完 12 篇后才走神的人极少,因此,别天真地指望阅卷老师会逐字逐句地阅读你的文章,毕竟你写的不是金庸的小说、徐志摩的诗呀! 你花了 40 分钟好不容易绞尽脑汁写好的作文,他们大概用十几秒钟大致浏览一遍就毫不留情地打下一个分数。这就是我们之所以有必要了解阅卷老师期待心理的主要原因。

母语为非英语的人学习英语时往往会将母语的思维和表达方式直接转移到英语表达当中。中国人学英语时往往会受母语根深蒂固的影响,最易造出 Chinglish,即不地道的、带中国腔的英语。现在我们举个例子:有人把"价格便宜"直接写成"The price is cheap",把"这件事小菜一碟"说成"This is a small dish",让人看后哭笑不得。因此要尽量摆脱中国式英语,方法看来只有一个:多看外国人写的文章,多多阅读。不难想象,阅卷老师如果在短短的二百字文章中到处看到的都是 Chinglish,他想给你很高的印象分都难。

四、审题构思

图画作文

(1)列出重要图画细节词

以 2002 年 1 月考题为例,图片中是一个美国女孩身着传统的中国少数民族服装,面带微笑。审题时果断列出可能用到的语汇如:traditional costume, ribbons, necklaces, earrings, majority group, sweet smile, charming features. 没有这些词汇的罗列,第一自然段的描述过程将耗费很多时间。

(2)以小见大联想把握象征意义

图画作文关键在于透过表面看实质,精确地点出图画的象征寓意,构思联想不到位会导致跑题或无话可说的尴尬局面。如前题的例子,要毫不犹豫地把图画和所定题目挂钩联想,并要以小见大把握象征意义,美国女孩代表着西方文化或西方人,传统中国少数民族服装则是个象征符号,指典型的传统中国文化。女孩面带微笑正好传达出西方人接受或热爱中国文化、世界经济文化融合和中国文化走向世界的深刻意义。

(3)把握背景原因和两条建议

联想的过程深入,很容易想到中国改革开放、加入世贸以及全球化(globalization)的国际大趋势。又可以联系到美国的 jeans, rock music, Hollywood movies, MacDonald fast food 等 cultural symbols 在世界的传播普及,进一步阐述"民族的就是世界的"这一命题。文章的收尾部分不妨参照考研作文模式提出两点建议:要保存珍惜传统民族文化;对待西方文化要"取其精华,去其糟粕",把优秀的文化发扬光大等等。缜密的逻辑构思足以恰当地表达出一个考研学生应有的理论素质。

图表作文

(1)选出典型的数据—纵横对位

面对图表应当首先结合主题,观察图表数据变化,如果表格、柱形和曲线都比较复杂,则需先确定典型数据,如最高点、最低点以及骤升骤降的时间变化范围,在表格和坐标图中精确地纵横对位,想象如何使用 demonstrate a dramatic change, increase dramatically, decline sharply, go up steadily, remain on the decline 这样的图表术语描述数据变化。

(2)把握变化—联系背景原因

想象这种变化和主题的必然联系,拓展思维确定出原因一二三来。如北京市民人均收入增加一定和近几年经济飞速发展、就业生存方式多样化和全面建设小康社会的国策相关联;沙尘暴次数猛增反映出中国西北土壤沙漠化、森林砍伐现象严重和城市房地产开发毁坏绿地植被的多元因素。

(3)建议或未来发展趋势

针对第二段分析的原因提出合理建议,基本思路可遵循以下两点:政府制定法律法规扭转(推进)现有局面;个人树立某种意识主动参与解决问题。最后展望一下人类解决问题后的美好明天,一篇议论文的格局已了然于胸。

下笔创作时应当注意:

①丰富提纲内容

有把握的同学可以立即动笔创作,把已定的思路充分表达出来。但思路还是不清楚、害怕跑题或无话可说的同学应把提纲丰富起来,如用汉语简单写出每段的三个方面,用简洁的词或符号代替即可,提纲具体化可以让自己沿着一个严谨的框架前行,避免天马行空、意识流主宰思维的危险。

②每段按一定句数创作

200 词的作文不等于长篇大论,又有明确的提纲控制,考生必须做到言简意赅。达到字数要求不难,要看自己有限的语言是否言之有物,表达切题且有力度。对规模作出合理控制只需有以下的意识:

3 段式作文开篇段落引出话题,评价现状或描述图画图表,尽量用 3—4 句完成任务,其中设置一个长句,使得第一段达到 50～60 个单词。

中间拓展段是论述主题并展现实力的黄金段落,要阐明图画图表寓意并且深刻分析原因背景,点出几个方面,结构有层次感,语言有闪光点和深度,写出 7－8 句比较合理,总字数控制到 80～100 字。

结论段不止下结论,还要提出 2－3 点解决问题的建议。并且设置一个漂亮的结束句,使用排比、强调、倒装、虚拟句型体现句式变化,写出 5－6 句不算太多,总字数在 70～80 字左右。

③创作有气势的开篇句

由于考研阅卷往往在写作第一段确定文章分数档次,最后一段往往被考官忽视,开篇的三句话要有爆发力,充分表现考生的语言水平和写作实力。因此要把平时积累的优秀句型应用到第一段开篇,如:

It is universally acknowledged that....

It is generally accepted that....

It goes without saying that....

As is vividly depicted in the picture, a lovely American girl is dressed in traditional Chinese costume....

The above graph reveals a dramatic decline in the production of... To be specific....

④注意 2、3 两段的段首句和层次感

英语议论文写作讲究拓展阐述部分有段首句和支持段首句的若干论据。分层次表达又要避免数字排列的机械感,讲究启承转合的多样化表达,因此 2、3 两段就有可以依据的优秀表达模型。

如:阐释原因段

Three fundamental factors can account for this sharp change.

Above all... In addition... Last but not least,....

建议措施段

To crack this hard nut, people have worked out many effective measures.

Not only can..., but... as well. More importantly...

⑤长短句搭配,每段构造 1—2 个长句

都是短句的作文略显水平稚嫩,写作功力尚需磨练,都是长句的作文又显得啰嗦冗赘,卖弄不成反倒做作。真正的优秀文章应做到长短句搭配合理,行文流畅,难简结合,曲径通幽,平实中见功力。大批考生缺乏写作训练,往往在作文中忽视运用长句。要试试在每段中设置出 1 个有特色的长句,如并列句、排比句、定语从句、状语从句等,使得文章流畅而不失难度。

⑥创作有特色的篇末结束句

文章的结尾不好,苍白平淡,则给人虎头蛇尾的感觉,很有可能因为一句话而减弱前面的文采印象,所以要有意识安排一个闪光句型在结尾,让考官读到结尾时能眼睛一亮。如:

倒装:

Only in this way can laid-off workers completely shrug off poverty and regain their dignity in life.

强调:

In conclusion, it is persistent work that is conducive to your grasping a large vocabulary.

虚拟:

Given all the above arguments, it is high time that the authorities enforced some reforms to convert traditional education strategies into quality-oriented education.

⑦注意笔迹工整

写作中笔迹是否工整美观直接影响考试成绩,因为没有时间打草稿,学生的创作基本上是一气呵成,如果字体潦草,则大大淹没了文字内容的魅力,极有可能一败涂地。所以要有细心落笔的意识,动笔节奏慢而沉稳,仔细写每一句话。只要具备了一定的句型知识,200 词的作文很容易完成。不要仓促下笔,一路狂草,造成悲剧结果。

最后一道工序:写作完成后不要急于放松休息,以下的语言文字润饰工作可以让你的作品锦上添花,不留遗憾。Taking every detail into consideration,让精心设计的文章突破 16 分也就有希望了。浏览检查不可能推翻全部内容,因为时间有限,也为了保持卷面整洁,修改工作要以纠正明显的语法拼写错误为主。为了避免用语单调重复,也可将若干机械平淡的语言替换掉,实现语言的丰富多变。

总之,我们只有40分钟完成写作。少些即兴冒险,多些理性沉稳,把握写作流程,突破自己的一般水准。希望考生们能超常发挥,把自己的语言知识精华展现在试卷上。

真题再现 ▶

2001 年研究生英语入学考试作文

Ⅴ. Writing(15 points)

Directions:

Among all the worthy feelings of mankind, love is probably the noblest, but everyone has his/her own understanding of it.

There has been a discussion recently on the issue in a newspaper. Write an essay to the newspaper to

1)show your understanding of the symbolic meaning of the picture below,

2)give a specific example, and

3)give your suggestion as to the best way to show love.

You should write about 200 words on Answer Sheet 2.

破题

　　本篇作文在提出文中必须要具备的三点提示前还有一段对揭示主题很有帮助的引文。学生如果仔细阅读并分析此段引文就会对给出的图画含义有一个正确的理解。虽然引文中第一句话的后半部分指出不同的人有自己独特的对爱的理解,但这些理解在本篇中都是基于对爱的正面的理解,因为前半部分已经给本篇要讨论的爱定下了一个范围,就是爱是最高尚的。这样一来学生的作文的范围就一下子缩小了。不是泛泛而谈,而是分析爱相对于其他种类的感情而言的价值和重要性。

　　虽然提示引文中提到有基于此的热烈讨论,但是从接下来的三点具体提示来看还是以表明作者本人立场为主。因此在考虑写本篇开头时也可以稍微提及一下不同人群的不同的观念,但应点到即止,因为这只是作为引出自己独特观点的一个引子,来吸引读者的注意力,通过对比,给读者留下鲜明印象。

　　接下来就是要来看一下文章的结构了。因为虽然三点提示非常清楚,但这还毕竟是一篇看图作文,因此一切观点要从图的内容与隐含的意义出发。先让我们来分析一下三点的内在联系。这三点内部是有一个层层递进的关系,必须由一点才能引出下一点而顺理成章。

　　如果要使文章层次更为分明,那我们可以将三点安排成三个不同的部分。即 introduction, body, and conclusion。

　　第一点可作为开头引出全文的论点(thesis statement)。突出其象征性的含义,而不是简单地描述画面的表面内容,画的布局只要略微提到即可,重要的是画上的那句话和画中的物品之间的抽象与实物的联系,可作为文中的论点。要突出爱在黑暗或有困难的地方显现出来的重要性。

第二点作为正文部分。用现实的例子来论证在什么样的令人感到前路暗淡的情况下爱发挥了巨大的作用。但是因为时间和字数的限制,举例部分不能太过冗长。

第三点作为结论部分。虽然向他人显示爱的力量可以无时无刻无处不在,各种各样,但是这篇文章最好是介绍一种或几种向他人伸出援助之手的方法,即要紧扣图画表现的含义和论点确定的范围来写。因为这毕竟是一篇看图作文,不能离开图画而天马行空。但要注意的是:如果作者在写第二点时,就已举例如何帮助他人,那么切记在写第三点时不要再重复了,几笔带过即可。因为并不是给出的三点提示每一点都要给予同等的篇幅,应该有侧重点。

优秀范文赏析

Love 爱

There is no denying the fact that love is the noblest and the nicest among all the worthy feelings of mankind. As is shown in the picture, a heart containing love is a lamp, which can light up the travel of life and direct one to go forward. What's more, the darker a place is, the brighter the light the lamp of love gives off. Such a lamp is indispensable to everyone.

Take an example of my own to explain the importance of love. When I was in Senior High School, I once suffered from a serious disease. At that time, the final exam was drawing near and I was very anxious and worried because I missed a lot of lessons. Hong, one of my classmates, visited me one day and noticed my anxiety. Then she helped me with my study every day. At last, I passed the exam successfully. I was very obliged to her for ever.

As far as the best way to show love is concerned, I think, the first thing is to be careful to others around you and find their difficulties in time, then try your best to help them, especially those in great troubles.

范文解析

本篇范文从接受爱者的角度来写,因为文中举的例子是作者本人接受他人的帮助而感受到了爱的力量。首先作者肯定了提示引文中的观点。但是作者没有简单地重复引文中的句子,而是用了"There is no denying the fact that"的句型。虽然 noblest 和 nicest 看似相似,但是两个词还是有一定的区别,是形容了一个事物的两个方面。既然是象征意义,那么肯定应该有物体与它的象征性。这篇范文用简洁的语言点出了灯与爱之间的联系和共通性。在做此对比时,作者运用了分词,非限制性定语从句,the more…, the more…等引导的句型,使句子变化更生动。另外运用了如 contain, light up, what's more, and, indispensable 等词,使文章看来更成熟。本文的开头一直用象征物来表述象征意义,没有脱离具体的事物。

正文中作者以自己的切身体会作为例子,更能说明问题。作者在文中注意了没有记流水账,面面俱到地描述事情的开始,发展和结局,而是用简短的几句话说明了在自己处于困境中感受到的爱的力量。

结尾作者阐明了 show love 的不同阶段和在不同阶段应做的工作和发挥的作用,简明扼要。并且没有忘记在最后一句又一次点题。

第二节 考研英语写作理论基础

一、基本句型

初学者写作文,最大的错误便是句子结构错误。所谓结构错误,主要就是句型错误。记得笔者有一次在阅卷时碰到这样一种情况,作文题目是:"Women's Role in Society"。有个同学开头第一句是:

"In old society heavy men light women."居然一个谓语动词也没有。当然,中国人大概差不多都能猜出他想说什么,可是,这不是英文句子。阅卷老师看了这样一个"句子",恐怕不会再往下看,打2分算了(满分为15分)。

另一个例子:有个男同学给女朋友写信,为了露一手,开头写了一句英文:Dear Ming Ming: I now very thinking you. 这根本不是个英语句子。没有谓语,状语放得也不是地方。

许多人先想好一个中文句子,然后逐个字译成英文,以为那就是英文句子了。这是大错特错绝对行不通的做法。我们写英文作文,每一个句子都必须符合英语规范的格式。

英语虽然有无数的句子,但可归纳为下面6个基本句型:

(1)Mr. Wang is a teacher. (S V C)

(2)He works at a university. (S V A)

(3)He has taught English for ten years. (S V O A)

(4)He asks us to study hard. (S V O C)

(5)He gives us English lessons. (S V Oi Od)

(6)There are 30 students in our class. (There "be" S A)

说明:Oi 为间接宾语(Indirect Object);Od 为直接宾语(Direct Object.);C 为表语或补语(Complement)。

用我们中国学生习惯的说法:

例1为:主系表句型(名词性谓语:系词+表语)

例2为:主谓状句型(谓语为不及物动词);

例3为:主谓宾状句型(谓语为及物动词,介词短语作状语);

例4为:主谓宾补句型(主语做的动作叫谓语,宾语做的动作叫宾语补足语),本句谓语动词 asks 要求复合宾语,不定式短语 to study hard 作宾语补足语;

例5为:主谓双宾语句型(该谓语动词要求间接宾语及直接宾语);

例6为:There be+主语+地点状语句型(存在句;表示"在某处有某人或某物")。

英语的一切句子都可以分解为上述6个基本句型,或这些句型的演化、扩展及组合。掌握这6个基本句型,对于我们分析和理解英语的句子结构,以及我们自己写英文作文,保证句子结构的完整,具有极其重要的意义。

说明:句型2和句型3中,状语(A)在实际应用中有时可省略。

二、扩展基本句型

我们首先要掌握英语的基本句型,同时也要学会把这些基本句型深化或扩展成比较复杂的句子。基本句型的演化,主要是指谓语动词的变化。谓语动词可有各种不同时态,及物动词作谓语,还有主动语态和被动语态之分。下面看几个演化的例子:

(1)Mr. Wang was an English teacher two years ago.

(2)Mr. Wang has been an English teacher since 1998.

(3)He has been working at our university for three years.

(4)He was asked to give us a lecture on how to prepare for Band-4 Test.

(5)There seem to be many students who want to pass Band-4 English in our university.

扩展句子的手段有如下几种:

(1)在名词前加修饰语:例如"Mr. Wang is a teacher."可扩展为:Mr. Wang is an experienced English teacher.

(2)在名词后加修饰语:Mr. Wang is one of the experienced English teachers of our department.

(3)在动词前后加状语:例如"He works at a university."可以通过加状语扩展为:He has been working continuously at our university for twenty years.

(4)加各种短语:One of my best friends, Mr. Wang is an experienced English teacher. / Having taught English for more than twenty years, Mr. Wang is an experienced English teacher.

(5)加各种从句:He works at a university that is famous for its computer science programs.

(6)加并列分句:He works at a university but his wife stays at home without a job.

以上6个句型,通过演化和扩展,组成英语文献中无数的句子。区分不同句型的关键是其中的谓语动词。"主系表句型"中的谓语动词为系动词;"主谓状句型"的谓语动词为不及物动词,有时候也可不带状语,成为 SV 结构;"主谓宾状句型"的谓语动词为及物动词,有时候也可不带状语,成为 SVO 结构;"主谓宾补句型"的谓语动词为要求复合宾语的及物动词;"主谓双宾语句型"的谓语动词为要求双宾语的及物动词;"There be 句型"的谓语动词为系动词"be"的各种变化形式。6个基本句型谓语动词都可有时态和语气的变化,及物动词做谓语时,可演化成被动语态。

我们在写作过程中,所写的任何一个句子,必须属于某一个基本句型。学习每一个常用动词的时候,也一定要弄清楚,该动词属于哪一个基本句型。例如,动词 give 主要用于"S V Oi Od"句型;动词 ask 可以是 S V Oi Od 句型(He asked me a question.),也可以是 S V O C 句型(He asked me to give him some food.);动词 work 则常用于 S V A 句型(He works hard.)。(请读者任意找一段文章分析一下每个句子的句型。)

通过上述的分析,我们应该深信不疑:英语的所有句子确实是由非常有限的几个基本句型深化或扩展而来的,因此,我们写作文时,就得按英文的规矩办,不能写一些无头无尾的东西。你想说"旧社会重男轻女,"变成英文,就得按英文的规矩说:"Men and women were not equal in the old days."当然,还可以有多种说法,但这个"主系表句型"是最简单的了,所有的单词都是初中阶段就学过的。

三、遣词造句的重要性

应当看到随着整体英语水平的提高,现在越来越多的大学生都能够写出几乎没有什么重大语法错误的作文来。但他们不会利用这个优势写出耐人寻味、生动和地道的英语来。把他们写的东西与英美人士写的英语相比,总感到缺了点什么。究其原因可能主要还是没有真正摆脱母语的影响。一方面在语言学习的环境中,他们在不断克服这一影响;另一方面,又有一种东西在顽强地抵制这个进程。这不仅仅指学习上的,还有教学上的因素。例如,在课上教师对汉英两种不同的表达方式及其组句特点讲得较少。要写出地道的英语(Idiomatic English),学生就要不断注意英语是如何来表达一个思想的。

例如从遣词方面来看,学生在写作的大多数时候依靠动词来组织句子。要表达"家庭生活使我感到幸福"的意思时,马上就会写出 family life makes me feel happy。不仅词序和中文句子的字序一样,而且所用的词性也相同。这显然是受汉语的影响。汉语组句的最大特点是通过频繁地使用动词,造成大量动词的集结来表达一个思想。往往在一个短短的句子里,集中了好几个动词,如:

老栓还踌躇着,黑的人便抢过灯笼,一把扯下纸罩,裹了馒头,塞与老栓,一手抓过洋钱,捏一捏,转身去了。嘴里哼着说,……。——鲁迅《药》

而英语则相反,组织句子时,它依靠的不是动词。一个再长的句子,主要动词只有一个,中文中的动词意思往往在英语中是用介词、分词、不定式以及由动词转化过来的抽象名词来表达的:

When Aunt Bette told me about her first sight of the bearded men in the stained blue uniform,she always used the same words.

贝蒂姨婆跟我讲起她第一次看到那个身穿血渍斑斑的蓝制服,脸蓄胡须的人时,她总是用同样的话说,……

——《大学英语》精读第三册

相比较来说,在写作中,除了动词,学生对使用分词、介词来组织句子并不陌生。正因为这一点,他们写的东西有点英语味:

In order to overcome the difficulties,every morning,standing by the window with an English book in hand,I read loudly,paying much attention to my pronunciation.

仔细分析,这与他们一开始学习英语时,教师就把语法当作重点来学习有关。

动词形式填空,介词填空,非谓语形式多项选择等等一直是练习的主要形式。而抽象名词的命运却完全两样,它一直是中国人学英语长期忽视的对象。抽象名词的学习和理解以及运用,一直是教学中的薄弱环节。不论是课本注释、练习安排,还是教师讲解,很少有它的位置。而抽象名词的使用,正是现代英语的一大特点,也是英汉两种语言的主要区别之一。试比较这两个句子:

(1)Family life makes me feel happy.

(2)Family life is a source of happiness to me.

两个抽象名词就使英语味道出来了。可见,由于抽象名词已暗含了动词的意思:source:a place from which happiness comes,happiness＝being happy,所以使用抽象名词来表达思想,能减少动词的使用,使文章更紧凑,句子更简练,从而写出的英语显得更老练、成熟、地道。例如上面这篇作文中的几个句子:

"City life is no longer thought of as the only source of comforts and the promise of success."

"Better communication and transportation makes for easy access to the city's benefits."

"The shift represents a dramatic break with the Chinese tradition of urban concentration."

显然,如果不用这些抽象名词,只能靠使用许多动词和从句来表达,这样就会失去英语独特的风味。再如下面的几个句子:

"Withdrawal from employment to complete domesticity has a profound significance on them."

"For a worker, retirement is associated with the gnawing awareness of a declining state of health, and with the anticipated deprivation of his participation in work which provides him most of happiness and contentment."

这些句子表达既简练又准确,正是这些抽象词才使其成为地道的英语。这样说,不算夸张吧。

下面再提供一些实例供学习参考。a 句是学生写的原句,b 句是改进后的句子。两者有时只是文体的差别,并不是 a 句一定不好。

(1)a. Our parents always expect that we should make progress in school, and will ask why if we fail to do so.

　　b. Our parents always anticipate progress and question its absence.

(2)a. The problem indicates that it is very necessary to modify the system of our higher education.

　　b. The problem points to the necessity of the modification of the system of our higher education.

(3)a. What our people wanted most was to end the uncertain situation.

　　b. What our people wanted most was to put an end to uncertainties.

(4)a. When I passed the entrance examination and was able to go to Fudan University, the whole family felt proud of me and even the whole village talked about me.

　　b. When I passed the entrance examination and was able to go to Fudan University, I became the pride of the family and even the talk of the village.

(5)a. In many cases, those unskilled labourers from the countryside bring a lot of trouble to our society, they contribute little to our economy.

　　b. In many cases, those unskilled labourers from the countryside prove to be a social cost rather than an economic asset.

(6)a. The minds of most Chinese people, countryside is a place where people are poor and sent to be punished. So they hold a strong anti-rural attitude.

　　b. A strong anti-rural attitude runs through the mainstream of Chinese mentality because of the association of the countryside with poverty and punishment.

(7)a. The mayor said he was very grateful because the construction workers were dedicated and competent.

　　b. The mayor expressed his appreciation of the dedication and competence of the construction workers.

(8)a. But it seems that people don't make any effort to conserve our limited natural resources.

　　b. But there seems to have been an absence of attempt at conservation of limited natural resources.

(9)a. By such methods, our teacher helped us to appreciate beautiful writing and improve our language.

　　b. By such methods, our teacher led us to an <u>appreciation</u> of beautiful writing and <u>perfection</u> of our language.

(10)a. The news made us no longer anxious but joyful.

　　b. The news turned our initial <u>anxiety</u> into <u>joy</u>.

(11)a. If we don't recognize the serious problem of growing population, we will make a big mistake.

　　b. <u>Failure</u> to recognize the <u>seriousness</u> of growing population will lead to a big mistake.

(12)a. He persisted in his work although people were indifferent and hostile to him.

　　b. He persisted in his work in spite of general <u>indifference</u> and <u>hostility</u>.

(13)a. This solution is welcomed by college students immediately.

　　b. This solution finds an immediate <u>welcome</u> among college student.

(14)a. This incident helps me to know the nature of human beings deeply.

　　b. This incident helps deepen my <u>understanding</u> of the nature of human beings.

(15)a. The first step is to make people realize the harmful effects of smoking.

　　b. The first step is the common <u>realization</u> of the harmful effects of smoking.

(16)a. I'm very glad that you will travel with me on the long journey.

　　b. I'm very glad of your <u>company</u> on the long journey.

(17)a. The notion has become more and more popular and accepted by more and more young people.

　　b. The notion has found its growing <u>popularity</u> and <u>acceptance</u> among young people.

【示例】

Directions：

A. Title：**Heading for the Country**

B. Time limit：40 minutes

C. Word limit：120~150 (not including the given opening sentence).

D. Your composition should be based on the OUTLINE below and should start with the given opening sentence："For the first time since 1949, Chinese people have begun to choose to live in the country. "

OUTLINE：

1. A new trend：Thousands of people moving from city to country

2. Possible reasons

1)More chances of success offered in small towns

2)The improvement of the rural standard of living

3. Its significance

范文赏析

Heading for the Country 走向村庄

For the first time since 1949, Chinese people have begun to choose to live in the country (Although in the late sixties there was a down-to-the-countryside program on a large scale, the movers were generally forced to, most of them leaving their families behind). Statistics show that in the past decade more than sixty hundred thousand people from Beijing, Shanghai and Guangzhou have moved to small towns in the countryside, and more flocked to those in coastal open areas. One of the notable characteristics of this migration is that the new movers are all well-educated and well paid people.

　　Why have people left metropolitan areas behind and headed for homes in small towns? One thing is obvious:city life is no longer thought of as the only source of comforts and the promise of success. There are more chances and hopes in the country. Since economic reforms,more and more industries and businesses are moving into small towns. The open door policies and preferential terms provided by the state have made it possible for foreign businessmen to invest capital in the rural areas where they can enjoy various favoured policies such as the lower taxes,the low-priced labour and materials,and the land-use right. The growth in joint ventures and foreign firms thus creates many job opportunities and,due to the promise of higher salaries,attracts many people from cities. For those people who are bound to remain on the lower rungs of the social ladder because of their unfavourable backgrounds,for those people who find no way to get promoted because the managerial positions have already been filled; and for those people who are frustrated because their ideas tend to get bogged down in the bureaucratic red tap,what these foreign enterprises offer are more than just well-paid jobs. They also offer rare opportunities to help them realize potentials and fulfil ambitions,and the chance for a flowering of authentic freedom.

　　The increase in the country's magnetic pull is also attributed to the rapid improvement of the rural standard of living as a whole in recent years. A two-storied house with a garden is a big allure for city dwellers who are suffering a serious shortage of housing facilities. Every family has a television set,and in some rural areas,private telephones,motorcycles and cars have outnumbered those of big cities. Better communication and transportation makes for easier access to the city's benefits. The problems that once plagued the country and frightened city dwellers no longer exist. Health facilities are developing quickly,and many good colleges are set up in small towns. All this change has freed people from the fears and worries brought about by moving to the country.

　　The heading for homes in small towns is only a beginning. But what is most significant about this trend is not so many people involved as the fact that the shift represents a dramatic break with the Chinese tradition of urban concentration. Its social consequences have been far reaching.

　　[注释]

　　1. metropolitan areas 大城市

　　2. preferential terms 优惠条件

　　3. get bogged down in the bureaucratic red tap 陷于官僚主义的条条框框之中

　　4. a flowering of authentic freedom 获取真正的自由

　　5. megnetic pull 像磁性一样吸过去

四、固定句式

　　英语有许多固定的句式。对于一些常用句式,写作文的时候,应该做到能够"信手拈来","恰到好处"。达到这个"火候",你就有了"自由",可以初步自由地用英语表达自己的思想和观点了。下面介绍 30 个常用句式,供读者练习使用。

　　(1)John is two years older than Helen. Bill is three months older than John.

　　(2)Bill is the oldest among the three children,and Helen is the youngest one.

　　(3)This room is as big as that one. Both of them are of the same size.

　　(4)The production of this year is twice as much as that of 1990.

　　(5)I told professor Wang that I didn't know how to translate that sentence.

　　(6)He asked me if I wanted a cup of coffee. (I said I would rather have a cup of tea.)

　　(7)When I was young,I used to work 14 hours a day.

　　(8)When I came in,he was reading a book.

　　(9)There have been a lot of changes here in the last 20 years.

　　(10)There used to be many old houses in this district of the city.

(11)I will stay at home if it rains. (I would stay at home if it should rain this afternoon. / I would have stayed at home if it had rained yesterday.)

(12)If I have time, I will go to see him. (If I buy that car, I'll have to borrow some money.)

(13)If I had time, I would go to see him now. (If you were a very rich person, how would you spend all your money?)

(14)If I should have time, I would go to see him tomorrow. (If it should rain tomorrow, I would stay at home.)

(15)If I had had time, I would have gone to see him yesterday. (If I had known you wanted to go, I would have called you.)

(16)Had I had time, I'd have gone to see him yesterday. (Had I known you didn't have a key, I wouldn't have locked the door.)

(17)It's difficult (for sb to do sth)... (for us to do this. / for me to make a decision without knowing all the facts. / for me to answer all your questions right now. / for the students to remember all these new words in such a short time.)

(18)If it is necessary (for sb to do sth)... (for us to know how to use a computer. / for him to come on time. / for our students to learn some history.)

(19)How long does it take (for sb to do sth)... (for you to do your homework everyday? / for the bus to get to the next stop? / for a graduate student to get a master degree in this university?)

(20)It took me... (three hours to finish all my homework. / a long time to make up my mind. / half an hour to solve that problem. / three months to write this book.)

(21)I'm sure/ confident/ ... (I've made a good decision. / you'll win. / he can do his job very well.)

(22)It's faster to go ... (by air than by sea. / by plane than by ship/ by train/ by bus/ by car.)

(23)I'm interested... (in learning English. / in buying a new car. / in starting my own business. / to hear your opinion. / to see what will happen next. / to know all the details of this matter.)

(24)Which would you rather have/ prefer/--fish or chicken? (I'd rather have fish. / I'd prefer fish to chicken.)

(25)Which would you rather do-go dancing or go to a play? / stay at home or go to a party with me? / wash the dishes or sweep the floor?

(26)I would rather (do sth. than do sth.)... (stay at home than go out this evening. / do it myself than to ask him for help.)

(27)I'd rather (sb. did sth.)... (you went now. / you didn't smoke here.)

(28)I'd like to (do sth.)... (have a rest for a while. / take a bath right now. / make an appointment to see Dr. Zhang. / change these shoes because they are too small for me.)

(29)Would you mind (doing sth?)... (opening the window, please? / calling me back sometime tomorrow? / waiting me here for a while?)

(30)I don't mind... (that you were late as long as you are here now. / if you don't come to my class. / whether we see the film or not.)

五、模仿

前面说过,我们既然要用英文写作文,就得按照英文的习惯来表述。要掌握英文的表达方式,模仿的办法有以下 3 种:

(1)**套用样板句**　在学习课文的过程中,把一些自己认为较好的句子分门别类地抄到自己的笔记本上或卡片上。这些句子应符合以下 3 条标准:1)意思相对完整,脱离上下文还能独立存在。2)其词汇和结构难度符合你当前的英语水平。3)作为一个句套子,值得你去模仿套用。假如你现在是大学 1 年级学生,那么下面这个句子就值得做一个卡片。

With the increase in road traffic in the cities, traffic lights have become more common.（随着城市道路交通车辆的增加，交通信号灯也就变得更加普遍了。）

这个句子是个主系表句型的简单句，但是前面那个介词短语 with the increase... 值得套用。如果我们想说，"随着科学技术的发展，计算机已经变得越来越普遍了"，我们就可以套用这个句型：With the development of science and technology, computers have become more and more common. 我们要表达"随着生产的增加，老百姓的生活也逐步得到改善"这句话，也可以这么说：With the increase in production, the life of ordinary people has been gradually improved.

（2）**听写**　听写主要是解决拼写错误的问题。初学者写作文时，往往出现大量拼写错误。如果你有学过的课文的录音磁带，不妨经常选 1、2 段来做听写练习。听一句，按暂停键，写下来，再听下一句。听写完之后，拿原文来对照，改正所出现的拼写错误。不要用结构复杂的、很难的段落，要选比较容易的，句子比较短的段落。有些初学者误以为，句子写得越长越有水平，有时候 30、40 个词才有一个句号，这是绝对错误的。以一个初学者英文水平，能够正确写出 11、12 个词的带一个从句的复合句就很了不起。千万别学那些专业教科书的文体，一大段文章才一个句子。即使你现在正做博士后研究工作，也尽量不要用很长的句子。

（3）**默写**　由于汉语和英语的发音体系有很大区别，中国人学英语，在初、中级阶段，免不了要大声朗读。当你把某一段课文朗读若干遍能背诵之后，不妨再前进一步，把它默写下来。你是否已经全面掌握该段课文，默写是最有效的检查手段。本来自认为已经掌握了的课文，一旦默写，就会发现各种遗漏：某个名词是单数还是复数，它前面有没有冠词，某个单词的拼写对不对。把一段课文看懂了，会朗读了，会背诵了，这都是耕耘，都需要花费很多劳动。然而，只有会默写了，才是学到手了，才是你的收获阶段。世界上只有最愚蠢的人才会只管耕耘，不问收获。

六、造句

【示例】

Directions：

In this section of the test, you will have 30 minutes to write a composition based on the following essay question.

The number of young people who live together before marriage has increased in recent years. The advocates say it is a good living style. But other people take a negative attitude. What's your opinion? Explain why.

范文解析

A Question of Living Together Style　同居的问题

Living together before marriage is now attaining a certain vogue, and becomes a national trend among young people. According to an official census, between 1980 and 1992, there was an eight fold increase in the living together style. Some people say it is a good way to test love before being formally married, other people suggest that it is a solution to the high divorce rate which has plagued Chinese families in recent years. They claim that by not making their relationship permanent they can avoid many problems brought about by divorce. In short they all believe, to eliminate the legal commitment of marriage is to eliminate the "bad" part of marriage. But I cannot share this point of view for several reasons.

For one thing, it must be recognized that a strong negative attitude towards the living together style runs consistently through the mainstream of Chinese thinking which, traditionally and morally, has placed a very high premium on marriage. Whatever life-style a single male or female chooses is a matter of individual's freedom. But since they live in China, the particular society, they have to take the social attitude into consideration. What they view as a marvelous, free lifestyle, the public may see as an abnormality even immorality. Of course they can turn a deaf ear to what others say behind them, but they can not escape the pressure from their families and society, the pressure they will experience anywhere and any-time. The day they enter into it, they may live in the shadow of the social censure which is a psychological burden they have to carry through their lives.

For example, a postgraduate failed to get the job he applied for, simply because the company, finding the girl he was living with was not his wife, felt that his life-style smacked of indecisiveness, instability and failure on his part to accept responsibility. Who is to say whether or not the company made the fair deci-sion? But what he may view as a sophisticated way to live, the company has the right to see as a career impediment.

When it comes to individuals, furthermore, the living together style can actually spoil a good relation-ship between two people who intend to marry eventually. Because it is entered into out of weakness rather than strength, doubt rather than conviction, drift rather than decision, it offers unnecessary obstacles. If marriage is what you want, why commit yourself to a shaky arrangement that keeps you out of the main-stream of life?

You may argue what you want is love not marriage. Then what is love? You cannot hope to find love by ex-perimenting biologically. Neither can you build love by creating a living situation designed to test it. Love is. And when you love you must commit to it—for better or for worse. Living together is not an act of love but a means of running from responsibility.

[注释]

1. attaining a certain vogue 正在流行

2. place a very high premium 非常看重

3. abnormality even immorality 反常甚至不道德

4. the social censure 社会舆论指责

5. smacked of 带有

6. a career impediment 有碍于工作

[讲评]

要写出地道的英语,不仅要注意词性的选择,还要注意句序的排列。英语句子和汉语句子的重心相同,一般都落在结果、结论、态度等上面。但是重心的位置却大不相同。英语的句子是前重心,也就是将主要的思想、信息放在句首,放在主句里来表达。而汉语则相反,一般为后重心,主要的观点往往放在句末。

这与两种语言组织句子的特点有关。汉语由于它的连词、介词等关系词不够发达,而动词较为丰富,因此汉语是扬长避短,主要依靠动词来组织句子。而用动词来组织句子,动作的顺序就得以时间先后、因果次序来排列:先发生的放在前面,后出现的置于后面;先罗列原因,后推出结果;先分析举例,后下结论;先提出条件,后得出假设;先摆出论据,后表明态度。意思一层一层下去,形成线性排列,重心的位置自然放在句末。

而英语则不同。它有着极其丰富的连词、介词、关系代词以及三大非谓语形式和 16 种时态。也就是说英语中的各类虚词要比汉语多得多。如英语介词有 280 多个,而汉语介词总共才几十个而已。英语的连词不仅数量多,而且使用频率极高。有人对英语冗余度做过调查,发现虚词使用率为 50%,这就是说有 50% 的词可以省去,只剩下动词、名词、形容词,仍不影响信息的传递和理解。如:

There is a great demand on the part of people for the acquisition of foreign languages
o　o　x　x　o　o　x　x　x　o　x　x　o　o　x　o　o　x

实词和虚词正好各占一半。但是英语正是依靠这些不传达任何信息或信息量较小的各类虚词所表示出来的关系 for, of, on the part of 把句子各成分连接起来,表达一个完整的意思。可见英语在写句子时,可以不考虑时间顺序、因果次序,而根据自己的需要,把自己认为最重要的信息如观点、态度、结论、结果放在句首最引人注目的地方来表达。然后运用各类时态,非谓语形式和介词、连词等表示出来的关系,把句子其他信息逐一表达出来。就如一棵大树,把主干这个主要部分让给主要信息,让原因、条件、背景情况等细节落在枝干上,在高低不同层次上得到立体表现。如:

I'm very glad to have received your letter after so many years of isolation.

在上句中先下结论——很高兴,后写原因——收到来信。但这个倒过来的关系和意思通过一个非谓语形式 to have received 和一个连词 after 表达得非常清楚。而汉语只能这样说:经过这么多年的互不通信,现在收到你的信,我感到很高兴。如按汉语这个顺序写英语句子则变成 After so many years of isolation,I have received your letter,so I'm very glad. 这就是汉语式英语。再如上面这篇范文中的一句:

A strong negative attitude towards living together style runs consistently through the mainstream of Chinese thinking which,traditionally and morally,has placed a premium on marriage.

也是先写结论:中国这个社会一贯对同居方式持强烈的反对态度,然后道出原因:因为从传统的道德观来说,我们社会看重婚姻。而这个关系通过关系代词 which 等表示得很清楚。如果用中文表达这个意思,句子则成线性排列:由于我们社会在传统道德上一向看重婚姻,所以对这种同居方式是持强烈反对态度的。原因在前,结论在后。如英语也按这种顺序排列,那么重心也落在后面去了:

Because Chinese society traditionally and morally has placed a premium on marriage,so people always hold a strong negative attitude towards living together pattern.

因此,要写出地道的英语,就要注意到汉语句子信息密度高,而英语句子冗余度高的特点;注意到汉语句子是按时间和因果顺序进行线性排列,重心落到最后,而英语句子却可以运用各类虚词着眼于空间的立体组合,把重心放在句首,不必拘泥于事件发生的时间顺序和因果效率,也不必担心其逻辑关系上的混乱。下面再举一些实例供学习参考。a 句是学生写的原句,b 句是改进后的句子。

(1)a. When I first visited Shanghai,I could not find any trees and flowers in the streets. I was really surprised.

    b. I was really surprised at the absence of any trees and flowers in the street when I first visited Shanghai.

(2)a. As long as the land encroachment continues by the growing number of structures,city greenery will be but a myth,can anyone question that?

    b. Can anyone question that city greenery will be but a myth as long as the land encroachment continues by the growing number of structures?

(3)a. Some shows will have a bad effect on children. But our parents fail to notice it,so they allow children to watch whatever program is on.

    b. Children are allowed to watch whatever program is on,with little thought on parents' part of the bad effect that some shows will have on children.

(4)a. In the summer vacation,I visited several places and met diffeent kinds of people. I can tell you many wonderful stories about them.

    b. There are many wonderful stories to tell about the places I visited and different kinds of people I met during the summer vacation.

(5) a. In this factory,all people from the cadres to the workers are devoted to their work. This has made a deep impression on me.

    b. I was impressed by the passionate dedication to their factory by all people,from the leadership down to all the workers.

(6)a. People in my hometown are friendly and ready to help. I was brought up in this small town,so I feel very proud of it.

    b. I feel very proud to have been brought up in a small town where a great sense of friendliness and voluntary service abound.

(7)a. When we consider the economic and social crises caused by the "Gang of Four",what we have achieved in the past 15 years is especially striking. I think no one can deny that.

    b. No one can deny that what we have achieved in the past 15 years is especially striking in view of the economic and social crises caused by "the Gang of Four".

(8)a. Money and power are what all children are taught to seek when they grow up. But I did not want them,so he was puzzled.

　　b. He was puzzled that I did not want what all children are taught to seek when they grow up:
money and power.

(9)A. As the final exam was drawing nearer I had to stay up much later.

　　b. I was forced to stay up much later by the coming of the final exam.

(10)a. In the city,I will have more opportunities for good education and well-paid jobs,and I can
enjoy more convenient transportation,good health service and various kinds of entertainment. So I prefer to live in the city .

　　b. I prefer to live in the city,because I will have more opportunities for good education and
well-paid job. Besides I can enjoy more convenient transportation,good health service and
various kinds of entertainment.

七、展开段落

(一)如何实现段落的统一性

　　首先,在写作之前对段落的主题思想要十分明确。段落的统一性是指要求段落的所有展开句都
必须紧扣主题思想。所以,如果主题思想不明确,含糊不清,后面段落的展开就没有明确的目标,当然
达不到"统一"。

　　其次,在确定好了明确的主题思想后,每一句话的构建都必须紧扣段落的主题思想,所有引用的
例证都应该支撑主题思想。

Example

Space Research 空间研究

　　People believe that space research has provided many benefits to mankind. They point out that hundreds of useful products,from personal computers to heart pacemakers to freeze-dried foods,are the direct or indirect results of space research. They say that weather and communication satellites,which are also products of space programs,have benefited people all over the world. In addition to these practical benefits,supporters of the space programs point to the scientific knowledge that has been acquired about the sun,the moon,the planets,and even our own earth as a result of space research.

←第一句提出观点:空间研究对人类有很多益处。

←对人类有利的第一个例证。

←对人类有利的第二个例证。

←对人类有利的第三个例证。

　　在这段中,第一句是主题句,接下去的三句展开句都围绕主题思想"has provided many benefits to mankind"展开的,因此没有偏离正题,也就实现了段落的统一性。

(二)连贯性

　　句子写作要求具有连贯性,段落写作也有同样要求。段落的连贯性指段落的每个句子之间应该
环环相扣、过渡自然、前后呼应、合乎逻辑关系。连贯性要求展开句在具体说明、阐述或支持主题句
时,能够合理、流畅、有步骤地展开。显然,要实现连贯性就必须遵循段落展开的一般规律,在紧密围
绕段落的中心意思的前提下,依靠一定的语言手段来完成,尤其要根据需要恰当地使用代词、关键词
语的重复和过渡性的词语或连接词。

Example

How to Protect Your Identity 怎样保护你的身份

　　The first thing you can do to protect your identity is to be careful when you dispose of any financial records, credit card statements(结算单)and offers. Don't just toss them if you no longer need them, buy a shredder and shred the documents thoroughly before you throw them away. Thieves can get your card number from the statements and use it for their own gain. If you receive credit card offers in the mail, make sure you also shred these mailings. Someone could use your pre-approved credit card and have it sent to their address. A good way to stop junk mail like these is to call 1 (888)567－8688, so you do not have to worry about these offers getting into the wrong hands.

←主要依靠代词 you、关键词语的重复和句子之间的逻辑关系来实现上下文的连贯性。

(三)主题句

　　一个段落中的主题句是对这个段落内容的高度概括,它所起的作用是引导读者准确地理解本段落的意思。英语写作与汉语写作不同,这是由思维模式的不同造成的。中国人表达观点的方式往往比较婉转含蓄,不是先抑后扬就是先扬后抑。而英语国家人士往往习惯于直接明了的表达方式。因此英语文章的段落大多以直接阐明主题思想的主题句开始,随后围绕主题思想层层展开。

Example

Malaysia will Import Foreign Barbers.
马来西亚要进口外国理发师

Malaysia is running out of barbers and needs to import foreign workers to keep the population's hair neat and tidy. The President of the Consumers Association of Penany(CAP), S. M. Idris, said at least 30 barber shops in Kuala Lumpur and the northern state of Penang closed last year due to a shortage of barbers. Malaysians are not interested in becoming barbers, forcing shops to turn to foreign labor. The Indians Barbers Association of Malaysia has submitted a request to employ 2,500 foreign barbers. "CAP appeals to the government to deal with this request urgently as the barber shops need to obtain workers quickly. Even a month's delay can result in another few shops closing down," said Idris.

←这句话是主题句,高度概括了全段的中心思想,下面的句子都是阐述和支撑这一主题思想。

　　第一句话是这个段落的主题句,它概括了整段文章的主要意思,即马来西亚的理发师严重短缺,而在此之后的全部句子都在具体而清楚地支持着这个主题句,换句话说,吃透了这个主题句也就掌握了全段的主要意思。

　　下面是由于主题思想不明确而导致段落不具有统一性的例子。

Example

> Joining the World Trade Organization (WTO) will bring us a lot of things. It will benefit ordinary people's life by reducing the prices of goods. It will create many job opportunities for educated people. Some people complain that it will hit the domestic industry and cause many companies to go bankrupt. Anyway China will have a bright future in its economy.

←主题句中心思想不明确，未能提出一个非常明确的观点。

←展开部分不符合逻辑，论述不统一。

　　首先是概括主题思想的主题句含糊不清，"bring us a lot of things"范围太大，不合适作为一个段落的主题句，也就导致下面的叙述模糊不清，一会儿说"利处"，一会儿讲"害处"，一会儿讲"ordinary people's life"，一会儿讲"domestic industry"，使得段落不具有统一性。

　　主题句是一个段落的核心，它揭示了段落的中心思想或主要内容。没有了主题句，段落就没有了主心骨，段落意义也就含糊不清了。段内其他所有的句子都围绕主题句来展开，通过它们来说明段落的中心思想。

　　首先，主题句必须是一个完整的句子。

　　其次，它只是一个段落的主题句，因此只能把它放在一个段落的背景下考虑。所以，主题句只能致力于一个单一的主题思想，且范围不应过宽也不应过于具体。例如：

　　China's entry into the World Trade Organization (WTO) will benefit Chinese people's daily life.

　　如果将这个主题句改为"China's entry into the WTO will benefit Chinese people's daily life and help many companies surmount difficulties"就不好了，因为如果这样，该主题句致力于两个主题思想，即 daily life 和 many companies，就很难使段落具有凝聚力，或者说根本不是一个主题句能概括的，甚至可以将 help many companies surmount difficulties 演变成一篇文章。再看以下两个主题句(1)China will join the WTO. (2)China and its trading partners have reached an agreement on the country's membership in the WTO. 其中，主题句(1)所涉及的范围太宽，没有把主题思想放在一个点上，靠一个段落是很难把主题句阐述清楚的，而主题句(2)范围过窄，限制了后面句子的展开，没有展开段落的足够的空间和余地。

　　总之，主题句要具体、明确、中肯、扼要并且范围合适、选词适当，这样才能恰如其分地构建段落。以下的句子均属于比较好的主题句：

　　1)Interest is a key factor to success.

　　2)Video games are a kind of wonderful entertainment.

　　3)Automobiles are playing a vital part in the daily activities of human society.

　　4)Being a teacher is the dream of my childhood.

　　5)Advertisement plays an informative role in people's daily life.

(四)支撑句

　　要写好一个段落，仅仅一个主题句是不够的，必须依靠更多的支撑句来帮助展开段落，表达段落的中心意思。换句话说，段落中不应该有任何与本段的主题句和主题思想无关的句子或短语，所有的句子和短语都应该有利于支撑这个主题成立。

　　写作支撑句实际上就是在紧紧围绕段落的主题思想，与主题句的展开方向完全一致的前提下以适当的方法来展开段落。展开段落的方法有以下几种：

　　1)按时空顺序展开；

　　2)按步骤顺序展开；

　　3)用比较和对比方式展开；

　　4)用例证和概括方式展开；

5)用因果关系展开;

6)用分类方式展开;

7)用定义方式展开。

对于不同的主题句,可以选择上述不同的方式来展开,例如:

1)When still at his high school, he began to show his outstanding talents in organizing activities. (用例证和概括的方式展开)

2)Compared with motorcycle, electric bicycle has more advantages than disadvantages. (用比较和对比方式展开)

3)Our teacher of IELTS writing is a responsible teacher. (用例证和概括方式展开)

4)In a certain sense, writing is a more important means of communication especially in the business case. (先分析,再用因果关系展开)

5)Interviewees have many different ways to ask about salary. (用分类方式展开)

6)Sociologists have reached a most specialist explanation of culture. (用定义方式展开)

7)After I graduated from my senior high school, I dramatically entered Cambridge, which was totally out of my expectation. (用例证和概括的方式展开)

8)According to management experts, a business must do two things to be successful. (按步骤、顺序展开)

Example

Advantages of Riding Bicycles 骑自行车的好处

Compared with cars, bicycles have many advantages. First, they are not very expensive and almost every family can afford to buy and repair them. Second, though they run more slowly than cars, bicycles are very handy and convenient. With a bicycle, you can go wherever you like and needn't look for a large parking place in a crowded downtown area or get a garage at home. Third, bicycles don't cause air pollution. On the contrary, they do good to your health. In addition, it's much easier to learn to ride a bicycle than or drive a car.

←直截了当点明主题。

←有步骤地展开论述、证明主题。

←例证充分,支撑句起到了支撑主题句的作用。

此例在第一句主题句"与汽车相比,自行车具有许多优点"的统领下,分为四个方面围绕主题思想进行具体说明。本例的主题思想范围很明确,即"与汽车相比自行车具有的优点",这就给后面的展开句指明了很清晰的写作方向。任何不属于此范围内的论据,如文章中的"Bicycle—riding, of course, is much faster than walking"(与步行相比,骑自行车有速度上的优势)就没有必要了。

展开段落的步骤

首先,不妨可以用中文简要地考虑一下这个段落的主题思想是什么,然后用英文写出这句话,这就已经是一个主题句了。

然后,判断一下这句话是表达了一种观点还是对事实或现象的总结和概括。要注意的是观点可能会有不同甚至完全相反的看法,如果是对事实或现象的总结则是不可以推翻的。例如:

After I got home, I found the walk-man did not work at all. (事实)

The speech contest has been very popular among the university students. (观点)

The beach party was a disaster. (事实)

IELTS can better reflect the candidates' ability of applying English language. (观点)

最后，如果是一个观点，展开时就要对观点进行分析或者说明，列举出几个原因，并且举例说明。如果是对事实或现象的总结，展开时要从各种不同角度给出更多的事实或现象加以说明。

（五）结束句

段落还需要结束句，这样才能给读者一个暗示，即本段落即将结束，同时还能使得段落比较完整。但是，考生在写作训练中要注意不要过度强调结束句的语气和效果，否则会影响它与主题句的关系，结束句应该顺理成章、自然而成。

八、妙用标点符号

考研英语作文主要从内容和语言两大方面评分。由于考研作文采用的是总体评分法（Global Scoring），作文评卷老师主要凭借总体印象打分，而中国的老师评卷时往往看重的是语言。因此语言的好坏直接影响到实际作文分数的高低。鉴于不少考生作文语言生硬平淡、单调乏味、缺少变化，本文将结合 2003 年考研作文"温室的花朵经不起风雨"，从标点符号这一常被大家忽略的方面破解考研高分作文的机密。希望通过本文的分析能对广大考生写作时提高语言表达有所裨益。

"逗号六剑法"的合理使用

所谓逗号六剑法，指的就是分句之间的衔接与连贯问题。句式的复杂多变要求一篇作文中既要有简单句、并列句，又要有复合句甚至复杂复合句。要构造句子结构的复杂多变就必须讲究分句之间的衔接与连贯问题。逗号六剑法实质就是逗号后（前）分句间衔接与连贯的六种技巧。为形象起见，美其名曰"逗号六剑法"。

第一剑法：非限制性定语从句的使用

（1）Nowadays, the call for quality-oriented education is becoming widespread and the drawbacks of test-oriented education, which have aroused great concern throughout China, are becoming increasingly apparent.

（2）The sharp contrast hinges on the protection of the greenhouse, which determines in a large measure the life and death of the lovely flower.

（3）This trend began during the Second World War, when several governments came to the conclusion that the specific demands that a government wants to make of its scientific establishment cannot generally be foreseen in detail.

逗号前后是我们写作时构造复杂多变、精彩生动句子结构的突破口。上述三例中我们合理巧妙地运用了非限制性定语从句，使前后两个分句有机地连接起来，显得连贯、自然。例 1 用关系代词 which（非限制性定语从句不能用 that）代替逗号前整个分句的意思。这样就把原本要用两个句子来表达的信息通过定语从句压缩为一个主从复合句，显得简洁、不啰嗦。例 2 用关系代词 which 代替逗号前先行词 the green house，通过非限制性定语从句进一步说明温室对于鲜花存活的重要性。例 3 中逗号前先行词是表时间，因此用关系代词 when 引导非限制性定语从句，将主要信息移置逗号之后，取得"尾重"或"末尾聚焦（end-weight）"的效果，其实考生们对于非限制性定语从句的用法不可谓不熟，但可能就是缺乏用多种手段衔接分句的意识。

第二剑法：非谓语动词做状语的使用

（1）By contrast, when removed from the greenhouse, the protective umbrella, it struggles helplessly against the sudden attack of storms, only to wither away.

（2）Parents are too eager to mold their kids, disregarding their individuality with a callous attitude toward their personal development.

（3）School-age children are often seen carrying bulging bags on their backs, weighed down on their way to and from school every day.

非谓语动词有四种表现形式，即动词不定式、现在分词、过去分词和动名词。利用这几种非谓语动词形式（动名词不能做状语除外）做状语，能很好地突出信息，取得信息"末尾聚焦（end-weight）"的效果。例 1 用 only 加动词不定式表示出乎意料的结果，做结果状语。从而将备受溺爱的孩子们不堪一击的惨状和盘托出。例 2 用现在分词做结果状语，表示一种必然的发展趋势，即结果在意料之中。

例3用过去分词做伴随状语,将饱受应试教育摧残的学龄儿童那苦不堪言的情形栩栩如生地勾了出来,辛辣的嘲讽宛然可见。当然这几种非谓语动词形式也可放在逗号前面一分句或句子中间,如:

(4)Weighing both these arguments, I can come to the conclusion that there is no need to take so drastic a step as doing away with this custom. (现在分词做时间状语)

(5)An old peasant, bringing his own food, volunteered as a guide for us. (现在分词做伴随状语)

非谓语动词做状语到底放在前还是后似乎没有绝对的要求。但一般来说,做伴随状语时可前可后;做时间状语时放在前面较多,间或放在后面;做时间状语时一般放在句子前部;做结果状语时一般放在后半分句;做条件状语时一般放在前面分句等等。

第三剑法:同位语或插入语的使用

(1)As is distinct from above, the number "13", a long-held symbol of ominousness in the eyes of most westerners, seems to be plaguing them.

(2)By contrast, when removed from the greenhouse, the protective umbrella, it struggles helplessly against the sudden attack of storms, only to wither away.

(3)Specifically, the number "6", as they strongly believe, is closely associated with smoothness in the Chinese culture.

同位语或插入语一般插在主谓语之间,一般由名词词组(如例1、2)、介词词组(如 in my opinion, in other words 等)、从句(如例3)、不定式短语、现在分词短语充当。它们能起到补充说明的作用。除此之外,插入语还可对整句话表示解释,如:

(4)There were twenty people present, to be precise. (不定式短语做插入语)

(5)Roughly speaking, these countries are the most densely-populated in Asia. (现在分词短语做插入语)

第四剑法:with 结构的使用

(1)We now live in a society where competition on the job market rages, with graduates and jobhunters from all walks of life scrambling for desirable jobs.

(2)As described in the picture, an American girl is wearing a Chinese costume characteristic of some minority group, with a sweet smile on her face.

(3)These children can set their hearts at ease, with everything well-arranged by their parents.

(4)With education on all sides being enforced, our young college students will grow up to be qualified not only in their fields but, more importantly, in moral cultivation.

(5)He entered upon the new enterprise cautiously, with his eyes wide open.

with 结构总的说来有五种形式,即:with+名(代)词+现在分词(如例1、4),with +名(代)词+过去分词(如例3),with +名(代)词+介词短语(如例2),with +名(代)词+副词或形容词(如例5),with+名(代)词+不定式。with 结构可表原因(如例1、3)、伴随或方式(如例2、5)、条件(如例4)等。

第五剑法:独立主格结构的使用

(1)Rosy dreams shattered, they are bewildering at the junction:"To be or not to be? That is the question"-Hamlet's perplexed monologue is echoing in their ears.

(2)"Just listen to this," she will say, her eyes glowing, her warm fingers pressed to my palm to hold my attention.

(3)The U. S. population expanding dramatically, the species of its wildlife has witnessed a corresponding decline in a span of two centuries (1800-2000).

(4)He went off, gun in hand.

(5)The floor was wet and slippery, so we stayed outside.

(6)The meal over, prayers were read by Miss Miller.

两个或两个以上分句间如果主语不一致时要用独立主格结构。所谓"独立主格结构"实质就是带自己主语的非限定分句和无动词分句。它按结构形式分为不定式"独立结构"、-ing 分词"独立结构"(如例2、3)、-ed 分词"独立结构"(如例1、2)和无动词"独立结构",即名(代)词+介词短语(如例4)、名

（代）词＋副词（如例6）或形容词（如例5）。

第六剑法：形容词做状语的使用

（1）Disillusioned and disheartened, they are most likely to collapse under the weight of life.

（2）Living in the warm nest, safe and sound, they are utterly free from external hardships and ignorant of what the bare reality is like.

（3）They swarm into the job market, curious and excited.

形容词常可单独或构成短语做状语，可用来表示原因（如例1）、方式（如例2、3）等。形容词状语位置比较灵活，可前可后或插在句中。

其他标点符号的独特运用

笔者从批改的大量的学生作文中发现，绝大多数学生在作文中只会一味地使用逗号、句号、问号和感叹号。且不说他们对这些标点符号的运用是否都准确到位，单就满篇文章四个标点符号密匝匝地堆砌，就可断定他们很可能压根儿不知道在适当地方可运用其他标点符号，诸如冒号（：）、破折号（——）、分号（；）等；或者不大了解他们自己常用的符号的特殊用法，如引号（""）、逗号（，）等的特殊用法。实践证明：标点符号的灵活运用不但能美化版面，增强视觉美感，而且更重要的是它们能节约笔墨，有时能收到"不着一字，尽得风流"的独特效果。为说明起见，现举例分述如下：

冒号

譬如，冒号主要用在列举的事物前面，将笼统信息具体化：

I believe that the most important forces behind the massive M&A wave are the same that underline the globalization process: falling transportation and communication costs, lower trade and investment barriers and enlarged markets that require enlarged operations capable of meeting customers' demands.

冒号还有解释提示下文的功能，用在附加的解释性的分句前面：

No clear-cut distinction can be drawn between professionals and amateurs in science: exception can be found to any rule.

分号

连接两个意思相关或等立的句子。

There is no denying that automobiles are indications of civilization, progress and development; nevertheless, automobiles cause the serious problem of air pollution.

破折号

有解释说明、归纳总结及穿插背景等作用。

（1）Rosy dreams shattered, they are bewildering at the junction: "To be or not to be? That is the question"——Hamlet's perplexed monologue is echoing in their ears. （破折号解释说明）

（2）In contrast, living near the countryside one can enjoy the clean atmosphere, the closeness to nature and the quiet, peaceful surroundings——the essentials of a healthy life. （破折号归纳总结）

（3）For example, in the early industrialized countries of Europe the process of industrialization——with all the far-reaching changes in social patterns that followed——was spread over nearly a century, whereas nowadays a developing nation may undergo the same process in a decade or so. （破折号穿插背景）

引号

除了表示引用外还可表示强调、讽刺意味。

（1）Historians, especially those so blinded by their research interests that they have been accused of "tunnel vision," （引号表示引用）frequently fall victim to the "technicist fallacy." （引号表示强调）

（2）If this approach were adopted, children would be strong enough to withstand any "storm" in their life. （引号表示强调，一语双关）

诚然，考生在真正应考时时间紧迫，心理压力巨大，不可能有过多的时间和精力去仔细揣摩每一字句，推敲每一字句的标点符号。况且，语言表达的技巧又五花八门，其变化多样远非本文所能穷尽。但是，正所谓"台上一分钟，台下十年功"，若在平时的写作训练中就着意训练，那必将大有裨益。长此以往，则考研作文高分不再遥远！

第六章　考研英语写作题型篇

第一节　提纲式作文（正反阐释题）

一、写作方法

正反阐释题型的写作往往使用比较与对比的方法。比较与对比是一种主要来说明相同点（likeness）和不同点（difference）的扩展方法。比较的目的是指出不同的人物、地点和事物在某些方面的相同之处，而对比的目的在于写出通常认为相似的人物、地点或事物在某些方面的不同之处。当比较事物的类似或相同点时用 comparison（有时这种写法同时意味着 comparison 和 contrast 两种含义）；对比事物间的不同、甚至相反之处时则采用 contrast。一般说来，比较、对比必须在同一类型事物之间进行。

在具体写作方法上，它们都可以采用不同的表达方式：

一种是：从总体上比较 A 和 B 两方面，可分别在不同的段落中讨论，也可以在同一段落中分两大部分进行，先把 A 讨论完，再讨论 B 的全部内容，如 A1，A2，A3，……B1，B2，B3……。

另一种是：通过取出对比双方要点中的每一项逐项对比，如：A1，B1，A2，B2，A3，B3……。

下面先分析一篇用第一种方法进行对比的文章。

（1）分项对比

The Difference between Living on and off Campus 住在校内和校外的区别

On campus living arrangements are quite different from off campus ones. In a dorm, the supervision is usually greater; it is more an extension of the watchfulness of parents, with other people noticing your comings and goings, establishing fixed eating times, sometimes restricting guests. Living on campus also means sharing with many other students, not only a room but also meals, showers, telephones, and soap operas. Privacy and dorm living are mutually exclusive, but loneliness is unlikely. Off campus housing, on the other hand, allows much more personal freedom. Whether or not you go out or come home is up to you. Eating or starving is up to you. Privacy is a constant option, but also the enforced privacy of loneliness is more possible. Off campus, you really notice when there's nothing to do.

这个段落开头先给出了主题句，然后在前半段写出了住在校内的情况，接着用 on the other hand 引出了与之相对比的住在校外的利弊。通过比较，两种住宿方式的利弊一目了然。

（2）逐项对比

Differences between European Football and American Football
欧洲足球与美洲足球的差异

Although European football is the parent of American football, the two games show several differences. European football, some times called association football or soccer, is played in 80 countries, making it the most widely played sport in the world. American football, on the other hand, is popular only in north America. Soccer is played by eleven players with a round ball. Football, also played by eleven players in somewhat different positions on the field, is played with an elongated round ball. Soccer has little body contact between players and therefore requires no special protective equipment. Football, in which players make maximum use of body contact to block a running ball carrier and his teammates, requires special headgear and padding. In soccer, the ball is advanced toward the goal by kicking it or by putting it with the head. In football, on the other hand, the ball is passed from hand to hand or carried in the hands across the opponent's goal. These are just a few of the features which distinguish association and American football.

在这一段文字里,作者用逐项对比的方法,讨论了 European Football 和 American Football 的异同,分析了无论是在踢球的国家,球队的组成及球的形状,踢球的一些规则要求上都分别说明了各自的特点,使人感到条理分明,内容清晰。

但通常比较和对比是分不开的,有时在同一篇文章中或同一个段落里可根据情况同时运用 comparison 和 contrast 两种扩展方式。

Where Americans pride themselves on a studied informality and openness, their Japanese counterparts employ formality and complexity. If Americans value time, the Japanese treasure space. While Americans have always enjoyed a sense of continental scale, Japan has developed its genius on the small. It seems appropriate for America to produce the world's airplanes, while Japan creates cameras and transistors.

But both, for example, have transplanted cultures. Each nation has a "mother" society-China and Great Britain that has influenced the daughter in countless ways: in language, religion, social organization, art, literature, and national ideals. Both societies, moreover, have developed the brokerage art, the business of buying and selling, of advertising and mass producing, to unprecedented levels.

上面第一段为对比型段落,强调两国的不同之处,如美国人不拘小节、开放;日本人意于礼节和繁复。美国人看重时间;日本人珍视空间等等。

第二段为比较型段落,强调两国相同之外,两者都有一个"母"文化——中国和大不列颠,它们的语言、宗教等方面都对"女儿"有数不清的影响。两国都发展了经纪业、商业、广告和批量生产。

在进行比较的时候,可以从某一方面逐一比较,如上例;也可以将某一对象的所有可比内容全部列出,再把另一对象的所有可比内容全部列出,形成整体比较。

对比分析时,必须在可比的方面展开,任何不相关或任何一方不存在的内容都不能纳入对比的范围。对比分析的具体方法与比较法相同。

二、常用的比较对照句型

(一)两者比较(注:"A"和"B"分别代表进行比较的两个事物)

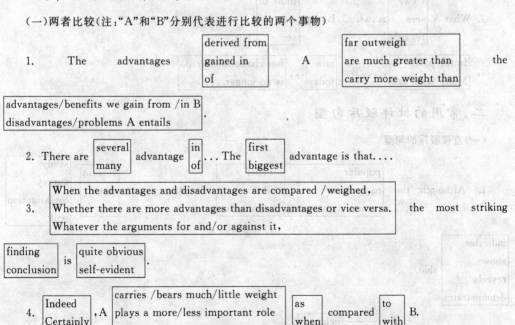

（二）两者相同句型

1. A $\left|\begin{array}{l}\text{is}\\\text{does}\end{array}\right|$ $\left|\begin{array}{l}\text{no less}\ldots\text{than}\\\text{as much}\ldots\text{as}\\\text{to}\ldots\text{as/what}\end{array}\right|$ B $\left|\begin{array}{l}\text{is}\\\text{does}\end{array}\right|$.

2. The same (thing) $\left|\begin{array}{l}\text{is true of}\\\text{goes for /with}\\\text{happens to}\\\text{applies to}\end{array}\right|$ B.

3. A is as $\left|\begin{array}{l}\text{much}\\\text{well}\\\text{good}\end{array}\right|$ as B.

4. A bears $\left|\begin{array}{l}\text{some}\\\text{many}\\\text{little}\end{array}\right|$ $\left|\begin{array}{l}\text{close}\\\text{striking}\\\text{startling}\end{array}\right|$ resemblance(s) to B.

There is/are little/some resemblance (s) between A and B.

5. A. . . . $\left|\begin{array}{l}\text{So}\\\text{Nor}\end{array}\right|$ $\left|\begin{array}{l}\text{is}\\\text{are}\\\text{can}\end{array}\right|$ B.

（三）两者不同句型

1. While on the one hand. . . , on the other hand. . .

2. $\left|\begin{array}{l}\text{A and B differ/are different in several ways.}\\\text{There are some basic/marked differences between A and B.}\end{array}\right|$ Unlike B, A. . . .

3. What A $\left|\begin{array}{l}\text{views}\\\text{sees}\\\text{regards}\end{array}\right|$ . . . as. . . , B may $\left|\begin{array}{l}\text{think of}\\\text{view}\\\text{see}\end{array}\right|$ . . . as. . . .

4. $\left|\begin{array}{l}\text{In the past}\\\text{Many years ago}\end{array}\right|$, ... But $\left|\begin{array}{l}\text{now}\\\text{today}\end{array}\right|$ . . . $\left|\begin{array}{l}\text{has changed/altered.}\\\text{is no longer.\ .\ .\ .}\end{array}\right|$

二、常用的批评驳斥句型

（一）直接驳斥的句型

1. Although the $\left|\begin{array}{l}\text{popular}\\\text{nationwide}\\\text{commonly-accepted}\end{array}\right|$ $\left|\begin{array}{l}\text{belief}\\\text{idea}\\\text{assumption}\end{array}\right|$ is that. . . , a $\left|\begin{array}{l}\text{current}\\\text{recent}\\\text{new}\end{array}\right|$ $\left|\begin{array}{l}\text{study}\\\text{survey}\\\text{investigation}\\\text{poll}\end{array}\right|$

$\left|\begin{array}{l}\text{indicates}\\\text{shows}\\\text{reveals}\\\text{demonstrates}\end{array}\right|$ that. . . .

2. Although it is $\left|\begin{array}{l}\text{widely}\\\text{commonly}\\\text{generally}\end{array}\right|$ $\left|\begin{array}{l}\text{held}\\\text{felt}\\\text{agreed}\\\text{accepted}\end{array}\right|$ that. . . , it is unlikely to be true that. . .

3. Most of us / The majority of people | have been | taken in by the notion/idea / under the illusion | that.... There is no such thing as the right / good ...for....

4. They may be | right / correct | in / about | saying/asserting the idea/belief | that..., but they seem to | fail / neglect | to mention / take note of / take into account | the fact that....

5) It is | perhaps / probably / maybe / very | true that..., but one | vital / critical / essential | point / fact | is being left out of our | thinking / consciousness / analysis / consideration.

（二）批评分析句型

1. To | claim / assume / suggest / say | that... is | to miss the point / wide of the mark / far from being proved / a gross exaggeration / the most obvious kind of nonsense |.

2. Such | suggestions / proposals / ideas / practice | are / is | actually a(n) | assault on / perversion of | the | right / system / value / spirit | of..., and | they / it | deserve(s) to be | rejected / thrown away | outright.

3. It makes no sense to | argue for / be in favor of | ...,but | object / opposed | to....

4. The | obvious / serious / fatal | flaw / drawback / defect | in the | idea / remark / view | is that it | fails to take... into consideration / happens to leave... out of account.

5. In many cases, / On some occasions, | public / general | dissatisfaction with / disillusionment with / criticism of | ... is unfair, for there is much we just take for granted.

真题再现

1992 年研究生英语入学考试作文

Ⅴ. Writing（15 points）

WHERE TO LIVE IN—THE CITY OR THE COUNTRY?

Directions：

A Title：WHERE TO LIVE IN—THE CITY OR THE COUNTRY?

B. Time limit：40 minutes

C. Word limit: 120 to 150 words (not including the given opening sentence)

D. Your composition should be based on the OUTLINE below and should start with the given opening sentence.

E. Your composition must be written clearly in the ANSWER SHEET.

OUTLINE:

1. Conveniences of the city

2. Attractions of the country

3. Disadvantages of both

4. My preference

Opening Sentence:

Many people appreciate the conveniences of the city.

破题

从这篇作文题目及其要求可以看出这是一篇提纲（outline）式控制性作文,同时又给出了第一段的起始句（opening sentence）,这就要求应试者紧扣题目,严格按照已给出的 outline 和 opening sentence 所限定的思路,通过扩展、充实、润色,写成一篇表达清晰、意思连贯、语言优美的短文。所给出的 outline 告诉我们,这是一篇对比型（又称"匹配比较型"）的论说文,应试者首先要客观地阐述城市与乡村生活的优点与不足,再说明自己偏爱的生活并陈述其理由。

文章结构看似简单,但有一点应试者必须保持清醒,并且自始至终地体现在作文里,这就是:前三段的"说长道短"必须尽量保持客观、公正,至少让人觉得是这样,同时还得与第四段的 my preference 保持内容与逻辑上的一致,从而巧妙地让阅卷人点头称是。这才是这篇短文能得高分的关键。当然。在整个行文过程中,还要注意全文的篇章布局与遣词造句。

就我个人而言,我现在生活在城市里,曾受过现代高等教育,城市的文明使我眼界大开。但我毕竟出生在乡村,对乡村有一种永恒的眷恋,所以一看到这个题目我马上确定了 my preference——I like country life better。但我知道,要写成一篇令人信服而且能得高分的应试作文,并非易事。对此,我必须精心安排,巧妙设计,让阅卷人"上当受骗"而不自知。

范文赏析

Where to Live—In the City or the Country 住在哪——城里还是乡下?

Many people appreciate the conveniences of the city. The city has better transportation service and health care. City dwellers can easily enjoy themselves in restaurants, department stores and concert halls. They are well-informed about what is going on at home and abroad, and have the access to better education, better jobs and more opportunities for business.

But country life is also attractive. With the fresh air, the green trees and the singing birds, country people are close to nature and live a quiet life. They can make friends with simple and honest men or wander about leisurely without any pressure upon their mind.

Both the country and the city, however, have their own disadvantages. In the country, educational facilities, medical services and transportation systems are still not fully developed. And the city also has many problems, such as heavy traffic, air pollution, great noise and poor housing conditions.

As far as I am concerned, I hate the terrible dirt and noise in the city. So, given the chance, I would prefer to live peacefully in the country.

范文解析

第一段:根据提纲要求,本段要说明城市生活的方便之处。这样就需要根据自己平时的感受激发联想,选取最有代表性的采样,对论点提供支持。比如交通便利、购物方便、娱乐场所多、卫生与受教育条件好、就业与投资机会多等等，便是这一段所要阐述的内容。

提纲如下：

TS：Many people appreciate the conveniences of the city.

A. Better transportation service

B. More restaurants, department stores and concert halls

C. Well-informed

D. More opportunities for better education, better jobs and business

E. Perfect health care

第二段：本段要论述"农村生活的诱人之处"，这对于我来说可是太熟悉了。湛蓝的天空、碧绿的禾苗、甘甜的井水、欢快的小鸟、冉冉的炊烟、郁郁的树林，还有永远飘荡在空中的乳汁般的泥土的芬芳气息……每当想到这些，我就激动不已。但我还是得静下心来，有条不紊、恰如其分地"慢慢道来"。农村生活的迷人之处总的来说主要有三点：一是贴近自然，鸟语花香，有利于健康；二是民风淳朴，没有太多的欺诈行为；三是生活悠闲，自由自在，没有太大的压力。考虑到 my preference，在这一段中我必须写出"小桥、流水、人家"的宁静与恬美和"采菊东篱下，悠然见南山"的和谐与欢快，从而让评卷人点头称是。

TS：Others are attracted by the country.

A. Close to nature

B. Simple and honest men

C. Without any pressure

第三段：城乡生活各自的不足之处。

无论生活在乡村还是城市，都有许多让人苦恼的地方。城市交通非常发达，可是一旦堵起车来，你也只好望"路"兴叹。城市汇集了现代文明，但其"副产品"也不容忽视，像噪声、大气污染、住房拥挤等等；而农村地区教育、医疗、交通的不发达，也着实叫人头疼。如果把这些内容有机地组织起来，并让阅卷人产生"乡村是有些落后，但城市生活中的某些方面更令人难以容忍"的共鸣，从而为下一段作好铺垫，这一段就算写成功了。

TS：Both the city and the country have their own disadvantages.

A. Heavy traffic, air pollution, great noise, poor housing conditions in the city

B. Underdeveloped education, medical care, and transportation system in the country

第二节　提纲式作文（阐释原因、方法、危害题）

一、写作方法

因果法是指人们在思维活动中，常常会根据某事物的原因推导其结果，或根据某种结果分析其原因。写作中的因果法就是这种思维方式的体现。由于这类文章的目的在于解释事物的原因与结果之间的关系，所以我们在写作中要特别注意使文章合乎逻辑和常理。通常，因果法有以下两种模式。

1. 原因在前，结果在后

It is difficult for workers to find employment this year. As a result, many recent college graduates are unemployed or are taking part-time jobs to meet expenses. Unemployment among high school graduates has meant that large numbers of teenagers are seeking unemployment benefits. The unemployment figures are the highest in decades. Finally, the Federal government must contribute large amounts of money to support the growing numbers of people who are receiving welfare assistance.

在段首指出"今年工人找工作难"，接着说明找工作难导致的一系列结果。

2. 结果在前，原因在后

There are many reasons why languages change. To start with, various languages that start from the same parent developed their own uniqueness after speakers drifted away from one another to establish isolated, independent communities. Language change is also due to the influence of and interactions with foreign cultures, often as a result of military conquest. Another cause for language change is rapidly expanding technology and new systems of communication. They bring all cultures and languages into closer contact and borrowing between languages has become a common phenomenon in the contemporary world. All languages change as the experiences of their speakers change.

在该段主题句中,作者首先说到"languages change"这个结果是由很多原因造成的。接着,作者列举了三点原因,该段是按"结果——原因"的顺序发展起来的。

因果关系较为复杂,往往是某一个现象是另一个现象的结果,而同时又是三个现象的原因,这就是链式反应,如 A→B→C,其中 B 是 A 的结果,又是 C 的原因,如:

As the price of everything from toothpaste to tuition increases, workers demand higher wages to keep up with rising costs. This can produce further increases in prices or a decreased demand for manufactured goods, or both. Since production tries to keep pace with demand, decreased demand is followed by decreased production. This, in turn, can lead to lay-offs and unemployment, which further decrease the demand for goods.

在段落写作中,可以给出原因引出结果,也可以先陈述结果再说明原因,这要视实际需要而定。还有一些段落可以只集中说明原因,因为结果是显而易见的。而另外一些段落则只涉及结果,因其原因不言自明。对简单的因果关系,一个原因对应一个结果即可。但实际写作中,许多主题往往一个结果需几个原因来解释,而有时一个原因又会产生许多结果。对这点考生常常忽视,只满足于给出一种解释,所以写出的短文有时缺乏足够的分析,显得空乏无力。

二、常用的原因结果题型

1. 基本原因句型

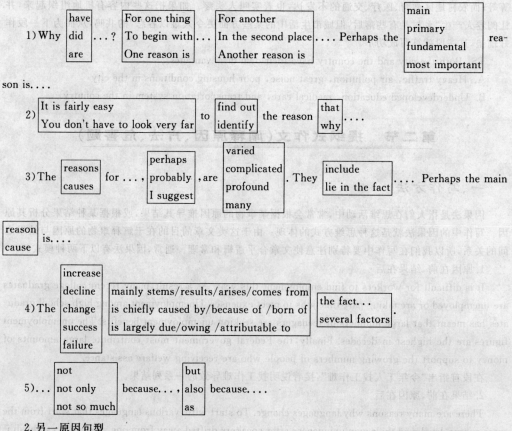

2. 另一原因句型

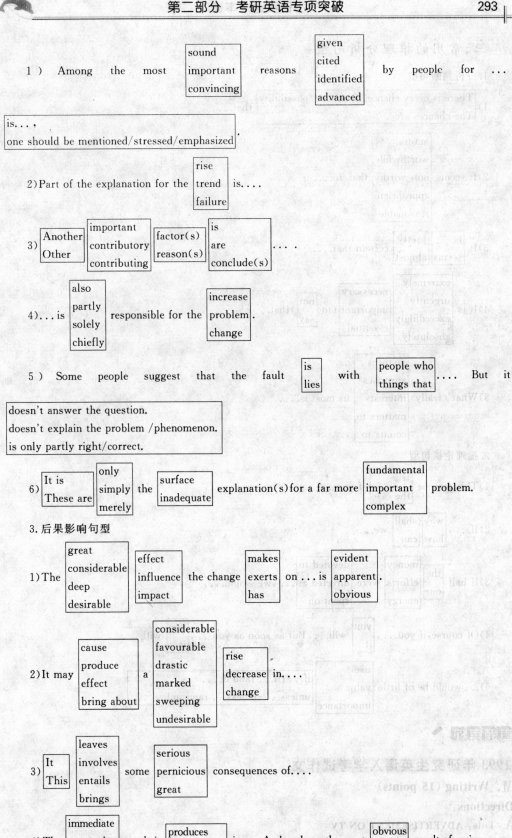

1) Among the most [sound / important / convincing] reasons [given / cited / identified / advanced] by people for ...

is... , [one should be mentioned/stressed/emphasized].

2) Part of the explanation for the [rise / trend / failure] is... .

3) [Another / Other] [important / contributory / contributing] [factor(s) / reason(s)] [is / are / conclude(s)] ... .

4)... is [also / partly / solely / chiefly] responsible for the [increase / problem. / change].

5) Some people suggest that the fault [is / lies] with [people who / things that] ... . But it

[doesn't answer the question. / doesn't explain the problem /phenomenon. / is only partly right/correct.]

6) [It is / These are] [only / simply / merely] the [surface / inadequate] explanation(s)for a far more [fundamental / important / complex] problem.

3. 后果影响句型

1) The [great / considerable / deep / desirable] [effect / influence / impact] the change [makes / exerts / has] on ... is [evident / apparent. / obvious]

2) It may [cause / produce / effect / bring about] a [considerable / favourable / drastic / marked / sweeping / undesirable] [rise / decrease / change] in... .

3) [It / This] [leaves / involves / entails / brings] some [serious / pernicious / great] consequences of... .

4) The [immediate / eventual / consequent] result it [produces / brings about] is... . And perhaps the most [obvious / direct] result of... is... .

三、常用的推理分析句型

1. 分析判断句型

1)
| There is every chance/likelihood/possibility | that.... |
| The chances are | |

2) It seems
| natural |
| worthwhile |
| noteworthy | that/to.... |
| appropriate |
| reasonable |

3) It
| is | pretty |
| seems | almost | certain that....

4) It is
extremely	necessary	
urgently	important	(to not say) that....
exceedingly	essential	
absolutely		

5) What (really)
| disturbs |
| surprises |
| interests | us most is.... |
| matters to |
| counts to |

2. 推理论谈句型

1) This may be
| true |
| the case | if you....

2) If...,
| why | shall |
| how | can | we...?

3) If half
the	money		devoted to
our	efforts	were	directed at ...,we would....
	energy		spent on

4) Of course, if you..., | you / it | will.... But as soon as you..., | you / it | will....

5) ... would be of little
| use |
| value | if...; if...; and if.... |
| importance | unless...; unless...; and unless.... |

真题再现 ▷

1993 年研究生英语入学考试作文

Ⅵ. **Writing（15 points）**

Directions：

A. Title：**ADVERTISEMENT ON TV**

B. Time limit：40 minutes

C. Word limit：120—150 words（not including the given opening sentence）

D. Your composition should be based at the OUTLINE below and should start with the given opening sentence："Today more and more advertisements are seen on the TV screen."

E. Your composition must be written clearly on the ANSWER SHEET.

OUTLINE：

    1. Present state

    2. Reasons

    3. My comments

破题

    本试题的题目本身定得很大,因此主要是要看提示中已经给出的开首句。让我们先来分析一下开首句：虽然从题目看起来,可能也可以写成对电视上的广告做一个描写,但从开首句来看,并不是要具体描写电视上的广告,只是要说明电视上的广告越来越多这个社会现象,并分析其原因。所以切忌将此开首句理解成侧重点在电视上,介绍因为电视事业的发展而使广告越来越多。相反的,这只是其中造成广告越来越多出现在电视上的一个原因。论点句还是开首句本身。写作文的时候,一定要首先搞清楚因果关系,论点与论据的关系,千万不要颠倒了。根据 outline 来看,这三点应该是个层层递进的关系,只有先说明前一点,才能进行到下一点。

Introduction：越来越多的广告出现在电视这种媒体上。介绍一下广告如何比以前要多,为何使人感觉比以前要多。在这一段可以表明一下考生自己的立场。虽然提示最后一点才进行到评论阶段,但是如果在一开始就没有一个准备,则中间正文的行文就有可能会观点不统一,造成文章散乱,最后一段就不好统一论点了。

Body：阐述为什么广告会越来越多地出现在电视上的原因。可以从广告业本身谋求发展和电视作为媒体传播文化有其特点和影响两个方面来讲。

Conclusion：考生得对这一现象做出评价。

范文赏析

Advertisement on TV 电视广告

    Today more and more advertisements are seen on the TV screen. Every evening a series of advertisements come immediately after the News Program is over, informing TV viewers of many different sorts of up-to-date products on the market. Besides, it often appears that while you are absorbed in a wonderful film on TV, endless ads interrupt you from time to time and make you quite annoyed.

    There are two reasons, I think, for the growing number of ads on TV. First, in a competitive economy, the consumer usually has the choice of several different brands of the same product. Thus, manufacturers are confronted with a problem as to how to keep sales high enough to stay in business. They solve this problem by advertising. Through advertising, each manufacturing company tries to convince consumers that its product is special and unique. Second, most consumers are interested in ads. They wish to get from TV ads first-hand information about new products, which enables them to choose what they like best. As a result, there is a sharp increase in ads on the TV screen.

    Personally, I am in favor of TV ads because most of them are interesting and informative. But there is no denying the fact that some of them are tedious and boring. Thus, I feel TV stations are faced with an arduous task to keep tight control of ads, to improve their quality and to make them more attractive.

范文解析

    本范文作者所持观点比较中庸,客观,从两个正反方面论述了电视上的广告出现的现象的好坏。本文论证主要是集中在广告的作用上,而不是重点放在电视上,在这篇文章中电视只是作为一种承载广告的媒体而出现。难能可贵的是,作者在使用具体的例子时,也没有给人以啰嗦的感觉,而是用一两句话结束描述。在阐述理由时,作者从消费者和生产者的角度去论证,比较全面。在结尾处,作者除了亮出自己观点外,还客观如实的表达出了在现象背后存在的一种挑战和责任。

　　文章做到了表达清楚,文字连贯,文章各段落根据提纲所确立的不同主题句来展开,而且各段落的主题句将段落的各个部分凝聚在一起,流利地表现出段落所要表现的思想,使读者能够轻松地理解段落中各部分以及段落之间的联系。另外本文的一些用词也值得学习,如:inform somebody of;up-to-date;be absorbed in;annoyed;enable;sharp;arduous;tedious 及一些句型的变化,连词的运用等,都使得文章更加生动。

1992 年研究生英语入学考试作文

Directions:

FOR A BETTER UNDERSTANDING BETWEEN PARENT AND CHILD

Title:FOR A BETTER UNDERSTANDING BETWEEN PARENT AND CHILD

Word Limit:120 to 150 words

OUTLINE:

1. Present situation:Lack of communication between parent and child

2. Possible reasons:

1)Different likes and dislikes

2)Misunderstanding

3)Others

3. Suggestions:

1)For parents

2)For children

Opening Sentence:

Nowadays there is often a lack of understanding between parent and child.

破题

　　看到这个题目,我不禁想到四年前与父母相处的那段令人尴尬的时间。当时正是备战高考的紧张时期,父母嫌我复习功课不专心致志,不厌其烦地述说他们当年高考前哪像我那样,电视照看不误,朋友聚会照样举行。而我,觉得他们太唠叨、太不理解青年人的心理。对于一个话题,往往说不上几句话就争起来,老是弄得不欢而散。后来,我有心里话宁愿找朋友倾诉,也不愿跟他们说。有一段时间我们一个星期说不了几句话,家庭关系紧张得"剑拔弩张"。最后,不得不通过咨询心理医生,才填平了这一家庭代沟。当然,今天的一切都已经完全正常了。对! 就以自己的亲身经历为素材来写今天的作文题。

　　本文属于"问题讨论型"模式。试题标题"FOR A BETTER UNDERSTANDING BETWEEN PARENT AND CHILD"对短文内容限定于讨论代沟问题。按照提纲所给出的三项,短文不妨安排成三个段落。第一段"Present situation"需着重描述当前两代人缺乏沟通的现状,第二段"Possible reasons"要探求导致这一现状的原因,第三段则应给出自己的建议。短文前两段之间存在因果关系,其中第二段显然属"因",而第一段的"Present situation"即是由此产生的"果"。

范文赏析

For A Better Understanding Between Parent and Child
父母与孩子相互理解

　　Nowadays there is often a lack of understanding between parent and child. Parents often complain about their children's "unreasonable" behavior,while children usually think their parents too "old-fashioned". Then,when a child has a problem,he usually goes to his intimate friends for sympathy and advice,leaving his parents totally in the dark.

　　There are some possible reasons for the present situation. First,the two generations,having grown up in different times,have different likes and dislikes for the things around them and thus have little in common to talk about. Second, parents and children, due to the misunderstanding between them, may even feel it uncomfortable to sit face to face with each other talking. Finally, with the pace of modern life becoming faster and faster, both parent and child are too busy to spare enough time to exchange ideas, even if they find it necessary to communicate. As a result, the gap between them is growing wider and wider.

To bridge this so-called generation gap, in my opinion, both parent and child should make an effort. The children should respect their seniors. The older generation, on the other hand, should show solicitude for the young. As for their differences, both generations should make allowance for each other. If they will take the first step by actually talking to one another, it won't be long before the arrival of a better understanding between parent and child.

范文解析

第一段：通过对当前两代人缺乏沟通的描述，向人们揭示代沟这一当前令人束手无策的社会问题。

提纲第一项 Present situation 后面的冒号引出较为具体的内容 Lack of communication between parent and child，在短文中起引导作用。这一内容实际是由标题 FOR A BETTER UNDERSTANDING BETWEEN PARENT AND CHILD 和写作题目所给出的起始句（Opening Sentence）中提供的信息 there is often a lack of understanding 所决定的。既然 FOR A BETTER UNDERSTANDING...，就暗示当前一定存在 Lack of communication...，而起始句更是明确指出 Nowadays there is often a lack of understanding between parent and child。

第一段提纲：

TS：Nowadays there is often a lack of understanding between parent and child.

A. Parents' complaint：children's behavior unreasonable

B. Children's complaint：parents too old-fashioned

第二段：在第一段讨论的基础上进一步讨论原因。所以，第二段与第一段之间存在逻辑上的因果关系，即第一段谈的是两代人互不沟通这一后果，而第二段讨论的是造成该后果的原因。第二段提纲给出了三方面原因：1）Different likes and dislikes；2）Misunderstanding；3）Others。这三方面的原因一定要围绕 Lack of communication between. 这一后果来发展。充实提纲如下：

TS：There are some possible reasons for the present situation.

A. Different likes and dislikes lead to having little in common to talk about.

B. Misunderstanding leads to unwillingness to talk to each other.

C. Others：Both parent and child are too busy to talk with each other.

T：Gap becomes wider.

第三段：我的建议，包括对父母、对子女两个方面。既然短文旨在讨论代沟问题，故 Suggestions 需针对父母与子女双方应如何努力消除隔阂、加强互相了解来发展。提纲如下：

TS：To solve the generation gap problem, both parent and child should make an effort.

A. For parents：show solicitude for the young

B. For children：respect the old

T：It won't be long before the arrival of a better understanding between parent and child.

第三节　提纲式作文（永恒话题）

一、写作方法

定义法。有时，我们需要用一段话来阐明某事物的性质和特征，这种发展段落的方法叫作定义法。通常，被定义的主题是一个需要特别说明的抽象的概念，或是读者陌生的专门术语以及做某种事情的方法或过程，或是容易引起误解的事情。这种方法在说明文、描写文和论证文中较为常见，但它不同于词典式的同义语替换。

一般来说，用定义法发展的段落包括两个部分。首先是定义句，概述被定义物的种属和种差。也就是说，阐明是一种什么东西，与同种属内其他事物有什么区别性的特征。其后，是扩展部分，展开叙述有关方面的内容，如：被定义物的来历、性质、结构、特征、原理、用途等。如：

Physics is a science. It deals with those phenomena of matter involving no change of chemical composition. Under this definition, physics includes the science of matter and motion, mechanics, heat, light, sound, electricity and the branches of science devoted to radiation and atomic structure.

这个定义不但指出这个术语的内涵，同时也指出了它的外延，即哪些领域的研究亦属于 Physics 的范畴。这样的定义一般称之为 extended definition（扩展定义）。在 extended definition 中，主题句是一个简单定义，其他部分则是对这个简单定义的展开。

另外，像这种使用段落下定义的方法，往往是要先把一个词限定为总属词类中的一项，再把这个词项和同类中的其他项目相区别。

在定义段中，作者还经常用读者熟悉的事物来解释对他们来说是陌生的东西。因此，定义法常常要和比较——对比、举例等方法结合在一起使用。如：

（1）简单释义

Homework is extra school work given by the teacher to be done at home.

（2）举例说明

Subject is something such as maths, chemistry, or English, that you study at school, college, or university.

（3）对比或类比

While burglary is the stealing of property from a place, robbery is the stealing of property from a person.（对比）

A hobby is an interesting way of spending your free time. It's an activity you turn to for pleasure, not something that you have to do, like helping with the dishes. It's more like a special friend that you choose for yourself. You spend your free time with it because it interests you and because you enjoy it.（类比）

（4）分析归类

Patriotism 爱国主义

Patriotism is a very complex feeling, built up out of primitive instincts and highly intellectual convictions. There is love of home and family and friends, making us peculiarly anxious to preserve our own country from invasion. There is the mild instinctive liking for compatriots as against foreigners. There is pride, which is bound up with the success of the community to which we feel that we belong. There is a belief, suggested by pride but reinforced by history, that one's own nation represents a great tradition and stands for ideals that are important to the human race. But besides all these, there is another element, at once nobler and more open to attack, an element of worship, of willing sacrifice, of joyful merging of the individual life in the life of the nation. This religious element in patriotism is essential to the strength of the state, since it enlists the best that is in most men on the side of national sacrifice.

一般说来，对一些具体的词像工具、动物等的定义都较简短而完整，越抽象的词，如 economics, normal, happiness 等越难以简单地定义。

请看在下面这个段落中作者是怎样给 Happiness 这个词下定义的：

Happiness 幸福

Happiness means different things to different people. For example, some people believe that if they have much money or many things, they will be happy. They believe that if they are wealthy, they will be able to do everything they want, and so they will be happy. On the other hand, some people believe that money is not the only happiness. These people value their religion, or their intelligence, or their health;

these make them happy. For me, happiness is closely tied to my family. I am happy if my wife and my children live in harmony. When all members of my family share good and sad times, and when my children communicate with each other and work together, I am happy. Although the definition of happiness depends on each individual, my "wealth" of happiness is in my family.

在这个定义段中，作者通过举例、对比，从多方面写出不同的人给幸福赋予的不同的含义，虽然篇幅不长，但内容具体充实。

由此可见，在写一篇文章或一个段落时，往往可以采用多种扩展方法和多种混合的支持主题句的技巧。

二、常用于文章开头的句型

（一）对立法开头句型

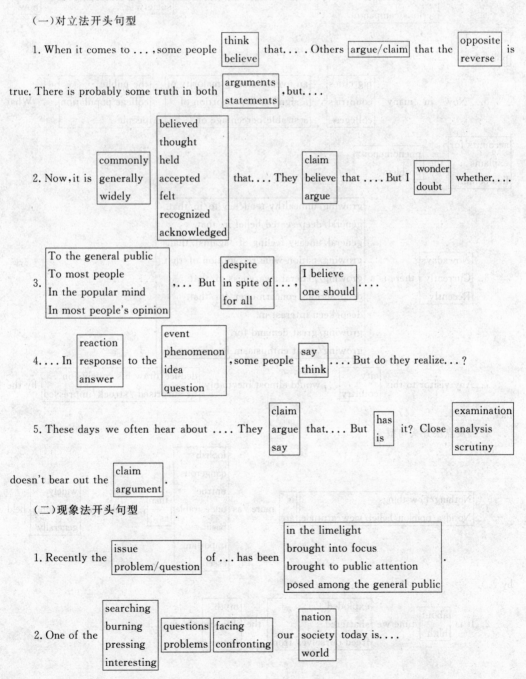

3.
| Now Perhaps | most | dangerous undesirable harmful | for our | nation society world college | is the | trend tendency phenomenon | of ... which is | apparent obvious evident pervasive rampant under way | in |

. . . .

4. A（n）
| virtual epidemic acute shortage serious campaign | of ... is now under way in this | country society | . According to a | recent new |

| study poll/survey | . . . .

5. Now in many
| big cities countries, colleges | an overwhelming majority of a significant proportion of a sizable percentage of | the public college population ... people | What |

| accounts for explains lies behind | the | phenomenon? problem? |

6.
| Nowadays Currently Recently | there is a | growing/unhealthy tendency to/in/that. general/deep-seated belief in/that. general/uneasy feeling of /against/that. growing/nation-wide recognition of/that. growing/general awareness of/that. deep/serious concern over/for/that. deep/keen interest in. growing/great demand for. growing/great enthusiasm for/among sb. | ... |

7. Any visitor to this
| city country | ... would almost inevitably | deduce/draw his conclusion be surprised /struck/impressed | by the

fact...

（三）观点法开头句型

1.
| Nothing/Few things No idea/opinion/belief/view/attitude | is are | more /as | foolish dangerous untrue undesirable basic important essential | than as | ... (which is | widely commonly generally | held

by...).

2. It is
| about high | time we | exploded shattered freed ourselves from | the | myth illusion fiction | about....

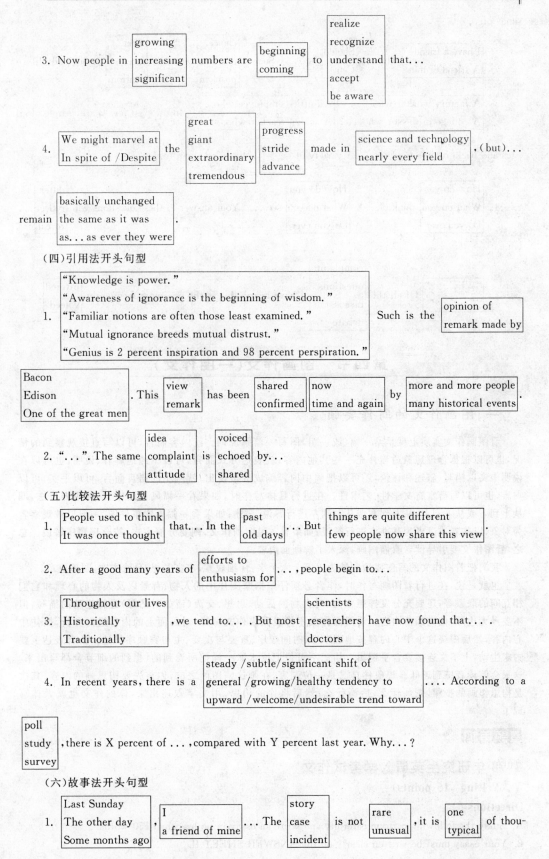

3. Now people in | growing / increasing / significant | numbers are | beginning / coming | to | realize / recognize / understand / accept / be aware | that...

4. | We might marvel at / In spite of /Despite | the | great / giant / extraordinary / tremendous | | progress / stride / advance | made in | science and technology / nearly every field | , (but)...

remain | basically unchanged / the same as it was / as... as ever they were | .

（四）引用法开头句型

1. "Knowledge is power."
"Awareness of ignorance is the beginning of wisdom."
"Familiar notions are often those least examined."
"Mutual ignorance breeds mutual distrust."
"Genius is 2 percent inspiration and 98 percent perspiration."   Such is the | opinion of / remark made by |

| Bacon / Edison / One of the great men | . This | view / remark | has been | shared / confirmed | | now / time and again | by | more and more people / many historical events | .

2. "...". The same | idea / complaint / attitude | is | voiced / echoed / shared | by...

（五）比较法开头句型

1. | People used to think / It was once thought | that... In the | past / old days | ... But | things are quite different / few people now share this view | .

2. After a good many years of | efforts to / enthusiasm for | ..., people begin to...

3. | Throughout our lives / Historically / Traditionally | , we tend to.... But most | scientists / researchers / doctors | have now found that....

4. In recent years, there is a | steady /subtle/significant shift of / general /growing/healthy tendency to / upward /welcome/undesirable trend toward | .... According to a | poll / study / survey | , there is X percent of ..., compared with Y percent last year. Why...?

（六）故事法开头句型

1. | Last Sunday / The other day / Some months ago | , | I / a friend of mine | ... The | story / case / incident | is not | rare / unusual | , it is | one / typical | of thou-

sands of...

2.　[I have a friend / A friend of mine]　who...　[Should / Can]　he...? Such a　[choice / dilemma / problem]　we often　[meet / face / confront]　in our daily life.

3.　[A factory worker who...; / A college professor who...;]　[An office employee who...; / A school teacher who...;]　In the past few years, people of all

ages and backgrounds tend to.... A variety of　[reasons / causes]　have led them to...

4.　[How do you / What do you / Do you ever]　think of...?　[How do you / What do you / Do you ever]　see...? Your answer to these questions will　[differ / reflect / reveal]...

but...

5.　["Why...?" / "Can...?"]　Of all the　[complaints / questions / discussion / debate]　I have heard, this is the one most frequently　[uttered / voiced].

第四节　图画作文（一图作文）

一、图画作文的写作要领

　　看图画作文实质上就是给一幅（或一组）图写一篇解说词。就内容而言，可以写直接观察到的情况，也可以根据合理想象适当补充一些其他内容；就表达方式而言，可以单纯地解释、说明，也可以在说明中夹以描写、叙述和评论，还可以把画中内容编成故事说出；就所用的语言而言，可以平实，可以典雅，也可以写得富有文学性、艺术性。在进行具体写作时，如果看一幅风景图作文，可用方位法，即从上到下或从下到上，从左到右或从右到左进行解说、描述；如果看一幅人物事件图，一般以被观察者为对象，以作者或读者为基准点进行解说；如果看一组图画作文，则要分清主次，按合理顺序解说。总之，看图作文要引导读者看懂图画，深入了解画面内容。

　　我们把看图作文的写作要领归纳为以下十六个字：仔细观察，丰富联想，分清主次，顺理成章。

　　也就是说，在进行看图画写作时，作者必须仔细揣摩图片中的人物、背景以及人物的心理和它们相互间的联系等，还要充分发挥想象力，对人物的活动、思想、交流（诸如对话等）进行生动的描写，但不要漫无边际，偏离画面内容。看图画作文不像看图表作文一样，对画面上的内容进行分析，抓住中心内容，然后围绕这个中心内容按地理顺序、时间顺序、重要与次要、主与宾顺序描述。语言表达上要力求生动，上下文连接要合乎逻辑。切记不可像记流水账一样把所看到的、想到的细节全都写出来，这只会使读者感到乏味。想象你自己是一位画家，在画这幅图画之前，你首先要构思画的内容；其次是构思作画的步骤，先画什么，后画什么；然后将你的构思，用文字叙述出来，你的作文也就大体写成了。

真题再现 ▶

1998 年研究生英语入学考试作文

Ⅴ. Writing（15 points）

Directions：

A. Study the following cartoon carefully and write an essay in no less than 150 words.

B. Your essay must be written clearly on the ANSWER SHEET Ⅱ.

C. Your essay should meet the requirements below:

    1. Write out the messages conveyed by the cartoon.

    2. Give your comments.

本母鸡承诺：
①本鸡下蛋不见楼见蛋皮，
②保证有蛋皮、蛋清和蛋黄。

如此承诺
各行各业兴承诺
欢迎监督不推托
原本皆为分内事
何需高唱"幸福歌"

破题

    本题给出的两点提示很简单,但图中的说明性的文字相对来说比较多,因此考生要特别注意不要机械地将图中的文字部分翻译成英语就算完成任务。与图表作文一样,考生也只需对给出的文字说明心领神会,然后据此归纳出一个论点。其实从 cartoon 的题目就可以看出本题涉及的话题,再从母鸡承诺的保证有蛋皮、蛋清和蛋黄来看,就知道是要让考生写当前的一种不正常的社会风气:承诺本是分内的职责,但很多个人和集体还要据此做出各种各样的承诺。这样论点就搞清楚了,然后就可以把主要篇幅放在考生本人的评论上了。

Introduction：首先将图中与主要论点相关的画面描写成文字。主要是母鸡的行为。然后提出母鸡这样做有什么不合理之处。

Body：将母鸡的荒唐做法与当今社会上的不良风气相联系,并提出论点。同时列举一些除本画面之外的具体实例,以证明这个问题的普遍性,但切忌描述具体例子。

Conclusion：重申考生本人的立场和观点。因为在第二段时已经间接表明了作者否定这种做法的态度,因此在结尾部分除了重申立场外,还可以提一些避免这种做法的建议。

范文赏析

Doing More Is Better than Promising More 做比吹好

    Recently, more and more people have seen varieties of promises either from TV, newspaper or from other media. As is shown in the cartoon, even a hen has learned to make blank promise. We all know that a hen's duty is to lay eggs which should undoubtedly play the most elementary part. But the hen in the picture promises what she should do!

    With the development of the society and the improvement of people's living standard, more and more attention should be paid to the improvement of quality of service. Therefore, many enterprises and departments promise to better their services so as to meet the people's need better. They are also pleased to invite people to supervise what they have done and will do. But much to our surprise, some of them just say something that they should do. These promises are only laughed at by people.

    In my opinion, doing more is better than promising more. Because people are willing to be served readily, we should lay more emphasis on what we do and how we can virtually promote better service.

Only in this way can we make people content with what we do.

范文解析

本范文没有直接从母鸡入手,而是从大家都熟悉的各种媒体上的各种承诺着手,引出其中一些承诺的空洞性和表面化。然后再用母鸡这样一个例子说明就连一般的动物都学会了承诺自己的分内事,可见如此承诺的普遍性。在第一段中用的较出色的一个字是"should"。(But the hen promises what she should do!)一个 should 十分传神的描绘出了 promise 与 should 之间的微妙的联系与对比。

第二段首先描述了一种令人振奋的景象,也就是人们的生活水平提高了,企业部门承诺要改善服务水平,这本是好事。读者看后也一定很高兴。但作者写到这里笔锋一转,用了"but"一词指出了其中一些并没有按照前面所说的去做的单位和个人,他们的做法令人失望。这样写就用了对比的方法更鲜明的突出了后面一种做法的危害性与荒唐性。

第三段作者提出了一些改进的意见和建议。

在行文中作者不光注意短句的正确处理,而且在写一些较复杂和较长的语句时也尽量注意语法正确性,如:so as to,被动句和倒装句的运用都符合语法习惯。

本文内容切题,文章长度符合要求。包括图画的全部信息;清楚表达其内涵,文字连贯;句式有变化,句子结构和用词正确。

真题再现 ▷

2002 年研究生英语入学考作文

IV Writing

Directions:

Study the following picture carefully and write an essay entitled **"Cultures—National and International"**.

In the essay you should

1)describe the picture and interpret its meaning, and

2)give your comment on the phenomenon.

You should write about 200 words neatly on ANSWER SHEET Ⅱ. (20 points)

An American girl in traditional Chinese costume(服装)

破题:

先让我们来看一下本试题的题目,从题目本身来看,可以涉及以下这些内容:文化的解读,文化与民族与国际的关系,民族的文化与国际的文化的分别论述,以及比较民族的文化和国际的文化孰优孰劣,或认为哪一边更能发扬光大。虽然有这么多内容可写,但这样一来反而难了,考生必须要在这些点中选出一个或两个重点,当然最好是集中在一点来写,把这一点作为论点来展开。考试切忌面面俱到,什么都想写,什么都写不好。

文章开头可描述一下这幅图的特殊性,它所表现的一个社会现象,也就是民族与国际的结合。在这幅图看来,分别阐述民族和国际不太恰当。而是应该强调二者在这里的结合,考生为了明确表明自己立场,可在第一段最后一句点出自己认为这样的结合是否恰当,是否更能弘扬文化。其实这里不需要花很多时间具体描述姑娘的外貌,点出含义就行了。

正文部分就可给出论据,论证开头论点。这里随着论点句的不同,也会有不同的具体的论证,也就是说作者自己的评论。1)结合利大于弊。2)结合弊大于利。3)各有利弊,互相影响。最好是能够有个明确的观点,在三点中任选一点。在这段中考生也可先点出时下大部分人的观点,或一些人的观点,然后在结尾处点出自己的观点,这样更能加深印象,突出自己立场,同时也分了段。

另外也可将利弊谁大于谁的观点分段,第一段一个观点,第二段一个观点,最后一段让读者来判断。

此外也可以开门见山先提出自己的观点,再客观地列举别人的观点,以求最后反过来证明自己的观点。

范文赏析

Cultures——National and International 民族文化和国际文化

A pretty American girl is presented in this picture. Interestingly, she is neither in Apple Jeans nor in Red Taps nor in anything typically American, rather, she prefers traditional Chinese costume. In my opinion, what the picture conveys is beyond a new fashion trend, and it carries cultural implications as well. On the process of globalization, to be national or to be international is a dilemma for almost every culture. While global economic integration has fostered thorough cultural interchanges and made purely national culture practically impossible, many countries with their distinct national culture still hold a conservative attitude toward being international for fear of losing their own national identity. Admittedly, as it is the reflection of the outlook of a people, national culture is especially to her people as priceless spiritual treasure and ought to be cherished and preserved.

However, there are also positive reasons to advocate an international culture. As the traditional Chinese costume in the picture adds some irresistible oriental glamour to her beautiful figure, the embracing of elements from other cultures will surely do great benefit to a culture. The fresh ideas coming in, controversial or even unreasonable as they may seem at first sight, provide a different perspective for us to observe the world, which is essential to social progress. It is multiculturalism in a society that essentially makes the society and its people diverse, colorful, vigorous, and open-minded.

As the picture raises the thought-provoking question in a light manner, the answer to the question is also implied in it. In my eyes, to be international is undisputedly the better choice if the nation wishes to adopt an open-minded way of progressing.

范文解析

本范文作者在描写照片的基础上,在第一段先提出了照片传达的意思:这不仅是时髦,也反映了一种文化倾向。接着,客观地提出了两种事实:民族的和国际的接轨的重要,以及保持民族的必要。在第一段内,看似作者是支持民族的是无价之宝,但到了第二段,从第一句我们就可以看出作者没有片面地摒弃国际的东西。在论证时,作者还是就地取材,用照片作为例证来证明只要二者搭配恰当,使用得当,就可以使民族的和国际的相辅相成。在结尾处,我们终于可以看清楚作者的真正意图,即要接受来自国际的不同的文化,以取长补短,这才是文明进步、开放的象征。提出论点的时机与一般的文章不同:论点句在结尾提出。如果能在前面行文时,可以把握得住不会走题的话,这也是一个好办法,且读者在将要读完之计,能够借此论点句将前面的内容融会贯通,印象深刻。本文表达正确,语言流畅,句式变化多样,用词面宽,如:neither … nor...; typically; convey; carries; integration; conservative; thought-provoking 等,虽有个别不妥之处,仍表明作者语言基本功较好,表达能力较强,长度符合要求。

练习

Directions:

Study the following drawing carefully and write an essay in which you should

1)describe the drawing

2)interpret its meaning

3)support your view with examples

You should write about 200 words neatly on ANSWER SHEET Ⅱ.(20 points)

终点又是新起点

破题

本文可由三段组成。

第一段,根据所给提示,简要描绘漫画内容,解释绘画者的意图并提出自己对漫画的理解。在本段结尾中引申含义,解读主题——我们时时刻刻都在参与竞争。紧扣主题,抓住关键词 race 和 finish line,按提示进行全面、概括、条理清晰的阐述。

第二段,以"In the race for success there is no finish line"作为 topic sentence,结合自己身经百战求学的经历,说明实现个人远大理想只有一个个新起点,没有终点,应该胜不骄,败不馁,持之以恒,奋斗终身。

第三段,采用提出建议的结尾模式,重申竞争是信息时代的特征,必须勇敢地参与竞争,使生命更有意义。最后用富有哲理的 Strong statement:"It takes as much courage to have tried and failed as it does to have tried and succeeded"结尾。

In the Race for Success There Is No Finish Line 在通向成功的道路中,没有终点

The drawing describes an extraordinary race,where the champion sprinter dashes off in next context immediately after he hit the finish line. No such race is available in any track-and-field meet,but that is the way it is when it comes to ruthless competition in our daily life. We get involved in intense competition everyday for academic excellence,for better jobs and for noble ideals.

In the race for success there is no finish line. In our lifelong journey, we all pursue something as ideals that invest life with meaning. I dreamed of being a good physicist like my father since I could count my fingers. As I grew up, I came to realize that my goal was no easier than Marathon Races, associated with fierce competition, unbearable hardships and painful setbacks. But I am not scared. I have been working hard to excel for many years. The tough challenges, formidable rivals and good opportunities fuel my courage to go for championships. My past achievement is nothing to boast about but the start line for greater success in my graduate study. Though I have a long way to go to be a successful physicist, I am on the right track and enjoy every minute of the race.

The Information Age is characterized by competition. Active involvement in competition makes the difference. We may build up our confidence if we win; and learn from others if we lose. It takes as much courage to have tried and failed as it does to have tried and succeeded.

写作特点：

(1)排比结构的重复使用。

1)形容词＋名词,如：

... for academic excellence, for better jobs and for noble ideals.

... fierce competition, unbearable hardships and painful setbacks...

The tough challenges, formidable rivals and good opportunities...

2)句子,如：

We may build up our confidence if we win; and learn from others if we lose.

这些 parallel structures 的修辞作用较强,它们使短文结构紧凑、语言精练、富于韵律、一气呵成,加深了读者的印象。熟练运用 parallel structure 是短文写作最常用的基本功,考生应给予高度重视。

(2)变通名人名言,为我所用。如：

In the race for success there is no finish line.

It takes as much courage to have tried and failed as it does to have tried and succeeded... ideals that invest life with meaning. 使语言更地道、更有说服力。

(3)词汇量较大,准确灵活地运用体育词汇、同义词、现代英语表达和学术词汇,体现较高的表达能力。如：

race/competition/contest, ruthless/intense/fierce competition(同义词)

champion sprinter, dash off, hit, track-and-field meet, finish line, start line, Marathon Race, on the right track, championship(体育词汇)

enjoy, fuel, involve, excel, have a long way to go, as much... as, tough, on the right track, boast about, when it comes to... invest life with meaning(时尚英语表达)

extraordinary, characterize, involvement, championship, academic excellence, challenge, opportunity, competition, Information Age, achievement(学术写作词汇)

文章整体给人的感受是写作规范,条理清晰,句子有变化,用词面较宽,语言简洁、流畅,有逻辑性。

通过对试题的分析不难看出,尽管考试的题型和主题有所变化,但英语短文写作特点是不变的。即:中间段必须有主题句;段落内容要借助过渡信号紧扣主题句直线扩展。另外还应该注意三点：

(1)短文扩展中不是单纯多写——"Write on and on",而是"Write in and in",内容层层递进,既有细节又有深度。

(2)不是你想写什么,而是你能写什么。要根据自己掌握的英语素材和写作能力扬长避短,尽量使用简单的修辞手法,部分发挥平时训练的真实水平,就会成功。千万不可眼高手低,自以为是,不考虑自己的写作能力,杜撰中国式英语。

(3)在考研作文中一定要坚持"**morally high**"的原则,且不可情绪消沉。

第五节　图画作文(两图对比作文)

一、写作要领

有时为了更清楚地解释一种不为人们所熟悉的事物,常把它与具有相同性的其他种类的事物相比,即对比甲和乙,揭示甲乙共有的某些特点进行推理,这种方法叫类比法。比如我们想解释什么是计算机,就可以把它比作"一种人造的电脑",这样就会使人们对计算机有一个较初步的概念。看下面两个句子是怎样以类比法定义朋友的:

"A friend is like a mirror."

"A friend is a safe port in storm."

再看下面这个段落,作者将语言比作地图,以这种类比给读者留下较具体、清楚的印象。

Language is like a map. It's not the territory itself, but it's a kind of representation. A map is a representation of the earth's surface, whereas language is, or should be, a representation of reality—including things, social relationships and more.

应该注意,比较对照的事物必须是同类,或具有某些共性,否则无法进行类比论证。例如,下面一段文字中,把弹劾(impeach)总统和动大手术进行对比,用的就是类比论证的方法。

Impeaching(弹劾)a president is like major surgery. It is an act that should not be done hastily nor emotionally, and only when it is necessary to restore the well-being of the patient, in this case the government of the nation. The purpose of surgery is not to punish the diseased organ; neither is the purpose of impeachment to punish a president. In both situations the only purpose is to remove a source of serious trouble and re-establish a healthy condition.

二、表比较的句型

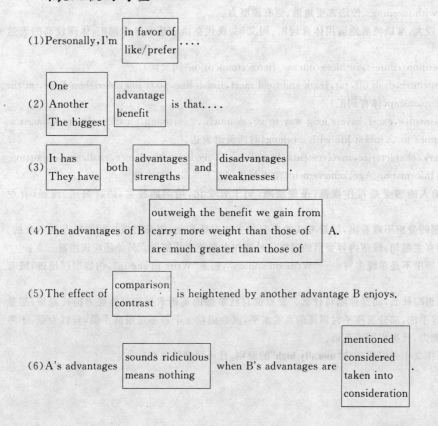

(1) Personally, I'm [in favor of / like/prefer]....

(2) [One / Another / The biggest] [advantage / benefit] is that....

(3) [It has / They have] both [advantages / strengths] and [disadvantages / weaknesses].

(4) The advantages of B [outweigh the benefit we gain from / carry more weight than those of / are much greater than those of] A.

(5) The effect of [comparison / contrast] is heightened by another advantage B enjoys.

(6) A's advantages [sounds ridiculous / means nothing] when B's advantages are [mentioned / considered / taken into consideration].

（7）When the advantages and disadvantages of... are carefully compared, the most striking

finding		self-evident
conclusion	is	obvious

.

（8）Although A

| has |
| enjoys |
| gains |

the

| distinct |
| enormous |
| considerable |

advantage of...,it can't compete... with B in...

（9）

| By contrast |
| On the contrary |

.....

（10）

| Despite these advantages, |
| Like anything else, |
| Good as A is, |

it

| also has |
| brings |

| its own disadvantages |
| problems |
| harmful effects |

.

真题再现 ▷

2000 年研究生英语入学考试作文

Ⅴ. **Writing**（15 points）

Directions：

A. Study the following two pictures carefully and write an essay of at least 150 words.

B. Your essay must be written neatly on ANSWER SHEET Ⅱ.

C. Your essay should meet the requirements below：

1. Describe the pictures.

2. Deduce the purpose of the drawer of the pictures.

3. Suggest counter-measures.

A Brief History of World Commercial Fishing

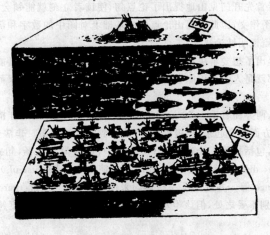

破题

　　本次试题的要求提示很简明扼要,相信每一位考生都不会走题。我们应该把握住的是写图表作文切忌将主要时间和力量分配于对图表本身的描写,这样一来就会沦于一般的说明文或记叙文。这是一篇说明性的论述文,因此主要篇幅应该还是在论述上。对图画的描写只是为了更直观地说明制图人要传达的思想和观点。所以考生千万不要先来个哗众取宠将图中的景物生动具体地描述一番,相反只要用几句表示对比的语句突出 1900 年和 1995 年的最明显的变化就足够了。然后主要的篇幅就要根据对比得出的结论来推断出这幅图本身所要揭示的一个观点或目的。但是要切记本题的提示所要求的不是考生个人的观点,而是本图的目的,虽然相信大多数考生所持的正面观点应是相似的。然后可在这以后表明自己的立场,来提供一些治理和杜绝这种情况的措施。

Introduction:点明论点——从 1900 年到 1995 年之间,捕鱼船越来越多而渔业资源越来越少。

Body:1)唤起世人注意这个严峻的社会问题。

　　　2)分析部分原因,但不一定要面面俱到,否则篇幅无法容纳。

　　　3)由这样的做法而有可能导致的严重后果。

Conclusion:缓解或有可能解决问题的方法。但切忌唱高调,空洞无物,如,讲我们要努力,要保护这样的空话。要尽量举出一些切实可行的具体的方法。

范文赏析

A Brief History of World Commercial Fishing 世界商业捕捞简史

As is shown in the pictures, we can see clearly that with the increase of commercial fishing, the number of fishes sharply decreased. In one picture, there were various kinds of fishes and only one fishing boat in 1900. On the contrary, in 1995 there was only one fish, but many fishing boats.

The purpose of this picture is to show us that due attention has to be paid to the decrease of ocean resources. Owing to overfishing, the number of fishes has obviously decreased. If we let this situation go as it is, we won't know where fish is in the future. By that time, our environment will suffer a great destruction.

Therefore, it is imperative for us to take drastic measures. For one thing, we should appeal to our authorities to make strict laws to control commercial fishing. For another, we should enhance the awareness of people that the ocean resources are very vital to us. Only in this way can we protect our ocean resources. Also, I believe that we human beings can overcome this difficulty, and we will have a bright future.

范文解析

在本篇范文中,作者首先开门见山地提出了论点句,使读者立刻就能领会作者的意图。然后作者还没有忘记这是一篇看图作文,因此在提出论点句的基础上对图中的数字和部分画面内容作了解释,这样就是名副其实的一篇说明性论述文了。

在论证阶段,作者提出了想要解决这一问题的迫切愿望。并且在指出可能出现的后果时,列举了一个通俗易懂的论据,那就是人们有可能会不知道鱼在哪里。这个道理大家都能明白,于是乎也更能引起共鸣。

在结论部分,作者从两方面着手,一个是制定措施的一方,另一方是遵守措施、制度,履行义务、权利的普通群众。只有两方面联合起来,积极配合,才能达到长远的效果。非常全面,客观。

另外本文内容切题,包括提纲的全部要点;文章通顺,语言简洁流畅,句式变化多样;用词较宽,如:commercial, sharply, due attention, owing to(不是简单地说 because of),obviously, imperative, drastic, appeal to, enhance 等。并且用了一些连词来使文章更连贯,如:therefore, for one thing,... for another...。虽有个别不妥之处,但该生基本功较好;表达能力较强;长度符合要求。

第六节　图画作文(多图作文)

一、用分类法写多图作文题型的作文

分类法就是按一定的标准对人或事物进行分组归类的一种发展段落的方法。

它既便于研究各种事物共性,又便于研究某一事物的特性,科技英语中经常会运用这种方法。读

下列段落，注意其分类法：

Education in the United Stated is usually divided into four levels. The first level is early childhood education. Its main purpose is to prepare children for school; The second level is elementary education. It is divided into six or eight grades, and children learn Reading, Arithmetic, Writing, Social Studies and Science. They also have Art, Music and Physical Education; The third level is secondary education. It is for junior and senior high school students. Some students take courses to prepare themselves for college. Other students take technical or vocational courses that prepare them for jobs after they graduate from high school; The fourth level is higher education. There are many kinds of institutions of higher education. Technical institutes offer two-year programs in electronics, engineering, business and other subjects. After two years at a junior college, students receive an associate degree and then they can continue at a four-year college.

美国的教育通常分为四个阶段，即学前教育、小学教育、中学教育和大学教育，而其中有些阶段又提供更详细的分类项。段落的这种分类法，条理清晰，易于为读者所接受。

另外，在使用分类法时，我们必须注意所分类范畴的合理性，要根据事物所具有的相同的特性把它归类。例如：我们不可将学生分成"成绩好的学生，不用功的学生，成绩差的学生"。因为成绩虽和努力用功有一定的逻辑关系，但它们不属同一范畴。

真题再现 ▶

1997 年研究生英语入学考试作文

Ⅴ. Writing (15 points)

Directions:

A. Study the following set of pictures carefully and write an essay in no less than 120 words.

B. Your essay must be written clearly on the ANSWER SHEET Ⅱ.

C. Your essay should cover all the information provided and meet the requirements below:

    1. Interpret the following pictures.

    2. Predict the tendency of tobacco consumption and give your reasons.

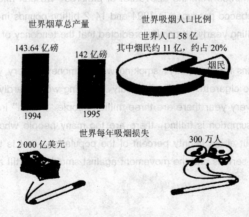

世界烟草总产量

143.64 亿磅　142 亿磅

1994　1995

世界吸烟人口比例
世界人口 58 亿
其中烟民约 11 亿，约占 20%

烟民

世界每年吸烟损失
2 000 亿美元　　300 万人

破题

本试题图表及数字都比较复杂，因此写作要在能看懂图和数字的基础上才能进行。图表中矩形和扇形图案表示各年数字比例关系。另外还有十分形象的图案来表示在香烟上花费的金钱和因为抽烟而死亡的人数。只要考生仔细审查每幅图上方的文字说明，就会很快明白各幅图案的所指意义。重要的是要找出各幅图之间的联系。另外还要找出图表和形象图画之间的关系。对这几幅图的表述可以有不同的侧重点。最基本的两种观点可以是这样的：乐观的和比较不乐观的。这里我们并没有说是悲观的，是因为其中一幅图中显示烟草总产量在减少，虽然其他情况不容乐观，但还是不应太悲观。否则的话,就太绝对了。第二点提示中要求考生写烟草的前景、趋势,如果是前一种写法,那么可以自下而上地描述四幅图画,先写每年吸烟造成的损失,然后指出这是由于烟民的数量多。最后点明虽然眼下的情况严峻,但是由于总产量的减少,因此也是有希望的。如果是第二种写法,那么可以自上而下地描述这四幅图画。先写好的趋势,再在这基础上严肃地指出情况也不容乐观,因为每年吸烟造成的损失也很惊人。而且这样使用对比的方法,就更能突出文章后半部要表达的意思。在行文中,也可适当点出重要数字,但有些数字,比如说年份等,在这篇文章中就显得不是最重要的了,因此可以不写入文章。

范文赏析

Tobacco Consumption and Harm 烟草消费与危害

Sample 1

About Tobacco Consumption, we meet smokers everywhere: in the streets, on college campuses, and in shops. There are 5.8 billion people in the world, and the smokers are about 1.1 billion, which makes up 20 percent of the world's total population.

Smoking is very harmful. I think there are two main aspects to the damage. First, smoking consumes a great deal of money. As is shown in the pictorial graph, smoking wastes 200 billion dollars each year in the world. Second, smoking does harm to the health of smokers, and it is the main cause of lung cancer. About 3 million people die because of the relevant diseases derived from smoking every year.

Because more and more people are aware of the great harm of smoking to humans, the amount of tobacco consumption is on the decrease. From the following figures we can clearly see the tendency. The total amount of world tobacco production added up to 14.364 billion pounds in 1994, but it dropped to 14.2 billion pounds in 1995. At the same time, many countries call on people to give up smoking. So it is certain that the number of smokers is to decrease.

Sample 2

About Tobacco Consumption from the above set of pictures, we can find that there were a total of 14.364 billion pounds of tobacco produced in 1994 and 14.2 billion pounds in 1995. Because the amount of tobacco production is falling yearly, it can be predicted that the tendency of tobacco consumption would also be falling yearly.

There are many reasons for it. Firstly, smoking wastes money. Every year there are two hundred billion dollars "burnt" in the cigarette "fire". Secondly, smoking would hardly do people any good and it can even cause cancer. Every year there are three million people "buried" in the cigarette "tomb".

Although tobacco consumption is falling, there are too many people who smoke. The population in the world is 5.8 billion, but about twenty percent of the population, that is to say, 1.1 billion people, smoke. So the situation is serious and the movement against smoking is still a difficult task.

范文解析

以上两篇范文就正好是两种不同观点,不同写法的代表。范文(一)是前一种乐观的写法,而范文(二)就是后一种写法。备考的时候可以对比着阅读。两位作者都选取了比较能说明问题的数字加以对图表进行分析。行文中运用的不只是简单句。如范文1在表达烟民的比例时,用了非限制性定语从句,"which makes up ...",使行文看起来更为成熟、连贯。范文(一)与范文(二)另一点不同的是:它在阐述各项子论点时,基本上都是先阐述观点,下结论,然后再举出相关数字加以证明。在范文2中,作者还动了一些脑筋使文章变得更生动,如:将"花钱"比做 burnt,将"抽烟"比做一场火灾,十分形象,又从另一个侧面揭示出吸烟的危害性。这就是所谓的闪光点。在用词方面,如:consume, derive from

等,体现出考生运用了一些中学以外的词汇。

以上两篇作文内容符合要求,包括对各图的说明,对趋势的预测及理由,数字表达正确,语言流畅,句式变化多样,用词面宽,虽有个别不妥之处,仍表明作者语言基本功较好,表达能力较强,长度符合要求。

第七节　图表作文(表格图)

一、写作要领(列举法)

列举法(也叫罗列法)是一种最常见的发展段落的方法。用这种方法发展段落,作者首先点明论点,然后列举一系列的论据对其进行陈述或解释。列举的内容可能是一连串的事物、事件、理由以及同一个问题的不同方面等。列举的顺序可以根据各点内容的相对重要性、时间的先后、地理位置的远近等关系来进行。请看下面这段用列举法发展的文章:

Basketball is popular in many countries. One reason for this is that it is inexpensive. A ball and a hoop are all you need. Moreover, it is exciting. There is always lots of action. Additionally, it is a healthful sport that both men and women can play. Furthermore, it is both an indoor and an outdoor game. In warm countries, the game is played outdoors all year. In cold countries, it is a winter game. In such countries, basketball is usually played indoors.

本段开门见山,指出"篮球在许多国家受欢迎",然后列出四点理由,最后得出结论:"The game can be played both in warm countries and in cold countries"。

在使用列举法展开段落时,最大的忌讳就是内容的重叠或罗列出与段落主题不相关或关系不大的内容。请看下例:

Time spent in a bookshop can be most enjoyable. Whatever the reason you enter a bookshop, you can soon become totally unaware of your surroundings. You can't help picking up a book. And the main attraction of a bookshop is to make you feel free and escape the realities of everyday life. In the bookshop you can buy anything you like. The shop assistant won't bother you when you browse(随便翻阅)。

此段主题句颇为生动有力,概括了一般读者的真实感受。但作者在段落中加入了"the main attraction..."这么一句多余的解释性的话,同时少了一个圆满的结尾,从而使整个段落显得参差不齐,缺少了应有的空间感和整体感。

所以,在点明主题后,列举的各项内容之间不妨留出一定的"跨度",让读者自己去联想,自然会增加读者的阅读兴趣。试比较修改后的段落:

Time spent in a bookshop can be most enjoyable. Whatever the reason you enter a bookshop, you can soon become totally unaware of your surroundings. You can pick up a book to read, and feel free from realities, or you can browse for as long as you like. You can buy a book if you are interested, or you can simply leave empty-handed if you are not. The shop assistant wouldn't care.

二、图表作文的写作步骤

(1)首先,不管是以何种方式出现,考生都应认真分析图表,要做到充分理解题意。花两三分钟研究,确定要解释和呈现何种信息资料,正如古语道:"磨刀不误砍柴工。"

(2)选择最佳次序、结构来表达你对图表的理解,因为一个图表可以从不同角度来审视。好的切入点意味着成功了一半。

(3)在下笔之前,首先要确定整篇报告的段落数。记住:欲速则不达。如果你确定了段落数,也就是,找到了切入口,并对图表有所理解;下一步是构思,因为只有20分钟时间,不可能写详细的提纲或草稿。一般来说,一篇报告3至5段较适中。

(4)在第一段,你应对整个图表进行总的概述或解说,引言段的主题句说明该图描述什么或包含什么信息。你应假设读者手中没有该图表,用自己的语言向他们讲述你所看到的。

【Note】One problem is that a suitable general statement may already be given as part of the question. In that case do not copy the sentence word for word. Instead, you should either rearrange the words to say what has been said in a slightly different way, and give additional information. It would be a mistake to copy this part of the task rubric to use as the general statement in the introduction.

【注意】考生经常会遇到一种情况,那就是考题中往往包含能很好解说图表的句子。考试中要记住,不能完全照搬考题中的句子,不管它多么合用。应该对该部分进行改写,或增补内容,完全照搬考题内容有可能令你失去部分分数。

(5)由于图表包含丰富的信息和各种各样的数据,要清楚有效地把它们描述呈现出来不是件易事,尤其是数据以及发展趋势的变化。考生应该熟练掌握常用套句和短语(本书为考生提供了大量有用套句。)。如果考生能熟练运用这些套句,自然信心倍增,对图表作文的恐惧也就消失了。

(6)考生应重视时态及语态的使用。如果是流程图或使用说明书,一般建议用一般现在时和被动语态。

如果图表是说明目前情况的,则使用现在时或现在进行时,必要时使用被动语态。

当图表传达的信息是过去某个特定时间的或过去某段时间内变动着的,应采用过去时或过去进行时(有时也可以用一般现在时来描述过去发生的事件,但建议还是采用过去时。)。在过去一段完整时间里发生的动作最好采用一般过去时或过去进行时。

有时图表信息时间跨度大,从过去一直延伸至将来。如果是这种情况,将需要运用表将来的相应时态。

(7)图表作文不一定要求单独的结论段,因为你不需就某个辩论下结论。当然,如果你完成200字都困难的话,那不妨写个独立的结论段,以便达到最低的字数。尽量如实地描述图表内容,让读者对图表有个准确、清晰的理解。

三、图表描述应注意的问题

对图表进行描述,应注意以下几点:

(1)要突出重点,抓住图表中的极端点,如:最大或最小、最多或最少、最好和最差、基本相同之处等。

(2)总趋势的描述必须准确,要看出总的规律、趋势,抓住特征,归纳增减速度。

(3)图表往往提供大量数据,考生应该仔细观察分析,从中选择有效信息,图表上资料、数据的描述必须选择重点,不能事无巨细,一一列出。

(4)充分利用图表中所提供的文字或说明,它们往往为我们提供了切入点。

(5)说明、描述图表时应注意动词时态,属于过去发生的应该用一般过去时,属于经常发生的应该用一般现在时。

(6)句子结构要力求有变化,不要总是一个句型。

(7)考生应该熟练掌握一些固定句式和表达方式。

(8)认真检查,由于数据多,注意别混淆,以免闹出"张冠李戴"的笑话。

四、图表作文的解题技巧

The table below summarizes one data collected by a college bookshop for the month of February 2000.

Write a report describing the sales figures of various types of publications, based on the information shown in the table.

You should write about 200 words.

	Non-Book Club Members			Book Club Members	Total
	College staff	College Students	Members of public		
Fiction	44	31	0	76	151
Non-fiction	29	194	122	942	1287
Magazines	332	1249	82	33	1696
Total	405	1474	204	1051	3134

解题步骤：

（1）仔细阅读题干

（2）阅读表格的信息并进行分析比较

图中有三种 Publication 分别是：Fiction，Non-fiction 和 Magazines。

消费者有两大类四种，第一类 Non-Book Club Members，里面有三种人：college staff，college students，members of public；第二类自成一种：Book Club Members。

消费的数量上抓住最多的和最少的。

（3）开始写作—首先开头一段介绍所写的内容。

What do the College Students Read? 大学生们在读什么？

The table shows the sales figures of fiction books, non-fiction books, and magazines in a college book shop in February 2000. The figures are divided into two graphs: sales to non-Book Club members and to Book Club members.

接着就具体介绍表格的内容，表格中包含了很多数据，注意除了列出这些数据外，更重要的是各个数据间的比较，见下面的黑体字：

The non-Book Club member's figures comprise sales to college staff, college students, and members of the public. College staff bought 332 magazines, 44 fictions and 29 non-fiction books. College students bought 1249 magazines, 194 non-fiction and 31 fiction books. More magazines were sold to college students than to any other group of customers. Although no fiction books were sold to members of the public, they purchased 132 non-fiction books and 82 magazines.

Book Club members bought more fiction(76) and nonfiction books(942) than other customers. On the other hand, magazines sales to Club Members(33) were fewer than any other type of customers.

第三部分，作一个总结。

The total number of publications sold for the month was 3134(1474 to college students, 405 to staff, 204 to the public, and 1051 to the Book Club members). Of this figure, 151 items were fiction books and 1287 were non-fiction. Therefore, magazines accounted for the greatest number of sales(1696).

（4）最后修改成文

注意：文章中如果要大量引用数据的话，最好使用不同的表达方式。

例题

The table below gives figures which show social and economical indicators for four countries in 1994, according to United Nations Statistics.

Write a report to your university lecture describing all the information shown in the table.

You should write about 200 words.

ITEMS	COUNTRIES			
Indicators	Canada	Japan	Peru	Zaire
Annual income per person(in US $)	11,000	15,760	160	130
Life expectancy at birth	76	78	51	47
Daily calorie supply per person	3,326	2,846	1,927	1,749
Adult literacy rate(%)	99	99	68	34

A Report about Social and Economical Indicators From Four Countries
关于四个国家社会经济指数的报告

The above chart shows four social and economical indicators of four countries in 1994, namely, annual income per person, life expectancy at birth, daily calorie supply per person and adult literacy rate in Canada, Japan, Peru and Zaire. Canada and Japan are among the developed countries, while Peru and Zaire are developing countries.

First, let's look at the figures for annual income per person. In Canada it is $US 11,100 and in Japan it is $US 15,760. These figures are much higher than those for Peru($US 160)and Zaire($US130).

Second, with regard to life expectancy at birth, there is a huge gap between the developed and developing countries. In Canada it is 76, which is almost the same as in Japan(78). However, in Peru it is only 51, and in Zaire it is only 47.

Third, looking at daily calorie supply per person, the developed countries also enjoy higher figures. In Canada it is 3,326, while in Japan it is 2,846. However, in Peru and Zaire the figures are 1,927 and 1,749, respectively.

Fourth, in the aspect of adult literacy rate, Canada and Japan boast the highest figure—99%. But for Peru it is 68%, and for Zaire only 34%.

From the chart, we can see that the two developed countries, Canada and Japan, enjoy high standards, while the two developing countries, Peru and Zaire, have much lower living standards. Moreover, the differences are huge. For example, the annual income per person in Japan is about 100 times of that of Peru.

解题步骤：

(1)仔细阅读题目要求

(2)仔细阅读题目中给出的信息

流程图的题目通常可以分为几个部分，例题中给出很明显的分段的标志：First Private Tutorial, Second Private Tutorial OR Study Group Discussion, Final Draft。这些构成了考生写作时天然的分段标准。

同时还要阅读每个步骤里面包含的内容，只要对这些内容进行稍微的修改和补充就可以成为文章的主题段落。

(3)开始写作

首先作一个总体的介绍；接着根据图中的天然分段标志进行段落写作。

(4)修改成文

流程图的题目相对而言比较容易做答，因为题目和图标中已经给出了很多的信息和现成的答案，考生只要好好地分段组织，进行必要的扩充和变化表达方式，就能很从容地完成这个小作文。

第八节　图表作文(柱状图)

一、写作要领

推理法。在一篇议论文(论说文)里,必须要有观点,又要有材料,还要通过各种论证方法,阐明观点与材料之间的必然关系,使之具有充分的说服力。常用的推理法有两种,即:归纳法(induction)和演绎法(deduction)。

(一)归纳法(specific to general)

从具体到一般的论证方法叫归纳法。这种段落往往先给出具体细节,或理由和实例形象,通过对各种具体的事实、现象的分析和判断,从而得出一般性的结论。例如:

In the future a young woman trained to be an engineer will not only improve her own life but may also make our country a better place for everyone. She may, for instance, devise a new kind of automobile engine that does not require gasoline at all. That would make our country less dependent on other nations for oil imports. Her invention would also serve the cause of world peace, because an America truly free from pressure by other countries would be stronger politically, economically, and militarily and would be better able to resist threats to world peace. Girls with interests in science and math should be encouraged to go to engineering school.

(二)演绎法(general to specific)

从一般到具体的论证方法叫演绎法。它与归纳法正好相反,是根据已知的一般原理推断出具体事物和现象的结论。写作时,往往需要以主题句开头,开门见山,点明主题,然后再给出具体细节,或是用理由和实例来论证主题。例如:

My ambition is to go to college, but my environment does not allow me to do so. My father has been in some difficulty in supporting me even in the middle school, so it is certainly a greater difficulty for him to pay my expenses in college. And I have five brothers in schools. if I go to college, the burden will be too heavy for my father. Moreover, I am poor in science, and perhaps this will prevent me from successfully passing the entrance examination of a college.

二、柱状图题型的解题技巧

(1)首先还是分析题目要求

时间和词数的要求一般不会变的。

(2)分析图中的信息

(3)组织结构,开始写文章

(4)修改成文

三、表分析的句型

写分析文章,也有一定的句型。如:

(1)First, ... Second. ... Worse still. ...

(2)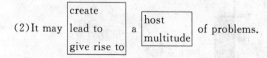

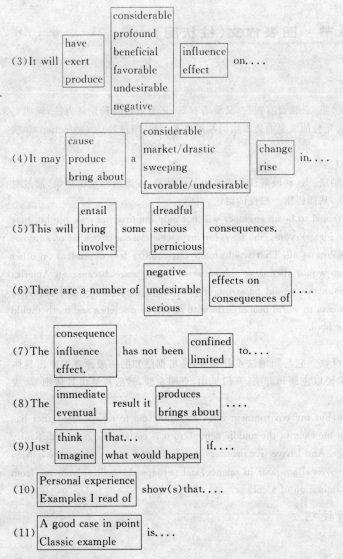

(3) It will { have / exert / produce } { considerable / profound / beneficial / favorable / undesirable / negative } { influence / effect } on....

(4) It may { cause / produce / bring about } a { considerable / market/drastic / sweeping / favorable/undesirable } { change / rise } in....

(5) This will { bring / involve } some { dreadful / serious / pernicious } consequences.

(6) There are a number of { negative / undesirable / serious } { effects on / consequences of } ....

(7) The { consequence / influence / effect. } has not been { confined / limited } to....

(8) The { immediate / eventual } result it { produces / brings about } ....

(9) Just { think / imagine } { that... / what would happen } if....

(10) { Personal experience / Examples I read of } show(s) that....

(11) { A good case in point / Classic example } is....

Directions:

For this part, you are allowed to write a composition based on the graphs below.

Health Gains in Developing Countries

1. 以下图为依据描述发展中国家的期望寿命(life expectancy)和婴儿死亡率(infant mortality)的变化情况

2. 说明引起变化的各种原因

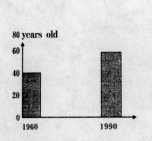
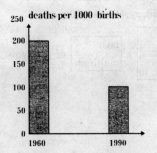

Health Gains in Developing Countries 发展中国家健康状况的改善

The developing countries have made great strides in the health conditions of their populations. The above graphs show that between 1960 and 1990 life expectancy in these countries increased from about 40 to almost 60. At the same time, infant mortality declined from roughly 200 deaths for every 1,000 births to around 100.

There are two main reasons for this improvement. The first is that the economies of those countries have developed rapidly in recent decades, and consequently there is more money available for health care. The second is that the governments of developing countries are paying more attention to education in hygiene.

If this trend continues, developing countries will soon approach the developed countries in terms of health care. People will live longer and healthier lives. The result of this will be happier and more productive populations.

第九节　图表作文(饼状图)

一、写作要领

劝导法。所谓劝导法就是通过实据、例证、驳论、引经据典、借助权威或预测后果等手段，说服劝导他人的一种段落发展方法。例如：

Passengers should refuse to ride in any vehicle driven by someone who has been drinking. First and most important, such a refusal could save lives. The National Council on Alcoholism reports that drunk driving causes 25,000 deaths and 50 percent of all traffic accidents each year. Not only the drivers but the passengers who agree to travel with them are responsible. Second, riders might tell themselves that some people drive well even after a few drinks, but this is just not true. Dr. Burton Belloc of the local Alcoholism Treatment Center explains that even one drink can shorten the reflex time and weaken the judgment needed for safe driving. Others might feel foolish to ruin a social occasion or inconvenience themselves or others by speaking up, but risking their lives is even more foolish. Finally, by refusing to ride with a drinker, one passenger could influence other passengers or the driver. Marie Fuillo is an example. When three friends who had obviously been drinking offered her a ride home from school recently, she refused, despite the driver's teasing. Hearing Marie's refusal, two of her friends got out of the car. Until the laws are changed and a vast reeducation takes place, the bloodshed on American highways will probably continue. But there is one thing people can do: they can refuse to risk their lives for the sake of a party.

段中第一句为主题句，指出旅客应该拒绝乘坐司机酒后驾驶的车辆。接下来十个发展句为说服人们这样做提供了四个理由。第一个理由以事实为依据，说明发生这些悲剧不仅司机有责任，乘客同样有责任。第二、三个理由实际上是对反面意见的驳斥，其中援引了权威人士的话，借以增强说服力。第四个理由通过一个具体事例，说明旅客公然拒乘司机酒后驾驶的车辆可以对其他乘客，甚至对司机本人产生影响。段落最后两句为收尾句，一方面预测了发生在美国公路上此类流血事故的前景，另一方面指出有一件事人们当前是可以做到的，那就是拒绝搭乘司机酒后驾驶的车辆。

尽管所有高质量的段落都或多或少具有劝导性，但劝导法仍被看作一种专门的段落发展方法。劝导法往往和其他段落发展方法结合使用，例如通过实据、例证、对比、特别是通过立论、驳论、引经据典、借助权威或预测后果等手段来发展段落。

二、饼状图的解题技巧

饼状图与柱状图的解题技巧比较类似。

A pie chart

Describe the trends in the following graphs.

Comparative Workforce Distribution
Great Britain, 1932 and 2000

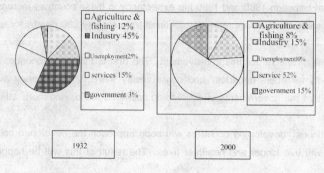

Comparative Workforce Distribution 比较性劳动力分布

According to the pie chart, there have been major changes in the relative size of the major employment sectors in Great Britain over the last 68 years from 1932 to 2000.

In 1932, 25% of people between the ages of 16 and 65 are unemployed. Of those who had a job the largest percentage worked in the Industrial sector, followed by those in the services sector (15%) and in agriculture and fishing (12%). The government employed only 3% of the workforce.

By 2000 major changes had taken place in the occupation of the working population. Most significantly perhaps, a far lower percentage of people of working age were unemployed (10%). The relative size of different occupational sectors had also changed significantly. The Industrial sector may only account for 15% of workers while workers in the Service Industry made up the largest employment sector. Agriculture and Fishing had also declined whereas the Government sector had increased enormously, employing almost 15% of all the workforce.

第十节　图表作文(曲线图)

一、图表作文的写作应当注意的问题

(一)结构要求

第一部分:开头部分

图表给出的时间段
图表的形式及数据的形式
图表研究的对象
注意点:不要照抄题目的内容,可以适当地变换说法和做必要的拓展。不要太长,简明扼要为妙。
建议写法:

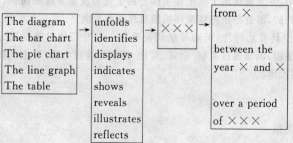

第二部分：主体内容

数据的引入：

小作文通常包含很多的数据信息，要截取其中重要的信息，把它们有机地融合到文章中去。切忌不要抽象地描述，要用数据来支持，同时也不要不分主次地列出所有的数据成为流水账。

趋势的描写以及客体间的比较：

由于数据通常在时间段上或者不同的实体间给出，因而时间段上的趋势和不同实体间的差别比较都是不可少的内容，通过这些描写可以更有效地说明问题。这也是获取高分的要求。

注意：

(1)在这个部分中引入数据以及表达趋势和比较的时候，表达方式最好不要过分地重复，经常变换一些说法，效果会比较好。

(2)只引用图中给出的信息，考生自己所掌握的知识点或者推理得出的结论都不要写入文章中。

(3)图表是客观信息的描述，所以千万不要出现 I 和 We 之类的词语。

第三部分：结尾部分

结论或者要说明的问题：

通过趋势的描写和实体的比较得出结论或者说明问题。

注意：结尾部分并非必需，但是从完整的角度出发，一个恰当的结尾可以起到画龙点睛的作用。

建议写法：

As the information indicates...

We can find from the above...

Overall, the chart demonstrates...

From the diagram it can be safely concluded that...

In conclusion,...

In summary,...

(二)图表写作中的常用词

1)文章开头

图表类型：table；chart；diagram；graph；column chart；pie chart

描述：show；describe；illustrate；can be seen from；be clear；be apparent；reveal；represent

内容：figure；statistic；number；percentage；proportion

2)表示数据

一般：have 10%；at 10%；over 10%

最高（低）点：peaks；reached a peak/high (point)

bottomed out；reached the bottom

变化：recover 略有回升；increase；jump；rise/rose；climb

decrease；fall/fell；drop；decline；reduce；fluctuate 浮动，摇摆不定

remained steady/stable；stay the same；little/hardly any/no change

变化程度：sudden/suddenly 突然地（地），意外的（地）

rapid/rapidly 迅速的（地），飞快的（地），险峻的（地）

dramatic/dramatically 戏剧性的（地），生动的（地）

significant/significantly 有意义的（地），重大的（地），重要的（地）

sharp/sharply 锐利的（地），明显的（地），急剧的（地）

steep/steeply 急剧升降的（地）

steady/steadily 稳固的（地），坚定不移的（地）

gradual/gradually 渐进的（地），逐渐的（地）

slow/slowly 缓慢的（地），不活跃的（地）

slight/slightly 轻微的（地），略微的（地）

stable/stably 稳定的（地）

表示范围：between... and...，from... to... 多长时间直到

表示程度：almost 几乎，差不多

nearly 几乎，密切地

approximately 近似的,大约

about 附近,大约,转向,左右,周围

just over 刚超过

over 结束,越过,从头到尾

exactly 正确地,严密地

precisely 正好;精神地;清晰地

比例:20 percent 20%

one in three 1/3

one out of every four 1/4

3)常用词

significant changes 图中一些较大变化

noticeable trend 明显趋势

during the same period 在同一时期

grow 增长

distribute 分布,区别

unequally 不相等地

pronounced 明显的

average 平均

no doubt 无疑地

corresponding 相应的,通讯的

represent 阐述,表现

overall 总体上讲

except 除外

in the case of 在……的情况下

in contrast 相反,大不相同

in conclusion 最后,总之

in comparison 相比之下

inversely 相反地,倒转地

in general 通常,大体上,一般而言

range from 从……到……不等

excessive 过多的,过分的,额外

lower 降低,跌落

elapse (时间)过去,消逝

category 种类

government policy 政府政策

market forces 市场规律

measure n. 尺寸,方法,措施 v. 估量,调节

forecast n. 先见,预见 v. 预测

(三)图表的几种常见形式

1) curve graph;2)bar chart;3)pie chart;4)table;5)sequence of events;6)a picture of an object showing how it works,目前仅考 1),2),3)和4)。

(四)图表描述应注意的问题

1)要突出重点,抓住图表中的极端点。如:最大或最小、最多或最少、最好和最差。

2)总趋势的描述必须准确,要看出总的规律、趋势,抓住特征。

3)图表往往提供大量数据,考生应该仔细观察分析,从中选择有效信息,图表上资料、数据的描述必须选择重点,不能事无巨细,一一列出。

4)充分利用图表中提供的文字或说明。同样,图表中没有的信息不能凭主观任意捏造。

5)说明、描述图表时应该注意动词的时态,属于过去发生的应该用一般过去时,属于经常发生的应该用一般现在时。

6)句子结构要力求有变化,不要总是一个句型。

7)考生应该熟练掌握一些固定句型和表达方式。

8)拼图比较形象、直观,常用来表示总体与部分、部分与部分之间的比例关系,一般以百分比的数字呈现。

9)曲线图一般说明变量之间的发展过程和趋势。

10)表格提供大量数据,应认真分析表格中各数据之间的内在联系,发现各项目的变化规律。

11)柱状图主要通过柱状的高度表示同一项目在不同时间的量,或同一时间不同项目的量。

12)认真检查。常见错误有:主谓不一致,时态,介词。

(五)标准化结构:(此部分仅供参考)

第一段:第一句:This is a _____ chart,which demonstrates the number of _____ from __ _____ to _____. 如果两个图,则:There are two charts below. The _____ chart describes the number of _____,and the _____ chart illustrates the figure of _____.

第二句:(所有题目适用)From the chart we can see that the number of _____ varies constantly/greatly in _____.

第二段:As we can see from the chart/It is clear from the chart that _____. 如果有两个图,则:the _____ chart shows that _____. /As we can see from the first chart, _____.

第三段：(如果两个图的话)It is clear from the second chart that...

第四段：结尾：From the figures/statistics above,we can see/conclude/draw a conclusion that...

第十一节　应用文

一、考研英语写作的应用文的类型

根据考研考试的样题和以往考试的情况来看,书信可以分成以下几类:

(1)抱怨信:提出问题、表达写信人对某些事情或现象的不满和抱怨。

(2)道歉和解释信:解释问题、说明情况,并就自己的某些过失或错误表示道歉。

(3)邀请信:邀请收信人参加一个活动等。

(4)请求和申请信:就某事或者某种想法向收信人提出申请或请求。

(5)建议信:以书信的形式向收信人提出建议和意见,可以是主动的信件也可以是回信作答。

应当说明的是公务书信与一般的私人信件有所不同,主要体现在**书信的形式、内容和格式上**,归纳起来说就是**语言风格的正式、严谨和格式的规范**。

题型举例

书信题目中包括以下几个方面:

Example　　A Complain Letter about Renting a Flat　　抱怨关于房子太吵的信

> You rent a flat through an agency. But it is very noisy as it is close to a public parking square. You have called the agency and expressed your hope of changing the flat. There has been no response yet.　　←背景提示
>
> *Write a letter to the agency to*
> ● *explain the situation*
> ● *describe the problem*
> ● *and tell them what you need them to do*
> 　*for you.*　　←作文的具体要求
>
> You do not need to write your own address.
> Begin your letter as follows:
> Dear Sir/Madam,　　←相关建议

二、书信写作的模式

书信写作模式一般为:

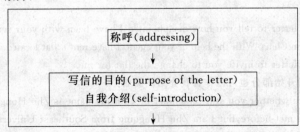

称呼(addressing)

↓

写信的目的(purpose of the letter)
自我介绍(self-introduction)

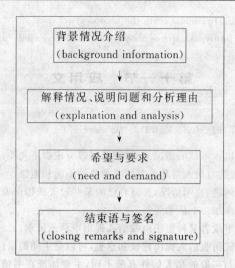

三、常用的书信开头称呼

Dear Dr. Green/Professor Green,（知道收信人的性别、职称、头衔和职位时使用）

Dear Sir/Madam,（不知道收信人的性别、职称、头衔和职位时使用，也是保险的用法）

Dear Mr. Smith,（已经知道收信的姓名、性别的男士）

Dear Miss/Mrs. Anderson,（已经知道收信人的姓名、性别和婚姻状况时根据情况使用）

Dear Ms Alice,（不管收信女士是否结婚均可使用，也是保险的用法）

Dear Department Dean/General Manager,（不知道收信人的姓名，性别等，只知道收信人的头衔、职位或职称等）

四、书信开头

对于大多数考生来说，书信写作的最大困难在于开始部分的写作。其实在开始部分只要直截了当但又简明扼要地表达写这封信的目的就可以了，这与汉语书信的形式有所不同，当然有时也可以非常简要地作一个自我介绍。

常用于书信开始部分的表达方法有：

I am writing this letter to...

I am writing to...

My purpose of writing this letter is to...

The reason that I write this letter is to...

I would like to inquire about...（常用于询问信）

I am very regretful to tell you that...（常用于抱怨信或道歉信）

I must apologize for...（主要用于道歉信）

例如：

I am writing this letter to tell you how disappointed I have been with your service.

I am a student from China. With the help of your agent, I have rent a flat located at...

I am writing this letter to invite you to change the flat for me.

如上所述，书信的开始部分也可以作自我介绍。例如：

I am not very sure whether you still remember me, but my name is Zhu Hongqing.

I don't believe we met before, but I am Zhu Hongqing from Southeast University of China.

但是希望考生注意的是，开始部分的介绍切勿过度，否则在第二部分背景介绍时就会有重复和累赘的感觉。

五、介绍背景情况

介绍背景情况的方法多种多样,但重要的是说清楚事情的原委和来龙去脉。例如:

I used to share a room with another student from China. Later on, I rent a flat and began to live individually.

I am the head of the IELTS training class, which began its first training course at last weekend.

I am from China, and I have just graduated from Southeast University at Nanjing.

Our university has established such a tradition that before Christmas of every year, all the foreign students and visiting professors are invited to attend a Christmas party held at the International Students' Center.

I was wondering whether your institution would accept any international students this year.

I am a sales manager working in an American company. So naturally, I seldom stay at home.

六、解释情况、说明问题和分析理由

这部分是整个书信写作中的重点,也最能体现考生的语言组织能力。但是要注意保证文章中解释和说明的重点必须清楚,不能拣了芝麻丢了西瓜。

Example　Explaining Why You Apply for the position 解释为什么申请此职位

> After my graduation from the university, I have been cultivating in the field of international marketing. As a result, I have not only accumulated much experience of international business, but also gained much confidence in intercultural communication...

←说明自己具备了何种能力,为进一步论证自己的观点打下基础。

说明为什么要申请国际市场营销部经理的职位,对这一特殊的职位来说,国际贸易和跨文化交际的能力是十分重要的。

解释和说明必须根据实际情况有条理地说明并用具体的理由来支持,切忌空话和大话,特别要说明后果、影响、意义等,这样才能说服别人。

Example　the Reason of Changing the Flat 换房的理由

> But the noise outside the flat day and night has greatly frustrated me. In the first place, I cannot sleep well at night, which, in turn, influences the effect and efficiency of my lessons in the daytime. Secondly, I usually need to write my papers in the evening, but now it is very hard for me to concentrate on it because of the noise...

←具体说明原因,充分论证自己换房的要求。

说明为什么要换房,这里所说的对于日常功课和论文写作的影响是非常实在的,因而也是十分有效的。

同时要特别注意,如果有两个或两个以上的内容需要说明,一定要有条理、合乎逻辑地排列组合好,避免颠倒、混乱。

七、信件正文的结束部分

这一部分主要是进一步明确提出写信人的具体要求,希望尽快得到对方答复,特别是要求收信人在收信以后所采取的措施等,虽然这是套话,但事实上如果没有这样的结束句,读起来会觉得信件不完整。另外,这样的套话对收信人有时也是一种压力,起到一种督促的作用,因此结束还是必不可少的。在信件中常用的结束语有如下几种：

I am looking forward to your reply. (注意 look forward to＋名词/动名词的用法)。

I am looking forward to your immediate/earliest reply.

Would you please take my request/application/suggestion into your earliest consideration and give me an early reply?

Please give us an earliest reply and we shall look forward to seeing you again.

Please be kind enough to take my request into your consideration. I plan to call/phone your office at this weekend.

If you can give me a positive reply, I would appreciate it very much.

If you need me to do anything else, please let me know.

If I can be of any help, please do not hesitate to tell me.

信件结尾签名的上面加上 Yours truly, Yours faithfully, Yours respectfully (特别尊敬和客气)，中间是亲笔签名，下面是打印的名字，正式信件则是全名。

八、一封完整的书信

下面将上述几种技巧综合起来并加以举例说明：

Sample 1　An Apologizing Letter 道歉信

> You have received a letter from an American professor invit-
> ing you to take part in a joint-research program at a univer-
> sity in the United States, You are very interested in it, but
> you cannot go there until next term for some very special
> reasons on your side.
>
> Please write a letter to him/ her.
>
> In your letter, you need to
>
> ●express your thanks
>
> ●explain the reasons
>
> ●and tell him/ her what you need him/ her to do.
>
> You do not need to write your own address.
>
> Begin your letter as follows:
>
> Dear Professor,

← 题目分析

← 背景情况

← 文章所要涵盖的内容，是文章的重点所在。

← 其他一些具体要求。

Sample Writing 1

> Dear Professor,
>
> Thank you very much for your letter dated September 28, 2003.
>
> I am very excited to know that you have been very successful with
> your application for this program. Besides, I have noticed that
> there are many excellent ideas about the next steps of carrying out
> this program. Frankly speaking, I am very interested in it and I am
> also very confident that the final achievement of this research pro-
> gram will cause a big surprise in this field.

← 典型的开头

← 这一段文字表面上看是表达自己对这一项目的极大兴趣，实际上是在为自己的托辞埋下伏笔，表明自己的态度是"心有余而力不足"。

But unfortunately，one of my important experiments is still under progress and I am afraid that it will not come to its end until this Christmas．Secondly，I have been preparing some important course books of civil engineering for our undergraduate students and I am supposed to finish the first draft before the end of this December，for which I signed a contract with the university press．And more importantly，two students of mine for MA degree of engineering are busy preparing their thesis，and they are in need of my advice and help．Apparently，it is very hard for me to tear myself away from our university at least for this term．

So，if you do not mind my straight forwardness，I would rather delay my arrival at your university till next term，when I can concentrate all my attention upon our joint-research program．Please take my request into your earliest consideration．I am looking forward to hearing from you soon．

Yours sincerely，

Zeng Dan

←说明自己不能成行的第一个理由。

←说明第二个理由。

←说明第三个理由，同时也是最重要的一个理由。

←用一种诚恳的语气请求对方同意自己的计划。

←写信人签名。

　　这是一封道歉解释信。文章完成了题目所规定的任务，条理清晰，说明理由展开得当，语言得体且规范，读起来流畅自然，是一篇不错的作文。

Sample 2　An Invitation Letter 邀请信

You are going to organize a semester-end party for the international students at your university．Please write a letter in the name of the Dean of the International Students' Affairs Office to invite a foreign student to attend the party．In your letter，you need to
● provide the background information
● introduce the participants and proposed programs
● and tell him/ her what you need him/ her to do．

You do not need to write your own address．
Begin your letter as follows：
Dear Sir/ Madam，

题目分析

←背景分析。

←内容要求。

←其他具体要求。

Sample Writing 2

Dear Sir or Madam,　　　　　　　　　　　　←格式正确

I am writing this letter to invite you to attend the International Students' Semester-end Party, which is going to be held at the International Students' Club at 7：00 in the afternoon of June 25(Friday).

←写信的目的。

←正式的邀请信中必须详细准确地表明活动的时间和地点。

Our university campus is covered with students of various colors from different countries. And it is our tradition that a special party for all the international students is held at the end of every semester, which, in fact, has become an important communication activity for them. Again, we shall invite some of the outstanding international students as well as professors to introduce their successful experiences in our country. Professor Cheng from China, is going to deliver a presentation upon. Intercultural Communication for Business Purposes, which will last only for 40 minutes. Besides, I am very glad to tell you that some of the other international students are going to perform some traditional and typical folk songs and dances of their countries. I believe that all of you will love it.

←介绍背景和本次活动的意义。

←介绍具体的节目安排。

←邀请信应当表现出热情和诚意。

By the way, you are especially encouraged to wear your traditional dressing. And if you hope to give any performance or presentation and you need us to do any special preparations for you, please do not hesitate to call my office.

←告诉收信人需做的事。

Please give us a reply before this Friday. And I am looking forward to seeing you there.

←常规的结束语。

Yours sincerely,

Jessica London

←照例必须签名。

　　这是一封邀请信。文章完成题目所规定的任务。文章条理清晰，结构合理，表现出邀请信应有的热情和诚意，且基本没有语言错误。

九、书信写作中的典型错误

(1)I am a talented, trustful and easy-going person.
　　(*trustful* 的用法不恰当，而且 *talented* 与其他词不属于同一类，因此最好改为 *I think I am an hon-*

est , trustworth and easy-going person .)

(2) I have come to Canada for two years.

（这种说法不恰当,可以改成 I have been in Canada for two years 或者 I came to Canada two years ago . ）

(3) I got bachelor of...

（这里没有清楚地表达出"学位"的意思,应当说 I got the bachelor degree of... ）

(4) I am writing for my telephone bill is unexpectedly higher than usual.

（表达写信目的的说法不规范,应当改成 I am writing this letter to invite you to re-check my telephone bill , as it is unexpectedly higher than usual . ）

(5) I am always responsible for all what I do.

（all what I do 的说法累赘,可以改成 I am always responsible for what I do 或者 I am always responsible for all I do . ）

(6) I would like to know whether you could exchange the walk-man for me.

（exchange 的意思是"互换、交换",用在这儿不确切,因此应改成 I would like to know whether you could change the walk-man for me . ）

(7) Frankly speaking, I have little interesting in attending this activity.

（interesting 的形式有误,对……的兴趣应用 interest,因此应改成 Frankly speaking , I have little interest in this activity . ）

(8) I believe that the major of computer will be more helpful and easier to find a job.

（该句中的"to find a job"的主体是 the major of computer,显然是不确切的,因此应改为 I believe that the major of computer will be more helpful to you. And it will be easier for you to find a job after your graduation . ）

(9) There are lots of students want to go abroad.

（这句话显然是中式英语"有很多学生想出国"的翻版,也是中国学生写作中常犯的一种错误,因此应改为 Lots of students want to go abroad . ）

(10) The volume button(of the walk-man) does not work smoothly, and the button of rewinding not, too.

（这句话后半部分中的省略不符合英语的习惯,应改成 The volume button does not work smoothly , and nor does the button of rewinding . ）

模拟试题

练习一

An Application Letter 申请信

You have just arrived in this country, and you plan to find a student job at the library of your university. Write a letter to the chief librarian to ● introduce yourself ● ask about the necessary information ● and apply for a student job. You do not need to write your own address. Begin your letter as follows: Dear Sir/Madam,	**Structure & Idea Aid** 1.申请信开始也是要先表达自己的目的。 2.考虑一下生活中找工作时最关心的几个因素。 3.确保题目中的每一个任务得以完成。 4.注意语言风格。 5.信的结尾要表达希望对方回信的愿望。

练习二

A Complaining Letter about Heating System 关于供暖系统的抱怨信

You rent a house through an agency.

The heating system has stopped working.

You phoned the agency a week ago but it has still mot been repaired.

Write a letter to the agency. Explain the situation and tell them what you need them to do for you.

You do not need to write your own address.

Begin you letter as follows:

Dear Sir or Madam,

Structure & Idea Aid

1. 介绍你已经做了哪些事。

2. 简单说明供暖的情况对你工作、学习、生活等方面的影响。

3. 说明你的要求。

练习三

An Inquiring Letter of Checking the Telephone Bill 一封关于查询电话账单的信

You received your telephone bill last month and found that the supposed payment is unexpectedly higher than before.

Write a letter to the municipal telecommunication bureau to explain the situation.

You do not need to write your own address.

Begin you letter as follows:

Dear Sir or Madam,

Structure & Idea Aid

1. 这是一封解释说明信，因此要遵循常规的书信格式。

2. 说明时应引用一些具体的、有说服力的例子。

3. 具体的要求可以是请对方重新确认，但要注意使用婉转的语气。

练习四

A Letter of Changing the Teacher 一封关于要求换老师的信

Your teacher of Linguistics is not a native English speaker, with a heavy accent in his/her spoken English. He/She is not so responsible for the teaching-being often late for the class, never correcting the students' papers, etc. What is worse is that he/she often flatters himself/herself in the classroom. Write a letter to the Dean of Academic Affairs Office to ask for changing the teacher. You need to give your reasons.

You do not need to write your own address.

Begin you letter as follows:

Dear Dean of Academic Affairs Office,

Structure & Idea Aid

1. 注意列举时的条理,并适当地用例子来支撑。
2. 遵循常规的信件展开模式。
3. 表达更换老师的愿望时要注意委婉的语气如使用 "Could you take our request into account?"、"Is it possible for you to change the teacher for us?"等问句。
4. 陈述理由时应说明迫切性,如"We are supposed to attend the graduate test very soon."等。

模拟试题参考范文

练习一

An Application Letter 申请信

February 16,2004

Dear Sir/Madam,

I am writing this letter to apply for a student job at your library.

I am international student. I have arrived here just for two weeks. Surely, it won't be long before I totally adapt myself to the university life. Besides, I believe that I still have lots of spare time. Very coincidentally, I have noticed your employment advertisement on the campus. To be frank, I am very interested in the student job at your library.

On one hand, I can gain some necessary financial support for my university education; on the other hand, this is also a precious chance for me to experience your culture. As for my English language, it is not a problem at all. I am confident that I will have no problem in communicating in English. Believe it or not, I am always a helpful person. By the way, I have prepared a resume for you. Please take my application into account as soon as possible. I look forward to hearing from you soon.

Yours faithfully,

Jiang Hong

练习二

A Complaining Letter about Heating System 关于供暖系统的抱怨信

Oct. 18，2003

Dear Sir or Madam，

I am writing this letter to invite you to have the heating system in my house repaired in the shortest time.

I am a student from Elon University. With the help of you，I rent the white two-story apartment near the western entrance of the campus. I moved into the house three weeks ago. On the whole，the house is pretty good——I like it. But unfortunately，the heating system in the house has stopped working. I called your office several times to tell you the problem last week. Every time the agent promised to send someone to come to repair it soon. Very disappointedly，nobody has ever been here for ten days. I have to emphasize that it would be very tough to live there without the heating system especially in such a freezing winter. Otherwise，I would think about changing the house or returning the house to you. So，please take practical measures and have the house repaired in the shortest time. I look forward to hearing from you before the end of this week.

Yours truly，

Lin Hongqing

练习三

An Inquiring of Checking the Telephone Bill 一封关于查询电话账单的信

Oct. 18，2003

Dear Sir or Madam，

I am writing this letter to invite you to check my telephone bill of last month.

I received my telephone bill of last month the other day，and I could not believe that the supposed payments is unexpectedly higher than ever.

First of all，I did not make any international call as I have not applied for and registered that special item yet. Secondly，I usually use my computer at the office and I never connect my computer with the internet at home. Therefore there should not have the payment for "Digital communication". More importantly，I need to stress that I went out of the town on business for over twenty days. How could I have made so many calls?

In fact, your bureau had the same problem about two years ago, so far as I remember, and you corrected it after it is rechecked. So, would you please check the telephone bill recording system for me again? I look forward to your reply soon.

Yours truly,

Wang Ming

练习四

A Letter of Changing the Teacher 一封关于要求换老师的信

Dear Dean of Academic Affairs Office,

I am writing this letter, on behalf of our class, to invite you to change the teacher of Linguistics for us.

We began to take the course of Linguistics from the beginning of this term. All the students in our class attach much importance to the course. Naturally, we expect a lot from the teacher. But, very unexpectedly, the teacher is not so satisfying though he has a pretty good academic record.

Firstly he is not like a native English speaker as his spoken English is difficult for us to follow.

We believe that the sense of responsibility of a teacher is very important. However, our teacher does not seem to have this qualification. He is often late for the class, leaves the class earlier, and often receives and extends calls in the class. And, he never corrects the students' papers. As a result, we do not know how well we write. What is most annoying is that he often flatters himself in the class. I need to clarify that most of us will have to attend the graduate test next month. If he maintains his teaching style, few of us will pass the test. So, would you please think about changing the teacher for us? We shall look forward to your earliest reply.

Yours truly,

Li Qing